Praise for *The Bottom of the Sky*

"William Pack genuinely and skillfully describes the insides of the financial services industry. Having been there allows him to tell it like it is and definitely keeps you on edge through to the very end. At this skill level, it is hard to believe this is his debut."

— David Standridge, retired Group President, Shearson Lehman Brothers.

"William Pack has written a powerful and poignant story that draws you into the saga of Levi Monroe's life and doesn't let you go. I fear it may be a long time before I find another book that captures my attention so completely. You don't have to be a Wall Street insider or a cowboy from Montana to appreciate *The Bottom of the Sky*."

— Theodore E. Gildred, U.S. Ambassador (Retired)

"*The Bottom of the Sky* is a powerful novel....[Pack] brilliantly weaves a 30-year saga....Pack's sometimes brutal writing captures the reader's interest and holds it to the very end....This book is recommended, not only for those with ties to Montana, but for anyone who enjoys a good read."

— Roundup Record-Tribune

"In *The Bottom of the Sky*, Roundup native William C. Pack has written a remarkably assured first novel."

- The Billings Outpost

Praise for *The Bottom of the Sky*

"*The Bottom of the Sky* is brilliantly written. I was drawn to
(the main character's) dilemma with the good and evil of Wall Street.
The character is both beautiful and tragic in his journey to top
management in the brokerage industry. This is a truly wonderful
read for anyone who enjoys the struggle and triumph within
and around our humanity."
—Donald Shagrin,
former Group President, Citigroup Smith Barney

"Bill Pack has written an intensely brutal novel about treachery – the
internal treachery that permeates the contemporary financial services
industry and the treason of extended familial sexual abuse. It is raw, but
redemptive, as Pack's protagonist Levi Monroe finds his final reward at
the bottom of the sky. It's a *goood* read; you'll recognize the landscape."
—Jim Gransbery,
former state editor for Lee Newspapers, Montana journalist

"Pack's novel is a poignant tale of loss and redemption as well as one of
compelling action and intrigue that has appeal for both genders."
Friends of Saratoga Libraries

THE BOTTOM OF THE SKY

A NOVEL

WILLIAM C. PACK

COLLECTOR'S ENCORE EDITION

RIVERBEND
PUBLISHING

The Bottom of the Sky

Published by Riverbend Publishing, Helena, Montana.

Printed in the U.S.A.

3 4 5 6 7 8 9 0 SB 15 14 13 12 11 10

Book design by DD Dowden
Cover photograph by Christopher Cauble

ISBN 978-1-60639-003-0

RIVERBEND PUBLISHING
P.O. Box 5833
Helena, MT 59604
1-866-787-2363
www.riverbendpublishing.com

www.BottomoftheSky.com

DEDICATION

■

For the righteous who endure and for those who cannot, for the
courageous truth-speakers, for the kind.

Community Overcoming
Relationsip Abuse
www.CORAsupport.org

3 6 7 6 9 7 6 7 4 4 4 5 3 5 8 8 8 3 6 7 3 8 3 7

ACKNOWLEDGEMENTS

The process of writing *The Bottom of the Sky* was so extensive that it's difficult to be confident that I'm thanking everyone I should. There were so many who gave me help and heart.

I thank John L'Heureux, a world-class novelist, professor, and friend, for his early influence and advice. A tough bird, a literary giant. If I look up and squint, I can glimpse him from here.

Thank you to my selfless readers, some of whom cared enough to be brutal, all of whom gave useful counsel. They include Liz Guy, Hopkins Guy, Kimberley Cameron, Bud and Suzanne Clarke, Elizabeth Evans, Pragati Grover, Angela Rinaldi, Todd Chestnut, Governor Ted Schwinden, Kaine Kornegay, John Baker, John Horton Sr., Carrie Chestnut, Scott Chestnut, Kerry Mohnike, Natasha Ritchie, and Greg Dufault. Thank you to Dale Alger, scholar and historian, for revealing the heritage of my birthplace. Thank you Irwin Zucker for encouragement and advice.

Thank you Mary Strobel, the best professional editor an author could have, for your frankness and unwavering skill. Amazing. Irreverent, sure, but amazing. A thousand times, thank you. We ain't done.

I benefited from additional professional editing and proofreading by Darrend King Brown, John Strobel, Beverly Dumas, Kevin McCaughey, and Barbara Fifer. Thank you.

Thank you to my early critics, who read the manuscript before it reached the Advance Review phase, so that subsequent professionals might venture a look. Thank you author Rosalie Maggio, journalist Jim Gransbery, executive Don Shagrin, journalist Jodi Upton, executive David Standridge, author Jean Lin, and U.S. Ambassador Theodore E. Gildred.

To my publicist, Richard Hoffman, a class act of great renown, thank you for teaching me and pulling me up. We ain't done either.

My very deep thanks to Chris Cauble, my publisher at Riverbend Publishing, for his vision, tolerance, courage, and patience as I learn. Thank you to Linda Cauble and Janet Spencer, the heart and soul of my Riverbend family, good folks all to ride the river with.

Thank you Melodie and Sam and Casey and Nathan and Kaine and Nicole, for believing and enduring when it was unreasonable to do so.

I most especially thank Clyde Allen Pack Sr. and Betty Ann Pack, my parents, who, when they had so little, gave all of it. From them I learned perseverance, sacrifice, forgiveness, and the durability of love – pretty much everything worth knowing.

Thanks be to God.

Make no mistake, this is a hard story. Know that absolutely all characters and events depicted in *The Bottom of the Sky* are purely fictional. Any resemblance to persons or events in the real world is unintended and coincidental. Seriously.

Love, like loyalty, does not die,
not the kind you give nor the kind you receive;
whether by neglect or asphyxiation, by poison or trauma,
someone has to kill it.

PROLOGUE

For her, Roundup, Montana, like Wall Street and Silicon Valley, never really existed in black and white or even sepia tone, though photographic images and personal retrospect may have recorded it that way. It had color and contrast. On thirty-below-zero days, the sky was always cobalt blue with a brilliant yellow bullet hole. After winter storms, the run-down Bull Mountains were blinding white, pocked with evergreen. The slough-green Musselshell River girdled the hills from tumbling north onto the plains. Grasslands that had sustained cattle since 1881—and the bison before them—were verdant in spring and gray-gold in summer and fall. The veins deep under Roundup ran coal black, and the ones above, crimson red.

Through the middle of the last century, most of the men in town were coal miners with Old Country names like Wilhelm Johnig, Kavka Bublivich, Cian O'Reilly, or Izroc Ketanna, and they went by Shorty or Red or Izzy. They named their children John or Kathleen or Betty or Charley. Some had never attended school, becoming trapped there in the mines by their ignorance and their accent, disoriented by their addictions, or buried beneath the propaganda and prejudice of two world wars. Straightforward and iron-tough, they bloodied each other regularly and their families occasionally. They drank and stayed married to resilient women of practical grace who saw to it that they wore their one set of church clothes when they were told to, who endured the profane to protect the sacred, and who rose above dispossession to hold up children so that they might see beyond shacks and mines and dreams played out.

Now, under sandstone hills, among weed-stumped plots, this daughter with a daughter of her own stands upslope from a pink granite cemetery marker. In one hand she holds a note written on waterproof paper, in the other, the hand of her child. "Thank you," she whispers to someone else. "Thank you." She pockets the note as though it were the heirloom it has become. In a swoop, she hoists the child to her shoulders, tickling the young girl's fancy. As they walk to the car, they point at big clouds and divine their magical shapes, marveling at the bottom of the sky.

PART 1

THE 1970S

1

The Caliber of Commitment

*Sometimes the lies you tell are less frightening
than the loneliness you might feel if you stopped telling them.*

Brock Clarke

Virginia had half a mind to kill the bastard, and it was talking to the other half, right there in the middle of a dead zoo.

A stop on U.S. Highway 12 beside the languid Musselshell River, Geno's Bar was, for residents of Roundup, Montana, a couple miles upstream and a couple miles closer to the United Mine Workers Cemetery. Half the county's population, about two thousand people, lived in town, and Geno's was the shortest drive that scratched the itch to just go somewhere. Some fancied their drink with other people. Some liked the pickled eggs. Inside this quirky clapboard box, between the stamped-tin ceiling, the hardwood walls, and the harlequin floor, was a menagerie of dead things. Dead things were good for business. Heads of deer, elk and pronghorn stared impassively, unafraid of a hunkered mountain lion, a marauding wolf. Mutant farm animals were favorites: a three-eyed sheep, a goat with five legs, an unlikely two-headed calf. Caged in Plexiglas, an albino coyote with a bootlaced gut guarded the cash register. Geno's Bar was a bona fide dead zoo. Virginia normally fit in there.

On a flop-hot Friday night in 1969, Armstrong, Aldrin, and Collins were on their way back from the moon. To celebrate, Geno had bought a round of drinks for the regulars – cowboys, coal miners and gals – who tonight had something to mark other than payday. That was hours ago. In the deep end of the saloon, the end without windows, 24-year-old Virginia Monroe had drunk five Seven-and-Sevens, two with Frank, her day-laborer husband, while laughing and talking across the bar with Geno – that big, happy son-of-a-bitch – and three by herself while Frank chatted up Laura Darling. Virginia would have graduated high school with Laura had Frank not made Virginia pregnant at fifteen the night she won a U. S. Savings Bond at the science fair. Now she had just about aplenty of having her skinny ass planted on this barstool, waiting for Frank to get back from the john. *Nobody takes this long,* she figured. Unconsciously she clicked her false teeth. They couldn't afford to have them refitted.

"Nothing matters more than family, does it, Geno?" Virginia's eyes cast an unfocused arc across the wall of elk the way a gambler rechecks his hand before he folds. She imagined one elk collapsing from the impact of a bullet, like strings blown off a marionette, its body beating its blood to the ground. "They had family, them deer. Elk." Still looking. "Now here we are."

"Yup. Nothing matters like family," Geno concurred.

"You think a family means more than people in it? Or the other way around?" Geno didn't say. "If one might kill the other one, which one would you save, Geno?" Geno didn't say to that either, and she was unsure if he was listening. "It must've purdy near killed you and Angela when her mother passed." Angela was nine now, friends with Virginia's oldest.

"Purdy near." He was listening.

Your Cheatin' Heart dried up like somebody had closed one sluice box and *Crazy* rolled out like somebody opened another. Pops and scratches warmed the air. Virginia watched for Frank some more. He had gone in back, allegedly to use the toilet, past the coal-smudged pool players but before the screen door that oozed smoke into the night. She picked at the small, itchy bumps that nerves pushed up on her face. Peering into the back-bar mirror, she fixed on the men's room door. She touched her eyeglasses, causing one of the bows to lift off her ear. No sign of her husband … or *her.*

"Her" was Laura Darling. After graduation Laura had attended Billings Business College and then got a job at a bank in Billings Heights – *la-te-dah* – and nowadays drove back to Roundup in her pinstripe work dress on Friday nights to enthrall Frank with how much of people's own goddamn money she had doled out that week, as if touching other people's cash was a big-ass deal. Then she'd sashay through the bar on her way out the front door, saying goodbyes to the hometown crowd as loud as anyone could stand. Degree or no degree, Laura Darling never really got out of town. Nobody did. Acting different was just bullshit. But Laura'd head out the door – like she just did – and Frank'd go to the damn bathroom – like he just did – and pretty soon he'd come back and tell Virginia to finish her drink and let's go home. Bullshit.

Geno dumped Virginia's drink and gave her 7UP.

"Angela's a nice girl." Virginia said and meant it. "She's turning out good." Her tongue felt a little heavy. "If anything was to happen to me, you tell 'em my kids should stay as family – you know – together. Like family. You tell 'em, will you?"

"Nothing's gonna happen to you."

"We'll see. But family's everything. Most important thing, right?"

"That it is."

"Even if a person ends up like me? Huh? Even if a father…" She looked away. A voice inside said shut up. *You shut up*, she thought back at it. "Even if you end up like me? You still do right for your family…" She was aware she might sound drunk.

"You want coffee? Have some coffee." Geno reached for a cup.

"Okay, buddy, I'll shut up. You're a good guy, you know that? Hey, I got something. Somebody over by where Jesus lived or somewhere over there's got a cave with a two-headed goat and a four-legged chicken. They charge money just to get in the cave."

"We don't have a four-legged chicken. But coffee's free."

She searched the mirror again. Geno lumbered into her view and stopped. Her eyes latched onto a button on his shirt. She was kneading her empty highball glass, working her anger. Her eyebrows crimped. Geno swapped her smoldering cigarette into a clean ashtray. "How you doin'?" he said.

"What?" She looked. "I got kids. Family. I can't give… But I don't want…" Geno's ears moved, his look pleading for her not to finish. Again she stared, over the pool table in back, at the doors marked "Bucks" and "Does." One of the pool players opened the Bucks' door and went in. That cinched it. The men's toilet was a one-holer.

Without looking away, Virginia slid off the stool, glass in hand. At 5 foot 1, she lost altitude. Her nostrils flared ferally and she hitched up her butt-saggy polyester pants. The pool player wasn't coming out – still wasn't. Suddenly, beyond the men's room, beyond the back screen door, headlights sliced open the dark, stirring up shapes. There. It was just a flash, but Virginia caught it. Pinstripes. "I'll be *go – to – hell!*"

Virginia could feel Geno watching the back of her head. She knew he saw what she saw. When she banged her glass on the bar, it launched him along the mirror to cut her off, but he guessed wrong. She swung about-face, toward the front, her hair launching eddies in the smoke-blue overcast. Geno pulled back.

Virginia shoved open the front screen door and plunged into the soggy, river-bottom air. *Skunk*, she smelled. The red neon from the rooftop sign scanned her hair, her back. By the time the door slammed, she was five steps into the gravel lot, barreling along pickup trucks and American sedans washed gray by bar-glow. She stopped at an ulcerated '58 Pontiac.

The driver's door groaned and the dome-light pitched hard shadows into the cockpit. She dove facedown onto the seat, groping under it as her stiff hair shifted like a helmet against the bench. Her fingers found the polished leather holster and dragged it across the floor mat. Like every man she knew, Frank called on obsolete tradition to stash a firearm under the seat. "Macho *bullshit*," she mumbled. Her trembling hands held the revolver waist-high. She blinked. She popped the snap on the leather thong, extracted the gun, and tossed the holster aside. Next she rummaged under the dash for a flashlight, then closed the door and waited for her eyes to adjust.

Gravel scrunched beneath her canvas shoes as she snuck around the building into the dark. Her gait slowed. Eyes searching, elbows out, she crept, ever slower, around the corner, until she saw the sifted light from Geno's back screen door. She concentrated. Whoever she had spotted earlier, from inside the bar, was still there, tucked in the shadow between bar and dumpster. She snuck closer, now fifteen feet away, now twelve. When she heard them, she froze, palming the slick handle of the .357.

Murmurs. Low, humming coos nested in dampened music. Inside, a toilet flushed. She risked another step.

"*Just a second*," a man whispered.

"*What?*" A woman whispered.

"*Just a second!*" Him again.

Only the arteries in Virginia's neck made any movement. *Sneak back to the car*, she told herself – *now* – or *back inside*. She could just make them out. *Look away – no. No, don't! No more!* One of them, the taller one, tilted toward the door, leaned into the light, peeked into the bar. *Frank!* His rawboned silhouette quickly fused back into the shadows.

Blood emptied from Virginia's brain to her gut, taking free will with it. She held her hands together before her waist, gun muzzle down, mindful not to drop the flashlight. She sent her left thumb to help her right thumb pull back the hammer. Two clicks, like Frank said. A deep breath. She held her index finger straight, outside the trigger guard. In her other hand, she found the button on the flashlight. She exhaled quietly and sucked in again, deep, as if preparing to submerge. Trembling, she raised the flashlight, and then the gun, and turned on the light. "You son of a bitch!"

A kiss broke roughly. Laura's hand flinched back from Frank's unbuttoned crotch. His hand yanked from under her skirt, his watch links snaring, stretching, exposing his smudgy forearm tattoo as some buried garment ripped. Laura stumbled towards darkness.

"Move, and I'll shoot yous both!" Virginia's dentures clicked as she jabbed the gun muzzle into the light beam to prove her threat.

Laura halted, arms locked down, fingers pointed stiffly at the ground. Her skirt was bunched in her garter, her nylon top torn. Her head sank forward, dropping her hair like curtains round her face, and she broke into a bawl.

Frank was feverishly stitching his pant buttons shut, tucking the shirt that hung long from his broomstick shoulders. "Dammit, Virginia! Please!! Please! ... Please."

"Please my ass, you *son of a bitch!*" Virginia's finger sledded the semicircle outside the trigger guard. She imagined the faces of her son and daughter. "Is this why our daughter's named Laura?" She sucked back some spit. "Were you diddlin' her all along? Six years? Huh? ANSWER me!"

Frank pumped his arms towards her as if doing standing pushups. "Hold on, wait!" Finally, palms up, he tried on an indignant *that's-crazy* face. "We never did it," he corrected, almost sternly. Virginia pointed the muzzle at his chest, and his shoulders dropped dead. "I swear."

Laura kept crying.

"Shut up, bitch!" Virginia commanded. "A bitch in heat. That's what you are. A bitch in heat. Aren't you! A bitch in heat. Well? Aren't you? SAY IT!" Virginia's teeth were skittering all over her mouth. "Bit-th! Aren't you! Huh?"

Laura whimpered and shook her head. "No, no, no ..." licking snot from her lip.

Something big eclipsed the light from the door. Virginia's eyes darted. It was Geno, blocking the exit, damming up chaos behind him. He called to her, and part of her wanted desperately to hear – wanted an out, a reason to pull up short.

Until she looked back. She saw Frank gently tugging at Laura's skirt – gently, to untangle it for her. At that moment, Virginia became her own observer. It was a strange, underwater calm. She knew Gino was talking to her but she couldn't exactly hear him. Nor did she hear Laura beg. She noticed Frank's arms extended, fingers up, palms out, and saw his reddened face – all popeyed and long – like make-believe. Make-believe.

Her index finger curled back and threaded the trigger guard. Her mind noted with interest that the barrel shifted toward Laura's chest. Her finger squeezed. She felt the hammer snap and simultaneously saw her children's faces shatter and crash down like so many heavy shards.

An instant later Geno's massive arms caved down on hers from behind, cinched around her, crushing her back against his chest as his hands swallowed hers. With the flashlight and gun dissolving from existence, Virginia's body rose roughly until she faced the stars. Ugliness drained through her back, leaving behind only relief. Nothing left to decide.

Laura collapsed, driving her knees into gravel and wailing as if she'd been shot. She hadn't, and in a thought thin as ether, it dawned on Virginia why. Frank always kept his pistol's first chamber empty. Then all thoughts were gone but her reason to be. "My family," Virginia mouthed to the sky. "My kids."

No one heard.

2

FOOL'S GOLD

Were you ever out in the Great Alone,
when the moon was awful clear,
And the icy mountains hemmed you in
with a silence you most could hear?

ROBERT SERVICE

In late August outside the tiny Main Street courthouse, the top two steps baked like stone griddles in the midday sun. Two ragamuffins, a boy and a girl, wore high-water pants and combed hair and sat on the steps and squinted at each familiar car and pickup that happened by. Nine-year-old Levi refolded the paper from inside his younger sister's worn-out shoe. At his shoulder, she balanced on one foot.

"This don't have to last," Levi said. "We'll get school clothes today."

Lam was dubious. "Who sez?"

"Me." He didn't look at her. He was sure.

"What if they put Mommy in jail?"

"They won't. Judge Rosario's got his bow in the truck." He pointed to a pickup, blurring it with his magic blue eyes, making it shiver. He stopped. "And camouflage. He wants to get going hunting. And there ain't no other cars here but ours and Mr. Granucci's. Dad says people won't say she did nothing bad. Dad says no one'll say it mostly 'cause they're all chicken-shit of her." He handed her the shoe. "Here. Put this on."

"Is Dad gonna say she did something bad?" She jammed her foot in, smashing the back.

"No."

"Well that don't mean we get clothes. Dad says we ain't got the money."

"There's lay-away, ain't there? Anyways, that's not why people buy things.

They buy things 'cause their feelings change. Like smokin' and drinkin'. Ever notice when Dad lights a cigarette or when Mom pours a drink? Ever notice if they been sad, they just got happy; or if they've been happy, they might've just got sad, or scared, or maybe not scared no more? It don't matter which – long as their feeling *changes*. That's when we get clothes. Or they get seat covers, or something."

Behind them, big county doors opened and Virginia rolled out on a wad of air-conditioned air, a step ahead of Frank. She tapped the kids' heads. "Levi, Lam, come on. We're going to Billings."

"Daddy calls me Lam," Laura protested. It was a play on her given name – Laura Ann Monroe. "Just Daddy."

"Not anymore," Virginia snapped. "Now we all like it. Me especially. From now on, we're calling you Lam." Virginia stopped and softened, getting eyeball-level with the girl, just for a moment. "Okay, Sweetie?" Lam looked at her mom until she trusted her and then nodded. Then Virginia said to Levi. "Understand? She's Lam now."

Levi nodded, too. At times, his diminutive mother seemed unshakably anchored, an outcropping on this big, sure land where she was born and where she bore him. Frank, his dad, seemed striking in contrast. Frank always said he had blown here in a dust storm as a boy. In his teens he escaped from his family – a Jesus-crazy mother and a no-good step-dad as old as a grandpa who traveled around selling salvation to folks. Frank said he spooked the bastard off, but it was Frank who seemed spookable, both in thin resolve and lank physicality. The only things constant about Frank were his perturbed weather-blown face and, on one strandy forearm, a crooked home-made tattoo of Christ's cross that looked about as sharp as an ink stamp on roast fat. But Mom wasn't iffy. Mom might act wild, but she was a sure thing – sure as Levi had been about this day. He grinned I *told you so* at Lam as he talked to his mom. "Are we going to Penney's? Or Sears? Or maybe the new K-Mart."

"The new K-Mart? We ain't putting on airs. Get in the car."

So Laura became Lam. By winter, the name was beginning to stick. Her teachers went along so kids went along. But as much as teachers helped Lam out, they were too skittish of her to give her full credit. They had reasons. They might have praised her flair for math had her brother not been a phenomenon. They might have appreciated her strength in reading had she not been prone to describing genitalia.

Levi Allen Monroe was one year older than Lam and proud to be named after the jeans that miners wore. His grandpa on his mom's side was a miner. Ranchers wore Wranglers. Miss McKenny – the split-grade teacher who was talking to his mom on the phone in the principal's office while he and Lam waited in the hall – had taught them all about local history, especially of the school, his best place. In 1910, women didn't have the right to vote in the U. S., but they did in Montana. In Roundup, twenty-three people voted to build a school. Like the Bull Hills, it was carved from sandstone: khaki-gray blocks as big as travel trunks, stacked formal and high. Central School became sixteen classrooms with plenty of windows and a bell tower tall as a grain elevator.

In school Levi and other kids did the same things at the same times each day. Predictable. Steady. Not like home. At school, grown-ups asked questions that had right answers. So Levi raised his hand a lot. At ten o'clock, everybody got a small carton of milk. On Monday the man from the Miner's & Merchant's Bank came by, and if you didn't have a quarter, you got credit for it anyway. Class smelled fun, like paste and crayons, and by eleven o'clock on Tuesdays the whole school smelled like hot lunch.

Levi and Lam sat on a hall bench under a fresh pine bough the janitor had hung on the wall. It smelled like Christmas. This was the night of the winter pageant. Levi absentmindedly massaged an odd ache on his palm. He couldn't wait for the night's program but here he was – waiting – with Lam, in coats and caps while their teacher gabbed on the party line loud enough for any passerby to hear. Miss McKenny was a strident woman of girth. She had seen nonsense in her time.

"I'm not necessarily saying he did that, Mrs. Monroe … I'm saying he's … well … unusual. Take that for what you will. All I'm saying is that we gave the class an Iowa Basic math test that even some sixth-graders have trouble with, and he finished it *very* quickly. *I* couldn't finish it that fast. By the time other kids barely got into it, he was just sitting there, done, looking glassy-eyed like he does sometimes… No, out the window. Anyway, I picked it up, and he had marked in all the answers. I asked him why he didn't show his work. He said he didn't use steps … he just '*saw*' the answers … with his eyes, in his head. So I checked it. On the back of the answer sheet he had drawn weird lines, and arrows, and symbols, but none of them made sense to me. He couldn't explain it. But *every answer was correct.* I know he's smart, but… No, I'm not saying that… I'm not *saying* he did anything! It's just not likely he did this without thinking, so the principal and I are resourcing another test – one he hasn't seen – Resourcing? It just means we're getting another one… Well, if he does poorly, we have a problem… No, we don't want a problem with you…Wait, I never said 'cheater'!"

Lam whispered accusingly. "Aww — *verr*…" like shame, shame. Levi rolled his eyes.

"We'll see, Mrs. Monroe, *but don't hang up.* That's not the only reason I called. I'm afraid Lam won't be allowed to sing in the pageant tonight… Please, please hear me out. We've talked about this before. Today, when the girls came in from recess, some of them were very upset. One of the boys was crying – because of Lam… No, Mrs. Monroe, I don't feel comfortable saying which boy… I understand, but *once again,* she was trying to… No, not Thelma Anderson's boy – and when he wouldn't let her, she called him…"

Levi bumped Lam. "*Aww – verr,*" he said. She stuck out her tongue at him.

Miss McKenny continued. "No, some other girls began teasing him, and when we separated the children and asked questions, we found out she told all the girls about, well, I'm going to say the word she said – boners. … Hello? … Hello?"

A moment later Miss McKenny palmed Levi and Lam's cap-covered heads, guiding them outside to a waiting school bus. The bus doors opened, issuing an earthy belch of mildew. They sat near the front, behind Angela, feet swinging, casting slush from black rubber overboots. Levi breathed on his window, blurring the winterscape movie outside. He tried to untie the gold ribbon in Angela's hair. She noticed. Soon the bus lurched to a stop between two crumbling snow-turrets that guarded the highway entrance to Geno's parking lot. Seven kids stumbled out and clumped up for safety, more or less, until the driver pulled away. One kid, Angela, lived with Geno in the cottage behind the bar. The others trudged off toward their homes, trailing blooms of fog that blew from their mouths into four o'clock twilight.

Levi and Lam plodded on crusty snow. One of her mittened hands gripped one of his and he jerked it back, rubbing his gloved palm on his leg. Like it hurt. He made a fist a couple of times, eyeing it confoundedly. Lam ignored it, latching onto his tatty corduroy sleeve. They walked. With his other sleeve, he periodically raked snot off his nose. Presently they climbed to a rail bed and hopscotched on the dark rail ties. Two hundred yards later, they bounced across a wide, wooden plank that straddled a litter-strewn ditch and ended at the gravel road. An old pickup loaded with coal rattled by. They walked in its tracks. Boots scrunched on hard-packed snow, the low vibration reminding Levi of grinding teeth. To shake the thought, he broke into song. "O Christmas Tree, O Christmas Tree…"

"Stop it!" Lam said, punching a mushroom of breath in the cold.

He sang louder. "O Christmas Tree, O Christmas Tree…"

"Stop it!" she cried and clubbed his shoulder with a round-housed fist. Levi could tell that once again his little sister dreaded going home. She herself had stirred it up. Well, he was eager for the evening.

"O Christmas Tree…" he yelled.

"STOP IT!" she screamed a little-girl scream. Thirty yards away, Old Man Pulaski's frost-faced dog, a black, thick skulled mongrel, barked and scrambled towards them through crap-pitted snow until its chain snapped back its head. Pulaski burst from his shack and beat the dog into quiet.

Levi issued a shit-eating grin that made him want to spit. Or sing.

Weeks prior, Miss McKenny told Levi he would be front and center at her holiday chorus because he was a star student and her best and loudest singer. She called him the golden bell-cow of her splendid, golden chorus, which would wear splendid, golden shirts – which parents could buy at a prearranged discount from the bowling supply store in Billings. Different classes would wear different colored shirts – green, red, gold – and, for the finale, all the students would form a giant Christmas tree. Levi, in front, in the place of honor, would lead the audience in singing "O Christmas Tree," always a crowd pleaser. No one questioned Miss McKenny's musicality. She and her sister had once made a record in Denver.

The shack in which the Monroes were squatters leaned very slightly away from the river as if to accuse the nearby outhouse. It had three rooms: two bedrooms with three cupped mattresses on squeaky steel bed frames, and a kitchen with a black-iron coal stove.

By 6:15 it was dark outside. In the kids' room, Levi smeared around a towel on his clean, damp hair. The house smelled of onions and tomatoes, potatoes and carrots, and seared deer meat – Virginia stew. It was a thick, gravied soup his mom made only from ingredients she herself had grown and chopped or shot and butchered. It beat rice and ketchup by a mile. When she made it, Levi liked the way she stood straighter and moved purposefully, with a kind of private cheer. Once he asked, "Why isn't it Virginia stew when Dad helps?" She answered, "Cause when other people decide, it ain't mine. Sometimes you have to make what you want, only from things you say, things you gathered your own self. Otherwise, you can end up sick." He didn't get it. Surely she didn't mean poison. So he asked her why not make Virginia stew all the time, you know, for health? She was slow to answer. "Most times, I just ain't got the ingredients. Or maybe I just been sick so long I'm afraid to try not to be." Now that, to Levi, made no sense whatsoever. She seemed fine, not counting drink. But his question. He hated the way it had turned the mood. He decided not to ask it ever again. He liked who she was when she was making Virginia stew and he ought not to poke at it.

Levi heard Frank in the kitchen, shaking down the coals in the firebox. With turned up cuffs, Frank hefted a bucket of steaming water off the stove-deck, slopping out liquid orbs that skittered like angry mercury on the hot iron. He lugged the pail across the tiny kitchen and poured the water in the galvanized washtub where Levi had just bathed. Frank wiped his forehead. "Lam, get out here."

In their bedroom Lam stood beside Levi, naked and rabbit-ear pink. She shivered and rocked against a skinny bed that issued metallic complaints. Levi dripped on the coiled oval rug, hating that rug like he hated the one just like it in their parents' room. At Frank's call Lam bounced back hard and launched through the room, careful to skirt the rug, watching it as though it watched her. Levi knew why. They never talked about it.

In the kitchen, Lam ran tippy-toed to her mom, who was sitting at the wall on a chrome chair, legs crossed, foot shaking. She lay down a beer and smoke and cloaked Lam in a towel.

Frank tested the water. "Okay, Lammy, your turn."

Lam advanced, peering at Levi's backwash. "It's steamy."

"That's 'cause it's cool in here," Frank said. He moved behind her and stripped away her towel. He traced his fingers along her upper arm. "See. Goosebumps."

She tested the bath with a finger.

"You want some Mr. Bubble?" Frank said. She did. He handed her the box. "Not too much."

She held it with both hands and dumped a cloud of pink powder into the water.

"That's plenty." Virginia took a swig.

Frank plucked a clackety eggbeater from an open drawer. "I swear if that kid don't start closing drawers I'll kill him." He gripped the stirrup handle, the tendons in his wrist banjoing up the length of his crucifix tattoo, and dipped the beaters into the water. While Frank steadied her, Lam jerked round the gearwheel knob, splashing spastically.

She let go and drew her hands modestly to her crotch, locking her elbows, watching Frank's eyes.

"You do it."

Frank cranked vigorously, launching a thick eruption of suds that caused Lam's knees to barrel-ring the tub with delight.

Virginia shook her foot more tersely, like it meant something now. "A little old for this."

Frank ignored her. "Hop in, little girl." He pulled a beer from the icebox.

In the bedroom Levi hopped on the rug, wresting fuzzy-kneed church pants up his sweaty legs. He sucked in his belly and snapped the pants. Next he rocked his feet into stiff shoes he got from a dead farm kid. Still shirtless, he entered the kitchen as Frank backed out the front door with the washtub. Arctic air billowed along the floor.

Virginia helped Lam dress. She handed Levi a damp towel. "Get the floor." She nodded at the puddle where the red linoleum had worn through to black. "And don't get your pants wet. I want you to look perfect when you lead the choir."

Levi mopped with his foot. "It's a chorus."

"Chorus, then. Go get your sister some underwear."

Levi went to his parents' room and dug through a basket of clean laundry, careful not to rip the new lint pad from the laundromat dryer. His mom was crazy for lint pads. She'd strip out the lint filter and press the pad in a warm, folded towel with all the reverence of saving a funeral flower in a Bible. At home, she would slip it into her pillow case, pulling out the one from last time and silently launching it into the river, Viking-style. It always sank. Levi touched the new pad. It dawned on him this was weird. He plucked out a pair of Lam's panties and took them to the kitchen, where his mom handed him a yellow shirt.

"Them shirts come out pretty good, if I do say so myself," Virginia said, smiling like it might be Christmas. "And Lammy, don't think you're never gonna wear that red shirt. I didn't sew it for nothing. It ain't nobody's fault but yours you ain't singing. You'll wear it 'til it falls off, by God, and you'll like it too."

Levi faltered at something on his shirt, his mouth open, his eyes disbelieving. Virginia looked. "Well. Put it on."

Dread gripped the boy. *Why didn't she call the bowling store? Dang!* He winched a sleeve up one arm and then the other. He buttoned. He turned away from her, focusing only on the black stove, giving the shirt a chance to change. But that stove was no ally. He distrusted it. To Levi the shiny parts were there to trick him into touching, like last summer when he took for granted what time the fire was usually cold and slapped the stovetop with his normal bravado, blistering his palm and all five fingers. Decorations can be lies, his mom said then, to make a dangerous thing pretty. It always seemed unclear if she wanted fancy things or not. Since his blistering, the nickel trim had only made the cast-iron block appear blacker, heavier. A little sinister. The silvery name plate in front was rainbowed from heat. "Castle Crawford," Levi whispered, evoking images of a gray, malevolent dungeon. His eyes darted away. Beside the stove, a coal bucket of garbage bloomed, topped with empty boxes of Rit dye.

"Well? You like it?" His mother asked.

"Yes, Ma'am," Levi was afraid he didn't, so he didn't turn to her. "I need to comb my hair." He excused himself to the mirror in his parents' room. He stood before it and held out the shirt's belly like a shelf. It was not golden. Not even strong yellow. And the stitching was … *orange. Ahh!* He slapped his cheeks, dragging his fingers down hard. From the kitchen, his mom called, "*Time to go.*" He blinked back tears.

The family spread out and put on coats, boots and hats – except for Lam. She had stalled on a chair, silent, somewhere else, seeing nothing. Levi caught it first. He moved quickly. Softly he said, "Hurry up, Lam." Levi had seen dogs dream with eyes half open but only while lying down. Sometimes Lam did it sitting up, even standing. Months ago his mom told his dad, *Lam needs help,* but Frank had bellowed, *Shut up!* And *Hard to fix crazy!* "Hard to fix crazy," Levi mouthed silently, recalling. Levi had recklessly whispered, *You shut up.*

He paid a price for that. He touched Lam's shoulder. "Laura, come on, hurry up."

Lam looked at him as if he had only just then materialized. "Don't call me that!"

The kids climbed into the back of the Pontiac where Lam held Levi's hand. The hand twinged, but he left it with her. Up front, Frank gave the gas two pumps and over-cranked the starter. He lit two cigarettes with the car lighter, handing one to Virginia. They headed down the gravel road toward Highway 12. From the back, Virginia's silhouette seemed to buoy in amber, dash-lit clouds. Her chronic cough rattled the air. Turning to Levi, she said, "You make me proud," which he took as a command. The fancy women would be there. That made her scared.

When they drove past Geno's, Frank said, "The Buick's gone. Geno and Angela must've gone to the gym already." Purposely or not, Frank had just broken the no-talking rule for this part of the road, the rule that existed ever since Virginia didn't shoot him. She refused to look. He drove on, into town, past squat houses hunched with winter. "Do you want me to drop yous guys off in front of the high school?"

"I don't care. I don't like crowds," she said. Levi heard her open the glove compartment and rustle around for the tiny, dark-pillow flakes she often used as mouth perfume before she saw anybody not in this car. "You want a Sen-Sen?" she offered Frank. To Levi, the name sounded dirty. Sen-Sen. He liked it better when she said mints.

Nearly the entire county turned out. The Monroes had to park a block downhill from the high school and hike up the glazed street. They joined a clot of people at the end of a corridor of lockers, by a table of bake sale pies and cookies where Geno and Angela yakked it up with other folks. Lam eyed the sweets. Levi saw Frank search his pockets, wishing for change. In good weather, Frank worked at the lumber mill, but things had been cold for a while. Levi urged his sister along. The family passed trophy cases chock full of ancient photos of pale boys in gym shorts or jerseys. Soon they stood inside the charged gymnasium where bleachers and folding chairs were filling with people dressed in parkas and down and good cheer. On the walls hung big, student-made decorations – gold cardboard stars, cardboard trees and toys, and boxes with bows. Levi saw his classmates assembling on stage. He instantly wanted to leave.

Too late. Miss McKenny spotted him. At rest, her big arms angled passively out from her round trunk as if the death bloat had taken them. But she commenced waving. She raised a hand, hoisting with it a heavy slab of underarm that jumped about haphazardly, at great risk of slapping something silly, which it did, and a thick velvet tsunami rippled through the stage curtain. She eyed it like it was the curtain's fault, thereby releasing Levi to bolt, but his parents' dumb bodies had sandbagged him in.

Miss McKenny was coming at him, heels clacking woodily over the din. She got there. Though a vocal teetotaler, she held her fire at Levi's smelly parents. Instead she ordered Levi and Lam with a waving flipper of a hand. "Scrunch together. I want a picture." They did as she told, and a camera came out of some fold and the flash cube on top of it exploded, implanting a vestigial blue dot in Levi's sight. Before it cleared, Miss McKenny clamped her flipper onto his shoulder, pointed him at the stage, and swatted his butt. "Get behind the curtain and get ready. You're my song leader, right?"

Virginia crouched, eyes to Levi's eyes, breathing all licoricey-Sen-Sen-boozy. "Make me proud!"

Levi climbed the stage stairs as if they were gallows, looking back once. His family had claimed three folding chairs near the front, next to Thelma Anderson, a rancher's wife Virginia disdained for her new clothes and her whispering.

Levi trudged behind the curtain, his hands pocketed, arms locking his coat against his body. Golden everywhere. Each giddy classmate a deep-golden shirt with one breast pocket. One! Angela ran up, smiling so full of Christmas her eyes nearly closed. She yanked at a sleeve of his corduroy jacket. "Come on, Levi, you're the middle!" Levi reeled to escape. A boy in new pants, Thelma's son, seized his other arm and yanked, giggling. Levi twisted and flung his shoulders. "Let go! Let me go!" A rip cried out from an ill-mended seam. They let go.

Miss McKenny pressed in, ordering Angela and the rancher's son back into the golden picket-line. "Levi, remove your coat and get in your place." She stared expectantly. His eyes began to sting and he sniffed hard enough to collapse his bottom lip. Slowly he unbuttoned the jacket and peeled it back, exposing bold orange double-stitching and twin pockets on a pale yellow shirt. "I see," Miss McKenny said kindly, taking a deep breath. For the next few moments she glared at the curtain that shielded Levi's parents. "Well ...

we have what we have. Get in line … but not in the front, okay? In the back. Trade places with Angela."

Levi hid behind Angela. He concentrated on the long, gold ribbon that trailed from her hair. The curtain opened. From nearby, he heard his mom cough. He did not look up. He did not want to see her red and puffed up.

The children sang. An adult tittered somewhere – at him, Levi was sure. He began to cry. When the song ended, Miss McKenny pulled him behind the curtain. She sat him on a folding chair at the side of the stage, gave him his coat, kissed his head. His lungs emptied. He didn't want to refill them. As other grades sang, he donned his jacket and zipped it clear over his nose. Staring close-up, cross-eyed, he lost himself in the cloth ribs and darkening tear-spots. Colors seemed to drain away. "No. No," he whispered fast. "Don't be gray. Don't be gray." The fabric smelled of cigarettes and mildew. Between two songs he sensed his mother on the move – the scoot of a nearby chair, fading footsteps in her gait, big doors reverberating. "I'm sorry, Mommy," he whispered.

"Levi." He flinched. It was Miss McKenny. "Take off your coat and follow me. Hurry."

"She's not proud of me."

"Hm. Well, everyone'll be proud of you when you're on top. Now hurry!"

At the custodian's closet she helped him blow his nose. The janitor waited there with a gold cardboard star, taller than Levi. Levi recognized it as one from the wall. "Stand still," Miss McKenny said. She balanced one star-point on each of his shoes and leaned the prop against his nose, marking the spot with her finger. Right there she cut out a hole the size of his face. At his waist she belted the star to him with a long gold ribbon. "Can you see?" He could. She led him back to the stage, behind the risers and curtain.

The janitor lifted Levi to the top row as kids formed below him in the shape of a Christmas tree. Miss McKenny handed Levi a large flashlight. "Wave this at the audience," she said. "You're still my star." Again Angela stood before him, her hair loose now and no longer his shield. Levi wanted his father and Lam to get a good look, imagining their pleasant surprise. The gym lights dimmed and the curtain opened. Levi's eyes darted for their chairs, eager to rope them with his risen mood. *About there*, he thought, just inside the dark. So he sang loud and strong at that spot. He waved big, beaming like a moonlit king-of-the-hill.

Ninety seconds later, to joyous applause, the curtain closed while the ROTC team organized for their tribute to local boys in Vietnam. Angela smiled up with crescent eyes. "Can I have my ribbon back?" He untied himself and gave it to her. "Did you do your Lewis and Clark project?" She expected an answer. "You have to before Christmas." Levi was grinning, still buoyed beyond the point of distraction. "I made a canoe from popsicle sticks. If you want, you can come over and I'll help you. I got plenty more. Not tonight, though." And then she touched him gently. "Your mom and dad left. We're gonna give you a ride home."

By the time Levi emerged from inside himself, he was outside his house, sitting in Geno's Buick. The Pontiac was gone, a bad sign. The kitchen light was on, so Levi headed toward the door while Geno and Angela waited in the car. He passed a stew pot strewn on its side in the snow, a frozen slick of stew flopped out of it like a dead thing's tongue. He cracked the door and waved back to Geno and Angela. Levi bumped through the door to the smoky kitchen.

Frank was straddling a back-turned chair, Cagney style, guarding the dark bedrooms behind him. His dingy T-shirt was flecked with ash, his arm-hair glowing orange from flames that danced behind the teeth of the firebox window. On the table sat a half-full ashtray and a half-empty bottle of bourbon. No Virginia. Levi breathed as shallow as prey, his stomach tight.

With palms on the door to shut it, Levi's boots rode backward on a knuckle of snow. By the time he turned and met Frank's eyes, Frank had loaded a fresh cigarette in his mouth. In a burst, Frank's thumb sprung the hollow lid of his Zippo and brusquely spun down the striker, driving flame to tobacco before slamming things shut with a virile sound that dragged with it the smell of lighter fluid. To Levi, these were moves and sounds and smells of men, grown men with unspoken man-skills, men to be revered – or feared – for indefinable reasons.

Frank took a drag. "I hope you're proud. They laughed at us real good this time. For Chrise-sake! It's no wonder we ain't got no money." The volume rose. "Goddamn kids!" He spoke as if he were a victim of some outrage. "You knowed we didn't have money for no *shirt* before you signed up for that show! Who do you think we are?"

Levi heard Lam stir in his parents' bedroom. He bent to pry off his overboots.

"Look at me when I'm talking to you! I asked you a question!"

Levi stood, bootless, motionless, socks growing cold and damp. He didn't know the answer. Frank's shoulders flexed into a hunch. His teeth gripped his smoke. His brow contorted under its own weight. Levi absorbed the glare. Blackness closed in and framed that menacing face. It's outline seemed to pulse with Levi's heartbeat. Frank's face cinched tighter, forcing Levi's eyes to break downward, having seen in his father, himself. A queer sensation unfurled from his gut, everything fading … *No. No.* He blinked. Blinked. Colors. *They're fine. Colors are fine.*

"You think we're rich like Geno, or those fancy-ass ranchers with new pickups?"

Levi's eyes hustled back to Frank. *Answer, answer. Answer!* He thought. There was risk in the answer. Levi was often told who they were *not.* "No, sir."

"You think those people don't cheat?" Frank yelled. "You want to be a cheater?"

"No, sir." Levi teared up.

"Are we pansies? *You better not cry!* Only pansies need all that fancy shit. And only babies cry, so knock it off, or I'll give you something to cry about! Damn baby."

Frank glowered; Levi dried up. He willed his breathing to smooth so as not to provoke. A contest of stillness was born. Time passed. Finally, low in the stove's core, spent coals lurched and Levi flinched. Frank rewarded himself by pouring more bourbon. He lit another cigarette. Nothing followed. After a while, Frank glazed over, retreating inside his past.

Levi eased into a lingering, creakless floor-dance toward the sweltering stove. Its smudge-bright trim stared at him; its heat felt his face. He slowly pressed against it, feet steady, risking only one quick rubber-banding sway of his torso to keep from casting a shadow of coolness on his father's back. Levi reached the bedroom's sill. He dared not close the door. He tip-toed staccato across the dirty coiled rug, lifting arms to lift his body above it, birdlike, high, higher, crossing in quickened form. But the rug won. It always won. Shame leached out from the oval mat, nastying his feet. Without undressing, he mounted his bed, sloth-like, so the tattle-tale frame wouldn't squeak. For a very long time nothing in the house moved. Then, from the kitchen, a lethargic rustle stretched over time. A light snapped off. Frank went to bed. And Levi wished Lam was here. With him.

As if a hiding animal, Levi stared at the fluid, orange glow in the kitchen and waited. Soon they came: metallic pleas from tortured bedsprings, the perverse proxy for Lam's silence until her body was settled on that other muting rug, the malevolent twin of the one at his bedside. The dull, low thud of grown-up knees telegraphed through the floor. Inside Levi's head formed dark, moving pictures he didn't want to watch, smells he didn't want to smell. *Think of something else. Something else.* Reaching for anything, finding his father's question, "Who do you think we are?" Who were they? It was hard. Levi didn't know who they were.

They were sad, he knew. They were afraid. And they were angry. They were poor, with clothes that made people laugh and made his mom too sad to stay home. Levi thought he would like to be rich – even if that made him a baby or a pansy, or even a cheater. No matter what. Then people would like them. And his mom would laugh. And he would laugh. And Lam would… *Lam.* The house had grown silent.

Levi wanted out of himself – out, from the inside out. Right now! He wanted to be new, like new clothes, not… *THESE!* His arms crossed his chest and stuffed his shirt pockets with tensed fingers. The muscles of his belly clotted. His face strained. He clenched at the pockets, plowing nails through young skin, craving physical pain, aching for it. Legs stiffened, arms contracted, hard, harder. The pockets tore, waking bedsprings. A fresh jagged breath and pockets tore more. He grabbed at the button-line and yanked. It held. He kicked and wrestled, madly, and bedsprings wailed as he stripped the shirt over his head. He ripped his arms from inside-out sleeves and jerked the cloth from his head. And then he panted. Beside him, in one hand, lay a newly made rag, all yellow and dotted with blood.

When he looked, the length of his arm seemed a prop, not of his self. His hand lay heavy and stone gray while the shirt in it broadcast loud yellow. The queerness took a moment to grasp. Color, no color. No color, color. His eyes widened in terror. In the space around him, tracers lit up, chasing firefly ghosts. "Not these clothes! Not these clothes!" he hissed. He stripped urgently, completely. He choked the bright shirt and popped off the bed, overshooting his feet, stumbling headlong into the sweltering kitchen. On his knees, he pounded across the floor, mopping dirt with the enemy garment. The heat from the stove folded around his face. He reared and gripped the hot coil handle on the firebox door, wrenching open its black iron mouth. Inside, red-orange pustules pulsed as if breathing his breath.

Without warning, from behind him a chair stuttered across the floor. "What the hell are you doing?" Frank slurred loudly. Deep-belly booze wafted out.

Sounds and smells did not form into thoughts. Levi did not turn. He stood up to the stove, raising his free right arm and its free right fist that was strangling a wad of cloth. Awash in firelight, the shirt danced at him, danced, while his flesh mocked him with its utter huelessness. He punched his ashen fist into the heat, forcing the shirt down the stove's black throat, dumping it there. Garish coals ignited in a hole of light. Liquid. Gray.

As the room swelled bright, Frank swooned drunkenly, tripping over little-boy feet. On the way down, the ink crucifix on Frank's forearm streaked past Levi's face. At the end of consciousness, a big hand opened, groped, grabbing for anything. Levi jerked in reflex, as if to rise, but Frank's body broke over him. The man's hand found the boy's, pinning it atop the scorching metal door, smashing it flat with the weight of a lights-out drunk. By the time Frank fell away, Levi could smell his own charred skin. He retracted his arm. He stared at the soot-fused brand seared into his palm. His burned flesh rolled back in a death curl, dark to light – but gray. All was gray. His hand. His arm. His body. Gray. Then the world went black.

Dawn fluxed numbly through the eastern sky as Virginia kicked ice from the kitchen doorsill. She pushed inside. There, on the floor, spooned behind his father, lay Levi's naked, moon-blue body. Suddenly sober, she scooped him up. Once straightened, she hunched her shoulders over him, using his weight as ballast when she drew back and punted Frank's ribcage with the force of their collective anguish.

3

MEANS

Not all wounds that harm us can be cupped in our hand. Examined.
Often they are not even our own. They are not so plain, so near.
Some are curtained by mysteries, at once invisible and opaque.
Like time. And distance.
And circumstances of which our own
give us scant reference to conceive.

— Clyde Monroe

A cab stopped before a two-story home on Chicago's North Shore. 23-year-old Gary Crawford listened to the radio announcer revel in Nixon's resignation. He smiled callously. He sure as hell wouldn't have enlisted if Nixon hadn't ended the war. Now this. So it's Nixon's fault.

Gary paid the cab driver and got out. He wore the uniform of a second lieutenant, U.S.M.C. He looked at the house, the big elm. The blinds were open to her office. He breathed deeply, once, through his nose. Shouldering his rucksack, he opened the picket gate.

For August it was cool, but his armpits were slick. He fumbled his keys, sending them jangling across a stand of empty milk bottles. Soon he was inside. From the entryway he heard faint noises in the office. Mother. Alone, no doubt, by mutual consent with the world. Even the maid wasn't allowed in there. Screw it. He entered without knocking.

A spider-armed woman sat in a stern dress behind a massive walnut desk, scribing in a ledger. When she looked up, her surprise gave Gary instant satisfaction. They looked at each other as she poked a finger into a small, metallic tin of violet-gray, pillowy flakes, forcing some out, popping them into her mouth.

In a diluted German accent, she said, "What are you doing home?"

"I'm out of the Marines."

"What do you mean you are out of the Marines?" As expected, her voice swelled.

He mustered a stare, ripening the moment as long as he dared. Finally he dropped his rucksack on the floor and shrugged his shoulders. "I resigned."

Her bony palm cracked on the desk. "What do you *mean* you resigned? You cannot just resign! Officers do not just *resign* when they finish OCS!" She screamed, "What did you do?"

What did you do? His mother had asked that question every day while Gary was growing up. She had asked it of Gary's father until the day he took his own life.

She had married him, a blue-blooded playboy, after WWII as cover for her German heritage – and for the money. He was on the board of a bank, after all. His ancestors had allegedly amassed a fortune by forging Castle Crawford cook stoves. By the time Gary was born, she had ridden the man hard, fueling his alcoholism. Then she practically arranged his affair with the wife of his best friend at the bank. She publicly exposed his philandering and the shame finished him. She replaced him on the bank board and leeched control of his other assets.

The day Gary's father committed suicide she asked the ten-year-old *What did you do?* Over and over as she beat him. She asked *What did you do?* when Gary failed to make athletic teams or performed poorly in school. She asked it when Gary was rejected by Annapolis and when he got suspended from Catholic University for spreading salacious lies about a priest and a brilliant rival student. She asked it when a prettier priest volunteered to intervene on Gary's behalf to get him readmitted. *What did you do?* Now Gary had to wash off the question until the context at hand become real.

Staring blankly at his mother, Gary reeled his fists closed. "I applied for a post at the Pentagon with Admiral Kuckens, as you instructed. One of my classmates applied, as well, some hard-luck story a congressman appointed. From one of those dirt states. A classless hick of poor breeding, lacking, as you say, birthright to position. So I stole his application before it got mailed and altered his papers." His tone said, *So there.*

She stood. "Idiot! You got caught. How do you expect to succeed, to have authority, if you are stupid?" Gary didn't answer. "So you resign? Like that? Your *Großvater* would have died of dishonor."

"They asked me to, Ma'am. And this is America. *Großvater* was a Naz –"

"– An aristocrat," she finished, "unlike your father." Her words were a challenge for him to choose his heritage.

"They asked you to!" she sneered. "They knew *you* altered the papers?"

Gary lacked the wind for the whole story. What did it matter anyway? "I used carbon paper. They found it in a trash outside our quarters. I admitted it."

"You admitted it!" she roared. "Even Nixon isn't that stupid! *Dummkopf!* Who could prove it was you? It could have been another. Why would you tell the truth when there was nothing to be gained by it?"

Gary lifted his bag. "I'm only here to pick up a few things."

"And what do you think you'll do now?"

"I don't know. I need some time to think."

"There's only *one* thing you need to know. You have failed – again."

His mother leaned forward and put both palms on her desk. "But I will not have you embarrass us further by malingering. People talk." She wrote on a pad of paper. "I can't put you at that bank. They won't want you. So take this. Tomorrow you will go downtown. You will talk to my stockbroker, Mike Sandler. He is..."

"I know…"

"…the manager of Bookman and Stuart. He's smart, not like you. A Jew. Good for something. He won't want to lose my business." She offered the note, softening. "Take it."

He walked around the desk, lowering his head as he approached her. When he extended his hand for the note, she slapped his face. It stung. He said nothing.

A moment later she brought her face to his, cutting his muskiness with the aberrant, concocted perfume that was her breath, a mixture of vodka and Sen-Sens. She kissed him on the mouth. "Now leave my office. And remove that stinking uniform before you come to dinner."

The next day, in a grand building near LaSalle on Jackson in Chicago's Financial District, a disgraced Marine in a charcoal grey suit of fine wool and silk was hired as a broker trainee at Bookman Stuart. Mike Sandler, the man who hired him, could not have known.

Gary Crawford became the best salesman Sandler had ever seen. He did all Sandler asked, quickly and enthusiastically. And he was a guileful competitor.

He often volunteered to cover clients for brokers who were out. Then he picked his moments to sabotage those relationships to his own advantage.

One night while Crawford worked late, the janitor left the door to Sandler's office unlocked. Crawford stole the master key from Sandler's desk drawer. By the following afternoon he had made a copy and returned the original. Afterward – sparingly at first, not every night – he let himself into "the cage," a restricted area where the brokers' overnight orders to buy and sell assets in client accounts waited until the wire operator arrived at 6 A.M. Crawford would thumb through the stack of "order tickets," pulling an occasional ticket or two that were entered or "dropped" by brokers he disliked. It worked. By the time the broker or client noticed that the order had not been executed, it was too late. The broker was embarrassed and had to pay for any loss. The client asked Sandler for another broker. Crawford received a growing number of reassigned clients.

Crawford sporadically lifted messages from other brokers' desks, and sometimes he took phone messages from other brokers' clients without identifying himself and then failed to deliver the messages. Brokers quit, or got fired. More clients asked Sandler to reassign them. When a broker left for another firm, it took less than an hour for management to ravage a broker's "book," handing out client holding pages to voracious salesmen who waited at the manager's door for reassigned customers, often calling them before the departing broker had cleared out his desk. To people who made a living by prospecting, this was free money. But Crawford's strategy was flawed. Accounts were redistributed, but not so much to him. Crawford was given only inactive accounts or, worse, he felt, blue-collar clients. It was embarrassing, standing in line for crumbs. After all, he was the one who ridded the office of undesirable brokers – not that anyone knew. At one reassignment, he finally complained.

"I work harder than anyone," he argued from the crowd at Sandler's door. Sandler said more experienced brokers got the bigger accounts. "I work nights," Crawford countered, and Sandler said in a warning tone that married brokers are more stable and more motivated. "But I come from money...I understand moneyed people," said Crawford, thoughtless of his coworkers' growing hatred. Sandler said he'd like to think they all understood money and to pipe the hell down. Crawford pointed to one broker and said "But he went to state school."

"And I went to Michigan State," Sandler responded coldly. Then he dismissed Crawford for the day.

For a while Crawford received no account assignments at all, but thanks to his mother, he landed some of the biggest clients in Chicago – the mayor, a Fortune 500 CEO, others. Over time, he produced monstrous amounts of commissions. Sandler forgave him, invited him to his home. Still, Crawford begrudged anyone with advantage over him, particularly brokers who were rewarded for simply breeding. At first, he retaliated. He invented flirtations between married brokers and staff and mailed anonymous, scented letters to wives. But he knew he needed to marry to advance. His mother harped on it.

After appraising the families at her club, particularly their eligible daughters, she selected a target, a pretty nineteen-year-old with Aryan cheeks who had recently moved back home, unable to hack it at Vassar. She also happened to be the daughter of Sandler's biggest client. The debutant was dumb and she was gentry. She was perfect.

It was little challenge to get her drunk on vodka, repeatedly. She threw herself at Crawford plainly and often enough, but he was unable to respond right away – an anticipated complication for which he had prepared a response. His impotence masqueraded as chivalry until one night he finally thought he could do it by getting her to spice her breath with vodka and Sen-Sens, a smell that bore for him base and sensual implications. He told her it was a trick to mask her under-age drinking. He also said not to talk. Just breathe.

It worked, and he asked her to marry him. She said yes. Crawford had already fantasized how he would ask Sandler to be his best man, and how his mother would simmer in self-satisfaction. To her, the wedding was insignificant. She thought of the future. Sandler would toast the joy of the day. Crawford's mother would toast what her son might become.

4

A Lump of Coal

That's the nature of women …
not to love when we love them,
and to love when we love them not.

Miguel de Cervantes

Virginia drove into town on a summer day that began brisk, green, and dry. The radio news said President Jimmy Carter had just invited the muckety-mucks of Egypt and Israel to Camp David to see if they could stop fighting. The distant disk jockey said the weather would turn bad, thunder and lightning, by afternoon.

Virginia was headed to get the mail, but first she wanted to find old Doc O'Brien. At the coffee shop she approached his regular table, her thin neck and bony head poking up from the slouch of Levi's letterman jacket, petitioning attention like an unstuffed scarecrow. Doc looked up from talking with his coffee buddies and his squirrel-tail eyebrows rose sharply under a head of white hair with an ill-sorted seam. From his misbuttoned vest he fished out a rubber coin purse and counted out a dollar. Then he led Virginia upstairs to an office dominated by a rolltop desk and an oversized Norman Rockwell print of a girl and a doll and a kind country doctor, from which he had long tried to cultivate his look. Now he was too old to much care about that, old enough to have attended Virginia's birth, those of her kids, and everyone else's in town for the past forty years.

The office window was open but his cigarette smoke made them both squint from behind their glasses. His stethoscope chilled her exposed brisket. He drew it away. "You're killing yourself, Virginia, sure as hell." He pulled the cigarette stub from his lips and crushed it into the ashtray. "Part of it's these damn things. The other part is your drinking." He held her blouse open and felt her breast. His eyes followed a sweat droplet as it streaked down her side. "I'm done." He sat back. "You're sweating."

Without meeting his eyes, Virginia angled her hands up her back and hooked her brassiere. "It's polyester – the wonder fabric. Keeps you cold in the winter and hot in the summer. Wonderful." Her capacity for banter was thereby spent. "How much do I owe you?"

His eyebrows collapsed across his glasses frame and he looked as if his breakfast was repeating on him. "Are you listening?" She was more waiting. "Your belly aches because you drink. You're skinny because you drink and don't eat. You're depressed because you drink."

"I don't need drink to be depressed," she said. "I do that plenty good my own self." She stood and put on the jacket. "I ain't going to no doctor in Billings."

Doc shuffled between her and the door. "You have to get the lump X-rayed. You need new blood work. Not for your liver this time. It's, well, in case of cancer."

"I ain't going to Billings." She slung the car keys from her coat pocket.

He rested his hands on her thin shoulders and bent to meet her eyes. "I'll see what I can do about the cost. But you have to go."

She looked away from him, wanting him to look away too, to get out of her way.

He said, more gently, "What happens if you don't take care of yourself? Will Levi stay with Lam if Frank comes back? Would he skip college? Or would Lam be alone with Frank?" His words bumped a grim prospect inside her, one she had kept covered for years, and her eyes suddenly welled with emotion.

Doc reached into a desk drawer and handed her a package of samples. "Take one of these when you're feeling anxiety or abdominal pain. Don't take any more than two a day. And *don't* drink with them. They may even help the diarrhea." He took her hand and made her take the packet. "I'll call Billings to make an appointment for you. Hell, I'll drive you there if I have to."

"I ain't going to Billings," she said again, lower.

On the way home she stopped at the Busy Bee Café to tell them she was sick and needed someone to cover. Ten minutes later, when she rolled up in front of the house, Lam was at the car door, antsy to the point of dancing. The girl had only been home an hour or two, having the night before called late to say she was spending the night at Angela's.

Lam hardly talked to her anymore, as if Virginia had no more to offer. It made Virginia sad. She got out and gave Lam the keys. She looked long at a daughter who would not see her looking.

As Lam pulled away Virginia heard shoveling. She turned. Levi was refilling the coal shed. He was a strong. Smart. *Good kids. Help them, God.* Virginia made for the kitchen, where she opened a beer and laid out two pills on the table. One made a run for it. "Quick. Get away," she whispered. It rambled off the edge. She took another from the bottle.

Levi finally stopped shoveling. The shed was full, the ground outside glinting gray with dust and chips. At seventeen and nearly six feet tall, he was built like the head of an axe and nearly as hard, but moving the truckload of coal, a gift from the United Mine Workers local, had heated him up. He smeared sweat along his brow and tucked longish brown hair behind one ear. He rubbed the gray scar on his left hand as he ambled toward the house. He shaded the screen door and peered in. "Mom, I'm going to Geno's."

Inside the kitchen only a square beam of dull light from the kitchen window cut the dimness. The faucet dripped. Flies flew. Levi saw Virginia's bra-strapped back. She sat hostage-still on a kitchen chair made of chrome and plastic and duct tape. He stepped inside, blocking the recoiling door with his butt. "Mom? What'd Doc O'Brien say?"

Levi knew his mother drank more when she worried and worried more when she drank. Either way, she didn't eat. At thirty-three, her skin hung like a sleeve at her backbone. Her shoulders were bony as bat wings. She struggled with her digestive tract and the persistent hives she always seemed to be picking at. She was short of breath. Levi had never known his mom to be robust, but lately there was something darker and more distant in her manner. Her elbow was planted on the table, flagpoling a lit cigarette up beside one ear, dangerously close to tangled hair. "If you're not careful with that cigarette, years from now folks will be telling each other where they were when they heard about the Great Aqua Net Fire of '78."

"Doc O'Brien don't know nothin'." She muttered. "He says I need to go to Billings, but he knows we ain't got *in*surance." She swigged beer from a can.

Levi considered her words. He stepped toward the rattling icebox and pulled the latch handle. There was Kool-Aid. He grabbed a jelly-jar glass and eased the cupboard door back, careful not to close it completely, a habit from a childhood of noiselessness. Noise might incite something. The sound of other people closing doors made him wince, as if ducking at their mistake.

Levi finished his Kool-Aid, rinsed the glass, and put it on the drainboard beside his spiral notebook. In it, he had drawn point-and-figure charts, like ones in the book on stocks in the school library. He usually got day-old quotes from the *Billings Gazette* that Geno kept at the bar. Levi tucked the notebook under his arm. "I gotta go get the car."

"Do what you want." Virginia took a drag. "Bring your sister home," she added softly. He touched her shoulder and kissed her head, and the light around him seemed to shift. He ignored it. He pushed through the screen door and took his frets on a walk toward Geno's.

Levi needed the Starchief. He was lucky enough to have landed a summer job cleaning up around Number 4 mine, as it was. Getting there required a car. If he didn't find Lam at Angela's, he would have to bum a ride from Angela or someone at Geno's Bar that was reasonably sober. He kept walking, lowering his gaze from the sun's glare.

The eyes of Levi's boots were choked with coal dust; the stitching of the bodies to the soles, frayed. Each time he hopped a rail tie, his feet slammed up into the toe-box like his socks had been greased. Heat shimmered from the rail bed, smudging from sight a distant locomotive that whistled to Levi with more promise than lament. At a break in a hedge of weeds, Levi veered off the tracks and shot over a dirt cornice, dropping into the borrow pit precipitously enough to enlist gravity to sling up the other side onto the gravel frontage road. He paused once to chuck rocks at long, gray grasshoppers camouflaged in the gravel. The bugs invariably burst aloft, flashing yellow under-wings that thrapped like a tersely shuffled poker deck. All the rock hit was dust. Though things had been dry, change was coming. Over the sandstone hills, a wreck of bruised thunderheads gathered, and beneath them advanced a smell of rain that hastened Levi's gait.

Inside the bar, Geno was restocking while Angela swamped a polished hollow in the planks, long since worn there by public consensus that this was the sweet spot of the dance floor. At seventeen, she helped with chores until the rosaceous-faced early-birds arrived. Then she went home – next door.

When someone outside strummed the window screen, Angela looked up. She knew it was Levi, and she ignored him. He opened the whining screen door and it chased him inside until it bounced off its frame. He slapped his notebook on the bar.

"How's my angel?" He was looking at the coyote by the register, not her, as he settled on a stool.

"I'm fine." Angela straightened up and stretched until she faced the stamped-tin ceiling, pushing the heels of her hands into the small of her back, distending her taut belly at him, her damp blouse sucked against it. With a soapy finger, she pushed her eyeglasses up, wiped an itch on her cheek. She handed him some newspaper, wet from her hand. "There. Business section." She turned and cracked a roll of nickels on the till drawer.

"Did you ever notice that nickels taste like blood ...?" Levi said. "When you suck on them ... a little?" He folded the *Billings Gazette* to read the stock quotes.

"Lam's not here," Angela said. Though Lam was her friend, it still annoyed Angela that Levi more frequently stopped by the bar looking for his sister than for her.

"I figured as much when I didn't see our car." Just then Geno plunged from the walk-in cooler like a great, happy bear with glistening jowls, towing a handcart of beer like a Hamm's commercial. "Where'd she go?"

"I'm not sure. She came in late last night, and I was in here when she left this morning. I see she used some of my makeup, which is fine, but she left my mascara brush out. Tell her she owes me a new one." She read his face. "Hey," she reassured. "She slept right next to me. She smelled fine."

Angela watched Levi finger circles on the urethaned bar that entombed silver dollars like bees in amber. "Your car drove by a half hour ago with her in it, but she wasn't driving. It might have been Tommy Zupick. I saw her drag Main with him last night. He's a nice boy." Angela smiled at Levi's blue eyes. "You wanna go for *a run* this evening?"

"I thought you had glee club tonight."

"Well, I'm not happy about it. So, wanna run? Get, uh, sweaty?"

Geno finished stocking beer and surfaced behind the bar, sucking air as if he'd gone for the record. "Levi, I hear you finally got a job." He muscled up a big, meaty smile. "So how's Mr. Big Shot coal miner? Angel, why don't you offer the union man something to drink? You're thirsty, no? Dry, like a popcorn fart? You want a beer, big shot?" Geno said happily. Levi didn't respond. Geno shrugged. "Okay, then. Get him a Coke."

Levi looked at his blackened fingernails and pulled his hands off the bar. "I'm no coal miner, Mr. Granucci." His words sounded sharper than he intended.

Geno laid his big hands on the bar to begin a sermon, but Angela stepped on his foot as she set up the Coke. "Okay, okay," Geno said. "So you just visit the mines, and do things…for pay. For money. Oh, yeah, I almost forgot. I did what you said with US Steel and Alcoa – called my broker at D.A. Davidson. Hey, not bad. Maybe you are a genius. So I made a buck or two." He shrugged. "I'm a tycoon. So how do you do that, anyway?"

Levi had won the stock-picking contest at school for three years running, and he *couldn't* explain it. Like the other kids, Levi kept stock charts – only forty or fifty at a time. But it wasn't that. He just *knew* – like solving a math problem without steps. He knew where stock prices would end up. The information came as images, icons that illuminated or darkened in his head. Or emotions.

One time in science class, Levi sat in a closet while another student held up symbols on cards – squiggly lines, triangles, circles and such. Levi guessed what they were twenty-one out of twenty-five times. It scared the bejesus out of his lab partner. The teacher gave them both Ds for screwing around and then lying about it. Afterward the students fitted Levi with a mildly freakish reputation. So he stopped sharing, especially since the whole *Star Wars* "force" thing.

"Levi records things, Papa," Angela said. "Like weather, and politics, and how people talk and dress and TV news, and the grain and pig report, and stuff. It's all in the magic book," she teased, shaking jazz-hands above his notebook and saying "Ooooooooo."

"Oh, good," said Levi. "This helps."

"Sorry, Obi-Wan. You know I love you. What got into me? I need a run or something." She winked at him.

Levi had fooled with assorted methods of charting and graphing, teasing out patterns and groping for the right questions to ask. He sought to divine what people felt, collectively or just one person, before they did. By knowing this, he could know what they would do, or he could prophesize what would happen to them if they did nothing. So went his theory. At night, on the floor in front of the iron stove, he would spread out the charts, rearranging them in various ways, trying to take in all of them at once, to *sense* them.

Lam had watched him. At a sleepover she told Angela he got googly eyed.

Later Levi told Lam his eyes weren't any googlier than hers. Glazed, maybe. Or shivery. But not googly. All this crystal ball gazing seemed a little silly to Angela, but she never said that to Levi. She allowed him this quirky path. She figured he needed it in order to hope his way out of his screwy home life. Besides, she didn't over-think their future. She had the hots for him *now*.

"I still want to know how you do it," said Geno.

"He *feels* things," Angela purred like Peggy Lee singing *Fever*.

"Hey, hey, little girl! Watch it." Geno fidgeted, then, at Levi, "You want money? With your guessing, you should be a stock broker." Levi scoffed. "Hey, smarty," Geno said. "Coal miners take home some free coal. Butchers take home meat. What do money changers take home? Huh? Be a money changer. So. How's your parents?"

A year ago Geno had caught Virginia dipping in the till. Embarrassed, drunk, and pissed off, she set fire to the mule deer trophy her father had given Geno decades earlier. The only damage was a sooted wall and the putrid smell of burned hair, but Virginia was finally banned from Geno's for good.

Frank Monroe was recovering from an alleged ruptured disc, and Geno's Bar was too public for his recuperation. He cashed his disability checks fifty miles away in Billings Heights and bought a used GMC pickup, bright orange. Levi hadn't seen it, but it had been spotted at honky-tonks. One local couple caught Frank huddled over a candlelit table with Laura Darling, his bank teller, at Wong's Village in Billings. So money was tight for Virginia and the kids.

At Geno's question, Levi turned on his barstool and looked at the empty, sooty space above one of the booths where a deer head used to be. In the soot hung a plaque: "*Fires and Firearms Strictly Prohibited.*" Levi turned back to Geno, smiled, and drank his Coke. Geno abandoned the question.

Angela hammered the till's Total key, releasing the cash drawer against her damp belly. Levi watched his girlfriend's butt and read the letters carved in her wide leather belt, A-N-G-E-L-A. She fingered out a quarter.

"Hey," she slapped it down in front of Levi, "why don't you plug the jukebox for me? How 'bout playing *Crazy?*" Every barfly couple in the Western world thought it was their ballad. For Angela, if she was crazy in love with Levi, his crazy family came with him. It helped to embrace crazy. "Got time before work?" she whispered.

He gawked deadpan at her. Then his eyes crossed, he cocked his head, and ejected his tongue to one side. Crazy. He scraped the quarter off the bar. On his way across the room big rainballs began pummeling the parking lot, kicking dust and fresh smells into the bar. He inhaled. *Good work, God.* He pressed Wurlitzer buttons, which snapped back at him. Soon, piano notes meandered through a simple introduction. Angela floated to him with confident grace and proud posture. Patsy Cline's voice filled the room.

Angela slipped one arm behind him. She kissed his scarred hand. "This brand is mine, Cowboy." Levi flexed the lat muscles under his arms, acting unconscious of it. She loved gripping him there when he was above her. Shifting in melancholy time, he watched over her shoulder for Geno, who disappeared with the handcart into the cooler. Angela tightened her hold, pressing her wet belly against him, then sneaking an arm between them. She plucked open her blouse, exposing a lacy bra.

"This just came in the mail. Do you like it?"

He groaned. "Boy howdy." His face flushed. When he looked up, her gaze volleyed dreamily from one of his eyes to the other. Her hand found his ass. "Your dad…" he said.

"He can't see," she whispered, raising an eyebrow. She folded his hand inside her blouse. She glided a leg between his. "Where are you?"

"What do you mean?"

"I don't know. You smell like wind. Where are you?"

"Hm. I'm here." Levi was anxious. Something was wrong. "I should go find…" Angela pressed her crotch against him, insistently. Persistently. He felt a rush of arousal.

From the thick cooler door came a loud plunge, then a thump. Geno materialized out of cooler-fog. "Hey. Hey! Hey!" he hollered as if breaking up a fight.

Levi blushed, but before they broke Angela squeezed his crotch and grinned, pleased by her work. "I love you like a crazy," she said.

"Huh? Yeah. Love you like I'm crazy." Levi faced the jukebox, pretending to select another song. Something was wrong.

Lam had a date to take Tommy Zupick to the Tasty Freeze. The night before, while dragging Main, they had passed each other under the town's only traffic light. They waved. Minutes later at the A&W, Lam left the Pontiac with a girlfriend and rode with Tommy for a while. Like Levi, Tommy was a jock, going to be a senior. This was the first time he had shown real interest in her.

They stayed out late. He had been a gentleman – disappointingly so – but he asked to see her the next day.

So today Lam rodded down the two-lane highway, checking herself in the mirror, unsure of her own desperate beauty. Her blush seemed dotty. She rubbed it, connecting the freckles, and she popped her lips to even out the frost. She wore her hair straightish, parted in the middle, just like the women in the tatty copy of *Playboy* that Levi hid in black plastic in the coal shed. Her hair was long and lighter than Virginia's, though just as maddeningly roguish. She had used Angela's big curlers to organize it. She also borrowed a blouse, a size too large and intensely blue, and buttoned it to the top like Angela did, unintentionally underscoring her pale skinny face. Her mom said the boniness was her dad's fault. *Antlers*, Lam thought. That had become her nickname at school, given to her in gym class by mean girls who said she showered up like a stack of antlers.

When Lam pulled into the Zupicks' place, Tommy's older brother, Donny, an on-again, off-again college freshman, was perched on the concrete steps like a stray dog on a gravestone. She had heard he was home for the summer. He rose and angled cockily toward her, advancing until his hands rested on her open window frame. He smelled like Camels.

"Hi-ya, Lam? Remember me? … *You* look all growed up." His teeth were dappled.

She smiled and shifted her rump forward a bit. "Hi, Donny."

"I regret to inform you that Tommy went to Horsethief with his crew to shoot rabbits. Now, don't get mad. It's a man thing. They go every week in summer. He already told 'em he'd drive, so I told him he gave his word so he had no choice. I told him I'd tell you he's sorry. Real sorry."

Her face warmed with embarrassment, her form shifting in the blouse like something breakable.

"Now, I said don't get all mad, little girl." Donny leaned in with a stern, humored look. "He wanted to wait and tell you hisself, but they made him go. I told him you was Levi's sister. You'd understand. Knowin' what's right runs in families."

She nodded. "I guess. Thanks." She slowly reached for the gearshift on the column.

"Hold on now! We don't want ya goin' away mad. Hell, I'll go to town with you. You shouldn't have to h've drove out here for nothing." He smiled, though it didn't help his case. Before she was sure, he opened the door and shooed her to the passenger side and scooted in behind the wheel. He avoided looking at her by adjusting the seat and babbling about doing right by pretty ladies. He kept his window down.

They drove up Laundry Hill, toward the one blinking traffic light. It began to sprinkle. The Tasty Freeze was left on Main, but he jabbered their way across Main altogether, past the Farmers Union Co-op, headed for the river. Lam monitored his mouth for her turn to talk. Finally he parked under a cottonwood tree near the bridge to the fairgrounds.

Years ago Lam had attended the Fourth of July Rodeo there with her grand-parents. It was the first place she tasted cotton candy and the only place she had ever ridden a pony. At home, on the wall above her bed, was a black and white photograph from that day, one she always saw in color. It showed vibrant, popping cottonwoods behind her, a little girl, steadied in the saddle by her bow-legged grandfather. He wore drab green work pants and shirt, laughing toothlessly. His thin oily hair was disheveled as he drunkenly pointed at the camera. Lam held a red cowgirl hat on her head. She still owned the hat.

Usually the fairgrounds brought Lam visions of fun – fairs, rodeos, Bump-and-Run car races – but there, sitting there next to Donny, she saw only the pool of dread where she so often swam. She offered but timid resistance. He took that as permission.

She was aware she laid on her back, stripped on the front seat. Her inside-out jeans were discarded onto wet grass beside the open car door. Her blouse was open, her bra shunted above her breasts. One bare leg had been pushed over the steering wheel, propped on the steering column. "I really like Tommy," was all she said as he pulled out her tampon.

"Yeah, me too. He's my bro," was all he said.

In her mind his tongue became pickle-like. She was vaguely thankful he only kissed her once. The last thing she felt of him was the rasp of whiskers on her temple. Then she deftly disengaged from any consciousness of the act itself. She noticed the hoses and wires under the dash, different colors. She saw caramel-brown smoke stains on the gray velour ceiling. She counted the eight-note piccolo of a western meadowlark. A gentle, sage-tainted breeze tumbled into the car, onto her face. She lost herself in the rain that collected on the windshield as droplets broke loose and ran down the glass like sweat on her father's forehead. When Donny finally rose from her, she had no sense of time passed.

As he sat facing out, feet in the mud, he pushed his hair back and lit a cigarette. With a finger and thumb, he hoisted Lam's sopped jeans from the ground and backhanded them to her without comment or glance. The rain drove down at a right angle, some drops exploding on Donny's knees, some draping the car with water and sound, unable to wash the sex-stained air within. Lam sat with her jeans in her lap, staring through the windshield.

At Geno's, in the scorch-marked booth, Levi sat watching Angela watch the slowing drizzle outside the screen door.

"Just think, Levi," she said, "this time next year we'll be getting ready to go to Eastern. Dad says I have to live in the dorms." Then, whispering, "They're *coed!* Can you believe it?"

Levi stared past Angela, down the gallery of animal heads. "I don't have the money for college. Besides, everybody who goes to Eastern ends up back here. Shit. I don't even know anyone who finished." His fingers blindly spun the ashtray. He never thought she really got it. She had always expected to go to college. How *could* she get it? "I just want to get the hell out of here and make some money before I end up like them."

"Like the deer?"

"Those are elk."

"Whew! 'Cause the deer in here are dead." Levi didn't laugh.

"Levi, the kids you're talking about went to Eastern to party." She paused. "You can work part time. Maybe get a scholarship. Hey, maybe you should come to church with me sometime. Then apply at Gonzaga or Santa Clara, or Catholic University. Catholics are first in line to get in, and if you can't pay they –"

"We've been through this. I'm not Catholic – or Baptist or Presbyterian or Buddhist or Caesarian, for that matter. Ange, I appreciate your faith, but it's all hocus-pocussy to me. Crosses give me the creeps. You won't get me in there – ever. Stop trying."

Angela let go a laugh. "Well. We wouldn't want people thinkin' you're all hocus-pocussy, seeing visions and shit! Get it? That's funny. Laugh. Okay, don't. But remember, God works out of his house."

"He also makes house calls. I don't – do – church. The only savings I need is the spendable kind."

Angela touched his foot with hers. He didn't look. "Don't worry, Baby.

You'll go. We'll go. It'll be great – okay?" She dipped her chin to the table to get his attention. "Hot."

"I don't want to go to Eastern *fucking* Montana College!"

Angela pulled her foot away and sat up. She teared up. Levi trapped the ashtray and cringed for hurting her. Now he wanted her to look at him, forgive him. "They're drowning me, Ange." She looked, and he tried to make her smile. "I'm sorry." He was sorry. He wanted her to say it was okay. At least smile. Before he could say sorry again, a sheriff's cruiser passed a window.

5

THE LUMP

It's hard for an empty sack to stand upright.

BEN FRANKLIN

Fading thunder called from the east, bringing with it the rush of car tires wading into the parking lot. Levi looked out the door and watched the sheriff lumber through the wet parking lot as if he didn't like walking, and then open the screen door. The man paused, looking at Levi as though he had found the next of kin.

Everyone liked Sheriff Tuffy Jankovich, including Levi. He was strong and practical. He stamped mud from his feet like he was digging in.

"Howdy, Geno," Tuffy nodded to the back bar. Then, to Levi and Angela, "What're you two doin' in the bar? Little early in the day for drinkin', isn't it?" He smiled wryly and the toothpick jutting from his mouth became erect.

"It's okay," Geno said. "They're still drunk from last night. That one's looking for his sister."

"Thought you might be. Why don't you come with me?"

Levi's stomach tightened. "Is she in trouble?"

"Not with me, she ain't."

Levi sat in the front seat beside a truncated shotgun with worn bluing. From the back seat, dirty-body smell wafted through the wire partition. They drove past the Farmers Union Co-op where, as a boy, Levi had drunk grape pop and listened to the men while his grandfather bought bags of concrete or chickenfeed. Next they passed the dump, where Levi and his father had scavenged for bicycle parts, then the drive-in theater where Levi and Lam had been smuggled inside in the trunk of their car.

Finally they arrived at the fairgrounds, nearing an oxidized car that shined dully, like a giant, muddied whetstone. Levi spotted Lam on the passenger side. On the driver's side a man sat with one leg out the open door, smoking a cigarette, his head cocked as if listening for grasshoppers.

Tuffy coasted the patrol car to a stop "Are you okay?" he asked.

Levi nodded, all the lie he needed, and got out. Tuffy got out too, laying his arms on the roof of the patrol car and letting the boy go ahead. Long grass whipped streaks into Levi's pants as he closed the distance. Donny flicked the cigarette into the grass and waved like a relative. Three steps from the car, Levi made out Lam buttoning her pants.

Levi measured his stride perfectly. You don't swing hard when you hit a home run. It's timing. He pivoted his hips and shoulder through a crushing right hook that drove Donny's head into the doorframe, dropping him like a heart-shot deer.

"Oh shit!" said Tuffy, scrambling around the cruiser. When the lawman hit the wet grass, his cowboy boots skated away with him, giving Levi time to swing his foot like a sledge and rock Donny's ribs like dead thunder. Then Tuffy was on him. A slap rang Levi's ear. "You dumb son of a bitch! What the hell's wrong with you? Get away from this car!" Tuffy body-checked hard and Levi dropped a knee in a puddle.

Donny's left eye was swollen and his right ear bloodied, but he was coming to and angry for meat. He lurched to his feet, trying to charge, but Tuffy collared him. "You mother-fucker!" said Donny. "You bastard! You're crazy as your fucking mother! I better never catch you alone, you son of a bitch – you or your fucking whore sister!"

Inside Levi a flash-fire ignited, propelling him at Donny, but Tuffy managed to block him. "I'll arrest *both of you* if you don't break it up! Levi, get your ass in this car and drive your sister home! Donny, get in the squad car! I'm taking you home. And if I hear any shit from either one of you later, I'll throw *both* your asses in jail! Got it?"

Levi snorted and pitched himself into the Pontiac. He slammed the door and fired the engine. Through the windshield, an ooze of fluorescence seemed to bleed through the treeline as if liquid sky found a torn seam. As he dropped the shift into gear, his hand and arm seemed gray. He shot Lam a look. "I don't know how long I can keep doing this." She neither focused, nor heard.

Levi drove back through town and out the other side, often checking the rearview mirror; for what, he didn't know. He drove past Geno's, crossed the railroad tracks, and headed down the frontage road, parallel with the wooded riverbed. Not until gravel rumbled beneath the tires and he smelled the sweet tang of fermenting silage did he relax enough to note his ripped knuckles atop the steering wheel. Finally he rounded a stand of chokecherry and lilac bushes. Home. He felt tired.

"You gonna tell her?" Lam said.

It startled him. It was as though a mannequin had spoken. "Nah," he pulled the keys from the ignition. "Everybody knows you're the future of the family. Why spoil it?" He gently put his hand on her damp knee. "Come on, we're home."

Inside, Virginia felt the muffled thump of a car door. Through a veil of eyelashes she peered down, at the table, at her yellowed cigarette fingers. A long cylinder of ashes had broken over them. The stub had fallen under her hand and burned itself out. Her arm was but a thing. She summoned it toward her body and felt the sticky skin of her forearm peel from the tabletop. Head down, she exhaled. Her breath burned her chest. Another breath, another burn, reminding her of the one she just forgot. She tried to focus. No bra. Her breast appeared dirty. As if from a great distance, she willed her fingers to her nipple. Dry. Flaky. Rough, but soft. Cool to her fingers. She slowly cupped it and pushed gently at it. Nothing. She felt nothing. It was as though touching something foreign. She lowered her chin and tried harder to focus. With the back of her wrist she plowed her glasses back up the bridge of her nose, but images remained bleary. She uncradled her breast, pulling tacky skin from skin. When finally she held her hand out to arm's length, she saw the blood. Behind her the screen door bounced against its frame.

"Mom?" She was sitting where Levi had left her hours earlier, but a stark rod of sunlight now stabbed through the kitchen window and hit her bare-knuckle spine. Her bra had died on the floor beside her. A thought hammered a sharp note down Levi's taut nerves. This wasn't just normal crazy. Something worse.

He edged up to her. On the table a toppled beer can had rolled in ashes. Next to it lay a boning knife – covered with blood – and blood on the table – and her breast. Terror scraped his insides. "Oh my God! Oh my God!"

"What?" said Lam.

"Shit! Get some bandages! Oh my God!" He dabbed at her splayed breast like it was something hot, frightened by red-yellow curds of fat. "Get some towels! White towels! And peroxide. And…shit! And tape – tape! Shit! Duct tape!"

Virginia tried to touch her breast, but Levi deflected her. "No, Mom. No!"

She cried feebly. "I'm sorry." Her teeth weren't in. With arms dangling from her shoulders, she looked down, bug-eyed, as if discovering the wound. "It's okay. I'm so sorry."

Lam returned, heaving supplies crashing across the table. Levi spilled peroxide on Virginia's chest, and her eyes rolled back as it boiled out of the wound to her waistband, forming a rusty gutter of froth. He hastily dabbed her with a towel.

"Lam, hold her hands."

Lam bawled, but did as she was told.

They slid her to the floor. Levi forced Lam's hands to the wound. "Press!" Lam pressed hard, moving only to let Levi pack in all the gauze they had. Again he doused her in peroxide, and then ringed her ribs with towels. Lam held them while he circled her with duct tape, careful to spare her skin. "Mom, we've got to get you to a hospital."

"No, kids," she whimpered. "We ain't got no money. We ain't … I'm so sorry."

Levi snatched Virginia's dentures and stashed them in his shirt pocket. "Lam, get the door." He gathered his mom and hoisted her, carried her outside. "Get a blanket. Quick!"

Lam bolted to her parents' room, hurdled the coiled rug, and stripped off the bedspread. Less than a minute later she was holding her mother in the back seat of the car, sobbing.

Levi drove madly away from Roundup, toward Billings. The prairie screamed vividly past – viridian and sage, sienna and buckskin – and the sky radiated cobalt. But held against it, curled atop the steering wheel, Levi saw two gray hands. In the mirror, flat, gray irises with charcoal pupils flexed at the sight of him.

At Billings Heights the car slowed and backfired. Only then, ten minutes from St. Vincent's Hospital, did Levi speak. "When we get there, you call Dad and tell that son-of-a-bitch to come get her. I'm done."

An hour later, behind an emergency ward curtain, a physician sewed up Virginia. She mewed, *I can't pay. I can't pay,* but he ignored her, the reserve of his attention allocated to scolding Levi for not fetching for biopsy the tissue she cut out.

Levi blinked. It dawned on him. This would be the exact instant of his release. "Thank you," he said, as if he were a beggar offered a meal. The befuddled doctor strode off disgustedly. Levi sent Lam to a pay phone. He stood a while, hearing public sounds of strangers' private pain. His legs shook as if used up. His mother drifted off. He kissed her forehead. "I'm sorry, Mom," he whispered.

A month later, in a crisp, early-autumn wind, Angela waited for Levi on the courthouse steps. Suddenly Frank Monroe forced the big glass doors open, blew by her and descended the concrete steps to his curbed car. As he sped away, Levi emerged.

In one, short hearing, the County of Musselshell had emancipated Levi Monroe from his parents. With the exception of the rights to drink and vote, he became a lawful adult. He could make legal contract – borrow money, rent an apartment, get married. He could leave.

Later that afternoon, sitting side by side on the cut bank of the tired summer river, Angela told Levi, "Dad says you can stay in the extra storeroom behind the bar until you finish high school. We can convert it." Her legs swung freely, pendulums of optimism and possibility.

"I can't believe your dad wants me to stay that close to you."

"That's why you can't stay in the house. I had to cry, as it was." She giggled.

"Oooo, pulled out the big guns, huh?" Levi tossed a rock in the water. "I'm afraid, Angela. Afraid to be here. I can't be near them anymore. I need to … get better. I'm moving away."

"You'll be fine. You won't have to be near them. Your folks don't go to the school and Dad won't let them in the bar. It's just for a while. One year, not even that."

"You don't understand. How could you? Ange, I need to get away, have to."

Next he said something he had never said out loud. "When I'm very upset … or very afraid … usually when they're nearby … I … I stop seeing color." Angela's legs stopped. She cocked her head as though trying to decipher him. He spoke carefully. "Not everywhere. On myself. I stop seeing color on myself. And sometimes on what I'm wearing. It's gray. Like this." He turned up his palm and touched his scar. She said nothing. He pointed at the skyline. "And the sky glows, around trees or hills, sometimes. I'm afraid. If I stay … I'm afraid…"

"Is this like the charts?"

"No. Different. The opposite. The charts don't scare me." A chill ran through his skin. "Fuck, I'm probably crazy either way. Please understand. I have to get away. I have to."

A day passed while Angela drove Levi around town to say goodbye to a few people. She went with him to pick up some things at his folks' house. Only Lam was there. He said he was sorry. "I will be there if you really need me."

She wore that faraway look. "I know." She had already surrendered.

He made her look at him. "I will be there."

Angela drove Levi to Billings. He would stay with an acquaintance while he got himself signed up for the high school equivalency exam and looked for work. She cried all the way home.

That afternoon, as the late-day sunshine warmed them on the porch swing, Angela buckled into her father's arms and he kissed the top of her head.

"Why wouldn't he stay?" she asked.

"He loves you," Geno said, "but people can only love as much as they can hurt. God help him now. God help him," he smelled his daughter's hair, "and those who love him back."

6

WHACK-A-MOM

The sick are the greater danger for the healthy;
It is not from the strongest that harm comes to the strong,
But from the weakest.

FRIEDRICH WILHELM NIETZSCHE

It was two years before Angela talked Levi into seeing his parents, and they drove out of Billings late because Levi had gotten hung up at the radio station. As his car slashed the rain-slickened, two-lane highway from the east, from Billings, they closed on Checkerboard. She was troubled that the last of the day's light was fading behind the Crazy Mountains beyond them as the peaks ripped holes in iron-colored clouds.

She had baited him to this scrubby, backwater outdoor sportsman's enclave. Frank, Virginia and Lam would meet them there, she said, for a weekend of camping and stream fishing. Lam was the bait. Angela knew it. So not until they were well down the 100-mile road, past the elbow at Lavina, did she tell him Lam had begged off.

"You have got to be shitting me."

"It's not Lam's fault," Angela said. "She's been throwing up."

"Maybe she should stop partying. Shit! I took time off for this?"

"Stop it. The radio station won't go off the air if you play hooky a few days. You'll sell plenty of ads later. And you can still draw your charts when you get home. Besides, I took time off from school. That's not convenient either, but it'll be fun."

"*Honey, let's go camping!*" he mocked. "*With your parents! It'll be fun!* Oh, yeah, those words go together. Kind of like *vacation Bible school.* I'd rather be beat with a brick stick."

"Come on. It's high time you saw your folks. They're still your folks, you know. It'll be fun! And I don't think that's why she's nauseous."

"Ange, if you'd taken a scholarship back east, you wouldn't be taking this time off. Neither would I. What do you mean about Lam? You don't mean …" Angela remained quiet. "Oh, for Chrisake."

She touched his hair, smiling. "I don't really know about her. She says the rabbit hasn't died yet. And if I'd gone east, I'd've missed all this fun with you. Ever think about that? Huh, Mister Happy Pants? Didja?"

"Where did you say we were meeting them?"

"At the bar."

"At the bar? The bar in Checkerboard?" She nodded. "Oh, that should work."

A few miles later, at a dark, ragged stretch of country highway, they came up on a few used-up cabins, a few vintage trailers parked in ways between purpose and abandonment, and the one going concern in Checkerboard – the bar. Levi rolled through puddles and swung the headlights toward the neon. There, nosed ten feet from the bar's front door, sat an old orange pickup puttering back exhaust that fogged up through the rain into the truck bed and then up a glistening back window grilled on the inside with a gun rack and a shotgun that didn't hide the back of what was most surely Frank's head. By the time they parked next to Frank, the man was slamming his door to come around and talk. It was clear he was pissed. Levi rolled down the window.

"Your goddamm mother," he started firing, without even a how do you do after these couple years, "started drinking the minute we left Roundup," at which point he threw an empty can he'd been holding into the truck bed of camping equipment, "and was drunk as hell by the time we got here and accusing me of sleeping with your aunt Frances, who I only kissed once in high school over twenty years ago before I even know'd your mom, which I told her. If I had any shells for this shotgun I'd shoot her, I swear to God!" It was May and hunting season was long passed, so he didn't keep ammo handy. He was panting. "Then she starting yelling at me for sleeping with women if she died, which she just might if she keeps it up, including that damn Laura Darling I ain't seen in a coon's age and don't intend to ever and I said she was being ridiculous and yous was coming here to camp so pipe down. So she says I'm sleeping around and I says I'm not and she says I'm a lying son of a bitch and don't I deny it! I do deny it, dammit!"

Angela looked at Levi who had been looking at his dad with no look at all and then looked at her with one that says *I've seen this stupid-ass show, and if you don't change the channel, I'm going to bed.* Then he looked back at Frank.

"Is she in the bar?" asked Levi.

"Hell no!" Frank said as if it were a dumb question, "She's took off walking, back to Roundup. I said she can't walk no ninety miles in the dark in the rain, and drunk, but she said, 'Don't you think I can't,' and she took the hell off. " He backhanded toward the highway.

"Why am I not surprised?" said Levi. "Did you try to stop her?"

"Hell no. I waited here for you," he accused.

"We got hung up," Levi said. Then he looked at Angela as if he needed to grit. "Why don't you go with Dad. One of us'll find her on the highway. Jesus."

So Angela got out. "I'm with you, Dad." Even under these circumstances, it felt good to call him Dad, now that she and Levi were engaged. It was the first time she'd said Dad like that, to Frank.

"Shit," Levi said.

They took both vehicles and convoyed east and west on the narrow blacktop in progressively lengthening legs, shining flashlights out the car windows into the ditches. Occasionally they'd sense her moving, untamed image a quarter mile beyond the frenetic windshield wipers, on the road ahead. Each time, by the time they got there, Virginia had disappeared through the weeds, out of sight in the barrow pit. They'd turn around and retrace, only to catch a distant glimpse of her … or a deer – something – before it melted into liquid ebony. Angela listened to Frank swear that if Virginia held still for any time at all he was going to knock her into next Tuesday. It was unclear if he meant to use the pickup. On each unsuccessful pass, to Angela's dismay, Frank would speed away as if leaving Virginia for dead – perhaps hoping – thinking the specter of abandonment would spook her to her senses. It did not. The more Virginia popped up and down, the more frustrated the men became. Finally the vehicles stopped side by side, windows down. To lighten things, Angela suggested they all just think of it as a game of Whack-a-Mom – like at the county fair with plastic rodents and a padded mallet. The men actually laughed, but it didn't last.

After midnight, Levi flashed his lights and stopped alongside Frank. They rolled down their windows, and Frank waited while Levi stared forward into grays and blacks, the only sound between them the hiss of rain. "Mom's gone," he finally said. "She's not out here anymore." Everyone knew the tone – that tone when Levi knew.

They followed a big rig to a bar in Harlowton. An old bartendress told Angela that a half-hour earlier she'd served a quick shot to a sopping, wild-eyed woman while her road-ripened companion hit the john. The man came out grinning, she said, eager to gittyup. Didn't stay five minutes, she said. A real pair to draw to, she said.

So the thwarted campers retreated to Roundup.

A big-rig was parked out front. They found Virginia sitting at the kitchen table, drinking beer and showing scars to a trucker. He was a sociable coot with a spark of mischief that misfired when the family arrived and snuffed altogether upon learning that Virginia wasn't a widow after all. About then, Lam's bed squeaked. He grinned and ill-advisedly asked if Virginia had a sister. Frank turned red. Virginia, apparently sensing the relative unattractiveness of her now-exposed marital circumstances, made a big show, telling Frank that he was dead to her – dead! – after which she angrily flung a pad of laundry lint into the coal stove to prove it. She stomped off to the bedroom. Slammed the door. Frank glared at the trucker with molten intent. The trucker left.

"I'm gonna kill the son of a bitch," Angela heard Frank say as he headed for the kitchen cabinet where he kept his ammunition. Levi blocked him. "You ain't that big, boy." While Frank warned, Angela heard a bump in the bedroom and slipped the door open a crack. The small curtains on the open window were waving at her, darkening with spatters of rain. *Not good!* she thought. She hastily shut the door and headed for the pocket of Frank's coat and his car keys. She had to get outside without the men, especially without Frank.

"I'll wait in the car," she said, trying to sound peeved and not alarmed. The men were fully bristling at each other, fists clenched at their sides, neither one willing to break the other's stare. She headed out the door, quickly, but short of telegraphing panic, just as the trucker's semi engine thrapped to life. She saw the top of Virginia's head in the passenger window and rushed to the door of the semi, but as she reached for the handle and lifted her leg for the wet sidestep, Virginia spotted her and slapped down the door lock. Angela hopped down. The big rig lurched into motion, jerking its trailer on gravel, back toward the highway. "Oh, my God." She looked back at the house. There was shouting. She bolted to Frank's pickup, fumbled to unlock it. She flung the door open and grabbed a shotgun from the rack. "No shells," she repeated to herself, but ran with it to her car and threw it in. "No shells."

She peeled down the wet gravel lane. It didn't take long for her to catch up and flash her lights, again and again, at the trucker. He ignored her. A quarter mile up, at the muddy T in the road, there were two choices down the frontage road, left and right. Either one got you to a railroad crossing to the highway. Equal distance. The semi swung wide and right. She'd never be able to pass him on this rutted strip. She laid her forehead onto the steering wheel. *What?* She whispered. She lifted her head and faced the fogging windshield. Mashing her hand against it, she wiped, slowly at first, and then with vigor. Then she cranked the wheel deliberately, left, and hit the gas.

A mile of gravel peppered the undercarriage, and she barely slowed for the upcoming turn and anticipated how the car would fishtail, using the slide, like driving brodies on ice. The car launched over the tracks and banked onto the highway. She steered against the slide, straightening it, and she accelerated up the blacktop toward the other crossing. At 200 feet from it, she could see the glow from the lights of the semi moving parallel along the frontage trough on the other side of the tracks. They were slowing, beginning to swing wide toward her. She punched it. As he crested the crossing, his beams angled up into the rain like searchlights, and she was already riding the brakes, just short of skidding on the pavement. She dumped off the side of the blacktop, onto gravel again, aiming at the tracks. Her leg pumped, dynamiting the brakes and blocked the big rig's access to the blacktop highway. She was getting out on the dark side of the car when he blasted his horn and bellowed out his window at her. He was honking the second time when she stepped into his lights and raised the shotgun at his windshield.

Inside the cab, the trucker's eyes got big, and even Angela could hear him yell "Get out!" Virginia said something and waved her arms, and Angela heard, more clearly, "Get the hell out of my truck! Now!"

When Angela pulled Frank's pickup in front of the Monroes', the first thing she saw was Lam silhouetted in the kitchen window by light from behind, dressed in what appeared to be her nightgown, peering out at something. Frank and Levi were outside in a standoff, both drenched. The pickup's headlights called them to action. Frank had his sleeves up, rifle in front, gripping the stock hard in one hand. On the other, his flexed and dripping, mud-green cross waved above the weapon in big-bodied gestures. Levi was pointing hard at Frank, all the while playing keep-away with his free arm pendulously hefting about a steel ammo box. Lots of yelling. When Angela stopped, they stopped.

Before Angela could kill the engine, Virginia, looking like she'd been dragged from the river, popped out and slammed the pickup door. She splashed between the two men on her way through. "You're dead to me," was all she said, this to Frank.

It was 3:30 A.M. Levi began driving back to Billings before Angela buckled her seat belt. The fireworks began as soon as they were on the highway.

"Now do you get it? Now do you understand why I don't want anything to do with them? Now do you see how fucked up they are?"

"I see what you see," she said calmly, as if she saw more. "It's a miracle they get by at all. I think if people are hurt long enough and deep enough, especially by those they love, they try anything. Or give in."

He waited. "What the hell does that mean?" he said. She touched his leg. "You don't get it! And what the hell do you think you were doing? Fuck!"

"Your Mom's home. The trucker's gone. Nobody got shot."

"*That's* the miracle. What the hell! *You* could've been shot. That gun you took didn't have any shells, and you knew it! Shit. What if he shot you? What the hell were you thinking?"

"I knew what I was doing."

"How the hell could you have known? Tell me that." He looked in the rearview mirror at a set of headlights, set higher than a car.

"I was raised in a bar, Levi. No piece of ass is worth getting shot over."

He winced. "Oh, please. She's my mom." Then it went silent for a mile.

"How'd you know?" she asked.

"What?"

"How'd you know she wasn't out there anymore? At Checkerboard. I … How do you know those things?"

He started to say something and stopped. Then, "We hadn't seen her in a while. Nothing mysterious." A moment passed. "And I'm not *going* to see her, or Dad, again. Don't ask me. I'll see Lam, but not if they're there. Don't ever ask."

"I won't ask."

Two miles passed. The windows fogged as their clothes and hair warmed.

Angela turned on the defroster. Levi looked at the rearview mirror; the headlights behind him had almost faded in the distance. He cranked the rearview mirror away until he didn't have to look.

"Do you see?" he said.

She looked. The dash lights painted his face as he stared down the highway. "Yes. I see," she said. Then, "I want you to know I'm truly sorry for my part in arranging this fiasco. I just wanted to bring the family together. I thought that could happen." She waited a moment. "I do love you, you know. Without condition. Forever."

Events raced through his mind and he raced alongside them, keeping up, keeping up, with clips and images, amplified – an hour ago, a decade ago, a lifetime ago. He looked at her, *beheld* her, his fiancée – his ... Angela, as never before. What came next took but an instant. Before him, right now, at this moment, she materialized anew, so *tangibly* anew, so ... physically so; yet more. He felt awe. And outside, the world raced. While inside – memories, memories, memories, and this moment! Racing, racing on now, disengaged from him, engaged in her, disregarding him, forgetting him. An instant only. But enough. To feel it. For the first time ever, events, past and present, dark and bright, dared to wheel past without his callous, strident resolve pressing them forward, matching their motion, contesting them as the true cause, contesting which drove – the profanities that had forever affronted him, happened *to* him, or what he believed he willed to come true in his life. For the first time ever he lost traction, lost the illusion of pressing events past him, seized still in the discovery of his Angela, a truth unmade by him, and in his arrest felt the great, dense yolk at the center of his life roll forward without aid or need of his accord. Something had ended. Something began. He – *beheld* her, anew. And there she was. And he knew that he had never trusted anyone so much. And it occurred to him that he had felt that way for a long time. Perhaps since grade school. He had taken her for granted. Discounted her. Unable or too selfish to sense the burgeoning wisdom beneath her sureness, the ballast her experiences had laid away, the depth that her character had quarried. In all the world, he had been unable to even imagine such complete admiration – for anyone – as that he felt for her at this moment. "Yes," he was able to say. "I do know."

PART 2

THE 1980S

7

Dance 'til the Coughin' Arrives

Buffalo gals, won't you come out tonight,
And dance by the light of the moon?
Anonymous

Over the next couple of years Virginia developed an uneasy but peaceful coexistence with Frank and with her body, which endured as long as she didn't look directly at either of them. So they might not have caught the cancer in time if the pigs hadn't gotten out.

The previous autumn, the rancher who had given Geno the stuffed armadillo died. In order to pay estate taxes the rancher's heirs sold the livestock and put the land up for sale. There remained a silo full of fermenting corn stalks, or silage, which was useless without animals to eat it. At the bar Geno happened to tell Frank Monroe that the silage was free for the hauling. From there, Frank's reasoning went something like this.

Pigs gotta have accommodations. The Monroes' house – more correctly, the county's house in which the Monroes lived – had an old dirt-yard chicken coop, strapped together by some long-forgotten inhabitant. With a little fixing, Frank reckoned it could hold a few pigs. Piglets were cheap. Silage was free. Grown pigs were money. So Frank drove over to Two Dot and bought piglets from his brother-in-law, Sam. On a crisp day, piglets were dumped into the ramshackle chicken yard that held up a mountain of sour silage. Winter came. Pigs grew.

On a snowy Valentine's Day, Virginia's sister, Frances, and her husband, Sam, drove over from Two Dot to double-date with Frank and Virginia to a dance at Riverside Hall.

That afternoon, the women dyed each other's hair. Sam made highballs from bourbon he'd brought. The kitchen thickened up with cigarette smoke, AM country music out of Billings, ammonia from a bottle of auburn Miss Clairol, and rinsewater. And rinsewater. Rinsewater. "Auburn" printed on the box might have been an estimate. The chatter and the fumes drove the men outside periodically, but men can only admire pigs so much. So finally they headed into town to the Model Grocery to buy candy-filled cardboard hearts and then over to Geno's for tap beer. By the time they got back, the women were lit and their hair was campfire orange.

"I'll be go to hell," said Frank. Virginia and Frances howled, pointing at each other.

"Yup," said Sam.

When it came time to dress up, Virginia and Frances cackled and zipped each other's dresses. Frances had forgotten her foam rubber falsies, so the gals went on about who should stuff their bra with Virginia's. They didn't have a real boob between them. They goaded the men to vote, but Frank and Sam weren't just married yesterday and would not. It was a tie. Ties went to the house. After all, they were Virginia's falsies. They each had their own nylons, high heels, and costume jewelry. The men put on bolo ties and Old Spice. Took three minutes.

Finally, about seven o'clock, after the couples had had a few drinks to get ready, Frank shuffled across snowy, moonlit gravel to start the car and warm it up before the drive. The engine cranked and an unearthly scream broke lose from under the car. A boar bolted across the headlight beams, hell-bent for a bare tangle of lilac bushes. Frank stared until his eyes adjusted. The ghostly snowscape between the car and house was pregnant with dark, meandering moguls that occasionally bumped and grunted, surging swift and brief. The chicken wire had given up.

For an hour Frank rodeoed the pigs while his friend, Sam, jigsaw-mended the coop with scrap lumber. Virginia and Frances screamed, "Run, piggy, run!" They laughed hard when a young pig bit Sam; harder still when Sam bit back. They delighted in the alliteration of *big balled boars* and called *sooo-weee*, each time more raucously than before, until the sport was over.

The men, triumphant and up-blooded in dirty slacks worn proud as grass-stained football pants at homecoming, feigned disgust as they washed up. Each sensed the forthcoming social esteem from a good story well corroborated. *They're smart as some people,* Sam said. *Smarter'n some,*

Frank said. Later, at the dance hall, the story was pitched with mighty power. Women loved it. It became grand and risqué fun for all the gals in attendance to gaily bawl *sooo-weee* at their men.

Inside, most of the revelers got pretty drunk, pretty sweaty. Outside, a cold front – an arctic freight train – raced down the west side of the Great Plains and collided with the Bull Mountains just as fate collided with Virginia. She chilled on the drive home. Between the early-evening pig wrestle and the freeze, something fragile in Virginia's throat broke. The soreness never went away.

Two weeks later, on a morning so dead-quiet that some snow in the air meandered up while some settled slowly to the ground, Doc O'Brien took a biopsy and mailed it to Billings.

Virginia had cancer of the epiglottis. When Doc O'Brien gave her the news in his office, a minute passed without words. She cried. Then she cussed at God; not so much at the prospect of dying as the thought of dying without ever finding enough courage and opportunity to save her family like she should have … could have. "Why. Why!" The doctor had heard the question so many times; the emotional charge always preventing it from sounding cliché. She dropped to the floor of the office, hard enough to bruise her knees. She implored again, "Damn you, God! Damn you! Why!" Had she known what had been set in motion by her disease, her words to Him might have been a thank you.

Doc O'Brien told her that he had arranged subsidized therapy at the cancer treatment center in Billings. What he didn't mention was that Levi and Angela provided the lion's share of that subsidy.

By late March, Virginia's larynx and epiglottis had been removed and she had suffered a round of chemotherapy. They gave her a diaphragm to insert in the hole in her neck so she could make noises that passed for talking, but she hated the mechanized buzz and refused to use the damn thing. People, women particularly, understood her needs well enough. It didn't take asking for Virginia to get an indoor bathroom. Early on Angela hired a contractor, unsolicited, and had it built. By May, Virginia's throat bore the tattoo markers of her second five-week radiation regimen. The irradiated tissue, when exposed to an astringent, was easily damaged and greatly pained, so Virginia stopped drinking alcohol. For good. The DTs ended, but the chemo made her sick and she didn't like people hearing her puke. And that's how she lost her teeth down the outhouse.

8

DEGREES OF HONOR

I had a little sorrow,
Born of a little sin.

EDNA ST. VINCENT MILLAY

Lam sat in the kitchen on a wobbly-legged chrome and plastic chair, her knees clenched so her baby wouldn't fall through the crack. She was feeding him a morning bottle and trying not to wrinkle her skirt. A threadbare diaper on her shoulder protected her blouse. At her feet lay a mounded coil of rug rope pancaked by a thousand footsteps, careful and cruel, the dirty strangled remnants of the oval rugs that had coiled hatefully on the bedroom floors as she clung to them, was forced to smell them. Never again. She and her mother had just unspun them, cut them to pieces. Lam's Aunt Frances helped. Barely a sound was heard but the snip of black-handled scissors and the shifting fire in a coal stove now ulcerated with rust. "I can't wait to see Levi."

"When we're done, Gin, hows-about we dye our hair again?" said Frances.

Virginia smiled at the nutty memory. Lam sensed her mom wouldn't have spoken even if she could have. Instead, Virginia kept feeding the past to the fire, her face sweating. On this bright spring morning, the room was hotter than anyone's liking, especially Frank.

Frank wore a blue work-shirt embroidered with the name *Tommy* and was perched eight feet away on an overturned coal bucket. He was thoroughly put out. "I don't know what the hell has gotten into the both of you," he said, smoking contentiously, but roundly ignored. "There weren't nothing wrong with those rugs." Still ignored. "I'll be go to hell." He looked at Virginia. "You want to tell me why we spent two weeks waiting for her," his arm swung toward Lam, "to come out of a loony spell, and then you help her cut up the rugs? How 'bout the furniture? Why don't we burn that too? If you ask me, you're both loony." No one paid attention.

The wall phone rang, and Lam answered it, snaking the exhausted yellow cord behind her back. It was the scheduling nurse in Billings, who was soon doing her best not to laugh as Lam explained. "Most people think that the pit of an outhouse is all slushy like one of those fiberglass toilets at county fairs, but it's not. It's cone-shaped. I mean the poop piles up into a cone in the middle of the pit. You even have to knock it down with a shovel sometimes."

"I see," the nurse said.

"And it's a good thing, too – the cone –" Lam continued, "or we never would've found her teeth. We missed 'em the first couple of times we looked, but they were right there, near the top. My dad was mad she didn't use the indoor toilet. He had to hold onto my waist so I could reach way down the hole and get 'em. It was just the uppers."

"I don't know if I could've done that," the nurse said.

"The worst part was trying to hold my breath." Lam tilted her head sideways to hold the phone, put the bottle on the table, and shifted the baby to her shoulder. "Anyway, that's why she missed her appointment. She wouldn't let us drive her over there without her teeth."

The nurse muffled the phone ineffectively as she guffawed, but soon recovered. "Well, you tell Mrs. Monroe that we understand, and she can come in on Monday," she burst into laughter again.

Lam laughed too, and Virginia's eyes were full of delight as she issued a great gaseous murmur, hard and quiet, snipping and laughing, laughing and snipping, until she dropped the scissors and wiped her mouth and tracheotomy hole with toilet paper and crossed her legs tightly and held herself so as not to pee, which she already had – a little – and they all noticed the spot and laughed harder, except Frank, who was disgusted.

Lam held the phone out and asked her mother if she wanted to talk, and the women laughed again, hardest after a one-off wheeze blew from Virginia's trache hole. Then, with a final sigh, Lam said, "She goes out there to puke because she doesn't want to wake the baby, okay? He has colic. Anyway, that's why she missed her appointment," and "Thanks so much," and "Mmm hmmm. Bye-bye."

Lam hung up. Virginia passed her a note that read, *When is my next appointment?* "Shit," Lam said. "I'll have to call her back," and laughter reignited in full as Lam dialed.

Five minutes later, Geno's pickup came to a gravelly rumbling stop in the driveway. When Lam rose and gazed outside, she saw Geno's arm, clad in a brick-hued leisure suit, reel a heavy branch ripe with lilacs toward the driver's window for a smell. Apparently satiated, he let the branch fling back. He flipped down the visor, probably to check his hair and clip-on tie. Geno was Lam's ride to Billings for Angela's college graduation ceremony.

Lam handed the baby to her mother. "I'll see you later, Mom. There's formula in the fridge. Thanks for the help, Aunt Frances." She picked up her purse. She shot her father a sharded look. "You're going to work, right?"

Frank leaned against the wall and scowled. He'd been working graveyard shifts at Zupick's gas station for over a year. This morning, he had only been home for an hour. "Station's closed Sunday nights. I thought I'd stay here, if that's okay with you."

Lam regarded him heavily before she turned to her Aunt Frances. "If you need anything, you can try to reach me at Levi and Angela's. Mom has the number."

"The hell, you say." Frank muttered and stood, tipping the bucket as he left the room.

Lam looked poignantly at Virginia, handing her the dead remains of flattened coil. "Thank you, Mom." They hugged, and a moment later the screen door slammed behind Lam. On her way to the pickup, she scratched baby spittle from her shoulder with her fingernail and pulled the padded shoulder to her nose, and then scrubbed a little more. Had she put on enough perfume? She wanted to appear sophisticated in front of Levi. As she climbed into the truck, she looked down to check her modest cleavage, which today was displayed immodestly.

The MetraPark Arena in Billings was a modern, yawning, concrete hockey and rodeo stadium. In its crowded inner lobby, Levi waited in a suit beside a begowned Angela. They stood beneath the Montana Poultry Fanciers Association trade show banner. She jabbered nonstop. Finally, when the turnstiles spat Geno and Lam at them, Angela's grin fairly crackled with current under her blue mortarboard and *magna cum laude* 1981 tassels. She kissed everyone and left for the staging area. Geno, Angela, and Levi secured passable seats in the mezzanine level and waited.

And waited.

Pomp and Circumstance looped mercilessly as the phalanx of graduates issued double-file from beneath the grandstands, bisecting a sea of banquet chairs and spilling left and right at the stage. From above, Levi spotted the white paper angel Angela had taped on her mortarboard. In due course, the graduates and audience were seated – only to rise and sit serially for the National Anthem, the college president, the valedictorian, and, as their keynote, the governor. Levi's paper program evolved into an accordion.

"*You* are our new leaders," the governor started, letting the words seep into the audience. "*You* set the new standards."

A baby bellowed from across the arena, and the crowd laughed. Levi was impressed with the acoustics.

"Well … not *that* new," the governor pandered, and the crowd responded merrily.

"Truly, you *can* and *should* be proud today of what you've accomplished over the last few years. As you target success in the world, be bold. Rise because you stand for something! The view is spectacular from there! Let those who are threatened try to shoot you down. And they might. But you will be proud of where you stood. And know that you did not rise alone. Give thanks, as well – to God and family – for the love and support they showed you in your journey of accomplishment…"

Levi's jaw tightened. *Support my ass.*

"Now it is your turn. *You* have responsibility – to those *you* love, to those who love *you, to yourself,* and to *our society…*" And so began the governor's traveling salvation show. The audience remained stoic, culturally disinclined to shout *Amen.* On and on. Levi numbed altogether until awoken by a change in the governor's tone that promised an end.

"…The *significance* of your future *depends* on your ability … *to love.* It is your turn, graduates!"

"What about my turn?" Levi muttered.

The governor stepped back slightly, arms raised, evoking sanctification from above. A short moment passed before applause budded low and sparse, and then bloomed up the grandstands as the audience grasped that he had finally concluded.

Names were called, diplomas dispensed. Pictures were taken inside. Outside, escapees scurried through the lot, into their cars, and onto the streets. Angela insisted on riding to her celebration lunch with her dad. Lam rode with Levi.

Lam looked at Levi's face as he drove his new Camaro toward downtown. He wore sunglasses. He had blow-dried hair and the shadow where he shaved seemed manlier. Everything he wore looked crisp: his sport coat, his shirt, his slacks. Lam pulled up the neckline of her blouse a little. She continued to look at him, but he pretended not to notice. "That was a nice thing that you did."

"What?" said Levi, keeping his eyes on the road.

"The house."

"No big deal." He was deadpan, but it *was* a big deal. It was a very big deal, and even though he sold more radio ads than anybody at the station, he would have to sell plenty more to pay for it. He remembered answering the phone a month ago and the surreal familiarity of a voice he hadn't heard in years. Without salutation Frank had said, "*Your mother has something she wants me to read to you,*" and he read the eviction notice from the county, followed by a short note Virginia had allegedly written, a plea for money. "I hear you're doing good, money-wise," it read, and, "It seems you could see your way clear…" Afterward Frank added, "It don't make me no never mind. It's up to you. She just don't want to be thrown out into the cold." The melodrama had been nearly laughable. Nearly. Levi was sure Virginia hadn't written the note and, when he asked Frank to mail it to him, his father hung up. Of course, no envelope arrived, but Levi nurtured guilt like a Petri dish, so Frank's words grew the intended effect.

Levi and Lam drove on in silence for a while.

"It's a big deal for us. Especially Mom."

With exaggerated weariness, Levi said, "Look, the county let me have it for back taxes. No big deal." As he checked the rearview mirror, he accelerated and shifted.

While she watched the road, the air conditioning cooled her face with the smell of leather. She looked down at her shoes, creased and puttied with polish. Pinpoints of a baby blue homemade half slip seeped through the seam of her dark skirt. Her belt had two misshapen notches – hers and the one her mother favored. "Thanks for the bathroom, too."

"Huh? Oh. That was part of the deal. The county says I can't let people live there without putting in a septic tank." He slowed at another driver's bumper and downshifted loudly.

"Well … thank you."

"No big deal."

A block passed. Two. "I'm sorry I couldn't make Angela's baccalaureate. How was it?"

"Fine I guess. I didn't go. I don't do church." Downtown they rolled into the shadow of a twenty-story masonry building, into its parking garage across the street. "How's your son?"

"Dusty? He's fine. He has problems with his ears. I'm supposed to bring him over here to Billings to get some tubes put in, and I was gonna come over when Mom gets her treatment, but I don't have an appointment yet."

"When does she get her treatments?"

"The next one's Monday, but we gotta get a ride. My alternator's out. Dad says it'll cost $63 for a new one. Why? Do you want to see Mom and Dad?"

"Jesus." Levi shook his head as he spiraled a little too fast up the garage before parking near the second-level skywalk.

"What?"

"Nothing. That's why I don't answer the phone."

"What?"

"Nothing. Forget it." He yanked the emergency brake and they got out and looked over the roof of the car at each other.

"No one's asking you to pay for no repairs, Levi. Wouldn't want *you* to feel used."

Levi closed the door hard and outpaced Lam into the Plexiglas skywalk tunnel.

On the twentieth floor at the fancy Lucky Diamond Restaurant, Levi and Lam saw Geno by the host station leaning against the oak paneling. He was apologizing to Angela for not sending her to Italy as a graduation present. Angela kissed her father's cheek and said, "I love you, Papa," and, "Let's go eat." On his way past the host station, Levi grabbed the section of the *Billings Gazette* that listed stock quotes.

Across a field of floral carpet, in chairs at the massive windows, Levi and Geno sat at a sunny table for four that overlooked the green Yellowstone Valley. To the north the Rimrocks, a great wall of sandstone cliffs, glowed amber with daylight against the azure sky. Fifty miles southwest, the white, vascular ski runs splitting the forest on Red Lodge Mountain had not yet melted into summer hazel.

As she opened her napkin, Angela beamed at her class ring. She caught

Levi looking at it too, but he quickly turned and folded the paper and studied the columns. He was happy for her, truly, but the ring seemed to sting him.

The waitress smiled. "What can I get you to drink? Coffee? Juice?"

"I'd like a Bloody Mary," Lam piped up. She caught a reproachful look from Levi.

"I guess it's gotta be noon somewhere," he said.

"I'll have a drink too," said Geno, his arms rising like a preacher. "We're celebrating! Do you have any champagne?"

"We might have some – left over from breakfast mimosas. It's pretty good. It's André."

"No problem. Perfect! We'll have a bottle of André. And four glasses."

"Three," Levi said, frowning at Lam. "I'll have coffee." He looked at Geno. "How are things at the bar?"

"The bar is wonderful. Same old same old. Lammy here is doing a great job." Geno patted the top of Lam's hand.

Levi looked at her accusingly. "Where's the baby when you're working?"

"With Mom and Dad. Why?"

"Well, that ought to work out great," he mocked. "It sure did for us."

As Lam started to reply, Geno dropped his double-barrel forearms between them and wove his fingers together as his head grew heavy on his neck.

Angela interceded, chipper and dismissive. "Leave her alone, Levi. I told you, your parents are doing great. You should stop by and see sometime."

On frequent trips to Roundup over the last four years, Angela had typically stopped to see Frank and Virginia. Levi never went along. It was Angela who had acted when the county threatened to evict his parents and auction the land. It was Angela who worked with the bank and the contractor who installed the bathroom and septic tank. Technically it was Levi's money, but he acted uninvolved and she figured she'd eventually share the debt anyway, when they married. She arranged everything. He simply signed the loan. $8,000.

The waitress set the Bloody Mary in front of Lam, and Geno insisted on uncorking the champagne, which he prepared to pop with great ceremony. "To the scholar, my Angel," his voice began to crack, "and to her mama."

"Aawh," Angela smiled as Lam patted Geno on the back.

As Levi looked out the window, Geno hugged the bottle like a fire hose trained at Levi's reflection and popped the cork, caroming it off the glass into Levi's forehead, causing him to jerk as if he'd been asleep at the wheel.

Everyone laughed except Levi.

The waitress poured Levi's coffee as Lam drained her Bloody Mary. Geno poured champagne for Angela, Lam, and himself, and then circled again to top off the glasses.

"To Angel!" Over the table three champagne glasses plinked against a coffee cup. Lam downed her champagne and gestured for more while she smiled coyly at a young man who walked by.

Levi ignored her. "Sorry," he said softly to the table at large. Angela kissed him on the cheek and gave his leg a little squeeze.

Lam watched Angela soak up the affection. She poured another glass for herself. Lam liked Angela – like a sister nowadays – but still wrestled with envy. When had Angela struggled? And now Angela had a college degree – paid for by the bar where Lam worked. Angela wasn't smarter or better, just luckier. No parent to care for, or a baby, or even herself for that matter, if she didn't want to. Levi was making enough money for himself *and* Angela. An image flashed in Lam's head of Angela and Levi in bed, and she immediately felt its poison and cut it off. It was Angela's day. Angela had earned it.

So they talked about Angela. They looked at her diploma, conferred with honors, as she itemized her favorite classes: child cognitive development, oil painting, human sexuality – ha, ha. They talked about her college friends (but not the boyfriends). They talked about student teaching and which grade levels no sane person could want – junior high. Angela liked *K* through *Three*. The vote was split on whether she should get a Master's right away.

And Levi kissed Angela's forehead.

And Lam drank. And she smiled at the busboy and looked sleepily at him when he was clearing a nearby table. She kept it up, wanting him to show he noticed, even more so wanting to make Levi notice, make him want her and need her, love her, the brother who'd rejected her and loved Angela, because Lam's reflexive, indelible certainty, at twenty, was that being loved was indistinguishable from being desired.

"Tell them about the interview," Angela said to Levi.

"No, it's not that big a deal," Levi said. He focused on his coffee.

"*Yes* it is. Tell them." Angela poked his ribs and blurted at Geno. "Levi has an interview to be a stockbroker with Bookman Stuart. They're opening an office here. He flies to San Francisco tomorrow. You always said he should be a money changer."

Geno looked impressed. "They got the right man, that's for sure – as long as you stay out of the temple." The Biblical reference wasn't lost on Levi. "Do you think they might not like so much you didn't graduate? Or is a GED okay? And you're so young."

That stung.

Lam put an elbow on the table and, as if she wasn't thinking, traced her sternum with a berry-colored fingernail. She waited until the busboy blushed before she smiled at him.

"Angela," Levi appealed and then looked at Geno. "I probably won't get the job." He meant to say if anyone had the balls to break the mold, it was him, but he didn't want to set himself up for humiliation if he didn't.

When no one was looking, Lam tucked her blouse in tighter, made it ride down. She poured the last ounce of champagne and hooked an arm behind her chair, straining the buttons. Angela sighed at Lam and looked put-out, but Lam ignored her.

"Of course, they want good salespeople," Levi said, "and I *am* the best salesperson at the station, even though I'm the youngest. Yeah, that's a problem, too, probably. I'm only twenty-one, I don't have a college degree, and I don't come from money. I mean, I *make* a lot of money – maybe more than your bar – but I don't *come* from money, not that that has stopped me. Besides, I still need to look up what bonds are..." and blah and blah. Long before Levi finished measuring his skills and guts in the process of hedging against his potential failure, Geno grew limp from hearing it. The topic finally died of neglect.

Geno nodded at Levi and Angela. "So what about you two? Do I have to keep mailing letters and packages to your girlfriend's apartment?" Geno knew she lived with Levi.

"What do you mean?" Angela smiled coyly.

"I'm just saying..." Geno smiled back.

"Excuse me," Lam interrupted, reminding the others of her presence. She unslung her arm and purse from the back of the chair and stood up.

"Oh. I'll go with you," Angela said.

"No." Lam headed for the restroom alone.

Conversation died. When Geno asked for the check, Levi touched the waitress's hand and said, "Give it to me." Geno let him take it.

"So, Levi, when are you coming to Roundup to see your folks?" Geno asked.

"I don't know. Not soon." And the table fell silent.

For a moment it seemed merciful when Lam finally breezed back in, her makeup freshly applied and looking as if she knew something worth knowing.

"You okay?" Angela asked, not that she particularly cared to hear otherwise right then.

"Yeah." She chirped. "Ready to go?"

"You bet," said Geno, discarding his napkin on the table. "I thought we'd go over and take a look at Levi's place before we head back home."

With smugness aimed at Levi, Lam said, "Oh. You go ahead. I've got plans."

Geno and Angela traded weary glances, and Levi's jaw tightened.

"I called Aunt Frances – she's staying with Mom tonight, and Dusty – I'm gonna stay in Billings. I'll catch a ride home tomorrow morning with Donny Zupick."

"We're *not* giving you a ride to meet Donny Zupick," said Levi. "Shit." Under the table he worked the gray streak on his palm.

"I didn't ask you for a ride. He's coming here. To the hotel. To pick me up."

Levi regarded the tablecloth for several seconds. He stood and walked around and put his face in Lam's. "I said I would be there for you. Okay, so far I haven't. Well I am now. Do not do this." Her eyes said he was getting through. Maybe he did owe her. He would renew his promise right now, keep it this time. "You don't have to end up like them. Please." It was working. Contrition was forming on her face. "You've already made one mistake."

He'd blown it. Embarrassment and anger blanketed her face. "My child is not a mistake."

"I didn't mean he, as a person, was a mistake. It's just that … If Donny shows up, I'll kick his ass."

Drunken stubbornness and pretend power stiffened her body. "Fuck off."

Levi straightened up, mirroring her attitude. "Okay. No problem." In an instant he imagined they had fought the current together, forever, and now, suddenly fatigued, he was just … letting go. Releasing her to drown of her own accord. With counterfeit calm, he said, "I'll meet you guys at the elevator."

9

SACRIFICIAL LAM

If I have only darkness
I must claim the light

David Whyte

Lam sat alone in the lobby of the Sheraton. Donny was late. She had already made two laps around the central elevator banks and twice examined the murals depicting the history of the town, including one rendering of Lewis … or Clark … one of them. Her buzz had worn off, and each time the nearby elevator doors opened she felt more conspicuous, so she would study the headlines and pictures of an abandoned *USA Today*. But mostly she stared past the whispering front desk clerks, through the large glass back doors that opened to the empty cobblestone turnaround. Finally Donny's Mustang rumbled to a stop there. He honked. She strode outside as surely as possible, climbed into his car, buckled in. He wore a *Stones* T-shirt, stubble, and sunglasses. With bright-cheeked hope, she smiled and raised her palms like *here I am*, and he bounced his eyebrows at her, beaming as if he had just won the pot at poker.

He pulled away, "Fuck, man! I can't believe you called! I was just talkin' to Harold about you. He's who answered the phone."

"Really?" she was wearing her smile a little too tight. "What did you tell him?"

"What?"

She smelled pot on his breath. She found herself watching the road for him. "What did you say to Harold about me?" she asked coyly.

"What do you mean, man?"

"You said that you were talking to Harold about me. What did you say to him?"

"Oh. I said you called, and you were comin' over. What did ya think?"

He laughed a fading, rhythmic hiss, as if letting air out of a tire stem by repeatedly poking it. She had almost forgotten that laugh.

"Before."

"What?"

"Before that. What did you say to Harold about me before I called?"

"When?"

"Anytime. What did you say about me anytime, any day, before I called?"

"Oh. I don't know. Just that you were cool – and hot. And that you had a kid."

"What'd he say?"

"Huh? Nothin'. We're going out tonight, and I said you were comin'. It's cool."

"How'd you know I didn't bring Dusty?"

"Huh? Oh. The kid." He shifted. "I figure you wouldn't have called me if you had him."

"Why's that? You'd like him, and…" She wanted to say "he'd like you," but held short.

"Cause he ain't mine."

"You don't know that."

"Neither do you. SSS-SSs-Sss-sss." She hated that laugh. "But that's cool."

As she looked out the window, she determined to remain cheery.

They drove through the rough South Side, nearly to I-90, and turned onto a narrow street. They parked at the curb in front of a small two-bedroom house long ago painted battleship gray over a layer of burnt orange. The peeling made it look rusty. The old sidewalk and concrete steps that led to the weathered-crackled door had become jigsaw aggregate. They were a block from South Park and rent was cheap. And access to I-90 was convenient to the industrial park where Donny had worked since his academic probation ran out at Eastern.

That afternoon they smoked some pot, the three of them, and Lam and Donny screwed before they went out. Early in the evening, they drank beer and shooters and played pool at the Red Door Lounge. Even with a wrinkled skirt, Lam felt overdressed. She sat on Donny's lap when Harold was shooting and talked with Harold when Donny shot.

Harold had sinewy limbs and ragged, mud-colored hair that mopped and smeared his thick glasses. Whenever Lam walked between him and the pool table, he bowed deeply and swept his arm as if to clear the way. It was sweet the first time. Then he began chanting "Lamb of God" each time, which mutated the gesture all the way to creepy.

Harold intended to make a fortune tying flies for fishermen, though he had never produced one fly and possessed no fly-tying equipment. As a commitment to his new career, he had quit his warehouse job with intentions to buy a vice, hackle pliers, and some bobbins and hooks. He had collected bird feathers from South Park, and a friend from Crow Agency gave him some pheasant hackle. His favorite fly was the Woolly Bugger. He delighted in making people uncomfortable by saying it.

About ten o'clock, they migrated to the Wild West Saloon so Lam could dance, which Donny avoided on account of he was lousy at it. He allowed her to dance with Harold. So she made the best of it, dancing with the crowd while Harold vibrated stiffly around the dance floor like some goliath insect with nervous wings. For her, regardless, it felt good to be out.

Around midnight, Donny insisted they swing by the Western Bar, an unpretentious, respectable saloon wedged between downtown and the South Side. As soon as they hit the door, Donny seemed to be searching for someone. The shuffleboard tables were shuffling, and the dartboards bristled as Lam and Harold bellied up to the bar and ordered shots of Jack Daniels. Donny hung back, nodding across the room to an acquaintance from work. He joined the man at his table. Before Lam and Harold had shot their shots, Donny had scored a gram of cocaine.

They drove to the house and Donny sat on the couch next to Lam. Harold cleared sandwich bags of bird feathers off the coffee table and Donny showed Lam how to cut the coke into lines with a razor blade on a handheld mirror. As anxiousness assailed her, Donny rubbed the small of her back. She watched Harold roll a dollar bill into a straw.

"Like this," Harold said. He bent over the mirror and held the tube to one nostril, collapsed the other with a finger, and snorted the first line. Then it was Lam's turn. Then Donny's. Then Lam again. Then Harold. Then Lam.

Lam's soft pallet grew numb and tasted bitter. She was drunk, and high, and her skin prickled, and she needed to grab and to touch and to rub and move her body so she wouldn't crawl out of it. In her malaise, she failed to object when Donny shoved the coffee table aside with his foot and maneuvered her to her knees. He opened his pants, leaned back on the couch. She balked at first, nearly contested, but with his fistfuls of hair he reined her until she acquiesced, letting her face be guided to his crotch. And her will collapsed utterly as Harold pulled her skirt and panties off and mounted her from behind. Her arm shot straight down, locking at the elbow, her palm planting against the floor to brace against his weight. Her fingers dug between the coils of the rug.

10

THE INTERVIEW

Please allow me to introduce myself,
I'm a man of wealth and taste.
I've been around for long, long years,
Stolen many a man's soul and faith.

MICK JAGGER AND KEITH RICHARDS

In the 1980s, Merrill Lynch and Smith Barney fancied an intelligent design approach to building a sales force, but Bookman Stuart was more Darwinian. Bookman Stuart chose to overpopulate its branches with all manner of brokerage trainees and let selective pressures – sales ability, emotional stamina, applied ethics – cull for survivors. Whenever the firm radiated into new habitat – like Billings, Montana – it exploited dynamic as well as marginal individuals; in this case, anyone who could sell anything – cars, canned goods, advertising, whatever. Unsuccessful adaptation was expected, and career mortality was high. When rookies failed, niches briefly opened. Levi chanced upon a niche – one he felt might finally and irrevocably allow him to ditch his contemptible heritage. So he applied.

First he withstood an academic test not much more challenging than the GED. It was proctored by the receptionist and designed to predict his ability to memorize answers to the general securities exams. He took another exam, after which he was assigned one of four personality profiles. They came in quadrants. A cursory, local interview followed, at which Levi described how he became the top salesman at the radio station. The station manager, he said, even offered him a raise if he would cancel the interview with Bookman Stuart. A week later, the Bookman Stuart manager's secretary called Levi to arrange a trip to San Francisco for more interviews. She'd been told to tell him he'd done okay thus far.

Levi bought a suit at JC Penney that hung on his body as smart as tent canvas. He wore it on his first airplane flight – *ever* – the early Delta Connection to Salt Lake City. From there, from a pay phone, he called the radio station and reminded the young receptionist – whom he counted on to tell everyone – that he was flying. On a jet. Two, actually, just to get there. And two back.

"I'm in Salt Lake," he said.

"You should go to Lagoon!" she said. "They have *the best* roller-coasters."

He tried to help her focus. He was becoming important. "I'm just looking forward to not having to hear Earl bitch anymore." Earl, a businessman of royal status about town, was Levi's biggest advertiser, his greatest source of commission. His greatest pain in the ass. Levi had already stopped returning Earl's calls. Surely the receptionist could realize Levi's impending importance. Or not. Like his parents wouldn't – not that he was willing to call them. He had hinted to Angela to call them. But what if he did fail? Next he called Angela and told her to hold off.

For the next two hours on a plane, Levi learned more than anyone wants to from a fiftyish salesman in the computer refurbishing game. On approach to San Francisco, Levi put his fresh *Forbes* and *Wall Street Journal* in his fresh-smelling briefcase. When he leaned against the window his fresh jacket rode his back like a tarp, slicing under the nape of his hair. Way down below, the water in San Francisco Bay winked up in careful concentric, ripples. Nice. They descended. Faster. Even faster. Okay, now, too damn fast. The ripples grew choppy, as if warning. Closer. Too close. Soon they raced mere feet above the bay. *Shit,* the land was over there. *Over there!* The salesman held *Reader's Digest* at arm's length, squinting. Where the hell's the runway? Levi whispered the *Our Father* the way Angela said it – with *trespasses* instead of *debts.* Finally a giant, charcoal tarmac raced out across the water, jutting out, jutting! It was a desperate, diving catch. "Jesus!" Levi jumped as the wheels touched down. The salesman read on.

At the gate, Levi asked an agent where the taxis were. He walked alongside the moving sidewalks because he was unsure where they'd stop if he got on. At the shoeshine stand he asked again about taxis. In the main terminal, someone finally pointed to the cabstand. The itinerary he'd been given gauged the fare to downtown at $25. Levi tried in vain to pay the Russian driver straightaway. When they arrived in the financial district, the man collected

$43. On the sidewalk, human eddies in suits and dresses flowed at the feet of sheer cliffs of polished stone and tempered glass. There were buses hanging on wires and vagrants simply hanging on. Levi knew he needed directions, but wasn't sure he could understand Orientals, and he didn't want to bother homosexuals – whom he imagined everywhere – so he walked around until he figured it out. Eventually he stood, briefcase in hand, before a fifty-floor façade of rose granite. Bookman Stuart was on the 45th.

Levi's appointment was at 1 P.M. At 12:45 he wedged into a revolving door behind a middle-aged Asian woman who promptly squirted out the other side and glared at him over her shoulder before disappearing into the crowd. There was a forest of elevators. Levi boarded one. Seven minutes later, back at the lobby, he got out. It was hard to imagine why anyone would design an elevator that didn't go all the way up. 12:53. He spotted the lady from the revolving door, now wielding a mail-tub, and sheepishly asked her for help. When he told her where he was going, she suddenly looked amused, coy even. She pointed and said only *good luck*. He finally arrived at the reception desk at exactly 1 P.M.

After waiting forty minutes, Levi was shown to a spacious office overlooking Market Street. From behind her desk, Joy Parnell, the divisional training officer, smiled too big with grownup lips on a child-sized face that was ringed with a shock of brunette hair that had been teased up into a vast brown cloud. She wore double-breasted pinstripes and a stiff blouse with the collar turned up, Elvis-style. She's too young, Levi thought.

Joy shook hands hard and told him to please sit. On her burgundy desk pad sat a box of mints and a burgundy pen on a burgundy Day-Timer. A picture in a rosewood frame featured her standing with three male golfers, sunglasses nested atop her head and a sweater draped piggyback style over her shoulders. Same oversized smile.

She asked about his trip and plainly endured his response. And she smiled, blankly now. Pleasantly suspended. As if waiting. For him? Oh. He looked out the window. "Is that the Golden Gate Bridge?"

"No," she said like a kindergarten teacher, "that's the Bay Bridge." She touched a paper on her desk. "You're from Montana."

"Yes."

"It must be cold there."

"It is during the winter," he spoke slowly too, for her.

"So what do you do with your spare time? In the winter, I mean."

"I like to play basketball. And racquetball. I like to read and get together with friends."

"'Get together' isn't really an action verb."

"Pardon me?" said Levi.

"Never mind," she said. "Let me shoot you a hypothesis. Let's say you're with your friends and it's too cold to play a sport. How do you kill your time?"

"Well," Levi stalled. Drinking and screwing probably weren't the right answers. Hm. Action verb. She didn't seem like a bowler. "I jump at the chance to play games."

She smiled and scribbled. Her index fingernail was cut short. "What kind of games?"

He thought. "Trivial Pursuit, cards, Monopoly – games like that."

More scribbling. More smiling. "Do you keep score?"

Is she kidding? "Yes, I *kill* to keep score."

"Excellent," she seemed genuinely delighted. "Do you like to win?"

She's kidding. "Yes."

"Excellent! I'm just nailing down the results of the tests you took. It's highly likely that you run competitive *by nature*. You use action verbs. Me too, and I've devoured board games all my life. I remember when I was young, my sisters and I..." and, "The reason I didn't want you to include athletics is because it's too easy for athletic people to..." and "I was athletic as a kid, too. I was a gymnast, and you can imagine what kind of shape I was in..." and "Now I play golf – it's quite civilized – do you play golf?"

"No."

"Too bad. Very civilized. Most managers play."

"Are you a manager?"

"I'm on the divisional management team, but Mr. Crawford hasn't assigned a branch to me yet. Have you met Mr. Crawford?"

"Not yet. I have an interview with him later."

"I'm sure you'll do well. I'll tell Gary – Mr. Crawford – that you passed inspection. He relies on me quite a bit." She nodded knowingly and then said, "What event in your life really threw you for a loop?"

"Pardon me?"

"Tell me something that crushed you – emotionally."

Crushed. Action. She smiled brightly at him, an idiot. "I can't think of anything."

"What's that dark streak on your hand?"

"Oh, this? Nothing. I burned it as a kid."

"Why is it gray?"

What the hell? He considered ending the interview. "The metal I burned myself on had some black grime on it at the time – coal dust probably. It stained the scar. Kind of like a tattoo. But I can't say it was crushing. Nothing *crushing* comes to mind."

"Really? Didn't you sue your parents? When you were emancipated? What'd they do?"

He stared disbelievingly at her. "I didn't think I wrote that down." He had mentioned it in the local interview. "Just one of them, really."

"Which one?"

A full minute passed in *don't go there* silence. He changed directions. "My grandparents died. I was quite close to them."

She perked up. "*That's* crushing. How did you feel?"

"Sad?"

"Perfect!" she said. "You don't have to elaborate. I was just confirming your autonomy, you know, your ability to work independently. Most people aren't aware of it, but autonomous people have an easier time identifying and expressing their emotions. People who *can't* work independently look for others in the group to tell them how they should *feel*. It's a very high correlation. You may have noticed that I easily express my emotions. I'm very autonomous. I have to be. No one holds the interviewer's hand in an interview. There's nothing wrong with showing how you feel. When I was a broker..." and, "Clients trusted me because..."

"How long were you a broker?" Levi eventually asked.

"We don't say broker. We're Financial Consultants."

"How long were you a Financial Consultant?"

"Almost a year before Mr. Crawford tapped me for this job. I'm highly autonomous. I remember when my cousin caught cancer..."

She liked that he had accomplishments independent of teams. She wanted to know if he'd overcome adversity. She asked if he could persevere. He said yes. She asked if he was empathetic. He said yes. She said he shouldn't be too empathetic and he promised he wasn't.

When the interview ended, Joy escorted Levi to the retail brokerage office where he role-played with experienced brokers. He played the broker and they were clients. Everyone discovered that salespeople like salespeople. Afterward, he returned to the reception area where he and the pretty receptionist waited for his four o'clock interview with Crawford. Levi sat in a deep chair for a long time. On a dark coffee table were copies of the *San Francisco Chronicle*, but he reread his *Wall Street Journal* – twice – holding it so passers-by might notice, which they didn't. He reread his *Forbes*. At 5 o'clock the receptionist offered him coffee. Levi said no, thank you, so she put on her grimy running shoes, said good luck and left.

It was 5:15 and Levi was booked on a 6:30 flight. He fingered the money in his pocket; wondered if there was $43. He stood and nosed up to the pictures on the walls, examining them as he furtively pulled at the elastic of his underwear.

"Levi?" Behind him, a warm, confident voice. He turned around to the square-faced Asian woman from the revolving door. "Yes."

"I'm Lily Fujiwara." She offered her hand. It was the woman from the elevators. She sounded so American.

He hastily wiped his hand on his jacket and shook. "I'm pleased to meet you ... I ..."

"I see you found us. I'm sorry we're running so late." She radiated sincerity. "I hope you've been comfortable."

"You're Oriental." He cringed at himself, knowing she already knew it.

"Actually, I prefer Asian. Or Japanese-American."

In his embarrassment he bumbled, "You must get that a lot. No accent."

"What?"

"I didn't ... That you're Asian. I mean. Maybe not here, though, I guess."

"I am Asian."

"That's what I mean." Again, he felt like an idiot, but she showed no sign of rancor. To the contrary, she seemed amused, as if a small child had noted the shape of her eyes.

"Mr. Crawford will see you now."

"I have a flight..."

"It's okay. I made tentative hotel reservations for you. Can you fly out tomorrow?"

He hadn't arranged that much time off. Screw it. "Whatever is needed. Thank you."

Lily handed a voucher to him. "When you finish today, give this to Jimmy, the security man in the lobby. You can't miss him. He's about six foot six. Some people call him Giant Jimmy. He played for the San Francisco Giants, I think. A Caucasian. For you, Italian-American." On the way to Crawford's office she stopped. "I heard Joy Parnell tell Mr. Crawford that you don't take notes," she smiled, "but I'll bet you do." She paused at her credenza, atop which she displayed a marbled, tombstone placard with three big gold Xs attesting to her thirty years of service to Bookman Stuart. Beside it was a WWII-vintage black and white photo of a young mother and infant in front of a small vegetable garden. Well into the bleak background were two squat stone and mortar sentry huts guarding a square lumber sign that read *Manzanar War Relocation Center.* To the left of the snapshot a small, flat box with a clear plastic door held the Purple Heart medal. Lily noticed him noticing.

"My father's," she said. "In Italy. In World War II." She opened the credenza doors. Stashed within was the Comstock Lode of office supplies. She apportioned a single legal pad and Bic pen for Levi.

"Thank you," he said.

Levi wiped his hand again as Lily showed him into Crawford's enormous office. Two of four walls were immense planes of glass, floor to ceiling, giving Levi the sense that the chamber might float into space were it not moored at its deep interior by a massive black walnut desk pinned down on either side by thick lamps that gleamed like polished nickel. Nickel on black...his parents' stove. As he stared, the light around the dark mass quivered. He curled his fingers until their pads stroked the scar. *No.* He blinked away from it.

The man in the room, presumably Gary Crawford, spoke to Mrs. Fujiwara. "Any word from the Bohemia Club?" Slender and fortyish, Crawford had sharp cheeks and austere hair.

"No, Mr. Crawford."

"Let me know if they call. Word is Kissinger and Rockefeller'll both be at Monte Rio on the Russian River this year." Then, at Levi. "Summer camp. For big boys. Up there." He pointed across the Bay. When his arm raised, his trim torso became straight as a pipe, the orderly line of 100-count pinpoint cotton shirt and creased trousers pulled taut from his pits to his Cole Haan loafers. "I'm on the waiting list. Unbelievingly, the next slot is between me and an Indian guy who invented rice that grows in salt water as a kid, an Untouchable in rural India, of all things."

"Abba Rice?"

"Right. His first name's Abba – Abhaya Ramakapur. Sold his rice company. Went to Yale in bio-something. Now he's CEO of a gene splicing firm. We do business, he and I."

When they shook, Levi's scalp retreated. He tried to slough the sensation. Crawford was speaking, motioning beyond high-rises, to the freighters and sailboats that etched the Bay. Levi focused, striving to appreciate the magnificence. The Golden Gate Bridge glowed orange above ultramarine. Behind it, in the mist, loomed the taupe Marin Headlands. Left-to-right, Crawford pointed out Sausalito, Angel Island, Alcatraz, Oakland. Then, abruptly, he turned and strode in a crescent that terminated within touching distance of the desk, like it was home base, Levi imagined, and some source of power. The tour had concluded.

"Take a seat," he said. Between the lamps rested only a notepad and a photo of a woman and teenage boy – her with cheekbones, the adolescent with a who-gives-a-shit posture. There was a second picture, a black and white head shot like a fashion photograph. The same woman, Levi presumed.

"Was your son born here?" Levi tried.

"They live in Chicago." Crawford didn't look at either picture. He grabbed the pad, pointed to one of the tapestried sofas. As he arced toward the seating area, his body seemed to swivel, staying no less than quarter-open to the massive, dark desk. "I'm from there."

"Do you have to go back every weekend?" Levi scrutinized the black and white. "Your wife is pretty."

Now Crawford looked. "That one's my mother. I never have to go back. But if my corporate plane is going there, I lay over sometimes. I have a house here and one there. I buy as many houses as I have to … so I don't have to be anywhere unnecessarily. Comes with the job."

The sofa was too deep. Levi repeated the last sentences to himself. How much money? Unreal. He watched Crawford claim a stiff wing-backed chair, draping one leg flaccidly over the other while his spine stayed military, his feet missile-skinny. The older man rested his manicured fingers on the pad. No ring. And then, like a stopwatch, he cocked his mechanical pencil. "What makes you think you can be a Financial Consultant at Bookman Stuart?"

Levi sat forward, feet planted, notepad at the ready. He pulled up a sock. He tried to hold his fingers as Michelangelo might have painted them; relaxed with big veins. "Well, I'm a good salesperson … I work harder than most people … and I'm smart."

"It says here you never graduated high school." Crawford slapped his pencil in his palm like a riding crop. Levi imagined him in uniform. Gray. Maybe a monocle.

"I can explain that…"

"You don't have to explain it. It is what it is. Besides, why would anybody tell the truth if there's nothing to be gained by it? Does your family have money?"

Truth? "No, sir, we don't. And I *would* tell the truth … sir."

"Do you know anyone with money? Does your wife come from money?"

Eichmann? "I'm engaged, sir … we haven't set the date. Her family owns a successful business." Levi said this quickly and instinctively remained circumspect about the bar. "I know a lot of business owners. I sell advertising to business owners and managers. I believe one of my strengths is that they trust me." Or Rommel.

"So – you're the kid that sells them advertising. Hear this. For years I was our top broker in Chicago, but I knew money going in. I assure you that you don't even *know* enough money to succeed in this business. You need to be able to talk people you *don't know* into giving you their money."

"I'm hoping that if my clients make a reasonable return, I'll get referrals," Levi had read that somewhere. Crawford smiled, barely tolerant.

"I have a … well … talent with stocks," Levi pressed on. "I keep charts … I know all brokers read charts … but I, well, have a knack … um. See, if you check my account … I have an account at Bookman Stuart…"

Lily appeared in the doorway. "Mr. Crawford, Mr. Ramakapur and his stock option administrator at EcoPulse is on the line."

"Ask him to hold." Crawford looked at Levi. "The rice guy. Now he thinks he's God and can save the world through science. Thinks everyone should help. Look. You had a better chance at the job until you said that. Every little-old-lady stock club has a system and we don't need yours. We're not a casino and we don't hold séances. A wiser man than you once discovered there are only three ethical ways to make money on Wall Street. Unfortunately, he was gored to death in a stampede before he could enlighten us.

"There's only one thing you need to know. My advice is to keep your radio job. No serious investor's going to give you money. 80 percent of brokerage trainees fail as it is." He tossed his blank pad on the table. "As a manager, I also built the most profitable office in the firm." He pointed to a plaque on the wall and waited for Levi to read the words, *Chairman, Branch Managers' Council, 1977-1979.* "That was two years ago. And that helped my boss get promoted to president. And I got his job. As a manager, I hired plenty of brokers. I know what I'm looking at. But I run a division now. So I don't have time to hire and train rookies. That's the local manager's job. My advice to local management will be not to hire you, but I'll leave it up to them. It's a new office."

"Mr. Crawford, I believe they should – will – hire me, and I believe I'll be the best hire they make. If they should pass, I will be hired by another firm – Merrill Lynch or Shearson or Paine Weber – and I'll be the toughest competitor you have."

They stared at each other.

Crawford took the lead. "Our firm has spent a hundred million dollars in the last two years convincing the public and our employees of our corporate belief system. You've probably heard it: '*How We Believe.*' Maybe even on your radio station." His voice rang with affected seriousness when he recited the slogan. "The spots go on about integrity, competence, research, and other ad-agency jingle-speak. As professionals, Bookman Stuart promises that we will deliver personalized service to our clients, no matter where they are. In my opinion, that's a mistake. It's a mistake for Wall Street firms to establish outposts in communities where potential clients think *stock* is something to be skinned, plucked, or eaten. If potential clients don't even get it, how can we expect to find any level of sophistication among broker candidates in those market areas? No, in the long run, that's not the image we're going for – and we shouldn't be buying spots to announce that we are. Nothing personal, kid."

"Advertisements or ads."

"Pardon me?"

"As professionals in broadcasting, we don't refer to them as 'spots,' but back to your ad campaign." Levi yearned to add the word *asshole.* Crawford's reaction said Levi had already made his point. "Why are you opening an office in Billings? Why not change the campaign?"

"Research says the baby boomer demographic will get a pile of money when they retire, and after they buy their Winnebagos, they'll be unable to figure out how to invest the rest. Our firm's president, Mike Sandler – Wall Street legend that he is – thinks Bookman Stuart should get a share of it. It's a mistake. It's like Sears buying Dean Witter – socks and stocks. Clients with real money will migrate to more … upscale firms. As for you, even if Sandler is right, someone with your profile would never have gotten this interview for a major market office." Crawford was repaying the jab, but in doing it Levi caught a note of respect. "Our warm-hearted, ma-pa ad campaign is misdirected, but now that we've spent the money, the office in Billings will open and you're here. There's no point in advertising a corporate belief system if we're not going to pretend to follow it." Then, "What is it you want? Ultimately?"

"I want to buy as many houses as I have to … so I don't have to go back anywhere I don't want to." Crawford looked surprised. "With all respect, sir, I am the real thing."

As Crawford stood, he softened, perplexingly so, and moved just inside Levi's space. "Are you staying in the City?" As he asked the question, he pulled a small tin from his suit jacket pocket, fished in it with a dry, white finger and pinched out a tiny, deep gray tab that he laid in his mouth, a mouth that closed too smoothly to be natural. Then he gently raised his hand to the level of Levi's chin, the movement itself crackling with electrical alchemy and raising the current in Levi's spine like a rheostat. Crawford paused, nine inches in front. Atoms filled the air, compounds, licorice cologne. The older one moved his face velvet-like, *You want some?* The willies shot through Levi's arm, causing it to raise, primally, a reflex unarrested until he tapped the man's hand away and the tin box shuffled. A black glint, an anti-flash, seemed to plummet into Crawford's eyes – *into them.* Levi went on autopilot.

"Oh, sorry. I … I meant to take it, the mint."

"They're not mints," Crawford backed off, his countenance armoring up now.

"I know," Levi offered a palm, recovering as best he could. "Sen-Sen? My Mom used these sometimes." *Should have said "liked these," not "used" … staying in the City? Is he asking? Suggesting?* "I'm going to try to fly home tonight."

"I see." Crawford snapped close the lid, re-hid the tin in a pocket. Cold. Colder. From a distance, he offered his hand. "Good luck." He waded back behind his black desk. Rejoined it. Levi again fingered the scar, slick now, sweaty. "Please excuse me. And please close the door."

And close the door? Did I ?... oh, come on! Levi stepped toward the desk and lingered as he pulled one of Crawford's cards from a tiny rack. The older man looked up. Levi spoke calmly. "You will succeed quicker in Billings with me than not. In a few days, I'll call Lily and set up a phone appointment, either to thank you for hiring me or to address any remaining questions you have." Crawford was unreadable. Levi turned away.

At Lily's desk he paused while she answered her phone. The voice on it was just loud enough to make stereo with the one from Crawford's door. *Did you see his suit? Get Billings on the phone!* "Can I call you back?" Lily was saying as Levi walked away.

At the elevator, Levi held the door for Joy and a companion. Then, almost thankfully, he became invisible to them as the man suffered forty-five floors of Joy's "mission critical value proposition." At the lobby, the man escaped. She shifted to Levi. "Hello ... you." She had forgotten his name. "I'd love to hear how it went, but I need to run," and she rushed off.

Levi found Jimmy, a giant, lantern-jawed young man in a uniform who called him Mr. Monroe. As Jimmy called for a limo, Levi noticed the big man's nose was slightly out of true with the rest of his big face. Levi could guess why. He tried to tip Jimmy, but the man said no, and we'll catch you next time. "Right," Levi said, feeling as if word of his failure had already seeped down.

The last place Levi wanted to sleep that night was San Francisco. At SFO, he wait-listed for the last plane to Salt Lake City. From a payphone, he called Angela. "I finally know what I want ... exactly," he began, "but I might have blown it." When he was done, he called Earl, the advertiser, to hedge his bets. "Hello, Earl? It's Levi. Sorry to bother you so late, but I've been thinking about your campaign..."

11

Sartorial Splendor

One's destination is never a place,
but rather a new way of looking at things.

Henry Miller

It was 1981. Levi was only twenty-one when he was hired by Bookman Stuart.

The DJs at the station bought Levi his first stock – a live sheep – which they put in his car. Others showed more faith. Earl the advertiser tried to sell him a new car. But the day came when, fresh from the sheriff's office, fingers blackened, fingerprint cards in hand, Levi stood in a brokerage office, in his future, smiling boyishly at the older brokers and secretaries who seemed reluctant to look back, let alone nod hello. Except Crazy Marilyn, the sweet 58-year-old sales assistant.

She rolled her chair with her old self in it out from behind the switchboard, halting his way. At least that's where it stopped when the castor got strangled by her long scarf. "I'm glad I was up front when you came in," she said. "I normally sit over there." She pointed to a small desk and then held up a key, waving it like a raffle ticket. "This is for you-hoo," she sang. Levi started to take it, and then drew back his head, eyes filling with discomfiture. "It's okay," she said. "Everybody asks. It's a squirrel's foot," she said, as though it would delight him. I am the keeper of the keys. Me. Oh, and I want to say: you – have – a – nice – color! Ooop-siee." She accidentally dropped the key and got on her knees to wrestle the chair for her scarf, ignoring him utterly.

Levi wouldn't be allowed to sell for six months. On his first day he sat in an unpartitioned bullpen, directly beneath a horizontal, ten-foot Trans-Lux ticker display that scrolled a thick black band past noisy vacuum jets that sucked over little yellow dots to form stock quotes. There were four clusters of brokers, each with four desks butted together at a single quote machine mounted on a Lazy Susan. Fifteen men and one woman – thirty-somethings, freshly ordained brokers – faced each other, smiling and dialing, barking with storefront confidence into phones, all the while wrestling for the quote machine and finger-stabbing its keys. It could display but one quote at a time. Nearby, the Reuters and Dow Jones News Service dot-matrix printers machine-gunned news stories onto unspooling, seven-inch-wide newsprint. The most important stories set off a bell, cuing Crazy Marilyn – or the newest trainee if Marilyn was, as usual, distracted – to rip and read it, announce it, and hang the ripped-off scroll on clipboards screwed to the wall.

Crazy Marilyn was assigned to type and file for the six newest brokers. She typed fifteen words per minute, flawfully, and no one gave her anything to file that they might need later. She had lived alone since her 27-year-old daughter died, and had thick, dimpled legs that poked from shortish skirts as stiff as lamp shades. She wore animal print scarves named Pongo, Boots, and Miss Kitty Poo Poo. While she worked, she hummed or softly sang old children's songs like *Hush, Little Baby* and *You Are My Sunshine*. Around noontime, she ate leftovers at her desk, except on Wednesdays. On Wednesdays, she took a two-hour lunch and had her hair tinted or shellacked at Billings Beauty College – her alma mater – and returned stinking of ammonia and varnish. The newest broker had to sit next to her. Levi sat three feet away, his elbows on his desk and his fingers in his ears as he tried to study a fat loose-leaf binder.

"I knew we would hire you," she continued from the week before, having rolled her chair next to his and waited until he finished reading page one of study materials. She introduced herself and said again. "I knew we would hire you."

"Oh, um. Thank you. Why is that?"

"You're the same color as my daughter?"

"I'm sorry?"

"My daughter. You're the same color as her. I watched you when you were interviewing ... through the window." She pointed as if peeking at the manager's office. "She was *wonderful*." Then she rolled back to her desk and hummed and worked and said nothing more and generally spooked him. For a week.

Between the mechanized sounds and everyone talking loudly (but not to him), and Marilyn talking (but not to anyone in particular), it was very hard to concentrate. One noisy Wednesday Levi was clipping charts from discarded chart books to take home where no one could watch him study them. It's something he did when he was too distracted. Marilyn, dressed for safari, had been back from the beauty school for about an hour and she stunk as if they might have dissolved her real hair – again. It got the best of him. "Why do you have your hair done so often?"

"The ozone layer." She pointed up. "Chlorofluorocarbons," she whispered. "They're in hairspray. Better once a week than once a day. Do you want to contribute?" She held out a soup can, the label of which had been stripped and replaced with one fashioned out of typewriter paper, colored pencils, Elmer's glue, and sparkles. It read, *Cash Out Chlorofluorocarbons!*

Levi decided it was better to be ignored.

Marilyn leaned forward and whispered, "You see things, don't you?"

"What?"

"You see things. In the charts. I see your eyes. Trancy. You focus at first, and then you don't for a moment. You take them home, don't you?"

Levi felt like he'd been caught in the outhouse with a magazine. "Yes. So?" *So?* Jesus. "I take them home, but frankly I don't have time to study here, and it's quieter there and…"

"My daughter said that noise didn't matter much when she saw things. She said she didn't hear anything. Anything at all. But she didn't look at stocks, though. She looked at people. Colors. Words too, I think. She said she could tell the unconscious mood of the world by words on television and in the paper and in public. Is that what you can tell?"

"Marilyn, I really don't…"

"She could – did."

"What did you say was in hairspray?"

"Chlorofluorocarbons. It was her gift, I told her." She looked serious, as if warning him. "No more than that, I told her. Just a sense. Like some people are sensitive to smell. No more." She smiled sadly. "She was smart. Like you."

A jolt of the yikes stopped him cold. He slid the scissors into a drawer and reached for safer topics, not getting as far as he aimed. "Marilyn, about the squirrels' feet. You don't, well, you don't kill squirrels…"

"Oh, that's just silly. I would never kill them."

As if in league to spook him, Levi's phone rang. It was the manager's voice. "Look over here," he said.

Levi sat straight and looked both ways, as if to cross a street. Through an office window, a man nodded and said, "If you've got time, come in here a minute." Levi quickly stood up. The boss was a kindly widower whose clean face and hands had grown squishy-white long before he transferred from Minneapolis as one last favor to the firm.

Levi walked through the boardroom, past the manager's assistant – navy blue outfit, perfect posture – and into the office. On his way to the sofa, he tried to walk confidently, but it was stilted, like he was trying not to step on a crack.

The manager halted him with a palm and casually gestured out the window at the boardroom. "Don't sit down. Look out there. Look what the brokers are wearing."

Marilyn waved, but Levi looked away. Brokers. Brokers wore … Levi felt his face redden. *Shit.* Navy blue, charcoal gray, pin stripes, club ties.

"Now look what you're wearing."

He didn't need to. It was an outfit he'd worn to sell FM radio. *Angel Flight* slacks with vertical seams down the front that bulbed at the knees and a dove gray sport jacket overlaid with a large gray and burgundy plaid. *Dammit.* He'd worried when he bought them. But that wasn't the worst. It was the scarf. It came with the outfit. He knew he shouldn't have worn it, not here, not under his lapels, and now it abbreviated their chat like a third party in the room. He pulled it off from one side.

"Levi, I want you to go home, and don't come back until you look like them."

As Levi retreated from the manager's office, Crazy Marilyn and Lynette, a farm girl come-to-town in a short, loudish dress which, despite self-conscious plucking, clung at the flesh above her leg warmers, were being similarly arraigned by the manager's assistant. Lynette appeared mortified, but Crazy Marilyn cheerfully took notes and sang "uh-huh, uh-huh."

A half-hour later, Levi was sorry to find Angela at their apartment, awash in construction paper apples, perusing a catalogue. "I thought you had kindergarten today," he said.

"The regular teacher got paroled early, so they sent me home. How about you, Cowboy?"

"They sent me home to…" He owed her more, and offered it begrudgingly. "… to change my clothes." She looked at him soberly until he pulled the scarf from his jacket pocket and threw it on a wet lump of coffee grounds in the kitchen trash. "They were talking to Marilyn and Lynette, the cashier, about their clothes when I left."

A moment passed. "They want you to wear big-boy pants?" She dead-panned it until a guffaw broke loose. She kept it up until his feelings got hurt. "Aw, hun-ney, don't feel bad. I was going to buy a little something for you today anyway." She held up the Frederick's of Hollywood catalogue.

"I need suits," he said, "not tawdry underwear."

"It's their bridal-slut-angel collection," she said dryly. "I'm pretty sure they mail them out clean." She tossed the catalogue on top of his scarf and grabbed her keys. "Come on, you big baby, let's go shopping. We'll spend our honeymoon savings on some big-boy clothes. But if you don't behave, you'll never peek at my *big girl* clothes again. Understand?"

12

MADE IN MONTANA

Sow the seed, and reap the harvest with enduring toil,
Storing yearly little dues of wheat, and wine and oil;
Till they perish and they suffer — some, 'tis
whispered — down in hell.

LORD ALFRED TENNYSON

After two months of solitary studying, Levi knew he wouldn't make it in the business. But because he had no other job yet, he got on the plane to New York. He and his trainee cohorts from around the country were herded there for a week of cramming that culminated in the Series 7 licensing exams. A typical trainee was thirty-four years old, married, male, and white. Most had been salespeople or athletes.

In Levi's group there were 112 men and 33 women. If they failed the exam once, they were fired. The ones who passed it earned nine more weeks in New York, packed three-to-a-studio in Midtown. Each day they rode the subway from Penn Station to 2 World Trade in the financial district for classroom training. Most charged cheap suits at Eisenberg and Eisenberg's or Mo Ginzberg's. On their $12 per diem expense check, they drank. They scammed free hors d'oeuvres at Harry's at the AMEX or Hanover Street and bought dirty-water dogs and pretzels from street vendors. And they drank.

By the third week, male or female, loneliness and alcohol had all but dissolved bonds and promises to lovers back home. Levi met a classmate from Denver he would remember as Cherry something. Her real name. Cherry. Hair like Dorothy Hamill. Plumpish. Thyroid, she said. He knew she wouldn't make it either. When ten weeks of surreality ended, so did the trysts, mostly at La Guardia or JFK. Some at Newark.

Once back home, scared new brokers proved wholly ill-equipped to competently value stocks or bonds – let alone find prospective clients – but most had an encyclopedic knowledge of the firm's high-gloss brochures on mutual funds and fee-based products.

New *registered representatives* were billed as Financial Consultants or Financial Planners or Financial Advisors or Investment Associates or Investment Executives or some other unregulated title that implied expertise. Apparently no firms employed salespeople. However, the success of FCs or FPs or FAs or IAs or IEs was measured by how many accounts they opened, how much money clients deposited, and what percentage of that converted into commission. It was called return on assets – or ROA – and managers received a monthly report detailing each broker's ROA. There existed no such report detailing clients' actual returns on investments. The truth be told, it didn't matter whether clients did well as long as they didn't sue.

New brokers' salaries fell at regular intervals until they were on straight commission. Less skilled salespeople simply starved out. The half-life of Levi's training class was ten months and three days. He kept track. On that day, Levi heard that the seventy-third broker in his training class lost their job. He made note of it, thought of his father, and got back on the phone.

Between 6 and 8 A.M. Monday through Thursday, Levi read research. At 8, he began cold-calling. He hated cold-calling. He was superb at it. Early on, to increase efficiency, he appropriated a country club directory. The club president soon called Levi's manager, also a member, who made Levi scuttle the list. Next he purchased names and phone numbers of households allegedly prequalified for wealth and income. Many folks on the list were dead. That's what their widows said. The wasted effort dispirited Levi. It inspired Crazy Marilyn.

"I know who the rich people are," Marilyn said.

He tried to block out her secret voice.

"My daughter showed me."

Now Levi looked at her, almost sure he shouldn't speak. "I thought your daughter was, well, dead."

"She is. That's how I know. I go see her all the time. When I save enough money, I'll buy her a bigger marker. A pink granite one. Like rich families." She smiled.

It took a moment. *Surely she didn't mean …* He said secretively, "Marilyn, I can't walk around graveyards writing down family names of rich dead folks and calling their relatives. I mean, I don't mind calling … the live ones …

but if I walk around graveyards and these guys find out..." he nodded to the other brokers.

She handed him several pages of scribbling from a legal pad. "No worries. They already call me crazy."

Levi stared in disbelief. "Yet, they made you mistress of the keys," he muttered. "How ... long ... how did you get the phone numbers?"

"Why, the phone book, silly."

"Marilyn, this is genius. Thank you." He felt seeds of shame for having judged her. "But even with this ... this list is fairly small."

"There'll be more. Since my daughter died, I've grown to like going to cemeteries. I clean up graves. It makes me feel good. And the history fascinates me. Lots of children died young a hundred years ago. Measles and mumps. The markers don't say, but I met a man there, an anthropologist from MSU — *nothing sexual*," she whispered. "I'm helping him measure patches of lichens on headstones because of how they grow different in different places, depending on altitudes and moisture and latitude, and grave stones have dates, so if you find other rocks somebody moved nearby you can measure lichen on them and know when that someone put it there because lichen doesn't grow on the bottom." As Levi stared, she waited for him to catch up, which he had no mind to do.

"We hope to eventually visit all the cemeteries in Eastern Montana," she continued. "He drives a van. It's no bother for me to write down the names on big headstones and bring you a phone book. Besides, then when you call families in little towns a hundred miles from here, maybe they'll do business without stopping in and seeing your baby face."

So she made lists and Levi called. It worked beautifully. They referred to it as his *very cold-call* list.

From 8 A.M. until 5 P.M., he called, one graveyard list at a time, seldom stopping to pee. He took a break when Angela brought dinner at 5 and then resumed until 9 P.M. He invited the living to seminars he gave in their town. The talks were well attended. Rural folks were curious about why an outside expert on something other than weed and feed would drive so far and buy coffee and Danish for everyone. On Fridays he didn't work after dinner – Angela insisted it was date night – but he normally clocked eight early hours each Saturday and Sunday.

Levi averaged eighty calls each day. He charted their profiles, time of day and responses, looking for patterns. Most prospects abruptly hung up, cussed at him, or talked about grandkids or the damn government until Levi said he had to go. His rate of opening accounts became astonishing, somewhat attributable to communication acumen common among bright kids of alcoholics. He was remarkably sensitive to subtleties in tone, cadence, and respiration – when to press, when to back off, when to empathize, when to take control. He instinctively knew what lies sounded like and wasted no time on liars. His kind frankness defused suspicion. He kept promises and was self-possessed in the face of abusers. He slept six hours a night and often dreamed about Roundup, waking up angry or scared. On those days, he called the biggest landowners he could find in the county records. One August day, he called a rancher north of Yellowstone National Park.

"Hello, Mr. Forbes." Levi had practiced an unembroidered presumption of rightful entitlement. "My name is Levi Monroe, and I'm a Financial Consultant with Bookman Stuart. I'm calling successful ranchers with an opportunity to own new investment-grade municipal bonds issued by the State of Montana that yield over 8 percent, state and federal tax free. Are you earning that much on your safe money now?"

Mr. Forbes said no thanks, and then asked for a quote on IBM.

"IBM. That stands for International Business Machines." Levi thought that piece of trivia might keep the prospect entertained while he wrested the quote machine from his desk partners. "Let me see here." His pulse quickened. He fumbled through a newsprint booklet on his lap – an S&P stock guide – not wanting to give another bad quote. "How's alfalfa this year?"

No answer.

Symbols were not always intuitive. The previous week he had given a client a quote on International Paper using I-P. International Paper's symbol was IAP. A purchase was entered, a complaint lodged. As his current prospect sighed impatiently, Levi fumbled the booklet to the floor. His desk-partner reclaimed the quote machine. "It's ironic that you and I are talking today, Mr. Forbes," Levi stalled, "and that we're talking about investments. Did you know that there's a preeminent investment magazine with your last name? It's Forbes. *Forbes Magazine.*" Just as he found the symbol – I-B-M – and swung the machine back his way, there was a click in his ear, followed by a dial tone. When Levi dialed back, there was no answer. He dialed again, waited, and slammed the phone down. He stood, looking at the ceiling.

"What's up?" asked Tom Wallace, the branch's top salesman, *as if he gave a tinker's damn.* Tom expected Levi to fail. Wanted it. You could see it in the rise of his fish-belly cheeks, the happy little pinch in the angle of their cusps.

Though pear-shaped and married, Wallace had nonetheless talked his way into bed with some of the younger secretaries. And he hated Levi, who, in front of those secretaries, had ignorantly asked Tom why the stock price on the monitor was often different from the price Tom quoted clients. What Levi didn't know was that Tom was hiding client losses. "Nice suit, Travolta," Tom had replied. "Was there a class ring with your GED?"

Levi took a breath, sat down, and told the story. Tom dropped a magazine on Levi's desk with a cover photo showing Elizabeth Taylor and Malcolm Forbes riding a Harley. "You mean *this* Mr. Forbes?" Tom said. The moment ripened. "You do know that he owns a ranch by Yellowstone, don't you?" Levi didn't.

Everyone laughed. Crazy Marilyn said she loved *National Velvet.* "Did you see her eyes in that movie?" she fluted. "They were just like velvet!"

"What?" Levi scrambled as laughter continued. He desperately wanted to know *something.* "Velvet was her character name – not her eyes. Jesus!"

Tom crowed. "My *God*! You two *deserve* each other."

"That's not nice," said Marilyn. "You know, Mr. Smarty, not everyone always thinks you're so special. But no one says so, because you're so mean."

"Oooo. Ouch!" Tom mocked. "Thus speaketh the jungle queen," he gazed below her skirt, "riding in on charging rhino legs."

Tom broke from the crowd and went into the manager's office, leaving the door open. "That kid will embarrass the firm," Tom bellowed, facing obliquely toward the window, toward his colleagues on the other side. "He *must* be stopped from calling influential people. Prospects should be matched with the broker's *experience*!" To prove it, Tom was willing to poll the other brokers in the office on the matter. He was yelling loud enough to pre-sell it. Then, if Levi wasn't stopped from calling influential people – or, better still, *any* person on a more senior broker's prospecting list – Tom would call Gary Crawford in San Francisco. "I talked to him about this at the award meeting in La Costa last month," Tom warned. Levi fumed. The manager said he'd talk with Levi.

That afternoon Levi worked out at the Y, making it back to the office before the air conditioning shut off and everyone went home. He took down $100,000 in Montana bonds from the municipal bond desk in Seattle. For all practical purposes, that meant he owned them and was responsible to sell them to someone. He'd keep dialing until that happened. Throughout the evening, clients weren't answering the phone. It was summer. Everyone was outside but him. Frustration compounded. He thought about Tom. *Protocol my ass,* he thought. So he tried to call Bob Hope in Palm Springs, but couldn't get through. The White House wouldn't take his call. Then he cold-called the governor's mansion. The governor answered.

Levi sat up straight. "Oh. Hello. Uh, sir, my name is Levi Monroe, and I'm a native Montanan, like you, but I'm calling from Billings – not Helena – but still Montana. Anyway, I work for Bookman Stuart – the brokerage firm? And I'm expanding my practice to accommodate a few new clients. Last May I heard you speak at EMC's graduation ceremony. I'd be proud to work on your behalf in *any* capacity you feel appropriate – money-wise, I mean. Anyway, is there a time when I could sit down with you? Buy you a cup of coffee?" *Coffee?*

"Did you just graduate?" the governor asked.

Levi said no, his fiancée did. He asked where Levi had gone to high school. Levi said Roundup. The Governor asked if Levi knew the Piccionis and the Adolphs and the Rodigarios. Levi did. "What made you think to call me?"

"Bob Hope and Ronald Reagan were busy. Malcolm Forbes hung up on me."

In an amused tone, Levi heard, "I'll be in Billings Wednesday. I'm free for lunch."

By 7 A.M. on a warm Wednesday, Levi was at his desk in his best suit, fondling the key to his manager's Cadillac in which he would drive the Governor – who used no entourage – from the airport to lunch downtown. Levi sat, foot bouncing, waiting for the call from Helena with the Governor's ETA. An hour later, Crazy Marilyn arrived cowled in a frayed, zebra-print neck-scarf named Stripes. Levi asked her to screen his calls and tell everyone except the Governor's office that he was in meetings all day. He made her repeat it back.

Hours passed. Levi was afraid to step away for coffee. He didn't want Crazy Marilyn leaving either. By 10:30, it was eighty degrees outside when she offered him steaming cider from her thermos. Another hour passed. Finally she answered a call and told him to pick up the line.

As he lifted the phone, Tom's eyes seethed from across the room.

"Levi Monroe."

"*Hel-lo-o.* This is your sister."

"Lam?" Levi looked dumbfounded at Marilyn's dented hairdo, but she was oblivious, pinching nutmeg from a baggie into a Styrofoam cup. "I can't talk right now."

"This'll just take a minute. I'm at the clinic here with Mom and Dad…"

"In *Billings*?" He rubbed his scar.

"…*Yes*… and when she's done, they want to come see your office … what it looks like."

"What it looks like?" On any day their presence would be unforeseen and unwelcome – but today. "Look, I'm pretty amazed at this call in the first place, but as it happens, I won't be here, and I'm *not* making this up. I have a meeting out of the office."

"When will you be back?"

"I have no idea." *As if that mattered.* He watched Marilyn pick up another call. "Not today. Just tell them I won't be here."

"Levi…"

"Just tell them! If you get a chance, you can call me tonight but I won't be here today. I love you, but I have to go." Marilyn had just said his name.

"But…"

"I have to go!" He and Marilyn hung up simultaneously. "Who was that?!"

"It was Angela. I told her you were talking with your sister. I didn't know you had a sister? That's so wonderful! I only had my daughter. Families are *won-derful.*"

Levi's head dropped forward like his neck had given out. *And now she'll cry. Crap.* "Please don't put through any calls like that. Just the Governor. It's important to me. Please."

Crazy Marilyn smiled. "I know it's important, Mr. Monroe. It's *so* important. I understand." She dabbed her eyes with Stripes, at once disarming and exasperating him.

"Look," he touched her shoulder. "I need to go to the restroom. Your hot cider is … well, let's just say it'll keep the doctor away today." She grinned. "I'll be right back, okay?"

He was, five minutes later, and Marilyn was on the phone.

"I'm sorry, Mr. Monroe isn't here."

Levi whispered, "*Who is it?*"

She smiled mindlessly, her attention fully allocated to the caller. "Oh he couldn't be expecting your call … he has an important day … out of the office. It's been planned."

"*Who is it?*" Levi repeated, futilely, as to a television.

She nodded only out of muscle memory. "Oh. Okay," she said sweetly. "Well, I'll tell him if he comes by. Thank you." She hung up, humming, *So Long, Been Good To Know Ya.*

"Marilyn, who was that?"

"She didn't say her name."

"She didn't say?"

"Huh-uh."

"What was the message?"

"What message?"

"I heard you tell her that you'd give me a message. What was the message?"

"Oh, it wasn't for you. It was for the Governor. He's supposed to go to the cow auction yard after lunch."

"That was the Governor's office? That's the call I've been waiting for!"

"Oh," she was happy for him. "That's wonderful! You were in the bathroom."

"Ahh!" Levi snatched his jacket and headed for the airport.

The Petroleum Club was a members' restaurant where old men ate what salty waitresses told them to and stayed late to play gin or poker. Under his boss's membership, Levi reserved a table. As Levi and the Governor walked in, Levi pulled his shoulders back but all eyes were on the popular politician, a wheat farmer and aging football star out of Montana State. Once seated, they were interrupted repeatedly by businessmen who either respectfully nosed their way up to say hello to the Governor or who brazenly strode there in odd-colored sport coats. Throughout, Levi sat dumbly, wholly ignored until the Governor introduced him. *Levi Monroe, this is so-and-so,* it went, *owner of such-and-such.*

Levi made mental notes of who he met, men he knew by sight but who had never taken his calls. He'd call them again soon. For now, he simply said, "Nice to meet you."

Levi decisively ordered Cobb salad on the premise that decisive was good, but it left an unbearable amount of time on his hands while the Governor read the menu. Suddenly Levi blurted, "Where do you keep your personal accounts?" *Crap!* "I mean, you know, do you have them with someone in Helena, or closer to the ranch?"

The Governor smiled congenially over the menu. "Why don't we finish ordering?"

Levi felt himself botching the biggest opportunity of his nascent career. His stomach agreed and protested against the lettuce and the bacon and the dressing. The Governor asked what his people did, and Levi joked evasively that he wasn't really like his folks. They led a ... simpler life, while Levi claimed a more "global perspective."

"Oh, really? Where have you been?"

"I lived in New York for a while – early in my career." There was that pang again. Definitely conscience.

"*Earlier.* Well. It doesn't get more cosmopolitan than that. How long were you there?"

"Ten weeks," Levi admitted. "But I made connections from all over."

"All over."

"It may be part of why I led my class at Bookman Stuart. It was the same when I worked in broadcast advertising. Things just come quickly to me. I've always thanked God for my native academic ability." That felt good: *native academic ability. Thanks, God,* he thought, just in case. "I don't know where I got it. I guess I'm the white sheep of the family." Levi grinned to make sure the Governor got it.

The Governor wiped his mouth on his napkin. "And all of this at twenty-two? Your parents must be very proud of you."

"Actually, twenty-three. I don't really talk about it much with my family." Levi said offhandedly.

"Oh, really?" The Governor laughed easily, at Levi's expense. Levi's face grew hot. The Governor leaned in. "Relax, son. You're as deserving as anybody in this room. There's nothing wrong with being from the boondocks." His cadence slowed. "It clearly worked for your parents. They had you."

Levi felt his scalp move.

The Governor leaned back. "In the mid-seventies, a tough guy who'd been in the Colorado prison system – I think his name was Lyle – got a chance to fight Muhammad Ali. Before the fight, a television announcer – maybe

Howard Cosell – went on about Lyle's background and asked him if he really thought he had a chance. Lyle said only one thing – something like, '*Judge me not by where I stand, but by the depths from which I've climbed.*' He didn't explain himself. *That* man had become a winner. He knew it."

"But Ali beat him."

"Crushed him. But Lyle knew who Lyle was. He was the best boxer he could be. But not every situation is so easy. Take politics. You can't get elected unless people vote for you. That's all some politicians think about – what do others *perceive* they are. And maybe that's all that matters if you want to accomplish something. You – me – everybody – has to decide, in any given situation, if it matters more for *you* to know who you are, or if what *really* counts is who *they* believe you are." The Governor uncovered a small basket. "Bread?" he offered.

Suddenly Levi's guest was again a public figure, opining that Montana needed to add value to its products. "We need to ship flour, not wheat … and steaks instead of cows." He talked about the size of the tourism industry and the folly of no sales tax.

Finally the Governor said, "It's always bothered me that Montana might pay brokerage firms too much in public finance fees to help us, the State, bring municipal bonds to market – to get our borrowing done so we can fund projects, or even operating capital until tax revenue comes in. Truth is, we don't let enough firms bid on the business, so we're probably getting gouged. Has Bookman Stuart ever approached us?"

Levi didn't know the answer, and, from the look on the Governor's face, he knew it. As a matter of fact, the only thing Levi knew about public finance was that he didn't know anything about public finance. So he went with that. "I don't know. I have no idea how to underwrite a bond. I'm not even sure who in my firm to talk with. So far, I just sell bonds to clients. But I'll get the answer. And I'll get the answer to any other question you ask, and I'll get it quickly, and I'll never lie to you. And if we're very fortunate, I'll save the state a great deal of money." Levi motioned through the room, "I'll save these people money. Ethically. If we work for them, that's our promise, isn't it? And maybe some of that money can be used to make them safer, or more comfortable." The Governor sat still, reconnoitering. *God*, Levi thought, *that was corny.*

Then, "Why don't you contact some of our department heads … see if they'll let your guys bid? Got a pencil?" The Governor ticked off the finance officials at the departments of Administration, Highways, Board of Regents, and Housing – departments that regularly floated municipal bonds. "If these folks don't call you back, talk with my assistant. She'll get you through – but I *don't* dictate who they do business with."

As Levi's eyes were in danger of swimming with gratitude, the Governor intervened, "And don't call my house anymore." The Governor's official residence was indeed just a state-owned house, a fairly modest one at that. "What the hell's wrong with you, anyway?" He smiled.

Levi was to hand off the Governor to some cattlemen at the Public Auction Yards for a forum on the reintroduction of wolves to Yellowstone, but they were a half hour ahead of schedule, and Levi wanted to show off the Governor to his colleagues – especially Tom. The Governor was happy to tour the Bookman Stuart office.

As they ambled through the lobby to the front doors, Levi spied Marilyn at the reception desk. She peered back with big eyes. When Levi opened the door, he smelled her freshly-shellacked head. To his chagrin, the Governor waded ahead, Levi scurrying to retake the lead, to control introductions. It was too late. Marilyn rounded the reception desk, straining the tether of her switchboard headset, which, at the depth of her curtsy, let loose and shot back, toppling her open thermos of cider onto the panel of blinking lights.

Unaffected, Marilyn held the somber pose. "Your Honor."

As he righted the thermos, Levi's face streaked with despair while the Governor executed a Renaissance bow. "M'Lady. To whom do I owe this pleasure?"

Marilyn popped up. "Oh, I'm Marilyn … and this is Stripes." She touched her shouldered scarf as though it were a pet parrot.

The politician laughed. "I'm pleased to meet you both." He offered his hand.

Levi raised his arm, motioning. "Governor, in the interest of time, may I introduce you to my boss?"

In the manager's office, the two older men joked about the Minnesota Vikings, flatlanders, and retirement benefits. Each glanced kindly at Levi as if they were teaching a young pup how it's done. The Governor eventually needed to get going. "You found a good one in Levi."

"We're proud of him," the manager winked. Winked!

"He's good stock," said the Governor, who looked as though he might wink, as well.

At that moment, utterly unannounced, Tom strode in and offered his doughy hand to the Governor. "Hi, I'm Tom Wallace…" he said as if it were good news. "Excuse me," he said pulling Levi aside. He pointed through a window into the bullpen and whispered, "Hey, Jethro, the Clampets are here."

In the field of desks, Lam was sitting in Levi's chair. Marilyn was sledding in an extra side chair so Frank could sit by Virginia, whose legs were crossed, her foot shaking, shaking below sweatpants that swung like arm flab. On seeing them, one of Levi's hands flexed involuntarily, open and closed, fingers to palm. In a collected voice, he said, "Would you mind doing me a favor, Tom? Would you tell Marilyn I need to take the Governor to a meeting, and I'll join my family later?"

Tom needed to wait but one, smug beat before the Governor said he wouldn't hear of it, and Tom added that he'd be happy to help out, give the Governor a ride. Truly. No bother.

Levi walked the Governor to Tom's car. As Tom absconded with the stolen celebrity, Levi reentered the office only far enough to hand Marilyn a folded piece of paper. "Take this to my sister," he said, and walked out. Twenty feet later, Lam read the note: "*Now take them home.*"

Over the next year, Levi drove to Helena repeatedly to give public seminars on everything from IRAs to managing investment risk. Before each trip, Tom howled that Levi was out of his depth. In Helena, Levi met with state administrators of public finance to convince them to meet the firm's investment bankers. Montana public officials generally mistrusted New York firms, and thus, Levi.

As a tactic to get Levi to go away, the state officials inundated him with questions, answers to which were either obvious but required in writing, or impossible to determine. Clearly the bureaucrats were comfortably entrenched in old relationships with other firms.

In an opposing universe within Bookman Stuart, Levi had incensed the firm's bankers with his presumptuousness, so they roundly eschewed him. In their view, retail brokers only hindered or queered sophisticated institutional relationships, so the investment bankers attempted unsuccessfully to contact the state without him. Both the seller and the buyer viewed Levi as an inexperienced meddler. But he persevered – dauntlessly, stubbornly and, in the opinion of his colleagues, stupidly.

Levi discovered what was important to state officials – avoiding scrutiny, saving money, and taking an occasional free trip – and he learned what was important to Wall Street investment bankers – money and winning. He arranged exploratory trips to New York for state officials and paid his own way to meet them there. He read five years of Montana bond prospectuses and compiled a summary of underwriting fees the state had paid and sent it to his firm's bankers, followed by phone calls in which he pointed out the prestige of landing an entire state's municipal bond business. He learned how to draft answers to *requests for proposals*, or RFPs, and he convinced Lynette and Crazy Marilyn – who revealed an astonishing aptitude for written detail – to type them at night for the price of a pizza delivery and a thank you.

Finally, Levi arranged a meeting in Helena between the Department of Administration and Bookman Stuart's public finance bankers regarding a $100 million municipal bond offering. To everyone's chagrin, Levi attended. The mood in the boardroom was cool at first, the administrators and the bankers viewing the other respectively as mules and serpents. After only twenty minutes of nonstop serpent-talk, the mules began packing their bags. Levi interrupted.

He handed out a spreadsheet Lynette and Marilyn had copied and tinted with colored pencils. He began with an emotional lay-up – that most Montana municipal bonds should be held by Montanans.

"Brokerage firms employed by the state for previous new bond offerings have placed only *some* of the bonds in Montana," Levi said. "The majority went to a mutual fund company in Boston. Not only has hundreds of millions in Montana bonds left the state in the last decade – reducing availability of bonds to Montana residents in an already thin market – but the underwriting fee and the commissions, millions in total, millions, for selling the bonds had been given to out-of-staters. To Easterners." He hung there. "And when the bond market rallies – which from time to time happens whenever interest rates drop – and these appreciated bonds are sold, there are capital gains to be taxed. But if the owners of the bonds live out of Montana, some other state gets to tax those gains." As one, the mules leaned forward.

"Bookman Stuart, though New York based, will not hoard the bonds at the expense of other brokerage firms in Montana. At the expense of

Montana citizens. At the expense of the state. Instead, we will distribute the bonds not only through our own Montana salespeople, but through a syndicate selling group that includes *all* Montana brokers, regardless of firm affiliation." One of the bankers glared at him for seizing such liberty. Levi loved it. "The spreadsheet I've provided details the amount of commission that would be paid to Montana brokers for initially marketing the bonds and how commission translates into state income tax," he said. "Additionally, it's important to note that part of the underwriting fee will be paid to Montana residents – including me. I will pay Montana, not New York or Massachusetts, income tax on that. I've also estimated taxes on capital gains if the bonds are resold in the next twenty years, given three different interest rate scenarios. Over the life of the bonds, the incremental Montana payroll tax alone could theoretically cover the entire cost of underwriting the bonds."

The Bookman Stuart bankers sat stunned. The public officials started asking questions, all directed at Levi.

A few weeks later, Levi was standing at his manager's desk, fuming. "What do you *mean* I'm to stay away from Helena?"

Levi's manager looked deeply apologetic. "I just got off the phone with Gary Crawford in San Francisco. He says I have to assign a more experienced broker to the State."

"Why? Did the investment bankers complain?"

"He didn't say that."

"Did someone in Helena complain?" Levi could see on his face that they hadn't. "Then why? At this point, there *is* no one more experienced up there than me. This is bullshit! Who does Crawford want? Tom?" The manager said nothing. "Fuck! You are kidding me!"

"I haven't talked to him yet, but he is the top producer, and he left me a note asking for it…as though he knew about Crawford's call."

"Of course he knew! He's been stroking Crawford behind your back."

In a rare break in decorum, the manager shared, "They're both pricks."

Levi looked out onto the bullpen. Tom was smiling and talking out the side of his mouth to colleagues gathered near him. "Tell Crawford if he gives it to that fucker, I'm going to Merrill."

"Levi, I'm retiring soon. If you don't stay, Tom will surely end up managing this branch." Levi had considered the possibility – a rung toward Crawford's job – toward the prize.

The manager's assistant popped her head in, looking coy, "You have a phone call."

"Can you take a message?" the manager asked.

"You want to take this one. It's Mike Sandler."

"You're kidding." She wasn't. The man stood to take the call from the firm's president. There was a series of *yes, sirs,* and *thank you, sirs,* and a bemused snort. "Yes, sir. Right here." He handed the phone to Levi.

Sandler gave Levi's name a traditional Jewish pronunciation – *levy,* like a tax. Levi corrected him. Sandler said how proud he was of Levi, thanked him for putting Montana on the map. "Some of the city kids could learn a thing or two from a country boy," he said.

"I don't understand," Levi said.

As the president of the firm informed Levi that Bookman Stuart had won the Montana bond deal, Levi's face radiated through the window into the boardroom, melting Tom's grin. When Sandler said Levi's finder's fee for the first deal would be $50,000, Levi's adrenalin surged. Levi would also be allowed to run, and received commission on, the "friends and family book," an allotment of municipal bonds from the deal that went to favored clients. "The State is yours," his dense voice rumbled. "Don't screw up our investment bankers on this. Listen to them. Good job. Now go back to work." He hung up. Levi threw his fist in the air and whooped.

"There. President trumps Divisional Director," the boss said as he shook Levi's hand. "I think Crawford'll be kinda mad."

"Kinda?"

At four o'clock that afternoon, Levi's manager had Marilyn dead-bolt the doors, leaving the key in the lock so people could let themselves out. He assembled the employees in the bullpen while his administrative assistant carted in three buckets of ice and champagne. The operations manager circulated through the crowd with a sleeve of paper cups. Bottles popped and wine poured. The manager stood under the sleeping Trans-Lux ticker and made a short speech about what Levi's accomplishment meant to the office, the firm, and how perseverance and hard work were no match for beginner's luck. Ha, ha, they said. He raised his cup.

"To Levi Monroe – a long-shot bumpkin who refuses to see where he shouldn't be. Lucky, to be sure, but no longer a beginner. Instead, a man from whom we can all learn." During the *Here-heres*, he looked at Tom. "And who now, incidentally, has the office record for monthly production. From now on, drinks are on Levi!" As the manager dragged Levi to his side to speak, people drank and applauded and laughed. Except Tom. Tom stood close enough to Lynette to smell her until she cheered. Then he peevishly trashed his cup and let himself out.

"I *do* feel lucky," Levi grinned broadly, vaguely aroused. "Thanks, everyone. And I know I was lucky."

"You bet your ass," someone said to everyone's delight.

"But I didn't do this alone. I'd especially like to thank my assistant, Marilyn, and thanks to Lynette. Every support person here helped, from answering my phone to typing proposals …"

"To changing your diaper," Marilyn blurted, sparking hilarity as she covered her mouth with a tiger print scarf named, of course, Tigger.

Levi raised his hand to quiet them. "As a gesture of my appreciation, I'm directing half of the finder's fee, $25,000, to be split appropriately among all of the support help." There were seven of them – over $3,000 each. The room broke into cheers. Levi looked at his astonished manager. "Call it a clothing allowance," he jabbed, and laughter erupted again.

Later, as she took her leave, Crazy Marilyn kissed his cheek and thanked him, setting the protocol for the other assistants. Reveling in warm recognition, Levi imbibed until most of the well-wishers were spent, at which time, in a fleeting moment of intimacy, Lynette, brandishing car keys and a crafty grin, kissed his cheek and whispered, "Would you like to see *all the clothes* I buy with this?" Before he could recover, she giggled and coyly made for the door.

Angela. He had forgotten about Angela. Minutes later, Levi bound to his car and tore like a kid from the parking lot, shouting above the radio, "Thank you, God!" and "Whoo-hoo!" and "Yes!" As he drove his arousal deepened and he squeezed himself once, through his pants.

At home he found Angela in the living room, still wearing a big teacher's skirt. Without so much as a "Guess what?" he told her the news.

"Fifty thousand dollars!" she said and threw her arms around his neck.

"Well. Twenty-five thousand. I gave half to the support help. But I'll get paid on subsequent deals too, and I won't need to share it if I don't want to. This first split'll buy plenty of favors."

"For twenty-five thousand? ... I'd give you anything you want. A-ny-thing," she winked.

He held her hand to his crotch. "A-ny-thing?"

"Ooooo. *I'll* be your support help, stallion. *You* get a big bonus ... *I* get a big bonus," and she unzipped his pants. "Seems like it makes us *both* happy." Holding him, she backed to the couch and sat down. Moments later she was lying back and her skirt was everywhere. Later that night they would make love, but winning made this embrace primal. Winning made him high. Winning was addictive.

13

POINT AND FINGER

He that has eyes to see and ears to hear
may convince himself that no mortal can keep a secret.
If his lips are silent, he chatters with his fingertips;
betrayal oozes out of him at every pore.

SIGMUND FREUD

"Do you know why I wore Chameleon today?" By their second year together, Levi had developed a sense when not to bite at Crazy Marilyn's questions – this one about a scarf she was wearing that changed from greenish-gold to goldish-green, depending on how she swiveled at you in her chair – but she always told him anyway. She waited him out until he looked.

"I'm told debate rages," Levi finally said.

"Changes in the powers that be are in the air! Ooopsie," she lilted, "I shouldn't have sai-eeed. But it could be you-ooo," she pointed at him with the side of her hair helmet.

Levi knew the possibility. He had surpassed Tom as the top producer in the branch, partly because of bond underwritings and partly because of a following that grew from his uncanny ability to anticipate major moves in stocks. He knew what that success meant now ... what it *might* mean, he reminded himself. The branch manager was retiring. A secret and official decision about succession was being made. In the industry, when a branch manager retired or got fired, it was customary to tap the biggest producer that had his hand up, notwithstanding that the two skill sets were largely unrelated and often at odds. Crawford actually came to Billings. He snuck in that afternoon.

Things looked good for Levi. He met Crawford's jet, met with Crawford in the airport coffee shop. An interview of sorts. Crawford was self-censored, even distant, but Levi stayed heartened by the sheer logic of his chances. After all, he was honest, smart, worked hard. He radiated results. He was, by all measures, the most successful broker in the branch. Respected.

Crawford and the old manager were clandestinely meeting for dinner that evening, according to Marilyn, at which Crawford would pretend to consider the retiring man's advice. So much the better, Levi thought. Levi respected protocol, that Crawford acted now like he hadn't decided.

The next morning, desks were clean and suit jackets were on. Tom arrived late, about 8 A.M., making it there just a half-hour before Crawford. On some level, Levi was surprised Tom showed up at all. When the manager introduced Crawford around, people pretended to be surprised. Crazy Marilyn, however, had crocheted him an abrasive vegetable scrubber with the letters GC in the center. She was asked to man the phones while the staff gathered in the bullpen.

Crawford gave a speech about the retiring manager's decades of service and loyalty and appreciation. An inspiration. A beacon. The manager took an aw shucks posture. Crawford smiled at each person and seemed to Levi to linger on Levi. So did the manager. Okay, Levi thought, *one step closer.*

"...but with each farewell, there is a new beginning, a new era, an exciting time of opportunity. This decision has been difficult. You deserve a skilled leader, a leader with respect, a *loyal* leader..." Levi tried not to swell, "a mature leader. At breakfast this morning, I asked Tom to take the responsibility for leading this office, and he accepted. So, people, I am proud to introduce to you your new manager, Tom Wallace."

Levi felt his face flush and pump redder with his colleagues' applause. He fought it, clapping along. He stayed only long enough to toast Tom and then lied about needing to see a client out of the office. On his way out, Crawford and Tom summoned him into the manager's office – Tom's office.

"I look forward to your support," Tom said. "I'd like you to consider being my assistant." Levi knew immediately it was cheap insurance to keep him from jumping ship to another firm. Tom needed him more than anyone. Managers' bonuses came from profit, which came from revenue. Furthermore, Levi needed a supervisory license to move up. As an assistant manager, he would get sponsorship to take the tests.

"Normally, you must be twenty-five to sit for the Series 8 supervisory exams," Crawford added. "If you accept, I'll see what I can do. Or perhaps you'd rather concentrate on the State of Montana – given that Mike Sandler gave it to you." It was a jab that gave pleasure to all parties, though for differing reasons. "I'm guessing you value loyalty. Like I do."

Levi showed nothing. "Sign me up," he agreed. That sealed it. He would wait. Study and wait. Shit like Tom can't float forever.

Despite his distrust, Levi initially enjoyed the added authority – approving trades, countersigning checks, moving millions. But soon he realized he had became Tom's cover, while Tom entertained clients, friends, sometimes secretaries, on long alcoholic lunches.

A year into Tom's regime, the tension between Levi and him was palpable. One morning at 7:30, Levi arrived late. Lynette was leaning over his desk with a stack of trade-corrections. She was already unusually nervous. Then she caught him looking at her ass. "Wow. New suit?" he said, trying to cover. It didn't work. "What are these?" Levi said.

"Tom told me to move all of the executions from your sale of stock of Abba Rice into the house account. He's asking New York to investigate."

"What! Investigate what?"

"Don't blame me. He says you sold all your clients out less than a day before the board of Abba Rice admitted they cooked their books and the stock crashed. Do you like that stuff?"

"What stuff?"

"Abba Rice. Seems hard, even when you overboil it."

"What?"

"Never mind. He's pissed."

"Who?"

"Tom. Everybody else in the office still owns it, especially Tom, and our analyst never put a sell on it. Yesterday Tom had me look at the phone logs and he saw a call you made to Abba Rice headquarters in San Francisco. He wants Compliance to investigate … sorry, 'interview you'… and look for insider trading."

"What! I *always* call companies before I make a major move in their stock. They refused to talk with me. I didn't know anything about their 'cooked books!' Give me the tickets." He snatched the papers from her hands and launched into Tom's office. From Tom's posture and tone, it was clear he was on the phone with someone of authority. There was a pile of time-stamped stock buy tickets on Tom's desk – the white copies had already gone to the wire room for execution. *Typical sleaze*, Levi thought. Tom had been out drinking the previous day. He could not possibly have called all these clients for permission before he entered orders in their accounts.

Tom looked smug as he hung up. "What's the problem?" Tom's lilt rang sardonic, his fish-belly cheeks already stung with alcohol.

"Good question. What's with these? You know I don't have insider information."

"Hm. Probably not. But as manager, I have to do the right thing, you know, treat everyone the same … fiduciary responsibility … per Gary Crawford." He nodded at the phone.

"Fiduciary responsibility, my ass! It's not *my* church pastor that's paid cash to help sell oil and gas partnerships to the congregation. Tell me, is that a charitable deduction if it never hits the collection plate?"

"Be careful."

"Careful? Of what? You're already afraid I'll leave. Did Crawford advise you to draw first, Marshal Dillon? If you stir up an investigation now, my license will get hung up for a couple weeks. So if I can't call clients, you can ask them to stay with the firm before I can ask them to move with me? Sure. Whichever of us the client says yes to first wins? We all know that's how it works with clients. Okay. But do you and your asshole buddy think that would stop me from leaving?"

Levi wasn't sure if he should bluff or not, but he sensed himself pushing too far too fast. Would they try to freeze his license if he left? Or fire him? He remembered the manager's name at Merrill Lynch, making a note to call the guy. For now, maybe he should back off, just in case.

"Wow. *That's* disappointing," Tom said. "You were thinking of leaving? We all know you're your own man. An investigation shouldn't scare you. But now that you mention it, it *would* stop your clients. I mean, if your license didn't transfer to a new firm, you couldn't call them, huh?"

"I haven't even talked with the competition." This was almost true. He had taken calls from Merrill, Shearson Lehman, and Paine Weber, but he never agreed to meet with them. *Call the guy at Merrill,* he reminded himself again. "What do you expect me to do about this trade? I have thirty clients I told to sell that stock. Most of them have already bought other stocks."

"Well. If Compliance decides you did have insider info, all of the trades will be busted. I'm afraid that for now, I have to move the trades to the house account."

"So you want me to call thirty clients and tell them that the stock I told them they sold, they still own – and at a 60 percent loss? By the way, Tom, it isn't lost on me that you'll keep these sales at higher prices for the branch house account and just buy the stock back at lower prices to balance the books – you know, cover the short position. And that will make the branch, what? $300,000? A profit that rightfully belongs to clients? And I also get that your bonus would bump $45,000 if you get away with it!"

"Wow. That's a pretty strong accusation from someone with a history of *mysteriously* guessing correctly when our firm's own analysts have no idea something's going to happen. You know, Crawford personally knows the officers at RICE," Tom recited the symbol. "He brought their employee stock options to the firm and he himself didn't know the stock was going down. What will you tell New York? You're a fucking mystic? The phone records show you're always making phone calls to these major corporations that you *say* won't talk with you, and then you place major bets on their stock. And you win way too often, *right?*"

Levi flushed of anger. He wanted to attack the bastard. "Crawford knows the founder. The founder's not there anymore. He heads EcoPulse now." Levi caught himself playing the knowledge game, and stopped. "As for my research, we've been down this road before." He grabbed Tom's scratchpad and scribbled something. "I don't get insider information. I just ask questions, do my due diligence. Someone should ask if Crawford gets paid off by Abba Rice."

"Whoa. Careful." He wagged a finger. "I repeat. I'm exercising fiduciary responsibility."

"What about the clients who can't afford to lose this money? Are you going to steal their money too?" Levi flopped the pad in front of Tom.

"I said careful. Crawford doesn't take prisoners. Neither do I." Tom scowled dubiously at the pad. Levi had drawn a long string of symbols. "What the hell's this?"

"Funny you use that word – prisoner." He spoke wryly. "It's a formula."

Tom snorted. "For what? I took B-school math. I've never seen some of these symbols."

"Some are my own. You wouldn't get it."

Tom laughed out loud. "Have an analyst call me."

"It's how I figure it out." Levi didn't mention phantom lights or color. "This RICE thing's even easier. Most of their stock's buy volume was coming from their own coffers – their corporate buyback program authorized by their officers. On the sell side, the stock *supply* was coming from the RICE officers themselves, who were exercising options and selling the stock into the market – which had artificially high prices fueled by the corporate buyback program. It couldn't last. The company's in a big-ass litigation because their rice causes allergies. Right now they don't earn enough to cover their dividend. It ain't fucking brain surgery."

From Tom's look, it could have been.

"And I know Bookman's agriculture and food-stock analyst is in San Francisco," Levi said. "Same building as Crawford. But frankly, I don't give a shit. What about my clients? Like Mrs. Thompson. She bought the stock because we recommended it for dividend income. She owned it three weeks, and Wham! She can't afford it. She's alone. She's too old to work at McDonald's!"

"Will she complain?" asked Tom.

"Maybe not. She trusts me like family."

"Then she won't sue. What's your problem?"

Levi made a fist. He stared until Tom fidgeted and said, "Fuck, this isn't an oat bran commercial, and you aren't Wilford Brimley. Giving away profit and bonuses isn't 'doing the right thing.' What about your commission? You sold it in good faith. Now, we need a reason to bust trades. Did you lie to her? Or me?"

For Levi, a fantasy flashed from the barrel of a gun. His tone lowered to a warning. "I didn't lie. She's afraid to outlive her money. She's like … Marilyn."

"Tell you what. If we bust this trade – like she never bought it – we have to report that you at least *inadvertently* misrepresented the investment to her. Are you good with that?"

"No."

"Who gives a shit? The NASD says the error report has to give a reason. It's the law."

"Regulation – not law." He wanted to add, *you moron.*

"And you have to take the error charge against your pay," Tom dug in a pile for Mrs. Thompson's ticket. "Market loss – hers – is about $12,000. The branch won't eat your error." Silence. "You take the error," said Tom, "and we move the commission away from you. We can't have a conflict of interest. Commission was $700. You pay that back to her too."

"You intend to take the commission!"

Tom smiled. "Oh, and one more thing – speaking of Marilyn. I've warned her before, but it's now only you and one other broker who are willing to work with her. I'm letting her go."

"You can't just *let her go*. She's got, what, two years until full retirement? Where else would she get a job?"

"She's not cost effective. If you'd learn to work the P&L, get on my team, you might get me promoted out of here, and this branch could be yours."

Levi's voice grew truly foreboding. "Not cost effective? I'll tell you what. You prorate the average number of brokers in here, per sales assistant. I'll take on Marilyn by myself and pay the difference in her salary. If I'm entitled to one-third, I'll pay two-thirds. And you're right. I may get this branch one day but I can do it without —"

"Fine. Two-thirds the benefits, too."

Again the gun fantasy. "I don't think so." Levi felt something snap inside. His shoulders flexed. Tom's eyes livened. Levi's arm bolted over Tom's desk, making the man flinch so his chair lurched. Levi's scarred hand dropped short, onto the desk, clenching a pile of yellow ticket copies with carboned handwriting, a whitening fist ripping them back.

"Listen," Levi warned. "The only part of this discussion we just had is that I'll pay Marilyn from now on."

In his head, the objective Levi recoiled, dispatching urgent, red signals to his mouth to shut the hell up before all was lost – everything! The job, the money, the ladder out! The other Levi, the raging Levi, screamed bullshit!

Clutching the ticket copies, Levi said, "I'll keep these, you son of a bitch. If you bust my trades, I'll have the Securities Exchange Commission and NASD reconcile the timestamp on them with the phone company's records of when you talked with clients. These trades are unauthorized, like always. They'll kick your ass out for fraud, and the world will be better for it. If you want to take me down, here's the fucking phone." Levi snatched the receiver and jammed it at Tom.

"Call Crawford now! While you're at it, ask him if he manipulated the research on Abba Rice."

Tom barely breathed, blinking. Blinking. In the silence, the objective Levi finally seized the initiative. As if to buttress a crumbling threat, Levi's fist bounced the receiver off Tom's desk. "Thought so." He pivoted and strode through the doorway, whispering, "What the hell did you just do?"

For weeks, the wound festered. Tom whispered, or kept his door closed. Levi tried to concentrate. He was trying when Marilyn bent on her knees behind his chair, rump-bumping it as she dove into his credenza drawers again and again, rummaging. She smelled of solvent. He kept his head down, drawing charts. He refused to ask what she was doing. Peripherally, two tubes of support hose ran along the carpet, terminating left of his chair where ankles muffined over sensible pumps whose toes were staked firmly in the rug. Bump. Bump. Finally, "What are you doing?"

"If I am sending anything to Mr. Crawford, it will be in order. Order, order, order."

"Crawford? What are you talking about?"

"Order. It's not just important to keep it, but it's just as important people think you keep order. It is the basis of all trust." With obvious discomfort, she cranked her neck to see him.

"What are you sending to Crawford?"

"His office asked for the yellow copies of your order tickets. I am putting them in order by day and time ... according to the timestamp. That way when he gets them he won't have to – well, Mr. Crawford himself probably won't be the one to…"

"Marilyn, why did Crawford…" he caught himself. "Tom! What did he ask for?"

"Tom doesn't talk to me. He…"

"Listen. Did anyone ask for anything else?"

She blinked back in time. "I think so."

"What do you mean, you think so?"

"Well I wasn't there, so I couldn't know."

"Know what?"

"If anyone actually asked Lynette for your phone records. But I know she's pulling them out, so I think someone asked for something, but I wasn't there, was I? You see?"

"Lynette?" he stood, stilt-vaulting Marilyn, and headed for the operation cage, hand digging in his pocket for the management key.

Lynette had become Tom's ally. The collateral damage of Tom's reign, particularly high staff turnover, had singularly benefited her. The once dowdy farm girl landed a stint as wire operator, and then as cashier, beginning along the way to dress beyond her means. It was inevitable. When the operations manager slot opened, Tom tapped Lynette. She had built experience. Of the support crew he inherited, she alone hadn't quit. Besides, Tom had told Levi, she and her husband were Mormon farmers – a low security risk – and she had "a nice set of pins."

Moments later, Levi keyed open the door to operations. He sidestepped two 2-foot pillars of phone bills rising from the floor. Beyond them, he closed on Lynette at her desk, her elbows straddling a mess of cancelled checks and bank statements, open palms supporting her forehead. He noticed something. His name.

"That's not my signature." He snatched the top check and looked at it. Someone had forged the second signature, the countersignature, on it. He looked down at Lynette's forearm on the rest of the pile. "Show them to me. Now." Her strained, waxy face peered up. She dragged her arm. Some of the pile hit the floor. He bent for them. "Who did this?"

"I don't know. I wasn't…"

"Bullshit. How hard do you want this to be?" He shuffled through the checks. A man's writing. He bent toward her face. "You know he'll hang *you*, if he can." One more nudge. "And he can."

As her eyes welled over, she said, "Can we go for a walk? Please, Levi."

He couldn't recall seeing such pure remorse. Through his anger bled an amalgamation of pleasure with rancor. This could be what he needed. Adrenalin and, what? He stirred. "Alright."

They walked quietly for several blocks. He hadn't seen that skirt before. Thin material. Very flattering. Finally, across from the courthouse on North 27th, Lynette crumpled onto a grimy park bench, new skirt and all. He waited for her to speak. She shifted her fragile eyes against a beggar on the lawn. Levi gave the man $20 to relocate. "Now tell me." He sat beside her.

Lynette watched the courthouse and talked. She explained that over the last few days, an officer at the local bank where the firm made its daily deposits called repeatedly, seeking assurances. He was worried about the balance on a Bookman Stuart brokerage account on which New York checks were drawn by a common client and deposited into that client's local bank account. Bookman Stuart bounced the checks back to the bank because of insufficient funds. The bank officer finally asked to talk to Lynette's boss, apparently unaware that Tom was both the client *and* the manager.

When Lynette passed the call to Tom "the manager," he guaranteed the banker that Bookman Stuart would pay the checks drawn on "the client's" Bookman Stuart account. Ultimately, Tom the Client bounced $275,000 in Bookman Stuart checks written to the local bank, all of which Tom the Manager guaranteed. Because of the guarantee, the bank allowed Tom the Client to draw funds against the local bank, and the $275,000 disappeared.

An hour ago the banker finally noticed that both Toms were the same, and now the bank was short the money and demanded that Bookman Stuart wire Fed Funds to cover the checks.

"It's check kiting!" Lynette burst into tears. "He stole $275,000!"

Levi's first impulse was that Lynette should be fired for looking the other way. But as he studied her face and form, he felt an unexpectedly strong desire to put his arms around her. "Don't worry so much," he said. He touched her knee and her skirt slid on her nylons. He leaned in front of her. Her swollen lips and wet eyes sluiced him into less vague desire, further heightened that she had chosen *him* as the vessel of her confidence. "If Tom guaranteed the checks, then it's Tom's problem. You'll be fine." He waited until she looked at him before he laid his arm across her shoulders. "Really."

"You don't understand. Either Tom will be mad at me for *telling you*, or if I tell Crawford's office, he'll fire Tom and me, God, maybe even arrest us! Or New York will fire me for not telling them sooner. My husband wants kids. We need this job," she sobbed.

"No one's going to fire you," Levi squeezed her shoulders.

"Crawford." Levi said the name like it was a joke. "I don't think muddying the water going through the division is the right way to go. New York won't blame you," though he believed otherwise, "and Tom can't."

"Levi, you don't understand." She took a deep breath and side-glanced at his face. "I've been seeing Tom, I mean, outside of work." She sobbed again. "I should have told the bank about the checks, but I didn't want to get him into trouble."

"Where's the money?" Levi asked mechanically, but his imagination flashed on Lynette naked with Tom. *Eww.*

"Tom has two personal accounts at Bookman Stuart – a checking account and a trading account – plus one account at the bank. It's a triangle. He ran the checks in a circle. In the trading account, he used the float on those checks to gamble on options in the market."

As she heated up, a couple walking by and looked. "He day traded for two weeks – using the float to play the market, and trying to sell at a big profit in time to cover the circle of checks! And it worked for a while, too. He bought me this dress!"

"Hold it down, okay."

"I'm sorry. Our home office never knew because the bank never sent the checks back to them. At first Tom would sell in his trading account and transfer the money to his checking account to cover the bad checks." She took a breath. "Then he started losing, and the bank...I'm so sorry!" She covered her face with her hands. "So he wrote *bigger* checks and made *bigger* bets. But he kept *losing*."

Her hands dropped, "God, I'm in so much trouble. I *knew* what he was doing. I asked him about it, but he got angry and said I didn't have to make a federal case out of it."

When they got back to the office, Levi circumvented the divisional office – and Crawford – and called New York Compliance. An auditor with a chainsaw voice ordered Levi to sit by his phone. A half-hour later, the firm's chief compliance officer called Levi back and confirmed that Tom had indeed stolen $275,000 and gambled it away. "Listen, you don't say nothin' to nobody, and the girl neither," he said. "We can't get out there for a couple days. Can you give us the number of your county's district attorney?"

It was then that Levi saw himself in the manager's office. *One step closer.* "I'll do you one better. Tell me what to do and in the morning I'll meet with the DA myself."

It was a long interview with the Yellowstone County assistant DA. Levi was amazed how many times he had to explain how Tom had stolen the money. The attorney seemed sleepy and said he was rusty on banking law. He asked twice if there was a weapon or "anything sexual" involved. Levi said no and felt oddly compelled to add, "I'm sorry." The DA said it wasn't Levi's fault. When Levi got to the office, Tom was gone for the day.

The next morning, in the lobby outside Bookman Stuart's double doors, a knot of people began to form around a cameraman and reporter, a young

East Indian woman who'd charmed the assistant DA into a scoop. She hovered impatiently, checking lighting and sound, practicing for bigger markets. Inside, Levi asked Marilyn to make a call.

"I'm sorry to bother you, Tom, but I think you should come down here. There are sheriffs here." The deputies had been there for the better part of an hour. She knew Tom knew it. She had seen him drive through the lot.

"Is anyone on the phone with you? Did they ask you to call?" Tom said.

"No, sir. Do you want me to get someone?"

"No, no. I'm sorry, but I can't come in right now. I'll try to make it later, and I'd prefer you not tell anyone you spoke to me. I have some things to take care of this morning, um, personal things, family things, you know … my kids."

"Oh, I hope they're all right, sir. I remember when my daughter …"

"They're fine. They're fine. It'll be fine, don't worry. I'll be in later. Is Levi with them?"

"No, sir, he's here."

"No, no, not with my kids. Is Levi talking with the police?"

"No, sir. The sheriff. They're in your office. Everyone is very upset. Suicide is so sad. I remember …"

"Suicide? What suicide!"

"Your minister, sir. I thought someone told you."

"What minister?"

"The one from your church. I thought you knew. It's awful, sir. They found him in his car, in our parking lot. It must have happened last night, poor man. He shot himself."

"Shot himself? You must be kidding!"

"Oh, no, sir," she said solemnly, reaching in her drawer and pulling out her soup thermos. "I would never kid."

"Listen, Marilyn, is the TV station still there?"

"Yes, sir."

"You've got to get ahold of Levi and tell him to keep this out of the press."

"I don't think I can, sir. Not with the note and all."

"Note? What note?"

"The Reverend. He left a note. I saw it. It had blood on it. It wasn't very long. It just said 'That was the worst damn advice I ever had.' Excuse my language, but that's what it said."

"Jesus!"

"Yes, sir. Jesus."

"Marilyn, have the press seen the note yet?"

"No, sir."

"Okay. Do everything you can to keep it that way. Go tell Levi right now! We *must* keep this out of the press. Uh, listen, I'll be right there. Please watch the back door and unbolt it when I get there. Don't tell anyone I'm coming. And *don't* let the police talk to the press before I get there. Can you do that? Can you do that, Marilyn?"

"I think I can do that, sir."

After they hung up, Marilyn buzzed the manager's office and Levi picked up. "I'm sorry to bother you, sir, but I just talked with Tom and he's on his way. He says the sheriff should wait."

"He's coming? He knows the sheriff's deputies are here?"

"Yes, sir. I tried to be salesy, like Tom is."

"Really? Easier than I thought. Thank you, Marilyn."

Ten minutes later Tom's car bottomed out as it raced into the back lot. Marilyn waited by the glass door and watched Tom run stiffly toward her, as if the blacktop were icy. By the time he reached the door, he was flush with exertion. As he raked his long wisps of hair into order with his fingers, she flipped the deadbolt key and let him in.

"Have they talked to the press?" he whispered breathlessly.

She shook her head. "I don't think so, sir. They're waiting for you."

"Good!" As Marilyn lingered at the door, he strode cockily through the office. People stood. They stared at him, mouths agape. "Come on, folks, back to work. This too will pass. Please, back to work."

Tom's pace slowed, gazing through his private office window. Two massive sheriff's deputies. A man in a suit – the detective, Tom presumed, as he dove in with billowing nostrils. "You must keep the note from the papers." Tom spouted. "For his family's sake. He was ill, after all, deranged, clearly. For his dignity. We owe him that."

"What note?" said the detective.

Tom answered with a look of bewilderment and his eyes quickly swept to Levi. The detective nodded at the uniformed men, and Tom suddenly got it. He bolted oafishly, retracing his path through the office with wisping legs, coattail aflutter. At the back door he still had the lead. He reached out, as he had a thousand times before, to flip the deadbolt. The key was gone, the door locked. He spun tamelessly and shot a beseeching look at Marilyn, vacuous Marilyn. While he fumbled for his pockets, his pale, sucker-eyed face lit hot for the TV camera, two hulkish silhouettes overtook him. They snapped handcuffs on his flaccid wrists while they read him his rights. Stoop-shouldered and burning with disgrace, he was escorted through the office – a new man's office. Someone muttered, "Good riddance."

A minute later Marilyn snuck up on Levi. He felt her press something into his hand. It was the deadbolt key. Her eyes brimmed with mischief. It took a moment for him to put it together. "Marilyn. Holy shit! You are *so* much deeper than people know."

"Not really, dear," she said sweetly. "Deep down I'm shallow. Screw the asshole." She turned away and Levi felt Lynette's hand on his back, an unspoken thanks.

The firm was also grateful. That is how, at twenty-five, Levi became the youngest manager in the Bookman Stuart system. He announced his own promotion with a tombstone ad in the local paper, as was custom in the business. The morning it came out, he found a sealed envelope taped to his office door. In it there was a clipped copy of the ad and a typewritten note that read, *Count on me if you need anything*. Acting busy at a typewriter outside his door, Lynette glanced at him, if only for an instant. Instead of acknowledging, he went in and closed his door. His office. At his desk, he placed the ad in a new envelope. To go with it, he wrote a note to Lam, telling himself he didn't care if she read it to their parents or not. Truth be told, he counted on it.

The phone speaker on his desk came to life. "Mr. Monroe, Angela's calling. Should I put her on hold or tell her you'll call later?" The voice was Lynette's. She smiled.

14

POACHING

Consider life: It is all a cheat.
Yet fool'd with hope, men favor the deceit;
Trust on, and think tomorrow will repay.
Tomorrow's falser than the former day

JOHN DRYDEN

Levi hadn't meant to get involved with Lynette. It was just that she was always there.

It began, he supposed, with her gratefulness for his protection when Tom was arrested. Levi successfully lobbied New York to retain Lynette, albeit no longer in the cage with direct access to money. He salvaged Lynette's career and some of her dignity by employing her as his administrative assistant, a role she instantly revered as a sacred trust.

Levi often worked late into the evenings and she often stayed late with him. Like all great assistants, she had frequent whiffs of intuition, often seeming to know what he needed before he needed it. She knew how he felt on management issues and she knew what advice he would give clients. So it was natural for him, wasn't it, to share his frustrations with her? And his triumphs?

Bookman Stuart unremittingly pressured local managers to recruit high-producing brokers away from the competition. Once an office is profitable, adding the revenue from clients of a newly recruited, experienced broker is *very* profitable. The incoming broker always told his or her clients an elaborate story about why the move was necessary. Sometimes they said the new firm surpassed the old firm in research and client service capabilities. Sometimes brokers insinuated that management at the old firm was unethical. Sometimes the incoming broker demanded an elevated, meaningless VP or Senior VP title so they could tell their clients it was a promotion. But it was always about the money. Always.

It was common for a broker who produced $500,000 in client commissions at their old firm to get a signing bonus of $400,000, and it was a seller's market. Reaganomics looked real. The Dow approached 2000 for the first time. Broker commissions had never been so fat. Bounties had never been so high. Levi courted brokers from other firms – Merrill, Smith Barney, UBS, Morgan Stanley. He knew if he offered a big enough signing bonus, he would hire some of them. It all came down to greed.

It was about money for Levi, too. If a new broker brought the office $500,000 in additional client commissions, about $175,000 would hit the branch bottom line, and the branch manager's bonus would increase by $26,000 – every year the new broker performed with the firm. Additionally, if lightning struck more than once, the local manager would be hailed by more senior officers as brilliant. Career talk might follow.

Levi and Lynette had been courting a million-dollar-producer at Merrill for months. They had met him for lunch and for drinks. They sent flowers to the broker's home on his anniversary. Lynette babysat his children. They had flown the broker and his wife to New York to meet Bookman Stuart's top brass and see *Les Misérables*. If they landed the broker, Levi's bonus would increase by $50,000 per year and he told Lynette he would allot part of it to her.

One afternoon the broker called Levi and said he had finally reached the end of his rope with his old firm. Besides, he was impressed with the availability of Montana municipal bonds through Bookman Stuart. He wanted to work for an up-and-coming manager like Levi, he said. He was an advocate for his *clients*, he said, not the firm, and it was only with *them* in mind he made this decision. And, for merely $50,000 over the usual deal, or nearly $900,000 in total, he would feel comfortable bringing his clients to Bookman Stuart. And, by-the-by, he and his wife just broke ground on a 10,000-square-foot home atop the sandstone cliffs that were the Rims. Levi called Gary Crawford for approval, and Crawford told him not to fuck it up.

What followed was an exciting and frenetic time. Beginning two weeks before the broker defected, every night after midnight, the recruit met with Levi and Lynette at Bookman Stuart. They copied the broker's books and client statements and prepared transfer papers to be mailed to the clients the moment the broker resigned from his old firm.

On the day the broker came over, Levi invited the entire office to drinks and dinner. On the moonless twilight ride to the restaurant, Lynette rode with Levi. He was unsure if it was the money or her presence that made him feel randy. She sat next to him at dinner. There was wine, and the more of it she drank, the closer she sat. Peripherally, Levi watched the eyes of his other employees. Above the table he seldom looked at Lynette, but below he brushed his hand along her skirt. Again. Again.

After the entrée, Lynette waited for a lull in conversation to announce to the table that she needed to straighten her desk at the office and get home to the farm, a twenty-mile drive, she said. Levi ignored the initial cue, but she persisted. Finally he offered her a ride to her car, leaving his assistant manager, Charley, to entertain the crew and pick up the tab. Anything they wanted, Levi said, just keep the receipt. Outside, a breeze stirred.

In the office lobby, while Levi unlocked the oak doors, Lynette visited the restroom. He entered his office and sat at his desk in front of his wall garnished with plaques attesting to his presence at Director's Club or Chairman's Council or some other internal boondoggle for big-commission producers. He was sorting through the pink message slips when he heard Lynette enter the reception area and lock the deadbolt. He watched out his open doorway as she sauntered barefoot across the carpet, sighing and waggling her pantyhose carelessly from one hand until she reached her desk outside his door and stuffed them into her purse. Levi picked up the phone to call Angela.

As he dialed, Lynette carried a file into his office. He felt her warmth when she shuffled behind him and laid it on his credenza. She closed the drawers that he had left ajar. Then she leaned against him and slipped one arm around his waist and the other around his chest. She pressed against his back, and he softly, almost imperceptibly, pressed back. Before the phone rang he placed the receiver back in the cradle and turned to her. They kissed, and she rocked her hips into him. He pulled back once to look at her face, all doe-eyed with admiration and urgency – for him.

After several minutes, kissing grew into indelicate groping. Levi pulled away long enough to close his office door and turn out the lights. In that moment, deep in his abdomen, beneath the sex and triumph, came a feeling of tightening, of …what? Fear? Premonition? Guilt? Before he could decide, she was on her knees in front of him. It was too late. They scooted the chair from behind his desk so they might not be seen, and he removed only one pant leg so he could dress quickly if he had to.

Ten minutes later Levi, while Lynette was in the ladies' room, was in the men's room washing and checking the fly of his dark suit for residue. He pulled up his pant leg and winced at the rug burn, unsure how he would hide it or explain it to Angela. Racquetball, maybe. When he emerged, Lynette was waiting in the lobby, sleepy-eyed. In a black night wind, he walked her toward an angry-looking muscle car he didn't know she owned. Old Chevelle. Her husband's, Levi presumed. The dark headlights glowered back until Levi looked away.

"You know, Angela's pressing us to get pregnant. I mean, not you and me, Angela and me, ha ha." Lynette laughed back. "Well, her more than me. But I don't want to yet, but … so we *won't* … I decided. But that doesn't mean I never want to have kids with her … I mean, my career's important, and her teaching is too, but …"

Lynette put a finger to his lips to stop him from talking. "Shhh." She kissed him.

"We shouldn't do this," Levi said. "Not again, you know …"

"I know. We don't have to. I mean, of course we don't *have* to … you know." They laughed. "But I'm not really sorry." Lynette kissed him like a spouse and got into her car.

In the accusing silence of his car, as Levi rushed his keys to the ignition, a gust stippled his fenders with sand. He turned the key; turned up the radio. At home he made love to Angela with a purpose he had never before fully embraced, letting himself imagine impregnating her, offering his all as an act of secret contrition. He was overwhelmed that she had given him the only home where he'd ever felt safe. He vowed to himself never to dishonor her again. Never.

But he did.

With every victory, every proselytized recruit, Lynette found a reason to work late – so much to be done! Levi was on a roll, and he began to put low producers on probation to make room for bigger hitters. It was like a perpetual game of gin, he told her. First you get a full hand, then you draw and discard until you have gin, and then they promote you and you play a new hand. "If you go, I go!" she'd say, sounding half serious. Angela seemed pleased enough with Levi's success and had no doubt taken the news to Roundup, but Lynette admired him and praised him continually. And it felt good.

Lynette went to most outside meetings, felt important and smart, like a partner. They stole more brokers from the competition. Prospective hires and clients regularly called to talk with *her*, ask *her* advice. Some days even Angela called and asked her about Levi's workload or disposition. Lynette and Levi achieved goals. They won. And it excited her. Levi excited her. Not like the farmer she had married – predictable, scheduled. Perfunctory. She imagined Levi as her husband, and once she told Levi so, but he withdrew from her for days afterward. Perhaps someday, she thought. He was different from other men. He even tasted different.

And so it happened. Plenty of times. But not anymore, he swore each time, not any more! At first he would argue with himself on the drive home. Then sometimes sooner, as he put his pants on. At last even sooner, when he was checking into the Super 8 or the Motel 6. Jesus, he was becoming like his father. No. He was not his father. He and Lynette were both married, and they both did want to stay married. He was sure of it. Well, maybe not Lynette. But it would have to stop! The guilt was too much, he would tell himself as he ground his way through traffic lights, fits and starts, toward Angela and home. Sometimes he'd turn on the dome light, checking his shirt, his hair, his fly. Did he wash his hands? What the hell was he doing? He wanted grander triumphs, bigger than Montana, with Angela, but now he couldn't even talk about promotions – not with Angela for fear she would tell Lynette – and *Lynette* never went home from the goddamn office until he did, DAMMIT, and she scared the shit out of him, and she'd just have to back off. *God, how do I get out of this?* He loved Angela. Wanted kids with Angela. Someday. It had always been Angela. His family. That's why he worked so late. And then he would realize that the voice in his head sounded salesy. And then more shame. For the moment, lust hid inside, escaping accountability, skulking somewhere. "Dammit! Why this?" Lust. Shame. Gorging on one and then the other. Twin addictions. Could both be quenchless? "Come on, God! Quenchless? You made both quenchless?" A voice in his head liked his word choice, wondered if God was impressed, hoping God didn't know his vanity. "God! Is this to get me to church? Like my father went? Well, hell no!"

15

HOTEL CALIFORNIA

The meeting in the open of two dogs, strangers to each other,
is one of the most painful, thrilling, and pregnant of all conceivable
encounters;
It is surrounded by an atmosphere of the last canniness,
presided over by a constraint for which I have no preciser name;
they simply cannot pass each other,
their mutual embarrassment is frightful to behold.

THOMAS MANN

In 1875, the splendorous Palace Hotel was finished, and its builder was found dead in a river. Since the very beginning, Levi mused as he stood in its lobby reading placards and looking at old photos in black and white and sepia-tone, shit happened there. In 1906 it shook and it burned, only to be resurrected. President Wilson celebrated the signing of the Treaty of Versailles there in 1919, and four years later, President Harding carried the secrets of the Teapot Dome and Prohibition scandals inside it and collapsed. He died. The hotel seemed a way station between the auspicious and inauspicious. Beginnings ended there. Endings began. Ooo-weee-ooo-ooo. At least that's what played in Levi's head while he waited in its high-brow lobby, too early to check in. Ooo-weee-ooo-ooo.

It was only early October, 1987, but back in Montana winter was already unpacking its drab wardrobe. So Levi welcomed the visit to somewhere green. It was also good to get away from the quote screen. Since the nosebleed high of 2700 in August, the Dow had been pounded down 400 points – 15 percent. Some said buy. Levi felt spooked. Perhaps a different perspective might help.

Just off Market Street in San Francisco, Levi and other Bookman Stuart officers were gathering at the Sheraton Palace for the western divisional branch managers' meeting. He had waved off the bellman, thinking no other man should carry his bags. Now, after a half hour of a strap digging into his shoulder, he regretted it. His footsteps echoed off soaring ceilings and marble and hardwoods, into the ferns and flowers of the cavernous glass-domed Garden Court Restaurant that had once been the central carriage entrance.

"I'm sorry, Mr. Monroe, the rooms aren't ready yet," the man at the front desk said again. "We're still programming in, per Ms. Oliver's requests." Ms. Oliver. There was a woman named Oliver on Crawford's staff. *Programming?* Levi didn't know enough to care. He walked around some more. He checked the time and then buttoned his suit jacket. He rode the escalator to another glass-domed area, the Sunset Court, from which he entered a ballroom set up for a conference. The Bookman Stuart crowd was gathering.

At the rear of the room, a pride of tall, suited, older men, the ones whose "back then" was the farthest back, circled a table of coffee and croissants like lions picking at a kill while the lesser predators had to wait. Their tone and manner said they knew unknowable things, a ritual meant to keep more junior colleagues feeling exposed for not knowing. Levi thought it was bullshit. He broke in and said hi in a voice that presumed they'd heard of him. As they responded, he gazed past them. Near a corner, Lily Fujiwara held the attention of a few young secretaries, all pretty, who had been sortied a few blocks to the hotel from Crawford's divisional office to provide support. "Crawford's corporate petting zoo," someone murmured.

Levi spotted Joy Parnell. She had told him she cut her hair. Not enough. Her hair-cloud was less billowy than when she interviewed him years earlier, but her face still got lost in it.

Joy was the division's only female manager. She was recently promoted to help run an operational complex on the San Francisco Peninsula, one that processed employee stock option business that Bookman Stuart administered for other public corporations.

Out of the need to attract and retain superior talent, Silicon Valley companies had reengineered a way to print money. Generous employee stock option grants were the currency, and brokerage firms like Bookman Stuart acted as virtual cashiers where engineers and salespeople could exchange options for wealth. Options gave employees the right to buy their employer's stock at the price the stock was trading on the day the options were granted. That price deal was usually good for ten years. If the market price rose, the employee only needed to contact whatever brokerage firm his employer had hired to execute the options for profit. If the employee had the right to buy 1000 shares at $10 and could immediately sell it at $20, then the employee made a quick $10,000 profit. It wasn't until exercise that the parent company incurred a like charge on their income statement. Because most employee options were exercised when the stock was high, all shareholders tended to look the other way and the expense and dilution of existing stock value went uncriticized. In short, a company could hire and hold top talent at an obscene cost without immediately revealing that cost to shareholders. With a wink and a nod, some companies even backdated the options to show lower prices so the employee (or officer) reaped an instant gain.

To execute employee options, Bookman Stuart charged corporations between six cents per share and nothing. It was a loss leader so that Bookman Stuart brokers had the opportunity to convince the option exerciser to invest the profits in something new – for a commission. Under Gary Crawford's nurturing, the option exercise business had grown so large in Bay Area offices that a processing center was built just to process Ex & Sell trades. Joy managed it. Early word on the street was that she was good at capturing client proceeds into accounts at Bookman Stuart. Maybe a little too good.

Levi noticed Joy watching him juggle his briefcase, a croissant, and coffee. In a light blue shirt with French cuffs under a pinstripe suit, she strode confidently toward him. "Can I take something?" She took his cup before he answered. "We may as well get used to working together."

"Thanks. Good to see you again. What do you mean by 'working together'?"

"Where are you sitting?" she asked. Levi nodded toward a nearby table that held his name card. "We're the youngest managers here," she said. "I've always been ahead of schedule. You should be proud."

"Well, I start slow, but I fade." He set his briefcase beside his chair and sat down. Joy bent at the waist to set his cup on the tablecloth, affording him a glimpse of her lacy bra. *Was that on purpose?* He looked away to her hand. "What's with the one short fingernail?"

She touched his arm. "I'd better find my seat."

Braids of suited white men untangled around white-clothed tables aligned in a room-sized chevron and punctuated with breath mints and water pitchers. With august airs, jackets were removed. Throats were cleared. Reading glasses were donned.

Up front, top executives perched behind a slightly elevated speakers' table. Several New York department heads had drawn the short straw for the San Fran trip. Crawford, their local host and EVP, sat in the middle next to Mike Sandler. Levi noticed that Gary wore a light blue shirt and French cuffs, just like Joy. *Oh, please*, he muttered.

As president of the firm, Mike Sandler was boss to all and legend to many. He was a dark, barrel-chested man in his sixties. He had heavy eyelids on a big face. Levi had heard stories, like the one in which Sandler flew to Atlanta to see a dying employee and, over a disputed cab fare at the hospital, tore off the taxi's door.

With a viscous voice that seemed three feet thick, Sandler's opening remarks evoked combat fraternity. Older managers lip-synched at "the best-damn-managers-in-the-business." Afterward, while other presenters spoke, Crawford presided haughtily, surveying the audience as though he suspected them of something. Occasionally he whispered in Sandler's ear and got a look. When the look became one of irritation, Crawford resumed surveying.

Periodically, reports were handed out, and the lofty panel pretended to discuss issues as they told the branch managers how things were going to be. The head of mutual fund marketing talked with his hands, his gold bracelet leaving circular, reflective tracers as he detailed how profitable it was – regardless of investment performance – to recommend the firm's own inside mutual funds versus outside funds managed by other companies. As a reminder, managers and salespeople would now simply take a pay cut if they sold outside funds. While he spoke, his assistant passed out sleeves of golf balls. "Outside funds? Fu-get-about-it," he said. Representatives of insurance and the municipal bond desk made similar pitches.

Eventually Crawford got around to pounding the table about recruiting brokers from other firms in order to bolster profitability and bonuses. "Some of you are better than others."

Emboldened by his success in this arena, Levi felt he had valuable insights to share. "But we need to be conscious of quality," he said loud enough to be heard, and then almost inexplicably felt the need to elaborate. "I mean, we should perform due diligence so we don't haul out our competitors' garbage for them by hiring their bad guys." The room quieted just long enough for him to stop feeling smart.

"I wasn't referring to you, Mr. Monroe," Crawford said into the mike, sparking laughter. "And don't worry too much about the rest of us. We've been around a while. Perhaps one of the older managers can elaborate during the break." Snickering. "Besides, if a top producer at the competition hasn't lost his license, he can't be all that bad." The assembly laughed.

Levi's veins stung with embarrassment. *Why bust my balls?* he wondered. *Because Sandler gave me the Montana muni business? Because Sandler promoted me? Because Sandler wants to meet with me later today? My success increases your bonus, asshole.* He took a breath and his mouth began to form when, mercifully, Crawford adjourned for lunch.

Before joining the herd for a plate of chicken-something and steamed vegetables, Levi escaped to his room to call Lynette. She gave him his messages and a market update. "Something feels funny," he said. He opened a *San Francisco Chronicle* to the stock pages and panned back his head, taking in the double-page spread as one image. He stared out the window in the same, holistic way. Then he took charts from his briefcase and asked her for prices and volume. He laid the phone on the desk, concentrated on patterns and colors, allowing his thoughts to melt and congeal. "You're here somewhere," he mumbled. "Lynette, listen. Something's wrong."

"Oh, here we go," she said.

"What?"

"You know what."

He wished he'd never told her. "I don't have time…"

"I'm not helping anymore until you tell me how."

She was burning time. She would burn more if he didn't tell her something. "Have you ever looked into deep water, trying to focus at some level in the middle? To find some object you suspect is there, knowing if your eyes find its depth you'll see it?"

Silence. "Fine. Don't tell me. But don't treat me like I'm stupid. What do you need?"

Levi plunged ahead. "This is why you're licensed. I think this market might collapse like a wet taco. I need you to call the key clients, stock clients, and tell them I want them to sell. Discount commissions to the bone. When they say yes, drop the tickets. As soon as you're sure the clients are out, sell every stock in my accounts." He checked his watch, wanting to get downstairs. "Yes, every stock… no, I'm not kidding.…I know you can't make recommendations. Just call them. I don't have time.…No, I'm not crazy. Listen, I've got to go. I'll call you."

After lunch Crawford introduced Deirdre Oliver, his division's Human Resources specialist. So that's Ms. Oliver, Levi thought. An angular, fine-haired dirty-blonde, she took post beside Crawford on the panel. She fixed only on her notebook, scratching in it with piano-fingers, scrutinizing with bruise-blue eyes, her thin lips giving away nothing of her thoughts.

In the afternoon, Crawford told managers how to avoid paying medical and retirement benefits to part-time employees by reporting that they worked only twenty-nine hours per week. Benefits kicked in at thirty hours. The head of New York Operations laid out how to cut costs for assistants by deliberately spreading the help so thin that desperate brokers would pay up to get an assistant of their own.

Next, Crawford wanted managers to hire their quota of women and minorities as broker trainees, even when the interviewer believed the candidate would fail as a broker. "Cost of doing business," he said, on the verge of a wink. He paused for Deirdre, his bony HR specialist, to get it in her notes. He lingered until she acknowledged him. Looking back, he smiled at Joy in the front row.

Next to Levi, an older manager smelling of cigarettes whispered, "CYA. He's padding statistics. The National Organization for Women and the EEOC are suing his ass."

"Mint?" Levi offered.

"No thanks. At a dinner last night he called them corporate herpes – women and minorities. Said once you get 'em, you can't get rid of 'em." Levi cringed at the man's lascivious smirk. "Personally, I think the pressure's getting to him. You're from Montana?"

"He said that? Exactly?"

"What I heard. I know people who pretend to have property in Montana."

In Billings Angela sat across the desk from her OB/GYN, squirming like a kid with a slow parent at Disneyland. He was older than her father, practiced at this sort of thing. If it weren't for his desk, she'd have hugged him again, just like she did before she was fully buttoned from the exam.

"Pay attention," he said. "I'm not kidding when I tell you to take it easy. You have the same congenital issues with your uterus that your mom had. She did what she was supposed to. You're proof of that, but her passing at your birth should be warning enough to you. I don't want to scare you – medicine's come a long way since her time. I don't think you yourself are at undue risk – but I mean it when I say take it easy. Understand?"

She burst with happiness. "Should I quit work, go on medical leave? I'm expecting a promotion. Should I turn it down?"

"You could work, but let's play it by ear. If there's trouble, you'll have to decide. If it's early, you can abort – not that I'm an advocate. If it's in the second trimester or later, I'll order you to bed. All right?" As she rounded the desk, he rose just in time for the brunt of her hug.

"Thank you! Thank you!"

After the break, Sandler's heavy voice fell through speakers like a bowling ball through a sock. He praised Crawford's ability to produce extraordinary interest income in the Bay Area offices. Levi thought it was overkill. Sandler joked that Crawford perfected his craft studying the EFHutton check-kiting days. "We've never lost a suit where Gary was named," he quipped. They all laughed. As Sandler concluded, a report was handed out. It ranked each office's interest income on margin debits and free credit balances. Crawford retook the microphone.

"Margin debits are how we get rich. We want clients to borrow against their investments. We also want their free credit balances to stay uninvested, so the firm can make interest on it. Most of these balances automatically earn money market interest for the client – but there are some free credit balances in certain types of accounts, such as credit balances of clients who exercise employee stock options, sell the stock, and wait for a check. The longer the client waits to cash the check, the higher the firm's interest income, and the higher your bonus…and mine."

As Crawford belabored the obvious, Levi focused on the spreadsheet – read it – resisting the urge to absorb it like charts. He circled a figure at the bottom. On average, interest income made up about 15 percent of a branch office's profit. However, Crawford's San Francisco and Peninsula offices earned more interest income alone than profit on all commissions and fees combined. "Impossible," Levi whispered and instantly ran the numbers in his head. Crawford's bonus on interest income must top … $1.37 million a year. A second report appeared.

"The Bay Area is home to the Silicon Valley." Crawford bragged "New companies are born here every day. We are at a unique time and place to profit from the revenue produced from new stock offerings – companies going public."

As he nudged Levi, the smoking manager pointed a yellowed finger to the line on the report. "Look at that. His offices are scalping the hot deals."

"Pardon?" Levi whispered. A chunk of croissant was riding the man's chin.

"Look how long they're holding the syndicate stock in client accounts." The manager pointed to the column again. "Just a couple days, on average. They buy on the offering and sell into the market as soon as the price pops. At least ten times as fast as any of the other offices. Crawford isn't placing these deals with investors. He's flipping them. Some favorite clients must be getting a sweet deal. Have to be. Probably Crawford's mother," the man grinned.

Levi had wholly forgotten that Crawford had – even could have – a mother. "Hm. He's got balls."

"I hear he's crazy," smoking manager solemnly shared. "Really. From the pressure."

By 5:30, when each manager had caught either narcolepsy or ADHD, the general session ended. Notes were stuffed into briefcases, the ballroom emptied. Most headed for their rooms to freshen up and make phone calls before the banquet. Mike Sandler stopped Levi at the escalator.

"Hang back for a minute," Mike said with low resonance that Levi felt more than heard. "You, Gary, and I need to talk about your career."

"Oh, Gary too? Yeah. Makes sense. Okay. I'll wait." *Shit.*

Mike disappeared into the crowd of managers who each carried with them some urgent question only Mike could answer, a question to be asked in close quarters, in a low, serious voice while others waited, a question honed and tailored to demonstrate how insightful the asker was or how uniquely important his particular business unit was to the firm as a whole.

Levi stood the outlier. The handle of his briefcase slickened as he switched from worrying about Sandler liking him to worrying about Crawford hating him. Working closer to Crawford would get him closer to Crawford's job – farther from Roundup. Closer would also make Levi an easier target. Decide now. Perhaps Levi could forge a friendship out of their strained past. These things happen. He had to piss. To stay available, he held it. As the crowd thinned, he shifted his briefcase from one icy hand to the other, air-drying his pink palm and then his soot gray one. He squeezed the handle into the gray scar. He felt graceless, loitering. Finally, he saw Gary follow Mike into the ballroom. A minute later, Mike waved Levi in. From the end of the table by the door, Crawford motioned Levi to sit.

Across from Levi, Mike leaned back, rubbing his eyes with his palms. "You've done a good job in Billings. Probably saved our ass. Now I understand you want a promotion."

How do these things get started, Levi wondered. He had never said to anyone he wanted a promotion. Outside of home, he had only wondered aloud about it once, on the phone to Joy. "Yes sir," Levi heard himself say.

"Gary thinks you're still too young. What are you, twenty-eight?" Levi nodded. He would be soon. "Jesus. Anyway, Gary needs some help. He's a victim of his own success. This thing down here has gotten too damn big for him to do everything. So we're creating a management job under Gary for someone to run the south end of Silicon Valley, the offices that don't do any stock option exercise business – San Jose and maybe Santa Clara and Carmel. Gary's got his hands full with Menlo Park, Palo Alto, San Francisco – the rest of this goddamn division."

As Mike spoke, Gary put on his reading glasses and perused a report, not looking up.

"You're married, right?" Mike asked.

"Yes sir." Levi's digestive tract churned with apprehension.

"Any kids?"

"No, sir." He swallowed. "Not yet." Thank God we agreed to wait, he thought.

Mike assessed him. "Don't take it so hard. It's an unrelated skill set. Anyway, whoever takes the job won't have time to wipe their own ass for a while, let alone raise a family."

"I'm sure that's true," Levi said, with no idea whatsoever why it would be.

"We have a couple of other people to consider before we make a decision, but you've got a good shot at it. Do you have any questions?"

"Not really. I need to learn about the ex & sell business."

Gary eyed Mike like I warned you and shook his head a degree or two.

"I told you," Mike said. "You won't be handling that. Any other questions?"

All Levi heard was the word 'won't.' Is this a done deal? "I'd like to see a P&L so that I can study the business mix of the three offices I'd handle, check the pay."

"Don't worry. " Mike said. "You'll make plenty. But remember, bigger money means bigger restrictions. For senior managers a third of each year's pay is tied up in stock that takes three years to vest. You leave, you lose it. Cost of housing is ridiculous here, too. Ten to one."

"I understand," said Levi, no longer thinking, but simply reacting, trying to stay cool.

Mike glanced at Crawford. "Do you want to add anything, Gary?"

Crawford didn't look up from the report he had been reading. "I do not."

"Don't worry," Mike said to Crawford. "Working with you will make him older. Ask anybody. Have Lily give him the P&L so he knows what the fuck he's looking at."

Levi held it all the way to his room before bursting joyously. "Thank you, God!" He laid the briefcase on a small table and went to the toilet, where he stood, too thick to pee. He laughed at himself. A minute afterward he sat on the bed and called Angela. It was 7:15 in Montana. The phone was busy. Just as well, he thought. It wasn't a done deal yet – was it? Better to surprise her when it was. What about Lynette? He pushed the thought of her into the shadows for now. As he hung up, his emotions broke adrift on welling vanity and arousal. He felt exquisitely alert as he circled the room, periodically glancing sideways into the wall mirror, trying to catch his reflection unaware. He fiddled with the TV remote, looking for nothing. Finally, he stripped naked and lay on the bed. Minutes later, momentarily spent, he looked at the alarm clock: still an hour until dinner. "Well, now what do you want to do? I don't know, what do you wanna do?"

At dinner in the grand ballroom, assigned seats at large round tables faced striking chocolate centerpieces of schooner ships – the corporate logo – cutting waves in beds of ultramarine orchids. Levi couldn't even guess at the cost. He sat near the kitchen entrance beside Joy Parnell, who was charming six other Northern California managers. The men talked wine. Joy drank vodka. Tuxedoed hotel staff swarmed in with entrees under silver covers, hoisting them with unified flare. Dining clatter nested into a thick gauze of conversation about kids and lawsuits and how business was more fun before the fucking lawyers ruined it.

"The whole damn industry's run by Compliance and Human Resources,"

THE BOTTOM OF THE SKY ▪ 139

complained the gray-haired manager from Oakland. "They tell us who to hire, what to pay and who we can't fire. They tell us what to sell and who we can't sell it to. I'm no virgin, so they can let go of my ears; I know what I'm doing." He led the laughter, and then feigning contrition. "Oh … sorry, Joy."

While a waiter presented flan to her, Joy gamely fired back, "My ears are generally left unobstructed, so I've heard it all." She was twenty-nine. "You forget I spent two years at the divisional."

"And so you remind us … again." Jim, the San Jose manager to her left, was a fortyish man with bloated eyelids and fingers that strained at his wedding band. "And we were just beginning to think you were one of us, or at least not against us." He flopped his arm across Joy's chair-back and looked past her at Levi. "Right, young man?" He winked.

Joy steeled, giving no sway, and stared at him. Once, at a meeting not unlike this one, she had made what Jim saw as an unaccountable pass at him. He didn't have the sense to pass it up. She took him to bed. He told her things.

Levi had no idea what the man was saying, but Jim was clear enough about being drunk. San Jose, Levi thought. So this is why the guy's job is being shopped to me. As happens in the presence of marked men, the table fell silent, partly out of collegial embarrassment that Jim might see they knew his fate and regarded it as shameful, and partly from wishing he would die, already, so they wouldn't have to watch it, much as a fundamentalist aunt at Thanksgiving dinner hates looking across the table at a gay nephew, home with full-blown AIDS. Then there was the fear of catching it. But Jim was focused on Levi's attention.

"I hear you done a good job, cowboy." Jim's tongue and lips had fallen out of sync. Levi was taken with his fork, hefting it for weight. "Lucky you're in Wyoming." Jim's eyes followed the fork. "You impressed with real silver? Don't be. Tarnishes the same, no matter the cost."

"Montana."

"Sorry. Montana. Lucky you're in Montana. From there you can't make too big of a difference. See, you don't want to make a difference … be noticed." He stared at Joy's earring as diners exchanged uncomfortable glances. "You think you make a difference to Crawford? You're wrong. You know why? 'Cause he isn't afraid of you. So you make no difference. You haven't even met Deirdre Oliver yet, have you?" Levi wasn't sure what he meant. "The death angel of Human Resources." He pointed to the head table.

Upfront, just before the giant screen with the corporate logo projected on it, Deirdre Oliver sat beside Crawford who sat beside Sandler. Jim darkened. "Hey, nothing personal. It isn't just that sneaky son of a bitch and his … Well … neither you nor anybody else at this table makes a fu'damn difference to anybody. This company's become too fucking big. No pillars of honor holding up this circus, either. It'll implode." His hands folded into each other, collapsing as if a tumbling tent.

One manager escaped for the restroom. The Oakland manager said, "Hey now, Jim, back off a bit. Okay?"

"We got no pillars." Jim said. "That's why Smith Barney, Merrill, Witter … they'll still kick our ass. They don't lie, cheat or steal. Generally. They care for people." Seeing Levi palm-signal the Oakland man to stand clear, Jim prattled on. "Just do one thing for me, Montana, and then I'll be quiet. It'll be fun. Will you do one thing?"

Anything to shut you up, Levi thought. "What's that?"

Jim showed his index finger. "Take one finger, and put it in your wine." Jim did it. Levi showed dubious tolerance. "Go on. One finger." Jim nodded toward Levi's wine glass.

Levi pointed his finger. He submersed it in wine.

"Now take a … another finger and put it in your dessert."

"Jesus, Jim, knock it off," a manager said.

Levi took his other index finger and poked it into his flan.

"Now pull them back out," and Jim took his fingers out and held them up.

Levi removed his fingers and began wiping them on his napkin.

"Now. Look at the wine … and look at the flan. Show me the holes you left behind." In spite of themselves, everyone looked at Levi's wine and flan. "One of these is thick and sweet, like your family," Jim said, "and, unless you're as big an asshole as me, you'll leave a void when you're gone. The other one is thin and intoxicating, like your job, mixed and blended with money, and titles, and authority. Important meetings, other bullshit. Now. Show me the hole that you left in your wine." No one said a word. "See, Cowboy, you're the finger. As soon as you're gone, no one will even know you were here." Jim stared contemptuously, as if he knew who his replacement would be.

"So which are you now, Jim?" asked Levi, "The alcohol or the flan?"

At the front of the room, from the head table at the big screen, Gary Crawford rose like a 3-D popup and rang a spoon on his wine glass with the vigor of command. Jim from San Jose stood as well. He tossed his napkin and walked out. Crawford clicked on the mike and waited.

Appearing among the diners as if from nowhere floated Lily Fujiwara in a silver dress that alluded to her hair. As Crawford's executive assistant, she would unobtrusively stage-manage the show. When she sailed between tables toward Levi, her wake alone quelled commotion on her way to idle the banquet staff.

As Lily neared the maitre d' at the kitchen door, Joy rose preemptively, appropriating his attention. Lily glided to a stop beside Levi. Even Levi could see Joy was encroaching. Joy whispered to the man and he signaled his staff to stop clearing dishes. Lily affected a look of kindly gratitude toward Joy.

"I'm glad to help," Joy whispered loudly enough. "Just because I'm management doesn't mean I can't pitch in. Besides, we're a team, huh? Like at the division."

With untouched dignity, Lily smiled, turned, and retraced her route.

Crawford, as usual, was as sober as he sounded. He was honored to host such esteemed colleagues, honored to work in an industry so crucial to a productive society at such a crucial time. Honored to be honored or some such thing. Honored to introduce his boss, Mike Sandler.

Sandler stood, looking lenient. He took away the mike. "I'm honored," he rumbled, igniting fun at Crawford's expense. "You people deserve every penny you make because of shit you put up with from the markets, from clients, from lawyers, from Compliance in New York, and from assholes like me and Gary." They cheered.

"Actually, your spouses deserve every penny you make for putting up with you." Big laugh. "Most of you wouldn't know if they ran off with it anyway, 'cause you're never home." Jocularity ebbed as he softened. "This job…No job is more important than your health and your families. Take your vacations. Go home at night to eat dinner." The audience sobered and murmurs muted. "But not tonight," Sandler broke out a rare, Cheshire grin. "The bar is open – but you damn well better be on time tomorrow." He raised his glass to a standing ovation.

During the hubbub, Joy leaned in close to Levi. "So, then. Do you want to get a drink?" Two portable bars had opened in opposite corners of the room, attracting the crowd like iron filings to magnetic poles.

"Sure," Levi said. "The price is right."

"Not here," she said, holding his eyes.

Low and dull, he felt an ache, his groin more sure of her meaning than his brain. "Nah," he said uncomfortably, "I shouldn't go out. Long day. I woke up in Montana."

"We could stay in the building?" she said.

Levi still wasn't entirely sure of her meaning, but he was sure he didn't want to be. "Ah, I better not. I'm tired. Need to call home." He tried to look gracious. "Maybe next time."

Joy's face flashed out and just as quickly she waded into the crowd toward Crawford, thirty feet away, who had his hand resting against Deirdre Oliver's back at the sharp ends of ditchwater hair and shoulder blades. As Joy approached, Deirdre intercepted her, guiding her aside with a touch on the arm as if to share something of import. Joy seemed to overact her interest.

Levi snuck out into the lobby and entered an elevator, presumably unseen. Inside his room, he shed his jacket and sat on the bed. From his briefcase, he pulled a photograph of Angela. "I'm not about to screw up, am I?" A vague fear stirred. No, he chided it back. Escape, not mistakes. He picked up the phone.

"Hello." She sounded groggy.

"Hey, Angel."

"Hi, Darling," she cooed. "I've been waiting for your call." He could hear her rustle for her glasses. "How's it going?"

"Fine." Moments passed. "How was your day?"

A tad woozy, she swallowed. "Good."

"How was school?"

"Good," she said softly. "It was too cold and windy to go out for recess, so the kids were a little rowdy." More moments passed. "I have some news," she teased.

For a reason he wouldn't let form, his stomach tightened. "What?"

"First you have to guess what I'm wearing. So ... what do you think?"

Levi could hear more rustling and wished he had waited earlier. "Not right now." As he sat on the bed, elbows to knees, his palm held up his jaw, he wondered where to start, his head dense with issues too complex to untangle this late in the day. Not the right time. "I've been thinking how much opportunity there is in bigger markets. There's so much money here."

Only rustling.

"Okay, fine," he said. "You're naked."

"Oooo. Bingo. Okay. Well, you know I'd support you in whatever you do."

"Yeah." His eyes blurred, searching for that distance. "It's just that I don't want to miss my chance. You know, to get far enough out." There was no reply. *What if she wouldn't go? She* is *family. Finally. My family. No. That's nuts. Of course she'll go. And Lynette won't, thank God.* "But I don't really want to leave home, either."

"Levi, you're already 'out.' Besides, we could make more right here. We'll talk about it."

"Not that easy. What do you mean we'll talk? What's so secret? I said you were naked."

She smiled to herself. "Well, you deserve some news." It was, indeed, some of her news – all the news she would give him on the phone. "Starting in a month, I am the new vice principal at the junior high. Is that cool, or what? They're throwing a party for me tomorrow evening – at the superintendent's house. It's at seven. You'll be there, right?"

He hesitated, but not long enough for her to notice. "Honey, that's great. I am so proud of you! Yeah, I should land in time. I'm sure I'll be there. Soon as the plane lands." Shit, he thought. Should he tell her now? Maybe he should just tell her. Maybe she can put the district off for a while, have them hold the job until he knows for sure. A party? Shit.

"Oh, good. Honey, I couldn't have done this without you. Get home. You worry too much. Like you work too much. Now let's just be happy for a while. We have our house, good jobs – now that I'll make the big bucks – good friends. I'm sure things'll work out great. God's always given us what we needed. I think you'd be happier if you relax a little."

"We have what we have because of skill and will, not some divine concierge service." He cringed at his own crass words. He heard her arm slap the bed. "I'm sorry."

Another long moment passed before she spoke. "Hon, I have to get some sleep. We can talk more when you get home. I'll pick you up at the airport."

"No, don't. Don't be late for your party. I'll take a cab." Before they hung up, they said their I love yous, and out of love, for now, each left something unsaid.

From the city outside, a muted honk from a MUNI bus oozed up from Market Street. He opened the window to the hiss and peel of tires along wet asphalt. Below, some of his colleagues crawled into a limousine. They hooted tipsily. He was thirsty, so he opened the armoire that held the refrigerated servi-bar. There were snacks, pop, half-bottles of wine. Diminutive replicas of Courvoisier, Chivas. Jack Daniels. He liked Jack Daniels.

As he checked for ice, his thoughts fell back to the dinner. What was Joy doing, inviting him for a drink? He should have gone, carefully, and listened. She knows something. Twenty minutes had passed. She could be in her room. Maybe… No. "Shit, Levi, you're a big boy. But no." He seized the phone, dialed the hotel operator.

"Hello?" It was her. Joy was in her room. Part of him was genuinely surprised.

"Joy, it's Levi. I decided I'm not so tired after all." He heard her hand cover the phone.

A moment later, "Great. I need to talk to you."

Need? "Okay." He rolled the JD bottle in his palm. "How about the lounge?"

"Can you come to my room?"

Levi sat on the bed again. He took a breath. "Well…"

"Levi, this is important. I'm in 628. Can you come for just a minute?"

That sounded straightforward enough. Maybe not so weird. Bad news? "628."

"Yes."

"Is it something…"

"I don't want to talk on the phone. Just come here."

"All right. I'll be there in a minute." He laid the handset in its cradle. He cracked the lid on the little bottle, drank half of it, sniffing fumes back. "Huh," he thought out loud. "Who's using who? Or is it whom?" He screwed the lid back on and set it down. At the door, he stepped back and finished the whiskey. In a pants pocket, he thumbed a mint off a roll – two – and popped them in his mouth. Three minutes later, at 628, Levi squirreled another into his cheek. He knocked. She answered, her blouse unbuttoned to there, bare feet below her skirt, and lip gloss.

"Thanks for coming," she sang. "Come in." Without breaking eye contact, she closed the door behind him.

"What's up?" Levi asked. Her bedding was pulled back in a triangle, not like turndown service does. On her table was a bottle of chardonnay and two full glasses, one with lip-prints.

"Nothing, really," she said. "I just thought if you're too tired to go out for a drink, we could have one here." Shifting her weight to one foot, prissily lifting her wine glass. Her head canting. She grinned, softly circling the rim of her glass with the finger with that short, red nail.

Levi's balls moved involuntarily. *This is too ... A drink? I don't need another drink. I should go ... now. No shit. But she was with Crawford when I left. She knows something. And Sandler stayed at the bar. Is this part of the interview? A promotion could change everything ... forever. Stay. But careful. Escape, not mistakes. With enough money, Angela can quit work, have kids – we could. Angela.* "I'm pretty tired. I don't think I could use another drink." He marshaled a sorrowful slump, as if he was tired and regretted it.

"Too bad. Then again, maybe you should rest. You'll need it, from what I hear."

Ah, here it was. "Oh? How's that?"

"I know why you talked to Mike and Gary this afternoon." Her finger wandered the skin at her breastbone. "Gary's a little concerned though. He bounces things off me. Wine?"

Levi looked at the wine. He looked at her. "Okay. One," he confirmed with one finger. She walked to the table and lifted his glass, waiting for him to come and get it. When the distance between them had stretched tight enough, Levi drew farther in, by the bed. "So what have you heard?" he asked. She was blocking the only chair, uncomfortably close now, so he sat on the corner of the bed. She sat on the mattress beside him, rotated her face and mane.

"Well, I heard Mike is making Gary take you as the manager in San Jose and Santa Clara." She paused for effect. "Gary thinks you're too inexperienced. He doesn't like how small Billings is. Says there's no..." She made quotation marks in the air, "'Miracle on 3rd or 4th Street' and that there's 'dust under your suit' – and you'll start breeding and get distracted."

"What?" *What could possibly motivate her to tell me this?* "First of all, I don't feel comfortable talking about this with anyone. It might not happen. And no one's ever accused me of not working hard enough."

"Oh, he didn't mean that." She touched his shoulder. "It's just that responsibilities of a magnitude that would pay you over a half-million a year usually go to more senior managers whose kids are grown. This topic never comes up with me. I'm not married and I can't have kids now. My choice. Career. Anyway, he knows you work hard. Mike says that. Everyone. Besides, until Mike retires, Gary'll dance like Mike wants. Then he'll inherit Mike's job."

"Mike's retiring?"

"I didn't say that." She leaned on him, ducking her head toward his lap and startling him. She pointed out the window. "Remember when I interviewed you? In that office?" She closed one eye and pointed as if sighting a rifle. "Did you know you can see our building from here?"

"Yes." He held stone-still, taking shallow breaths of her hair. Vanilla. Something flopped in his abdomen, tensing his butt. When she sat back up, he took a courtesy sip of wine and stood, setting his glass down. "I need to get to bed," he said, regretting the double-entendre.

Instead of standing with him, she lay back, pressing her elbows into the bed. Her eyes closed as she rolled her head to please her neck. "Mmm. No kidding. Long day."

"Why don't we sit together at breakfast?" he offered.

She looked up. "Okay," she chirped. She sprung upright and continued to the door as if by force of momentum. She held it open until he was several steps down the hall.

Crawford leaned against a massive burled desk in the Presidential Suite as he spoke into the phone. "Did you take care of the copies of the billing from the hotel?" He knew she had. Deirdre, his HR specialist, was very thorough, and discreet.

"Yes, sir," said Deirdre. "I'll receive copies when everyone checks out tomorrow. I'll wait for them myself so they aren't mailed to the office. Lily won't see them. Do you want a copy of Mr. Sandler's room charges as well?"

Crawford thought a moment. Oddly, he hadn't considered it. If anyone asked, he could say it's a mistake, one made by Deirdre. "Why not? Give that one to me. For the rest of them, all the managers, I want every phone number they call identified and collated. I want every drink they charge, including the servi-bar, what movies they watched." As he said it he felt a compulsion to add something, something to inject integrity into his motives. The feeling evaporated as quickly. The good thing about Deirdre is she didn't care. She expected quid pro quo, and maybe he'd advance her career – maybe – but otherwise she didn't care.

The other line on his room phone rang. "I need to go. We'll talk tomorrow." He punched the other button.

"Gary?" It was Joy.

"That was quick. How was it?"

"He just left. We didn't do anything."

"What do you mean?"

"I mean we didn't do anything," she said.

"That's unfortunate. I was hoping for a story." She didn't speak, for fear he'd want one anyway. It didn't matter. "Well, gather your things and come up. I'll leave the door ajar."

"I'm pretty tired."

"I'll see you in a minute." He hung up.

Joy placed the phone in the cradle and sighed. She cracked a vodka and drank from it before fishing a tiny paper Sen-Sen packet from her purse. She slipped her naked feet into her shoes.

Between the stomach cramps and trying to figure what Joy was up to and dwelling on when and what to tell Angela, Levi didn't sleep well. By morning he was drained and sweaty. While packing he had to sit down to rest. He decided that unless he got definitive word about the promotion today, he wouldn't tell her until after her party. He'd tell her right away that they were probably moving. Rather, he'd discuss it with her. They'd decide together. Then she could give up her job before she started it. That would be better.

He schlepped his suitbag to the ballroom and dropped it in a corner with the others. Crawford greeted him curtly. During breakfast, Levi sat with Joy and three other managers. She ignored him, opting instead to work the table. Finally he offered, "So you stay in the city and work while the rest of us fly home?"

She paused. "Work is my home." She glanced across the room and Levi's eyes followed. Deirdre was handing Crawford a cup of coffee. Joy looked away.

During the morning's presentations, at the front of the room, individual speakers hawked their wares. Something about charitable remainder trusts. Another thing about hedge funds for rich clients. A staff economist talked in circles, the point being – as always – that brokers should sell some stocks and buy some other stocks. Cash was bad, Levi thought, for commissions.

As he considered the potential changes in his life, the initial fluidity of excitement and hopefulness slowly congealed, taking on a surface tension that strained until it roped up. From a mind furrowed by the past, a sludge of dark bewilderment seeped along, unwelcome, unstoppable, infecting his hope with fear. "Act normal." His lips formed words without sound. "Normal."

From across the room, Crawford was watching him. Levi held his gaze, purposefully, pulling in emotion, resharpening the moment. How hard can this be? Look at you. I'm smarter. I'm ethical, he thought loudly. Surely Crawford heard, like he could hear Crawford's thoughts.

When the session ended, Mike cornered Levi with the low rumble of a hangover. To preserve confidentiality, he stood very close. "You want this job?"

"Yes, Mike. I do."

"'Cause I don't want any bullshit if we offer it to you."

"Don't worry." *Oh shit*, Levi thought. *This is it.*

"Go home. Talk with your wife. We'll get back to you." Sandler turned and shook hands with others.

16

CHOICE

No seed shall perish which the soul hath sown.

JOHN ADDINGTON SYMONDS

"Sorry for the turbulence, folks. They say the planet's getting warmer, even with the sun down. We're going to try another vector to see if we can get away from these convection currents and find some smoother air."

With his right hand, Levi tendered the small, empty bottle and four dollars across a sleeping passenger to the flight attendant for another red wine. He cracked the foil seal and poured it into the plastic cup on his tray table. When he swallowed, the glow in his mouth, throat, and stomach felt particularly gratifying. He exhaled long and slowly. He took another drink. He rooted his wallet from his hip pocket and pulled out his business card. Levi Monroe; Vice President; Branch Manager. Soon it might say First Vice President or Senior Vice President.

A long way from Roundup, Levi thought. He drank again. One step closer to the divisional job. To Crawford's job. To EVP. To dignity. He dug his elbows into the armrests, lifting his weight slightly off the seat in an effort to alleviate the involuntary but not unpleasurable effect the plane's vibration was having on his scrotum.

It was twilight over the Rockies. Past the window, sitting just outside the plane, Levi saw the spectral face of a successful young businessman. He raised the plastic wine cup. They toasted each other.

Back home Angela was watching someone's mouth talk as she stood by a window at the party in the district superintendent's house. She was remembering a fight she and Levi had about having kids – their only real fight. Not loud – more like pushing opposing magnets against the invisible ball between them. He was afraid – irrationally, to her thinking – of stifling his career or ending up poor, or whatever. What she feared was ending up childless because what if she had inherited her mother's uterus? Anyway, the fight was months ago. Accidents happen. She had forgotten to take the pill on certain days. Holy Moses, she thought. She was pregnant. She caught herself touching her tummy and smiling at the cliché of it. She told herself Levi would be okay with it. At worst, they'd fight, and then make love. After this party.

Angela looked at her watch. Levi would be landing about then. She got butterflies. She'd have to watch for him, catch him at the door, to tell him her – their – news before someone here at the party let it slip. She had only told Lam in Roundup and a friend in Billings. But word got around. And that's another thing the superintendent had been sweet about. He simply congratulated her and talked about balance in one's life. What a great guy. The face before her had stopped talking. "I'm sorry?" she said.

For an hour Angela stayed near the front window, letting well-wishers circulate around her, wrap her in a blanket of good will. By the time Levi arrived, she was holding a warm glass of sparkling cider and a paper plate of snacks, staring heedlessly at the animated face of the a lightning-witted, ageless woman with a voice like Velcro, the union shop steward at the junior high to which Angela was being promoted.

Angela hadn't seen the cab pull up, so when Levi crooned "Hi Darlin'" in her ear, it startled her. They kissed lightly, and she tethered him to her side and made introductions. When the union rep took a breath, Angela begged her pardon and stole Levi aside. She was bursting with news, wanting to find somewhere quiet, which seemed impossible.

"It is so great to see you," she said, kissing him again. "Was your plane late?"

"No," he said as if asking what she meant.

"Oh, it doesn't matter. I'm just glad you're here. How was it?"

"There are some changes coming, not all of them good for clients or employees. People don't have the courage to speak up."

"I don't doubt it. Did you piss anybody off?"

"Who, me? Mike Sandler was there – the president? – and he didn't seem pissed. Crawford? Maybe not so smooth. I'll tell you later."

"I thought you'd be in a suit. Did you put your bag in my car?"

"No, I dropped it at the house. I changed there." He looked around the room and smiled. "Glad I did. Wall Street's a little formal for this crowd."

She laughed. "Can you tell we're teachers? Free food. Great turnout. I didn't remember packing that. Did the cab wait at home while you changed? That was nice."

"Oh, I didn't end up taking a cab. Lynette gave me a ride."

"Lynette?" A surge of circulation hit her face. Levi saw it.

"Hey, I was as surprised as you are. Nice of her, I guess. When I called in for messages I must have mentioned that you'd be here. She said she was in town shopping anyway."

"Really? I see." She was trying hard not to sound as irritated as she was, a level of peevishness that surprised even her. *Hormones?* "So, did she wait for you at baggage claim?"

"No. At the gate."

She tried to shut up. She felt herself running at the edge a little too fast. But an hour late? "She waited at our house while you changed clothes?"

"Well, yeah? Is that okay? I thought it was nice. Hey, it's not that big of a deal."

"Did she wait in the car?" She tried to force a slight smile in case anyone was watching them from across the room.

"Oh, come on."

"I've got to get back to the party." Her news could wait. This isn't how she wanted to feel when she told him. She turned, squeezed her eyes shut tightly for a moment, and determined to look pleasant and relaxed. It'd pass. Probably just hormones.

Another half-hour of chatter brought a steady rise in volume until someone brought in a white sheet cake emblazoned with, "Congratulations Squared, Mrs. Monroe!" scrawled in sapphire blue icing. Drawn in the corners were sugary party hats, blowers and passable fireworks explosions. Everyone topped off their plastic champagne glasses.

"You all know why we're here," the superintendent said. *I don't,* someone who'd already hung a sheet or two to the wind barked, and laughter broke out. "Okay. Almost all of you. We're here to honor a woman who, at twenty-eight, has shown the skill and leadership that some of us didn't achieve until much later." *Or never,* the same voice called, this time with less success. "Yes. Or not yet. But tonight is not our night. Tonight is that of Angela Monroe." He turned to Angela. "I want to congratulate you, Mrs. Monroe, on the first of two things."

Angela's stomach tightened. *Oh, Christ*, she thought, *not now*. She looked for Levi, but he was behind her.

"First," her boss went on, "let me say how much I look forward to working with you as the new assistant principal at Will James Junior High School. You are the youngest assistant principal I have ever appointed, and I have appointed no one in whom I have more confidence. Here's to you, Mrs. Monroe."

Cheers bloomed, as did Angela's eyes. Oh shit, she thought. In spite of her wishes, the noise died down to hear the second toast.

Now the superintendent cocked his head coyly. "If you've had the chance to read the cake, you may have noticed that it says 'Congratulations squared, Mrs. Monroe.'" Everyone looked at Angela knowingly, glowingly. She landed at Levi's querying eyes. She shrugged, palms up, an instant before the superintendent said, "While I was never good at math—"

"That explains our paychecks," the union rep chimed.

"I'll ignore that. While I was never good with math, the sentiment on the cake was meant to point equally – no, more importantly – to the fact that Angela will be taking time off not long after she starts her new job. Here's to Mrs. And Mr. Angela Monroe – and baby makes three." Wild cheers erupted.

All arms raised and Angela lost sight of Levi. By the time they lowered, his lips were tight, his eyes pissed.

It was a cold ride home. The porch light had burned out. Levi fumbled the key. "Dammit."

"Do you want me to get it?"

"No." He finally found the slot and slammed in the key. His shoulder hit the door an instant before the lock released. Then they were inside. "When did you know?"

Angela would have to handle this carefully. He'll come around, she promised herself. Just be kind. Just be patient. No matter how mad he is. She sat on the couch. "I suspected before you left."

"What do you mean you suspected? Did you take a pregnancy test?" he tossed his coat on a big chair.

"I hadn't seen the doctor."

"That's not what I asked. Did you take one of those home tests?"

"What does it matter? I saw the doctor yesterday, and he confirmed it. That's when I knew I was pregnant."

"When did you intend to tell me? Huh? When? After everybody else in the world knew? After you made an ass of me at your party? After I told Sandler I wanted a career beyond Billings? And Crawford. Shit, Crawford."

"I didn't want to tell you on the phone. I was going to tell you as soon as you got to the party, but … I had to tell the superintendent. For crying out loud, he has the right to know."

"More right than me?" Levi fumed. "I thought we were waiting. I thought you understood that I don't want to end up like them."

"Having a child will not turn you into your parents. Jesus. Get over it."

"How did this happen?"

"What do you mean, how did it happen?"

"You were on the pill."

She sat up straight. "I got pregnant. It happens." This was good news, right? If this were a movie, there would be music. Strings.

They sat silent. The thermostat clicked on. The toilet tank drew some water. Something inside Angela contracted, just a flutter. She still hadn't removed her coat. "Excuse me." Levi walked into the bathroom and closed the door. Silence rang in Angela's ears. Eventually the water in the sink ran, too long for hand washing. The toilet never flushed. After a while, she heard the door open and the light click off.

Remorse seemed to stir behind Levi's face. "Angela. I want us to get far enough away – and I don't mean geographically – that our children never have to worry about ending up here … or there." He pointed north, to Roundup. "If we have kids now, I *can't* take a bigger job, not now. In the first place, I'm young, and if they think I'm distracted, they'll never give me a chance. I need them to consider me now. When we're set, we can breed like Osmonds."

She sat forward on the edge of the sofa cushion and swiveled to face him squarely. Her fingers shook. She slipped them into her coat pockets. "That's bullshit."

"It's not bullshit." He didn't sound like he convinced himself. He seemed panicking.

She stood and turned her back on him, heading for the coat closet. She knew he hated arguing with a moving target. "I thought we agreed we wanted a family."

"We did agree. At least you did. I thought we agreed my goal was Crawford's job."

She spun and looked at him like he was daft. "What about my goals? I got a promotion. Remember? The party?" She snatched a coat hanger from the closet. "Do you want this baby?"

"Do you?"

She closed the closet door and parked her hands on her hips. "I'm pregnant!"

"Congratulations! How long did that take?"

"What? How can you think … What the hell is wrong with your head?"

"Maybe I received it unassembled. Oh, forget it!" He strode for the dining room.

Angela followed. "What are you saying?"

"I'm saying that my whole life other people have taken control. Why should y… this be any different?" He popped a dining chair out and sat on it. "Dammit!"

She stared disbelievingly. "It's *our* baby, not just mine." But it had been her decision. It showed on her face. "You can't always time things like this. Sometimes God gives you …"

"God?" he snapped. "I don't think this was God's decision."

Levi's eyes briefly lost focus. He seemed to be watching himself and hating what he saw. He stood abruptly, stormed into the living room, snapped his coat back on, and gripped his car keys. He didn't look at her. "First them and now you. God dammit, Angela! How long can you be thrilled collecting Cabbage Patch dolls from Rimrock Mall?" He slapped his hand against the wall. "God dammit! I'm going to the office." He opened the door and left.

At some hour before daybreak, Levi stealthily rode a beer-buzz into the darkened house. He stood in the hallway and peered into their bedroom. He heard Angela rustle and saw her hand strobe before the lighted numerals of the alarm clock. He stalled there, futilely wishing she would call out to him. Fine, then. The farthest bed from her was the sofa, so he'd sleep there. He opened the hall closet and gathered a pillow and blanket. In the dark he lay down and drifted off, deep within himself.

I am standing in the oozing gray-green Musselshell River below a sandy cutbank higher than my head. I hear Angela on the ground above, singing sweetly, but I cannot see her. I hear laughing behind me, on the far bank, men in suits, and oddly think I am here to give a seminar. I am late, but I need her, or need to tell her something, to make her understand. My chest wells with anxiousness. The thick water rises to the crotch of my pinstriped pants, coiling, sucking at my groin, and I strain to stretch above it, but my bare toes sink in the mud. Above the cutbank, inches above my eyes, the bottom of the sky shimmers and dances, and over the lip of the embankment I sling my hands like grappling hooks and claw into grass with tense, knotty fingers. As I strain to hoist my body, Angela stands above me, on the edge, holding a barkless length of river-polished cottonwood. She is pink. Girly. I smell her clean. "Grab the branch," she is saying. When I reach for it, she laughs and steps aside, unaware of me. "Grab the branch," she says again, but she is not offering it to me.

Near my waist, peach-naked human torsos periscope out of the coiling current, arms slicing into the air beside me, hands and arms, tearing at the tree limb. I command my arms to compete, to seize the branch for me, for me, but my limbs are sensationless, gray, and do not move. Angela laughs as the other bodies saturate with color and engulf the branch, smother it with bright nakedness that makes me squint. I pull harder at the clumped grass and I begin to win, rise from filthy spiral water and feel the luminous, viscous blue belly of the sky – welcoming, beckoning – and Angela delights in rolling the branch my way, it now cocooned in lurid forms. They are winning. They are taking my limb! I must rise! I pull harder at the sod.

Jealous slabs of sand sheer from the bank and heavy, heavy earth collapses onto me, filling my shirt with dirt, gunmetal gray, gray to my waist, gray to the coil, sinking me. "No! No!" I say. "Spread out! You're caving it in!" and a vortex of thick water turns dry and dirty –the rug! – and it sands my belly. "Get away!" I scream at them, and Angela cries and rolls the branch on my back until garish faces press against mine with smudgeless, tawdry colors and a smudged tattoo. I smell one breath of tobacco and booze. Another, Lam, tears at my shirt and drives her head into my chin, a naked thigh to my groin, and the branch disappears, for the stripped, faded stem becomes … me! They are clinging to me, all of them, and I cannot, do not want to bear them. The severed horizon floats away from me, away. Angela's sorrow cascades into me. Beside her stands a child with pleading eyes who is Dusty and then is not. A child not yet born. Angela says please. Lam says please. I reach, and the child is of the sky. I reach, and a tattooed arm reaches with me, and there are bar smells and pleas, and I can no longer order my scarred hand to hold. The bank crumbles on top of me and I am plunging. And I reach for one of them, to save… I am in the torrent...

Levi awoke with a sharp, desperate breath he held until he knew he was looking back from his couch. "No!"

In the early morning darkness Angela heard Levi rise. She heard him shower. She stayed wrapped like a pupa, the blanket clutched to her throat, keeping her back to him and laying stock-still when he rummaged in their closet for a clean suit, shirt and tie. There was a long, quiet moment before he left the room. She heard the front door open and close and then the muffled thud of the car door. She was alone.

She lingered in bed, crying, until her alarm intruded at 6:30. Her legs made tiny zipper sounds on the sheets as she swung to sit up. Her feet scratched the floor for her slippers. She sighed, hoisting herself up. Her nightgown stuck to her behind and she grabbed to pull it loose. That's when she felt it, warm and sticky on her butt, her thigh. She snapped on the lamp, her head craning around at her ass, her thighs, the mattress – the blood. What sounds came next were pressed to the walls by dread.

The doctor waited a day, just to be sure. Then, on the wintry Friday morning the following week, Levi drove to Angela's school. When he peeked in her classroom, he saw walls plastered with third-grade cornucopias, leaves and jack-o-lanterns. The children, charmed by Angela's voice, didn't notice him. She was sitting on a stool before the blackboard, reading out loud. Kids stared out windows at snow flurries. Behind Angela's desk was a young woman, presumably the substitute teacher, reviewing a folder of papers.

Angela spotted him and closed the book. "Maybe Mrs. Flanagan can finish the story for you," she said with optimism. "Right now *Mr.* Monroe is here, and it's time for me to go." The kids turned in their chairs and examined Levi like the incongruous curio from their teacher's secret life that he was. It had always amused Levi how kids seemed shocked to catch her grocery shopping or attending a movie. "Can you say hello to Mr. Monroe?"

"Hel-lo, Mis-ter Mon-roe," they chanted in singsong.

Angela collected her coat and purse and told the class to be good and thanked Mrs. Flanagan. Without talking, she and Levi marched down the hallway and pushed outside into winter. Wind needled their faces with ice crystals, and they turtled into their jackets.

They drove toward the hospital in silence, east on Lewis Avenue to 17th, north to Poly Drive, east again. A gust buffeted the car, breaking the mood enough for Levi to regard Angela. She ignored him.

"You okay?" he asked gently. No response. He drove farther under an undulating canopy of frosted elm trees and stopped at a light. "How are you feeling?"

She looked at him incredulously, then back at the road. It was a long light.

"Have you heard from your dad?" She didn't respond. "Ange?"

"I heard you." Silence.

"Maybe we should get away for a while after this. Maybe Hawaii." He wished he hadn't said it.

The wind launched a crystalline cloud over roadside cornices, prickling the windshield, leaching warmth through the glass. "We'll try again. Okay? It'll be fine … great, even." The light turned green.

"How much do you need?" Her voice was almost imperceptible.

"What?"

"What's the number?"

A shameful nerve burned. "That's not it, and that's not fair." He breathed. His frame and voice softened. "It's just that it was such a surprise."

She was expressionless. She rested her elbow on the door handle and tilted her forehead to her shaking fingers. It *had* been a surprise to him, hadn't it? He would resent her – and the child. But why? They already had more money than her father had ever had, and as a child she had never felt dread.

"Dusty's poor," she thought out loud. "He laughs all the time. If you'd go to Roundup with me, you'd know. You wouldn't be afraid of the stain." Dusty was six, living with Lam and Virginia and Frank. With Virginia frail and Frank working graveyard, Lam had grown to depend on Angela to take Dusty overnight from time to time. The boy was generous with laughter – and in love with Aunt Angela. She stared out the window. "You're your own boogieman."

The accusation deflated his voice. "If you grew up with monsters, you'd fear monsters."

As they turned south on North 29th Street, she fingered the beads in her pocket and missed her father. In Roundup, only Lam knew so far. Probably. Hell, they probably all knew. They continued past St. Vincent's Hospital to Deaconess Hospital.

"Drop me out front while you park," she said, and he did.

By the time Levi joined her at outpatient registration, her eyes were dry, her face sober, her voice even. Levi sat next to Angela in a side chair at the registration desk. He felt conspicuous. Ashamed. He wanted desperately to share her burden – or at least be seen as sharing it. He, too, felt anguished and sorrowful. He did. So he blurted the answers to the insurance questions until she said she could handle it, a message to be quiet. It wasn't his deal now.

A few minutes later he had shrunk enough to fit in a small plastic chair in a tiny room with three walls and a curtain. Angela lounged uneasily on the gurney and chatted like pals with a sweet, thirty-something nurse wearing a butterfly-print smock that Angela said was cute. No, the nurse hadn't made it herself, but she was flattered to be asked. They went through a checklist. Angela hadn't eaten or drunk since midnight, she hadn't taken a sedative yet – so she could sign the consent form – she didn't need to pee, and she could leave her jewelry and other valuables with her friend.

"Oh, this isn't my friend," said Angela. "This is my husband."

When the nurse checked her clipboard again, she looked up with a brief, little smile. "Oh," she said. She looked at the ring on Angela's left hand, then checked Angela's face and wrapped her in a warmhearted look. "Why don't you leave your ring on? We can secure it with tape." Sisters now; Levi became invisible. The nurse adjusted the incline of the gurney and covered Angela with a warmed blanket. As she fitted Angela with terrycloth booties, she and Angela talked about which shoes felt best for people who worked on their feet all day. Then she bandaged Angela's ring finger, giving it a little squeeze at the end.

While the IV was started, Levi caught himself admiring the nurse's panty lines and shamefully looked at the wall. A sign by the blood pressure dial read, *For patient safety, glove balloons are not allowed.* There was a soap dispenser, but no sink. He looked back as the nurse gauzed a trickle of blood from Angela's arm. He cringed and reread the *air, vacuum* and *oxygen* labels on the wall jacks. Soon another woman, the anesthesiologist, appeared and administered a sedative.

"You'll have to wait outside now until she's out of recovery," the doctor said optimistically. "Someone will come and get you."

Levi stood and brought his face over Angela's. He said, "I love you," like it hurt.

Angela's face reddened and a vein on her forehead swelled. She squeezed his hand and tried to make her quivering lips smile. "I'm sorry, too." Her eyes closed, squeezing out a tear.

He squeezed her hand and kissed her cool lips. "I'll see you soon," he whispered.

Levi walked outside to clear his head. He sat in the car for a lost amount of time, watching small snowflakes melt on the windshield. He would not pray. He turned on NPR. A breathy twenty-something social scientist was reading an essay detailing the folly of the Laffer curve. Finally the national news came around. The stock market getting creamed – off over 100 points for the first time in history, on record volume. A pundit said this was the market climax he'd been waiting for since the decline began in August. Levi shut off the radio. He stared into the distance, imagining the charts and trying to feel what people ... out there ... felt. Colors changed.

Two minutes later Levi called the office from a payphone. "Hey," he said to Lynette, "how's the market?" He was squinting at a TV screen across the hospital lobby.

"It's getting killed. At least your clients are happy. Some want to buy."

"Don't let them. On Monday the gamblers will be selling to meet margin calls and the moms and pops will sell their mutual funds because they don't like being afraid. So mutual funds will be dumping shares at the same time the margin selling is happening. No, Monday won't be good. At least one more day."

"If it is bad Monday, won't the same logic apply to Tuesday?"

"Maybe. But eventually margin debt's paid down. Nervous investors are out."

She gave him his messages. Some were clients. One of the brokers in his office wanted approval to enter a large options order. Mike Sandler's office had called an hour earlier.

"Shit. I've been waiting for that call." He looked at his watch. "It's nearly five o'clock in New York. Did they say what he wanted?"

"They were confirming dinner with you next week. Here. In Billings." There was a needling silence. "I didn't know he was coming here."

"Yeah," Levi stalled for a moment. He was staring past a massive aquarium stocked with live rainbow trout, through the glass doors, into the gloom outside. "I just found out myself. I guess he's doing a swing down the West

Coast and he's visiting a few offices on the way there." His peripheral vision blackened around the doors. Like many winter days, outside seemed only cold and pewter.

"And he chose Billings? Is there something I should know?" she asked.

"No," he said a little too quickly. *Not until I'm out the door.*

"You also got a call from Gary Crawford."

"Oh, yeah, he's coming too. I think they're traveling together."

"No, he's not. He said to tell you he has more pressing needs elsewhere, and that, quote, 'Sandler can do this one by himself.' I asked if you should call him back and he said no and hung up. That's all he said. Just no. Are you in trouble?"

"No, no. Things are great. He's just that way." *Great. If I get it, I'm the bride in a shotgun wedding.*

Lynette was still on the phone. "Is Angela okay?"

"Yeah. She'll be fine."

"What's she having done, anyway?"

"Oh, I don't know. Girl stuff. You know."

"Hm." There was a curdle of jealousy in her tone. "Who's her doctor?"

Please, not now, Levi thought, but answered instead, hoping it was the quickest route out of this conversation. "Johannson."

"Really? Mine, too. I see him next week. Must be something in the water." Levi closed his eyes, refusing the bait, which hung out there a full ten seconds. "Did you hear me?"

"Yes," he said sharply.

"Oh. Kay. Well then. Are you coming back in?"

"I don't know. Maybe later tonight. Probably not." Just then Levi was distracted by a familiar figure entering the lobby.

"Listen, Lynette, I gotta go. I won't be back today."

As Lam entered she unzipped a beige coat resembling a sleeping bag. Levi met her at the door and walked with her. "What are you doing here?"

"Angela asked me to come."

"Why?"

"She didn't know if you'd go back to work," she said matter-of-factly.

He frowned before deciding to move on. "Where'd you get that coat?"

"Do you like it?"

"Like homemade sin."

"Mom and Dad got it for me for Christmas.

"Hm," he said. "Do Mom and Dad know?"

"They thought it looked nice. So do I. And it's warm."

"Not the coat. Do they know about Angela?"

"They know."

"What about Geno?"

"She hasn't called him?" Lam surveyed Levi's wearied shoulders. "Is she in there?"

He nodded.

"Hm," she said, and wrapped her arm in his. "Buy me some coffee."

They walked to a bustling cafeteria with fake ficus trees, a soaring wall of windows, and a central chow line. In line, they scooted trays forward like it was prison or school, purchasing coffee and donuts. They settled in a booth.

Lam spoke first. "I'm co-managing the bar. Geno's having problems with his back and blood pressure."

They ate their donuts. When Levi finally asked about men, she reported exuberantly that she had met one – slowing briefly to add caveats about it being early in the relationship, yadda, yadda – a strong, thoughtful man, Russ Johnson, thirty-two years old, a third-generation rancher, never married.

"Hm. An older man. What about Donny Zupick?" Levi asked.

"Oh, that's over. I broke up with him last year. Anyway, Donny came in the bar drunk a few weeks ago. Expected me to go with him. But Russ picked me up at the end of my shift."

It was snowing outside. "How'd that go?"

As she considered what answer Levi might expect, she craved a cigarette. She popped the last piece of donut in her mouth. "Russ walked me to the pickup and went back inside. I don't know what he said, but I don't hear from Donny no more. That should make you happy."

Levi sighed. "I'm thrilled beyond belief."

As Lam described how much Dusty liked Russ, and how much he adored his Aunt Angela, she dug through her purse for a picture of Angela and the boy. She hesitated with the photo below the table, knowing it might hurt Levi to see it during Angela's D and C. Then again....

Levi was quiet for a moment. "He's beautiful," he said, and then handed it back. "I want him to go to school. To do well. In case you can't ... well, I started a college fund. No matter how kids come about, they deserve a good shot." They simultaneously cringed.

"Oh, Levi."

"I said I'd be there. Maybe if I had…" He moved on quickly. "How's Mom? Angela says she won't go in for a checkup."

"She doesn't think she needs to. Says she feels fine. Besides, she's embarrassed."

"Embarrassed? About what? A checkup, after what she's been through?"

"They don't have any money, Levi. She's embarrassed."

Levi looked at the walls decorated with outsized nature photographs taken by local artists. He looked at a man with the earflaps on his hat. Bland people enjoying bland food. "I thought the clinic checked her for free."

She gawked at him. "I can't believe you're the smartest person I know."

"What! I've helped plenty! I'm not throwing money at them just 'cause they're embarrassed. Besides, I came from there, too. I get it. We clipped coupons."

She spoke calmly. "I still can't believe it." She put the photo back in her purse. In the kitchen, a metal thing rattled. "You don't 'get it.' No one who feels the need to brag about clipping coupons 'gets it.'"

"I'm not going back there," he whispered. His finger swabbed for crumbs.

With utter void of passion now, she studied him. "Get over yourself." Lam drank her coffee, staring blankly, making him fidget. She reopened her purse and retrieved a ragged page from a tiny spiral notebook. "Last week I tried to get Mom into the car for her doctor's appointment." She handed him a note scribbled in cursive. He read: *I ain't got no good panties.* Lam seemed satisfied at his recoil. "She was crying. So we didn't go."

"Jesus Christ, Lam!" Levi dropped the note on the table like it was nasty. He leaned back. He rubbed his face, sighed heavily and looked at the ceiling. He dug in his pocket, pulling out his money clip. "Here! Here's forty dollars. Get her some underwear, for Christ's sake!"

"I took care of it," Lam said.

He held out the money but she didn't play. He sighed. "How's Dad?"

"Fine. Working." Her vision bled beyond Levi. "He's changed." She added, "Smaller."

Levi snorted, watching people crowd the buffet like winners of an all-inclusive cruise. Looking back at Lam, and for just an instant, behind the woman, he saw the little sister he left behind. "I should have been there. Like I said."

"Don't worry about it. Mom says God is saving you ... you know. For something."

They finished their coffee in silence. An hour later, as Angela warmed in recovery, it stopped snowing. The air outside turned cold enough to break. When she was finally released, Lam followed her and Levi home. While Levi helped Angela out of the car and into the house, Lam gathered a vase of flowers and a Beanie Baby that had been left on the porch. The card read, *Get Well Soon – Lynette.*

17

No Choice

Yet sometimes, when the secret cup
Of still and serious thought went round,
It seemed as if he drank it up,
He felt with spirit so profound.

William Wordsworth

"Do I look all right?" Angela asked. It had not yet been a week since her D and C. She stood in the dining room, looking into the living room, waiting.

Levi lounged on the couch in his suit pants and tie, watching CNN. On Black Monday – the Monday after her D & C – the stock market had dropped horrifically, 23 percent. Since then Angela had watched Levi argue more with the television.

For having called the crash, Levi's cocksureness might be justified, but he'd become uncharacteristically vocal since Crawford's accusation. After the sell-off, Crawford made Levi forfeit some of the money in his and Angela's own accounts – something about selling before clients did, *selling ahead*, she thought Levi called it. Or *front-running*? Either way, Levi called it bullshit. He was also reprimanded for having Lynette relay recommendations to clients while Levi was in San Francisco. *Should I have let the clients fry because I'm out of town?* Levi had griped to Angela. *The asshole is out to get me.* She thought he was overreacting. So he barked at the TV, "You bet your ass, Paul," after Paul Kangas of *The Nightly Business Report* recited new money supply numbers and quoted Fed Chairman Alan Greenspan. Levi kept his eyes on the screen and hesitantly rotated his head. Finally he looked at her.

She ran her hands down her sides to smooth the black dress.

"You look fine. Great." His eyes bounced to the TV again, then back. As usual, she wore her schoolmarm glasses when she was getting ready but would soon replace them with her contacts. She wondered if her hair was too big. It's not as if he would say so. Still, her figure was okay. Maybe still a little thick. But fine.

"Are you sure?" Her voice lilted.

"Yeah. I'm sure. You look great." He smiled.

She sighed and returned to the bedroom. Pearls or no pearls? Twice Angela draped them against her neckline, and twice she pulled them back. It had been her mother's strand. Though they might not be real – she had decided not to find out – she loved them. Pearls, she decided. She fingered her armpit to check for deodorant.

As she fastened the *Cartier* watch, a wedding present from Levi, she remembered how crestfallen he had been when she mispronounced the brand in front of the Justice of the Peace. She said the blue stone on the stem made it pretty, even nicer than her Timex. To this day, Levi retold this *You can take the girl out of Roundup* story to new acquaintances, but she never let on that it embarrassed her.

This was not the time to hurt, and she searched her head for velvet memories. She recalled their honeymoon tour of Western Montana and she smiled into the mirror. She had dreamily played with his hair while he drove. It hadn't mattered then – not much, anyway – that Levi visited clients and prospects along the way. She had romanticized that he was building their future and visiting clients together somehow authenticated their union. He appeared brilliant, respected, confident and, for all that, more desirable. Once, near Butte, a wealthy prospect with gray chest hair shoved drinks in their hands and withheld his account until everyone had drunk to his satisfaction, or as close to it as his wife would allow. Then he stood close enough to Angela to massage her bra strap while he handed her a $1 million check that she was to hand to Levi. At that point Mrs. Chesthair abruptly ended the meeting. When Levi and Angela were five miles down the country road, he pulled off and made love to her. She reflected on his energy, how physical he had been, and how much that excited her. Now she wondered if it was her or the money that aroused him.

She looked down at her wedding ring, then back into the mirror. She flattened her hand against her tummy, pausing as she smoothed the dress again. She entered the living room cradling a cashmere coat like a sacred totem. On their first anniversary Levi had taken her to Seattle and bought it for her at the Nordstrom's. He was also on a business trip. It was camel-colored with burgundy silk lining, and when she wore it, she felt drenched in romance and elegance. She reached for a tissue and leaned back toward the mirror and dabbed at the corners of her wide-open eyes, and then went to the bathroom to put in her contacts, pee one last time, and put an extra pad into her purse. "I'm ready."

Levi was in full regalia – a navy blue suit, power tie and pocket square – his hands crossed behind his back, watching M*A*S*H. He turned off the set, walked to the front door and put on his shoes. They wanted to make the carpet last long enough to trade the house for one in a more exclusive neighborhood. Angela had said she wanted new carpet anyway. He said they'd never make it back on resale. She had gently pointed out that they had already accumulated enough money to pay off their modest mortgage, but he said she didn't get it. Sometimes she wanted to pop him one. So she never removed her shoes.

As Levi drove, Angela watched the flashing lights of an airliner disappear over the cliffs on its way to the airport. She remembered with amusement how apprehensive Levi had been before his first flight to interview in San Francisco. It seemed forever ago. She still enjoyed his romantic urgency on nights before he left, as if there was some unspoken, noble danger that he may not return.

When Levi started the car, he switched the radio to NPR. Angela laughed. "What?"

"Nothing," she said.

"I listen to NPR."

"Sure you do," she mocked in a breathy, soothing tone. "Good times … good times."

He pulled out and they drove on streets wet with snowmelt.

"You know which one Mike Sandler is, right?" Levi said. He had talked about Sandler practically every day since he had become manager. "He's the president." He may as well have added, "...and that makes this meeting, and me, important."

"I know who he is, Babe," Angela said warmly, allowing him his moment of pride.

He looked into the mirror. "Is my hair messed up in the back?"

She looked. "Nope. You look great." She touched his hair.

"I was laying on the couch." He turned his head and looked again.

They parked in the garage across from the Sheraton but walked across a different skywalk into the historic manila brick Grand Building. Years ago it had been the General Custer Hotel, a local landmark, but it fell into disrepute. For a while the rooms had rented by the hour. Angela remembered when the building's owner had been gut-shot in the hotel bar by a patron with a .22 pistol. The gunman should have used a bigger gun. The wounded owner chased him out onto the street, caught him, and beat him senseless. Downtown had since enjoyed a Renaissance. The Custer became an office building with a ground-floor brass and fern restaurant called Jake's, replete with mahogany millwork and rich floral carpet. Just lovely.

They came off the skywalk at the second floor. Midway down the grand staircase, Levi slowed. Angela held the handrail, descending gingerly toward the lobby. He asked quietly, "You okay?"

"Yeah, I'm fine." She was being cheery.

Mike Sandler was planted like a boulder on the tiled lobby near the restaurant's host station. He was talking with Charley Peterson, Levi's tall, bespectacled assistant manager. They had been in the adjacent bar which overflowed with a tangled score of happy-hour voices and long glasses with clinkety ice. As Angela took the last step, Levi held her hand and they crossed the lobby toward Mike and Charley.

"Mike Sandler, this is my wife, Angela," Levi said.

Compared to Levi's hand, the older man's felt warm and dry, and Sandler smoothly folded his other one around hers. He stood just inside her space, powerful and gentle.

"It's wonderful to meet you, Angela," he crooned deep and warm, like sweetened thunder. "I'm impressed with your husband, but I didn't anticipate that his spouse would be so beautiful." He looked in her eyes and meant it.

Angela inflated involuntarily and shined as she glanced briefly at Levi, who showed no sign of being sore. He was holding hands with himself at his belt buckle. Modestly, she said, "Thank you, Mr. Sandler."

"Call me Mike." His voice remained rich but devoid of impropriety.

One hostess took their coats and another showed them to their table and waited with menus as Levi held Angela's chair. Soon a waiter arrived and recited the specials. Mike asked Charley what was good here, and Charley said you couldn't order a bad steak. Mike ordered a bottle of cabernet.

Mike laced their early exchange with comfort. He told Angela how he, too, had come from a small town in the mountains – Appalachia, actually. He, too, had gone to college at a state school, and he made fun of those private school bastards, excuse the language, but one shouldn't hold it against them for being pansies. They laughed. The real conversation arrived with the entrée.

As he looked at Levi, Mike spoke to Angela. "You must be very proud of this guy."

"I am." She touched Levi's leg under the table. It was bouncing. She beamed at him.

"It's not often we put so much confidence in someone so young, but the scrappers I trust the most are the ones with empty pockets." He looked at Levi. "You've done a helluva job, kid. This place could've gone straight to hell. Right, Charley?"

Charley tilted his head, eyebrows up. "I tell you what."

Sandler turned back to Levi. "You've earned it. Don't forget who you are." Then he looked at Charley again. "After the shock wore off, Charley and I reached an agreement. He says he didn't know a thing." Now in-the-know, a big dog, Charley nodded seriously. Back to Levi. "How many people outside of this table know?"

Levi looked at Angela as though he'd been caught. At first her eyes widened slightly and blinked, *know what?* But she quickly reclaimed self-awareness and drew the slack from her jaw.

"Uh, nobody," Levi said. He hooked his foot around the leg of his chair and though he talked to Mike, he collaterally explained to Angela. "I kept a lid on it. If you tell one person in a town this size, everyone finds out. The competition would've been all over us, trying to hire our brokers." He tried to make it sound momentous. As he faltered one solemn beat, Angela crossed her arms. Levi concentrated hard on Mike's face. "Also, I didn't want to celebrate too soon."

"Well, you did a good job," Mike said, and he raised his glass. "To Levi. The next manager of our Silicon Valley complex."

Angela's mouth gaped, measuring the distance between her and comprehension. She watched Levi raise his glass without looking at her. Charley raised his glass too, grinning, listing a tad. She suddenly realized they were waiting for her, and she saw her arm raise a glass as well.

Levi gave Angela a pleading look. He touched her thigh under the table, and she lifted his hand and moved it away.

The next toast was to Charley, a big grinner now, who was to be the next manager of the Billings office of Bookman Stuart. Charley promised Mike that the success of the office would continue, even bigger with Levi out of the way, *ha ha*, and he appreciated the opportunity, and he was sorry his wife couldn't be here, but his kid had a basketball game, and he was thankful to Levi and would find good homes for Levi's clients, and of course he would want Lynette to stay on as his assistant because she knew where the skeletons were buried, *ha ha*, and so on and so forth until he realized that Mike was bored and he should shut up.

"Where exactly *is* Silicone Valley?" said Angela.

Levi tittered and Mike smiled so Charley did too, but it was clear he didn't know why.

"It's silicon, Honey, not silicone." He put his hand on the table, but stopped an inch from hers. "Silicon is brittle, sili*cone* is oily or −"

"It's south of San Francisco," Mike said warmly.

"*You* know that," Levi still wanted to pass her off as a kidder, but her look wasn't kidding. "South of the San Francisco airport. The opposite way as the City."

Mike watched Angela and touched her hand. "Thank you for lending us your husband. I've been doing this a long time. Sometimes these young guys think they're Superman, but I've never seen one worth a damn that didn't have someone like you. He'd better be thankful for it."

Instinct told her to soften her look − *shit, for what? Levi's sake?* That she now felt an impulse to protect him was itself an offense − and the thought that he might be sitting there … counting on it … even in betrayal! There must be more. Something Levi would explain. She mustered a tentative smile.

"Oh, I'm thankful," said Levi. "She's the best."

"Moreover," Mike continued, "what you youngsters do now will change your lives forever. It's the perfect time for you. Levi told me that you weren't sure if you wanted kids, but until they come along, you'll be glad you put in the sacrifice now. You'll see …"

As Levi winced visibly, Angela stopped hearing words. Her lips scarcely parted as her eyes fell to the table, holding her steak knife. Her stainless knife with its stainless handle and blade. Like surgical steel. Glinting. Mocking. She pushed it away, just an inch, and it flashed at her. She looked up at Sandler. "You're right, Mr. Sandler. This timing is perfect," she said confidently, amicably. She put her napkin on the table. "Would you excuse me?" When she rose, so did Sandler and the others. She lifted her purse, nodded, and walked toward the restroom.

Levi told Sandler that Angela hadn't been feeling well and that she had just come through minor surgery, nothing to worry about, and he hadn't wanted to burden her with too many details.

"Rethink your strategy," Sandler advised.

Angela returned and led the table in declining dessert. Sandler asked if anyone wanted to join him in the bar for a nightcap, and Levi looked to Angela for a favor he had no right to ask. *What the hell did he want from her?* "Sure," she chirped. It didn't sound sincere, but it was all she could muster.

"Don't feel obligated, dear," Sandler said to her.

Grief unexpectedly clotted in her throat. "It's just that I've been under the weather."

Charley proved not so blind after all. "I can give Levi a ride home, Angela, if you trust him with me. It's on my way."

She welcomed the opportunity to escape. With this stone on her chest she could endure no more chitchat, especially with Levi. "That's nice of you, Charley. Thank you."

The men stood with her, and Mike, again, took her hand in both of his. "Thank you, Angela. Dining with someone so charming and lovely has been a special pleasure."

His voice was genuine but scarcely a curiosity to her now. Any luminosity it had aroused in her earlier in the evening had become an artifact. Still, she felt oddly grateful to him.

Levi walked Angela up the grand staircase and toward the skywalk. She hit the glass doors ahead of him and cold air surged into the building. Her coattails flapped back at him like a warning. Finally, when they were pacing above the street, Angela spoke.

"What the hell was this? Retribution? I embarrass you, you embarrass me? Haven't I paid enough?"

"No," he protested.

"When did you know?" She stared straight ahead.

"I wasn't sure until tonight."

"You're lying."

"Angela …"

She arrived at the car, hand in her purse.

"I hope you're digging for a reason to understand," he said.

She unlocked the car door. "Just don't. You got what you wanted." She flung herself behind the wheel, slamming the door shut on her cashmere and silk. She opened the door to the foot-long hash of black road-grime that had been driven into the camel-colored overcoat. She gathered it protectively and began to cry.

Levi squatted to inspect the cloth. "Hey," he said gently, and reached for her face. "It's only a stain. If it doesn't come out, you can get another one."

"Get a-way!" she screamed and popped his shoulder, causing him to tilt clumsily onto his butt. She slammed the door and drove away.

Fifteen minutes later, she parked in their driveway with no memory of driving home. She sat a minute, cradling the soiled skirt of her topcoat to her belly as though it had passed on. Once in the house, she pulled a rocks glass and a bottle of Jack Daniels from a kitchen cupboard. She poured three fingers of whisky. On her walk to the family room, she swung the bottle pendulously and welcomed the weighty feel of ice cubes lurching through booze at her glass. She set the bottle on the end table, by a photo of third-graders. She crossed the room to the fireplace mantle picketed with picture frames, frozen slices of time ordered by significance to her. There was a shot of Levi in blue jeans. There were shots of weddings, shouting echoes of cheer. One was black and white, her parents before a simple altar. Beside it, a boastful print of an outdoor wedding – Levi's and hers. Geno looked older, but no less happy. Then came an image she took at this very fireplace of Frank and Virginia and Angela and precocious little Dusty. Levi was gone that day. Whenever his family came to town, he had clients to see. The next shot had been taken a minute later, of Angela standing in stiff-legged A-frame, her thighs wish-boned apart by four-year-old Dusty's pudgy arms to make room for his face with its ice cream grin. She touched the glass of that frame as though it were broken. She began to cry.

The following morning, Angela went searching. Near the edge of old downtown where narrow streets of Victorians spliced into blocks of the original business grid, she sat still in her car, flat light filtered through dull clouds and bare trees and her windshield. She stared from the steeple to the concrete steps to the massive doors of the old St. Patrick's Cathedral. God's house. She liked St. Pat's. It seemed older and perhaps bigger than her problems. In it she felt less desperate, as if whatever she decided, over time, would become right, like the feeling she got with her father felt when she was little, or even nowadays. But she couldn't go to him to know the answer this time. Not yet. She had to decide this alone. About her marriage. About Levi moving to California. She got out.

In the winter muffle, the close of her car door seemed dense and sure. At the steps she looked up. The steeple's cross held up an aluminum sky. On one level, she was unsure why she came. It's not as if the Church viewed divorce as an option. Maybe that was it. Maybe she didn't want the option. Of course, she didn't want a divorce, of course not. Did she? It wasn't that. Was it? Then what was it? Sanctuary? To lock some hurt out? So she could decide easier. And now was the time to decide. She heaved at the big door.

Near the entrance, by an ornate baptismal font fatter than a rain barrel, Angela dipped her fingers into a bronze bowl of Holy Water and made the sign of the cross. A drop trickled down her forehead. She liked the sensation, a tickle of childhood. Cool. The more felt, the more real. Past the nave, about halfway up the empty pews, she genuflected and slid in to kneel and pray.

It was a long talk. She took time out to look at her hands, unbutton her coat. She talked some more, careful not to ask for anything, not before she had done all her thanking. She thanked Him for everything she could think of: health, her dad, her job, friends, food, snow. The day off. Her coat, even with its smudge. This great church and its great stained glass windows all around. Her house. Food, she already said that one. And yes, Levi. Levi's family.

She sat back. She wasn't ready to ask the big question. She knew what God would probably say – stay together. But she wanted children. She wanted her husband to want children too, while she still could. She wanted a husband who wanted what she wanted, a family, more than God, money, or title. It was so cliché! But so what? That's what clichés are. Common. Her thoughts were babbling. Something gnawed deeper. If God was true, He could see it anyway, so why not say it? She wanted her husband not to be nuts. She wanted a husband and a father of her children who wasn't nuts. No matter what. But she loved Levi. Only Levi.

After a while, she slid to the center aisle. She wasn't sure she wasn't ready to ask God yet – ask herself – if she would go. Not this moment. Instead, before she left, she would walk up front, to the right of the altar, to the nook that was the Chapel of the Shrines. Yes, that was right for now. She would light a candle in the chapel and say a prayer, and go home. She would stop at

Albertsons. She would come back tomorrow.

As she entered the small chapel, she stopped short and her mouth dropped. Sitting in a suit, mere feet from the candles, was her husband. He stirred at her approach, and as he stood, it was clear that he was as surprised to see her as she was to see him. He was first to stumble through their pause.

"I … I figured it couldn't hurt."

She was hearing, but barely believing. "You don't do church."

"I talked to God outside. I lit the candle in here for you. Uh. You aren't going to get all Lordy on me are you?"

Before she could reply, his vibrant blue eyes peered beyond her at the altar, then nervously shot back. She glanced behind her. Just the usual – an altar, a cross. In his face it was clear he felt agitated, but he had something else to say. "Angela, I'm so sorry. I love you. More than anything. More than anything. Do you understand? I want you to know I called Mike Sandler. I left a message for him to call me. I'm telling him that I'm staying here."

Her mind raced to assemble parts. "But Mike made Charley the manager."

"And he still will be. It's okay. Charley can be manager. And you can be an assistant principal. I have plenty to do with clients. Maybe when you're ready again, we can talk about a family."

Suddenly Angela was not sure where the parts were. Had she turned down her job offer yet? No, she recalled, not yet. Get pregnant? She couldn't think about that yet. She was even unsure about that.

All at once, she was not unsure about Levi. As she looked at his face, she saw a calm in him. He meant it. He meant it. And that meant the world to her. She was not unsure anymore. "Call Mike back. Tell him anything you want, but don't tell him you're staying here. You're going. I love you. You've earned it. You're going, and I'm going with you. I love you."

They embraced, holding onto each other. "You're trembling," she said.

He self-consciously cleared his throat. "Well, I don't do church well."

Yes. Now she was sure. Freeing one arm, she lit a candle. "Thanks," she whispered before turning to Levi. She took his hand and walked him. "You're cold?" He said nothing. She squeezed and walked back down the aisle with him, slowly. She was pleased for the corny symbolism, hoping he got it, smiling shyly at well-wishers watching from the stained glass.

"Ange, I'm sorry I hurt you so," he said with a sincerity that struck her with sweet, raw pangs, at once unexpected and inexplicably welcome.

This, she thought, was the pain of love. "We're fine, honey. I love you … so very much." What had her father said? You can only hurt as much as you can love? "I have lots more room to hurt." She had stumped him, but her look told him not to think. All was good. Very good.

Past the last pew, at the big, round baptismal font, Levi wavered queerly, staring distantly into black water, swimming away in it. She scanned his face, trying to read what she never could.

"What?" she asked as the wedding fantasy evaporated. "Oh, Levi. Don't."

PART 3

THE 1990S

CONFIDENTIAL

Personal note – Do not add to visible employment file.

Human Resource Business Unit Executive Summary

BOOKMAN STUART SECURITIES
JANUARY, 1990

To: Gary Crawford, Executive Vice President
Divisional Director/Western Division

From: Deirdre Oliver, First Vice President
Director of Human Resources/ Western Division
Re: Silicon Valley Complex
Manager: Levi Monroe, Senior Vice President
Administrative Assistant: Position unfilled at this time.

Per your request, I completed a one-week review of the Human Resource issues at the San Jose office of the San Jose/Santa Clara/Carmel Complex. While there I:

Addressed issues of benefits, both in individual meetings and with group as a whole, in order to gather Beta information so that the firm may more efficiently tailor its benefits packages with an eye toward cost control.
> **Results:** There was no material resistance to the new health benefit pricing structure, though it was unclear, even after group and individual meetings, whether most employees fully understood the differences between the proposed pricing matrix and the one we are using at this time. The same holds true for our current defined benefit plans versus the proposed defined contribution plan.
> ***Recommendation:*** The firm would meet little resistance from rank and file by implementing the proposed, more cost-effective benefit plan.

Made myself available to counsel any employees who might suffer with residual fears from the earthquake in October in an effort to head off any claims of Post Traumatic Stress Disorder. As you know, the new benefits package excludes health-related claims for psychological issues going forward. No one in San Jose took advantage of my counseling, so I think we're in the clear.

<u>Interviewed veteran and newer brokers as to the competency of management and morale of the sales force.</u>

Result: All investment executives in the branch are impressed with the investment recommendations Levi Monroe has suggested to the sales force over the last two-plus years, particularly the brokers and trainees Monroe has hired into the branch (about half the sales force). However, some senior brokers (some of whom you hired and have called you regarding this issue) are suspicious that Monroe may be so accurate as to engender suspicion of trading on insider information. Further, in their opinion, Monroe has been overzealous in his supervision of them vis-à-vis industry compliance, ignoring the spirit of Rules and Regs in favor of a more literal interpretation. Conflicts between Monroe and brokers primarily center around:

- 1) issues of client suitability of investment recommendations (per the "Know Your Customer Rule." Monroe dictated that an updated personal and financial profile be submitted on every client, which senior brokers consider onerous).
- 2) brokers exercising unauthorized discretion (some claim client verbal or "pocket" discretion to trade accounts and Monroe only recognizes written discretionary authorization).
- 3) documentation (there are rumors of forged client signatures on new account paperwork, particularly the arbitration clause).
- 4) velocity of trading ("churning").
- Note: New York Compliance loves Monroe because of his conservative stance, so we should be careful.

<u>Interviewed female support staff, both in office and at private dinners, to determine grounds for your concerns that Monroe might condone or be participating in inappropriate behavior.</u>

Results: Female employees showed unusually strong support for Monroe. Coached? However, at least one is concerned that Monroe hired a sales assistant who purportedly works nights as an "exotic dancer" at a club called the "Pink Poodle." Based on the firm's Code of Conduct, Monroe has allegedly discreetly forbidden male brokers from visiting the club. One might construe this as favoritism to the dancer/sales assistant. I will interview the woman in question at my first opportunity. The same female employee who cited the dancer joked that Monroe only closes his door when he gets an outside call from a "mystery woman."

<u>Reviewed phone records of local management (conducted off premises).</u>

When I compared the incoming and outgoing call-tracking report for Monroe's lines to our master Best Practices surveillance list for his market area, I found that Monroe has made to and taken many calls from the competition, including Smith Barney, Paine Weber, Morgan Stanley, various regional firms and, most particularly, Merrill Lynch. As you know, Monroe has an uncanny record of recruiting, so one might expect this. What is anomalous is that the incoming report shows a large number of calls from Merrill management phone numbers, though I found no other evidence that Monroe might defect.

Of note, Monroe receives daily calls from Joy Parnell's number in our Peninsula Complex. These calls tend to be longer than his 2 min 42 sec average. Monroe makes no calls to Joy from his office line. He may be calling her from his cell, but refuses to turn in the cellular bill, opting to pay for it himself. I will follow up and download the call-tracking report from Joy Parnell's office and check her cellular bill for incoming calls to attempt to render this pattern more lucent. Perhaps on a related note, Monroe appears to work late on many evenings. About a third of the time, one of the last phone calls he makes from his office phone is to an 800 number. When I called the number, I found it was a calling card. It appears that this call is meant for neither our eyes nor does he want it to appear on his home phone.

By considering Monroe's personal profile against known phone numbers and area codes, it appears he has at least 1 personal call with his home or his wife's place of work (an elementary school) each day, generally incoming. These calls have about a 50% correlation of happening within 5 minutes of calls with Joy Parnell. (Per the firm's Fraternization and Collusion policy, I will follow up with Parnell and Monroe's separate T&E reimbursement filings to see whether they are claiming meals, hotel charges, etc. from the same locations/times).

Monroe seldom calls Montana, but receives calls from his birth town of Roundup about once or twice a month. Investigative Services tells me the calls are originating from one of two residences on which Monroe has taken a mortgage (I have heard he owns the houses in which his parents and his sister live). These calls are short.

Lastly, there have been occasional dense clusters of calls to one particular number in Silicon Valley. Upon calling that number, I found that it leads to the CEO of EcoPulse Biotech, Mr. Abhaya Ramakapur. I am aware that you brought this client to the firm, both Investment Banking and Employee Stock Option business, and Monroe's business units do not handle this business for the firm. One cannot help but wonder if Monroe may muddy EcoPulse "relationships" to his benefit and at the expense of others.

As you know, the firm uses an insurance company to process health claims, but since the firm is actually self-insured, HR has access to employee medical files if we deem we have "vested cause." Your concerns about Monroe's leadership fitness constitute vested cause. <u>I checked his health reimbursement claims against call-tracking records</u>. Monroe regularly receives incoming calls from the two medical offices – a gastro-intestinal internist and a psychologist. The calls are likely appointment confirmations. (The diagnoses from both doctors are stress-related and could bring into concern the level of responsibility assigned to Monroe. We must tread carefully here). Note – Monroe and his wife also seem to be addressing fertility issues, though that is less clear.

As prescribed by Securities Acts of 1933 and 1934 and the NASD, NYSE, SEC and firm guidelines, Monroe appears to abide by the prohibition of employees having unapproved investment accounts at other firms. His investment account at Bookman Stuart, as you know, has both check-writing and VISA Card privileges. In conversation, he told me this is his and his wife's only checking account. Though regulation does not specifically demand it, <u>I used this opportunity to review Monroe's checking and VISA transactions through the firm.</u>

> The Monroes write regular checks to three mortgage companies – one for his California residence, two for Montana properties. He writes intermittent checks to "Laura Ann Monroe" and "Virginia Monroe" and an annual $10,000 check to "Laura Monroe for the benefit of Dusty Monroe." Employment files indicate that Laura and Virginia are his sister and mother. The Monroes also write regular checks (some monthly, some annual) to various charities, the total of which is in the tens of thousands annually. I will check if these organizations have accounts with Monroe's offices and determine if he is inappropriately buying investment business from or through charities.

> Regarding their personal charges, the usual grocery, airline, gas, clothes, restaurants, etc. show up. Only three charges in a year to a liquor store, Kelly's Liquor of Saratoga, CA.

In response to Rules and Regs pertaining to correspondence supervision (per the SEC and the Acts of '33 and '34), <u>I have reviewed Monroe's written correspondence files and his emails, both incoming and outgoing, for the last six months.</u> (The "upgrade" in his personal computer has been downloaded and I should have the printout next week.) While Monroe received several sensitive emails, both securities related and personnel related which could be interpreted unflatteringly so as to lay grounds for further investigation, no correspondence clearly indicates regulatory misconduct, personal misconduct, or malfeasance. Monroe's responses to incoming correspondence are precisely worded and leave little room for exposed interpretation. One must wonder when this level of precision is a matter of course. Hereafter, I will check Monroe's emails daily (on your and the firm's behalf).

On a final note, I have a call in to Bob Cohen, our General Counsel in New York, to get clarification of our "obligation" to check the contents of any personal computer that managers or employees keep on Bookman Stuart premises. I will keep you posted.

I should tell you that Monroe's diligence and skill can appear both remarkable and robust. This engenders palpable loyalty for him among some employees. By the time we next meet, I will provide an addendum hereto detailing his supporters.

I presume that my efforts meet with your approval and satisfaction. If there is anything else you need, please don't hesitate to call on me.

18

FAMILIAR CONTEMPT

A piece of advice always contains an implicit threat,
just as a threat always contains an implicit piece of advice.

JOSE BERGAMIN

Lily Fujiwara listened in on Gary Crawford's telephone conversations for more than an hour. Her ear ached. She removed her earring. She listened, barely. She had stopped taking notes and was numbly surveying the divisional office from her desk. It could be any brokerage office in the West, many of which she'd visited, or any in America, for that matter. As with law offices and casinos, the mood-baiting guise of brokerage offices had long since become formulaic. Crawford liked hunter green carpet, the hands-down favorite in financial services, and wouldn't sign off on dusty eggplant or blue and tan. During any remodel or build-out – and there were plenty since last year's earthquake during the 1989 World Series – centralized New York design teams interviewed local managers to determine unique design matrixes based on area culture, client mix, and office personality. Then, no matter what, they ordered the dark furniture and a corporate art package: Old World maps, botanical drawings, fox hunt prints, maritime scenes, or lithographs of Wall Street. In the Western Division, that was that. Crawford disallowed personal art and had once threatened a manager over a lamp.

In San Francisco even the secretaries had a look. On any given night they might eat Top Ramen in shared studio apartments, but in the morning they dressed in deep-colored suits and dresses, the only whimsy appearing in accessories. Unneeded eyeglasses were big among the younger ones. All were pleasantly guarded around high-paid executives, but occasionally, despite age and rank, they included Lily in their shared frets, baked goods, and sex stories, and it delighted her more than she let on.

As divisional administrative assistant, Lily was as much traffic cop and village priest as she was expeditor. And when Crawford called from his car, to her consternation and disgust, she turned into both operator and eavesdropper. Early on she refused to illegally tape his calls – like the urgent calls he asked her to place to Michael Milken to discuss junk bonds just before Milken was indicted on racketeering in junk bond schemes last year. After that, Crawford insisted she silently conference him with whomever he asked for and take notes of his conversations. When one call ended, Crawford would remain on the line while Lily connected another.

Amid the regular business dialogue Crawford would routinely bait unwary colleagues: "You must feel (about controversial issues)…" or "Don't you think (about someone)…?" or "I notice that you and so-and-so (about a questionable activity)…" He would angle for disparaging remarks about women, minorities, rivals – any poisons he could stockpile and re-brew later into contrived combinations to destroy alliances or careers if he had to. He particularly savored a party's self-disclosures of business or romantic indiscretions. These were easier to extract than one might expect. Crawford would simply imply that big dogs – meaning him and the other party – *discreetly* took advantage of opportunities. Most Wall Street men wanted to be thought of as big dogs. Lily despised the tactics and the low confessional tone with which Crawford professed appreciation for his quarry's judgment and sly bravado. Then he would caution discretion and tender off-the-record guidance and sponsorship to keep the confessor out of danger…and lure them into deeper disclosures.

After these calls Crawford would demand Lily's notes, often puffing with crimson exasperation at her omission of incriminating passages he had so deftly rendered. From Lily's perspective, Crawford's very employment sullied her firm. She all but dared him to battle her openly over the transcriptions, a fracas he cleverly sidestepped by having Deirdre Oliver of HR issue Lily a probationary warning for an unrelated transgression – "misappropriation of company property." She had taken home outdated stationery to use as scratch paper.

After her reprimand, when Crawford called from his car to be connected with someone, Lily would blurt, "Hold on!" and, before he could speak, put him on hold. She would stare at the blinking light until she thought he might hang up. She'd pick up, panting, and say, "Sorry. The phones are ringing off the hook. Go ahead." If he seemed irritated, she'd say, "Hold that thought!" and start again with the blinking light. As for her notes, they became even more cryptic, and sometimes she wasn't there at all to patch in a new call. Sometimes she was there, on mute, grinning and hearing, "Hello? Hello? Dammit, Lily, are you there?" and then she'd say, "I'm sorry, Gary, I just picked up. You were saying, 'Dammit, Lily?'" The truth be told, she would have been both extensive and accurate in her minutes if Crawford revealed his own indiscretions. But he was careful. Except when he talked with Dr. Abba Ramakapur, CEO of EcoPulse Biotech. And that's who Crawford was talking to this day, while Lily contemplated corporate art.

Abba was a wily businessman, a Yale Ph.D. in genetics who had earned millions in genetically engineered rice before selling his patents and co-founding EcoPulse Biotech. Like all good scientists, he demanded detailed and precise communication. He seemed to take pleasure in pummeling Crawford's rhetorical veneer with interruptions.

While Crawford sped toward Sacramento spouting slick, bureaucratic doublespeak, Abba cut him off, again and again. Lily could almost hear Crawford's hands strangle the steering wheel as his voice bored into the microphone, demanding the upper hand. But Abba showed no patience for snobbish ambiguity. Abba's voice projected both force and tedium as he laid out how much stock option business EcoPulse would direct to Bookman Stuart if Crawford in turn directed hot stock issues to Abba's friends.

Lily picked up her pen.

"For every four million dollars in market value EcoPulse or its employees transacts through Bookman Stuart," he said with a trace of Hindi accent, "Bookman Stuart will only need to direct *one* million dollars in IPO stock to the accounts we've discussed. Don't deny you can do it. I know some of your customers. You do it for them. As they say, you are already pregnant, right? So, as you require…"

"I never said I require anything! Be careful what you say to…"

"May I continue? I will give you the names of the people on the new accounts, and you will never have to worry. I guarantee the funds will be there. And as always, none of them are direct employees of you – or me. None of them use my name, and I have never mentioned yours. Never, my friend." He began naming the people who were to be directed hot stock. "Are you writing this down?" he asked at one point, and Lily laughed out loud, relieved that her phone was muted. She was amazed when Crawford said to wait while he pulled over. Had he forgotten she was taking notes? Lily heard paper rustling and then Crawford said to go ahead, dammit.

"If you please," Abba said, "our research could change the world. What's money if you save the world? You can call these names your *Friends of Gary* list. It is legal to direct stock." From his silence, Crawford was either unsure or thought Abba was full of it. In fact, Abba's mission statement was to save the planet. But for now he stuck to the issue at hand – distributing payoffs to people he needed. As his list ended, he said, "I'm not an ungrateful man. We will help you delay payment on stock sales to our employees so you can earn the float. You can hold up their money for more days." Lily copied and underlined the words. "And now I will tell you the names of other senior executives in The Valley with whom you may make this same arrangement."

"That is enough!" Crawford said. "You need to know one thing. You will not dictate business to me! I don't think you appreciate who I am. I don't *need* this arrangement with you."

Abba spoke darkly: "I know my colleagues, Mr. Crawford. I have made it a habit to study the … affairs … of my strategic partners … even back to your military service." There was a dense moment of dead air. "But with you," he lightened as if he had discovered himself off-topic, "with you, I know how you do business with others in The Valley. If you are not interested in EcoPulse business, so be it. We will take it elsewhere. I will pray that if your firm accidentally does anything upon which the SEC would frown, it will never be discovered."

"This call is over," said Crawford, and the line thumped dead in Lily's ear. At first Lily thought he had forgotten she was listening. But when he didn't call back, she knew he was driving back to the office. Within the hour he stood at her desk.

"Give me your notes," he said, palm stiffened at Lily, "and all the copies. All of them."

"I didn't make any copies," she lied, and handed over the originals. That was the last time he asked her to take notes. For almost a month, she thought she had won.

Then Crawford hired a second assistant, Karl, a theater dancer with a finance degree. Months earlier, Crawford had targeted Karl's father, an old-money publisher and rumored friend of William F. Buckley Jr., as a potential sponsor for Crawford into the Bohemia Club, an organization Crawford mistakenly took to favor but one creed, his creed – power. Crawford had abandoned Catholicism to shadow Karl's father at the man's Lutheran church. After a luncheon prayer meeting in which the man confessed his son's sin of loving a man named Kevin, Crawford saw his opening. He offered the man a ride to his office, during which, as a favor and in wise tones, Crawford agreed to offer Karl "a real job." The men spoke of how this might have some curative effect on Karl. So Karl was hired. It quickly developed that Crawford mentored and playfully teased Karl, which regularly galled Lily into closing Crawford's door.

By the end of his first week, Karl was forwarding instructions to Lily about what reports were to be mailed and what supplies ordered. One afternoon while Karl double-checked the numbers on branch budgets, a task that had for years been Lily's exclusively, he asked her to get someone in New York on the phone. It was innocent enough – Karl felt she had the clout to get through where he didn't – but the faux pas incensed her. She left for the day.

The next morning Karl brought her flowers. With palpable repentance, he twice asked her to lunch at Hotel Nikko, a favorite of his and Kevin's. She finally said yes.

At first, not much was said. Karl ordered sushi. "I love Japanese food," he offered. She ordered a salad. He fiddled. Lunch came. Finally he bleated, "I can't help it if Gary likes me!" As he spoke a small slab of maguro tuna waggled sportily at the far end of his chopsticks until it broke for it, belly-flopping into a shallow pool of soy sauce and slapping back a rebuke of tobacco-toned drops onto Karl's tie where they bled out like gossip. "My new tie!"

"Selzer, please," Lily cued the server. "Here," she said to Karl, signaling impatiently. "Take it off. Give it to me." Karl did as he was told.

Lily's hands worked quickly, quietly. Karl watched, then abruptly announced, "He knows I'm gay." She gazed up at him like a put-out mother, then back down to her work. "You don't know what it's like! He doesn't judge me."

"Here." She handed the tie over, having performed a small miracle. "I guess we should stay positive. Okay. Mr. Crawford possesses low homophobability. There. Now eat?" That confused Karl enough to keep quiet for a while. Until he chased a piece of ginger across the table cloth as it lured the tip of his tie into the same, now wasabi-clouded pool of soy sauce. His shoulders fell, dispirited. Lily laughed. "I like you too," she said.

Afterward Karl began to avoid Crawford's door, instead asking Lily and other senior support staff for his assignments while helping them with theirs. He proved smart, genuine, and he quickly became appreciated by all. Lily couldn't help but like him. They began to take coffee together at the Starbucks across the street. She decided it was working out wonderfully.

A few weeks later, late one day, Crawford called Lily into his office. She sensed why.

"I require that you respect me," he said, "publicly and in all facets of work, at all times."

"Your concern is unfounded. I always pretend to." That's when he swung back.

Lily emerged from Crawford's office with death in her eyes. Crawford had declared a divisional *reduction in force* – a layoff – and Lily, a lifelong San Francisco resident, was offered an administrative role with Levi Monroe in the San Jose office. It was that or be laid off.

Karl was racked with unwarranted guilt and outrage. He headed to Crawford's office to resign but Lily stopped him. He should stay, she said. It was best for him. The slow spawn of a dark idea had already begun in her pre-consciousness. Like instinct. That vague awareness of an imprecise thought, the one that arouses the human need to horde assets, even if they are of no immediate use. Lily cared about Karl's well-being, yes. And she just might see if he cared back someday.

19

BONDING

The flame is not as bright to itself
as it is to those it illuminates:
so too the sage.

FRIEDRICH NIETZSCHE

A t 1 P.M. in sunny San Jose, Levi poked his head into a broker's office to remind him and the others crowded around the broker's TV that the sales meeting was about to begin. The on-the-scene reporter was practically yelling into the microphone. "September 11 is a day that folks here won't soon forget and experts say the worst may not be over. It may take weeks to assess the toll in life and property. President Bush has already alerted FEMA, and the National Guard is on its way. No, people will not soon forget the name Iniki, the strongest hurricane to hit Hawaii in some 90 years, and on the heels of Hurricane Andrew in Florida and Louisiana, the second major hurricane to batter the U.S. in the early weeks of the 1992 season. "

"It's time," Levi said to the brokers. One barely nodded. *Good, they're watching,* Levi thought. At the opening of sales meetings, Levi normally had some of the more seasoned veterans present ideas on stocks, retirement planning, or muni bonds. Not today. Today he would push only two ideas – Crawford's first, and then his own.

As with every sales meeting, Lily ferried trays of sandwiches to the already bustling theater-style conference room. As she passed Levi she paused. "That woman who wants to build a shelter keeps calling," she said in soft tones. "The one who helped our hooker. If you're really thinking of pledging $100,000 a year, let's talk about my bonus. And Mr. Ramakapur is here."

"Already? Sure seems like a pushy bastard. Tell him he'll have to wait."

"Be careful. He talks to Crawford. And Angela's here, looking beautiful. Happy anniversary. Oh, and I almost forgot, Marilyn from Billings is on hold."

"Crazy Marilyn?" He checked his watch and watched folks file into the conference room.

"You promised me you wouldn't call her that. You also said she's the only person you'd always take a call from. And do me a favor; take your gym bag home. It stinks."

"You're just like Angela." He hesitated and motioned to an empty office. "Send the call here." A moment later the phone buzzed. "Hi, Marilyn."

"Hello, Mr. Monroe. How are you?"

Her fluted voice made him grin. "I'm very busy right now. Did you need something?"

"Yes, sir. Money for parvovirus."

"I'm sorry?"

"Parvovirus. I got a dog."

"You got a dog?" All of his colleagues were now waiting. "Does it have parvo?"

"No, sir. But some dogs do. Puppies."

"You need money for shots?"

"Oh, no. Humans don't get parvo."

"For the dog, Marilyn. Do you need money for the shots for the dog at the vet?"

"No, sir. My dog has shots. I need money for other dogs."

"Marilyn, I have to hurry. What other dogs?"

"All other dogs. Parvo gives them diarrhea and can make puppies vomit. I saw some at the pound – poor things – I…"

"How much do you need? I'll send a check." Right then he would have sent any amount.

"Five dollars, sir."

"Five dollars? Marilyn, that isn't…" She started to speak. He smiled at her and talked fast. "Marilyn, I'll send you a hundred bucks. I have to go now. I'll call soon." He hung up to Lily's face grinning from the other side of the glass.

Although the room was packed, the top two or three salespeople were absent – an industry custom whereby senior brokers underscored their unimpeachable expertise as well as management's indebtedness to *them*. They were half-right, Levi knew. Commissions did pay the bills. Other veterans stood near the back door, and Levi knew some were there chiefly to score a sandwich. Even in 1992 the average W-2 in the room was $170,000, but, just like minimum wage earners, brokers better tolerated meetings that offered free food. Levi made a mental note to have Lily bring the sandwiches late from now on. Centrally seated on stackable chairs was the base of the hierarchy – new and used salespeople who were not yet or only marginally successful. Most of them paid attention.

The crowding was no mistake. Irrespective of the floor plan, Levi had amplified his "plant capacity" in the San Jose, Santa Clara, and Carmel offices by hiring more experienced recruits and trainees than he had offices. By packing less productive producers two-to-an-office, he was able to increase sales without increasing fixed costs such as rent and leasehold improvements. Same plant, more capacity. He likened it to when McDonald's launched breakfast service in the 1970s – they already owned the plant and equipment, so incremental breakfast revenue brought 25 percent to the bottom line, though McDonald's margins otherwise averaged 19 percent. And for Levi, the strategy further served to spur employees to increase personal productivity in order to earn a private office.

When word of this Spartanism got around, Crawford admonished Levi for poor judgment and then scoffed to Mike Sandler that Levi had shortsightedly undercut decorum. "Erecting bunk-desks in an investment house," he scoffed. "Like pouring gravel in a crystal glass. Well, one might expect as much." Crawford had basked in his boss's laughter until he realized the joke was on him. Sandler loved competitive conflict. "Brilliant!" Sandler had thundered. "Tell him, have at it." The wound got salted when Sandler publicly praised Levi's horse sense on Crawford's weekly managers' conference call. The lemon juice came when he said, "It's just possible that San Jose will surpass the record growth rate Gary Crawford set in Chicago. And that makes me and Gary happy, right Gary?" A quick moment passed before Lily's voice broke in, "Mr. Crawford had to step away. He'll be right back."

Now another sales meeting was starting late. Deirdre Oliver from HR was supposed to be in the room, ostensibly to explain how the company was about to screw people out of benefits – again. Levi started with sales ideas. To his perverse satisfaction, the crowd groaned at the rehash of the firm's managed-money program: financial consultants were to direct clients to money managers who charged an ongoing fee – about 2 percent per year – that the firm, broker, and money-manager split. This strategy, to the firm and broker, was ultimately more profitable than selling mutual funds. Quarterly client billing flattened out commission flow. "If nothing else," Levi said, "it'll keep most of you from pretending to be both analysts *and* salespeople."

"But we have a time-tested strategy for investing," one broker called out. "Ready! Shoot! Aim!" Everyone laughed.

"Okay, now *I* have some recommendations." Levi took on a more serious tone. "I want you all to be careful about buying stocks. The market feels heavy to me. If I'm right, your trading money should go to cash … *or* … I have a muni bond idea."

A veteran broker in the back said, "Ah, come on! Not this again." Levi knew the man was a snitch, a crony who Crawford had hired, a man who was dirty from the Hutton check-kiting scandal. Levi expected another call from Crawford. The thought pleased him.

"I know," Levi said. "You all heard that Crawford told me to stop making stock recommendations. But you also know my record, and you know I never used insider information when I said to sell EcoPulse. And Mr. Crawford has a relationship with the company. Enough said." *Maybe too much*, Levi thought. "Well, I am *not* making a specific stock recommendation. I *am* recommending that you stand aside *on all stocks*. Just for a while. And it's not because of my '*voodoo charts*'." They laughed. "Besides, it's math, not magic..." (He knew they didn't believe in either, but luck, well, luck was different.) "...or astrology, or tea leaves, or bunions." This drew smiles. "My *buy* recommendation is Kauai municipal bonds."

They looked at him as if there would be a punch line about Iniki.

"Seriously. Three weeks ago I took down $10 million worth of uninsured Dade County Florida general obligation bonds for this office – water and sewer. The bonds had been dumped on the market by weak hands because of hurricane news. Even mutual fund managers sold because they didn't want to be asked why they owned them. It took our newer brokers one day to sell them – and now they're up 20 percent because the market realizes you can't rebuild an infrastructure after a disaster without water and sewer, and a municipality can't fix its water and sewer if it doesn't make payments on its bond obligations. Further, no politician is going to let a beloved community in the U.S. go without being rebuilt. It's political suicide. Politicians – local and national – must, will, and ultimately do guarantee the bonds at whatever level is necessary. So the dumped bonds go back up in value. Hurricane Andrew put the bonds underwater. Now they're high and dry." His cornballism drew groans. It was beginning to smell like onions. He had told Lily no onions.

"Now it's Kauai's turn. Different bond owners. Clients and brokers are dumping bonds on the market because they can't understand their risk. Fear and greed. The bonds are down *twelve points in two days* – from $980 to $860 per bond – about 13 percent. These bonds won't default either. I don't care *who's* in office. The state and/or federal government ultimately *has to* guarantee infrastructure. The bonds will rally. Your clients get tax-free interest while they wait. You can sell at a profit as soon as Bush or Honolulu makes assurances. Sell the Dade bonds and buy Kauai. $10 million becomes $12 million, which becomes $13.5 if the Kauai bonds just go back to where they were last week. In two months, that's 35 percent profit *plus* tax-free interest for every day held." The room stirred. *By the time Crawford sees this one,* Levi thought, *Sandler will be making another congratulatory call. Crawford can stick this one up his ass.*

"And don't buy the insured Kauai bonds. *Insured* bonds don't drop much in disasters. The market gets irrational with *uninsured* bonds. Look, everyone wins here. The client profits and you make commission, in *and* out." Crawford's man left with his sandwich.

In the administrative portion of the meeting, a top broker complained that some of her clients were forced to work with other Bookman Stuart offices – the Peninsula offices – in order to exercise employee stock options. Then the bastards wouldn't release the clients' money on time. Clients were defecting to Smith Barney. Maybe she should too. Levi said he'd look into it. Then, as the general meeting concluded, he said what he always said. "We succeed because we work harder than we have to. We don't lie. We don't cheat. We don't steal."

"Praise Jesus!" someone mocked.

"On that note, I don't know where Ms. Oliver from benefits is. I guess she'll walk around the office to see you all." It got a cynical chuckle. "Anyway, at the end of the day, all that matters is who you love and who loves you."

"Praise the Lord!"

"All right," said Levi. "Thanks everyone. Rookies, hang around."

Ten careworn rookies stayed behind. This week, Levi would preach about how not to measure success by commission but by the number of successful conversations – an old sermon.

"Problem," said a woman with runner's calves and mustard on her face. She opened a small bag of chips. "How do I define and track successful conversations?"

The man she had screwed in the restroom at the holiday party answered. "A successful conversation is one when your mouth isn't full." He reddened at his own wit.

She looked at him as though he needed professional help. She ate a chip. "The training department makes us track 'prospects, new accounts, assets, and commission.' Not 'successful conversations.' I spend half my time filling out their idiotic form."

"No shit," someone confirmed.

"No-o shit!" said another.

Levi saw a point to rally around. It was as important to good meetings as sandwiches were. "Throw away the tracking sheets." Brokers loved blasphemy. "If New York trainers were decent brokers, they wouldn't be trainers." The woman led a cheer. "Listen, tracking is secondary. The best producers never get off the phone, and most importantly, in every conversation, in every meaningful relationship, they express an expectation. You do too, whether you know it or not. You express expectations with your significant other, your children, maybe your God." I should write this down, he thought. "I want you to express expectations with clients and potential clients in every conversation. By the way, they expect you to. Expect something."

Just as he began to bask, all eyes moved to the front doorway, to Angela in a sleeveless, cotton dress. She liked the rookies, had thrown a barbecue for them. As she waved and smiled, Levi wilted. She approached him and kissed his cheek to a chorus of ooo's and ahh's and said she'd come back, leaving behind an alluring whiff of her perfume. He threw his hands up. "Where was I?"

"Something about expectations," someone luridly offered.

"Yes. Well, I clearly haven't expressed mine to Angela very well." They laughed. "I'll cut to the chase. Ask for something every time. Information, an appointment. Doesn't matter. Just don't call to bullshit. Salespeople do this because they're afraid of rejection." They were listening. "Try this. Try to get to a point in every conversation where you say 'I strongly believe.'" They stared more blankly. "Okay. First, discuss what you called about. Then say," Levi wrote on the whiteboard: "'Mr./Ms. Client/Prospect, given what we've just discussed, I strongly believe you would benefit by meeting/owning/selling/other action.

I'd like you to do this today/other specific time." He looked back. "Then stop talking. Let them respond. You might request information, an appointment, an order to buy or sell. But always express an expectation. Otherwise, don't bother people. As far as keeping track, make hash marks on a scrap of paper every time you say 'I strongly believe...' If you get to thirty marks in a day, go home – not to that pole-dance hall I don't officially know about." They laughed.

Again Angela appeared in the doorway and waved. "Mr. Monroe, if I may interrupt." Laughter blossomed as Levi swooned. What was she thinking? She went on. "I know how hard you all work and that you can't get by without him," she floated toward him on a wave of laughter, "but it's also important to keep balance in one's life." She put his marker in the tray and hooked arms with him. She looked at the board and cleared her throat. "I strongly believe you would benefit by *spending your anniversary in the wine country with your wife.* I'd like you to *begin that right now.*" He looked at her. "Hey, it's who you love and who loves you." This, to great general amusement.

Damn, she was cute, Levi admitted to himself. To a standing ovation, she led him through the doorway. As they walked past sales assistants he whispered, "Angela, I can't. I'm booked. Besides, I made dinner reservations here."

"I always forget how many trainees there are. No wonder it's so crowded in here."

"Well. Most of them will give up. Training's like stacking water – but frankly, recruiting has gone a little *too* well. Those three brokers at Merrill want to come, and I have nowhere to put them. And I got *another* call from their divisional guy wanting to hire me. He thinks I'm pretty."

"Do you like him?" she teased.

"Well ... he does have a pert-y mouth. Seriously, I like the guy, but he's only playing defense. He's trying to pick off the sniper. This time he offered a million signing bonus."

"Why don't you take it and let's get a bigger house. I wouldn't want to move pregnant ... you know ... if it ever happens." Levi didn't respond. Nearing the desk of one ordinary looking young woman, Angela whispered, "Is that her? The one from the abuse shelter."

Levi winced and hustled her forward. "Shh. If you can call it a shelter. It's awful."

"She didn't hear me. She looks so ... normal, for a pole dancer. Does it make you hot?"

"I am compelled to say I have never taken note of how the potential plaintiff looks. But hot?" He looked around. "The third bullet point on her résumé read: 'What the fuck should I put here?' Clearly she was getting help. Lily hid it from me. Anyway, I *had* heard about her night job, but I'm still glad we gave her a chance, though she scares the hell out of me. She's got a kid, too."

"Is that why we gave her $500?"

"Shhhh." God, he didn't need anyone to know *that*. "You know why. The firm fucked up her first paycheck. She still had to pay rent. And stripping isn't what mommies want to do. Something happened to her – probably a lot of somethings. I just wish the younger brokers would stay out of the Pink Poodle."

"Does that make you hot?" She pinched his arm and grinned.

"She's a great assistant. That's all I care about. And she smells like soup."

"You like soup." No response. "Sheesh. It's *definitely* time we got away together," Angela said as they approached Lily's desk. "Ms. Fujiwara, can Mr. Monroe come out and play with his wife for a few days?"

Lily looked at the calendar and turned the page. "Let's see. As a matter of fact, he has nothing scheduled until Monday." She slyly gazed at a suspicious Levi. "I moved all of your appointments into next week, except Abba Ramakapur." She waved her head toward Abba, who was standing in the reception area with his back flared to them, like a soldier in full dress uniform.

"One more thing," Lily said. "Karl – Field Marshal Crawford's manservant? – he called and said Crawford wants your brokers to cease calling employees of any company with which the firm performs stock option services. Oh, and Crawford's having our phones audited for personal long-distance calls. Karl says he's 'on the rag' about you again." Levi's worry must have shown. "Don't over-think it," Lily said. "You scare him."

"Scare him?" Levi said as Angela tugged his arm. "Can I get my jacket?"

When Levi walked into his office Deirdre Oliver swung around to face him from his own chair. Behind her a technician was closing up Levi's computer – his personal computer. Levi stiffened.

"Oh, hello," Deirdre said. "The firm is upgrading. You were in a sales meeting, and someone has to be here when the tech makes the upgrade," – the tech smiled at Levi – "so I stayed. I hope you don't mind." Levi didn't say.

"Oh, and I had him blow the dust out of your personal computer while he's here. No charge," she joked. "Well, I need to get started talking with people." She closed her laptop and walked confidently out the door. "I'll check back later."

His bottom desk drawer was open. *Did I leave that open?* He wasn't sure. From it he lifted out a small, blue Tiffany's box and two chart books: one a large paperback subscription of *Daily Graphs*, the other a thick pad of graph paper on which he had drawn lines and points and figures and moving averages and volume bars with red and blue and green ink. The inside cover had complex, color-coded formulas inscribed in columns, and on at least thirty alphabetical pages were statistical diagrams labeled AGM, for Angela, and then GS, JP, LF, LAM, MS, ME, and so on. As he put on his jacket, he gazed out at Angela talking with Lily. She was so damn pretty. He pocketed the blue box and returned the chart books to the drawer and locked it.

Levi quickly unlocked the drawer and ripped out a few blank chart pages, grabbed some colored pencils, and relocked the drawer. As he looked up, he was startled at Abba Ramakapur standing in his doorway. Levi had read Abba's history in the press. They said he was headstrong, a dusty kid from central India who forged his renown as a high-tech prodigy, a personality to rival the giants.

"Don't blame your assistant, Mr. Monroe," Abba said. "I insisted." He stepped to Levi's desk and offered his hand, which Levi took with equal firmness. "I am Abba Ramakapur. Our companies – your firm and mine, your boss and I – have a, well, delicate relationship. I need my business done in a certain way. In order for that to happen, I need it done in your option-exercise processing facility on the Peninsula. My vice president of human resources told you this." He pointed out Levi's window, through the distant haze, toward Palo Alto. "I know your Mr. Crawford also agrees. As a matter of fact, unless the business is processed in the way Mr. Crawford desires, I am unable to get the service I need from your firm, and the benefits my associates require from trading the markets with your firm will not be offered. My associates are the finest scientists in the world. They can work for anyone. If they do not receive the benefits I have arranged through your firm – through your boss – they will leave my team."

Levi raced to process this information as fast as he could. Lily's warning was right. Whatever this guy was talking about, he was in cahoots with

Crawford. It had to be crooked. But something about this guy felt solid, almost familial. No matter. If it's crooked, Levi could bring Crawford down! Levi couldn't help but, for an instant, imagine himself succeeding Crawford. He pushed it aside. First things first. Keep him talking. Whatever it takes. Levi looked at Angela who pointed at her watch and signaled with pleading eyes. That's when Abba took an unexpected tack.

"You were very poor, but you also rose from it."

"What?"

Abba nodded at a small, framed picture Levi kept on a corner of his credenza, a photo Levi never noticed anymore, a black and white of him and Lam in ragamuffin coats at a school Christmas pageant many years ago, her looking sad and clinging to his arm, him glaring through dread into old Miss McKenny's instamatic camera.

"I grew up poor," Abba said. "My life too has been blessed with good fate. Because of it, I can reach back for people. Help them. Perhaps you do not understand that need. Perhaps you do."

Levi audited Abba's eyes, trying to read them. He thought of his promise to Lam – to be there. How could this stranger....

"As I said, perhaps you do," Abba continued. He gestured out the window. "Mr. Monroe, it is the efforts of my scientific associates that may lead to this air being clean one day. It is their efforts that may turn back global warming. With them, climatological disaster might be averted. Without them, millions of people, including the villagers where I grew up, might starve. Even at that, it costs money to implement global environmental strategies. Billions. What is our planet worth?"

Global warming? Who said anything about global warming? Levi had scarcely heard of it, mostly through news reports on tree-hugging hippiephiles in Berkeley and Santa Cruz. But this guy didn't seem like a nut. Everything about him seemed genuine, strong.

"You want me to make sure your employees do business in the office up there," Levi pointed through the smog, "but it is not your money. It's your employees'. If they want to exercise options through a broker in this office, I welcome them, no matter what you and Crawford want." *Probably should have left Crawford's name out,* he thought.

"Further, I understand that proceeds checks to your employees out of that office are being delayed. On behalf of the firm, I apologize. I'm sure your employees would rather make interest on the money than give it to us. I'm sure you agree. I'll look into it." It was clear in Abba's eyes that Levi had guessed this part right. "As far as 'benefits' for your associates, I don't even want to know what you mean, and I should tell you that it might be in your best interest not to tell me." Levi let that hang there.

Abba only smiled. "Did you know that if one seeds iron dust on the surface of the ocean, phytoplankton will bloom? Did you know phytoplankton absorb atmospheric carbon dioxide at a voracious rate? Did you know that trees from temperate forests can be genetically manipulated to grow at the rate of bamboo?" Abba paused. "Tomorrow my board and I will authorize various stock option awards in EcoPulse shares. It is routine, a formality. I appreciate the service you have already given my employees. For that, the vote will include a grant for you. No strings. If you find in the future that it may serve my employees to work with the office that Mr. Crawford and I prefer, I'm sure you will direct them there. Should I tell Mr. Crawford we spoke?" He offered his hand again. "Crawford and I are not friends. We do business. I cannot help but admire you. Perhaps you would consider leaving this firm?"

"Tell Crawford whatever you want. Do not give me any stock options."

"Then let me give you this." Abba laid a business card on Levi's desk. "This is my private number. Not even my secretary has it. We all need options. Someday." Abba turned and walked out.

Levi knew Angela meant business. When she buckled her seatbelt, she exposed a flirtatious length of thigh, leaving it that way. An hour later, while they drove up Hwy 101 in Marin with the sunroof open, she popped in a mixed-CD of sensual songs by Toni Braxton, Melissa Ethridge, and Barry White, and fed him grapes and crackers with brie, and they laughed at the cliché of it. She pronounced him handsome. That evening they strolled in warm, russet light along dormant, knuckled vineyards before watching the winter moonrise from the porch of a bed & breakfast. He gave her a Tiffany's bracelet and she gave him a Rolex.

How she woke, Levi wasn't sure, but an hour before daybreak, Angela flipped on the lamp and produced two kooky pair of aviator goggles. At sunrise, standing in a wicker gondola below a roaring propane burner, they launched in a hot-air balloon and rode the wind smack into a hilltop row of merlot rootstock, upon which Angela cut her hand and said fuck, for which she was embarrassed. They finished the ride so the chase car could drive them to the walk-in clinic where the doctor said merlot was overrated.

While she stitched Angela's palm, Levi called the office from a payphone at the bread and cheese shop across the street. Later, at a winery, he snuck another call from the hired limousine while she visited the restroom. At the mud baths in Calistoga, she wrapped her hand in a bread sack as they jabbered from side-by-side concrete basins. Afterward he showered quickly, creating time to make another clandestine call to work. Back at the B&B they dozed heavily, spooning naked atop fresh linens.

Sixty days prior, at exactly 10 A.M., Angela had booked a reservation at the French Laundry and then a limo. Levi managed to look engrossed as the waiter described the first wine, a sample of well-oaked pinot with overtures of blackberry, tart red cherries, coffee, cola, and generous Asian spices. Levi and Angela smirked more openly each time the sommelier described his wares, until it became a thing, out of their control. By dessert they fairly squirted laughter, splashing unintended insults on staff and other patrons alike. They were sorry. Best damn food and wine they'd ever had – seriously. The best. No kidding. Good service, too.

In the limo back to the B&B they closed the privacy glass. At the hotel the driver got out, but instead of opening their door, he unaffectedly leaned against the hood and smoked while they giggled and arranged their clothes.

Inside their room, Angela lit a squat candle and produced a bottle of vanilla massage oil. "Me first," she said. They kissed deeply, and with exquisite restraint, he peeled back the lace she had perfumed for the night. As he proceeded, she felt his breath between his hands, moving down until she was for him the barest of bare. He massaged her back, straddling her, and she felt his hair and his arousal. "Not yet," she playfully slowed him, undulating to roll him forward. "First my massage, then – after that – I can be a *very* good tipper." A half-hour later, after he had used every massage stroke he knew and a few he made up, she traded places with him and began with his feet and calves, then his hands. "Our life is almost perfect." She oiled his scarred palm.

"Almost?" his dampened voice groaned from between two folded pillows.

She started to rethink herself, but blurted it out before it took hold. "I want to have a baby with you." There. There it was. Lying there between them. She hoped she had only risked the perfection of one night, albeit a rare one. A moment before, Levi was heavy and deep on the mattress, but now his body took on a new stillness. She breathed shallowly, bracing for payment, but he rolled over gently and took her hand. He pressed it to his disfigured palm.

"Sometimes, when I'm … threatened … afraid … I… Things look gray."

Gray? The word was unconnected to anything … his scar? He seemed to search her face, deciding whether to give another piece to her. She waited. He looked at his hand. She looked with him. "I thought that stopped, a long time ago."

He was quiet.

His eyes seemed to moisten, and his arousal subsided, though she remained hopeful enough not to look at it directly. Was he afraid *now*? "

Everybody feels gray sometimes," she said

"No. I don't just mean a dark feeling. I mean *colors* go away. Especially mine. My … Anyway, things become the color of my scar."

Angela saw that a tiny fissure to a deep, private compartment had opened again, and now, with its revelation, she was fearful to acknowledge it. She hoped she had misunderstood what he said. She wanted to ask him to explain. Then again, not. Any question might become wedged into the frail opening, sealing away this secret place that she, his wife, should know about. Worse, the wrong question, applied too firmly, might rupture it wide open, spilling out ugly things and forcing decisions she didn't want made. She warmly stroked his palm. "You are a good man. You'll always be a good man." She kissed it. "Your scars are only gray on the outside, like the husk on a pile of hot coals. You glow inside. You wear a scar on your hand. Inside, it's time to let go, you know. Shake down the embers."

She smiled and then touched his penis. It moved. "Let the flame burn as bright as it will. You're a wonderful leader and a wonderful husband." Then, whispering loudly, "And you're a wonderful lover. You'll be a wonderful father." She kissed him, and lingered, and laid herself on him, and they kissed harder.

That night, right then, in the candlelight, they decided to make a baby. The hours that passed before dawn transcended sex in a way and magnitude they never imagined. In the end, Angela cried. At breakfast outside, in the rich morning sun, Levi choked up and tried poorly, yet perfectly, to tell her what she meant to him. She had never seen him so sweet.

On their way to Opus they stopped to buy water, and Levi bought a *Wall Street Journal.* "The market dropped big yesterday," he said excitedly, and the smile abandoned her face.

During lunch, Levi pulled from his pocket a pencil, a blue pen, and a green pen, and drew all over the newspaper. Angela caught him scooting and pulling the paper various distances from his unfocused eyes. Inside another hour, at a gallery, he had fidgeted her into doing what he wanted.

"It seems like you want to go back," she said.

"We don't have to. But I do have responsibilities." He added a smile.

She took his hands in hers. "I know you. We can go, I love you."

As he drove, Angela smiled at her bracelet and dug a small pair of scissors from her travel kit. She twisted tight a yarn-thick cord of hair behind her ear and cut it off.

"What are you doing?" Levi asked.

"I'm weaving you a friendship bracelet."

"What?"

"A friendship bracelet. The kids at school exchange them. You tie it around your wrist and wear it until it falls off. Only you're my *special* friend, so in addition to colorful thread, I'll weave in my golden locks — okay, highlighted locks. Do you love me? Check yes or no."

Levi shook his head in amusement. "You've got to spend more time with grown-ups. You want me to wear a strap of hair around my wrist?"

"I'll weave a sleeve of thread around it. It'll be pretty. Yes or no? Tell me, tell me!"

"I love you like I'm crazy."

She smiled. "I love you like a crazy."

20

Made in Manhattan

Drink and be thankful!
What seems insignificant when you have it,
is important when you need it.

Franz Grillparzer

From the back seat of a limo, Levi gazed out the window. It was 33 degrees in lower Manhattan and spitting snow that scarcely wet the windshield. Classical radio was playing something recorded at Carnegie Hall. He returned to reading an article in the *Times* that treated Clinton's reelection as a foregone conclusion. A passage caused him to mark something in the charts in his briefcase. The *Times* was right, he concluded. Later he hoped to meet with the head of the firm's research department but he was still unsure whether he should reveal his method, which had twisted over the years. Levi barely did the math anymore. Though he avoided admitting it to himself, he relied increasingly on visions that came ever more frequently, more tangibly.

Levi knew he probably shouldn't show the charts he'd kept on people. Stocks, yes. People, no. He'd keep those to himself. But the patterns in them said it was a good day to meet Sandler. Not so much Crawford.

He flipped through the current *New Yorker*, noticing an advertisement for the B&B in Calistoga where he and Angela had stayed three summers ago. He rolled back his sleeve to touch the frayed friendship bracelet and to read the Rolex she had given him. He checked the time and noted the date, his thirty-fifth birthday. The limo stopped downtown and Levi signed the corporate voucher, marking in a liberal tip. "Thanks, Mr. M.," said the driver, and Levi joined the swell of pedestrians that flowed from Church Street through the World Trade Center.

He was drawn, as always, into the Plaza between the Twin Towers, breaching the vast ring of ten massive concrete planters, cusps that encircled the central fountain where sheets of water usually flowed over forty feet of black granite, seeming to spring from under the colossal, twenty-five-foot-high bronze *Sphere*. A center for world trade made possible by, perhaps enabling, world peace. That was the idea, Levi heard.

Levi had always found calm here, among the chaos of 50,000 workers. But today the fountain was off, the black water still, reflecting the sky, reflecting the Towers straining up at a vanishing point not yet reached … outlined in … black? The water lay eerie. Still, but not calm. Ambient sound was… the *wrong* sound. He shook his head. Relax. *It's only a meeting.* God. He gazed past the sculpture to the base of one tower. The lower façade, its glass and steel rising three stories in cathedral shapes that ate light, perhaps twenty of them, slender, the illusion propagated by strong, elegant rivers of steel flowing upward, freezing tri-pronged, like a row of giant tuning forks. Ever since training, Levi had fantasized about their harmony, their 'om,' his inner voice called it. Of course he knew he couldn't actually hear the sound, or the one now. The discord. One of his hands flexed on the handle of his briefcase. The wind gusted and the water shivered, atomizing the reflection, dissolving the shapes – and the sound was gone.

For two years, ever since the WTC parking garage bombing in 1993, acquiring a guest pass had become more cumbersome. Security called upstairs to Mike Sandler's office. They checked Levi's briefcase and issued him a blue paper badge with the date, his name, company, and the building number. It said V I S I T O R in red on the bottom. Finally, he passed a metal detector.

At the center of the North Tower he and twenty others herded into an elevator the size of his parents' kitchen. They faced the way they entered as the car accelerated, whistling and rocking up the shaft. His ears popped. At the 78th-floor sky lobby, the passengers exited the opposite side and relayed into other elevators. Two minutes later Levi sat in a reception area filthy with leather and immense, cracked oil paintings, their frames too gaudy to be a joke. *So this is what the CEO's office is like.* While he waited for Sandler, he talked with Lily on a cell phone the size of a chalkboard eraser.

"Happy birthday," she said. "Have you unwrapped your promotion yet, so *you* can commute to *my* city by the Bay?"

"First of all, San Jose is not *my* city."

"Tell that to the lady from the shelter."

"Secondly, I'm not getting promoted," he said offhandedly, hoping he was wrong. He'd wanted it for years. "Crawford won't stand for it."

"Your doctor and Angela won't be so happy about it. Crawford should find pleasure in it though. He'll hate you for it. Contempt arouses him."

"Lily!" Levi lowered his voice. "Is this still the Karl thing? Don't be jealous. There's nothing contemptuous about Karl." Less than a month earlier Crawford had moved to Manhattan as Bookman Stuart's new president, Karl in tow.

"You know I like Karl." Lily said. "Anyway, you'll be fine. You're white, you're young, you're a man." As Levi listened, a familiar, athletic young man in a new suit approached him with unaffected enthusiasm.

"Well, *hello*, Mr. Monroe."

Levi smiled and stood, holding up one finger as he teased into the phone. "Bitter, bitter. Hey, gotta go. You won't guess who's standing here. Yes, Karl! I'll call you."

"Call as soon as I can burn my Caltrain pass. And tell Karl he owes me a call."

Levi pocketed his phone and extended his hand. "I heard you moved here."

Karl grinned hugely. "I wouldn't have, but Gary offered me a job. I thought it might be my big chance to get on Broadway. And Kevin's applying with NYPD! Can you believe it?"

"Good for you! Well, if you can make it here et cetera … and I'm sure you will."

"Thanks, Mr. Monroe. Hey, listen, we're backed up, so we really need to hustle."

Karl handed off Levi to a boxy headmistress type with gray hair piled high, Seuss-like, with painted-on lips and a warm whiskey voice that implied *you ain't got nothin I ain't seen.* She led him into an office the size of a large loft, replete with a wood-burning fireplace and a panoramic view anchored by the Statue of Liberty. Sandler, robust and coatless, filled one thick chair with restrained impatience. The double-breasted Crawford perched regally in the chair beside him, legs crossed, casually observing a commuter plane cross Jersey City and the Hudson. Levi settled in the trough of a green leather sofa. The assistant eased a third jade coaster on the coffee table and filled china cups from a heavy silver pot. Levi fished in his briefcase for a notepad.

As much as hearing it, Levi *felt* Sandler's voice throb with praise for the extraordinary job that had been done in Silicon Valley. It took a half-step to realize that Sandler meant him. Semiconsciously Levi counted verbs, categorizing them. He noted clothing, making private symbols on his pad under *MS*, under *GC*. Sandler pinched his cup like a grandpa playing tea party, saying how Levi "hired and trained more goddamn brokers than anybody" and all the while waved his coffee cup in a way that made Levi sure the man would scald himself. "Kept our ass out of court, too," Sandler said, and "made a shitload of money doing it." He said Levi helped make Crawford look good too – "not that Gary needs any goddamn help" – and "how the hell *anybody* can deal with those fuckin' flakes in California is a mystery." As Sandler spoke, Crawford eyed the tired, homemade bracelet on Levi's wrist, mockingly it seemed, thinking Crawford thoughts. Crawford recrossed his legs and dangled a skinny foot at Levi.

Levi fought the impulse to clench his teeth, to swallow. He'd be damned if he'd hide a lock of his wife's hair! As Levi forced himself to meet Sandler's eyes, Crawford's hostile silence crowded in, clotting the words that found Levi's head, splaying light between incandescence and shadow.

Concentrating, Levi eked out tiny swirls on the pad with his fingers, thinning, thinning, until... "And that's why," Sandler was saying, "I brought Crawford back here to help run this clusterfuck – though he'll live to regret it. So someone has to step up to the divisional job in San Francisco. I think it should be you."

What? Levi refocused.

"Crawford can't goddamn shuttle from coast to coast forever," Sandler said. "I want an answer now."

Levi's mouth moved. It said yes. He had dreamed of this hundreds of times, thousands. Sandler put down his cup and tension ebbed a bit.

"Something else," Sandler said. "There's been a lot of concern over the years about your stock and bond trading – both in your own account and in your recommendations to brokers who work for you. We don't need any goddamn scrutiny from regulatory agencies because we employ a senior officer who guesses correctly a little too often. There are only three rules to making money on Wall Street, young man – three." He held up three fingers.

So this is where Crawford got that. "And no one knows what they are?" Levi said.

"Including you. No one's right more than 60 percent of the time, long haul."

"Yes, sir. Well. I'm not always right. My house is worth about a half-million less than I paid for it." Levi chuckled but Sandler was looking testy.

Levi sobered. "Actually, with stocks I'm right about 85 percent of the time. But it's mostly math-based. And I only trade my retirement accounts – where the firm holds my money hostage." Again, Sandler missed the humor. "After this, I'm meeting Jack Copland, in research, to show my methods."

Sandler's voice thumped. "You aren't listening, and you *aren't* bothering Jack. He's got a business to run, for Christ's sake."

Sandler lowered his heavy voice. "I don't give a shit if you're Mother Teresa, Stephen Hawking, and fucking Nostradamus rolled into one. I'll hang your ass out to dry if a regulatory agency or the press accuses you of insider trading, and if you run a division, you'll see and hear things other people don't, and I don't need an EVP accused of insider trading. I don't want any bullshit. If you want the job, you have to turn over your accounts to one of our money-managers as a blind trust. Your house, your problem. If I were you I'd buy a bigger one. With Clinton and the Fed letting Smith Barney and Citibank merge, the laws separating banks and Wall Street are being thrown out. If brokers get their way, any bum will be able to borrow any amount they want to buy a house, whether they can pay or not. Real estate'll peak like stocks in 1929. God help us.

"Anyway, about your money. The blind trust is Gary's idea. I like it. Even if you don't want the job, it's probably a good idea. You savvy?" Levi savvied. "And dammit, stop giving investment advice. We pay plenty to people who do that.

"And one more thing," Sandler said. "Up to now, a third of your pay has been in the form of restricted stock. From now on it'll be half. And it'll be locked up for five years, not three. Other than that, the restrictions are the same – if you leave the firm during the lockup period, unless you're dead, we keep the stock. But what the hell do you care? You're young."

Young, Levi thought, doesn't mean unencumbered – the California house, Lam's house, his parents' house, their medical bills, Dusty's education fund, Angela's pet charities and his. As he worried, he again sensed Crawford's malevolence. Levi's stomach said to duck the promotion, stay low. Let Crawford pick another target. With limited liquidity, Levi and Angela wouldn't last six months without his job, without selling something – *without ending up like them*. He'd have to survive the new job long enough to get his restricted stock – millions. He hesitated. "Can the firm hold back less of my pay? Less the first year and more later?"

"No," Sandler said, manhandling his china cup. "And I hope your listening isn't going to be a problem. Maybe I'm making a mistake here. If I am, we better stop it now."

"No, no," Levi said. "It's just that I'm young. I mean, Angela and I haven't built up much cash."

"What's your monthly household budget?"

"About $25,000." Levi flushed at saying it out loud, but no one else flinched.

Sandler faked a woeful look at Crawford, pointing a thumb at Levi. "He's young, poor bastard." He grinned back at Levi. "You'll be fine on cash flow. Don't worry. You'll get old. And while you wait, you also need to bump your contribution to the firm's Political Action Committee. I can't tell you to, officially…" Levi's look must have tickled Sandler because a laugh crawled out on a growl. "Welcome to the big leagues."

They stood and shook hands. "Make sure Angela's on board," Sandler said. "It's a team effort, and she's better than you are. On your way out find Gary's assistant … uh..."

"Karl?"

"Yes. Karl. He'll get you a limo to the corporate hanger at Newark. You'll be riding back with Gary in your division's Gulfstream. You two can talk then."

Sandler's eyes might or might not have twinkled as Crawford shifted peevishly, but the words expanded to engulf Levi like magic vapor – *your division's Gulfstream!* Holy shit.

"Close your mouth. You get the keys – but you don't own it."

"Yes, I know," Levi said, businesslike, and thanked Sandler. Then, when Levi shook with Crawford, he sensed color siphoned from his own body, from his clothes. Stolen. He forgot his grip. Crawford regarded Levi as if he knew he was the thief. Then Levi left the older men alone.

"For the record," Crawford needed Sandler to hear it again, "I still disagree. And he coarsens our culture." Sandler shot a look of warning. Crawford looked away, quick to acknowledge the discussion had ended. Once again he hadn't prevented Sandler from promoting Levi, and this time the insult was nearly intolerable. But Crawford knew he was not yet entrenched as Sandler's heir apparent, despite his ace in the hole, and he dared not spend his new currency before he was sure of its worth. Besides, there might loom a bigger problem out West.

Levi walked outside and the sight and sound of the Plaza pulled at his pallid skin. He crossed West Street and continued through the World Financial Center to the Hudson River. The sky was colder. Pewter. Out of habit or need for purposefulness, he dug from his briefcase the fat cell phone and called Lily. He wrestled inside with the color-sucking fantasy – it *was* a fantasy – hating that he *had* such a fantasy, until he reddened, realizing his briefcase held homemade charts – on *people.*

"There's a message from Marilyn."

"Crazy Marilyn?"

"Levi..."

"Okay, okay. Just Marilyn. What did she say?"

"She said to call her. She needs some money."

He sighed. "Look, can you call her for me? Money for what?"

"You said you'd always take her calls. Scoliosis. *Money for Scoliosis,* she said."

"She must mean the cure of it. Does she have scoliosis?"

"I don't know, actually. She didn't say. But it's not for a cure."

"I'm sure I don't get it, but I'm not calling her. What's it for then?"

"She wants to have everyone in her office screened for scoliosis. She's hiring a health care professional to come there. $150."

"She wants to have everyone screened?"

"Yes. $150. Her manager won't pay. She doesn't want anyone having it undetected."

"Lily, please call her for me. Tell her I'll send $1,000. Tell her to give what's left to any charity she wants. And please mail her a check from my account."

"Levi, it's not the money, you know. She calls you."

"Please, Lily. I don't have time." Four seconds passed.

"Listen, there's one message you should take," Lily said. "Your sister called and said to tell you that your dad's bypass surgery went well."

A pang of anger and its guilt arose inside him. His parents, forever uninsured, denied him the ability to feel – or *be* – financially safe. "Cha-ching!" he blurted.

Lily gracefully ignored him. "She also gave me a message about your mom."

"My mom?"

"Yes. I'll read it to you exactly as she said it. 'Mom freaked out when Dad went into surgery. They found her in a snowbank again. She's not dead. She thawed out again.' That's what she said. Word for word. Is your mother okay?"

"Well, she's not dead ... again." He sighed. "It happened before, when we were kids. As I've said, she's colorful when she drinks." *Colorful.* He imagined his parents sucking color from him, from Lam. "Did Lam say if she took Mom home?"

"She said your mom and your dad are in the same hospital, Deaconess, but your mom will be out of observation today."

"Cha-ching!"

"Stop it," Lily said, and gave him Lam's phone number. She asked him if he'd been promoted, and he said yes. "Good," she said, "now go schmooze some department heads while you're there – Trading, Syndicate, and General Counsel. You'll need them."

He walked to a garbage receptacle while she looked up what floors they worked on. He pretended to write it down. After they hung up, Levi rested his briefcase on a receptacle and opened the lid. He gathered his hand-drawn charts. Long ago he had decided never to plot these with a computer. He told himself the nuance of the process demanded his hand. But there was something else. People might find them, judge him, think he was sick, like a father drawn to porn sites. *Why do I care?* Caring bugged him. He pulled out the charts and balanced them on the edge of the trash bin. It had taken years to figure out how to predict people's behavior based on trends and facts at hand – their verbiage, their clothes, their birthdays, the change in the tint of their skin, the broadcast news, the hue of the sky. He looked up and something dawned on him. He pulled a colored pencil from his briefcase and shuffled the charts to the one labeled *GC.* He extended a line. Then he checked his notes on Sandler's word choice and flipped another chart, counted up the y-axis and then across. He held his finger there while he found a different colored pencil, then made two dots. He held the two charts side by side. Concentrated. "One good, one not so good," he mumbled, and suddenly felt a rush of embarrassment. "This is bullshit!" He slapped the charts roughly against the greasy rim of the trash bin. His fingers slid. Stopped. He looked away at the slate colored river. At anything. He didn't watch his hands jerkily shove the graphs in his briefcase and lock the lid.

For the next hour or so, Levi strolled the river walk at Battery Park City, trying to assimilate what was happening, thanking God, noticing colors and forms and patterns. *Stop it! Maybe I should tell more to my therapist. What for? Same meds.* The skyline wore a luminous corona, as eye-tricks can do. But the outline of the Twin Towers appeared in photographic negative. He blinked it away and hurried along. Time to meet people. Later, from the corporate hangar at the airport, he called Angela. She was teaching. He didn't leave a message.

A man in an understated uniform approached and introduced himself as the pilot. Next he introduced the copilot, who took Levi's bag. The attendant escorted Levi forty yards across the tarmac to the portable stairs for the Gulfstream IV. As he stepped up, the two rear-mounted turbines whined to life, drawing his glance. A shiver seized him. At the mouth of an engine cowling, like dandelion petals spun on a stem, turbine blades chased a circle, faster, faster, and at its center, a painted cone, white spiral on black, screwed to life – coiling, coiling. Like symbols from his charts that only he could read. Private meanings. The other engine screwed the other way, opposing directions. Reversing, like a rug flipped over, *hide the dirt, hide the dirt.*

Dammit! Levi blinked hard, peeved. Intellectually he knew he had made it where he had wanted – *had* to get – and he never had to go back. *No!* He fought the creeps. *Should've dumped the charts. First chance, back home.* He set his jaw. It crept back. *Hard to undo crazy. My ass! Not anymore. Not anymore.* He ducked into the fuselage.

Inside the eight-passenger cabin Crawford alone occupied one of the leather recliners at a modest, burled table. He was reading. With scant eye contact, he motioned for Levi to sit across from him. Levi exhaled, stealthily, stayed loose. "Imagine seeing you here," he said.

Crawford kept reading.

The attendant offered Levi a drink, but Crawford didn't have one, so Levi declined. He quietly gawked around the cabin. Eventually the attendant sat nearby and warmly recited safety instructions as though he were her overnight guest and the towels and fridge were just down the hall. Next she brought hot washcloths to wipe their hands. She said he could choose dinner from filet, chicken, salmon or vegetarian, and he could eat whenever he was ready. "So then, Mr. Monroe, you're our new boss," she said.

Levi looked to Crawford, who continued to read. "I ... I guess so. Call me Levi." He was thankful when the plane finally lurched. The acceleration and takeoff were amazingly smooth Levi thought, for a small aircraft. When the captain said they were at cruising altitude, Levi used the interruption to begin conversation. "I'd like to thank you for the vote of confidence, Gary. I won't let you down."

"Your thanks is misdirected," Crawford said. He ordered scotch and held off until he got it. "There's one thing you should know, Mr. Monroe," he said as if chiding a child, "I did not endorse your promotion. In fact, your pedigree and judgment don't support your *current* position. But you have managed to fool Mike – for now. I am profoundly displeased to have him make my first major appointment *for* me. Are we clear on that?"

Levi's lips tightened. The expressionless attendant faded into the galley.

Crawford continued. "Over time I will gather anecdotal evidence to validate my assessment of you. I know, better than you ever will, the managers who will report to you. And *you* will report to *me*. Not Sandler. Verstandlich?"

"Pardon?"

"Understand?"

Levi tried again. "You've been my leader a long time, Gary. I'll carry forward your initiatives. You can count on me for results, though your division is already doing exceedingly well. I intend to gain your respect and the respect of the professionals in the division you built."

Crawford's eyes flashed. "Don't try to manage *me*. Managing *up* is not a skill I admire. Do you think respect – *veneration* – is something you can simply rub on like so much … liniment?" He began to boil. "Your managers will have an open channel to me, without retribution from you. If incidents surface that call into question your character or judgment, they will be addressed – without attribution of the source of information."

"You mean you'll encourage people *to tell* on me, with the promise of anonymity? And their accusations will go unquestioned? You're kidding." Levi wished he'd phrased it differently.

Crawford leaned forward. "Cross me again and I'll have your balls. Now perhaps you'd be more comfortable at another table, Mr. Monroe."

Levi gripped the armrests tightly before he pressed himself to a standing position.

"One more thing," said Crawford. "I've not yet decided whether stock option Ex & Sell will report to you. I'll consider other alternatives." Crawford went back to reading.

At his first step, Levi's feet flexed as if to set an anchor with his toes. As he moved past Crawford, his right arm wanted to slug the bastard's head. *Just pull the trigger.* But he didn't. *Not anymore.* He made his way to the table at the back. Once seated, Levi turned off his overhead light and willed the sky to darken. The attendant smiled sweetly and offered him a dinner menu to think about, but he declined and asked her for a pillow. He could hear, feel, the engines spinning up, coils against coils. In the air, he wanted to sleep, but his stomach had been provoked and he was up and down to the restroom. Off and on he talked to God, once about the flight, but mostly about why the hell he accepted this job. Acquiring it had been his focus for so long. For so long he knew he would get it. It hadn't mattered to him whether Crawford moved up or out to make room for him. If Levi was to move up again, he decided, to the presidency, it would have to be with Crawford's demise. That black thought felt good.

21

Secret Seeds

The world leaves no track in space,
and the greatest action of man no mark in the vast idea.

Ralph Waldo Emerson

O n Market Street, on the third floor of an unremarkable office building
with no view of the Bay, Fran Abondolo walked off the elevator and
stopped at the locked glass doors, again without her card-key. She clutched
the door handle and waved to the receptionist, who waved back at the
beautiful, slightly fuzzy Mediterranean face and buzzed her in. Like most
mornings, the small lobby of the NASD office had two spare clusters of
people in courtroom attire huddled as far away from each other as possible,
whispering, waiting for their arbitration to begin.

The National Association of Securities Dealers handled most legal disputes
between clients and brokerage firms, and for years the NASD offices hadn't
had enough conference rooms to handle the caseloads. Many disputes were
heard in conference rooms at the Sheraton Palace or the Saint Francis or
some other hotel. There, like here, innocent clients faced off with innocent
brokers, once trusted friends, and avoided eye contact with each other by
listening to their respective attorneys tell them why they were right, and by
answering softly posed review questions designed to keep the claimant or
the respondent loose and confident. The only courtesies exchanged between
parties were in the lobby during periodic breaks when each side attempted
to cede the receptionist's bathroom key to the other so as to appear reasonable
in the presence of passing arbitrators who also had to pee. That's what was
happening as Fran, an investigator in the enforcement division, walked
through the small lobby to the bland, interior door for which she did hold a
key. She unlocked it, entering the restricted sanctum of investigative offices and
cubicles. Then she unlocked her private office, hung her topcoat on the coat

tree her husband bought her at Wal-Mart, and picked up the paint-it-yourself coffee cup on which her daughter had brushed, *I'd Rather Be Gardening*. Before addressing her burgeoning inbox, she fetched a cup of coffee.

The top item was yet another large, sealed, manila envelope with no postage and no return address. It merely bore Fran's name in now familiar handwriting. It was the third such delivery this month. She opened the envelope and removed a copy of a letter to Gary Crawford at Bookman Stuart.

Dear Mr. Crawford,

I have called your office several times for a year, and you have not returned my calls. I don't know who else to talk with so I am writing you.

I am a 22-year employee of EcoPulse in Mountain View. For many years our company struggled because we couldn't get enough money. Sometimes I even worked for IOUs (which my company always paid) and I got stock options. As a single mom you can things were tough, but we made due, and I borrowed money for a house and my kids to go to school. They're out now.

Finally my ship came in. EcoPulse got the money it needed to become a real going concern and our stock went public. Boy was everyone happy.

Last year in February, we had a meeting. We were told to call your company if we wanted to exercise our stocks. I called and talked to one of those machines where you press the buttons so I could trade my options for stocks and sell some. I told the machine to sell some because I wanted to pay off my kid's school loans and we planned a vacation. I got a note in the mail that you sold some, but no check, so I called the number on the slip and I got a recording. So I called the operator and asked for a phone number at the address on your slip in San Mateo and I called it. I asked why no check? They gave me to a broker named Chad who told me it took longer for this kind of thing. He said I would get my check in a few more days and I did. He also said I should keep the rest of my stock with him and not to sell it because I would have to pay taxes so I didn't. He said I should buy more stock but not in EcoPulse because I already had too much, but other things would go up and I could borrow with my good EcoPulse stock. I did what he told me to do. The things he bought me kept going down and down so he made me sell some more of my EcoPulse to pay him off. I sold some extra and asked him to send me money for my kitchen and he did, but took his time too.

Now I get a letter from the IRS saying I owe them $341,215 because I made my options into stock and that was a big gain. Only I don't have $341,215 *because the things I bought all went down and I had to sell me EcoPulse (and when it was low too) and pay you guys for what I borrowed. I told the IRS that I made a big gain but I made a big loss too so how could I owe so much? They said I have to pay taxes on all of the gain because it was the first year but I can only count $2,000 of the loss each year until it's all used up because it was the next year. I don't have any money to pay them and my son says I have to live to 400 to use up my $2,000 per year.*

Now the IRS wants my house and they treat me like a crook, all because I did what you said. I don't even like to remember the vacation we took. I called Chad to ask for help, but he went to sell real estate and no one else wants to talk. I talked to a manager named Joy and she told me it's not your fault. She felt real sorry for me (ha, ha). I asked her to sell everything I have and send me the money, but she said it isn't much and I haven't got a check yet.

This has been going on for 1½ years now, and no help. It's making me sick. My kids say I should sue (I don't want to). What should I do? Please answer me!

Yours Truly,

Mrs. Roberta Andonian

On the floor next to Fran's desk were cardboard file boxes labeled *Bookman Stuart, Option Exercise and Sell, Abondolo*. Fran opened one and filed the letter under *EcoPulse*. There were other files for other Silicon Valley companies that used Bookman Stuart's employee stock option services. Each file had client complaint letters about Bookman Stuart. Some claimants had hired attorneys who alleged violations of the Securities Act of 1933, the '34 Act, and the Investment Advisor Act of 1940. Plaintiff attorneys tended to take a kitchen-sink approach – alleging lack of client risk suitability, inappropriate tax advice, unauthorized trading, churning, and lack of supervision. What they all had in common, however, was that the initial client transaction at Bookman Stuart was an employee stock option exercise and sell – and all of the complaint letters mentioned that Bookman Stuart didn't send out checks in a timely manner.

Fran also had sub-files for each company that detailed the corporate officers who were responsible for hiring Bookman Stuart to service their company's employee stock options. Each sub-file listed those officers' purchases of initial public offerings of common stock, particularly hot issues – EcoPulse, EBay, Yahoo, Krispy Kreme, Global Crossing – and there were many purchases of the same IPOs. Most were made through Bookman Stuart.

There were only two possibilities. Either Bookman Stuart used illegal favoritism to distribute IPO stock without divulging that favoritism to the issuing companies, or many of the corporate officers who hired Bookman Stuart to service their stock option exercise business had been astonishingly lucky in their personal accounts. Fran didn't believe much in luck. It was time to call Julie Pennington, her counterpart at the Securities and Exchange Commission in San Francisco.

"Julie, Fran. Hi. I've got a pattern emerging at Bookman Stuart here in the Bay Area that looks a little funny. They may be manipulating stock option exercise & sell clients, stealing the float on other folks' money, among other things. I've got anonymous tips. And it gets weirder.

"Normally Bookman flies way under our radar. Their last boss out here tried to stay invisible. Never heard from him. But they've got a new EVP here and the new guy – um, Levi Monroe – sent me a letter on *private stationery* alerting us about something the firm was about to do. Apparently Bookman intends to move all their retail clients' money out of money market funds into some new product called a Bank Deposit Program that pays about half the interest. They're in bed with a Chicago bank. Bookman pockets the difference. It'll increase profits a billion a year, he says."

"Shit, it's all because Congress and Clinton repealed the Glass Steagall Act. Who decided it was a great idea to let bankers and brokers remarry in the same firm? Where's their history? FDR must be rolling over in his grave. Where's their heads? This won't accommodate the American Dream, it'll create indiscriminate lending for fat fees and build the American nightmare."

"It'll be convenient for clients. And loosen up lending."

"It'll destroy the banking system. Or am I just old?"

"Are you on hormone replacement?"

"Very funny. If this flies, the whole Street will gather at the trough. What the hell, lawsuits keep us employed. Anyway, Monroe's letter says the firm only intends to inform clients of the bank deposit program through a statement stuffer that implies that the new deposit program is safer. Monroe claims it is not. He says the client money will be deposited, roundabout, in the bank that Bookman's in cahoots with, and that that bank will use the deposits to make subprime home loans, which will be sold back to investors through Bookman. Everybody makes commission, but clients get set up to take an enormous, unwitting risk.

"In his letter – which, again, is *not* on the firm's letterhead – he says he protested to his boss, Gary Crawford, the guy who was Monroe's predecessor out here and is now president of Bookman in New York. But Crawford gagged Monroe on this topic. Are you getting this?" Pennington said she was.

"Now get this, Monroe's asking that we help pressure Bookman to hold off until each client gives individual and informed consent to move their money to the bank deposit program. He says informed clients will pass.

"Frankly, I don't know what to make of Monroe. This guy either has enormous cajones, a death wish, or he's nuts. No matter what, he'll get his ass fired if Bookman finds out he's tipping us. By the way, I like big cajones, so I say we don't tell them. Regardless, I don't think we can help him. The law doesn't require a firm to inform clients with anything more than a statement stuffer – which no client reads.

"My bigger problem is I'm also getting *anonymous* tips from inside Bookman about this potential option exercise & sell scam. Great morale over there, huh? How about coffee?"

22

DEFERRED DELIVERY

A little kingdom I possess, where thoughts and feelings dwell;
And very hard the task I find of governing it well.

LOUISA MAY ALCOTT

It was 105 degrees in the Bull Hills, another record. As usual, Lam was wearing short cutoffs. The unusual part lay in her born-again belief she could stay true to Russ. She had help. First of all, Dusty was working for Russ on the ranch. Boys talk. And so do folks in a small town, not that they hadn't always, but now she cared. She had something to lose. Despite that, some days that low, primitive ache in her belly made her pace – like the day she saw the UPS guy making deliveries on Main. They waved a couple of times as he drove around and finally said hi at the dime store. She told him he had cute legs. To show her that hers were better, he stood beside her, looking down, so close the hair on his calves touched her skin. She leaned a little, crowding its softness, almost imperceptibly. Almost. When she followed him outside she caught herself keeping that distance in the neutral zone of gossip, not that anything might happen. She couldn't help but note the truck was from Billings, not that she cared if his other life was a safe distance away.

A week later Lam was sunbathing in the backyard. She went in the house for another beer and saw the UPS truck out front, through gauzy kitchen curtains. The driver had just made a delivery next door to Mr. Pinsky, who sold pinball parts out of his garage on eBay. He was bent into his truck, rearranging his packages. Yup. He had nice legs. Very nice. Lam leaned into the sink and before she knew it she was touching herself. He stayed just long enough.

The next day Lam caught herself looking out the window often. It paid off. Mr. Pinsky got another delivery. After about a half-hour of thinking and a beer, she flipped through mail-order catalogues, whispering, "What can Brown do for you?" She finally called Spiegel and asked if they shipped UPS. She ordered a dress she didn't intend to keep. With working nights at the bar and Dusty at the ranch, it was easy to arrange a delivery when she was home alone.

The morning the package was to arrive she was nervous, so she drank a beer. Okay, two. She showered at seven and put on a thin robe. At mid-morning when he parked the boxy truck at her curb she quickly dampened her hair and answered the door as though he had surprised her. She peeked out. "Oh, hi! I can't believe it's you!" she said. "Would you mind stepping in?"

She stood too close to him, and for too long, without signing anything, until she stared him into kissing her. "Kiss me hard," she said, and he did, and without saying anything important, she gave him a blowjob. Then she turned and braced her hands on the wall. He took her passionately, launching ripples of flesh across her ass that broke into the small of her back. They never left the entryway.

She never opened the package. It aged for a week until her shame fermented with such randiness that she called for a UPS pickup. They did it again, this time on the kitchen floor, her cutoffs slung around one ankle.

Afterward he asked to see her again, to meet her in a week or so on a day off, probably late afternoon. When she asked if they could meet earlier because she worked nights, he stammered before he said no. His wife was scheduled for a Caesarian section that morning. He said he should be there. *What*, she said. He had been afraid to tell her, he said, and never would have consented to another child if he had met Lam first. She said please leave. *Now*.

As he drove from sight, her chest deflated, her shoulders rolling in on it like a scroll. Walls caved close again. Standing in her tub, she showered, grating her skin with a loofah until she drew blood and pain through the surface and the scalding water ran out and turned cold, but she didn't care. Finally, she buckled to her knees, straining fiercely from her abdomen and bawling, "Get it out of me! Get it out of me! Please, God! Get it out of me … get it out… "

It had been that way since puberty. The lovers – mostly men – the cravings, the toxic shame, and, ultimately, pouring more lovers in to water-down disgrace with pleasure, to make the act common. But sex was a caustic placebo, and she despised the inevitable, blistering degradation that followed.

For a period before Russ, Lam had connived to *make* the users – her bastard neighbors and barfly customers, the married ones, the fathers – crave her sex by getting them all hot and hopeful with counterfeit leers and contrived touches, keeping it up until they had nothing but shit for brains. She could make men sneak and sniff around for weeks. Years even. Only when they had sacrificed all of their will and prudence to her crotch – only when she knew she could hurt them – would she ration sex to them. On *her* terms. It never worked. They just spilled acid on her soul and disappeared. And the stain was impossible to wash away.

Later that summer, during one of Angela's visits, over a blender of margaritas, Lam confided about how many men there'd been, how often, and how she hated most of them. After Lam's anger and self-loathing had boiled dry, she fell silent, and Angela finally spoke.

"I love you," she said. "It hurts to see you in such pain, but I don't understand. You're telling me you *seek out* these guys … you *find* people who use you. Why don't you just stop?"

Lam hesitated. "Remember the Pulaskis? Remember they had a big, black dog that Mr. Pulaski beat all the time? Mean-ass dog. It used to chase me and Levi all the time. It could never quite catch us, but it kept trying, every chance it got. One time, when I was about twelve, it chased us home. Dad was out front shoveling coal. I fell down just before I got to Dad, and the dog bit my foot. Dad dropped that shovel and yanked the dog by the collar, but the dog didn't let go. Fortunately my shoe came off, all bloody, but he didn't let go of the dog then neither. He made a fist and showed it to the dog's face. The dog jumped at it. He was gonna get bit for sure. He wanted to. When the dog opened its mouth, Dad shoved his fist down the dog's throat as hard and as far as he could. Practically up to the elbow. He went crazy, cussing and shoving. The dog drew blood, too, but couldn't bite that hard with Dad's fist down its throat. It just made Dad shove it deeper, with all he had. Pretty soon the dog was gagging and making ungodly sounds and scratching like all hell to get away. But Dad hung on. I thought he'd kill it, and pretty soon the dog's eyes went from this crazaround pushing-out-to-the-white-parts look to all the sudden dull. Like it was dying. When Dad finally pulled his fist out, the dog ran off. It never bothered us again. I remember we drove to town for tetanus shots, and when Doc O'Brien stuck Dad, he never even flinched. Not even when Doc sewed up the gash bleeding out of Dad's cross tattoo. He wouldn't take anesthetic. I tell you what, that was weird."

Lam's eyes drifted back in time, "But when Doc O'Brien stitched my foot? To this day that's the only time I ever saw Dad cry."

Angela ventured, "First of all, men aren't dogs. If you hurt one – I suspect you haven't hurt anyone as much as you think – and hurting one sure doesn't stop the others. Besides, they can't *all* be assholes."

"They're not the dog." Lam's eyes remained elsewhere. "I am. I thought if I stuffed the fist far enough down my own throat, I'd get hurt enough to lay off it."

She flashed back with Angela. "But you're right about assholes. Russ isn't one. He looks at me like I'm clean, and he listens like I matter … and he don't go away when I lie. He just calls bullshit, like he's brushing lies off me. So I don't sleep around so much now. A while back – when I did? – when they were finished, I'd call Russ and tell him how much I love him and want to wake up with him every morning for the rest of my life. He listens – all quiet – almost like he knows what I did. Then he says he loves me too, that he wanted that too. Then he asks '*How are you doing?*' in a way that makes me sure I'll never do it again. I try not to."

23

Hunters in the Dead Zoo

Mishaps are like knives,
that either serve us or cut us,
as we grasp them by the blade or the handle.

James Russell Lowell

Yet another summer morning and Lam was splayed in bed, stomach down, rousing to nervous semiconsciousness by a vague, pulsing pressure on her shoulder. Thick light bled through her eyelids, and her hot breath nested in a wad of hair and pillowcase and stunk like stale cigarettes and *Clairol* dark apricot. The effort to suck air back in hardly seemed worth it. Exhaling was easy. Her head hurt. She felt the pressure again, four or five shallow, rhythmic nudges pressing her torso against the mattress.

"Mom?" Her teenage son bounced her shoulder again.

"I hear you, honey." The pillow was wet. She cracked open one eye, but the other one stuck. "Would you uncover my legs?"

He did as she asked. "Have you seen my Wranglers?"

Her head hadn't finished rebooting. It took a second. "I thought you said they made your crotch hurt."

"Have you seen them?"

"Wear your Levis."

"Where's my Wranglers?"

"Why?" The second eyelid finally broke loose.

"I'm going to Billings."

"What?"

"I'm going to Billings. With Russ. To buy cattle."

She opened her eyes wider and blinked at the clock. "Shit. What time is it?"

"Quarter to eight."

Lam had forgotten that Russ would be by at eight that morning. With some effort she rolled over until her feet flopped to the floor, pausing to marshal the strength required to sit up and steady herself, one palm on the bed and the other over her eyes. She chewed at a nasty thickness in her mouth and noticed mascara on her pillowcase. She finished a plastic bottle of water she kept on the nightstand. "Fill this up, would you," and she waited for Dusty to take it so she could use both hands to stand. Her ankles popped. She stepped into her slippers and consciously threaded her hands into the armholes of her robe. "Did you check the laundry basket?"

"Yup."

On the way to the bathroom, her feet snapped and complained about standing behind the bar all night. As she stabbed the toothbrush into her mouth, Dusty peered beseechingly at her in the mirror. "How 'bout the dryer?" she said – the dryer Russ had given her two years ago when she and Dusty moved into this cottage that Angela had insisted Levi purchase.

Lam spit and rinsed her mouth, then brushed her hair, stopping to sniff it before she banded it back with a scrunchie. She washed her face and misted herself with eau de toilette. In the kitchen, she put on a pot of coffee as much to fill the room with its aroma as to drink it. Dusty followed her there and dropped his cowboy hat on the table and his boots on the floor and sat behind them.

"Ain't *you* cowboyed up?" she said. As he tugged on his boots, she admired his shoulders. Football training was under way and he would wrestle again this winter. He went undefeated his junior year, but this year he'd have to move up a weight-class – or two.

Lam heard a rig pull into the driveway and plodded to the window. The engine cut and she watched Russ sit for a moment with his head and Stetson bowed in concentration. He was on the phone. Out on the ranch they used walkie-talkies and a land line, but a spotty rash of phone cells had erupted in Roundup, a godsend for ag-folks in town on errands. Russ' call gave Lam time to pour the men a thermos of coffee, and when he finally strode across her sunlit lawn, she took several quick swallows herself, hoping to mellow her breath.

When he walked in he removed his hat. "Hi, Darlin'."

She hugged his waist with affected luster, held her breath, and kissed him. She pulled away and smiled at him for what felt like a respectable amount of time and then turned her head as if, out of the blue, she'd remembered something on the other side of the room, and exhaled.

"You doin' okay?" he asked.

"Oh, yeah. Just thinking." She pressed her cheek to his chest, gave him a squeeze. "I'm great … now." As she disengaged, she leaned back on the counter and seized her coffee cup.

Russ turned to Dusty, who had a copy of *The Billings Outpost* open on the cluttered table so that Russ could see him reading the farm and ranch report. With a shrewd air, Russ snatched the paper, sending half a dozen pads of dryer lint lofting to the floor.

"I was reading that," Dusty complained.

"The hell you say? What exactly were you reading? If you can tell me, you can drive."

"'The success of *Abba Rice of Utah* has put the renegotiations of water rights in California's Central Valley and Owens Valley in turmoil.'" The boy became self-satisfied.

Russ looked at the paper. "I'll be damned. Good thing we're not in California." He handed it back and forfeited the keys. Then he bent and picked up the lint pads, variously speckled with blue, gray, and red. He raised his eyebrows.

"Grandma wants them. Sometimes she keeps lint."

Russ was deadpan. "I didn't realize she was a keepsake kinda gal."

"She's making something for the fair in Billings, I think. Some kind of display or quilt, I'm not really sure."

"I believe she intends to make a jacket," Lam offered.

"From lint?" said Russ.

"Apparently it involves lint … that's what she said."

"I see. Okie-dokie, then." Russ scanned Dusty from feet to head. "You ready?"

"Yes, sir."

Lam put the lint in a Ziploc bag and handed it and the thermos to Dusty, who started for the door.

"Don't forget your coat." Russ pointed to the jean jacket on the back of a chair. The boy plucked the coat and stood, intending to wait, but Russ said, "Why don't you go adjust the seat."

Dusty sauntered out the door before he smiled, as happy to drive as to leave Russ with his mom, not wanting to jinx either one.

"At least if you take him in the summer, he won't miss school," Lam said.

Russ let go a laugh. "That kid wouldn't get a B if I took him for a month." Then his voice became more serious. "Hey. I'm sorry I didn't make it in last night. One of the guys pulling fence bummed up his hand, and I had to finish with them."

"That's okay."

"You sure?"

"Yeah." She smiled.

"How'd you do?"

"Fine."

"You sure?"

She became exasperated. "I'm sure. You don't have to baby-sit me just because I work at a bar."

Russ regarded Angela, 1,400 miles away, as Lam's only close friend, but Lam's other intimate friend, albeit a jealous one, was alcohol. As an addict, alcohol's potent role in her life seemed to have become ordained by the very drug itself – surreptitiously willed into being over time – absent Lam's consent. She flirted with hating it, but her terror of abandonment always spiked her into secretly guarding the relationship, in all its profanity, as sacred. On jagged days it alone heard her plea; it alone offered warm absolution from ridicule, from shame, from self-doubt. And when, on occasion, her affair with booze was challenged, it demanded eradication of all rival relationships.

"It's my pleasure," Russ said. "I always wanted a fixer-upper girlfriend, long as she's no more than half a bubble off plumb. Besides, I come to Geno's for the floorshow. Wouldn't miss it. Fools on Stools. But you've got to stop serving me Coke, the caffeine's killing me. Maybe you could keep lemonade at the bar. Or herbal tea."

"Herbal tea?" She shook her head. "And you call yourself a cattleman. If your folks were around today, they'd rue the day they let you go to college in California. Stan-furd."

"Mom drank herbal tea," he played wounded at first. "Seriously, though, we're going to stay overnight in Billings. You okay?"

"I'm fine. I'll be fine." She paused. "Even better if I was sleeping in *our* bed."

He changed the subject. "Hey, I saw another announcement in the paper about Levi getting promoted. How does the *Billings Gazette* know what's happening in—"

"Be nice. He may have found success, but he ain't found him*self* yet."

"Okay, but why do I have to look?"

"Stop," she sheepishly cut him off. "Listen, about the rent…"

"Hm. I'll send him a check," Russ said.

"No. Don't. I don't want him to think…"

"I can't believe you have to pay him. He owns the house."

"Well, the bank owns it. Besides, I pay him less than half the mortgage, and he doesn't *make* me. It's my choice. Angela told me he banks my checks for Dusty, for college."

"All right, all right. Give me a deposit slip. I'll stop at the bank."

"I'll pay you back."

"Why yes. Yes you will," he said suggestively.

She put her arms around him, her cheek against his chest. "Hurry home." He cupped her ass with both hands but differently than other men had, intimate, to be sure, but loving. The first time he did it was on their third date. After driving back from a movie in Billings, she had invited him in for a beer. She had put on Toni Braxton, and they sat on the couch and, as she'd hoped, made out. After ten minutes, he stood and she stood with him, willing to go where he wanted. The kissing became more passionate, but still soft, and she got that low ache in her belly, but he was simply saying goodnight. Her stock script said to act disappointed, but he had made her feel … safe … by touching her ass – confidently, but as though it were … *hers.*

Now he made her look up at him. "We'll have our time. When you're ready." He wrapped his arms tightly around her. "Count on it."

"It's just that it's been years." She could tell he was listening, truly listening, as always, and it irritated her some. As if he understood her and still knew what's best. She kissed him perfunctorily and slowly spread his arms with her elbows. She backed up until she was against the counter again. "Don't let him drive in the dark."

"He'll be fine. I love you."

She knew it was true. It had been for a long time. Even when she faltered. Even when she hurt him. He never gave up – but he never gave all. "I love you, too."

As Lam watched them drive away she wondered if she "craved a soulmate too much to hold onto one." That's what her mom had written. She'd heard it on TV. Corny as hell and Virginia even spelled soul as "sole," but the point was taken. Worth considering. Exhausting. Lam went back to bed.

For a while, she forced herself to lie still, but the hangover gave her legs the heebie-jeebies, and the longer she laid there, the heebier and jeebier she got and the more she considered how to take the edge off. She began searching her memories of men she'd been with. She couldn't hold any one image for more than a half a minute, and finally the UPS guy popped in and she decided this wasn't helping and stopped her hands. Her head hurt when she moved it. At last she slipped off her panties, closed her eyes and thought of Russ. It didn't take long. Afterward, she let her body go limp, but the noise in her legs returned and crept higher until she couldn't lie still for more than a minute or so. Finally, she gave up and got up and poured another cup of coffee, leaving some room at the top.

For a while she carted the coffee up and down a path in front of the cupboard, never quite sipping. She toted it into the backyard and stood by the juniper bushes and closed her eyes and adjusted her angle to the sun to spread its warmth like balm across her jitters. The heat didn't sink in so fast and the cup kept picking at her, so she pivoted it to the periphery of her vision where she could have some peace and still keep half an eye on it while she gave the sun another shot and smoked a cigarette. Afterward she hauled the coffee back in the kitchen and made it wait on the counter while she went to the bathroom. Maybe it would grow cold. She returned to the counter and faced it. Finally she opened the cupboard doors above the refrigerator, moved a box of Abba Rice and some Wesson Oil, and, on tiptoes, reached in deep for a bottle of Bailey's Irish Cream. She topped off her coffee, leaving the bottle out. She could nap until her shift started at Geno's.

The cattle auction at PAYS, the Billings Public Auction Yards, wasn't to be held until the following morning, and Russ and Dusty had been to nearly every jewelry store downtown. Next they headed to Rimrock Mall on the west end. Dusty was still driving, and Russ nonchalantly draped his left arm across the back of the seat to make it look like it didn't bother him.

"The Four C's, huh?" said Russ. "Color, cut, clarity, and what?"

"Cash," said Dusty.

"I tell you what. We'll have to forgo a few other Cs – cattle – if this keeps up."

"Boy howdy." Dusty's hat was tipped back, and he was riding large. The windows were down and they were rolling west on Central Avenue, a four-lane thoroughfare.

"You think she'll be surprised?" asked Russ.

"I think she'll be shocked that you finally got off your ass … sir."

The pickup was drifting a bit. "Apparently thinking taxes your mind too much to simultaneously hold the interdependent concepts of lane-lines and turn signals," Russ taunted lovingly. "Why don't you stop thinking for a minute and drive?"

"Yes, sir." The pickup straightened out.

"You're a ballsy little shit."

"Yes, sir." Dusty grinned and aimed the rig and checked his mirrors with a nervy head-twitch.

By the time Lam woke at 5:15, she had forty-five minutes to make her six-'til-closing shift at Geno's. She rinsed her cup and put the Bailey's back in the cupboard. She wanted to bathe in the claw-footed tub, but she showered because it was quicker. She put on low-rise jeans, a crop-top, and a little mascara. With no time to blow-dry, she left with what Dusty called ditch-water hair. Didn't matter. On the way out, she opened the junk drawer, fished out a thick rubber band, and slipped it onto her wrist for snapping.

She spent the early evening serving some of Geno's regulars – several ranch hands who lived in town, a couple who owned one of the grocery stores, and some on-again, off-again oilfield workers. A survey crew from the USGS, in town to update maps of the fallow coal mines, dutifully fed their day's wages into the poker machines that flanked the pool table in the back, and one of them hit a straight flush, instantly making new friends in the bar by buying a round before she fed it back into the machines. Lam filled her time between orders by watching ESPN on satellite TV – because that's what Geno was tuned to at his house next door. Geno wouldn't let her turn on the sound, on account of he wanted patrons to play the jukebox.

About 7 o'clock Lam was sitting on a barstool at the deep end of the bar listening to a patron, thinking of slipping some rum into her Coke. She was snapping the rubber band on her wrist when a hunky survey crew foreman, who had just returned from showering at the Big Sky Motel, came in. She stubbed out half a cigarette and stepped behind the bar. The foreman stood across from her with his short-sleeved shirt unbuttoned two buttons. As he assessed the ornate walls, he pressed his forearm heavily onto the bar and acted unaware that he was flexing at her.

"Last year I shot a muley bigger than any of the ones hanging in here," he said.

"You don't say," she said.

He did say. "Yeah, I only regret that I didn't have the head mounted. But I wasn't a foreman yet, so I didn't have the money. Too bad I didn't shoot it this year, but being the boss doesn't leave as much time. What're ya gonna do?"

All of this registered vaguely with Lam as she made eyes at the rum bottle and guessed the smell of his toiletries. Just as she was settling on Red Zone, her train of thought was derailed when, from the front door, Donnie and Tommy Zupick invaded, advancing deliberately and perching one stool down from the deer hunter. She turned as if to straighten the glasses and glanced at herself in the back bar mirror. As she walked behind the bar and toward them, her finger tugged at her thong in back. "I heard you moved back to town," she said and laid a coaster in front of Donny.

"You heard right for once," Donny teased. His hair was neatly trimmed and his polo shirt was buttoned to the neck, but he was thin and his eyeballs were the shade of old newspaper.

"Stop tearing me down, genius, I already escaped. Why do you keep showing up?"

"Well, darlin', you got under my skin and into my heart and you've been growing there ever since."

"My dog had that. We put him to sleep. What can I get you two to drink?"

Tommy spoke politely. "MGD, Ma'am. Thank you." He wore a uniform from the gas station he inherited when their father died. Tommy looked fit and as big as Donny nowadays.

"And a Moose Drool," said Donny.

She came back with beers and mugs, picked up the money in front of Donny and turned to the till. As she made change, she looked through the coyote's plastic case and into the mirror. Donny was gauging the other patrons when the surveyor asked if he was a hunter. Lam quickly slapped the change in front of Donny, diverting his attention.

"You married yet?" Donny asked as though there was a fat chance.

"Nope. You divorced yet?" Donny laughed through teeth that had never been pretty but had come to look as if they'd been exhumed. *Meth mouth,* she thought. On the few occasions she had smoked it, she had suffered oral skin burns from the vapors, but never damaged her enamel. After all, she never got *that* bad. Thank God. He coughed ugly. "You are pathetic."

His smirk attenuated as he poured his beer. "Yeah," he said, "I s'pose I am."

Tommy looked disgusted. "Oh, shit. This again." He slid off his bar stool. "I'm gonna plug the jukebox. Any requests?"

They shook their heads.

Lam leaned her butt against the beer cooler and crossed her arms, exposing her midriff. She watched Donny until he finished pouring and looked back.

"Janine and our daughter stayed in the house in Billings," he said.

As Lam assessed the bitterness on his face, he stood and pulled a pack of cigarettes from his pants pocket. He tried vainly to tap a cigarette free and finally pushed a finger into the pack and smeared around until he forced one out. He offered it, but she declined, so he lit it up.

"You a hunter?" the deer hunter asked again. He had turned toward Donny and now he was leaning hard on his other elbow.

Donny shot him a look of utter disgust until Lam leaned over the bar a bit. "Now Donny, it ain't like he shit on the carpet. Everybody around here's a hunter. Right?"

Donny looked at her as if to insinuate the interloper was *her* dog. "Hm. Yeah." She raised her eyebrows at him and cocked her head a little. As a favor to her, he relaxed and took a drag.

The deer hunter stood straight, squared his shoulders with the bar, and winked at Lam. He downed his beer, ordered another and nodded toward the restroom. "Save my seat, Darlin'?"

Lam smiled and he headed past the pool table for the room marked "Bucks." For the next few moments, she waited for Donny to talk.

"Last week I moved in with Mom and Tommy until I find work. It's weird, but it's good to be home." His voice was tired. "Really, it is." He drank some beer and stubbed out the cigarette. "How's your folks? Tommy says your dad works at the station once in a while."

"Yeah, it was nice of Tommy to hire him. He's doing okay. His heart bothers him, but he's doing good. Mom's not great."

"How can you tell?" He sounded self-pleased.

"What do you mean?"

"She never did exactly cook with a recipe." Donny scouted the room for

Tommy as Lam folded her arms. Tommy was talking to some local men in a booth. "How's Dusty?"

"Why would *you* care about *my* son?" The score didn't feel even yet. "He's fine. Great student. Great athlete. Don't smoke, or drink, or take meth. Today he's in Billings buying cattle – with Russ." There. That felt about right.

"Good for him. How's Russ?" The question was disingenuous.

Lam picked up Donny's bottle and poured the remains into his mug. Without looking, she threw the empty into the plastic barrel under the bar. "Anything else?"

"Can I buy you one?"

He must be shitting her, she thought. "*Huh*-uh."

She returned to the deep end of the bar and stood post under the TV. She began watching a muted episode of *CSI* she had seen before, intermittently scanning the evolving crowd for signs of thirst or drunkenness or rancor.

The deer-hunter-surveyor drank and chatted her up and got more talkative every time she came out from behind the bar and smoked a cigarette on the stool next to him, at which times he turned his back to Donny and Tommy so he could give her deep eye contact without competitive scrutiny. He sat splay-legged, now, dressed left, she noted. Whenever she ignored him, he ordered a beer.

"A buck-fifty," she'd say, and he'd hand her a five or a ten and say, "Keep the change." She'd grin and bang a coin loudly on the bar and say "Thank you very much" and put the dollar bills in the tip-jar she had moved near Donny, to whom she offered the quarters if he'd plug the jukebox. He scowled each time as if she was an asshole, and she just looked at him like *What?* Then she offered them to Tommy, who passed, so each time the deer hunter plugged it. Early on he played *Slim Shady*, an act which Donny told him if he did again, somebody was gonna fucking kill him. Deer-hunter laughed, but Donny didn't, so Deer-hunter spun away as if to dismiss Donny. But he didn't play anymore hip-hop. Worse. He decided to help Donny out.

"Earlier I couldn't help but overhear that you were looking for work," the deer-hunting-surveyor said. "How about I put you on my surveying crew, see how you do. Nothing technical. You pretty much just have to hold a stick." Tragically, the blunder sounded as earnest as it was.

As Donny stood, Tommy stepped between the two men and faced Donny's reddening countenance. "Don't," Tommy said quietly and sternly. "You're on probation."

"I ain't got no weapon … and she lied."

"It doesn't matter. Janine'll fuck with your visitation."

Lam hastily pulled a bill from the cash register and gave it to the deer hunter. "Here's five dollars." She nodded in the direction of the poker machines. "Why don't you play, and if you win, you pay me back and keep the winnings?" She nodded again.

"Hey, I didn't mean … sorry." He took a beer and went to the machines. Things eased. Eventually the surveying-deer-hunter handed Lam $5 back and said thanks and that he knew good music, little of which was in the jukebox. He'd do his best. He leaned over the machine for quite a while, remaining there well after *Desperado* began to play.

Lam said to Donny, "Hey, if this song ain't you, I don't know who it is," and, from across the bar, she touched Donny's hand. Everything got fairly relaxed for a while, and might have stayed that way, but the deer-hunting-survey-foremanning-music-aficionado played *Desperado* five times running, and Lam said, "Ain't that you?" all five times to Donny, who wasn't the only one getting irritated, because a local pool player finally unplugged the goddamn jukebox, and Lam had to plug it back in and tell the pool player to give her a dollar, which she gave to the wounded deer hunter and told him to play something else.

Finally the musical-deer-hunting-surveyor gave Lam a twenty and asked for four fives. Over another half hour, he ordered four imported beers, one at a time, without drinking the one he had, letting five bottles line up in front of him, just so he could say "Keep the change," which, to Lam's surprise, she grew tired of hearing. Still, Donny didn't need to know that, so Lam laughed harder every time and called the big tipper a moron, and tried not to but did look delighted to irritate Donny. She said out loud that she could go on like this all night. That made the big-tipping, deer-hunting, musical boss of dumb-ass surveyors smile, and she smiled back, and Donny got off his barstool and grabbed his change off the bar and pocketed it.

"Ohh. Where ya going?" Lam sounded disappointed but felt sadistically gratified.

Donny didn't look at her. His bottom lip slackened as he tucked in his shirttail. "Tommy's gotta work in the morning."

Deer-hunter sat a little straighter and watched in the mirror.

"Come on," she whined. "One more. I'll buy." Maybe she could grind it in a little more. "I'll be good," she whispered. "Come on." She winked.

Donny and Tommy ordered a couple more beers, and Deer-hunter offered them two of his but quickly apologized before Donny fired up again.

By midnight the standoff had become boring. Donny was due back from the restroom as Lam sat on the stool between the rivals, resting her elbow on the bar, nearly knee-to-knee with Deer-hunter. She slowly rubbed her fingertip inside a small jar of Carmex before she applied it to her bottom lip and handed the jar back to the deer hunter. "Thanks."

"What songs do *you* like?" he asked.

"Why?"

"Just tell me."

She laughed tiredly and drank her Coke. "I've heard 'em all too many times."

"You haven't heard me play them. On the jukebox, I mean."

She considered him. "I don't know. I like *Boogie Woogie Choo Choo Train* by the Tractors. I like *Stairway to Heaven*. Anything by Garth Brooks; *That Summer, The Dance, Shameless*." Lam watched Donny return to his seat, sit backward, elbows on the bar. Including Tommy, who had wanted to leave hours ago, only the four of them remained in the building.

The deer hunter smiled at Lam and put his hands on her knees and slid off his stool toward her. When he stood, his knees brushed her thighs. "I've only heard of one of those tunes. My dad likes *Stairway to Heaven*."

"Play *Shameless*," she said.

"I always do," and he turned and started toward the jukebox.

"So you're a big hunter, huh?" said Donny.

Lam tightened, but the deer hunter ignored his antagonist and continued to the jukebox.

"What'd you shoot your deer with?" Donny called to him.

Tommy put his hand on Donny's arm. "Hey. I gotta open the station at six. Let's go."

"Hey, Deer-hunter. What'd you shoot that big buck with?"

Before selecting a song, the deer hunter turned around, relaxed and confident, having made a decision. "A lever-action .25/35. Remington model 1894. It was my grandfather's rifle."

"Well, I'll be go to hell, Deer-hunter. I do believe you're full of shit."

Lam slid off her stool and walked behind the bar. She ran her hand under the counter by the till, looking for a button.

Deer-hunter stood, feet shoulder-width apart, and folded his arms on his inflated chest. He was bigger than Donny and younger.

Donny unfurled from his stool and stared at the younger man. As Donny spoke, Tommy reluctantly put his car keys back in his pocket and stood beside him. "The '94 is a Winchester, stud, not a Remington. I been listenin' to your bullshit all night. Trophy deer, my ass."

Lam's eyes darted toward the back door.

"You know, I think you're right, Donny. The rifle *was* a Winchester. My mistake." Deer-hunter hooked his hands low on his hips. "And you're right about that deer, too. It was no bigger than Bambi. I apologize." He smiled. "You got me."

Having his provocation dulled only made Donny fume until he coiled to strike.

Tommy grabbed his arm. "Let's *go*, Donny. Shop opens in six hours."

The deer hunter raised his hands, palms up, and nodded to Donny. He wasn't looking for a fight but wasn't afraid either. Dealer's choice.

Donny clenched his fists and his jaw pulsed.

No one heard Geno, in his slippers and his sleeveless undershirt and his pajama bottoms, as he passed the poker machines and rounded the pool table. Then, like Charlton Heston as Moses, Geno raised a pool cue like a mighty staff and drove the butt of it to the floor. The world flinched. "Closin' time," Geno bellowed.

Donny glared at Geno, then at his rival. Finally he rolled past Tommy toward the door.

Tommy laid $10 on the bar. "Thanks, Lam." He nodded aside. "Geno."

Geno locked the front door behind them before facing the man by the jukebox. "Closin' time."

Lam intervened. "It's okay. He's okay. Let him finish his beer while they clear out."

Geno walked ponderously through the barroom and returned the pool cue to its rack "Lock yourself in. I'll wait up until I see you drive off." He meant, *don't keep me up all night.* She locked the back door behind him.

As Lam returned, the young man gestured toward the dance floor. "Can I play one more song?"

Lam hesitated, and then smiled and nodded.

He punched three buttons on the jukebox and walked toward her, stopping before her as *Shameless* began to play. He took her hand, and they began a self-conscious box step. "I really did shoot a big buck," he said, and she laughed.

He stepped left, and left, and left, and did it with such tenderness that she consigned to him the trust to hold her close. Soon they surrendered into the slow, tranquil rocking of couples lost in unguarded affection. For that moment, her eyes closed. She smelled him, felt his hand find the skin of her back. His fingertip traced above her waistband. It wasn't until the song was ending that he tried to kiss her. That broke the spell. She tentatively pulled away. "Sorry," she said. "Closing time." She let him kiss her forehead.

"Closing time," he said gently, and they walked to the bar holding hands. "Thanks for the dance." He took a drink of beer and waited to see if she'd change her mind.

"I'll let you out," she said, and she walked with him to the front door.

He dawdled. "Must be someone pretty special."

She opened the door to a stark pulse of tepid night air, full of honesty and quiet. "Goodnight," she said. He kissed her forehead again and walked out as she looked beyond him, checking for familiar cars. Relieved, she closed and locked the door and went back to work.

Lam placed the few remaining glasses in the empty sink, policed the pool table, and stacked the dirty ashtrays on the bar. She paused and checked the rows of call liquor on the back bar. Everything was in its place. An able bartender, her muscle memory made it unnecessary to actually look at the bottles when she poured drinks, and frankly, she had disciplined herself not to. It wasn't that hard until she was alone with them – the bottles. When Russ closed with her, it was easier to ignore them. But Russ wasn't there. She pulled a bottle of Jack Daniels from the upper shelf and set it on the bar. Next, she iced a rocks glass, held it on the bar beside the bottle. As the glass cooled her hand, her organs heated and crowded her ribs like restive inmates. Her brain packed up against her forehead. She clumsily mauled a chunk of ice from the glass and fed it to her mouth. She pulled on the rubber band, snapped her wrist hard. Again, again – until it welted – and again! Finally she lifted the glass and flung the ice at the sink, and without addressing the bottle, returned it to the shelf.

Suddenly cramped and alone, Lam skipped restocking the beer cooler and fled. Geno was waiting to go to bed anyway. She shut out most of the lights, set the alarm and exited through the back door. She got into her car and started the engine. She locked the doors. When her headlights went on, Geno's kitchen light went out. From the rearview mirror hung a delicate gold chain bearing a medallion of St. Jude Thaddeus, the patron saint of desperate causes. Russ had given it to her. "Thank you," she told it.

Tommy drove Donny to their mother's house and went to bed. Donny grabbed a beer and went back outside to smoke and stew. He finished the beer quicker than he started it and got in his Firebird and drove back into town. In a pitch-black alley behind old houses, he parked along a fence lined with juniper bushes that partially obscured Lam's home. From there he could see the back screen door. He could watch her driveway and smoke and indulge his resentment.

First he imagined knocking on her front door with a decent reason for her to let him in. Maybe he'd ask for a beer, and maybe she'd give him one. Maybe not. He played out several scenarios in his head, each ending in rejection, and each imagining made him more pissed at her. It wasn't as though her precious son was home, he thought. Who the hell'd know? Fifteen minutes passed, and each one gave her a bigger excuse to be tired, or unfriendly. "Dammit, where are you?" he growled. Part of him wanted to forget the whole thing, to leave, but each time he touched the keys that dangled from the ignition, his hand recoiled. He looked at her driveway. "I came here to be nice!" He ripped open his fly and handled himself roughly. It was no good.

A half-hour passed. She was probably doing the deer hunter, Donny supposed. He imagined meeting her in her driveway or at her door. She'd act all stiff and pissy, like she ought to be scared of him instead of just being nice. He bet himself that, with Russ away, she fucked that freak. Wonder how Russ'd like sloppy seconds. Arrogant son of a bitch.

In the end, Donny dropped the delusion that Lam might let him into the house, and that was all that had checked him. In the end, he hopped the back fence. He crept across the yard as though creeping mattered and slowly clutched the handle of the screen door. It was latched. *Dammit!* He stomped angry divots into the lawn on his way back to his car. He jammed the keys in the trunk lock and popped it open. He seized his hunting vest and rummaged in the dark, through its pockets until he held a four-inch knife handle, smooth except for an engraved Z that he traced with his thumb. His ex-wife had bought it for him. He closed the trunk, hopped the fence one more time, and strode back to the door. He cradled the stained ivory and pried open the thick blade. Before he would pocket it, he sliced a six-inch hole in the screen, reached through, and unlatched the door.

Confident he was alone in the house, Donny took his time, crouching or wedging himself here and there, assessing the vantage points. Finally, he settled between the couch and the hinged side of the front door. From there he could see the driveway. He rested his butt on the arm of the couch and loosened his belt. He only had to wait a couple of minutes until headlights pulled into the driveway. As a car door closed, Donny removed the knife from his pocket and opened it. He pressed his cheek on a door hinge. He unbuttoned the top of his jeans. As the screen door strained, he leaned back and held his breath. Keys jangled. The door unlocked.

24

WANTS AND NEEDS

O ruthless, perilous, imperious hate,
you can not thwart
the promptings of my soul.

HILDA DOOLITTLE

In San Francisco silver-haired Lily Fujiwara gazed over her glasses and answered a call on Levi's line and then put it on hold. She walked to his office. "I'm sorry to interrupt. Levi, your sister's on the phone."

Levi stood behind the black walnut desk that he hated, the one Crawford had absurdly ordered not to be moved from the premises, by which Crawford meant his old office. Crawford had said the desk, like the pewter, stovepipe lamps that jutted from the credenza behind it, was furniture befitting the "Office of the Divisional Manager" and might help Levi "appear more presidential." Lily said it was part of the firm's *Evil Empire* collection, but to Levi the whole ensemble reminded him of a coal stove. It creeped him out to lay his hands on it or tuck his legs under it, so between the desk and credenza, beside his chair, he erected a nice cherry wood tray table on which he signed what needed signing.

Levi was locked in conversation with Deirdre, the bony string-lipped blonde from Human Resources, who was gawking judgmentally at the wall he had shingled with award plaques, making him think Lily had been right about less being more. When he talked with her, he stood, one hand touching cherry wood for balance and the other hiding in his pocket.

Deirdre used decorum like a guardrail against all classes of employees. Years earlier, Levi had grown wary of her when Crawford insinuated her into his San Jose branch for a week "to conduct beta interviews for a national HR benefits initiative." Afterward, the employees reported that the only questions she asked concerned his conduct and popularity. They were asked to keep her queries hush-hush. She was there to help. No one bought it. Crawford had anointed her Divisional Director of HR in what was now Levi's division – a fact unchanged when Crawford moved to New York as president. If anything, Levi knew that made her more dangerous. So Deirdre and Levi had fashioned an unspoken arrangement. She pretended she worked for Levi, and Levi pretended he didn't know otherwise.

To Levi, the office was the size of Crawford's ego, not his own. He was embarrassed on some level. Alternately it was often surreal that *this* office – in which, long ago, he had interviewed, an interview from which he was relieved to have escaped – *this* office, with its sacred Bay view and its profane work station – was *his* office. He felt that way now as he regarded Lily, still waiting for an answer in the unhandily distant doorway. "Please tell her I'll call her back."

Deirdre sat down and opened the laptop everyone had come to see as a permanent appendage. Levi continued. "Are you saying I can't promote her? Karen's one of the most competent managers I know, and the brokers and staff alike respect her."

"I hear you." Deirdre said it like a question, uptalking like some vacuous teenager whose every tone asked if you understood.

"Then what's the problem?" Levi had a senior management position on the Peninsula in Palo Alto to fill, and Karen Rasheed, an $80,000-per-year branch operations manager in San Francisco, was, to Levi, the obvious choice for the $500,000-per-year senior vice president of both operations *and* retail sales.

Deirdre engaged her squishy-soft, Human Resources voice, the one designed to cast an illusion of empathy. "My understanding is that there are concerns that she has no sales experience."

By this date Levi realized that the very existence of HR departments was to mitigate the cost of labor, benefits, and employee lawsuits, and to surreptitiously do the firm's bidding, often through disingenuous conversations that were cleverly documented after the fact. But even if Deirdre weren't Crawford's operative, the phony uptalk of her voice alone was enough to make him suspect her.

"You gotta be kidding me," Levi said. "Karen's a black, Muslim woman with a high school education who polices a bunch of privileged, white college graduates in a white-dominated industry. Every day she has to bust the balls of brokers who think they can break the rules with impunity because their egos are bloated from eating their last kill. Yet any one of those guys would murder for her. She's that good. Neither you nor I have ever *met* a better salesperson!"

"I never realized you Montanans were so liberal," as she quickly tapped on her laptop.

"What? Montanans elected the first Congresswoman four years before suffragists won the vote. And we're fascinated by ethnicity. We can't hate anybody. Think of us as trickle-down Canadians. But liberalism isn't the point."

"Anyway, I meant no *formal* sales experience? And Karen's experience is light in stock-option business? Gary doesn't think she's a good fit for Palo Alto?"

"I can't tell when you're asking a question. Are you asking or telling me?"

"Positing." She liked to use words as a means to absorb reason.

"Look, despite how we sell option ex & sell service as mysterious, it's less complicated than Mexican fast food. There's only about five ingredients no matter what wrapper we use. Look, if Gary's concerned about clean hands – and the way the NASD's been acting, he should be – Karen runs the cleanest legal and compliance operation in the firm. Look," he held up a *TIME* magazine with a picture of Ivan Boesky on the cover. "Boesky gets busted for perhaps the biggest insider trading scandal ever. Lily tells me our correspondence files here are full of letters from Crawford to Boesky." He let that settle. "Crawford can use people like Karen. If anyone's dealing favors out the back door to get the business, she'll stop it." ⸜

Deirdre stopped tapping on her keyboard. "Are you saying you suspect a compliance problem in ex & sell, or that you're … un-com-fortable with how … to … supervise it?"

Her comment smelled like bait. Whether she knew something he didn't was up for grabs, but he made a mental note to ask Joy for the detail of the ex & sell audit reports at her location. "I'm not saying that. I'm just saying we should be vigilant." Levi tried to hide his frustration as she began typing again. "Besides, didn't the settlement of *Gary's* discrimination suit call for promoting underprivileged classes of employees? Including religion, Karen's a statistical trifecta. And she didn't set off the bomb in the World Trade center garage, she didn't bring down flight 800 in New York last month, and she didn't set off the bomb at the Olympics in Atlanta a few weeks ago. She was here working hard during all three. We'll look good. If you want, I can ask her to limp." At that point, Deirdre blotted all will from him with a banal smile that lasted as long as Levi wanted to look at it. "Okay. Who does he want?"

"I don't know. Maybe Joy? That's between you guys."

"Jesus. Is he going to let me run my division or not?" Levi mumbled. No answer. "He's always talking about judgment. If he thinks Joy has better judgment than Karen, then *he's* got judgment issues." Even as his stomach lurched at his misstep, Levi maintained a steady countenance. He wondered how much Deirdre or Crawford knew about him and Joy. Joy's relentless self-promoting *out of bed* stuck out in emails, phone messages, and queries of Lily about what Levi was thinking – all of which went unanswered. She had to be calling Crawford too … or doing him too.

Unable to give up the argument, Levi tried another tack. "Karen would fit great on the Peninsula. It may be elitist there, but it's also ethnically diverse. Hell, isn't Stanford supposed to be the most ethnically diverse private university? Didn't Condoleezza Rice run Stanford for a while?"

"Depends on whom you talk to. She thought so."

Lily reappeared in the doorway. "Your sister says she'd like to hold. And Lynette from the Billings office is on line two."

He looked at the blinking lights on his phone and imagined the women on the other end. Lam was inconvenient, but Lynette… "Huh. My old assistant. It's been a while," he smiled like he'd be darned. "Tell Joy I'll call her back."

Lily looked puzzled. "You mean Lynette?"

"Huh? What'd I say? I mean Lynette. I was thinking of Joy, I mean, we'd been talking. Just take a message, please." What the hell could Lynette want? It was lamentable to him how getting a promotion tended to leach relationships from his past into his present. Particularly lamentable in this case. He looked back at Deirdre, who'd been waiting.

"I hear you saying that you're frustrated." Deirdre said flatly. "You'd like to help Karen. I understand how you feel. I've felt that way many times." To Levi it felt like she was assessing his judgment, what he knew or didn't. *Crawford. Threatened again?* She went on. "Your logic and passion are interesting. I see why Mr. Sandler is impressed with you. But you know, I've found that if I'm patient, things have a way of working out. Perhaps we can revisit this."

Levi sighed and looked at Lily. "I'll be with my sister in a minute." He looked back at Deirdre. "Please don't '*feel-felt-found*' me." When she stiffened, he knew he had annoyed her, and it pleased him to have made it show. "I don't believe we'd be having this discussion if Karen's name was Karl … or Joy."

As her impenetrable air reformed, Deirdre said, "Why don't I get back to you?"

"Thanks, Deirdre." Levi came out from behind his desk as Deirdre closed her laptop and stood. "I didn't mean to sound so harsh." In fact, he had held back. "Maybe you should paraphrase when you talk with Gary." They laughed. "Anything else?"

He offered his hand but she seemed not to notice. "The three managers whom you put on probation have all called to complain. They claim you want to replace them with younger people."

"Oh, bullshit. Younger people," he scoffed. Then, "I thought calls to HR were confidential."

Deirdre nearly smiled. "I'm not the only one they called?"

"Listen. I'm working with these guys. I meet with them regularly."

"That's another issue of some concern. Gary feels … *managers* have felt … that you're in their offices too often? They're not used to so many visits? From the divisional guy? They say it makes them look over their shoulders? Like you might pop up at any time? Like you're digging for something? They say you undermine their authority in their branches?" This time she sounded like she actually *meant* them as questions – or prodding – to get Levi to admit … what? "And then there's the matter of you canceling all country club memberships?"

"I didn't cancel anybody's membership. I just said the firm won't pay for them. So, are these the managers who tolerate sexual harassment, or the ones who use travel and expense reports to steal? Or are these the same guys who collect personal commissions on ex & sell business they appear to have nothing to do with, you know, the same guys who get allotted more than their fair share of hot issues and then flip the stock in the same few client accounts? Incidentally, as the 'divisional officer,' I'm supposed to sign off on the appropriateness of that syndicate allocation. You know. Like Gary Crawford did."

Levi had meant to get her goat, but Deirdre seemed more satisfied than surprised. "I'm not sure how all that stuff works. I'm just letting you know. And, oh, on another note? I found out that insurance doesn't pay for in-vitro fertilization. Sorry? Please tell Angela?"

"I'll tell her," and Levi stepped back behind his black desk and sat down. It irked him that the company, Deirdre specifically, was privy to his personal matters.

"What's that?" In the corner by a rumpled, bulging grocery sack was a melon-sized rubber shell from which rose five droopy, upside-down cones, green and purple, each dangling a jingle bell.

"Oh. It's a jester's hat. The San Rafael office is having a costume party this afternoon."

She tipped her head back. "Ah," and then walked out.

With one hand on the phone and the other on his abdomen, he winced and waited for her to be gone. For months the cramps had been growing more frequent, more severe. He picked up the receiver. "Hello."

Somewhere in her house in Roundup, Lam sniffed. "Hi."

Levi grabbed a handful of paperwork from his cherry-wood tray and dropped the papers on the desk and scanned for places to sign. "What's up?"

"Not much," Lam labored to sound even. On a step-stool in her kitchen, wrapped in a frayed Turkish robe, she sat, twisting the rubber band on her wrist. From an overcast summer sky, flat light pressed through the windows and stuck on her body. Donny's attack the night before had driven her into that thick, nowhere place. Outside of it her body moved, but more as her proxy. "Just miss you." She peeled the collar of the robe back onto one shoulder, away from the whisker-burn and the hickey. As she gingerly held her knees apart, her elbows upon her thighs, one hand pushed the phone against her head while the fingers of the other raked the hair off her puffy face. She breathed through her mouth and carefully exhaled so he wouldn't hear.

"What's wrong?" He kept signing and turning pages.

"Nothing." She smiled when she spoke to make it sound truer. "I just hadn't talked to you in a while."

Lily entered the room and held a document in front of Levi. As she turned the pages and pointed, he signed. He pivoted the phone away from his mouth and whispered several instructions to Lily before he noticed that Lam had stopped talking. Lily turned and left. "I'm sorry. What did you say? I had someone in front of me."

She forced another smile. "I'm just checking up on you."

"Well. Here I am. Everything's pretty much the same. Job's busy. Angela's fine." Levi signed a few more papers.

"Are you coming home this summer?"

"I am home."

"You know what I mean."

"I don't know." He knew he was being dismissive but he didn't apologize. *You'd think she'd get it by now.*

Lily poked her head in and whispered, "Joy Parnell's on the phone."

Levi nodded, held up one finger, and continued with Lam. "Hey, Angela keeps the calendar. Why?" Then he put his hand over the phone and whispered, "Joy doesn't have my new cell number, does she?"

Annoyed by the insinuation, Lily frowned at him and left.

On the other end of the phone, Lam's eyes filled with tears. "It'd just be nice. Dusty'd like it. So would Mom and Dad."

"Dusty was just here for spring break. He can't miss us that much."

They both stopped talking.

"You're my big brother, Levi." A tear dripped from Lam's jaw. "I'm feeling pretty crazy."

"Most of us are pretty crazy – and the others would be if they knew we wanted to kill them." Levi stopped signing and listened. "Did you and Russ break up?" *Please say no*, he thought. She'd been less burdensome since Russ. Well, not for him so much as for Angela – Lam hadn't called her so much.

A sad, sudden laugh popped out and Lam sucked it back. "No. At least not yet. I haven't seen him yet today. He and Dusty have been in Billings." She sighed. "No, we're fine."

"You don't sound so fine." He was watching the blinking light of his other line.

She sat up straight. "I just have a cold." Then, more firmly, "Levi, I'd really like you to come home for a visit."

He looked at the quote screen on his credenza. Green and red stock symbols; mostly green today. Up-market. He checked the volume of Bookman Stuart stock versus the time on his Rolex. Up on early volume, a comforting sign. "You sound down. Do you need some money?"

"No. I don't need money." She slumped on the stool and mumbled. "You and me used to cling together like tissue in rain. I need that."

"I'm sorry, I can't hear you. Listen. Do this. Give Angela a call and discuss it with her. She knows the calendar. Besides, she has summers off. If she figures out a time and I'm not too busy, I might come with her. Okay?"

Lam's eyes were tearing. "The Bump-N-Run races are today. We're all going."

"There ya go! That'll be fun. Wish I was going." he said, hoping another tack might cheer her without making it look too much like he wanted to get off the phone. "Watching other folks get slammed 'til they can't move. Always makes me feel better," he said optimistically. It wasn't working. "Look, there's no hurry with Angela. Call her anytime. Soon. Okay?"

"Yeah," she conceded. "Fine."

"No promises, but I'll try. And don't call too early. She's been working late, tutoring or something, I'm not sure. Why don't you call after six your time? I'll try, okay? I can't take much time now." She was too quiet for his comfort, so he fumbled to ease the moment. "I know I'm no big deal. Maybe I should save the trip for another time. Hey, didn't Mom always say God was saving me for something big?"

"Something big. Yeah. I guess."

"You okay?" His finger poised above the blinking phone button. He was tired of avoiding Joy's calls, and now he wanted to get it over with so she'd back off for a few days.

"Yeah. I'm fine."

"Okay. Listen. I gotta go. Call me when you know more. Okay?"

"Fine."

"I love you, little sister."

Lam looked down at her raw flesh and began to cry. "I love you, too. Bye."

Levi pressed the other blinking button. "Joy?"

"Yes." As she spoke, Joy removed the manufacturer's tags from her new, oversized executive chair, one she would submit a receipt for. Reaching over her desk, she handed a coffee cup bearing a *Porsche* logo to her new Vietnamese assistant and motioned the nervous young woman to fetch about two inches worth of coffee. "Not too hot," she whispered. Joy inhaled the leather on the chair back.

"What's up?" asked Levi. "You called."

"Will I see you tonight?" Joy's house was in Palo Alto just off the 280 Freeway, on Levi's way home. She nested her butt into the chair.

"I'm not sure. I'm going to San Rafael for their Halloween party." Levi had had sex with Joy only once in the past month, at the Fairmont Hotel after a manager's dinner he hosted. It felt like he was on an installment plan, and he resented what he was paying for. Now that he was the boss, it was difficult to slip out of meetings before her. Given his new position, it was ludicrous for Levi to continue hoping she would cultivate another mark, so he was left simply trying to hide and it was pissing him off. He had changed his cell phone number. Lily screened his office calls and removed his schedule from the company's internal web pages. It didn't work, and now that he was a bigger asset to Joy, he had reason to sense that she was about to call in her markers. For one thing, she phoned way too often, especially since her superior on the Peninsula had retired and she wanted the position.

"It doesn't matter how late you are," said Joy. "I'll shoot home around five. My staff can handle any aspect that's mission-critical. I'll be available all night."

Levi put his pen down and leaned back in his chair. "I don't know. I'm pretty swamped. I might even stay in the City tonight."

"No problem. I can come to the City. I just want to talk about that promotion. I won't stay if you don't want. You need to hear me, strictly on business. You need to hear my value proposition."

He hated himself for getting into this position, and this jousting made him physically sick. As he threw his head back and closed his eyes, fluid quagged through his intestines. "I've been reviewing the client complaint files. The file for your office, specifically the ex & sell operation, is two inches thick. Is there a problem?"

"Why are you reviewing this office? I thought I still officially reported to Gary, at least until you select the new manager of this complex."

"Yeah, well, that's a little fuzzy. So, what about the complaints?"

"What about them?" She spoke like a spouse accused of overspending.

"Why are there so many? And why do most of them allege that we don't pay clients promptly – *on time* – after they sell their stock? And why did we talk so many clients into going on margin during this Internet bubble? The market is already overheated by any prudent standard."

Joy leaned forward. "Have I done something wrong?"

"Joy, I'm your boss. Don't bust my balls for doing my job. We've got a mess to mop up in *your* shop and I need some answers before you and I talk about promotions."

"Okay, but consider this. We rifle through tens of thousands of exercise transactions down here every month, and every receptionist and janitor with a million dollars in option gains acts like a goddamn millionaire."

"Well?"

"This isn't the Gilded Age. When Howard Hughes was alive, only 4,000 Americans were worth a million dollars. Now there's 2.7 million – one in a hundred people. And they want special treatment and they want to spin the wheel again because now they're a fucking investment genius. They don't listen, they don't get it. So we give 'em what they want, and when they lose their ass they act like slaughtered lambs."

Levi sat up straight. His voice became exceedingly controlled. "That is my point. Some people *don't* get it. They have no idea how the market works. Yes, they just got lucky and now they have money. But *we* have the fiduciary responsibility. Our revenue should be a *byproduct* of doing the right thing, not the object of our advice. At the end of the day, *it's not our money*."

Joy tapped her pen on her desk. She closed her eyes and bit her lip. "I can launch a plan to catapult this Peninsula operation to record profitability," she offered. "For instance, we could haircut our payroll expenses. We don't need all these people answering phones and we don't need a chainsaw consultant to tell us that. Technology has given us a new paradigm...."

"Jesus, Joy! Haircutting payroll expenses in this division won't be done by Sweeney Todd. Besides, I thought we had trouble sending clients their checks on time as it is. Isn't that what the NASD's pissed about? Those back-office folks you'd fire are the ones fixing these errors."

"Computers are *quicker* than people. And that NASD thing's just a few clients pissed because they can't buy their new Hummer fast enough." Joy's assistant handed her the coffee, and Joy whispered, "*Skim milk*," and handed it back. She continued with Levi. "Why don't we talk about this in the City tonight, okay? I'll keep the topic mission-critical."

He sighed. "Why do you talk like that? Clichés."

"Just because people say something all the time doesn't mean it's a cliché. What about, 'I love you'?" There was an awkward pause. "Well? Can we meet?"

"I'm going home." Levi urgently needed a restroom.

Joy stood up and opened her mouth but stopped. She sat down, removed a nail file from her lap drawer and began to file her index fingernail. "When would be good for you?"

"I don't keep my calendar. Check with Lily." He really needed to go. "Joy?"

"Yeah. I'll check with Lily. Maybe I'll have dinner with Gary instead." She grabbed her Blackberry and began thumbing an email to Crawford.

"Gary?" He couldn't stop from sounding out of the loop.

"Yeah. He's in town to take a few managers to dinner. You knew, right?" They both knew she took pleasure in being the one to tell him.

Levi hurriedly gathered the remaining papers in both hands and bounced them to order on his desktop and then re-deposited them into his in-box. "Listen, Joy, I really have to go. Set it up with Lily. I gotta go. Bye." He hung up.

Levi stood and walked stiff-legged to Lily's desk. "Did you know that Crawford's in town?"

"What did Joy want?" She peered over her glasses.

Clearly she was avoiding the question. What was unclear was if she meant to signal some oblique disapproval. "She wants a promotion. Pushy as hell. I shut her down."

"Be nice. Her shell only seems thick. That's why she keeps it painted."

"Damn good paint. Did you know that he's having dinner with some of my managers?"

She removed her glasses. "That's what I heard."

"Do you know which ones?" His mind was a highlight reel of the debates and confrontations he had had with various managers who were once his senior, and then, until recently, his peers. Over the years he had drunk plenty with the best of them and the worst of them, and now he was determined to improve or eliminate the latter group.

Lily looked at him gently. "I'm not sure. Almost everyone in the region likes you, admires you. But…"

"But what?" He was still in discomfort but stood closer to her desk.

Lily's look told him to settle down. "I don't know," she said evenly. "At your first meeting with the managers as their boss, the one where you said you wanted no empty desks and no empty suits, you had most of them. Then you gave your 'We don't lie, cheat or steal' speech. I don't think they ever thought of themselves that way. Everyone applauded, but some were offended."

He inhaled as if loading his lungs with ammo, but stopped. He had, until recently, blown off outrage in front of her, particularly before he faced the employees or clients he was mad at. But when he found himself constantly apologizing, he agreed he would break the habit.

"I think they thought you were arrogant. Maybe out to get them," Lily said.

"Fuck 'em," Levi said, and then cringed. "Oops, Sorry. Really. Sorry. The old guard sits on their asses, riding their office's short-term profitability into retirement, and not training new brokers because it costs money. In ten years, those managers will be gone, and those offices won't *have* senior brokers. Some of them already have six or eight empty desks, and half of the remaining cronies are unproductive, unethical, or both. Hell, even *Crawford* calls one old-timer 'the forger.' With his protection, I can't fire *anyone* unless they draw blood in the office." He inhaled. "And these managers can't pressure brokers because their offices aren't full, so they allow shitty performance as long as not too many clients complain – so shitty brokers keep great accommodations. If the managers trained quality, productive brokers, it would push the sloppy, unproductive ones into smaller offices. They'd get embarrassed and sucker some other firm into paying them up-front money to jump ship. Problem solved. But the way it is, the only way to get them out is if Crawford drops dead." That's all the time his stomach allowed him. He started toward the restrooms, but Lily stopped him. "Sorry," he repented.

"Levi?"

"I'll be back," he took another step away.

"Levi," she said, looking over her glasses. She rattled a small paper bag over her desk.

He looked inside the bag and laughed. "Toilet paper?" He whispered. "You're amazing."

"It's very soft."

"You're too much."

"It was on sale. Quilted. 24 double rolls for $10.88. Either Costco or Wal-Mart."

"*That's* why this is a full-service firm. You don't get this service at Schwab."

"Schwab? I have a friend there. You can read the newspaper through their toilet paper."

Levi laughed and then his face abruptly screwed up. "I need to go."

"Wait! One more thing. Lynette, from Billings? Remember? She called."

Levi became more uncomfortable. "Ah, man. You'd think she'd take a hint."

"She has something urgent to discuss with you. She wants you to call."

"I left Montana a long time ago, and it's time for Montana to *leave me.*

Throw the message away."

"She also wanted to let you know that someone died, but that wasn't what she wanted to talk about," Lily said.

"Did she say who died?"

"Yes." Lily took a breath. "Crazy Marilyn. Levi, I'm so sorry. She left the time and location of the funeral. Lynette says that Marilyn left something for you with her. She wants to talk with you about where to send it."

Levi pulled the message from Lily's hand, read it, and gently handed it back. "Please don't call her that. Send flowers for me. No. Yes. Do that. And call the funeral director. I'm sure she's being buried next to her daughter at a place called Sunset Memorial Gardens. As a personal favor, could you arrange to have a large, *pink granite* headstone made for Marilyn – and one for her daughter, if it's not there already?" Lily looked like she was afraid to ask. "If there's just a plaque, ask them to replace it – unless there's family that feels otherwise, but I don't think so. Use my VISA. Please."

Lily paused and made a note. "What about what Lynette said Marilyn left for you?"

Levi knew Marilyn. She would have called. He knew Lynette, too. Marilyn would never have left anything with her. "Ignore it. She just wants me to call. And that reminds me, Jimmy downstairs's mother died. Please send him something, too. I forgot."

"The building's Jimmy? Giant Jimmy? The security guy?"

"I never called her back," he said, absentmindedly. Then, "He's my gumba."

"Gumba's pejorative. I think Italian-Americans might prefer 'paisano.' But what would I know. I'm O-ri-en-tal." Pause. "Are you okay?"

"He's my friend." Then, nearly a whisper, "She was brave." Pause. "I gotta go!"

As Levi sat in the bathroom holding the roll of paper, he vexed over Crawford's visit. Occasional footsteps reverberated on the tile while he held quiet. He gaped at the floor, blotted his clammy forehead. His peripheral vision grayed in, darker, until he stared through a tunnel to the snowy, night-streaked marble. From stone veins emerged a dog's head. Then a long barrel, bent, as if in an illusionist's bobbing hand. He saw a melting face – an ape? – mournful and pocked, forehead distorted and pinned to the toilet's base.

Electric fingers, each invading from the next stall – two of them stabbing, stabbing down across the linear reflection of fluorescent bulbs. A chart? He moved his head, fore and back, to shift the bright mirrored lines. Two others, perhaps a forefinger and pinky, jutted then swirled darkly like photographic negatives of Van Gogh stars, wrapping, pinching the graph, rotating opposite each other. Which was higher? Which? Which tighter? Is the clockwise rotation the stronger, or the counter? Where's the thumb? Does the thumb rotate? If it does … He couldn't see the thumb but was sure it was implied. Sure. Maybe in the next stall. He bent down to look and saw, between him and the sink cabinet, black, very skinny black shoes, pointing away.

25

ONE MAN'S JOY

A negative judgment gives you more satisfaction than praise,
provided it smacks of jealousy.

JEAN BAUDRILLARD

With freshly manicured thumbs, Joy was accessing Crawford's cell phone number on her Palm Pilot when Minh Nguyen, her assistant, stepped into her office.

"Ms. Parnell…"

"Have you seen these?" Joy flashed her new PDA. "Second generation. Very civilized."

"Yes. You showed me. Mr. Ab … Abha … ya Ramakapur is here to see you."

"Christ. Not now." She looked at the Tiffany desk clock that had been mailed to her by an internal auditor with whom she had slept. It had been a last-minute barroom tactic that kept her from failing the audit. As long as they were both discreet – a likelihood with him married – she passed her audit and he'd keep his job. No harm, no foul. It was 4:45. A new email from Crawford popped up on her computer screen. "I'm a little busy," said Joy. "Wait with him until I'm ready."

"I'm very sorry, Ms. Parnell, but I can't," the young woman demurred. "I have a five o'clock class at Cañada College."

"Where?" Joy knew where Minh attended.

"Cañada College. In Redwood City." Minh became embarrassed. "It's a junior college. I'm hoping to transfer to Berkeley next year."

"How will you go to Berkeley and work here? It's an hour away. Whatever. All right. Send him in." She pulled out a drawer and swept a nail file into it. As he entered the room, Joy stood to greet Abhaya Ramakapur of EcoPulse BioTech. His sunglasses were nested atop his black hair. "Hello, Abba. I'm surprised to see you." With chest out and shoulders back, she extended her hand.

"I was on my way to the City. I decided to stop by." Joy had only observed Abba in expensive suits and footwear. She was never able to imagine him as the dusty, untouchable boy from India, or wherever the newspapers said he was from. Perhaps it was because, whenever he occasioned by her office uninvited, he was utterly void of naiveté and patience. "May I speak with you alone?"

Before Joy could walk to the door, Abba closed it. She returned to the manager-side of her desk and pasted on a smile, motioning Abba to sit on the opposing side.

Abba remained standing. "I assume you value the business from EcoPulse."

"Of course we do, Abba. And I enjoy our friendship."

His eyes seemed to grow darker. "We do not have a friendship, Ms. Parnell. Our business is, as you are fond of saying, a value proposition, and I see little value in continuing it."

Although her spine stiffened, her voice smoothed out. "I don't understand, Abba." She commanded her arms rest on the desk, and her hands commenced elegant gestures. "We don't charge your employees anything to exercise their options. Not a penny."

"Yesterday Bob Nelson, my VP of Human Resources, provided you with an updated electronic record of the cost basis of employee stock options. Is that correct?"

Given the potential legal snares, his boldness on the issue took her aback. "Yes. He did. And according to him, the new records that you want us to upload into our computers lower the price at which officers – only the *senior* officers – of your company can buy stock when they exercise options. Coincidentally, the new records indicate the options were dated – were granted – on the very day that the stock hit its 52-week low two months ago. With all due respect, it looks like back-dating."

"Ms. Parnell, it's not for you to question how we grant options to officers."

Joy spoke carefully. "Actually, Abba, the NASD and SEC feel otherwise. But before you get angry at me, I did not make the decision to delay uploading the new database. Our attorneys just want you to shoot us a letter declaring that your board approved the back-dating of stock options. Then it's perfectly kosher – not that you're Jewish." *Shit*, she was nervous. "Anyway, we're okay with it as long as they agree and shareholders are informed, in your 10-K filing or something like that. I need a letter from our people in New York giving me the go-ahead too."

"Do you know what EcoPulse does? What we have engineered?" It was a rhetorical question. "Ms. Parnell, do you read any science or watch science television?"

"Uh, no…"

"Global warming is not a myth. If you ever had children – not that you would not have become a good mother … I presume …"

What? flashed through Joy's mind. *How could he know I can't have children? Surely Gary wouldn't…* Before she could answer her thought, she was interrupted.

"Are you listening? They might die of hunger, or riots, or natural disasters, due to global warming. We may all die in a nuclear war over oil. Global warming *will not* be stopped by lip-service from energy companies. The world doesn't work like that."

"Uh, maybe, Abba, but I'm just talking about the options."

"No! We are not just talking about the options! You can't halt global warming now by shutting off some pollution valve, because people *will not* shut it off. Even if they would, the planet will take centuries to heal, maybe longer. We must *actively* clean the atmosphere, replenish the forests."

"Hey, I hate global warming. I've recycled for years. But I'm sorry…"

"Listen! The biotech, engineering and government team I am assembling has the potential to clean our atmosphere, maybe in less than 100 years. We can *bioengineer* it. We have engineered trees – common temperate zone and tropical trees – that grow twice as fast and, listen – *listen* – regenerate the atmosphere at *seven times* the rate! The chemistry would bore you. We have also engineered near-microscopic plants that in a decade can be produced and released in millions of tons in the troposphere – where we breathe – and the lower stratosphere. For practical purposes, these plants are lighter than air. They *eat* pollution. And they seed clouds, act as a nucleus for raindrops. We think they are benign to surface life, but we will need more tests. Ms. Parnell, I am talking about saving our planet!"

"Would you like a soft drink. Or coffee?" She felt *decaf* went without saying.

"No! But the riskiest element is not the biology. It is holding together a scientific and political team who can make this happen – biologists, industrialists, government officials. Don't look so shocked. Bureaucrats like money too. Ms. Parnell, you … you … *you* have a chance to help save millions of lives, and that only counts *our* species."

His voice lowered. "I cannot take back-dating stock options to the board, or the shareholders. We cannot involve the public. I don't have time. If the authorities look for bent rules later, which is unlikely, their investigation will take years. By that time the technology to arrest global warming will be out there. This stock business will seem trivial." He paused. "*You* have this chance, Ms. Parnell!"

It took fifteen seconds for Joy to speak. Abba waited. Finally, she said, "I wanted to be a scientist for a while. I took AP chemistry and biology in high school – they called it 'honors' back then – but I thought I could make a bigger difference in people's lives in finance. I don't know. I could be wrong. But here I am. I do know that I need a letter to change the price where your officers can buy stock." Hearing her own voice on familiar ground gave her a semblance of surety. "I'm sorry, but Bookman Stuart doesn't…"

"I am not a fool, Ms. Parnell, and Gary Crawford never took me to be one." His feet were planted shoulder-width apart. He brushed back his sport coat as he put his hands in his pockets. "Almost five million shares of EcoPulse stock were exercised and sold through this office in the last year, and almost none was processed at the other wirehouses. At about $30 per share, that's $150 million that went through your office. When my employees sell stock, the law compels you to pay them in three days, and you do, indeed, cut the checks on time, but it takes you seven days from the date of sale to deliver them to our company for distribution. For your benefit, my staff delays distribution for two more days by pretending to verify their accuracy. Last year, these delays gave you over $120,000 in profit on the float. There's more.

"The only time you don't steal the float is when you convince my employees to leave the money with Bookman Stuart to buy whatever heavily-loaded investment product your company recommends. Our records show that $90 million stayed at your firm last year. If you charged 1 percent per year for your advice, that's $1 million in commission. But that's not all. You have convinced some of my employees, the imprudent and ignorant ones, to borrow against their investments in order to gamble in the market, and you make additional interest on the loans and commissions on unwise trades. You, Ms. Parnell, get a large bonus on all of it. Currently, Bookman Stuart and you make a fat profit, but it would require only one memo from me to channel all of our employee business to Merrill Lynch or Morgan Stanley. Do you understand why I do not write that memo? Do you understand our … *value proposition*?"

"Abba, there hasn't been any stock available in hot issues lately."

He pulled a pack of cigarettes from his pocket. As he struck a match, he said, "You are a liar, Ms. Parnell." As she recoiled, he lit a cigarette. He shook out the match and laid it on her desk pad. "How small do you think Silicon Valley is? I will tell you. Very small. I know that you directed hot stock to my counterparts at other companies that do option business with you."

What she felt wasn't quite fear. Something else. Regardless of his accuracy, bullies had recently, finally, become anathema to her. Only since Crawford had moved to New York had she fully realized how he had oppressed her, and she had only just begun to feel confident in making decisions without first calling for his criticism. And she was tired of being steamrolled and fucked over. Enough. She decided to filibuster. So she watched him smoke, and waited … waited until he laughed.

"Do you think that staring at me shows your balls, Ms. Parnell? You have already failed to show courage."

She swallowed. "Crawford doesn't keep the syndicate book in this region anymore. He doesn't decide who gets hot stock. His successor does. Mr. Levi Monroe."

Abba grinned. "I know Mr. Monroe. He managed your business units around San Jose. I saw him once to tell him my employees would deal only with your office and not his. He said my employees' financial affairs were none of my business." He laughed heartily and took another drag. "I have to admit, I liked him." He tapped the ash from the cigarette into his palm. "Yes, I know about Monroe." Then he turned dark again. "Tell Crawford to fix it. Either my key people buy IPOs from you, or I take EcoPulse business elsewhere … stock options, corporate banking, investment banking, everything. Other Valley companies will follow my lead and leave your firm. You might be fired, maybe worse. I hope I am clear."

Abba took the step to her desk, emptied the cigarette ash from his palm on her desk pad, and offered the lit cigarette butt to her. "Perhaps you can find a place for this." She took the butt.

"Thank you for your time. Later today I'll see that a letter is faxed to you for your file. Mr. Crawford's office will send you a permission letter as well. So tonight you will upload the new data. Tomorrow some of our officers will exercise. Understood? Incidentally, I personally have no account with your firm. There *are* no more decent causes."

She stared with him, unsure how afraid she should be, unsure until he left the room, then she dropped the cigarette butt into her tepid coffee.

That evening, Joy and four other managers joined Crawford in a private room at an old-school Italian restaurant in the North Beach district of San Francisco. At the door, Crawford pulled Joy aside and said only, "Abba called. Get it done. I don't want to hear one more word about it."

At the table, Crawford produced half-sized reading glasses with red frames and declared the *Drouhin* pinot and the *Vin de Pays d'Oc* chardonnay pretentious. He ordered Opus One cab at $200 per bottle and an overpriced Stag's Leap chardonnay. He whispered to the sommelier to give each diner both red and white and keep all wine glasses full. Bring him tea. And bring the lady a vodka martini.

Straightaway, Crawford said he was interested in improving relations between the local office managers and local senior management. When he looked away, managers exchanged quizzical, nervous glances, waiting to confirm wind-direction.

Some wine passed.

"There's one thing you need to know," Crawford finally said. "No one will ever suffer retribution for bringing … concerns … to my attention. I value courage, and I value judgment. Unfortunately," he said as an aside, "not everyone has good judgment. However, this is a meritocracy, and observations and suggestions that bear merit are actively appreciated."

The men at the table became serious and thoughtful. Some nodded.

They ate entrées, drank more wine.

Joy listened as the conversation rattled around the topic of Levi Monroe; how Levi disrupted decorum with unannounced visits; one manager, on probation for forging logs of client conversations, said Levi created "sexual tension" in one office; a manager who'd been outed for sexual harassment complained. At that comment, more than one of them glanced at Joy.

By the time dessert was served, someone had heard that Levi was unwell, losing weight, and everyone hoped it wasn't serious. Smoking-manager from San Rafael said he didn't know how anyone could handle the pressure of Levi's job, or who'd *want* it, (though he had twice lobbied for the position).

It could drive the best of men nuts, he said. Take this afternoon, he said, when Levi – that silly bastard – wore a jester costume to the San Rafael office and met the landlord regarding the lease. While smoking-manager shook his smelly head, he failed to explain that he himself had sponsored the employee costume party to which he had invited both Levi (costumed) and the landlord (not costumed).

In his lap, Crawford was working his mechanical pencil on his little notepad. In her mind, Joy took notes of equal detail, whether she needed to use tonight's information against Levi or against Crawford. Either way. She was simply sick of waiting for her turn, and someone was damn well going to give it to her. Someone would be grateful for her help. Maybe even Sandler.

By the time the check came, everyone agreed that Levi was obviously talented – based on performance numbers alone – and clearly a fine man. It was Levi's "judgment" that perplexed Crawford and therefore perplexed everyone else, too, though judgment about what, they weren't sure. In the end, Crawford magnanimously begged the managers for patience … for the time being. People agreed that people get out of their depth – not that Levi had – and they really didn't want to see anything bad happen to him.

Finally dinner ended and everyone stood, smiling and shaking hands and damn happy to get out of there. Crawford excused himself and crowded in on Joy so the others were at his back and unable to hear, though they would linger until he dismissed them.

"Here," he handed her a tiny box of mints. "Meet me at the Nikko."

She looked at him plaintively, but he lowered his eyebrows and turned from her. He took a limo, and as was their routine, she waited fifteen minutes before driving herself there. Minutes later she strode through a white marble lobby against perfect feng shui.

On the elevator to the 24th floor, Joy put two Sen-Sens in her mouth. In the beginning, she didn't mind them, but she had grown to hate the flavor, *hate it,* as she did all of Crawford's fetishes. When he opened the door to his suite, she tried to hand him a tiny zip-lock envelope, the size one might store a ring in. He looked peeved and wouldn't touch it until she was inside and the door was closed.

Joy sat alone on a love seat, weighted with regret. He would take several minutes. She removed a nail file from her purse and filed her one short fingernail, dulling the edges so as not to slice his membrane. She gazed out the window at Coit Tower, all tawdried up in night-lights, as Crawford washed and brushed his teeth and combed his perfectly parted hair. She heard his long sniffs, three times. Four. She hated the narcotic taste dissolved into his spit. His voice echoed from the bathroom only once, to say that a fax from him regarding EcoPulse options had been sent to her office and that she would never put him in this situation again. Then he walked out of the bathroom in a towel and held his hands and head as if to ask her why the hell she was still dressed. So she stripped and lay back on the one pillow he allowed and assumed the position, whereupon he put his tongue in her mouth, with its bitter numb, its wicked perfume. She managed to turn her head as he unceremoniously mounted her and ground his bony, hygienic hips against her and prodded with his sober whisky-dick.

"Tell me about Levi," he said.

"Gary, no."

"Tell me. How does he do it? Tell me. What's he like when you taste him?"

She resisted at first, though she knew he would persist as long as it took. He guided her finger to his ass and grunted into her hair, his half of the pillow. She fantasized about the next day when he would get out of her car at the airport – *for the last time, dammit* – and she would drive the hell away, away, away. As he utilized her flesh, abusing what she had always traded to him, invited him to take, she hated him for taking it. The shock of his weight rolled through her, again and again, and her outrage began to unhinge. Finally, it broke loose, tearing away with it her fear. That's when she knew. This would never happen again. Not ever. Whatever it took.

26

BUMP - 'N - RUN

Everything is like a door swinging backwards and forwards.
Everything has a little of that from which it is most remote
and to which it is most opposed
and these antitheses serve to explain one another.

SAMUEL BUTLER

Russ and Dusty returned from Billings on an amber Saturday morning smelling of fresh-cut, late-summer hay. Russ dropped off Dusty at home before he checked on the ranch, and when he returned in the midday heat, he was announced only by the bounce of the screen door.

Dusty's frame was slung in the couch, his untied running shoes propped on the coffee table. Russ couldn't see the boy's face because he was holding the *Roundup Record-Tribune and Winnett Times* like a big menu, under which a headphone-cord snaked out to the CD Walkman Russ had bought him and that now rested on the belly of a T-shirt with a hash-mark, below which was printed, *You Must Be This Tall to Ride This Ride*. A rogue puff of breeze rustled the front page. Dusty said, "Did you know spotted knapweed spreads 27 percent a year and grows to three feet and cattle shouldn't eat it?"

"You don't say." Russ took off his cowboy hat, laid it on the coffee table by Dusty's feet and sat next to the boy. "It's upside-down," Russ said. On the back page Russ saw an advertisement for today's Bump-N-Run Racing at the fairgrounds.

"Farmers say it's dry as ash," Dusty said. "That'll stunt the knapweed crop."

"It's always dry first week of September," Russ said. "Get your feet off the table."

Dusty complied. "They mean this year. Some say they'll stop planting and run sheep."

"Hope not."

"Good noxious weed abatement, sheep. Beats herbicides."

Russ smiled. Dusty apparently had been reading the magazines Russ gave him. Russ tugged Dusty's earphones down. "It's dubious ecology and bad economics. Sheep are puppy-chow for coyotes – and wolves will eventually be here from Yellowstone. Maybe ten years. Either way, there'll be too many dead sheep and farmers will go back to farming. The government won't pay farmers to stop planting sheep like they do crops. And when the sheep are gone, the coyotes and wolves'll still want to eat, so they'll kill calves instead – our calves."

"Yeah? So why don't the farmers know that?"

"They do, it's just desperate talk. Forty years ago, the average farm family had five people – now it's two, partly because of birth control and partly because more farm kids go to college now and don't come back. That creates a labor shortage at the same time technology allows big corporate farms to operate at much lower costs. Family farms don't have the liquid capital to buy million-dollar combines. And if they have a bad crop year, what little they have is gone. So farmers'll consider any supplemental cash crop – sheep, emus, pocket-puppies – anything. They don't know whether to shit or go blind. However, if they hang on, I'm guessing they'll be okay. Might even get rich in another decade or two."

"I don't get it."

"I've got a theory that might be bullshit. For the last thirty years, Roundup has averaged an inch more rain per year than the thirty years before that. Warmer oceans evaporate more readily. The higher humidity moderates air temperature so our average winter temperature is a degree higher and our summers are a degree cooler than thirty years ago. Oddly, global warming might be good for our part of the continent. We might be one of those spots that actually *benefits* while farmland halfway around the world is taken by saltwater or drought. Maybe old-timers are right when they say 'You don't know what hot is,' or 'You don't know what cold is.' I swear, farmers would bitch if they were hung with a new rope."

Even with the bathroom door closed, Lam could hear their voices as she stood at the sink. She pulled her hair aside one more time to see in the mirror if her makeup hid the hickey and the thin, raw line. By this time she had examined it too many times to be sure. She rinsed her fingers and gently toweled them, careful with the broken fingernail. She wrapped it in a Band-

Aid before slipping a tube of cover-up and some lip gloss into her purse. When she entered the family room, she smiled cheerily at Russ. "Ready?"

He admired her figure and grinned up at her. "Bump-n-run, Baby."

Dusty covered his face with the newspaper. "Ah, please!" He stood and held his hand out to Russ with a give-them-to-me motion in his fingers. Russ forfeited the car keys.

Lam sidled up to the couch, bent, and kissed her man. "We need to pick up Mom and Dad." As she said it, she felt him glance at her neck – but his eyes were still soft. She anxiously swung away. From the kitchen table she lifted two *Roundup Panther* stadium cushions and a large, Zip-Loc bag of lint pads. "Zupick's gas station entered a car and Tommy asked Dad to help in the pit," she said as she marched to the door. "Okay. Let's go." She pushed outside.

Dusty whispered to Russ, "Did you bring it or did you chicken out?"

"Get your ass in the car," Russ said.

Dusty flinched playfully and followed his mom.

As Russ pushed off the couch, he spotted something white between the cushions. He slipped his hand into the crack and found a thick pocket knife with a stained ivory handle. It was inscribed with a Z. The blade was open. As he stood up and adjusted his Stetson, he examined the knife. He closed the blade, opened it, and closed it again. He turned it over in his hand a couple of times. For the time being, he thumbed it into his pocket next to the small jeweler's box and then walked out of the house, pausing to lock the door behind him.

At the curb Dusty sat at the wheel of the idling Tahoe with his sunglasses on, his head bobbing in rhythm. He took the CD from his Walkman and loaded it in the dash. Lam sat in the back. Russ climbed in at shotgun and grimaced at the music.

"*Smashmouth*," Dusty hollered.

"It will be if you don't turn it down." Russ turned it down.

In the kitchen of the house by the river, Frank stood chicken-chested and knocked crumbs off his yellow *Pit Crew* polo shirt and sniffed once, dryly and confidently. He put his plate in the dishwasher. The room smelled like bacon. He picked his coffee mug off the new countertop, leaned against the cabinet and sipped. He had become the sort of man who used sugar. In front of him, in a kitchen chair, Virginia was folded at the waist, putting on tennis shoes. Her hair had grown back coarse and gray as pencil leads. She tightened one Velcro strap and sat up to catch her breath. Cancer had metastasized into her lungs and liver, and the chemo had probably just bought time. They'd see. Her dentures looked bigger behind hollow cheeks, and her thick, ever-smudged glasses made her eyes seem too big for her head.

"You want some help?" Frank asked plainly.

Breathing hard, annoyed by the inconvenience, she waved him off and bent over again.

Frank went to the entryway closet, a tall box of unpainted sheetrock with a raw hole the size of his fist on one side. The contractors had installed three coat hooks. From one hung a stiff, new Levi jacket with a leather collar, into which Virginia had pinned flannel lining. It was Frank's size, but he'd been instructed to leave it alone. From a second hook he lifted her sweater, and hanging from the third rung was a soft, nylon harness with an unused, fifteen-inch oxygen tank. "Hope they finish the house before winter," he said. "Did Lam bring the mail yesterday?"

Virginia pointed to the counter, next to a small quilt of clothes-dryer lint.

He began sorting a stack of envelopes. "Is there a check for the contractor in here?"

She shook her head and picked up a pencil and wrote on a spiral pad. *Angela mailed the check herself. He already got it.* She handed the pad to Frank.

He read the wrong side; something private she had scrawled to God in the dark the night before, at this very table. *Is this why?* It read, *is this why? Is this why?* Over and over. He looked up. "'Is this why,' what?" Frank asked. With impatience, she gestured for him to turn it over. "Oh. He got the check. Did he tell you that?"

She pointed to the spare bedroom. On Angela's last visit, with hopes that she and Virginia could have two-way conversations, she arranged for a second phone line and set up Virginia with a computer. She taught Virginia how to retrieve email, but Virginia seldom responded beyond "OK" or "LOVE YOU'SE GUYS."

"She emailed you?"

Virginia nodded.

"Financing must've come through. Did she mail *our* check?" Frank asked.

Virginia pointed to the envelopes in Frank's hand.

From a quarter-mile away they heard tires rumbling through gravel. Frank looked out the window and nodded at them. "I'm gonna ask Lam to go to church with me this weekend." As he turned to her he hooked his left thumb into his back pocket, hiding his tattooed forearm against his body. "I'm asking you again, too, but I'm asking her." Virginia didn't so much as look at him. "This month's sermon is on forgiveness."

With that she snatched her notepad and wrote so hard he could hear it. "Don't!"

"I been going a long time now. Virginia, I might spend forever in hell, but I'm asking that it don't start now. I got some things to say to the both of you. Maybe if yous could just listen …"

Her hand slapped the table hard. "DON'T!" she scratched. She stood and shouldered a tan leather purse the size of a saddle bag into which Frank had tooled roses and her initials. He had taken a correspondence course in leather craft.

Frank stuffed a pack of cigarettes in his shirt pocket and a tin of nitroglycerin tablets in his pants. He took her arm. "Yous going to church ain't just for me. It's also for purpose and whatnot." It was clear he should stop digging. "You want your oxygen?"

She shook her head disgustedly.

"Of course not," he mumbled.

As the Chevy Tahoe pulled to a stop in the gravel driveway, they walked out the front door, leaving the house unlocked. Virginia shook Frank off her elbow and shuffled to the rear door, which Frank opened, causing Lam to move to the middle, eyes catching him sideways like he had a bug she didn't want.

Before Frank made it to the other side, Lam dropped the bag of lint in Virginia's lap, straddled her panting mother and hopped out of the car. She looked back at Virginia. "You sit in the middle, Mom." Their eyes locked for a moment. "Makes me carsick," Lam offered, and then looked toward the river and waited.

Virginia sighed and scooched next to Frank, and Lam climbed back in.

The impressive wooden grandstands at the Musselshell County Fairgrounds had been erected generations earlier between the willowy south bank of the Musselshell River and the piney, sandstone mountains. The seats were broad, terraced planks, each row thick and 200 feet long, painted evergreen and mottled with pigeon droppings. In the middle was notched a thirty-foot central platform for bands and dignitaries. Balanced along the lofty back row was the long edge of a lazy-A-frame roof that jutted out high above the cascading benches, held aloft by two alignments of massive white pillars, a foot-square each, one growing high out of row nine, and a taller one jutting from way down at row one, by the rodeo grounds, which, on this day, had changed into a spastic figure-eight dirt track.

Local clans flocked into their traditional seats, long since designated through squatters' rights, their kinship for the day defined by affinity for one contestant or another, who in this case would drive a rasping car with a bad paintjob. Kids were eager to hit the snack counter under the grandstands, and moms were happy to pay them a few dollars to stop hounding them. A respectable thirty yards west of the main structure, men wearing caps and cowboy hats gathered at the beer shack, a sawed-off patio porch with an over-hung roof and waist-high walls, to ritualistically lie and laugh at each other.

On the track, between the logs and tractor-tire barriers, a tank-truck made laps, laying out a skirt of water that glued down the dust before the first race. On the far side of the arena an announcer climbed into an elevated cabin above six rodeo chutes and a small Conoco sign. He leaned out a big window-hole and talked on the PA system to the volunteer firemen a hundred yards away who were making exaggerated, comical body gestures from a steel-pole fence.

Dusty drove slowly, parting the crowd of pedestrians, all the way onto the grounds. He stopped at the grandstands to drop off Virginia and the others before he made a U-turn to go park. From the concession line, Lam watched as Frank attended Virginia, who labored up the flight of stairs to the stands. They were holding up some high school kids who didn't seem to mind.

"She'll be fine," Lam heard Russ say as he took her hand. He lifted her hand waist-high. "What'd you do to your finger?"

Lam released his hand and folded hers like a child's fist. She stepped to his other side and took his other hand and began to read the menu-board out loud to the pigtailed high school girl behind the counter. Finally she ordered hot dogs and pop.

"So, what did you do to your finger?" Russ asked again.

She released his hand again and touched the blood-spotted bandage. Without looking up, she said, "I don't know. I'm so clumsy." She nervously fiddled with the rubber band on her wrist. "I like your braids," she said to the high-schooler. "How much is it?"

"What do you mean you don't know?" Russ said.

"Five twenty-five," the attendant said. "Oops. No. Six twenty-five. Sorry."

While Russ paid and thanked the girl, Lam picked up the tray and started for the stairs. Russ caught up with her and took the tray. At the top, just as Lam feared Russ was about to ask a third time, they found Frank standing with an armload of stadium pads at the rail below a grandstand of people and Virginia breathing hard and holding onto the rail and looking up with a face that said *I want to get out of people's way, but I can't.* She could climb no more, and the lower seats were taken. Lam pulled Russ close. "Can you check the other side?"

Just then Dusty arrived and a knot of people formed, waiting. As Virginia's eyes said *Get me the hell out of here,* Frank smiled and pointed down the front row. "Looky there."

From the looks of Thelma Anderson, Virginia's high school nemesis, and her family, they'd bought out Eddie Bauer, but at this moment they were as compassionate as they were well-dressed. They vacated a ten-foot swath of the first row, clearing to the left, right and up a couple of benches. Thelma beckoned to Virginia but Virginia looked away until Thelma marched right up and, like a sister, took her arm. Virginia smiled sheepishly and mouthed *thank you.*

Everyone sat except Frank, who stood before the stands as though he was about to deliver a preflight briefing. He looked only at Virginia, sniffed once, and declared too loudly, "I gotta get to the pits." His eyes quickly inventoried for listeners. "Wish us luck," he said like a big shot and kissed Virginia and left.

As they settled in, Russ talked with Thelma, and Lam was glad to see Frank cross the track, heading for a dirt stretch by the rodeo chutes where the salvaged race cars, including Tommy Zupick's, were strewn. Tommy was milling around his vehicle. And so was Donny. And cracks began to form.

All day Lam had known her rapist would be there. Dreaded it. Closed her eyes. Contained it, as she had on 10,000 days. But not this day. The vessel broke. The stark weight of his existence, right there, in daylight, just as real as she, was unendurable. The brittle dike she had patched and patched and patched finally shattered, and the timeworn blackness of her past was everywhere, swamping her in malevolence, drowning her in what it made her, what she had always felt she'd been. She felt it hold her to the foot-worn coil, rough against her face. Rage turned outside-in – *Enough! Enough!* – And she forced herself down its throat – *Fuck you!* – Plunging violently, greedily, in profane memories – *Is this what you want! Do it! Do it, dammit! Do it!* And she *made* them do it … *she* was in control. She seized the memories, made them hers, any … way … she wanted! *There! … There! … There!* Lam's skin grew dank, her senses blunt – her only movement, imagined. Blackness.

Virginia felt Lam change before she saw it. When she turned, her daughter was already drifting into that other place. She shook Lam's thigh, but the younger woman's eyes were unfocused, her mouth uttering incantations. Virginia pinched her, hard, and pinched again, but nothing. Virginia's heart raced, and she wanted to yell, and she held her teeth in with her lip. Beads of sweat were rising on Lam's forehead and neck. Dear God, no! Frantically, Virginia scrawled HELP on a notepad and then dropped it, having neither the time nor means to explain to anyone. Desperately, Virginia swung at Lam's face, but her angle and strength were poor. Finally, in a great, fisted half-circle, she stabbed Lam's thigh with her pen.

A jagged breath raced into Lam, and her eyes fluttered wildly. Her face reddened. By the second breath, she was wide-eyed, staring, disconnected, at the small dot of blood on her thigh. Virginia cupped Lam's face tightly and commanded her eyes. As Lam came back, Virginia locked an arm around her neck and pulled her close.

"What's wrong," Russ asked, and Virginia signaled him to leave them alone.

A minute later, Virginia gouged "I'll kill the bastard" into her note pad.

"No," Lam whispered. "I saw the rugs. In my head. The ones we burned. But it wasn't him! It wasn't him. He didn't do it this time." And she couldn't help but cry.

Virginia looked back across the track, and her face became dark.

By then Russ had bored in on Lam and Virginia. His jaw tightened. "What happened?"

The women were hugging, and Thelma was acting as if she wanted to help. When they broke, Lam wiped her face and said, "We're fine," and took a breath. "Really. We're fine."

Russ poked a thumb in his pocket and touched the knife.

Across the way, scattered at the track's perimeter, four volunteers, each holding an orange flag in one hand and a plastic cup in the other, signaled the starter that they were paying enough attention to identify a hazard in the inevitability that a collision caused one. The announcer rallied the crowd. The starter dropped the flag, and the roar from ten straight-piped beaters rattled Lam's chest and rousted a sortie of pigeons from under the grandstand roof.

Amateur drivers, charged with adrenaline, ground gears as their cars body-checked each other, and the crowd cheered. One coupe blasted through a tractor-tire barrier. Another took out some logs. Dusty cheered, and Russ cheered, and Virginia waved her arms, and Lam watched. The cars bellowed around the figure-eight until six of the seven survivors earned a berth to a later heat. Tommy Zupick was one of them.

Lam watched Tommy rattle into the pit area and climb out the driver's window to be back-slapped by Frank and lofted, bear-hug-style, by Donny. Them. Celebrating, without a thought or a care. It sickened her. Then, as Tommy removed his helmet, Donny and her father turned to each other and high-fived. Both hands.

Russ stopped clapping and sat down next to her. "What's wrong?"

"Huh? Oh. Nothing. I'm just tired." Lam held a napkin to her thigh with one hand and, with the other, raked her hair until it screened her neck on Russ's side.

"Do you want a Coke?"

She wanted a beer and knew he knew it. "I don't know." She fiddled with the rubber band.

Russ leaned forward and looked beyond Lam's lap. "Virginia, do you want something?"

Virginia nodded.

"A beer?"

She nodded again.

Russ smiled kindly at Lam before he turned to his other side and looked at Dusty's mustard-stained face. "Did you bang your face on some food?"

Dusty touched his mouth and grinned. "Nothing for me." He licked his finger. "Really. I'm good."

"Mmm hmm." Russ stood and turned back to Lam. "Do you want something?"

"No," Lam said softly. He was staring at her neck – too long. His face changed. He looked away, frowning, and began to leave. "Wait." With her bandaged finger she reached and touched his hand, wanting to beg, *I love you, Forgive me, Please love me!* But instead she smiled bright and brittle and said, "Get me a beer," and reached in her pocket for money.

He merely looked at her. "Not today." Then he walked away, broad-backed and careful, like he didn't want to scare off trouble before he found it. As she watched Russ start down the stairs, Frank topped them with a beer and a swagger.

Frank plopped down next to Lam and patted her knee. "We did it!" She stood coldly and moved her cushion to the other side of Dusty. "Oh, for crying out loud," he said.

Donny and Tommy leaned along the beefy plank counter that girdled the beer shack, the edge of which had been beveled by a thousand belt buckles and a dozen layers of paint. Donny's arm was stretched up over Tommy's shoulder, and his free hand soaked in a puddle of spilt beer. "Two MGDs," Donny said, interrupting the concession volunteer who was bent and wrestling a keg.

"How about just one?" said Tommy. "One of us has to drive the next heat." He liked that his coveralls smelled of petroleum. He stared at the long scrape on Donny's temple and cheek. Donny seemed to notice and hooked Tommy's neck in like a knucklehead, knocking Tommy's hat askew before he wrestled free and self-consciously surveyed the men nearby.

"Yup, little brother, one of us does. One beer ain't gonna hurt nobody."

Up and panting, the vendor handed over the beer. "That's $3."

Donny gave Tommy a tight-ass grin. "You're the one who owns a gas station."

Engines revved and rasped, pounding conversations to death, heralding the next heat.

The beer attendant shook foam from his hand and took Tommy's money. He smiled and nodded at a cowboy waiting behind Donny and held a finger up. "I'll be with you in a minute," he yelled, and he squatted for round two with the keg.

Donny pinched Tommy's neck and raised his beer. "Here's to you, little brother. We're still in it, though by the skin of your ass. I bought *us* in the Calcutta, and I can use the money, so I'm thinking *I* oughta drive the next heat. Nothing personal, but, hey, who taught you to drive?"

A swell of blue exhaust rolled in and choked the spice from the river-bottom air.

"We don't need a Braille driver," Tommy hollered.

"What?" Donny shouted.

Tommy shook his head. It wasn't worth it. As Donny pinched his neck again, harder, Tommy turtled and seized Donny's arm and easily rolled from his grip as the last car passed and the noise ebbed. "That's enough!" Tommy could see in Donny's eyes that he knew he was no longer the bigger brother.

"Just 'cause you're taller than me don't mean I can't kick your ass, you skinny shit."

"I'm just saying you been drinking," Tommy said, "'n you weren't home 'til dawn. Think I'll drive."

"Ain't nothing I did last night that'd bother my driving. Ain't you heard that it helps to blow the carbon out once in a while? You get my meaning? Ha-hah! Maybe not." Donny delighted in teasing Tommy about women. "Or are you just jealous?"

Tommy was looking over Donny's shoulder at a cowboy with sharpening eyes. He knew it was the exact wrong time to laugh. When the cars came around, under a camouflage of sound, Tommy captured Donny's elbow, leaning in. "Come on. Let's get ready for the next race."

But Donny pulled off, unready to stop spurring his kid brother. "You had your chance in high school, bro. Blew a lay-up. R'member? 'N she'd screw a woodpile if there's a snake in it."

As Tommy watched, the cowboy squared with Donny's back. Tommy hastily pulled his brother's arm, "Time to go." But Donny jerked away, popping Tommy's chest with his palm.

"What'sa matter, pussy?" Donny grinned, open-mouthed. "I bet you never even saw her naked." By this time, men were gathering. Mistaking it for a pep-squad, Donny hooted, "Didja?"

Tommy inhaled and looked down. His family blood was thinning. Looking past Donny to Russ, he tucked a hand in a greasy coverall pocket. He sipped his beer. With reluctance, he placed his beer on the counter. Russ tightened to take them both. "I gotta go."

"Hah! You didn't! Didja! Hell, I saw her naked *back then*." Donny talked bigger. "Don't feel bad, little bro, you didn't miss much. I seen her plenty of times – more than that *farmer* has. Like last night. Hot as hell. Rougher the hotter, baby, and sweaty-ass naked. Well, all except for that little rubber band..."

"Jesus." Tommy bowed his head till the bill of his cap blocked his eyes. He turned away.

And that's when it happened. Donny felt someone at his shoulder and swung around, unable to pull up before Russ's driving forearm shattered his nose. Blinded, he felt his shirt pulled up over his head, trapping his arms. Through it someone grabbed his hair, jerked him upright. In an explosion, sharp white pain bolted from his balls through his lungs, lifting him off his feet. The last thing he heard before blackness was the melon-like *thwok* as his head hit the ground.

Some while later, the first thing Donny could perceive was men's voices and roaring engines. When his eyes burned open, nothing was discernible. He was unaware of the ambulance crew tending his face and crotch, and the fact that he was naked from his waist down. From the ground between his thighs, an inch from his scrotum, they had already extracted the pocket knife with the ivory handle. He didn't know how close he had come. As he tried to blink clear, a new sound bled through. Men laughing. Men laughing.

As Russ waited, Sheriff Tuffy Jankovich interviewed those who were there, some of whom swore they saw Donny throw the first punch. Some didn't see a thing. As they loaded Donny in the ambulance, he asked Russ. "What the hell was this about?"

"He called me a farmer," Russ said.

"That's not good enough, goddammit!"

"Well, we could've had a bake-off, but…"

"Dammit, Russ! You think this ends it? Huh? You know him? Shit. I'm too old."

Russ waited until the Sheriff became his friend again. "Tuffy, would you mind giving Lam and her folks a ride home? Think it's time for me to go."

Tuffy's eyes started to ask, but then didn't have to. They softened. "Sure thing."

THE BATH

...because finally
after all this struggle
and all these years,
you don't want to any more,
you've simply had enough
of drowning,...

Davidseg Whyte

Deep in a crisp, early autumn night, a time-beaten house exhaled lightly through a dark window. The furnace was firing for the first time in months, and Dusty lay on his bed breathing the hard-earth smell of burnt summer dust. Across his chest, the white sleeves of his letterman jacket fluoresced with moonlight, his hands joined over his heart. For hours he prayed, undistracted by far-off dogs and late-night trucks, as the moon descended along run-down crests and settled on the vast flatness of the basin.

He thought about the fight. About how it had always been just his mom and him. How their ranks had closed once more. He prayed she would heal, be okay again, saying *Please, God*, bargaining away college, vowing to stay.

Once, before morning, he heard her stir and his spirits rallied. He crept to her bedroom door and peered into the blackness. He sniffed one time, to make a noise. He saw the cherry of her cigarette trace an arc through velvet darkness and pause as it brightened, before collapsing under the prison of its own ash. He sighed heavily. Nothing. They said nothing.

The next morning was thick, and the tiny house got smaller. Dusty skipped football practice. He did their laundry, mowed the lawn, and fiddled with his Walkman, but none of the music seemed to understand. At two o'clock he heated soup and made grilled cheese sandwiches. He did the dishes. As much as possible, he stayed where she could see him, hoping she'd want to talk. For hours she lay on the couch, spiritless, the lights off and shades drawn, the fitful strobe of TV illuminating her face and threadbare robe. Finally, near twilight, she stirred, rising to run a bath, and Dusty used the interlude to get outside, to shoot baskets in the driveway. Inside the house, the phone rang. He trapped the ball and listened. It stopped. A minute later it rang again, only two rings, and he exhaled when he heard Lam's muffled voice. Whoever it was didn't get to talk for long.

A half-hour later, in the murk of dusk, Dusty was panting from imaginary one-on-one when Russ's rig pulled up. He hung the ball on his hip and walked halfway to the curb while Russ got out. "Hey."

"Hey," said Russ. He slipped his fingers into his pockets. "How's your mom?"

"Quiet." Dusty smeared his forehead with a grimy hand.

A moment passed. Russ took the ball with both hands. He slowly turned it. He looked back at his friend. "How are you?"

"I'll be all right."

Russ hesitated. "Do you have plans tonight?"

"I thought I'd hang around here."

Russ looked into a man's eyes. He turned the ball. "Would you do me a favor?"

Dusty looked at him.

"Would you mind staying at your grandparents' tonight?"

Dusty retook the ball. He drew a hopeful breath. "All right," he said. "Allow me to gather my fine toiletries," and he grinned, but Russ didn't smile back.

Russ waited in the front room while Dusty got his things. It only took a minute. They said goodbye, and Dusty drove away, leaving the fate of him and his mom to God ... and Russ.

Russ stayed seated for a couple more minutes. Slowly he re-gathered the thoughts he had brought with him, arranging them in the same order as before. What would come next would be difficult, but it was right – at least for him. Finally he rose and walked to the bathroom door. He knocked lightly with one knuckle. Inside, water moved. "Lam. It's me. May I come in?" He slowly turned the handle.

More water sounds, fainter; a sigh. He eased open the door and inched into the humid room. Before him, over the rim of the claw-footed tub, hung a ragged veil of tired hair. He gently closed the door and sat on the toilet lid. As he replanted his boots, he skirted a fat glass of whiskey. Her eyes were closed. Water had beaded on her face, and a damp, open washcloth clung to her chest.

For a long while they were still. Occasionally the toilet ran. The ice in her glass settled.

In time, Russ knelt beside the tub and sat on his boots. He rested a forearm on the porcelain and waited for Lam to open her eyes. Minutes passed. When he drew a smear of hair off her cheek, tears welled along her eyelashes. After a while, his legs tingled, so he shifted, and a teardrop escaped down her cheek.

He reached across her for a bar of soap. With an open hand he gently, so gently, met the washcloth on her chest. When his touch had settled, he slowly drew the cloth down, floating it in water. Her brow swelled with pain, and she angled her face away. He towed in the washcloth and lathered it with soap.

Next he slipped his arm under hers and buoyed it from the water, and he began to stroke her, slowly, tenderly: the curve of her shoulder, the delicate hollow of her mid-arm, the slight rise of bone at her wrist. He released the cloth and soaped his hands. He wove his fingers into hers. When he had finished, he leaned over her and cleansed her other arm.

With the cloth warm and heavy, he caressed her collar. She shrugged deep to one side to cover the bruise Donny left. He rinsed her and re-soaped the cloth. With one hand he cradled her jaw, coaxing her face toward his. Her eyes stayed closed. He washed her neck as if it were sacred, and the tears of a thousand mistakes quietly flowed down her cheeks.

"All my life…" she started, but it pinched into a muted whine.

With bare hands he washed her, gently pausing along the cruel, red line. He soothed it with warm water from cupped palms. And she cried. When there was nothing left to wash away, he rested his hands on her, leaned in and kissed her forehead. And she cried. She draped a wet arm around his neck and began to shake, so he wrapped her shoulders and head in his arms, hid her in the darkness of his chest. Without letting go, he crawled over the side of the tub and into the water, on his knees, straddling her in boots and jeans. She bawled, from long ago and now, and he held her forever, until she could cry no more.

When he released, she clutched his shirt as if to forbid him, so he kissed her head and embraced her once more, until, again, she slackened. Then he rose smoothly, and for an instant she lay limp, resigned, he thought, or at least spent. But she wasn't. With raisined fingers she clenched his buckle and popped it loose before he could trap her hands.

"No," he said.

He was looking now into eyes at once sad and savage, and it was he who needed to hold her this time, and he tried, but she grabbed and unzipped him, roughly. He seized her forearms. "Lam. That's not why I'm here." Her pulse coursed beneath his fingers, insistently at first. Then slower. She was watching his mouth. He thought she was listening, not waiting.

"I'll do anything you want!" she said. "Anything!"

When he sighed, she thrashed and he stopped her. Finally they released, and she lay back in the water, exhausted. He cradled her face once more, and kissed the corners of her quaking mouth. As he leaned back, she finally searched his eyes. He rose from the water, fully on his knees. He held his belt with one hand as he reached into his wet pocket with the other. He pulled out a small jeweler's box and fumbled it into the water but quickly recovered it. He opened it toward her.

She threw her arms around his neck and collapsed in his embrace, sobbing.

28

HAPPY ACCIDENTS?

The beauty of the world has two edges, one of laughter,
one of anguish, cutting the heart asunder…

VIRGINIA WOOLF

Levi was no help to Angela's assimilation in the new home in Silicon Valley. Even when he was there, he was never there. Monroe Manor, she called it, was a showcase of pillars bought in a hot market. Overkill. Eventually Angela had unpacked and fussed plenty, not that she ever completely unpacked. She was lonely, and boredom made her squirrelly. She tried aerobic classes to make friends, but the mother's club wouldn't let her out of the back corner. At Levi's urging, she hired a housekeeper, so on Wednesday mornings she watched out the window for Gabriella's car and tried not to wag like a puppy when the woman came in. She also liked seeing the gardener and the pool guy. To the casual observer things stayed nice. Tidy. Quiet. But like the San Andreas Fault beneath her, energy mounted with no place to go.

In the 1990s, the Monroes lived in the Santa Clara Valley near San Jose. When Hewlett met Packard, it was a Del Monte prune and apricot town at the south end of the Bay, long before the birth of microchips and Intel and Apple. The city grew to become the capital of Silicon Valley, eclipsing San Francisco in both population and sprawl.

The Valley was a dichotomy. Oak and amber grass on the east, redwoods on the west. The east side was home to thousands of immigrants from Vietnam and Latin America – some documented, some not – many working in agriculture or service jobs catering to the well-to-do in the west side cities of Los Gatos, Saratoga, Cupertino, Los Altos, and Palo Alto, where the gravity of new dynastic wealth pulled in the world's best and brightest. The privileged. Long-time local gentry stood against a tsunami of highly-educated, high-tech pilgrims, families from China, India and the Middle East. Office complexes bloomed on farmland. Schools went up. Older residents took to saying they could "remember when it was all orchards," but their lament was white noise to the modern-day prospectors.

The environmentally conscious had pretty much protected the west side coastal mountains, the Santa Cruz range, from overbuilding, turning the dewy, redwood canopy into a sort of demilitarized zone between builders from the Valley and builders from the beach. A few custom estates and wineries stood sentry in the forest. And tucked against the edge, Saratoga became some of the priciest real estate in the world. A far cry from Roundup.

One sunny Wednesday, after Angela and Gabriella made tamales while watching *Oprah* (it had become their way), Gabriella left with her share and Angela went back to the kitchen to stare at a PBS fundraiser on KQED. She wondered how one got to be a telephone volunteer. It could be fun. Meet some people. She called the station and flipped through a Pottery Barn catalogue as it rang. She and the store's interior designer had already staged her house with most of their collection. Just like in the pictures. Maybe too much so. Now she was making fast friends with the woman at Thomasville.

Something on TV distracted her enough to hang up. It was that white guy with an afro and a paint brush, that old hippie. She was sure it was recorded some time back. Bob Ross was mesmerizing to her. He was a gentle man with the soothing delivery of a preacher trying not to spook a toddler before he baptized the hell out of it. "Welcome to Bob Ross's *Joy of Painting*." As he painted, he talked about the years he had lived alone in the Alaskan woodlands – more alone than her, she thought, and apparently much longer, until he emerged as the high televangelist of oil painting. He was a nice man with a nice system by which nice people could produce nice paintings in about half an hour. At show's end the fundraiser guy said the man was dead. Bummer. She felt bad for thinking ill of his hair. She called the station and donated $1,000 in exchange for the *Joy of Painting* instructional videos, now on DVD. So began her painter period.

Always alone when she painted, except for Bob who was there in video and in spirit, she took to talking like him. "It's *my* painting," she would softly repeat in Bob-voice, a warm blend of hum and whisper. "I can put in *a–ny-thing* I want." As she jabbed trees into being with a fan brush (perhaps Bob's favorite), she yielded to his mysticism. "If I *want* a little friend by my cabin, I can *put* a little friend there," and she'd switch wands and paint a squirrel on the forest floor. "*A—ny-thing* I want. No mistakes … just *hap—py accidents*."

It became her way, after sessions, to remove her spattered and smudged clothes in the studio and walk naked through the kitchen on her way upstairs. She imagined that Bob painted naked in the Alaskan woods, at least on warm days. Stripping in Monroe Manor kept paint off the carpet. And it felt sexy. One afternoon she was particularly pleased with her work and grabbed a bottle of Chardonnay and a glass before padding up to the master bathroom to shower and primp before Levi got home. As she lighted the makeup mirror, she began to talk like Bob. "*A—ny-thing* I want," she said dreamily, nudging at her crow's-feet. "*A—ny-thing* I want." Soon she had blended rosy blush with foundation into the color of sunset. She pensively streaked fingers of it across her forehead, studying the wide smear before selecting the eyeliner. With it, she drew down the length of her face, making what she deemed to be reasonable tree trunks. Next, she imbued her fan brush with green eye shadow and stabbed in branches, herringboning them at the trunk, working down the left side of each tree and then the right. She became owned by the process. By the time she was drawing a varmint by the pond of blue eye shadow, she was startled at the sound of Levi downstairs.

"Hello?" he called into the house at large.

Her first impulse after she jumped was pleasure that he might be taking the doctor seriously by knocking off early. Then she stared wide-eyed at her face. Then her naked body. "Oops. Is it Bob, or is it Angela? Or both? Blenderful." She grinned as a new thought took hold. She scampered through the bedroom and ducked behind the bedroom door as Levi came looking. The door moved. She jumped. He flinched, hugely. Then she laughed at him and herself, and he laughed at her and himself, and they laughed until they couldn't.

"And they say I'm nuts," Levi said.

"Uh-uh. Not yet. Remember. You won't snap until something big happens," she playfully bit his chin as she loosened his tie. "And this might be it, Bob Ross style." Her voice changed. "*There are no* mistakes," she said, "just *hap—py accidents. A—ny-thing you want.*"

That night in bed, they Bob-talked and laughed, and the sex was fun again – really, really fun.

The glow had not fully dissipated when they awoke the next morning. Not at all. To her great satisfaction, it built again, big as ever, and it was hot that the pillow cases and sheets smelled of sex and linseed oil. Afterward she decided she'd wash them, but she sure as hell wouldn't throw them out. Now they were special.

Levi uncharacteristically lingered past 7 A.M. They showered together, and she felt like dressing up. While he shaved, she rummaged in the closet, rearranging Tiffany's and Gump's boxes and his gun case for better access to her jewelry box. She looked at his back and his cute butt. He'd been generous, really, with his labor and money, if not his time. Time would come. And this was the moment Levi's cell phone began to vibrate on the dresser. He couldn't hear it above his electric razor. Angela hesitated, and then read the caller ID. "JOY CELL." Her face fell. She opened it and listened.

"Hey, fella. Coffee's on. Are you coming by or what? If not, I should shoot in … Hello?"

Angela held her breath as the ripple of betrayal rolled out from her heart. She said nothing, torn about wanting to hear more, until Joy hung up. She paused. She walked the phone to Levi. "Your phone rang. I answered it, but they hung up. I think it was Joy."

The razor snapped off. "Joy who?"

She stared at him.

"Oh, Joy Parnell. I'll call her back later."

"Sorry I answered it."

"Oh, no worries. I agreed to meet her at a restaurant. Forgot all about it."

"A restaurant?" Angela watched his eyes, thinking he was trying to read hers.

"I think it was a restaurant. I'd have to call Lily. I wrote it down, I think. My Day-Timer's at work." On the last word his eyes broke away and he kissed her as if he had this great spontaneous urge to, a kiss delivered a little too zestfully.

"Do you like it here?" It just came out of her.

"Do I like it? In the Bay Area?" He began tying his tie in the mirror. "I don't know. I guess. I don't like Crawford. He could fuck up a wet dream."

"Why don't we move back? To Montana. Go to work for another firm." She fielded his dubious look. "I know you think about ways back. You never really let go."

His arms dropped. "I got over my folks long ago. I don't think about 'ways back.'"

"Then why don't you ever completely close drawers and cupboard doors?" They both looked at the bathroom vanity. Each of his drawers was open two or three inches.

"What?"

"Either you don't want to make noise … because you're still afraid somewhere inside … or part of you thinks you might want or need to come back."

"You still amaze me." He gave her a peck. "I've left no doors open with my family. At least not on purpose."

"No. You have me for that. I'm the door you've kept open to them. I depend on you, too. Completely."

He finished with his tie. "You think too much. I'm late."

That morning Angela enrolled at San Jose State to earn her California teaching credential. For Angela.

29

TROPICAL DEPRESSION

Is it possible to succeed without betrayal?

JEAN RENOIR

From inside the island villa, Levi watched Sandler's muted silhouette not move. The older man was staring through the glass door into a bright tropical haze. Past the ostentatious Grecian pavilion, Levi guessed, even past the swimming pool where the bikini-clad, 28-year-old, fire-haired wife of Levi's top salesman, a 50-something broker, jiggled unnaturally above her trophy-husband's shoulders, having a camel fight in the water with a younger man and wife. Sandler didn't seem to notice them. He seemed to stare beyond the cloudy, Caribbean horizon. At what, already? Thinking what? Levi feared he had just fucked up. Sandler's shape grew a halo that made Levi squint. From an island shirt, the CEOs head jutted, stiff and fixed, like a blocky Bermudan version of the idols on Easter Island, pasted against the bright sky. *What the hell is he thinking?*

"A goddamm waste of time and money. You know how many of these sales award clubs I've had to host? The IRS says we have to have at least a half day of meetings. In the old days, brokers would stay in the ballroom, in their chairs, the whole morning, half out of courtesy and half out of fear that we'd fire their ass if they didn't. Now, if they sell enough to get to this boondoggle, they think they're bulletproof. So now the room is empty by the 10 o'clock speaker because these arrogant, overpaid bastards are keeping a tee time or going sailing or getting a goddamn massage. We can't do a damn thing about it." Sandler said, as if to himself. "And we worry about other firms raiding them away." Then his tone changed. "Do you know how big the home mortgage market is?"

The question was wholly disconnected from the threat Levi had just dropped in Sandler's lap. "I'm sorry?" Levi queried the back of Sandler's head.

"Trillions," Sandler said. "If we were in that business and captured a shard of it, we'd make billions. We'd all be rich. And stockbrokers' balls would get a little smaller."

"I don't understand." But Levi did know some. He had sent that letter to the NASD, after all, and he suspected where this was going.

When the silhouette turned, it offered only linebacker eyes and deep bass voice. "We don't need to lend out the firm's money. What we need is a bank. One to merge with, or partner with. The bank makes the loans, but doesn't have to lend the money for long. A few days. So they won't worry about loan risk. As a matter of fact, the riskier the loan, the higher interest they'll charge the homeowner in interest and fees. We can buy the loans they make, bundle them into packages, and sell them like bonds on the Street. Then, just like the bank lays off risk on us, we lay off the risk by reselling them before the homeowner's first payment is due."

"If we package a bunch of loans together, even junk loans, the pieces of that package we sell – bonds – get the highest of investment ratings from Moody's and S&P. So we get to sell bonds that pay low interest rates, backed by mortgages that charge high rates, because rating agencies presume someone along the line still gives a shit about credit risk when the loans were made. Naïve as hell. There's big profit between gouging risky borrowers and then marking up the value of a basket of sub-prime loans and reselling pieces to bond buyers as if they're high quality bonds just because S&P rubber-stamps them that way. We can arbitrage that all day long. The fucking bank will lend to anyone if they can sell the loans to the Street. Collect fat fees when the loan is made, collect commission when the bonds are sold; we all get rich. And struggling apartment dwellers get the American Dream – to borrow enough to buy any home they want, whether they can afford it or not, because the lender doesn't give a shit if they can pay it. Let the borrowers hang themselves. Broke people have always been willing to be overcharged to acquire what they can't afford. Hell, we'll cut a fat hog helping them do it. Then, bond-buyer beware. It's brilliant. It's Gary's idea."

"I don't see what this has to do with Gary running an illegal stock option…"

"Do you know the name Ilsa Crawford?"

"No." Inside he said, *Oh, no.*

"Sometimes she uses Englehardt, her maiden name. Ilsa's on the board of the third largest bank in Chicago. About a hundred years ago her husband committed suicide. He owned a chunk of the bank. She inherited it. Over twelve years ago, in the crash of '87, Bookman Stuart needed cash badly. She arranged a bridge loan for us. Since then, she's been on our board too. She can make this mortgage business happen for us. Make our shareholders rich. You and I, through stock and options, are big shareholders. Without her, the firm would give away too much to partner with any other bank or merge. And without competing in this arena, we'll lose market share to Merrill, Smith Barney, UBS. Do you understand?"

"I understand what you're saying. I've never met Gary's wife. He never brings her along. But if she's like –"

"Ilsa is Crawford's mother. It was for her I hired Gary in the first place, back in the seventies. I have to admit, he's made us money. She backs me, like I back you, with the board. Understand?" Levi nodded. "Ilsa throws her weight around. She's a tough old broad. So. Now you want me to fire her son. You know, he's not the only subject of rumors."

What? "I'm not saying fire him. I'm saying there may have been fraud in the West while Gary was there. You must see how seriously I take this. I might be putting my job on the line here, coming to you." Levi waited for Sandler to dispute it. He did not.

The doorbell rang. Sandler answered it, releasing hot, thick air into the entryway and sitting area, dosing the villa with a fog of salt and faint lagoon rot. Then that voice.

"Hi, Michael. I'm really sorry, but I when I changed for the pool, I realized my sunglasses weren't in my suite. I think I left them here." Joy's eyes caught Levi, deep in the room. "Oh, God. I'm sorry. I didn't know … I mean, thanks for critiquing my strategic plan for product penetration, and chopping fixed costs, costs are important. Well, um, I can see you're busy, Mr. Sandler." Despite her discomfort, Levi only observed, long since void of the passion to think her a slut. It was simply Joy.

"I am. Please excuse us," he said gently.

"Oh. Okay. Well, see you this evening, then." Then, louder, "See you Levi."

"See you later," Levi said, as if he'd witnessed nothing. Sandler closed the door.

"I have some things to do," Sandler said. "Please excuse me." Taking his cue, Levi walked to the door, which Sandler held until he got there. "We'll talk. Give Angela a kiss for me. Please tell her I'll see her at tonight's prom."

"I will," Levi said, barely finishing before Sandler closed the door behind him. Twenty yards away he saw Crawford standing on the patio of another villa. Crawford removed his sunglasses and nested them into his hair. Eyes locked. "That's right, asshole," Levi whispered. Then the sliding glass behind Crawford opened. Deidre Oliver emerged wearing a bikini top and sarong, cradling an open laptop.

30

Riders on the Storm

God moves in a mysterious way
His wonders to perform;
He plants his footsteps in the sea
And rides upon the storm.

WILLIAM COWPER

In their villa, dressing for the formal dinner, Angela put on new underwear. She sauntered flirtatiously, brushing against Levi. "Why don't we sneak back early tonight and see what they left for our pillow gift. Crystal, jewelry. Or I can leave you a pillow gift. The last night's gift is always the best." The fact that she had never succeeded in luring Levi early from a party didn't daunt her. While he leaned into the mirror wrestling his bowtie, she sidled behind him in bra and panties. A glass of wine in one hand, she explored his boxers with the other. "Know what I'm thinking?"

"Uhhm, liquid squirrels ... Velveeta car-seat covers ... uh, pomegranate music."

She put her glass down. Hooking her finger in his ravel-bare friendship bracelet, she towed his hand to her ass. She cupped his crotch. "How about now?"

"Happy circle people ... paisley puppies ... and teenage diaper products."

"No!" Her arms fell like popped balloon animals. "From the feel of things, you really *don't* know what I'm thinking." She reeled in her hand, snapping his waistband. She grabbed her wine. "I thought we'd enjoy some intimate time *before* cocktails."

"I'm sorry, Babe, I was thinking about this morning. And this afternoon."

"Oh! Hey. Don't worry about me. I just thought you might want to help me out with, no, *out of*, something." With embellished tedium, she straightened her thong and grabbed a half-slip from the bed. She held a palm up like a traffic cop. "But I got it. Whew. That was close." She grinned at his bright blue eyes in the mirror. "All right. Tell me about this morning?"

"I'm going to be pretty busy for a few weeks."

"Gee. I'll make arrangements." He ignored her sarcasm.

"We're considering getting deep in the home loan business. Lending money to people who shouldn't be borrowing, then selling the risk to people who don't know what they're buying. We could make jillions. I don't like it"

"Oh, dear God! Not that! Anything but home loans!"

"Stop. This is serious – and probably unethical. Most investors won't get it. The risk is invisible. Brilliant. It might add billions in profit, a hundred million in management bonuses." He struggled with his tie. "My bonus would get huge."

"Levi, I don't pretend to understand, but if it's wrong…" He caught her disapproval.

"If one big firm does this, every firm on the Street will follow. It's too profitable to resist. If the market drops big – and this irrational exuberance and related commissions *will* dry up – we'll all pull the trigger on this new revenue. Presto, chango – we're mortgage banks, making sub-prime, meaning 'bad,' loans for big commissions. Like Crawford says, it's better to ask forgiveness than permission. This is his initiative. Asshole. He's banking on the fact that it's easier to hide if you steal from people by giving them what they want, like houses they can't afford, and sell the hidden risk to other greedy bastards. But it's not okay. Clinton should never have let brokers and banks get married again. I'm going to talk off the record with a woman at the SEC, but this will go live before the SEC or the Fed or Treasury or whoever can stop it. In the meantime, you can donate that portion of my bonus to the child and spousal abuse center, as if we weren't already overcommitted."

"Hey. The center deal is yours. You're the one who cosigned the two million dollar loan on their new building – speaking of loans. No one named a building after me." He didn't seem to hear her. She untied his tie, indicating he should start again.

"This afternoon I met with Sandler and told him what's going on. I told him we were out of compliance and that's why some Silicon Valley branches are so profitable. I insinuated that Crawford built it on purpose."

"Jesus, Levi. Crawford will…" She studied his eyes for signs of that thing that happens.

"Hey, I told Crawford before – twice – once in writing, via email. He ignored me. So I met with Sandler today. Crawford wasn't there."

"Isn't that a little ballsy? Going over his head?"

"That's what Sandler said. Loyalty is everything to Sandler, huge. So I showed him the email. He got quiet. Spooky quiet. Then he told me Crawford's mother was on the board. I missed it. She uses her maiden name. She's a friend of Sandler's."

"Shit. Are you in trouble?"

"I'm not sure," Levi said. "Joy showed up, and we ended there." Angela told herself to ignore the name. "Then, when I left, Crawford saw me from his patio." Angela inhaled through her teeth as if she'd been pricked. "Deirdre was with him." Having tied a passable bow, he turned. "Okay. Ready to go?"

"Did you bring your prescription?"

"I told you I won't take it. Nothing's going to happen."

She told herself to believe it. He had never taken anything before. He was always fine. And he never mentioned hallucinating any more, not since the appointment. Besides, this night could be romantic. It was okay. Okay, then. Back to her husband. Her sexy husband. "Zip me up?" She arched a little and a better kind of tension tried to come back. Her zipper rose from the crack of her otherwise naked ass. "So Crawford knows?" The words felt toxic, threatening to poison her chance for intimacy.

"Are those your mom's pearls?"

"Why, yes. What with the island theme, and all. Might be a fertility charm, too."

"I don't know if Crawford knows. Sandler's pretty solid, but who knows. Crawford'll have to explain sooner or later." Then, offhandedly, Levi said, "I wonder who Sandler'd promote if he sacks Crawford."

"And you say *I'm* the idiot." She took his hand and leered naughtily at him. "How 'bout we come back early, discuss it more?" She French-kissed him. "Or … not."

"What time…? Crap. Let's get to cocktails. Brokers are pissed. The bank deposit thing."

She stopped him. "Wait." She slipped her fingers under his tux lapel and uprighted his corporate pin – a red enamel schooner cutting through blue waves. "There. Perfect."

They crossed manicured grounds pocked with underpaid black men in absurdly formal uniforms making perpetual raking motions. Men whose slow strokes and faces held no expression save gauzed contempt. The salty evening breeze strengthened, the surf heaving bigger than before. They looked past palms waving like construction paper cutouts against a flagging golden sun. Menacing clouds on the russet horizon. At a hundred feet from cocktail fun, beyond the marble Poseidon, the pool surface shivered under a hot, heavier breeze. "Think something's brewing?" Angela asked.

"Yup. They've already named it Tropical Storm Hillary."

"If it blows harder, will it become Hurricane Monica?"

"Funny. We've got this Indian client who says he can fix that – global warming."

"Ah. Okie dokie then. Not to worry."

They breached a picket of nervous tiki torches. "Corporate cocktail redux," Angela said. She always said that. It was another resort party strewn with brokers brandishing non-corporate senior VP titles, granted for marketing purposes only because they had produced the most commission. "Should be fun. Do I look okay?" He said she did. His eyes and ears were fixed on the cobweb of conversations from poolside, no doubt seeing flows and patterns where she could not. Last year, at her school's holiday party, he accurately predicted where three disparate people would stand and when. It was freaky. But here, as with any veteran senior officer, he would mostly deploy where other top brass weren't. As his sweeper, Angela would drink buttery chardonnays with bands of women she had stood with at any number of previous parties, women freer than their husbands to bitch about the firm; women who knew everything about everyone yet still needed to read her nametag as they asked if they hadn't sat next to her at dinner last year in Scottsdale. Or was it Puerto Vallarta? Levi kissed her cheek.

"Work your magic?" he said. She nodded.

To Angela's relief, Sandler saw her at that brief alone moment and parted the crowd to greet her. Joy washed along in on his wake.

Across the pool stood the Grecian pavilion, obliquely lit in amber to exaggerate its plaster relief of Odysseus resisting the call of the Sirens. Beside that, four eyes observed Angela. They saw Sandler kiss her cheek, watched Joy pull two chardonnays from a server's tray and hand one to her.

"Mrs. Monroe must be unaware of Mr. Monroe's extramarital activities," said Crawford.

Deirdre was both surprised and flattered that he spoke so frankly. His manicured fingers slowly worked his juice glass, rotating it. But did he take her for a fool? It's not as if the world didn't know Joy was sleeping with him as well, had been for years. No matter. Better, even. Joy was over there, and she was over here. What relationship Joy had with Levi or Sandler didn't matter. It only mattered that Joy's ties with Crawford were severed. If Sandler pulls Joy from Crawford, so much the better. *Nature abhors a vacuum,* she thought, and she could profit by filling Crawford's void. Crawford, not Sandler, would choose the next director of corporate human resources in New York. The current director, her other direct report, had a case of prostate cancer that was killing him. It was a fortuitous fact for her, nothing more. HR eats their dead. She wondered if she should be drinking wine. Crawford wasn't. She waited for his glance to delicately adjust the thin strap of the tiny purse that hung from her bare shoulder. Tease a little. *Made you look,* she thought.

"I wonder who's the greater sycophant," Crawford said aloud.

"You mean between Joy and Levi?" *Or Joy and me?*

"That too. But I meant Angela or Levi." He looked annoyed, even suspicious, as if Deirdre had eavesdropped on his thoughts. He went on. "The only reason Levi is still with this firm is his relationship with Sandler … and Sandler's relationship with the fair and wholesome Mrs. Monroe. Sandler prefers wives who show well. Two assets for the price of one."

"I understand your concern, but in my experience…"

His head snapped briskly at her. "Save it. We are not children, you and I. You're ambitious, you're smart." She took it as fact. "I would think you'd get the picture. After all, you met with your counterpart at EcoPulse repeatedly … and their employee stock option administrator, Bob…"

"Bob Nelson."

"Yes. Bob Nelson. Ramakapur's man. Another of those absurd Silicon Valley tech-idol worshippers." He pondered. "If Monroe fully assimilates what happened out there, his Boy Scout righteousness could cause me … difficulties." He checked to see if she was with him. "To wit, if *I* am not in New York, *you* never will be. If I leave the company and Sandler promotes the wrong people," he looked over pool water at Sandler, spitefully; at Angela;

at Joy, "how do you think your career will go? How is your relationship with Mr. Monroe, Deirdre?"

Her already slim abdomen tightened to the verge of sunkenness. Just then an old Crawford crony from Chicago approached to glad-hand. Deirdre embraced the interruption. Had she not thought it through completely? Had she not planned? Covered her own tracks? She took inventory of events. She was sure she had never said anything specifically illegal to anyone. Just played along, that's all, with Crawford's … irregularities. Yet she did know that Ramakapur's people – "*friends of Abba*" – were getting hot stock. She knew Bookman Stuart was illegally holding up money that belonged to EcoPulse employees. Someone might ask how she knew. How, then? Too many conversations – all documented, meticulously, she reminded herself, on her computer. Her eyes darted in the direction of her hotel suite, her laptop. What was said? To whom? What if Levi … Did she have enough on Levi to get him fired? Maybe not. And Angela, Angela was perfect, in everyone's estimation. Despite herself, even Deirdre liked Angela. And even if Deirdre did stop Levi, what if Crawford got caught? What if some EVP from Denver or Atlanta became president? She had no dirt on those people, no control. No. Crawford *had* to stay in power. Levi could not be allowed to jeopardize that. Jeopardize her goals; jeopardize fifteen years of hard work since Stanford. It was her turn, high time. A server with a drink tray drifted by. She finished her wine and set the glass on the tray. "Please excuse me," she said to Crawford and his friend. "I'll be right back." They barely noticed her.

Deirdre started around the pavilion for the grassy side, the side with the sea and the restrooms. Thinking. Past the pillars and dressing rooms. As she rounded the corner, the pavilion became a sound-wall to the party. She gazed across a proper lawn, fifty feet wide, flexed against the Atlantic surf with the ineffectual authority of a velvet rope. Alone now, hidden from all but the groundsmen and other irrelevants, Deirdre could focus. Plan her assent. She tumbled her thoughts in the distant surf, washing them of emotional clutter. She sorted the pieces, big to small, heavy to light. They were as interlocking blocks. Angela, Joy. Sandler and Levi. Crawford's crimes. Remove one, weaken another; harden one, shape one. "Pull a piece, leave the ladder," she told herself. "Probabilities, not people. Pull a piece, leave the ladder. A game. Like Jenga."

"Are you happy?" A Caribbean voice, the voice of molasses, spoken softly, oozing up under nature's noise.

Deirdre palmed her purse to her side. The happy gums and teeth of a young groundskeeper, perhaps twenty, flashed at her. "I beg your pardon?" she said, edging toward one plantation-shutter in a row of doors to private ladies' rooms.

"You are a beautiful woman. More beautiful when you are happy, yes?" She puzzled, mildly galled that he would think her attention within his reach. He gazed toward the party, checking, and then pulled something from his pocket. A baggie. Two. "You want to relax, or you want to be happy?" One was pot, the other pills.

"I don't smoke," she said and started to turn away.

"Ah, then you want to be happy. You are a happy woman? Your husband, he likes you happy, yes? Happy like ecstasy? Like E?"

"No," she said, firmly, and opened the plantation door to a restroom. She stepped onto marble and bolted the lock. "Waste my fucking time." To refocus, she turned on the tap, washed her hands, trying not to wonder if the young man was still outside. The pieces: Sandler, Crawford, Joy, an HR boss in chemotherapy. Levi and his perfect wife. Suddenly it snapped together. In a jerk, she killed the water and grabbed a hand towel. She yanked open the door before she was dry. The groundskeeper loitered a few feet away. She homed in on him, wondering if this is how Crawford bought his drugs. "How much? Two tabs. How much?"

Less than a minute later she ducked back into the restroom. She crushed the ecstasy into a tissue, stashed it in her purse. She reapplied her lipstick and set out.

Around the pavilion, at the edge of the party, Deirdre seized two chardonnays from a server's tray. She stepped behind a pillar, set the glasses on the ground. Her hands shook as she opened her purse. She emptied the contents of the tissue into one glass before discarding the tissue. "Just a game," she mumbled, "Jenga." She stirred the tainted wine with a trembling finger. Stirred more, causing it to overflow. "Okay. Good enough." She poured from the clear glass to even them up. She melted into the crowd, sighted her objective, and moved in.

"I suppose I've tied you up long enough," Sandler said warmly. Angela supposed he was right. Across the way, Levi was standing next to the top broker from his division and Red, the man's new wife, all boobs and jabber.

He cast Angela a look saying *Get to work.* There were more than forty couples from Levi's division here, and he couldn't alone make each one feel special. Sandler read her thoughts. "He's a good man. Ballsy son of a bitch." Angela wasn't sure what to say, what she should know. "Tell him to relax. You're better at it than he is. Tell him I said so."

Beside Sandler, Joy's eyes worked, looking for an opening. "I remember when I first began to work these things. Frantic. But you just get used to it. Mike, you're the best. To you. Sir." She raised her glass. Sandler barely looked at her. Joy had already given up what he wanted: information that confirmed something smelled in the ex & sell business. He'd put up with her until this trip was done, but he would not encourage her, especially publicly. Angela was not fond of Joy, but that didn't keep her from being embarrassed for her. So Angela finished the last sip of wine and set the glass on a marble table.

"Listen," Sandler said. "Why don't we split up and take care of business." He was looking at Joy. "We all have constituents here. Let's work." With that, he kissed Angela's cheek and traversed a short radius to his employees and guests and groupies.

Left alone with Angela, even for a moment, was clearly outside Joy's comfort zone. She met Angela's eyes for only an instant, pasting up a chipper face. "Well, I better charge at it." And so she did, into the crowd. Angela scanned for Levi.

"Hello, Angela." Deirdre materialized from her periphery. "I'm glad I spotted you. Looks like you could use one of these." She offered a glass of wine.

"Oh. Uh, thank you. I was just going to find my husband."

"Oh, he's working. He's an extraordinary talent, you know. Smart. Brokers love him. You must be proud." As Angela opened her mouth to respond, Deirdre raised her glass. "Here's to Levi. Here's to the privilege of working with him, side-by-side. It is my honor." Deirdre drank. How could Angela not?

"Thank you, Deirdre. That's so nice. He is smart, and he works hard. I hardly see him." She took a breath to tell Deirdre goodbye.

"If you have a minute, I have news on your insurance coverage."

"I'm sorry?" This wine wasn't as good as the first glass.

"Well, I know that you guys are working on having a family. I know that you are exploring options, you know, fertility clinics. I've done some research on your health benefits. I may have discovered some additional benefits, even access to renowned experts, which may come with being an EVP. Can we talk about them?"

Now that's out of the blue, Angela thought. *Has Levi been asking?* She liked that thought: Levi asking about fertility options. She glanced hesitantly at the crowd. "Well. I suppose. We're hosting a table at dinner. I can work the crowd then."

By the time the maître d' sent a man around the pool with dinner chimes, Deirdre had finished her explanation – thank God. Angela had to pee. She discreetly tugged at the armpits of her dress. They were a tad damp. "Is it getting hotter?"

"I think it is," said Deirdre. "I think it is."

Angela touched the glow on her forehead. "Whew. You don't look hot. We better hurry at the fertility clinic. I'm having a flash." Angela laughed, and Deirdre smiled. Maybe Deirdre wasn't so bad. "Can you excuse me? I better go before dinner."

"Ah! First a toast. To the fertility gods."

Oh, what the hell, thought Angela. "To the fertility gods." She finished her wine. "Do you need to go?"

"No, no. Unless you want me to go with you…"

"No, no." *What a nice woman,* Angela thought. She headed toward the back of the pavilion. As she rounded the pool, the water twinkled so clear, lit from below, its giant nautical mosaic, its preening marble Poseidon again, all sparkling with clean blues, crisp greens. The water never seemed so damn fresh. Quenching. She swallowed. The restrooms were full, so she waited, staring at the ocean, pushing the breeze with her body, swaying. She imagined swimming in it with Levi. Stark-ass naked. It made her laugh. A young groundskeeper asked her if she was happy. *What a hotty.* "I am!" she said. "What about you?" Why had she asked that? A slatted door opened and she scurried into the bathroom. In there, she washed her hands and forehead. She noticed her temples in the mirror, the muscles pulsing. She was clenching her jaw – news to her. "Whew. I gotta slow down." She ran her tongue at the roof of her mouth. Cottonmouth. She stuck it out at the mirror. She drifted. She jerked. "Whew. Gotta get to dinner."

At the entrance to the ballroom she passed under decorative fishnets hung from the ceiling, hammocking glass balls and starfish and a treasure chest of coins and necklaces. Crawford was standing at the table farthest away, by the stage, making opening comments into a microphone, saying, '*the one thing you need to know.*' One of the travel people with a clipboard whispered that she and Mr. Monroe were hosting Table 12, and pointed. Seven of the eight chairs there were full. Levi was there. And young Red. As Angela fairly tiptoed into the ballroom, Crawford was watching. *What a funny man*, she thought. *If he were naked, I bet I could see his ribs.* He seemed to eye her as she walked, turning with her movement, only not actually turning, like Levi says the posters in Victoria's Secret do. Angela reached the table as Crawford finished and dinner began in earnest.

No sooner had she sat down than Joy appeared from nowhere, standing between Levi's chair and hers. "May I take your husband? I have a P&L issue, boring stuff."

"Only if you can replace him for one of equal or greater value," said Angela. Levi leaned to her ear. "Are you okay?"

"Yeah, yeah." She licked her lip. "Salty. Go schmooze. I got this table." She thought she had whispered. The look from an older woman said it carried. "Hey. Red. Haven't seen you since you hitched with us on the jet. Leona, right? The new wife."

The beauty lit up and pointed. "Bar owner's daughter from Montana, right?"

"Boy, howdy," Angela said and grabbed a glass of water, downing half of it. She came up for air. Levi was still looking. "Go, go. Really. I'm good." Under table height, she pinched inside his thigh. "Go." He looked as if he wished he had a choice. He stood. Joy seemed to crowd him, touch his shoulder too long as they walked off.

"You want me to kick her scrawny ass?" Leona whispered. Angela laughed a good laugh. *Oh, Leona. Leona.* The other three couples at the table remained really erect. Must not have heard.

Angela didn't remember much of the table talk before Levi and the entrees arrived. She drank champagne because it was colder than the water. Leona drank Jack Daniels. Leona's husband, on Leona's other side, matched them drink for drink. "You're young," Angela said. Leona laughed. She sucked on Leona's ice. Hooyah.

During the entrée, Levi kept touching her every time she wanted to talk. Answering for her. She tried to touch him back, but he kept returning her hand to her own lap. One time she fiddled with the upside-down schooner pin in his lapel. *Angela, please*, he said. *It's sinking*, she explained. Finally, dessert came. The sound of a spoon against glass rang through the din. Or was it several spoons and several glasses? Up front, Mike Sandler was standing at Table #1. Angela shushed Table #12 and beamed at the thick man admiringly. She leaned into Leona. "He's just a friend," she blurted. Levi squeezed her thigh, so she whispered. "He is pretty sexy though, for an old guy."

Leona winked at her husband, who winked back.

Glasses clanged. Sandler cleared his throat. At Table #1, Crawford and Deirdre looked up at him from one side, Joy from the other – two seats away, to buffer rumors.

Angela had heard this year's speech in several other venues. She liked it, had unwittingly memorized the parts she liked the most. So she mouthed the words '*the best in the business*' in synch with Sandler. This delighted Leona. So Angela began mouthing catch phrases and tag lines and generally tickling Leona with the trick. Sandler said the brokers in this Council were "*the backbone of the organization*," but the "*spouses deserved all the money and credit for putting up with them*." Occasionally the synch was perfect, on words like "*meritocracy*" and "*core values*." Angela and Leona covered their mouths in delight, Leona's face ripening to the hue of her hair. On one long pause, they failed to notice Sandler look toward them. The others at Table #12 squirmed. Levi whispered *knock it off*. Angela was inclined to comply until she noticed the ship on his lapel pin was upside down again. She rotated it. "God," she whispered, "I hope this doesn't mean we're going under." Now the humor was lost even on Leona. A moment later, Sandler and Angela mouthed "*take your vacations because no job is worth your health*." The assembly, Angela included, courteously applauded. When the applause subsided, Sandler held, appreciating the room, acknowledging individuals with his eyes. Just as the hush reached a warm ache, Angela said to Leona, too loudly, "Now he'll cry." She twizzled her pearls and bit her lower lip. Bit her lip. Bit her lip.

As with most public calamities, those nearby looked away. Those on the fringes asked in whispers what happened. Leona paled. On some level, Angela sensed something wrong. She searched the faces by hers in succession. Each bumped out the memory of the last, restarting her daze like a hiccupping record. She recalled no gaffe.

Across the room, good fortune inflated Crawford. Deirdre leaned up to feed him a secret. She had poisoned Levi's sustenance – Sandler's patronage. Better yet, she had caused Angela to do it. As for Joy, she sat stiff, looking aghast at the Monroes and Sandler and back. Sandler did not cry. Nor did he acknowledge Angela. He smiled, gracefully, utterly void of discomfort and sentiment. He thanked the room. He said to enjoy the rest of the evening. The band by the pool was top-notch, he promised. He'd see them all in the morning. And don't miss your flights! A storm's coming.

Outside, the band struck up *Margaritaville*. Angela asked Levi to dance. She was bewildered why he didn't answer. She licked her lips. More salt. She forgot what she had just said to Levi, and it scared her. She was hot. He wouldn't look at her. He rose and strode from the ballroom to the crowd outside, some of whom were already shuffling to the music. She didn't know he was in triage mode, thinking damage control.

"Girlfriend," Leona said. "You need to find Sandler now and apologize. Now."

What was this girl saying? "For what?" Angela said.

"Oh, my, you *are* in trouble. Now listen to me. You need to drink water – nothing else, you understand? And you need to find Sandler. When you do, just say you're sorry. Do you understand? Find Sandler, and say you're sorry. Don't say why, just say you're sorry. Drink water! Then go to bed. Right away. Understand?"

Angela repeating it in her head. *Find Sandler, say I'm sorry.* "Okay." The walls were closing in, throbbing with music. She was burning up. Wanted to move.

"Now," Leona said.

By the time Angela circled the pool, she had forgotten why. The inside of her thighs slickened with sweat. She was in a party. *Hoo-hoo!* The band chanted *I Shot the Sheriff*. People danced. Levi was there, on the other side of the pool, talking with Red and brokers, his brokers. He was surrounded by brokers she knew, and wives. Beyond him was Sandler. *Find Sandler. Say I'm sorry. For what? Doesn't matter.* The music moved her head, her spine, her guts. She slid between dancers, wanting to dance with them, but they stopped. Always stopped. She pivoted a corner of the pool like an architect's compass, trying to focus on Levi, move toward Levi. Her face and chest were on fire. One corner to go. The sides of her dress were cusped with perspiration. Her temples hurt, teeth ground. Cottonmouth. The pool, so clear! Blues, greens.

"Cool, cool, cool." she said. Her dress itched her to the point of pain. Levi. Sandler. People. Music. Everything at once. Levi – looking now. Looking so hot. Cool pool. Blue and cool. "Clear, clear." She stilt-walked another corner, going to him, touching no one. Her dress was hot. His eyes got big. The music. Move! "Hot, hot." Seams burned her pits. And water. "Cool, cool." She leaned out, each pebble in the pool-bottom mosaic becoming crisp, pulsing under music and wind. A sear of heat raced the small of her back. She jumped.

The water above her deadened the beat, swallowed the white noise. It was cool. Quiet and cool. She saw only Poseidon, flaunting his brilliant dimples of blues and greens, splendid and cool. When she surfaced, she spit. The music egged her into long, languid strokes. When she reached the edge, Levi was there, his face stretched wildly. She smiled, wonderful, and people laughed. *Woo-hoo*, hollered Red. Angela waved Levi in. He looked back, over his shoulder. Sandler's back was turned, moving away. "I love you," she chimed, grinning. Levi surveyed the audience. "It's so cool. Come on," she waved. Her temples hurt, teeth ground. *Yeah, go on!* cheered Red, who gathered a tuxedoed man under each arm, yelling *Jump! Jump! Jump!* The cheer spread like light through the crowd. *Now she knows how to have fun!* a man yelled. Levi searching, she saw, for someone, something, not seeming to know who or what.

Cool. Wonderful. Angela back-floated, drinking a mouthful, and swam to him again. Crawford was well behind Levi, observing, beside Deirdre. Levi spotted them. Angela shifted away, treading water. The cheer crested. Levi took two steps toward Crawford and turned to the pool again. Then, with an aw-fuck-it gesture, he jumped. *Cannonball!*

A moment later, beneath the water, her mother's pearls caressed her chin and she was with him. Cool. Cool. Touching arms. Quiet lasted only a second before a muffled crash squeezed her ears and a Red bullet of hair shot by, trailing billows of ballgown sporting nipples and legs. A third plunge came quickly, and then more, even quicker. Surge after surge. When Angela and Levi rose for a breath, laughter was everywhere. Black suits everywhere. Dresses bobbed, undulating as if gay-colored jellyfish. Nine of them. Levi's friends and Angela's. Now ten. More. The band played *Under the Sea*. "I love Disney!" Angela squealed. "I love kids!" People sang. Her head rolled forward, cutting the arc the body would follow, spooling her trunk cross the surface and down in a languorous crack-the-whip, through the cool, the blue cool. By the time she stopped, Levi was gone.

An hour later, the music had finished. Most conventioneers had retired to their suites. The wind was blowing hard. It was after pool hours, but easy money paid for the pool and bar and hot tub to stay open. Some people were naked. "Nobody fires revenue!" was the rebel call. And this night, Angela had been revenue's princess.

In twin Turkish robes round dissolving formalwear, Leona walked Angela along mean-breaking waves. The sea sucked back, undercutting sand beneath Angela's feet. It tickled. The sensuous became sensual.

"Me and Levi have never done it on the beach," said Angela. Her imaginings rushed surf over Levi's naked back as if he lay on her now, waves washing them, sucking back under his hands and her ass.

"It's not what it's cracked up to be," said Leona. "And neither are drugs."

"Drugs? Yeah, but sex is." Angela decided to stay in sex, though she did hear herself say *Uh huh* when she should. Her mind was on stripping off her wet dress or feeling Levi do it.

Leona left when Angela unlatched the door to the villa. Levi had changed into an aloha shirt and shorts. He was slumped in the big chair with a rocks glass, watching CNN and rolling a small rum empty on his thigh. His chart book was splayed on the side table, pens scattered around it. Angela stepped in front of the television, blocking his view. She dropped her robe. She planted her feet a yard apart and pulled the hem of her sopping gown dangerously high. He craned to look around her. She peeled the dress from her breasts, one side at a time, and touched them. He stared beyond her. She rolled it farther down, exposing the full, tender swath of skin between pearls to pubes. He stood up.

"I'm going for a walk." He turned away.

"No!" she said, grabbing his hand, pulling it toward her body.

"No," he said, pulling it back. Then, softer, "Give me a few minutes." He turned his face before she could read it. She moved to drop her dress altogether, but he didn't turn toward her again. In an instant, the heavy door closed behind him.

She looked out the peep-hole as he disappeared. She turned, pacing nervously. "He said a few minutes. A few minutes. A few minutes." She checked her body. Fluffed her pubic hair for him. "A few minutes." Minutes passed. Occasionally she touched herself to ward off negative thoughts, stay

up for him. He wasn't back. "A few minutes." *Stay up for him.* She reached in
the mini-bar and cracked the twist of a Bailey's Irish Cream. Drank from it.

She held the thought of sex, letting the images roll in her head. Levi. She
went into the bathroom, looked, imagining him more than waiting now.
"He's not coming," she said, "but if he were…" She could be with her man.
She could be, even if he wasn't there. Like so many times. She started the
shower. She closed the bathroom door. Again, she stood before the mirror,
thinking of them. She stepped closer, trying not to see that she was closing
in on how she had become. What they had become. She paused and wiped
the fogging mirror. Studied herself. She raised the Bailey's, draining it onto
her tongue. Eyes on the mirror, she let her hand float down, releasing the
empty in the sink. She leaned against the wall. With the pad of one finger, she
skimmed atop her pubic hair. In her head, the image of them pulsed strongly,
and faded. She relaxed where she could, kept tension where she must.
Pleasure pulsed again, and she held it for a while, but lost it to … to sadness.
She pushed off the trough of her mood, rallied once more. Twice more. But
each pulse crested lower, dimmer; each trough became deeper. For fifteen
mechanical minutes she tried, tried to empty her head of noise, to trick her
body. Twice she came close. Twice she stopped to catch her breath. In a final,
desperate clench, her slick chest reddened and her brow strained hopelessly
to hold their image. Finally, she burst into tears, unable to continue. As she
hit her knees, a strangled longing surged from her throat.

The takeoff in the divisional jet bordered on violent, and then the plane
broke the cloud ceiling and settled to a whisper. Red – Leona – looked much
older than on the way there, her husband, plain old. After breakfast, no
talking. People slept. Angela sucked on ice from her orange juice, unable
to tie enough fragments together to be sure who all had been in the pool.
Couldn't remember. Surely not … Crawford, Deirdre, Joy – they had all left
early, caught a ride to New York with Sandler. Ahead of the storm.

Angela sat across the table from Levi while he worked his charts, checking
numbers and symbols written in columns, erasing, drawing. "I won't do this
anymore," she nearly whispered.

He didn't look up. "Do what?"

"Travel thousands of miles to be alone with these people." He said nothing.
Angela looked again at the older broker and his younger wife. "I won't keep

painting myself and waiting so long for you to notice that by the time you do, I come off as some old diaper-butted clown carcass. Or you trade me for a newer model." She still didn't have his attention. "Levi, don't you see? I wasn't drunk. I think I was drugged." Though that possibility had been trying to draw her attention since she awoke, her instinct said to ignore it. Trouble. Saying it now gave them no choice but to deal with it. Yes. She was drugged. The shame and embarrassment had redoubled this morning, but they would pass. They could now. With his help.

"Oh, for crying out loud." He scowled at the page, shaking his head at her ... her – what? Silliness? Concocted alibi? As the urge to smack him rose in her chest, she noticed his bare wrist. Her heart sank. "Where's the friendship bracelet I made you?"

"I don't think you have to go on anymore trips. Let's just hope *I* get invited, shall we?" He glanced at his wrist as if to remind himself. "It's in my bag." He returned to his charts.

31

THE DANCE

O remember in your narrowing dark hours
That more things move than blood in the heart

LOUISE BOGAN

It was sticky for May, even for the South Bay. Teachers and youngsters were hot. Folks who remembered when it was all orchards had never seen it so hot. So into each portable double-wide classroom roared the dirty-sock smell of window mounted air conditioners. But things were changing. Fifty feet away, behind a chain-link fence, workmen were pulling cable through the skeleton of a new, state-of-the-art elementary school.

Angela's twenty-five third-grade students had been sleepy since lunch, and the white noise from the fan further desensitized them. As she checked the clock, she clipped her hair up off her neck, exposing a gray root or three, and shut off the air conditioner. She was glad it was nearly 3 o'clock, dismissal time. Besides, she had a date.

Well, not a date, really. It wasn't like *that*. Brandon Cole, a fourth-grade teacher, had invited her for a drink. He was a colleague. And thirteen years her junior – nearly a boy. So why, she chided herself, had she chosen today to wear something lacey and new under her summer skirt? *So what*, she thought. *People do.* The class was looking at her. "Okay, everyone, 3 o'clock! Let's clean up!" Bantam arms and legs suddenly became animated and randomly percussed against diminutive desks. She drifted toward the door and caught a whiff of crayons and tempera paint. She loved that smell. Shiny swabs of black Asian hair bobbed around her, punctuated by errant tufts of sandy or blond. She rechecked the time. "Take your seats, everyone." She opened the door and stepped into the sunshine where she would give each child a goodbye hug if they wanted one. The bell rang and Angela hugged. As she patted the last child on the back, she spotted him – her non-date – and rolled her eyes.

Brandon was lunging frenetically between the portables, pinballing down the row like an inmate bolting through a WWII *stalag*. Wearing a baseball mitt. He was Steve McQueen in *The Great Escape*, sans the bomber jacket. But just as hot. Okay, hotter.

Sure of her attention, he crouched – bare hand on one knee, gloved one on the other. Ready. "Runners on first and second," he barked loudly. "A tremendous rip!" He dove left.

Angela plucked the clip from her hair and pocketed it.

"And Cole comes from nowhere to snare a bullet!" He popped the glove with his fist and raced to his right. "Cole tags out the runner heading for third, turns, challenging the runner approaching second ... who vainly scrambles back, no match for Cole's world-class speed!" Brandon sprung and faked another tag. "*An unassisted triple play! He's done it again! And the babes go wild!*" And he ran toward her, arms held high, into her classroom, spinning her against the door sill as she hooted and clapped. He stole a victory lap around the desks. He halted before her and playfully pulled her inside the room, walked her back a step against a bulletin board papered with planets ... and kissed her.

She did not reciprocate, at least not much, before ducking back into the sunlight. She craned to look over her shoulder. "Do I have paint on me now?" she said sternly. "Well?"

"A little. On your butt. You want me to brush it?" His voice was less sure.

Angela was momentarily transfixed by the single velvet eyebrow that mantled the rest of his square face. "No." She hoisted her chin over her shoulder in a futile attempt to see her back. Finally, she rotated her body around under her head and squared off. "I told you not to do that. I'm serious."

He faked a pout, but she knew he knew she meant it. She felt a maternal pang, and the fact that it bothered her bothered her. *No. Maternal is okay! He's a kid! Okay, a hot kid.*

"You know, your eyes dance with more light than any woman I've ever known."

"Oh, God. Maybe your vision will get better as you grow up. Or your pick-up lines."

Angela knew the type. The good looking, hometown jock who forever had women assure him of his specialness. She'd even heard that after

Brandon graduated college his mother wrote a stern letter of inquiry to each minor league baseball team that cut him at tryouts. Then his aunt, the School District human resource director, hooked him up with a teaching job. Now his coworkers were all women. He was special again. It was said he had seven tattoos. Rumors varied as to who had seen them. She wondered where they were.

"Sorry," he said. "Can we still have our second date?"

"Sharing Cheetos and Red Bull is not a date – nor is this." She turned and straightened an aisle of desks, wondering if he sensed her wrestling the dull ache low in her belly. "I invited Kathy and Mandy to join us." She stopped and looked at him, but saw no reaction. "So I'll see you there." She returned to making perfect rows.

"You want to ride in my Civic? The *seats* recline…" he teased.

Angela eyed him reproachfully. "Stop it. Persistence don't always fix dumb."

"Doesn't. Oh, I get it." So he cocked his head and lifted his long eyebrow. "*Hmmmm?*" he begged. She couldn't help but laugh. "Okay, see you there," he said, touching her hand.

She watched him walk away. "*Hmm?*" She hung behind and checked her makeup in the mirror over a sink splashed with tempera paint. "What?" she said to herself.

Chevy's Mexican restaurant brought gaily painted south-of-the-border adobe to a shopping center parking lot. On hot days the patio tables filled up early. Brandon had gone ahead to secure one. Sweet boy. From where Angela parked her Lexus SUV, she could see his back over the purple half-wall. He was greeting Kathy McDermott, a veteran fifth-grade teacher, when Mandy drove by and parked.

Mandy's car door opened and two thick, fleshy pillars swung out and rolled upright, balancing her big rump atop them like a miracle of Stonehenge. Above that rose a svelte, tan torso and the face of a runway model. To Angela, she was sex in abstract. Whenever Mandy said hello, her sensuous lips stretched out a mischievous dare Angela swore not to take. Mandy taught fifth grade as well, her first year.

On the shaded patio, Brandon floated his sunglasses on his damp-looking hair. He wore fresh cargo shorts and sandals and a tight, cashmere polo that showcased his pectoral muscles. "Hey, just in time," he said and moved to get Angela's chair. He ordered four margaritas from a waitress who smelled like fresh tortilla chips.

"I haven't drunk since Lent." Kathy said it like she was sorry.

"Big ones," Brandon said to the waitress, flexing as he held his hands, one above the other, to show the drink size. "Top shelf. I'll buy," he announced. "Everyone likes salt, right?"

"You mean you brought money *and* your ID? That's a first," Kathy said. Like Angela, Kathy was well into her thirties. She was a single mom who wore a crucifix and a grudge for an ex-husband who went to work at eBay after their divorce but before it went public. He had a young new wife and she had two difficult teenagers in Catholic school on needs-based scholarships.

"It's okay," said Brandon. "Jesus'll forgive me." He stretched his arms above his head as if to stretch his back, and his shirt rode up, exposing the thin geyser of hair on his stomach.

"Cover your pride, stud," said Kathy. "This isn't a PTA meeting. We've seen it before."

"I haven't," said Mandy. Kathy rolled her eyes. "Well, I haven't."

Kathy turned to Angela, "So when do you and Levi go to Mexico?"

"Oh, God, never, I hope," Angela said. "At least not for work."

"Ahh, you poor thing," said Kathy. "Whatever *will* the gentry do for vacation?"

"Actually, I'd rather be in Montana. Levi doesn't really take vacations, but I'm going to make him go to Italy with me. He's gone so much that he doesn't even like to go out to dinner."

Mandy weighed in. "Why can't he take time off? I thought he was king, or something." She grinned slyly at Brandon, took a drink, and touched her teeth with her tongue. "Hm. Salty." One of her fingers dallied at her smooth, modest cleavage.

"Yeah, Angela." Kathy taunted playfully. "Why *do* you think men are on the road all the time?" Brandon sat taller, eager for Angela's answer. Kathy turned to Mandy. "Quit playing with your tits." Mandy closed her hand, speechless.

Angela spun the stem of her glass. "That's not him …" she said softly. "He works hard."

"Hell," Kathy said, "what for? You can already buy half of Monta-a-a-ana," she bleated. "Wall Street hillbillies. Rural royalty meets high society. To

Angela Monroe," she toasted, "goddamn Queen of Montana!" Even Brandon laughed. "If I didn't love ya, I'd hate ya. Ah, hell. Why not spend it? You don't have kids—" She instantly winced at herself.

In the last two years, Angela had been pregnant three times, all ending tragically. The doctors eventually decided she was unable to produce enough progesterone to grow an adequate placenta. They said they could supplement her progesterone, but now her uterus was prematurely senescent – by which they meant old. That's when she stopped paying fertility specialists.

"Ah, shit," Kathy said. "I'm sorry, Angela."

"Hey. No big deal," Angela deflected the gaffe. "I don't have to worry about birth control anymore. And no more preparing romantic meals at home."

"Woo-hoo," said Mandy, well into her second margarita. She nudged Brandon under the table. "What kind of meals?"

"Let's move on," Kathy said.

"No, I'm serious." Mandy took a clinical tone. "What kind of meal *would* one prepare for a man you want to make you pregnant?"

Kathy's face tightened in disgust. "Oh, God. What's the opposite of oysters?"

Angela poked Kathy. "Jesus, Kath, maybe *you* need to get laid." That's when Mandy cleared her throat like she knew something. Angela raised her brows at Kathy. "What? You? Come on, give it up."

Kathy threw her straw at Mandy. "His name is Bob Nelson. He's a VP at EcoPulse."

"*Aaand ...*" said Mandy.

"And I met him on a Christian fellowship website for singles. There. Okay?"

Mandy laughed heartily and Angela said *ick* and Kathy said it wasn't like that. Brandon asked if she used an anti-virus program, and the women said shut up in unison.

"Bob is ... big," Kathy said in all seriousness. "You know ... tall." They laughed some more, but Brandon particularly drew Kathy's ire. "Listen, stud, unlike some here, he's old enough to stay in a long time."

That drew a reproachful *ooooo*'s until Angela said, "Yeah – or until a girl coughs," and everyone laughed as one again.

After his third margarita, as the sun set over JC Penney, Brandon said it would be fun to go dancing at Mountain Charley's, a raucous kids' bar in Los

Gatos. Kathy said bullshit. Only after Mandy pled that she didn't want to be the only girl did Angela agree to go.

Both chic, Los Gatos was unlike Saratoga Village. Saratoga was sedate, where wealthy families and the over-forty crowd dined and were home by ten. But Los Gatos was prowled by trust-fund babies and corporate climbers, most young or pretending to be. Casual and upscale, after-dark players packed micro-breweries, lounges, and bars to drink, dance, and hook up.

Behind an unassuming door on the main sidewalk, Angela followed Brandon up a long, narrow stairway as music thundered down the walls. Two girls in tight tops squeezed past Angela and then whispered and giggled, looking back up on their way down. Brandon paid the cover charge. Inside in the din and diffused light they faded into a deep, blue-jeaned line of kids pressing a battered, ornate bar and bellowing into bartenders' ears. As if misplaced, deer, elk, and moose heads jutted from the walls. *Just like home,* Angela thought, *but not.* On a tiny, low stage before a heavy, black curtain, a DJ played deafening music, all bass and drums and nasty. Angela felt it beat her chest. The crowd on the dance floor dry humped. Brandon's hip rubbed hers. He bobbed his head and bellowed, "Classic."

She nodded. She'd never heard the song. Angela spotted Mandy across the room, holding down a dark, wooden table, and yelling sociably into the upright crotch of the blond-haired guy who yelled back down at her. Finally Mandy noticed Angela and waved them over.

About when Angela noticed that Mandy's cleavage had become sparkly, the DJ played another hump song and the atmosphere ratcheted up even farther. Brandon snared Angela's hand and dragged her through the mob to the dance floor and commenced gyrating around her – on her? – accelerating toward full rut. She self-consciously looked to see if Mandy was watching. She wasn't. Angela imagined Levi in the crowd and felt suddenly naked. Then she imagined him working the crowd, uninterested. When the song finished, she pulled Brandon to the table.

Mandy had set up two Red Bull-and-vodkas and two shot chasers – each. "Bottom shelf. The railest vodka they got," she hollered. Brandon hooted and lofted one shot glass, grinning mindlessly. He held another for Angela, standing close. She could smell his body. *I'm in trouble,* she warned herself.

They danced again, and she let him be behind her this time, let him touch a little. She'd heard high school teachers complain about freakin'. What if they saw her now? She gave herself to it. And she drank. She surged with the core of the tribe, and more and more, as her hair melted on her face, she rocked her ass into Brandon's crotch. Other breasts brushed against hers. Splendidly. Anonymously. For a time she was faces with Mandy whose blond guy was drunk with her ass, and the women's necks and chests glistened and smelled of sweat and before long Angela, too, sparkled with body-glitter. No speeches, no banquets, no rules.

Mandy leaned into her ear. "You're freakin' hot for an old chick, I mean, cougar." Angela wanted to kiss her. Mandy motioned for Angela's ear again. "Now try dancing in time with the music." They laughed. She motioned again. "Look, if you're okay, I'm outta here," and she rolled her eyes toward the blond guy. "He wants to get a booth at The Black Watch." It was a dark lounge where folks drank their liquor. "I don't think we'll make it there." Angela's eyes said, *You can't leave! What am I supposed to do with…*, but Mandy grinned and leered toward Brandon and back. "Relax. It's the new millennium." Then Mandy looked at blondy.

No speeches, no banquets, no rules, thought Angela. "You go, girlfriend!"

"God!" Mandy shrieked with delight. "You *are* old … and hopelessly white … *girlfriend*." She laughed and jerked the blond guy by his belt buckle to stop his humping for a minute. "See you tomorrow." And then, "Be good …. or tell me about the tattoos."

By then it was after midnight and the bar was its most crowded. Angela thought about leaving but chose not to decide. Usher played, and Alicia Keyes, and Mary J. Blige. And they danced. "Classic!" Brandon yelled, and she leaned back against his chest. His fingers found her belly, slid down until she wondered if he felt her hair. At last the tempo slowed, deep and heavy, and Brandon faced Angela and wrapped her in. She stopped thinking as she straddled his leg, pressing down, and simply felt. And hung on.

"Follow my car," he said, and she nodded. He led her out. She followed his car, listening to hip-hop radio, playing it loud and not deciding. She parked on the street by his condo and listened until he opened her door. In the entryway, he paused only to close the door before kissing her, salty and deep. His hand gathered her skirt until his fingers were between her legs. She stopped him. He unbuttoned his pants and unzipped. He guided her hand. His skin was hot. She squeezed him once, pushed her tongue in his mouth, and pulled away. Three times they kissed passionately, her skirt rose, and the scent of sex grew stronger. Three times she regathered herself. "I have to go," she said, over and over, and finally, agonizingly, she meant it. He held her face, and she smelled herself on his fingers. She kissed him hard and said, "I'll see you tomorrow," and he walked her to her car.

All the way home, her body buzzed. It buzzed while she scraped the mail from her big mailbox, while she unlocked the door of her house. She disabled the security alarm. She turned up the lights on the Monroe showroom and dropped her keys on the kitchen table, still holding the mail. There was a bill-sized envelope from the Stanford Fertility and Reproductive Medicine Center. She didn't open it. Not yet ready for reality, she decided not to open anything. She checked the answering machine. There was a message from the lawn guy, a reminder from her hair stylist. Then Levi's voice. He was sorry he missed her, but he was spending the night in – Angela pushed the erase button.

On her way to the bedroom, she removed her shoes and let her naked feet feel the carpet. In the master bathroom, she peeled away her damp blouse and pants and dropped them on the floor. She looked at herself in the mirror and replayed the night in her head. The dancing. His skin. Hot. His skin. She held her hand to her face. Imagining. Finally, she closed her eyes and went to him. To Brandon.

32

Role Playing

Hope is a pathological belief in the
occurrence of the impossible.

H. L. Mencken

Levi stood in a suit beside a date palm outside a hotel near LAX. Through the man-made funk from car exhaust and oasis landscaping, he swore he could smell jet fuel exhaust from the sky and urine from the guy by the planter. He jammed a finger in one ear and held his new phone, which seemed much too delicate, gingerly against the other. His elbows jutted out to vent his pits because it was 90 degrees at 10 A.M. All summer he had been coast-to-coasting and puddle-jumping, and every day *USA Today's* weather map showed nothing but red, New York to Los Angeles. Maybe Abba was right, he thought. "I'm sorry, what?" he asked Angela, even as he marveled at a valet bringing around another $80,000 car and handing the keys to a trim, twenty-something blonde with an improbable figure. Nothing here was straightforward. Nothing.

"I miss you," Angela said.

"I'll be home tomorrow." He scanned his watch. He had five minutes to get back inside.

"Aren't you tired of me saying that?"

"I miss you too, honey. I love you." He delivered his lines, trying not to sound hurried.

"Levi, I'm tired of California. I want to go home ... with you."

"You know I can't take time off right now."

"No. I mean it's *time* to go home. We need to *go home*. To *live*."

"Oh. Can we talk about this later?" Silence. "Angela, I can't quit now. We'd lose millions. You know that. And if Crawford goes down, I..."

"When, then? When will it be time? It *never* all vests." She seemed edgier than usual.

The truth of the words hit Levi unexpectedly hard, and ever-stalking doom touched his back. *My God*, a voice called within, *what if it WILL never be time?* From nowhere, his father's face loomed inside. He erased it. *Not now.*

"I don't know," Levi said. "Not now. Besides, if Montana is what you mean by home, what town do you have in mind?" A plane roared over. He checked the time. "Billings? With all the seedy little casinos, it might as well be Elko. And I don't want to go to Roundup. And speaking of Roundup, what the hell will *they* do if we quit giving them money? If I quit now, everyone suffers. And what about the Monroe House?" He started walking. "Listen, Crawford's waiting."

"The shelter is already named after you. And they have other donors now. What about Italy?"

"Named after *us*. And what about Italy?"

"If we can't go home, let's travel. Just us. Let's see where my dad's from. Anywhere."

"I'm trying. Things are wild. Maybe in a while." He heard nothing. "It's for us."

"While you're up on that cross, look toward your own house."

"What? What does *that* mean?"

"It needs to be shorn up."

"I can't…"

"Our phone records arrived today," she said as if fishing.

"What phone records?"

"I thought maybe you'd tell me."

"I have no idea what you're talking about."

"A big envelope came in the mail today. It was a record of every phone call we've made for the last six months – from home, from my cell, from yours."

"You're kidding. Why would they send us that?" Immediately he tried to imagine anything in the records he couldn't explain to her. Joy? No. He could cover that. *Everything's related to business. But what about time of day? What if she looked at times? And who the hell asked for records? Maybe she's baiting. No. Not Angela.*

"The cover letter says 'Per your request.'"

"I never requested anything. They made a mistake. Listen, I'll call you at the break."

"I'll be in class, then the gym. I'm going out later with Kathy, Mandy, other teachers."

"I'll try later then. Leave your phone on." He listened for a reply. What other teachers? "I have to go. Okay? Goodbye." He heard nothing. "I said goodbye."

"I said goodbye."

"I couldn't hear you. Okay, goodbye. I … goodbye."

"Goodbye."

Inside, crossing the lobby, he tried to imagine Angela moving with him to New York if Crawford got sacked – *when* Crawford got sacked. It was inevitable. Sandler *can't* be so blind. President. It could happen. Why not? What's with the phone records? He tabled the thought. Outlast Crawford, he thought, and Angela would move with him to New York. Wouldn't she?

Deep inside a farcically large, near-barren banquet room of modular carpet and movable walls, at a long, draped table, Levi took his seat in the line of five executive observers. As always, Gary Crawford sat on the left end next to Deirdre Oliver from HR, so Levi had snuck in early and dropped his briefcase on the far right. Between them were two of Levi's counterparts, divisional directors from the Heartland – older, honorable men, men with perspective. Deirdre provided each panelist with a three-ring binder. The hotel furnished coffee and pastries.

At the distant center of the chilly room was a small table with two stackable chairs – a "simulated office." From time to time a candidate for management training, often a broker with flagging sales who fancied management as a safe harbor, was shown in and sat on one side of the table and pretended to be a manager sitting at his or her desk. Across the fake desk, a corporate trainer, usually a former broker who'd done even worse, would play the problem employee.

The *problem employee* role was always one of five or six stock characters such as a big producer who demanded too much, a female employee who felt harassed or discriminated against, or an under-producing employee who needed to be disciplined. The management candidate was to solve the hypothetical conflict, and they were told to be natural because there were a myriad of valid solutions. But Crawford, it was known, recognized only one or two. He would nix candidates with original thought. "Poor judgment," he was fond of saying. So as word got around, Crawford found that good judgment abounded. In fact, he was singularly unaware that before most candidates were assessed, they would practice Crawford's role-play solutions with their hometown managers until they had memorized good judgment. Even a cheat sheet was in circulation. All the other panel members were amused by Crawford's witless smugness about the high caliber of management applicants under his leadership.

This day Crawford had instructed housekeeping to keep the room cold, the idea being to distract the candidates and "ratchet up the fear factor." Next, he had Deirdre remove the tablecloth and skirt from the role-play table so there would be "nowhere to hide." The water pitcher on the candidates' table was empty, and the pencil lead was broken. "Let's use props, not crutches," Crawford admonished.

Ten minutes before each role-play, in an adjacent room, a nervous candidate in his lucky suit was handed a two-page printed summary about the hypothetical history of a theoretical office and the background of a simulated employee. The candidate was to quickly assimilate the proposed scenario. Once a role-play started, it lasted exactly twenty uninterrupted minutes, during which the panel members ranked communication skills, poise, judgment, job knowledge, professional appearance and such on a scale of one to five. Afterward the candidate remained seated at the little table for debriefing.

The first candidate, Ken Ogfasu from Oakland, was sponsored by Levi. When Ken's role-play ended, Deirdre, who wore friendly pastel sweaters at these drills, gently appeared from behind her laptop and lobbed in her stock question. "How do you feel that went?"

"I thought I did well," Ken said. She invited him to sit, but he declined. The 32-year-old stood squarely, relaxed, brandishing confident, smart eyes.

Deirdre's fingers just met her keyboard. "What would you have done differently?"

"I would have spoken louder," Ken said. "I sense that the panel had trouble hearing me over the air conditioning."

Levi laughed, ending Ogfasu's chances with Crawford.

"The question, Mr. Og-fa-su," Crawford said, "is would you have fired your most important producer or let him destroy the morale of your office?" In Crawford's mind, he had asked a question to which he would deem either answer wrong.

Throughout the day, every time Levi's candidate came before the
panel, Crawford discharged one unsolvable question after another at him,
dismantling the man's prospects of approval before the three otherwise
neutral – but subordinate – assessors.

In the end, the assessors had each dutifully scored fifteen role-plays. At
5 o'clock, they gave their score sheets to Deirdre. The tabulation would be
revealed to the reconvened executives at Gary's favorite restaurant off Pacific
Coast Highway in Malibu. The anticipation alone quelled Levi's appetite.

The air seemed hot and sloppy when Levi climbed in the limo with the other
two divisional directors. Everyone made cell calls. Levi had one message:
Angela reminding him that the balloon payments were due on the Saratoga
house and one of the Roundup houses, and did he want to refinance both or
just one? Could they sell any stock yet? She said don't call back because she'd
be out with the crew. She loved him.

During dinner they sat at a picture window overlooking the surf. Crawford
knew the sommelier, Mitchell, and made a show of ordering an obscure label.
For himself, he chose decaf.

As they discussed the candidates, Levi played as if he were engaged but
relaxed. Like his counterparts, he offered Crawford colorless observations,
void of sharp points on which he could be skewered. *This candidate definitely
has potential,* or *That candidate is fairly unique,* or *The way she handled the
scenario merits thought.* Trying hard to say nothing made his guts ache.

During the entrée Levi escaped to the restroom, which was temptingly
close to an open back door. Outside, a Mexican kid in an apron and paper hat
was smoking. Inside, as Levi washed his hands, he saw a thinner face in the
mirror than he expected. He peevishly tucked in his shirt, cinching his belt a
notch tighter. When he exited, the Mexican kid smiled invitingly enough, so
Levi paused and ducked outside into the orange sunset and bummed a red-
box cigarette – *Montañas.* The humidity made it burn slowly, thickening the
smoke. He needed to use the bathroom again. Once back at the table he acted
fine, just fine, thanks, while he waited, endured the time, until Crawford
finally, mercifully, signed the check.

As the valet captain signaled a limo, Crawford pulled Levi aside. "It's time
we had a talk," Crawford said forebodingly.

"Okay," Levi tried to sound fearless. "When?"

"Back at your hotel."

"Should I meet you downstairs or in your suite?" Levi asked.

"I'm not staying at *that* hotel," he said as if Levi didn't get it. "How about your suite?"

What an asshole, thought Levi. "Great."

"Fine. We'll meet there."

Levi again shared a limo with the other directors.

Deirdre stayed behind with Crawford, who signaled for his limo.

"I think I have a solution to our NASD problem," Crawford said.

By the time Levi entered his suite his forehead was waxen and his guts were processing a ball of nails. His charts would have to wait. He washed his face. As he dried it, the door bell rang. Midway between the love seat and wet bar, he grimaced. He blew out a deep breath and opened the door to the watery white noise of an indoor courtyard. Against the balcony railing, six feet away, Crawford held a regal pose, as if the echoed voices three stories below were his tribute. He turned fluidly.

"May I come in?" he asked with palpable warmth.

Smiling? Perhaps this wouldn't be so bad, Levi thought. With a soft, open palm, Crawford insisted Levi enter first. Behind them, the heavy door fit its frame like a vault, smothering the noise inside with quiet. Crawford walked comfortably to the bar. He drew a wine bottle and studied the label. "Do you drink martinis?" he asked offhandedly. Levi said he didn't. Crawford reconsidered the wine. "Hmm. This is okay. Mind if I open it?"

Levi touched his abdomen. "All right. But I always assumed you don't drink."

Crawford smiled. "There's a great deal you don't know about me, young man."

"I'm not surprised." Levi walked behind the bar and handed a corkscrew to Crawford. By the time he pivoted for two glasses from the upper cabinet and turned back, Crawford was standing by the sofa. He was holding his little fingers clear and twisting the corkscrew down the throat of the bottle. He motioned for Levi to sit on the couch. He pried out the cork, offering another smile as though he was in no danger of running out of them.

"To be more accurate," Crawford said. "I don't drink during business."

This isn't business? Then what? Friends? Levi placed the glasses on the table and sat on the love seat as Crawford poured. Instead of taking the matching chair, Crawford sat beside him.

"How do you think today went?" asked Crawford.

Business – thank God, Levi thought. Maybe Levi was in a stronger position than he had presumed. Maybe Crawford needed *him.* Nevertheless, Levi would not abandon caution. "I believe it went well. Several of the candidates have strong potential."

"I think so. Perhaps not your boy, Ken." Crawford took a mouth of cabernet as he coyly draped one leg over the other, pointing his foot toward Levi. "Was I too hard on you today?"

Levi turned toward Crawford and crossed his leg, showing Crawford the sole of his shoe. "I appreciate that this is a serious business. I guess you kept me on point."

Crawford laughed lightly through prim lips. "I don't know about that. But you're learning." He drank heartily, then stood from the sofa, removed his jacket, and threw it on the chair. "I have to admit, *I'm* learning to appreciate *you.*" Levi flashed on his charts, wanting to check them. The bedroom was impossibly far away. Crawford's orderly shirt seemed stitched to his pants. He lifted his glass again and sat, resting his elbow on the back of the sofa, letting his hand dangle limply. He shifted his weight to the hip nearest Levi. "You're a complicated man."

"I'm not so complicated." *Games like this are what's complicated.*

"I'm not the only one in the boardroom who thinks so."

Who else? Sandler? Levi had barely spoken with Sandler in months, since the island fiasco. When he did, Sandler seemed fine. Levi was careful to appear neither malicious toward Crawford nor covetous of his job. Meanwhile, behind the scenes, he worked an internal investigator in their New York Compliance office, a friend from the Billings days, attempting to glean what's-what regarding Crawford's past practices in the Western division. Compliance had sandbagged him, revealing nothing. Had they tipped Crawford? Levi would call Sandler tomorrow, find an unrelated reason, and get the lay of the land. For the moment, on the love seat, each waited for the other to talk. Levi sipped. Crawford drank.

Crawford re-primed the pump. "You can send mixed messages. For instance, you coach – well, some say 'bark at' – managers and brokers about best-practices on sexual harassment issues and responsibility with their personal finances, yet you gave $500 to a sales assistant who moonlights as a stripper."

How the hell did he know that? It was cash. "She had just started working for us. We failed to process her first paycheck. She's a single mom. Her rent was due. Even Angela knows."

Crawford smiled again. "Still, it's against policy, and it's poor judgment. Word gets around. People can misperceive your motive. Then there's the issue of decorum."

"What issue of decorum?"

"Well, you ride the managers about professionalism in their offices—."

"I don't think I *ride* them."

"...yet you wore a *costume* to a lease negotiation?"

"Oh. San Rafael. It was Halloween, Gary. People wear costumes, regardless of policy. And the office was demoralized. The manager, your friend, invited me. Half the office wanted him fired and had told me so. You only allowed me to put him on probation. Some folks were threatening to leave. They had no leadership – in their opinion – and their lease was due because – in their opinion – we wouldn't sign it. It sent a pretty gloomy message."

"You say their manager didn't show leadership? What were you?"

"At the time I was their divisional director, but I can't be there for morale every day."

Humored, Crawford touched Levi's foot. "I meant, what was your costume?" Levi's disoriented look seemed to tickle him more. Crawford pulled a small, square envelope of Sen-Sens from his pocket. "Mint?" Puzzled or embarrassed or ... something, Levi took one.

"A court jester," Levi said, "with a sign hanging from my neck that said '*lease negotiator.*' The employees thought our sincerity in negotiating a lease had become a joke."

Crawford laughed delightedly.

So this is why he doesn't drink. "They didn't even know where they'd be working. They thought we were closing them down. As I said, they were about to jump ship."

"Did you wear *tights?*"

Levi couldn't decode Crawford's intent, but the way he was mining details was creepy. "I wore the whole costume." Crawford smiled lazily. "Gary, I wore it to loosen them up. I was going to change before popping in on the landlord, but he showed up. He got a kick out of the outfit. We took pictures. The next week he met our terms. Net-net, it was good for morale."

"A court jester," Crawford repeated. He refilled his wine glass and leaned back toward Levi. "Tights! No wonder you moved from Montana." He sighed. "I bet you looked good in tights, though," he laughed pleasantly. "Do you have the pictures?"

At once Levi became windless. "I wouldn't know where to look for them," he managed.

"Don't be so glum. Sandler doesn't know this one. You might mean well, but you need to be more *presidential*. Don't take it wrong. You're just not ready. You'll get there. I'll help."

This one? What did he mean, this one? Did Crawford mean for him to be insulted or grateful? Or afraid? Was Crawford drunk? "Frankly, I wasn't so concerned about being presidential," Levi carefully explained, "as about building goodwill with skilled colleagues."

"No, no. I understand," and Crawford sounded, at first, as if he did. "San Rafael's worth saving. Though bedroom communities are a poor return on time." He took a drink. "Sandler doesn't know you cosigned a two million dollar note for some charity, either."

"It's a child abuse center. Children and women."

"Well, you didn't reveal it on your financial disclosure. It's a shame to have you take a strike because you didn't tell us, not to mention the risk. Sometimes you seem to have this pathological need to save the unwashed. You'll end up dirty," Crawford said. Levi was speechless, not from Crawford's crassness, that was constant, but from the realization that a background check was being run. Phone records? Crawford sighed. "By the way, have you found a sponsor for the Bohemia Club?" Crawford was still a member thanks to Karl's father, though he intended to drop Lutheranism. Bookman Stuart's board had more Jews. "They've loosened up. Jimmy Buffet's in, and Colin Powell."

"I've been pretty busy. Besides, I'd rather work."

"You're a tough one, Levi." On *tough one*, he threw a little jab with his fist. "But I'd bet there's a certain warmth inside." On *warmth*, he rested his open hand on Levi's knee.

Levi looked at Crawford's manicure. His boss's palm was warm on his leg. Crawford offered another mint and stared. *Just do something, move, anything!*

Levi took it, but immediately something inside of him wished he hadn't. *I don't fucking believe this*, thought Levi, as he scrambled for an out. "What do you think of Ken?" Except for his mouth, the rest of Levi's body was frozen.

"I'm sorry?" Crawford didn't move his hand.

"Ken." Levi slid his leg off the love seat and anchored his feet on the floor in front of him. "From Oakland. Has he got any chance with you … to get through assessment?"

"It's still possible, my friend. It's just a question of skill and desire … and discretion." Crawford scooted forward on the sofa and picked the bottle from the coffee table. "More?"

Levi stared straight ahead at his wine glass. He looked at his scar, felt it. The gray bled outward. "Can you excuse me?" he said. He walked to the bathroom and closed the door.

To buy time, Levi lifted the toilet lid until it struck the tank for the noise. He looked in the mirror. He was thin, pale, with fearful eyes. A boy again. *Dammit!* He needed to get a grip. "It's the neon," he hoped in a low voice, knowing hope was no strategy. He held his breath. Strained. In his head screamed *Dear God!* until his face felt pregnant with blood. But his reflection only looked darker. Darker. He drifted. *Hm,* he mused. *Look at that vein.* His forehead closed to two inches from the glass. His eyes – pupils on irises, coals on gunmetal. Suddenly he flinched back, exhaling. He struck a strong posture and face. He could handle this. He was a grown man, for crying out loud, physically stronger than Crawford – why did *that* matter? Forget that. Okay. *Be* presidential. He unzipped and stood in front of the toilet, tightening his stomach to pee with some force, make some strong noise. Buy more time. He couldn't relax his buttocks enough without fear his colon would betray him. He should sit. *No!* No hole-noises. That *sure as hell* wasn't presidential. All right, he wouldn't pee. He felt nauseous. The Sen-Sen. *A fucking mouth of perfume.* He spit it into the toilet. *Zip up.* He crowded the door and zipped loudly. He flushed and turned on the tap and washed his washed-out hands – *it's the neon!* – and his gray, gray scar. The soap was still pink. Okay. But in the mirror his face was *not* pink. His face was *not* pink! Dammit! With palms on the vanity, his head dropped. *Shit.* He checked his shaving kit. No pills.

At last Levi reentered the sitting room. He remained standing.

Crawford had moved to the big chair. His suit jacket was on. He sat erectly, a leg crossed in a powerful triangle. His skinny foot drew circles in the air. His hands overshot the armrests, one of them twisting the stem of a near-empty wine glass between forefinger and thumb. "Are you well?" he asked.

"Yes. Fine." Levi smiled. "Thanks." He sat on the sofa and looked for his glass.

Crawford's voice had turned clinical, his eyes mean. "As I mentioned, you're complicated. Employees seem to respond better to you on a local level. You also seemed happier in a branch office."

Levi would give him no ground. "I'm pretty happy in my current position."

"What do you think about yourself, about *you*, when you consider how few people get to do what you do, how few people, even on Wall Street, make this kind of money? From Round-up, Montana," he said *Roundup* with a derogatory drawl, "how did you get here?" Crawford kept twisting his glass, now swabbing his teeth with his tongue.

"We were a mounted people."

Crawford was unaffected.

"Look, I know I'm good, but yes, sometimes I wonder who invited me to this party. I'm thankful. Okay."

Energized, Crawford sat forward. "*Now* we're getting somewhere."

"What?"

"You still haven't filled the management slot on the Peninsula, the one in exercise & sell that Joy wants."

And now we're talking about jobs in exercise & sell? "I realize that we've gone eight months with no one in that position, but I still think Karen's our best choice. You like Joy. Okay. You're the boss. I'll go with Joy." Levi hoped to deflect whatever was coming.

"Forget Joy. *You* enjoyed local management. And you can make a healthy bonus in that position. It's close to your home. You could sleep with your wife ... every night." Levi stared at the man incredulously. "Further, that office may have some regulatory problems. Perhaps they're Joy's problems. Joy can be transferred away from you. Maybe you'll fix it, be the hero." Levi was not biting. Crawford continued, "I don't see any reason to inform Sandler of these ... issues."

"What issues!"

"Joy. Costumes. Playing with receptionists. Stability issues, really. Need I go on?"

Joy, Levi thought. *Did she tell him? The phone records! Of course. You! You fucker.* Levi had heard of pretexting – calling the phone company, giving a Social Security number, getting copies of records. They could do it. Crawford could hire someone to do it. Like at Hewlett Packard. Shit, HP did it to board members!

"Stability?" Did Crawford know about his shrink? Instantly Levi decided to change tacks. "The costume was a matter of honor. We implicitly promised we gave a shit about those employees, and a little comic relief launched the beginning of honoring that promise."

"People don't want honor out of leaders. They think they do, but they don't. What they want most is dignity. Honor is incidental. In leadership, dignity trumps honor any day. Winners project dignity." Crawford held his head a tad higher, raised his chest.

"So instead of 'What's the right thing to do?' I should ask 'How'm I lookin'?" Levi's hands fisted; his nails dug at his scar. "Are you threatening to ruin my marriage? My career?"

"You'd be wise to know I have no patience for histrionics."

In a low, private voice, Levi murmured, "I lose this, I become them."

Crawford groaned. "I can only imagine who 'them' is. This conversation is over. You have no choice. You *will* end up in that branch." Crawford set down his glass and stood.

"What about the NASD inquiries in that branch? Word is the SEC is already involved. Those aren't my deals." *This is not presidential.*

"There is a great deal to do."

"I don't see myself back in a branch," Levi asserted. "I like working on a larger scale, and I've had excellent results – revenue growth, bottom line, recruiting, retention…"

As if to block him, Crawford squared with Levi, two feet away. "It's time you took direct responsibility of *only* the exercise & sell business. There's one thing you need to know, Mr. Monroe," Crawford condescended. "Making you a senior executive was a mistake. Period. Maybe it's cultural conflict, your background, maybe not. Doesn't matter. It is what it is."

"No. What this *is* is wrongful termination! How do I know you won't try to use the same things against me later? I'd like to talk with Deirdre Oliver. No, not her. Mike Sandler."

"You have reached my limit! Remember, the SEC, the New York Stock

Exchange and the NASD require us to have *branch managers* in every branch
– it's the law – but they don't dictate how many *division directors* we have. *I*
do. Give that some thought. You are dangerously close to being out on the
street, mister." Then he walked to the door.

"I have options, Gary. And they're not all with this firm."

Crawford smiled humorously. "You must mean the job Abba Ramakapur
talked with you about – as their staff investment banker? I wouldn't count on
it. I'm having dinner with Abba tomorrow." Then he left.

At 3 A.M., in his suite, Levi lay naked at the perimeter of lamplight, on his
side, knees drawn up, bedspread clutched at his throat and knotted around
his cell phone. He had tried to call her cell phone, but it wasn't on. So he
was listening again to Angela's voice on their answering machine at home.
"Where are you?" he whispered. He panted and blinked so he could make
another wish on the floaters in his eyes.

As his vision caved in, his shallow breath halted. He became mesmerized
by the wood-grain of the nightstand. He saw microscopic cells, boxy and
pithy. New cells burst forth from old ones and then arrested. His mind
panned out to behold a menacing mountain where stands of age-silvered
pines stood dead. He saw himself on the mountain's sheer face, suddenly
there, eyes cast up at a winter-gray branch with two branches of its own
curved off in a flexing cross, around which his whitened fingers choked a
slipping, crumbling skin of bark. The limb cracked from the tree's crotch.
A kind, beckoning sky swiftly darkened, grew indistinguishable from the
malevolent rocks. He dare not reach. Frantic, he peered down. His stomach
and legs dulled and smudged as though half-erased. He dangled alongside
sheer winter stone, a thousand feet high, over leafless, ashen beds of rigid
willows, accusingly pointed and hard, blunts rust-smeared of feces and
blood, pointing, pointing, threats in a row, wrapping outward, coiling,
coiling, again and again. Endless. Stop! No! Never again!

He drew a sharp, desperate breath. *Where?* Heartbeat in Levi's eyes. A
hotel bed. *My heart. Naked.* He didn't move for fear of falling. Very still. His
rational self watched, coaching him back. Eyes. Moving eyes would be okay,
if he was careful. He'd focus hard on something close … a bubble of snot
grew and shrunk from one nostril. One eye closed. He marveled at how
much mucous sinuses could produce. Limitless. Maybe. He opened both

eyes, looked cross-eyed at the bubble, breathing through his mouth. He exhaled from his nose and the bubble burst. A foot farther, his cell phone. "Please, God, make her call."

PART 4

33

Employee Assistance

The screwin' you get for the screwin' you got.
Colloquial saying

All weekend Charley Peterson's stomach had clotted with dread, and now it was Monday. The lanky, bespectacled manager of the Bookman Stuart office in Billings pulled his summer-tan suit jacket off the coat tree in his office and put it on. He always wore his jacket when someone was in trouble. He straightened his tie and glasses and sat behind his desk. His new operations manager, Laura Darling, of the Roundup Darlings, was perched in one of the guest chairs, armed with a legal pad. She was sixtyish and trim, an unintended spinster who wore tight dresses and Wonderbras, and she had come to the firm after an ill-fated affair with the president of the bank in Billings Heights where she had worked forever. She looked at Charley expectantly. He took a deep breath, picked up the phone and summoned his administrative assistant, Lynette Brigham, from the desk just outside his door, the same desk she sat at when she worked for Levi. "Lynette, could you come in here?"

"As soon as I finish this letter." Her head pounded. She had no particular letter in mind. As she held her desktop for ballast, she reached under it for her purse where she kept gum.

Charley's voice again. "Why don't you save that until later? Come on in."

Lynette opened her compact mirror and checked her makeup. She had applied it at stoplights this morning. Her eyes looked tired, and the gray roots at her temples were showing. She grabbed a spiral notepad and trudged into Charley's office. She looked at Charley and then at Laura. She looked at Charley again. She knew this drill. "Can this wait? I've got a pile of work." At that point she watched Charley check Laura's face for instruction before leaning in and resting his forearms on his desk. "I guess not." Lynette sat in the empty guest chair.

Charley cleared his throat. "Lynette, Laura and I continue to be concerned about your ... well ... behavior. Laura tells me you were late again this morning."

"I was not! I was in the bathroom. Can't I even go to the bathroom? And since when do I report to her?" She pointed her pencil at Laura's chicken-skin cleavage.

"Corporate guidelines now deem that all support personnel report to the operations manager," said Charley. "Laura's the operations manager."

"I've been here seventeen years, Charley, and the manager's assistant has always reported to the manager. That would be you. Laura's been here three months, and that guideline is just a guideline. I assume they didn't print it on Bible paper." A moment passed. "Sorry. It's not you."

Laura smiled condescendingly. "You should never assume, Sweetie. You know what they say, assuming only makes an ass out of you" – she pointed a wicked finger at Lynette – "and me," and pointed at herself.

Lynette stared with bewilderment. How could Charley listen to this bitch, and why did she keep one pen in her hand and another in her hair? She looked back at Charley. "I *was* on time today, and you know things are difficult. I had the kids last night, and they're out of school today, and I had to drive them out to the farm to spend the day with their dad – who doesn't even want *to see* Caleb, the older one – treats him like a stranger." She closed her eyes and raised her eyebrows. "He even wonders who the father is. God knows why." Suddenly Charley looked away, Laura gloated, and Lynette's face reddened, wishing she could pull that one back. It seemed that everyone in the room made the same guess as to the *why*, a guess Lynette had toyed with for years.

"Laura said she saw your car on her way to work this morning ... outside the Wild West Saloon."

"It was not!" Lynette sat bolt-upright, selling her outrage. "And since when is it anyone's business? If I wanted rocks thrown at me, I'd go to a church picnic." She glared at Laura.

"Professionals in financial services do not hang out at bars," Laura said in a maternal tone that only fed Lynette's ire, "but you're right. What you do in your off-time is up to you. Unless it breaks the firm's laws."

"Policies," Lynette said, exasperated.

"What?"

"Write this down. Governments – make – laws. Firms – make – policies. It'll be on the general securities exams, if you ever take them." She didn't add, *you stupid bitch.* Lynette looked pleadingly at Charley, who smiled back painfully.

"Lynette, Laura noticed that one of our clients wrote a check from his account to you for $500."

Her face drained as though a gut artery had burst. She closed her eyes and took a deep breath before she opened them. "That was a loan. We were dating." Lynette's face grew red. "Since the divorce began, I haven't had access to money. It's tied up in his family's corporation. The kids and I live on my salary. As for the $500, I didn't ask for it," she glared at Laura, "and I didn't *do* anything for it. I'll pay it back. Did he complain?"

"No, but taking money from clients is a big no-no," Laura said.

"'*A no-no?*'" Lynette's distain for the woman was too rancid for her to taste Laura's insults.

"We have $300 million in this office," Laura continued, more sharply, "and the company trusts us with it. I, for one, won't jeopardize that. Do you realize that I receive and disperse checks for at least a million dollars a day?"

"I *know* what you do. I used to do it. For years."

Charley sat wide-eyed, taking breaths, but not talking.

"So I've heard," said Laura. "But Levi isn't going to be there for you this time. I noticed you e-mailed him a couple of times and he hasn't replied."

"So, Charley, delegating mail supervision to an unlicensed party?"

Charley reddened. "Lynette, you had Marilyn go through and copy all incoming and outgoing mail before she went in the hospital, and she wasn't supervisory licensed. I hardly think that with Laura – who will be licensed – supervising the mail is an issue."

"I trusted Marilyn. Besides, I reviewed all mail after she opened it, print or electronic."

"By the way," Laura warned, "I've known Levi since he was a boy, longer than you, and if he's anything like his father, he'll … avoid you. So you can't *cozy up* to management this time – if that's what you want to call it – to get them to look the other way."

"That's it!" Lynette stood as she yelled, and by doing so launched a sour fog of last night's booze. She saw them smell it. "I don't know how you know Levi's father – I can imagine – but if you don't back off I'm gonna kick…" She gritted her teeth, narrowly averting disaster as Laura stared at her triumphantly.

Charley cleared his throat again. "Hold on, Lynette, settle down." Laura began to speak and he shook his head. "Have you considered the employee assistance program?"

"What are they gonna do, Charley, give me money? Settle my divorce? Drive my kids to 4-H? Build a file of private comments so when *she* cans me," she pointed, "*you* can defend it?"

"I understand how you feel…"

"No you don't! I helped build this office! Give me a break!" Lynette gazed through the glass into the main office. Employees were gawking.

A moment passed, then Charley handed Lynette a piece of paper. "I need you to sign this. Last week Laura warned you verbally. Isn't that right?"

"I have my notes," said Laura.

"Now I want you to sign this." He began to read a copy of the warning letter.

"Dammit, Charley, spare me! I *wrote* that damn letter. I've printed it dozens of times." Lynette turned, letter in hand, and marched out of Charley's office.

Laura looked at Charley. "You're doing the right thing."

Lynette felt eyes, humiliating eyes, as she marched past several desks to her own. She opened a drawer and rummaged, moving aside a small, flat box the size of a sandwich. She'd been keeping it there since Marilyn called her to the hospital and asked her to mail it to Levi. Marilyn made her promise to tell Levi it was coming. But the bastard never called back. Lynette thought maybe she should open it now. She fingered its grocery-bag paper, addressed to him in Marilyn's hand, probably a day or two before she died. Lynette slipped a fingernail under the tape. No, she thought, it would not be right. She wanted to, but not as much as she wanted to respect her wacky dead friend. She moved it aside and went for the employee handbook. She hauled it into an empty office and closed the door behind her. She tapped on a computer terminal and got Levi's phone number. She dialed, angrily this time, knowing he wouldn't take the call, pissed she was trying. On the other end Lily took a message. Years ago, when he first moved to California, his indifference had hurt. She still loved him. He didn't even return her call when her first boy,

Caleb, was born. Back then she cried when she was alone with the baby. For a while, she learned to rejoice in her family. Then Levi ignored her again when she called to congratulate him on his promotion to the division. She had wanted to show she had moved on, was ready to be happy for him as a friend. Fine. She let it all go. Until she called him on Marilyn's behalf. And except for the desperate thoughts on days like today. She was sick of desperate. Time for furious.

As Lynette girded for what she was about to do, her vitriol churned to the surface. Why shouldn't she have vengeance now, now when he once again refused to give so little of himself, when his slightest regard for her might – no, would – save her this last indignation. He had the power. She remembered, as she had so many times, when she was at hand for him. When he rose. *Could he have even done that without me?* Missteps or not, her actions too, not only his own, put him in management. Her actions, too, her dedication to his work – in between blow jobs and cum-stained skirts – made the difference between him being adequate and him being a hero. When it was handy for him, he had taken her adoration, her body. But had he ever truly taken her affection? Truly given his own? Across 1300 miles she thought of him – *yearned for him!* – as she delivered her first child. But he did not so much as take her call from the recovery room. He had moved on. Did she still love him … or the opposite? No, not the opposite. The opposite of love is apathy, not hate, or whatever this was she was feeling. He accepted nothing, nothing! It was he who reached apathy. It was he who gave nothing. So now why not take, take from him without regard, and in doing so save herself? Why not? Hell with him. It was time for vengeance.

At the terminal, she pulled up the directory for Human Resources. The head of HR for the western U.S. was one Deirdre Oliver. The 415 area code and 772 prefix were the same as Levi's. That pleased her. She picked up the phone and, as hot tears fell, she punched the numbers.

34

GUT SHOT

Suspicion is the beginning of wisdom, and of madness.
MASON COOLEY

In San Francisco, forty-five floors up, Levi was subconsciously, perhaps semi-consciously and if so, okay then, irrationally, afraid that the big black desk would burn his legs. But there it was. He sat, as always, sideways behind it, legs vaulted out stiff to the floor like lumber off a saw horse. This time he was gazing at the sailboats on the azure Bay while he cradled the phone in the crook of his neck. He fished a pill from a prescription bottle trapped on his lap. Week's end brought a beautiful Friday morning – highs in the 60s at the beaches, 80s on the Peninsula, 90s inland. He reached across himself and hit a speed dial button on the phone.

On the Peninsula, Minh answered it with something in her mouth, "Ms. Parnell's office."

"Hello, Minh, this is Levi Monroe. What's for breakfast?" He liked Minh, and he liked the idea of embarrassing her a little. He heard rustling.

"I am so sorry, Mr. Monroe."

He smiled. "That's okay. But what is it? What are you eating?"

"Fried rice, sir."

"I love fried rice! Did you know orange zest – grated orange-peel – is pretty good when you sprinkle it in with fried rice? I mean while it's frying, of course. Make the zest fresh, and don't scrape your knuckles. Not too much. You need to have plenty of egg and either pork or chicken, and of course soy sauce. The low-salt kind is best. Probably Kikkoman, not Chung King." The line went silent. "Minh?"

"Yes."

"Did you hear me?"

"Yes."

Levi got the sense she wasn't taking notes. "Is Joy there?"

"I'm sorry, Mr. Monroe, she is unable to take the call. She is meeting with our operations manager and our sales manager." Minh had been watching through Joy's office window as Joy talked and gestured to her management team. "May I take a message?"

"That depends. Has she seen my previous messages?" He threw the pill in his mouth and carelessly lofted a cup of hot coffee to chase it down, scalding his tongue and making him grimace.

"I gave it to her right after you called, sir. The end of the week is very hectic."

"I thought you got accepted to Berkeley?" He stuck out his tongue and sucked air over it.

"I did, sir. I decided to defer."

Between pants he said, "Why?"

"Oh, the timing isn't good for my family, sir, and Ms. Parnell offered me a bonus if I stay."

"Minh, you can *always* come back to work for us. Not everybody gets into Berkeley. Maybe you can work part time in the Oakland office, and we can help you with tuition."

"Yes, sir."

"Call Deirdre Oliver in Human Resources and ask her about tuition assistance, okay? Tell her I asked you to call. If Lily answers, let her know I said to call." Levi looked at his watch. "In the meantime, please let Joy know I called again. Tell her I need her response to the NASD."

"Yes, sir."

"Be sure to say NASD."

"I will, sir."

As they hung up, Levi stood and sucked more air in and out. *What the hell's the deal with Joy?* He opened his chart book to "JP", studied it and extended the red line by a centimeter before he slipped it into a drawer. He picked up the phone and pressed buttons. "Lily, could you come in here?"

At her desk Lily carefully finished cutting an uncanceled stamp from an envelope. She tossed it in a drawer with others. Out of an old picture frame on her credenza, her mother and baby Lily were watching from Manzanar long ago. She fingered dust off the glass. Then she gathered a pencil and a notepad she had fashioned from used copy paper. She trudged into Levi's office and flopped limp-limbed onto his sofa.

Levi was still standing behind his desk, tongue out, fully engaged in cinching his belt a notch tighter. "You know," he talked toward his feet, "you don't have to stay late every night just because I'm here." Finished, he rounded the dark box and stood at the leather chair.

"I know."

His shirt was ballooning from his waist. He fussed with it. "Does this look funny?"

"Didn't they have anything in your size?"

"It's an old shirt." He gave up and sat down, feet planted, legs spread. "Have you seen your husband lately?" He left his mouth open to better pant cool air over his tongue.

"After forty years, I know what he looks like. Doesn't Angela get lonely for you?"

"Good question. I'm not sure. She hasn't said in a while." It was uncomfortably true. "She's talking about going to Italy without me." He felt a pang of guilt for putting her in that light. "To be fair, she's asked me to go. Several times. I just can't, well, don't take the time. We aren't that romantic anymore." Time to change topics. "Do you like fried rice?"

"I can't believe that. She's goo-goo over you."

"That's gaa-gaa. Anyway, I don't think she likes the smell of Imodium on my breath." He touched his tongue again, babying it.

Lily rolled her eyes. "Hard to blame her."

"I burned it." He stuck his tongue out for her to see.

"You don't say? Don't do that. It hurts."

Levi raised his eyebrows and nodded. Then, soberly, "Is something going on out there? My managers aren't returning my calls." If anyone knew, Lily knew.

"Hmm," she offered, and then went quiet.

"Hmm," he said back. "Let's address communication on Monday's conference call."

"There is no conference call. I talked to Karl, and it's cancelled."

"Our Karl? Crawford's Karl?"

"Yes."

"How's he doing?"

"He couldn't talk long. He sounded unhappy – but I guess he's dancing in 'Lion King.'"

"Huh. Well, I'm glad he's in a show. Wow. 'Lion King.' Good for him. Anyway, I don't mean the senior management call. I mean *our* call, with the managers in our division."

"That's what I'm talking about. Crawford's office cancelled our reservation with the conference center."

"You're kidding?" He could see she wasn't. "Who cancelled it?" She simply looked at him. "He can't cancel *my* call with *my* managers. Call the conference center and tell them we're still having one."

"I already called them. Then they called Crawford's office to confirm, and Karl was told to cancel it again." Time passed. Lily finally spoke again. "Karl wasn't supposed to tell me until Monday." More time passed. "Crawford's flying in. Here. Word is that he's having another dinner in the Bay Area on Monday. I thought you knew. I saw it on Deirdre's calendar." She paused. "I looked up Crawford's schedule on the executive page, and he's supposed to be here all week." She paused. "I'm sorry. I thought you knew."

"I met with Deirdre an hour ago. She didn't mention it." Quiet. An image of Crawford's death, an impact explosion of his head, flashed in Levi's mind. Lately he'd fantasized about it often. The venue varied, but it always involved a gun. "You think I should call Sandler?" He knew the answer, and from the look on her face she did too. Lately Sandler hadn't returned his calls.

Levi looked out the window. The Golden Gate radiated orange, and the deep blue bay was speckled with sails. He looked at his watch. 10:30. "Please call and cancel my spot at the Bohemia Club dinner tonight. I don't think I'll be joining." He rested his elbow on the arm of the chair and his jaw on his fist. He looked at Alcatraz. "Is Deirdre still here?"

"Yes."

The phone on his desk rang. Neither of them moved. It stopped. Without looking at her, he said, "Are they playing telephone? The managers? Speculating about my demise?"

"You know how it gets. If one thinks he spots it first, he wants to be the first to yell out. It's like slug-bug."

"Or skunk." Levi stared.

Lily laid her pencil down. "You gave them what they said they wanted. Honesty. Accountability. Profit. You can be proud of that. Those values prevail."

"Scared people get dangerous, Lily. I'm an easy target."

"Well, that explains those concentration camps. But I don't get you. Who? Crawford?"

"Some of these managers and some of the top brokers have been around a long time, and they're used to doing things in, well, a certain way. Especially the ones Crawford recruited during the Hutton check-kiting scandal. They're particularly loyal to him. They make a lot of money and enjoy a certain lifestyle ... and a certain self-image. Sometimes, when people make a million a year and have authority long enough, they *become* the job – the image. If you threaten that image, question it – even by rolling your eyes at their vacations or cars – it's like you've threatened *their very selves*. Like you're stripping them naked, publicly."

"Is that what you did?"

Her tone asked if that's what he intended. Was it, he wondered? "I thought I could change the culture. Make it more honest. So far I've just made people uncomfortable. Scared. So it's tempting, when they find out my superior is trying to bury me, to grab a shovel and throw some dirt my way. Especially if they can do it with anonymity." His hackle began to rise. "I never directly threatened *anybody* – without reason, anyway – without using formal probation – and even *that* is redundant and well-documented. And I couldn't give two shits what they buy or where they vacation! I never said anything unkind or unreasonable. I just believe that..."

"Please stop. You're doing it now. People don't remember what you *say*, Levi, at least not exactly. But they *do* remember how you made them *feel* – forever." As she leaned forward, she looked hurt for him. "If Crawford wants to undermine your reputation with Sandler, he'll only ask the people who feel threatened by you. The preening pretenders. The more humble among us will vouch for you." She looked as though something dawned on her.

"What?"

"Nothing. Well, something. It occurs to me that you're an easy target, from a legal standpoint. You're the profile nobody likes."

"Nobody likes me?" *Why did I say that? – like I'm nine?*

She touched his knee. "No. That's not what I said."

"I wasn't out to make them like me. By demanding that brokers and managers be more ... humble, or more ... forthright, I inadvertently insulted them, scared them. So be it. If a broker has been trading a client's account for twenty years without calling the client first, and I send a letter to the client asking them to sign off attesting that all trades are authorized, I not only scare the broker but embarrass him – well, what's the alternative?"

"But…"

"Let me finish. If a manager has built an office on locker-room decorum, and he's the beloved coach, and I warn him about blue jokes or not hiring enough women or giving women smaller offices, I might threaten his world … and embarrass him. But the good-ol'-boy system only works for the good-ol'-boys. And good-ol'-boy fear and embarrassment becomes anger – especially in men. Okay, I shouldn't scoff at their vacations, their country clubs, their cars. Their concubines and their kids' elite summer camp. Their props are their shields. Their public scorecard. Tempting as it is, if I disparage their props, they'll find reasons to disparage me."

"That's the part I'm talking about. Disparaging you is pretty easy."

"Et tu, Lily?"

"That's not what I mean. I think that in the ultra-liberal Bay Area, you're an unprotected species, an opportunistic target – even for other rich white guys. You're a young – young*ish* – upper-management male. You pay white men more than dark women." Levi wanted to protest but Lily held up a hand. "Those who feel underpaid – like secretaries and operational personnel – resent your *profile*. They might not take any chances to stand up for *you*. And the other overpaid white guys don't respect you, not at their core, because you're trash—you're not formally educated and you don't belong in their club – though they seem fascinated by your success."

"I'm fascinating? That's encouraging."

"Glad I can help. By the way, Crawford doesn't want you in the Bohemia Club. He wants you *rejected* by it."

"How do you know?"

"Never mind. I just do."

Karl, Levi thought. Good ol' Karl. Levi's jaw slackened at Crawford's treachery, but his next thought, on a base level, was some odd measure of relief that he wouldn't be joining a club. He suddenly longed for simple. "Do you know that headcheese is one word? I saw it in Draeger's. Their deli has everything."

"That's nice." Lily said. "Pretentious, but nice. And you laugh at brokers for getting their pictures into the gloss-magazines next to real-estate agents and cosmetic surgeons at charity parties. If you're getting us sacked, we better shop at Costco."

"I was just joking…"

"And now we need a shield and you don't have one. You aren't Muslim, Buddhist, Jewish or Hindu. You wield authority with strong opinions, piss people off, and like it or not, you *are* unprotected. Unfortunately, because you're not female, brown, gay, disabled, old, or practicing a minority faith, you're on your own. You're just a plain white male. The EEOC won't care, the ACLU – no one – if men *just like you* want to cut your legs off, and Crawford and the firm's lawyers know it."

"But you can't come from much further from the other side of the tracks than us," he said.

"It's 'farther'. And get over it. You don't live anywhere near the tracks anymore. And I'm here by choice, paleface. You're part of the hegemony."

"The what?"

"The hegemony. It's the dominant power of one group; influence; political sway."

"Did you go to Berkeley? Sounds like you went to Berkeley."

"Oh, grow up. You're indefensible because you're in the hegemonous group. And I'm the cabin boy on the *Titanic*. Thank you for the job."

"Don't complain. Just when I'm cured of the poverty, I catch the hegemony." He flopped his head back and wished she was wrong … wished himself the fuck out of here.

Lily softened. "But inside, *know who you are*." They said nothing for a while. "It could be worse. You could be an old, Asian, Buddhist woman, born in a concentration camp, who must type letters and answer phones for the white male oppressor, hoping to survive to full retirement." She smiled lovingly, and he did feel loved, and he wanted to hug her.

As silence grew, Levi felt the scald from the black desk spread across the floor toward him. His stomach moved. Intestines lurched and crawled, calling for his attention. "Maybe I can get you a spot in the lifeboat," he said from somewhere far away. "Can you excuse me?"

"Of course," she said, and they stood. She stepped close, looking to hug him, but before he noticed he had already crossed his arms. She touched his elbow. "Can I get you anything?"

"Huh? No." As he tried to smile, he teared, and his stomach tightened and his head began to sweat. "Thanks," he said. She left him alone.

Levi walked behind his desk, sat and tapped on his keyboard. He checked the balance in his brokerage account, did some math. With his parents' medical and living expenses, Lam's home, Dusty's college fund, California household expenses, and the charity supplements, his monthly budget was about $22,000 – about $40,000 pretax. He could last maybe six months without a job. Because he'd been forced to sign a three-year non-compete agreement, no other firm in the business would touch him, leaving him no chance to make that kind of money outside of Bookman Stuart. If Crawford succeeded in ousting him, Levi would have to sell someone's house – his parents', Lam's, his own – and forget Dusty's college fund. *Fuck it! They could all learn to care for themselves or go to hell. I'll be fine. I have my fucking GED to fall back on.*

Levi hit a few more keys and accessed his deferred compensation and benefits page, an internal web page that, to the embarrassment of the sales and marketing department, received more hits each day than any other in the firm. He typed in his PIN, and his personal information jumped onto the screen. First he reviewed the Bookman Stuart stock options he'd been granted – particularly their current value and how long he had to wait to exercise them. "I don't *have* years," he whispered. Like all the inmates, he knew the numbers by heart, but he printed the page anyway. Next he accessed how much restricted stock was "held for him" – shares the firm forced him to buy from his paychecks, shares the firm would confiscate if he terminated employment before vesting. He printed that page. He looked at his 401K and his retirement plan, large portions of which would be worthless unless his age plus his years with the firm added up to at least seventy-five – "the Rule of 75" – before he left. Even after nearly twenty years, because he was so young, he was nowhere near meeting "the Rule." And he sure as hell wouldn't retain medical insurance.

Levi printed out every phantom benefit the firm had designed to keep him indentured, and he stacked them neatly on his cherry-wood TV tray. He tallied what he would lose if Crawford fired him or he quit. $3 million. That, Levi thought, was the value of his execution. He hurled the printouts into the room, and as they settled to the floor he felt his guts move. Three million dollars for which the firm had charged the bottom line of *his* business units over the years and, therefore, reduced *his* profitability bonuses by nearly a half-million dollars – to fund *his* retirement on which he would *never collect!* A \$3 million expense that the firm would never actually incur! He laid his palms on the black desk but jerked them back as if it were hot.

From his outrage rose an epiphany – Crawford's bonus was *also* based on profitability, including that of Levi's division. Crawford could *increase* profitability by \$3 million if he fired Levi, recapturing Levi's deferred comp, and booking the number back in as profit! *Son of a bitch!* Levi lifted a calculator but didn't need it. If Crawford sacked him, the bastard's bonus would increase by *\$400,000!* "Son of a bitch!" he yelled. Levi hurled the calculator at his wall of awards, blasting a plaque loose, launching a rain of plastic shards and circuitry across his credenza.

Sound fell dead. Levi wanted to throw up. Give up. He pinched at his clothes and laughed quietly, painfully. He roughly stripped his tie off and tossed it into the room. He couldn't be happy with these clothes on. Had *never* been happy with these clothes on! He wanted old blue jeans, wet with river water as boys have when they fish with their fathers, leapfrogging each other for the first cast on the upstream hole. *He had, hadn't he, fished like that? With his dad?* Oddly, he couldn't exactly recall, and the blank spot made him laugh coldly. He must have, he thought. Maybe not. In his head he heard his father, "Don't you *ever* jump in front of me!" The voice rose big inside, resonant at first, but quickly growing flat, like pulling a towel inside the shower. The words, the memory, were from indoors. Closed. Not fishing. A smell. Anger, fear, shame. What *had* his father taught him? Not nothing. No, not nothing.

As he lowered his head atop his expensive tray, rested it on letters with impressive letterheads, he closed his eyes. Work had always been his sanctuary, a place where he knew he was good. He *was* talented. He looked sideways at a fallen plaque, a prop attesting to his worthiness, his membership. "*For dedication to…*" it read. *That* was his dues! Dedication and integrity and profitability and family forgone were his dues! Suddenly he felt sick. He dragged the trash can from under the black desk and puked in it. He lifted his head, eyes bleared with moisture. He wiped his mouth on a mutual fund brochure and dropped it in. He gathered the top of the trash bag and knotted it.

He opened a drawer and dug for an address book. He found the number and called. Several times he said he'd like to hold. Finally, "Dr. Hussein? I'm sorry to bother you, but I was hoping you could do me a favor." They talked less than two minutes.

Levi took the trash bag to the restroom. Ten minutes later he leaned against the wall by Lily's credenza and watched the FAX machine.

By the way Lily went at her keyboard, not looking at him, he knew she'd heard his commotion. "You don't need to wait," she said. "I can get it. Who's it coming from?" Finally she stopped and regarded his face. "What's wrong? Where's your tie? Are you okay?"

Levi smiled softly, suddenly sleepy, and laid his hand on the FAX machine. "It's okay. I got it." He yawned.

Lily looked at him a moment longer. "How many pages?" she asked.

He smiled again. "I'm not sure. Not many. Maybe two."

She opened a drawer chocked full of hotel mints and a cellophaned bundles of teeth-whitening gum. She broke the cellophane and handed him a packet of gum.

"That bad?"

As he opened it, she reached under her desk and fished three sheets of fresh copy paper from an open bundle. She slipped the sheets into the FAX paper-feed, atop the upside-down sheets she was recycling, and went back to typing.

While he waited, Levi looked out across the corpus of the office. He saw young MBAs in suit jackets, some brilliant, most afraid of thoughts and whispers. Some would walk in a veteran's office from time-to-time and pick up fading pictures of foursomes, or children, or sailboats, or the old guy standing with bygone CEOs, and smile and say, "Wow. That's amazing," but actually be thinking covetously about the view of the Bay. The veterans worked in shirtsleeves, waiting for their victory lap, after which some would spend their healthy years traveling with the love of their life before they took up buying art. Others will travel for only a month or two seeing relatives they don't really know and then ask the firm for a courtesy desk where they can sit for a couple of mornings every week because they desperately need somewhere to feel safe.

Electronic chatter gargled from the FAX machine and Levi jerked like he had awoken on the freeway thinking, *My God, how did I get here?* It was a short note from Levi's internist. Lily looked at Levi curiously as he read it to himself. He smiled at her.

A minute later at the copy room Levi waited while a new secretary with rabbit eyes and turquoise barrettes used the machine. When she recognized him, she began to blink and stutter and offered to interrupt her work to make copies for him. He wouldn't hear of it. While he waited he learned her name was Mercedes, and she was from a farm near Fresno. When he told her he was from Montana, she said she liked country-western music, but she didn't tell most people, except the fund analyst she had just moved in with – maybe she shouldn't have said that. She was tickled that Levi knew *Breathe* by Faith Hill and they both liked Tim McGraw and George Straight – who were *so* hot – oops. When it was Levi's turn at the copier, she hung around. She was surprised he'd never drunk Jägermeister. As she went on, Levi motioned for her to walk him back to Deirdre Oliver's doorway where Mercedes apologized for talking so much. She said he wasn't scary at all. He said that was good to know.

Deirdre was on the phone and held up one finger. She spun in her chair, away from him, and, in low tones, told the person on the line that she needed to go. She spun back around and hung up. "What's up?" As she stood, she closed her laptop and slipped it into a case.

"Have you ever been to the Gilroy Garlic Festival?"

"No. I haven't"

She looked impatient, so Levi spoke more slowly. "Neither have I. It's this weekend. You know, it's true what they say, that there's no such thing as too much garlic. I love it, though it has to be cooked. Al dente is a little harsh for me. I especially like to roast an entire head, elephant heads, and spread it on toasted French bread with olive oil. They say to use one of those terra cotta garlic roasters because the terra cotta soaks up the oil, but I've baked it in a small pan, and I can't tell the difference. I'm going. This weekend. When I worked in downtown San Jose, at least once a year during the harvest, about dawn, I could smell garlic, and it must be, what, twenty miles away? I'm going to go to the festival this year. They even have garlic wine. Amazing. Can't be that good."

"I don't suppose." She sounded peevish and hurried. It pleased him.

"I have something I need to discuss with you."

She saw the paper in his hand and then looked at her watch. "Hmmm," she said. "I'd love to talk later, but it'll have to wait." She avoided eye contact on her way toward him and the door.

Levi stepped to the center of the doorway.

She glared, a reprimand. "Excuse me?" She coldly invaded his space.

"Surely you aren't rushing to meet Gary's flight. He always rents a car." He didn't blink.

Deirdre slowly set her briefcase down and took the paper from him. "What is it?"

"As of this moment, I'm out on a medical leave of absence." There. He'd done it. There.

She read the note and one heel unconsciously rose out of one of her shoes. "This'll have to wait until Monday." She handed it back with a snap.

Levi put his hands in his pockets. "No, Deirdre. I am out on leave as of *this moment.*"

She pulled it back in. "I didn't know you were sick."

"That's simply untrue," he said flatly. "You couldn't have missed it."

Where most people would stiffen at being called a liar, it simply told Deirdre which part of her script to use. First she acted surprised, unable to grasp. A friend, mildly hurt, but forgiving. "I'm sorry you feel that way. I didn't mean to be insensitive. And I'm sorry you're so ill." She lifted her briefcase and suspended it between them with both hands. "Is there anything I can do?"

"Just place me on medical leave ... as of now."

"What, exactly, are your medical issues?" she asked softly. "This note doesn't specify."

Levi couldn't help but grin at the game. "No, it doesn't," he said, just as softly, mocking. At this point, why not? "As you know, in the state of California, the doctor isn't required to be specific with my employer while I'm out on short-term leave. If I'm out for more than three months, he'll provide more detail."

"Oh, don't even *say* that." She touched his arm. "What day *can* we expect to return?"

Levi laughed out loud. "As you know, Deirdre, I cannot – and am *not required* to – tell you what day I'll be well enough to return. Honestly, you slay me sometimes."

"Levi, I am *so* sorry," she continued. "Can we refer you to a specialist?" This made him laugh again, but she pushed on with her role. "One of those digestion doctors? I can never remember what they're called. Or a counselor?"

"Not at this time. Thanks, though."

"Are you seeing a counselor?"

"Are *you* seeing a counselor?"

She smiled. "Okay," she said and slipped the doctor's note into a side pouch of her briefcase. "I'll let Mr. Crawford know. If you need *anything* you can call me. Please." She no longer sounded sincere. "And I encourage you to call the employee assistance hotline. Lily should have the number."

He laughed until his eyes watered. "I'm not laughing at you..." and he laughed more. Levi gathered himself and let her by, briefcase clutched, eyebrows knitted. He guffawed. He didn't want to, really he didn't, but he did. He laughed. He laughed until he needed to go to the bathroom, where he sat and laughed.

35

DATE NIGHT

Once drinking deep of that divinest anguish,
How could I seek the empty world again?

EMILY BRONTË

Angela turned her ear to the bathroom mirror as she tried to slip the back onto her pearl earring. She could see into the master bedroom where Levi was slumped in the overstuffed chair, his head back, staring up at nothing. He wore a sport coat, as close as he'd been to a suit in two weeks, and he had become gloomier while he dressed, not that it made much difference. "We don't have to go out," she said over her shoulder, and meant it. Frankly, she'd grown weary of shoring up a framework on which to hang some thin gauze of normalcy.

"No. I want to," she heard him say.

She secured the earring and stood straight, pulled at the sides of her dress. For months she had been working out daily. It showed. She entered the bedroom. "Okay. I'm ready."

He followed her downstairs. While he tried to decide if they needed an umbrella – it had rained a record twenty-eight of the last thirty-one days – she opened the beveled glass front door and headed for the dry cobblestone driveway, arriving quickly enough so he wouldn't hold the door. A moment later he slid in behind the wheel of the giant BMW she wished he hadn't leased.

They drove in silence between heritage-sized oaks, redwoods, and sycamores for which the neighborhood gentry kept arborists on retainer. Jogging in place was a wiry, prematurely bald man in running tights whose leashed terrier was shitting on a neighbor's lawn.

"Why do they wear those?" Angela asked.

"What?"

"Those holsters with plastic water flasks. They're all over Los Gatos. How far do they think they'll run, anyway?" She was making an effort.

Levi looked in the mirror and smiled. "I think the object is how far will *other people* think they run. That or an irrational fear of bypassing potable water."

Three hundred yards later, they rolled to a stop near a stand of eucalyptus trees on Highway 9, an old stage coach route and the primary foothill artery between Los Gatos and Saratoga. "Don't you think wet eucalyptus smell like B.O?"

He chuckled. "Yup. I still do. Which way?"

"You pick," she said. After all, it was supposed to be a date.

He looked left and right, quizzical. "I don't know. We could go to the Plumed Horse. I don't know if Table 43 is available, but we can ask." He looked at her for approval.

"That's fine," *if you like Tony Bennett.* They sat for another moment. He sighed heavily. "Come on. I chose indecision. I'm sticking to it." They sat. "Or do you want to try Forbes Mill in Los Gatos?" He looked at her. She pretended to check something in her purse.

"That's good, too." A Hummer pulled to a stop behind them, and Levi squinted at the lights in his mirror. Angela took a breath as he turned toward Los Gatos. At town's edge, they passed an enormous, stunning Victorian with a long driveway of pavers. "I love that house. Is that where Steinbeck lived?" She knew it wasn't.

"No," he said.

They turned onto North Santa Cruz and parked on the street in front of the Black Watch. It was Thursday, the first party night of the weekend, and proximity to the bar's entrance made her feel conspicuous. She knew the crew from school was going out tonight. She was sure Levi had never been in there. Before he had even killed the engine, she was out. At the crosswalk, she lingered for him. They crossed the street together and entered Forbes Mill, a trendy steak house, where pretty people drank martinis at the bar, waiting to be seated.

"Reminds me of a *Morton's*," Levi said.

"You've mentioned that."

They were seated among dark wood and white noise at a small table next to the sidewalk windows. They unfolded napkins in their laps and then ran out of things to do. The waiter arrived and told them the specials. The waiter left. Someone asked if they'd like something to drink. Levi said they wanted wine, and the server waited for him to select one. Levi said he supposed he should pick a Chardonnay. Angela knew he didn't like Chardonnay. He ordered Chardonnay.

Levi's elbows were spread out on the table, hands folded in front of him. She watched him as he looked out the window. He watched a man with a dog on the sidewalk. He studied the dog as it passed.

"I wonder what kind of dog that is?" he said.

"It's a chocolate Lab," she said.

"I've never seen one that color. Seems too red."

They drank some wine. They buttered some bread.

Levi looked at the menu. "They don't have beef-steak tomatoes like Morton's."

"No, they don't."

He ate some bread, his second piece. "How was school?"

"It was fine," she said. "The same." She considered asking how his day went, but she didn't want to rub salt in it. As usual, he hadn't left the house. "Have you thought anymore regarding Italy?"

He looked at her and took a breath. He looked at the stem of his glass. "I can't go," he said. "I'd love to, but I can't. I'm thinking of going to college." He looked up. "As long as I'm out on sick leave, I don't want to give them an excuse. Besides, I am sick."

"You're not that sick."

"I've had diarrhea for a year."

"That's not sick. You're just less full of yourself now. Joke. Can't you be sick in Italy?"

"It could be questioned."

"I don't see why. You can be sick anywhere. Your shrink would back you up."

He returned to looking out the window.

She looked out the window, too, toward the Black Watch. As though she had willed it, the bar door opened and Brandon appeared and someone followed him out. It was Mandy, sexy even at a distance. They kissed and then walked up the street. Angela turned back and straightened her napkin. Levi was looking at her.

"No one knows I'm seeing a shrink," he said, "and my guts are the problem, not my head."

Angela said nothing.

He continued. "Besides, if the worst happens, we'll need the money. That is, if I get fired. Actually, if *the very worst* happens, you'll be fine. Financially. I'll be dead, but you'll be fine."

"Hmm. Well, the hotel rooms are guaranteed. We paid for them whether we go or not. And there'll be a penalty to change the airline tickets."

"I can't," he said. "There's too much at stake. Can't you see?"

"Hm," she said again. She looked at the menu. "Do you want to split an hors d'oeuvre?"

He picked up his menu. "Do you?"

She put the menu down. "I'm going to Italy."

"Fine."

She picked up the menu again. "Maybe I'll take Dusty. I'd take Dad – he'd love to go – but he needs to watch the bar. Lam and Russ will still be on their honeymoon when we leave."

"So you're going to take an eighteen-year-old?"

"Why not? He'd love it."

"Isn't funding his college enough?" Levi looked at his menu. "Jesus!"

They skipped hors d'oeuvres, and they didn't talk while they got the entrée over with. Throughout the meal Angela watched an old couple, all dressed up in expensive old clothes, pushing food onto their forks, seemingly incognizant of each other or anything out of arms' reach. The waiter interrupted Angela to offer dessert, but neither she nor Levi ordered any.

As the waiter walked away, she said, "I don't want to be them."

"Who? Them?" Levi nodded toward the old couple.

"Yes. Them. I don't want my world to contract until I'm all that counts to me. I don't want sending my tongue out like an advance party to escort food into my mouth to be more important than talking with the man who took me to dinner. I don't want to publicly ignore each other every Thursday night because that's what we do on Thursdays."

Levi signaled the waiter and asked for a doggie bag. Angela looked across the street again. When the waiter returned Levi was already holding his charge card.

As they left the restaurant Levi held the door, and she walked without pause to the corner and across the street, Levi in tow. Without breaking stride, she turned toward the car.

Levi caught up with Angela. He looked…sad? Disappointed? "Are you sure you're okay?"

"Yeah. Yeah, I'm fine."

They drove in silence, viewing separate windows. As they closed on their house, he spoke.

"You know why I don't favor hiring jocks?" It was a rhetorical. "Because they're often charming in the sales process – the hunt – but lousy at maintaining client relationships. It's all about winning, possession … then they need another fix." Then this, "Are you seeing someone?"

At first her heart raced, the heart of a little girl caught holding chunks of fresh-broken shame. At the same time she stared inside at much more, much more that had become brittle, something bigger that cleaved away in her hands that had held it too hard. Anger sprung from inside to cover her, to defend her, commandeering her thoughts to think, *The gall! What right had he? What right!* When he killed the engine, she was already strangling the door handle. *Am I seeing someone?* "Only when I close my eyes and concentrate." She popped the door as he touched her leg.

"Is it me you see?"

She removed his hand. "It's always dark." She exited and slammed the door.

36

Is It Warm In Here?

*The true way to be deceived is to think oneself
more clever than others.*

Françious, Duc de La Rochefoucauld

"Are you ready?" Fran Abondolo at the NASD office in San Francisco spoke into the mike on her speakerphone.

"I am," Julie Pennington, Fran's counterpart at the SEC, replied from across town. It was her habit at times like this to twirl the brass knuckles her husband had given her as a key chain.

For months the two women and their staffs had prepared for the confrontation with Bookman Stuart, and this would be the first conference call with Gary Crawford's New York office. They had briefed Bookman Stuart's general counsel that they had evidence suggesting the firm used the syndicate calendar to bribe corporate officers in Silicon Valley in exchange for corporate option exercise and sell business. They were further concerned that Bookman Stuart was illegally profiting from the float on other people's money.

As Fran applied glue to the broken handle of her *Gardening* coffee cup, her secretary hit the conference button and dialed a New York number. Someone named Karl answered. "Hello. This is Fran Abondolo of the NASD, and I have on the line with me Julie Pennington of the SEC. Is Mr. Crawford available?"

In less than a minute, Fran's cup handle held on tight on one coast as the speaker phone went live on the other.

Crawford leaned over the walnut conference table. "Ms. Abondolo, Ms. Pennington, can you hear me?" They could. Crawford looked out toward Liberty Island. It was a clear day. "I'm here with Bob Cohen, our chief counsel, and Deirdre Oliver, a senior executive in Human Resources." Cohen sat forward, staring with predator eyes. Deirdre worked her laptop. After greetings, Crawford spoke again. "We received your inquiry regarding our exercise and sell business and our syndicate practices on the West Coast, and we're attempting to respond in a timely manner. I'm embarrassed to say that these issues caught us by surprise, and unfortunately we've been slowed by our inability to contact some of the involved parties."

"Mr. Crawford, this is Julie Pennington. We feel that you have had ample time to respond to our query, and we would prefer to avoid issuing a subpoena for more records at this time."

"Ms. Pennington, this is Bob Cohen. I assure you we are doing all we can. Regrettably the supervisor who's responsible for the ex & sell business and the syndicate calendar in the Bay Area is out on medical leave and is incommunicado. To wit, he doesn't return our calls."

Fran had been blowing on the cup handle. "This is Fran Abondolo. Are you referring to Levi Monroe?"

"We are," said Cohen, staring down the speaker.

"Our understanding is that Mr. Monroe was not responsible for these business units during the majority of time in question."

Crawford shot Cohen an *I told you so* look.

"This is Bob Cohen again. It's true that Mr. Monroe did not have his current job during the entire time in question. However, he had supervisory responsibility over several Silicon Valley offices for *years* prior to his current position and his lack of cooperation hinders a complete and comprehensive internal investigation. Though we are confident of our internal controls, it is theoretically possible that Monroe breached supervisory responsibility without our knowledge."

It was silent for a moment.

"This is Julie Pennington. Mr. Cohen, that begs the question of whose responsibility it was to supervise the activities of Mr. Monroe during that time. But setting that question aside for now, do you have any evidentiary reason to accuse Mr. Monroe?"

"Bob Cohen again. At this time we are accusing no one of anything and we believe our officers and firm are free of wrongdoing. However, one of our corporate customers, EcoPulse BioTech, has recently expressed concerns that Monroe and one of Monroe's subordinates, Joy Parnell, an office manager, may have purposely delayed payment of checks to their employees. We have a letter in hand on the letterhead of EcoPulse's CEO, a Mr. Ramakapur, outlining their concerns about Monroe. We have not yet talked to Mr. Ramakapur."

Fran lifted the cup and the handle immediately broke off. "Can you send us that letter? This is Fran Abondolo."

The boardroom went quiet for another moment. Deirdre eyed a copy of the letter on her laptop screen. She had composed it, printed it and mailed it unsigned from the Bay Area, leaving open the possibility of an anonymous whistle-blower. Crawford smiled at her. She could be the next national director of Human Resources. Crawford looked at Cohen and nodded.

"This is Bob Cohen. We'd be happy to provide each of you with a copy. In the meantime, we will press Monroe further for his cooperation. There's another point of concern. In checking records sent to us by EcoPulse, preliminary reports from our Peninsula office show that Mr. Monroe may have been personally granted stock options directly from EcoPulse while he was running our San Jose office. Further, it seems his office there continued to process business for EcoPulse employees after the date of those options. We're trying to verify this with Mr. Ramakapur."

"This is Fran Abondolo. Are you suggesting Monroe was somehow paid off?"

"We cannot speculate at this time."

"When do you expect Mr. Monroe to return to work?" More glue.

Deirdre stopped typing and Cohen nodded to her.

"Hello. This is Deirdre Oliver, senior vice president, Human Resources. We are unsure about Mr. Monroe's health. We are concerned about him physically and, well, in other ways. Additionally, we are currently reassessing our corporate structure on the West Coast. I guess this is my way of saying that I don't know the degree to which we can depend on Mr. Monroe."

Things were quiet. Deirdre smiled at Crawford. She took a box of mints from her jacket pocket. She opened it, put one in her mouth and smiled again.

"This is Fran Abondolo. We'd like to thank you for your time. It may be necessary for us to have a more extensive meeting in the near future. I believe that I speak for Julie when I say that we would like copies of your syndicate logs and your disbursements-versus-settlements from the exercise & sell business conducted through your Bay Area offices…"

"Bob Cohen here. You must realize there are tens of thousands, perhaps hundreds of thousands, of ex & sell transactions during the period in question. It will take time."

"Do you have electronic copies?" It was Julie Pennington.

"Well, I'm sure we must…"

"Then just prepare it digitally. I'll have our IT guys contact yours. It shouldn't take more than a day or so. If you need a subpoena, let me know. We also look forward to copies of the salient correspondence from EcoPulse. Anything else, Fran?"

"Yes. We would like copies of your procedures manuals and your internal audit reports of the subject offices covering the last five years. I anticipate that we'll be back to you in the next week or so to schedule an on-site audit."

"This is Gary Crawford. We look forward to providing you gir–, uh, your people … with anything you need. Just let us know how we can help."

"We certainly will," said Julie. "That ends our conference call. Thank you for your time." Then, "Fran, can you call me back on an outside line?"

"Yes. Thank you all."

Less than a minute later, Fran and Julie reconnected. Julie took the lead. "Fran, from the ammunition in the documents you've sent me, their story already limps. I think it's time you, your sources, and I meet in the same room at the same time. Maybe *us girls* can take closer aim."

"I don't think the sources are aware of each other, and I don't think they're lying. I'll have to tell them about each other. I'll let you know when I can get them here."

"What do you make of the letter from Ramakapur?"

"Shit."

"What?"

"Oh, I just broke the handle off my cup again. Oh, well. Anyway, Ramakapur came to us. He likes Monroe. It doesn't hang together. No way did he write that letter."

"I agree. And liars don't survive when the bullet hits the bone. Maybe some Fed boys with real guns can lend us a hand."

"Have you been to the gym today? You should go to the gym. Truly. Soon."

"I'm just saying."

37

ACCESS DENIED

Those whom God wishes to destroy, he first makes mad.

EURIPIDES

With grass clippings nettling at his greasy shins and the house phone at his ear, Levi's ass and thighs stamped a sweat print on his leather office chair. He stared at his computer screen until sunscreen burned his eyes and then wiped his face with a sloppy company T-shirt that hadn't seemed so big last year in Maui. Now he tasted the sunscreen – piña colada. On the walls around him hung girders of unworked leather-bound classics purchased on sale at Barnes and Noble. The old gal there, Mae, had quit to move closer to her kids. In New Mexico or somewhere. The new gal was a skinny nineteen-year-old with weed-whacker hair named Lucy. Kind of nasty looking. Levi made a note to go to Barnes and Noble today. As he held for Deirdre Oliver, he had a stare-down with his insolent computer screen. It taunted, *Password expired, Password expired, Password expired ….*

Finally Deirdre's voice broke cool and dry. "Hello, Levi. Long time no hear."

"Yeah, it has been a while. I've tried to call. Did you get my messages?" He was ready with a yellow pad of paper. He heard her keyboarding.

"I did. It's just that your three months aren't quite up yet, and we didn't want to hurry you. How *are* you feeling?" She could hardly have sounded more patronizing.

"If possible, I'd like to discuss that with you and Gary. I know he's going to be in town for the Managers' Council. I thought we could schedule a meeting. I called him but couldn't get through. If not during the day, maybe we could meet after the formal dinner."

"Uh, yeah. Hmm. Mr. Crawford's office told me that you wanted to meet, but they said to let you know that his schedule is very tight and…"

"I know he's busy, Deirdre. Once again, if he's booked during the day we could meet after one of the dinners. It wouldn't take too much time. Given that the meeting is hosted by my division, I thought I'd attend the Friday night dinner anyway."

"Hey. I hear what you're saying… but, we don't feel it's appropriate for you to attend a company function as long as you're ill. You know how careful we have to be, and besides, you should just concentrate on taking care of yourself. Nothing's more important than your health."

"It isn't going to kill anybody to meet. Why don't I just come to the dinner, and we'll catch as catch can."

"I'm afraid I have to ask you to stay away from the function, Levi."

You fucking bitch. The phone went silent for a long while as they made notes. Levi finished writing and looked at his bare feet. "Don't do this to me."

"No, no! You misunderstand. We just want what's best for you. You just get well."

Levi took a deep breath. "All right. All right. Will you tell Gary I'd like to meet with him?"

"Of course! Maybe we can work something out. How's Angela?"

Levi smiled as he frowned. "She's fine. Can you pass me to Lily?"

"Ooo. I'd love to, but I'm not very good with this phone. I'd probably just disconnect you. Would you mind calling back in?"

"No. No problem. Goodbye." He hung up.

Deirdre waited until the line Levi had come in on was no longer lit. She pressed another button. "Are you still there?"

"Yes," said Crawford. "Go ahead and set up a meeting with him while I'm out there, but not until after the announcements. See if you can get that woman to fly in."

"I'll try."

"And one more thing. I need you to pick up a little package for me. I don't want to fly with anything. Call my friend there. Same number."

"Gary, I can't…"

"Can it. You proved your abilities in the Caribbean. Now goodbye."

A minute later Lily picked up the phone. "Mr. Monroe's office."

"Hi. It's me."

"Hi." She sounded genuinely pleased to hear from him. She was watching strangers all around her, men with handcarts there on Crawford's authority, riffling through the file cabinets.

"I can't log on to the system."

"I know. They shut off your access. Deirdre said they do that for anyone on sick leave."

"God dammit I'm not just anyone! I'm an executive vice president! Son of a *bitch*!" he yelled, unable to help it. "I'm sorry, Lily. You don't deserve this."

"No, I don't," she agreed. "But don't worry about it."

He felt the veins in his head pulse and worked to control his voice. "You know what? Maybe I should just come back in. Maybe tomorrow I should just *show up*."

"I'm not sure that'll work."

"What's all that noise?"

"Movers."

"Movers?"

"There are people here, Levi, people from Crawford's office. They're boxing up records and marking most of them to be shipped to New York – some to L.A."

Blood drained into Levi's abdomen. He pressed his palm to his forehead. A finger quaked. *So this is how my career ends, without sensation, the silent heart attack.* "What do you mean?"

Lily talked cautiously, pausing when anyone came too close. "I mean I think our division is out of business. Or at least you and I are. I'm not sure." Someone pushed a handcart of boxes past her. "I've heard the SEC is threatening to subpoena records. These guys assure me they'll handle it." He didn't respond. Someone walked by with an empty box. She changed the subject. "You've only got a few calls; most of them are Lynette in Billings. Do you want the number?"

He was trying to assimilate the subpoena news. "No."

"Do you want me to call her for you?"

"No. Thank you." She was the last thing on his mind. "Just throw the messages away." His nose began to run and he walked through the house looking for a Kleenex. "Lily, if they take those records, they'll be scrubbed before the SEC ever sees them. You know that."

"I know that," she said. "Are you okay?"

He laughed and sniffed, breathed through his mouth. And laughed. *Am I okay? Funny.*

"Levi?" There was more concern in her voice now. "Will you be okay?" He did not answer. "I've never asked you, but do you have a spiritual leader, a reverend or priest you could talk to? You've never thought of anything crazy, have you?"

"Ooo. No clergy. Men with crosses are unlucky for me. I don't really do church. And suicide? Come on. It's been done to death. Though I *could* use a little divine interference."

"You mean intervention."

"Yeah. I'll be fine. Listen, I better let you go. Hey, don't let them take my toilet paper."

"I won't. I want you to call me for any reason, no matter how small. I need you to check on *me*. Okay?"

"Sure. Hey, Lily?"

"Yes."

"I've been trying to get ahold of Abba Ramakapur. He hasn't called there, has he?"

"No. I'm sorry."

"That's okay. He's probably just busy. How about the divisional guy at Merrill?"

"No." She sounded conciliatory. "Do you want me to call his assistant?"

"No, no. That's okay. I know him. It's just that I left a message. But he'll call. No big deal. He's probably out of town." A pause passed. "You know I can't intervene from here, divine or otherwise. But someone can. Someone." Silence at first, enough for him to wondered if he had offended her. Maybe she hadn't heard him. "Lily, what matters most?"

"Levi, there's nothing I can do. The boxes are on their way out."

He could think of no way to say it without just saying it – but he would not, not to his friend, his dear friend. Who was he to suggest committing a crime, to put her job at risk, her dignity, perhaps even her freedom. Not for him, a man already lost. No. He realized then what she was to him. Lily had become family, as surely as Angela, and he loved her as such. But Lily was also a woman in full, a mentor, a cunning warrior. A survivor. Lily could damn well decide for herself. And he could damn well let her. "The boxes aren't the only records. Deirdre keeps records."

Lily walked to a south-facing window. She stood for a long time, gazing into infinite haze, trying to feel Levi, forty miles away, wondering if he was safe. She thought about his words. What matters most? What is right? She wasn't sure what "right" was anymore, let alone what she owed to it. She'd given plenty. She wanted to just retire and forget it. Honor. Loyalty. It would be easier to plant a garden with Yoshi. Right? She returned to her desk and lifted her phone. She called her home near Geary and Fillmore in Japantown. "Hello, Sweetie. Did you take the movies back? … No, I left a note. They're two-day rentals … Yes, both of them. … Fine, we'll sign up for that mail-order one. Yoshi, Sweetie, would you do me another favor? Would you cancel our appointment in the Valley? We can see the property another weekend. … No, I am fine. … Work is fine. … It is finally time for me to see my ghosts. … Yes, there. I want you to take me. … I love you, too, Yoshi-San.

38

Set the Table For...

I'll eat my head.

Charles Dickens

"Ha, ha! No duh!"

Levi was sitting on his bed all dressed for dinner guests, needing a haircut, crowing like a kid. Four months had passed since he had reported to work. He reread the certified letter informing him that the insurance company had denied his long-term disability claim. Insurers knew that some denied claims would be dropped because the claimant simply didn't have the strength to pursue them, *particularly* claimants of mental illness. Most particularly if they were actually sick. Other claimants would accept less as they ran short of household money or couldn't afford a lawyer. The most callous truth of all was that a calculable percentage of denied claims could be tied up long enough for the sick to die, thus terminating the claims – unpaid. Levi hadn't yet decided which kind of claimant he was. He grinned and wondered how much in bonuses he made over time by tacitly endorsing the tactic. Being self-insured, Bookman Stuart management directly benefited by withholding benefits. Rank and file never knew.

Downstairs, Angela was glowing from wine and from scurrying around the kitchen without Gabriella's help. Out of friendship alone, her former housekeeper would have been happy to prepare the meal, but Angela felt guilty enough, having let her go. She was reading her checklist when the doorbell rang. Angela took off her apron and wiped her hands and tapped across the marble entryway in black pumps under white pearls, stalling at a big mirror as much to create an air of nonchalance as to check her lipstick, hair, and figure. The time at the gym showed, and no detail gave away how harried she was in working to make this evening perfect – perfectly normal – so much so that she had snuck a cigarette or two in the garage. She exhaled into her palm and sniffed, took a deeper breath, and opened the door.

Kathy McDermott from school stood next to her Internet boyfriend, Bob Nelson, and beamed. Kathy had become serious about Bob. He was a full-size man with pleasantly dulled features, a gem, by all accounts.

Kathy and Bob had ascended to the Monroes' A-list. In fact, they *were* the A-list. In the past decade the rare times the Monroes entertained were purposefully tied to Levi's career. Those people were busy nowadays. Over the last several months, Levi's few non-business acquaintances had become uncomfortable with his sullen demeanor, so now only Angela's friends returned calls. Levi called them his friends-in-law. Tonight Angela was relieved, and a little nervous, that Kathy and Bob had accepted the invitation.

"Angela, Daaa-ling, it's been too long," Kathy joked. "How *have* you been for the last," she checked her watch, "oh, four hours?" The ladies laughed and hugged. "You remember Bob."

"Of course, I do, from the open house at school! You and Levi hid out together. Welcome." She stood on her tiptoes and kissed him on the cheek.

"My goodness, Angela, you look beautiful," Bob said, and he handed her a bottle of wine. "We got this special. Two-buck Chuck. I think it needs to breathe." He laughed. "So. Where's the man of leisure?"

"How thoughtful, Bob," she said, and then whispering loudly, "I'll open it, but I should tell you, the doctors asked Levi not to drink because of *his condition*." She made a comical smile.

"I'm right here," Levi said from the stairway, "and my hearing is just fine." He grinned and descended the stairs. His pants were cinched around a shirt and T-shirt – he had taken to wearing T-shirts for bulk – over which he had layered a cashmere sweater.

As Kathy hugged Levi she shot Bob a look of concern. The host was a bag of bones. The men shook hands and the women headed for the kitchen where Angela said something that brought snickers and then clanging.

Levi led Bob to the living room and lit the gas fireplace. "Scotch?" he asked. Bob said yes. Levi poured two glasses, though his was just for show, and they sat on sofas on opposite sides of an expensive coffee table that now seemed an embarrassment in its sheer size. What was he thinking when he bought it? Levi stretched his arms casually across the back of the sofa and crossed one leg easily, ready for a chat with Bob, his new friend, who knew almost nothing about him; *tabula rasa*, as it were, a white canvas, a fresh piece of paper. They sat, drinks in hand.

"So, how's business in the Valley for you guys?" Truthfully, Levi couldn't remember exactly what Bob did or who he worked for. Something high tech.

"Great. We've survived the tech-bubble bust. Actually, if a couple of deals drop, we'll have a record quarter, God willing." Bob fished out a chunk of ice with his finger, sucked on it, and spit it back into his drink.

"Refill?" Levi leaned forward.

"No, thanks." Bob sucked in another piece of ice as he surveyed the room. "You've got a great house."

"Thank you." Levi searched for a topic. *Shit*, he thought. *I know nothing, nothing outside this house. Nothing that's not on TV. Nothing that's not on AOL's home page.*

Bob looked at a landscape painting above the fireplace. "That's beautiful."

Levi tittered. *I tittered!* "Angela did that. It's a Bob Ross, the TV guy, but don't tell her I told you." *Dammit! How would I know Bob Ross?*

"You're kidding? Very cool. I wish I had that kind of talent ... and time. I should start classes now. If our stock pops, I'll get *too* busy. Good busy. Or maybe I'll just retire like you."

"How's that? Become too busy, I mean. I guess I'm not sure what you do, exactly."

Bob laughed. "A lot of people say that." His finger was in his glass again. "I work in benefits at EP."

"EP? EcoPulse? For some reason I thought you were at HP." *Shit. EcoPulse.* "You're with HR? What, like health insurance? Retirement?"

"Yeah, some of that. But not HR exactly. We split them out – benefits and HR. I do benefits. Actually, we're a big customer of yours. Well, not *you*, but Bookman Stuart."

Levi nodded. "How's that?" Levi's breathing shallowed.

"I'm the company's stock and option plan-administrator. We do our executions through you guys. Though maybe not for long. The NASD seems to be mad at you." Bob chuckled.

Levi reached for his scotch, stomachache or not. "Really? I'm not too sure what's going on out there. I've been a bit out of touch." He took a small sip that heated his mouth.

"Good for you. It's been a pain in the ass. My staff spends all their time copying records and responding to subpoenas." Bob chewed a piece of ice.

"Still, if the stock gets hot – from what I hear upstairs, it's about to – we won't be able to process all the employee transactions. They'll all want to get through the door at the same time. You know, exercise."

Levi swallowed scotch. "Do you work for a guy named Abba?"

"Yeah! You know Abba?" His big, grinning mouth churned ice more busily.

At that moment Angela opened the kitchen door and the rich smell of baked lamb rolled through the room. She and Kathy brought a plate of fruit and baked brie to the cocktail table and sat next to their men. Angela was jocular, smelling of wine. For months, as Levi's ego collapsed, she had struggled to hold it up, and in the process her spirit had steadily compressed. Now, encouraged by alcohol and a sympathetic audience, it expanded unevenly. With her hand on Levi's thigh, she sat erectly, shoulders back. "I know you don't need fruit, honey, but maybe the cheese will … you know, help." Angela looked at Kathy, who grinned when Angela giggled.

Levi's face grew red. He had assured Angela that he felt comfortable with Kathy and Bob, but, *Christ, Angela!* Concentrating, turning to Bob, he forced himself to move smoothly. "Yes, I know Abba, but I believe my predecessor – my boss – knows him better."

"Great guy!" said Bob. "Brilliant. Wants to save the world. Too bad you didn't get to know him better before you quit or, well, whatever. Retired."

Lately Levi's fight and flight had become too tightly strung and intellectually he knew it, so as he felt the mean grow inside him, he forced himself to smile. "I'll probably go back to work in the next week or two. I haven't decided. Actually, I've enjoyed the time off."

"Oh, *honey*," Angela sounded disappointed. "Your shrink's gonna hear about this one." She opened her eyes wide and put her hand in front of her pursed lips. *Oops.*

Kathy squirmed. Bob stopped chewing.

Levi stood, empty glass in hand. "I'm getting a drink, Bob. Get you one? Lots of ice?"

Bob shook his head, "No thanks." He smiled sympathetically, and Levi blamed him for it.

Angela touched Levi's pants leg as if a mother slowing a child.

Pursing his lips and looking at no one, Levi calmly walked into the kitchen. He lifted a bottle of scotch, exited the other side of the kitchen, and escaped upstairs.

A half-hour passed in which Angela babbled nervously and laughed with big-limbed gestures. It wasn't until dinner could be held no more that she finally acknowledged what her guests were agonizingly aware of: Levi hadn't returned.

"You go get him," Kathy said optimistically. "I'll put the food on the table. Go."

Angela found Levi standing bare-assed in the master bathroom, hunched over, pants at his ankles, fiddling with something in his briefs which he held stretched open at his knees.

"Get the hell out of here!" he said.

"We have guests!" she said. "Are you okay? Are those my panty liners?"

"I said get the hell out!"

"I wondered where those had been going. I thought you were getting better? Do you use those every day, or just certain times of the month?" She laughed uproariously. "Oh. Sorry. 'M a little tipsy."

Levi could take it no more. "Now!" He lurched oafishly, shoving her through the doorway, popping the strand of her mother's pearls and netting her pant pocket onto the doorknob, ripping it open. He tripped on his underwear and fell, slashing his knee on a door hinge. Blood streaked and smeared across cold marble as he scrambled to get up, to cover his ass.

"You crazy bastard!" Angela seethed. "How can I love you? I hate you!" She started at the pearls and held up short, driven from the room by loathe.

Levi dropped to the floor, disoriented, echoes pushing him against the cabinet. *I hate you! I hate you. Crazy. I hate you. I hate you. I hate ...* Immeasurable time drifted by, floating him into eye-games with the marble floor. He made out foreboding mountains, vague genitalia, *hate you*, and the cold, malevolent face of a man. A tattoo. *I hate you.* Levi waited for the madness that would take him, for once unafraid. He invited it. As it crawled through him, he insolently yanked it, forcing it in, this ... color-sucker. "Hard to fix crazy, huh? Come on, you fuck! I *own* you." Now it was his alone! His *private* madness, his intimate acquaintance. *How can I love you?*

Levi's body became so much meat, and a sense of comfort settled in the dullness. He kept things in the closet across the room. Dangerous things. He traced his limbs, found the sticky liquid on his knee, scrutinized its leaden coagulation. His head conjured a science show, PBS in monochrome, *NOVA* body shows in black and white, the camera's eye diving into arteries at the moment of crisis – jetting along tubes beside dimpled, gray corpuscles that clustered wildly at his wound. *How much per minute does it cost to make that? Maybe not that much anymore, now that the computer programs are written. How much commercial time can ya sell? Twelve minutes an hour? More? What does that make? A million a minute? Is that enough? Two million, maybe, for NOVA. Then there's reruns. And syndication. Like Seinfeld. It's a fucking gold mine.* Next he noticed his drab finger, the tip looking as if covered in liquid tar. Use it, he thought. He angrily smudged the cool stone image, checking pearls aside, until a burst of scarlet desecrated the cruel, male effigy. A rage screamed within him, he bore down with his palm and drove his stain into the likeness, again and again, imbuing it forever with his blood. From his throat, a voice rasped, "Be DEAD!" He was unsure who had said it.

Angela, too, heard the voice. She was standing two feet from him, having returned for a safety pin. "What?" she asked. But he could not sense her presence.

Her pants pocket pinned, Angela stepped bravely from the bottom stair. She took a deep breath and felt her heart with her palm. She sat at the table with Kathy and Bob. "He's pretty sick," she said, blinking and smiling and breathing through her mouth. "I'm so sorry."

Kathy asked that they hold hands and pray. She thanked God for the food and asked Him to help Levi and Angela. For the next ten minutes they made awkward conversation and politely moved food around until Angela cried and Kathy asked Bob to wait in the living room. Ten minutes later, Kathy and Angela rejoined Bob, and Angela had a duffle bag.

"It's time to go," said Kathy. "Angela is staying with … at my house tonight."

"Oh." Bob said lightly, flashing a glint of confusion and disappointment. "Okay,"

"Oh don't look so disappointed." Kathy said to him. "I sent the kids to their dad's tonight for a reason. God and Angela both know we're having sex." She turned to Angela. "Ready?"

Angela nodded, and looked up the stairs. She heard the closet door open. She wanted nothing of him right now but distance. "I'm ready."

39

A Flower in the Desert

Honor the spirits, but keep your distance from them.

Chinese proverb

Lily and her husband left in the dark. It took a little over six hours to drive the 337 miles from San Francisco, just as AAA said, time enough to appreciate Yosemite and the Tioga Pass. They gassed up in Bishop and stopped at Schatt's to buy a loaf of their famous Sheepherder's bread which, for a short while, made the car smell content inside. They slid farther south down the 395 through the Owens Valley, beside the urgent eastern Sierras, momentum and memory tugging them in. A little over five miles past the county seat of Independence, isolated on the parched desolate valley floor near Mount Whitney, it slackened. Nothing here. Nothing here loudly. From the highway, though only shoulder height, a lonesome obelisk the color of whitewash dragged her attention through the scrub manzanita. It pointed at the sky.

They pulled off and rolled past two squat stone and mortar cubes, guard huts that marked the entrance, and past the square lumber sign strung between posts, tight from its corners by flatiron and chain, as if it had done something shameful. A low, three-wire fence marked the perimeter. An empty sequestered parking lot petered out next to a hollow hulk, a derelict sun-shot ruin, the old auditorium masquerading less as a visitor center than an abandoned warehouse. The long-gone canvas barracks of block four, the barracks of all the blocks, left building-sized holes in the desert sky. From ash-gray dirt, heat rippled up wetly to whisper its lie, transporting closer the white-capped image of cathedral mountains, using awe like a promise. At a shorter distance, a remnant of a dead orchard jutted from the soil like a giant, wooden long bone. Their car crept a bit deeper into the grounds and stopped. Lily got out. The dry, hot air shocked her cheeks and forehead, her nose, her lungs. Yoshi stayed in the car. With a small flat box in her hand, she walked out toward a white pylon.

She felt them, those she had come to see, more acutely than she had anticipated. There is a fine distinction, she thought, between hallowed and spooked. Holding at bay her thoughts of silliness, her urge for self-reproachment, she gave herself to it, let this place wash over her, take her. Listen, she told herself. Try to hear. After all, wasn't that why she came? To listen for her answer? From them? From him? A car whined by on the highway well behind her, and then a truck, the other way, and she heard the air fill its tunnel.

The gleaming little monument, scarred with Japanese characters, marked only six graves of the 150 internees who died at Manzanar War Relocation Center during World War II. Most of the dead were cremated. Most, who were released after the war, some 10,000 Japanese-Americans, had by now died wherever it was they went to live. But Lily could feel them here, now, the ones who'd left their spirits behind, as if they were holding the spot until a proper memorial to their sacrifice was erected, little enough to ask for the redistribution of families and assets. Why had they taken it?

Lily snapped open the clear plastic door of the box and extracted the Purple Heart medallion, felt the raised letters on the back: "For Military Merit." She put it back in the box and laid it at the base of the obelisk so that the medal faced her. She closed her eyes. She began to clear her mind of all grasping thought, to observe, without mental comment, what is real. As her mother had taught her.

Time passed. In the wind she could almost hear the voices of the adults playing pinochle, the older children playing baseball. She tried again, as she had throughout her life, to imagine, judgelessly, the conversation her parents had in the dark the night before her father left here for the Army, for Italy. She liked to imagine his hand on her mother's protuberant belly, two inches from Lily herself, due to be born soon. What had they said, this husband and wife, these unborn parents who shared the values of earnest immigrants? How had they justified the possibility of their baby's life without a father? Had it been as her mother told her, all those times? *In loyalty, honor.* What had her mother not told her? What had they said after they loved each other the last time? What wisdom was in that deep, gentle pain? Lily had always taken her mother's account of their farewell at face value. She had *honored* it, that word her mother gave her, as big enough to justify the loss of a father. Big enough to fix mistakes, to forgive or at least tolerate human weakness. She had adopted it as her credo.

Her thoughts were getting in the way.

Again she listened, determined to do so for as long as it took for the answer to grow stark. She wiped a bead of sweat from her temple, another from her hairline. She knew they were here, he was here, and somehow the answer would come. She felt the sun penetrate through, to her meat. Yes, they were here. He was here.

Her father's remains were overseas, in or near the Alps, a decision made by the Army. Her mother's were in Oakland, a decision made by necessity last year. It didn't matter. For Lily, their spirits were here, at Manzanar. She had imagined it all her life, and she believed her mother thought that too. So here she was. Once more she asked, wondered, if in that final instant before his death, he had reconsidered the word she so revered. Once more she listened, between the wind and the weeds and the highway and Yoshi starting the car to run the air conditioning. She swiveled calmly at the hip and issued him a stern look. He turned off the car and opened the door. He pulled the keys out and the ringing stopped.

Lily turned to the Purple Heart, its ribbon speckled with grains of hot sand. She closed her eyes, opened her mind, allowed her thoughts to move without tendrils of the past, without leaving a trace of their presence. *If in loyalty lies honor, must one sacrifice honor for loyalty?*

Minutes later, the wind whispered, cooling the sweat on her forearms and chest, raising goose bumps on her skin.

She got in the car without saying a word, her face reddened, her hands empty. Yoshi started the engine and let the air conditioner run full blast without putting the car in gear. She held the tail of her blouse up to the vent. "Whoooow," she whispered.

"Did you get your answer?"

For a while the question went without response. Then, "Yes."

"You don't have to talk about it … Did you learn anything? From your ancestors?"

She looked quizzical, as if trying to decide. "Yes. I think I did."

In a careful voice, Yoshi said, "And?"

"There's a reason no one lives here." She wiped her brow. "And dead is dead. Wait here," she opened the door, "I forgot the medal."

Back on the highway, she watched the obelisk until it was no longer possible, and then turned her eyes forward, seeing clearly what she needed to do.

40

So. Who's the New Deceptionist?

It is a pleasure to deceive the deceiver.

Jean de La Fontaine

Deirdre Oliver had just returned from a two-week, office-by-office, employee benefits road show, and she cockily exited the elevator in San Francisco at the forty-fifth floor, laptop clutched beside crisply whispering pant-legs. It was the annual benefits enrollment period, and her PowerPoint presentation had once again successfully made opaque the fact that next year employees would pay more for less insurance coverage. By jumbling combinations of major medical, emergency, dental, optical, deductibles, health maintenance, PPO and HMO, most employees gave up and just picked one. Deirdre had even coordinated the actuarial committee, which determined that, by switching long-term employee retirement benefits from defined-benefit (a check every month until death) to cash-balance (one big check upon retirement), the firm could cut its retirement benefit costs by about 40 percent. Employees contemplating retirement were consistently blinded by the specter of a big check, unable to imagine themselves old and broke, unable to do the math. A few were caught unaware that companies may arbitrarily and legally change or freeze pensions for non-union employees. Statutes don't require companies to offer a pension in the first place, so there is no requirement to keep them – or even pay pensions that were promised for decades. To divert attention, Bookman Stuart introduced a laughably nominal contribution to 401Ks and an even smaller employee stock option grant called the Prosperity Plan. Meanwhile, the company devoured several smaller firms that had dutifully socked away money each year to fund, even over-fund, retiree lifetime payments. Then Bookman Stuart converted the incoming plans to lump-sum distribution – presto chango – and stripped out tens of millions of leftover dollars. Management bonuses rose proportionately, including Deirdre's. But on the road, to her amusement, employees loved her. They still didn't get that she, a SVP of HR, was the equivalent of management's Gestapo.

Lily Fujiwara looked up from a seed catalogue and watched Deirdre offer her greeting like a door prize at each secretary's desk. Whenever an employee said, "How are you?" Deirdre consistently replied, "How are *you*?" so it had become sport among the staff to ask Deirdre how she was and afterward, in the break room, laugh at her. Deirdre stopped at some Mylar balloons and congratulated a woman on being one year closer to cashing in, *ha, ha.* Lily cringed.

Lily knew the clock until full retirement. Ever since the authority of the division had been unceremoniously reassigned to the L.A. office, there was nothing much to type or file. Further, Levi's old phone lines had been forwarded to L.A., so Deirdre's calls were the only ones Lily answered. She supposed they'd cut her job soon and offer her a two-hour commute to Lodi or Modesto or some other God-forsaken branch, hoping she'd quit. As Deirdre approached, Lily swept a small, plastic device the shape of a pack of Juicy Fruit into her middle drawer. It was a wondrous innovation, a computer jump-drive storage unit.

"Good morning, Lily." Deirdre stopped uncomfortably close to the front of Lily's desk. "Did you have a good weekend, dear?"

She was *not* Deirdre's dear! "I did," Lily said sweetly. "And how are *you*?"

Deirdre smiled sweetly. "How are *you*?"

Lily smiled back. "Fine, thank you."

"Do I have any messages?"

"They're on your desk. Your boss's funeral is this Thursday." That seemed to pique her interest. "I suppose you'll apply for the job?"

"Please, Lily. I hadn't even considered it. Let's allow the man some dignity."

"Would you like me to schedule a flight to New York?"

"I've already taken care of it, thank you."

"And there's this." Lily casually handed Deirdre an official-looking envelope. "It was delivered late Friday."

Deirdre opened the envelope and her smile fell. "A subpoena?" she said. "From the SEC. Why would they include *me* in a subpoena? I'm HR," she said like it was a minor outrage.

"It mostly asks for documents – electronic or printed – but, as you know, there isn't much here. I faxed a copy to Bob Cohen's office. They said to gather what I could. Before we turn it over to the SEC, they'll send counsel here to review it. I told them that Crawford already had many of the documents shipped from here weeks ago, but I wasn't sure where."

Deirdre turned cool. "You told Cohen that? Great. Thank you. Be sure I see what you've still got before Bob's people get here."

"Bob said not to. He probably just wants to keep you above the fray." Lily smiled and handed Deirdre a message. "And Levi still wants you to call."

Deirdre became sweet again. "Thank you."

Lily watched Deirdre's back as she walked into her office. She watched with interest as Deirdre pulled out her laptop and plugged it in. Deirdre looked up, smiled from across the room, and held her laptop as she walked to her office door and closed it.

As one of Deirdre's phone lines lit up, Lily reopened her drawer. She retrieved the oblong plastic tablet, pulled off the cover and touched the USB plug. She thought of Levi, wondering if she should have told him. It might have lifted him. No, she thought. Better to protect him from any more fire. Instead, she had asked Karl. The jump drive was the model Karl recommended – the Lexar four-gigabyte – and over the weekend her husband bought two for her at Fry's at $289 a copy. Lily opened her purse and unfolded the notes of Karl's instructions. Yesterday, from the phone in his New York studio apartment, he had helped her practice. His unambiguous new bloom of dislike for Crawford was palpable, even distracting. When she asked why, he became pissy and reticent, but she decided not to take it personally. Lily could think of plenty of reasons for Karl's anger. She suspected one in particular. Finally Deirdre's phone lines went dark, so Lily dialed Levi and asked him to hold. She buzzed Deirdre. "Line one."

A voice came back. "Who is it?"

Lily pocketed the jump drive and instructions and walked away from her desk. She heard Deirdre ask again. She didn't want to be at her desk to answer.

Irritated, Deirdre rounded her desk and opened her office door. Lily wasn't there. She presumed Lily had gone to the restroom. Back at her desk, she answered the phone. "Deirdre Oliver."

"Hi, Deirdre, this is Levi."

Deirdre's shoulders slumped. "Hello, Levi. I've been meaning to call you. Sorry, but I was on the road. I only have a minute right now. What's up?"

"I've got some problems and I really need your help." He sounded frustrated. "As you know, Angela and I have always put the lion's share of my pay into company stock and options. You also know that the vast majority of what income I *do* get in the form of a check is from my annual bonus, not salary. What you may not know is that we spend a lot of money helping my family – my parents, and my sister and her son. My mom is very sick again…"

"Oh, I'm sorry."

"…and my dad has heart trouble, and they have no insurance. And now, because *I'm* on sick leave, the firm isn't giving me my annual bonus because the firm's rule is that I can't be on long-term disability the day it's paid – even though I wasn't on long-term disability for a single day during the period in which I earned it." He sounded out of breath.

"Okay. I'm not sure what you're asking."

"I'm asking for cash. Angela and I are running out of cash, but I have some stock vesting in a year or so. Is it possible for the firm to lend me money against that stock?"

"Hmm. Yeah. That's a big one. We haven't done any employee loans in quite a while, but I don't think it would work in your case anyway. You're on medical leave." Deirdre wedged the phone into the crook of her neck, opened a file on her laptop and started typing.

"I can't think of a better reason to help an employee."

"Oh, I agree," she said quickly. "It's just that we don't know if you're coming back." She took satisfaction in that lie. She knew it would be never.

"Of course I'm coming back."

She stopped typing. "I'm *so* glad to hear that. When would that be?"

"I don't know the exact day –"

"I see."

"But even if I'm out longer, the stock and options will vest, and I can pay the loan back."

"Ooo. I don't think so. See, the vesting clock stops while you're out on long-term leave. We can't make any distributions until you return and the clock resumes and completes the vesting period. Even if you come back, we don't know if you'll be staying. I'm *so* sorry." She typed some more.

"Deirdre, that's crazy. The minute I went from short-term to long-term leave, you guys … Crawford … eliminated my division. The job I had doesn't exist anymore! And I can't come back as a broker because I don't have any clients! What am I supposed to do, come back as a mail clerk in one of the South Bay offices?"

"Actually, that won't work either. Firm policy prohibits you from stepping down from a position and working in an office that you supervised. You may need to relocate."

She looked at her watch and craned to see if Lily was back yet. She was.

"So you won't let me work in California or in Billings. Jesus! Did you know that I got subpoenaed a couple of weeks ago? So did Joy Parnell. By the SEC."

"I heard that."

"Do you know that the firm is refusing to defend me? Are you aware that I have to hire my own attorney? Does Joy have to hire *her* own attorney? I bet not. Since when *doesn't* the firm represent its senior officers? Doesn't that seem a little odd to you?"

"I don't know, Levi. I don't get involved in those matters." She was typing quickly.

"Deirdre, I'm already selling my sister's house. Luckily, she's getting married. I took out a home equity loan so I could hire an attorney for an SEC investigation that I know virtually nothing about. I don't want to sell my *parents'* house. Is there *anything* you can do to help me?"

"I'd like to, Levi. If you think of anything that's possible, I'd be happy to help." Deirdre thought he might be crying. She wasn't surprised but didn't want to listen to it either.

His voice lost energy. "Who's to say that if I do move – and take a mailroom job in Phoenix or Denver or Biloxi – that Crawford won't find some reason to fire me? Then I'd lose disability pay *and* my deferred comp?"

She wouldn't be trapped into answering him. "Are you saying you're no longer ill?" She typed in the question and another moment passed.

"There is something you can do," he said. "Lily told me that Crawford's coming to town." To this, Deirdre frowned. "I want to meet with the two of you. Together."

"I'm not sure that's possible," she said.

"Deirdre, I've given my life to this company and I've made it a ton of money. I moved across the country. I delayed starting a family ... I guess that's good. Now I'm sick. I have no family here, and everyone I know works for Bookman Stuart and acts like I have smallpox."

"...as if..."

"What?"

"...*as if* you had smallpox. Sorry. I don't mean to be a grammar Nazi. Go on."

"I can't even go to work for another firm. You've taken my health, my career – everything. What can I lose?" His voice began to rise. "Because of the firm, *I personally* have to employ an attorney – an expensive one, dammit! You're destroying my life. What you're doing amounts to constructive termination – wrongful termination – and you know it! We could stop playing this game, settle, if you just give me my money. I don't think either of us wants to go to court!"

"Arbitration."

"What?"

"Your employment agreement states that we don't have to settle employment disputes in civil court. We settle them in NASD arbitration. You know that."

"Dammit, people like you are not just destroying *me*. People like you – like Crawford – are destroying many others. You destroy support people, you destroy good, honest leaders. You destroy families, children. You can't just rape chil..." Two malevolent faces flashed in him, and he tried to choose quickly. That one. That one was Crawford. "How much damage? For how long? Who will stop you if you don't stop yourselves? Can't you see? Don't you care?"

Rape? Deirdre did not feel an impulse to respond. Indeed, she did not care, though she found his passion interesting from the standpoint that he was clearly unable to be rational. Irrational. Gary was right. Levi blew his nose. She heard him sigh.

"What about the meeting?" he asked.

"I'll ask Gary. Listen, Levi, I am so sorry things seem so difficult for you right now. But you should concentrate on getting well. That's most important. Now, I hate to do this, but I have to go. I have two other lines blinking," she lied again. "I promise I'll get back to you."

When the light went out on Deirdre's phone line, Lily buzzed one of the secretaries and told her that now would be a good time to sing happy birthday. When most everyone in sight was rounded up and herded toward the break room, she rang Deirdre. "Deirdre, there's a birthday celebration in the break room. They're going to light the cake."

Deirdre picked up her phone. "Thanks, Lily, but no thanks. I've got a lot to do."

Lily palmed the jump memory device and once more quickly read the instructions she had written. "They're already in there, and they're waiting for you before they light the candles."

There was an exasperated sigh. "All right. I'll be right there."

When Deirdre opened her door, coffee cup in hand, Lily was pretending to be on the phone and plugged her other ear. Deirdre paused before her, so Lily held up two fingers and waved for Deirdre to go on ahead. As soon as Deirdre rounded the corner, Lily stuffed her dog-eared notes back into her purse and scribbled a phony pink message and carried it toward Deirdre's desk.

Deirdre's laptop was open and on, and the USB ports waited along the back of it where Karl said they would be. Lily inserted the jump drive. She rounded the desk and clicked into Windows Explorer where the removable drive showed up under My Computer. She moved the cursor to My Documents and dragged its contents to the drive and dropped it. The data began to transfer, but the progress bar grew much slower than when she had rehearsed. From outside the room the sound of a stapler startled her. She couldn't see who was there. She rotated the computer so she could see the screen from the center of the room and stepped away where she could alternately monitor the screen and spy for signs of Deirdre. Two minutes elapsed, then four. Laughter, singing and more laughter wafted from the break room. At one point, a young analyst burst from the adjacent office and Lily flinched. He stared at her, and she pointed. "That way. There's cake!" A minute later the screen showed the task was finished. Lily sidled to Deirdre's desk, removed the device and closed Windows Explorer. She repositioned the laptop as Deirdre had left it, lifted the phony message, and turned to the doorway.

Deirdre was standing there with a paper plate of cake. She looked at Lily's hands, Lily's eyes. A heavy, sick moment passed before Deirdre smiled sweetly. "We missed you."

"Oh, I got tied up. Levi called. He needed someone to talk to. I was just going to put a message on your desk." Lily suddenly realized that the jump drive was in one hand, so she held up the other one and waved the pink message.

Deirdre looked. "Don't bother. I've talked to him enough today. If he calls again, tell him I'll talk to him after I talk with Gary."

Lily wadded the message in her hand. "Will do." Back at her desk she waited five minutes, and then, from her cell phone, she dialed Karl's in New York.

"Did you do it?" Karl asked, ducking in an empty conference room on the executive floor.

"I think so."

"How'd it go?"

"Fine. Now what?"

From a thousand feet up in WTC 2, Karl looked northeast, up the brood-blue East River, counting back bridges like stitches – Triborough, Queensboro, Williamsburgh, Manhattan, Brooklyn. He'd miss the view. "Call me this weekend. I'll talk you through copying the files onto the other jump drive. Then just FedEx mine to my apartment. Hopefully we'll both find what we need."

Lily looked again at the small device in her hand. A tide of remorse was rising in her. "Karl, I don't want you to get into trouble. I was born in a jail – not that I remember – but the reviews from my mother weren't encouraging."

"Oh, don't worry so much. No one's going to find out. I'm gay. I can keep a secret. *Now* let's see if Crawford can blow me off. Human-resource *this*, you assholes!"

41

GIANT MISTAKES

For our struggle is not against flesh and blood,
but against the rulers, against the authorities, against the powers
of this dark world, and against spiritual wickedness in high places.

EPHESIANS 6: 12

For the third night in a row, Levi got plastered at home, but he finally had a plan. He'd have to get up early. Angela was in Italy, with Dusty, and without her here he was afraid of sleeping in. *No problem*, he thought. He'd stay up. Be home by noon. So, in the small hours, he packed his briefcase. He threw in some aged Bookman Stuart performance reports – reports that proved he was good at his job. He included two small pill-bottles – Wellbutrin for depression and Buspar for anxiety – and a couple of Light Days panty liners. Then he decided to shower and dress before his body crashed. So tired his chest hurt, he lay back on the couch, just for a minute, and crossed his arms. For three hours, he pressed a second-hand look into his suit and tie.

At 8 A.M., minutes before the limo arrived, his neighbor's gardener woke him with a leaf-blower. His skin hummed like a tuning fork. His eyeballs hurt. With a start, he remembered what he decided the night before. He repeated it. "I *will* return to work. When I do, Angela will come back. We'll be like before. I'll return, doctor's note or not, and Crawford, Deirdre, and the neighbor's fucking gardener can kiss my ass." When he rose, his forehead ached as if knuckle hit bone. On the way out the door, he grabbed a bottle of Gatorade. He'd take his pills in the limo.

For the next hour Levi dozed fitfully as they drove north on Highway 101. When the car stopped in the financial district north of Market Street, Levi signed the voucher to charge the fare to Bookman Stuart, but the driver sheepishly told him that he wasn't on the list of parties authorized to charge to the firm. So Levi paid cash and told the driver he'd call when he was finished. He entered the building and swiped his card. The turnstyle remained locked. He swiped it again … futilely.

"May I see your card, sir?" said a security guard with an out-of-true nose. Giant Jimmy.

Levi looked annoyed out of eyes cupped by great, dark circles. "This is nuts. Remember me?" He relinquished the card. "That's an Inner Circle Card. You're Jimmy. Remember?"

Jimmy swiped the card through a different slot, reserved for security guards. "I'm afraid it's expired, Mr. Monroe. Why don't I call upstairs and get clearance from your floor?"

"You do that," Levi said, insinuating something foreboding about his own powers.

A moment later Giant Jimmy hung up the phone. "Thank you, Mr. Monroe. Here's your day pass. Please keep it clipped to your jacket." He handed Levi a card. "I'm sorry," he added.

When the elevator reached his floor and the doors opened, Deirdre Oliver was there to meet him. As she escorted him to his former office – Crawford's old office – Levi moved with self-conscious fluidity, a scant veneer. As he crossed the field of desks, only the rabbit-eyed secretary from Fresno acknowledged at him. She waved shyly, cutting it short when Deirdre spied her. Lily stood and hugged Levi. She whispered something. "Who?" Levi mouthed. Lily's chance to warn him evaporated. Before she could answer, Deirdre said Mr. Crawford was ready. Inside, Crawford presided in the overstuffed chair. Deirdre sat on the sofa in front of a full cup of coffee, a legal pad, her computer. Levi sat at the far end of the couch. His desk and bragging-wall had been cleared of his personal items, and against the wall were three boxes too heaped for lids.

"Thank you for seeing me, Gary," Levi said.

"You're welcome." Crawford barely looked at him as he shuffled through a handful of messages. "How's Angela?"

"She's fine. She's in Europe with our nephew right now. How are things around here?"

"We're making do." Crawford sat back and touched his chin. "You wanted to speak with me. Speak."

"Yes," Levi crossed his leg. "I think it's time I returned to work and I want to explore how I can do that."

Deirdre stopped writing on the legal pad and took a quick sip of coffee as if it were fuel.

"How has your time at home been?"

"Good. Nice. But now I'm a little stir-crazy. I'm ready to come back."

Crawford gazed out the window. "I'm not sure that's possible." He looked at his watch.

"I think it'll be okay," Levi reassured. "I'm feeling quite a bit better. I know the division has been dissolved – and my job eliminated – but I'm qualified to do anything. I haven't talked with my doctor yet, but I'm … hopeful, pretty sure, actually, he'll release me."

Crawford looked as though he resented every word of this game. "You look thin."

"My health is fine. Well, fine enough." Levi lifted his briefcase to the coffee table. It was time to make them see, make them remember how good he was … *is*. Crawford looked at his watch again, out the window again. Levi removed a manila folder. "I took the time to collate my performance, as reported by the firm's own internal reports, in the various jobs I've had over the years." He held the folder out to Crawford. "I outperformed my peers at every stage, and I have a clean compliance record. As you know," he pointed to the boxes, "I've won many awards and I—"

"Stop!" Crawford sat straight and glared at Levi, ignoring the folder. "I told you long ago not to *manage me*. There's one thing you need to know. Your record is *not* as clean as you think it is."

"What do you mean? I've never had a compliance complaint or a human resource complaint. Never."

"You are mistaken, Mr. Monroe. As you know, the NASD and the SEC have concerns over your supervisory record. *I* have concerns. Even *Mike Sandler* is concerned about your supervisory record."

Before he could stop himself, Levi said, "Any supervisory problem with exercise and sell business in this division was *before* my time. *That* would be my sworn testimony." Next to him, Deirdre's writing became manic, drawing everyone's attention. "For Christ's sake," Levi said, "who are you, Madame Defarge? Buy a Dictaphone. Or is accuracy counterproductive?"

For a long moment, the contempt in the room crowded out dialogue. Crawford scowled out the window. Pure hatred, the purest Levi had known.

Deirdre sipped her coffee, wrote more words, any words she wanted.

Levi began to feel sick. There was a sharp pain, and he stifled a breath and put his hand on his abdomen. "I need to excuse myself for a moment." He stood and left the room.

In the restroom stall, Levi felt faint. He hung his head over charts, Van Gogh stars and melting faces. He focused. Took a pen from his pocket and drew on the marble, tracing the coils, studying them – catching himself with a start.

Afterward he washed his face. He steadied the counter and looked. The ghost in the mirror scared him. Was him. The melting ape. A rational self said, *Maybe you* should *stay on sick leave. If I'm allowed to return, it'll merely be so Crawford can fire me. The son of a bitch wins. No. Fucking Nazi. No giving up. Frozen out is constructive discharge, is wrongful termination! Besides, he's the crook. People will see. They have to, and I'll be vindicated. No. I'll* demand *to be reinstated, in any capacity, anywhere, and if Crawford dismisses me on some trumped-up crap, I'll sue the bastard. Either way, I'll see that the SEC throws his ass in jail.*

Levi dried his face. His hands were cold. He ran them under hot water. On the way back, he stopped at each and every secretary's desk and said hello. It took a while, but so what? In due course, he walked into the office. Crawford looked callously from the big chair. Deirdre was still in her place, but another woman was sitting where Levi had been. Levi could see only the back of her head, but she seemed at once familiar and out of context. Her hair needed dying. *Oh, shit* – his open briefcase had been moved, closer to Deirdre. *Shit!* The pills and panty liners were there – right there! – in plain view. He lurched closer, short of a lunge. The woman turned. Levi's mouth slackened even as the veins of his face became engorged.

Deirdre spoke first. "Levi, I believe that you know Lynette."

His mind churned without traction for the meaning of her presence. "Hi," he said.

She didn't answer.

Deirdre continued. "Lynette has some concerns of a, well, delicate nature. Instead of handling them through an attorney, she's chosen to take advantage of the employee assistance procedures?" Again Deirdre was talking in questions, as if asking a child if they understood. Deirdre gently touched Lynette's hand, as if to say it was okay. *What was okay?* Levi wondered. She smiled sublimely at Lynette. "Do you want to explain what we've talked about?"

Lynette looked at her own lap. "No, you go ahead."

Deirdre proceeded with obvious pleasure. "Lynette tells us that, during the time you worked in Billings, you asserted your authority so as to … sway her … to have relations with you?"

Levi's jaw dropped. Lynette couldn't look at him. *This can't be real! Why would she strike out now?* Doesn't matter. She *was* striking out. He blinked long and hard. Dammit! Deny it. Of course, deny it. It wasn't true! … was it? Like Crawford says, why tell the truth when there's nothing to gain? Why *now?* After all these years? Lynette couldn't prove *anything,* and *everything* he'd worked for was at stake. "I don't even know what to say." No statement could have been truer. Levi moved to the other side of the coffee table. "You…" looking at Lynette, trying to grab her eyes, "I mean … This is ridiculous!"

Pen in hand, Deirdre raised her eyebrows. "Am I to take it that you deny Lynette's claim?"

"Of course I deny it! This is incredible!" He wanted to say, 'She seduced me!' He looked at Lynette again. "What could you possibly gain by striking out at me like this?"

Crawford rose. "Dignity, Mr. Monroe. Dignity. I think it's time to end this meeting."

"No," said Levi. Then, arm extended, pointing a finger at Crawford, "You have sunk *too* low. I've never understood why you hate me, but I don't give a shit anymore. I'm going to sink your ass." Then, yelling at Lynette, "Can't you see you're being used? This guy is a *crook!*"

"Get out of here, Levi," Crawford said evenly.

Unfinished, Deirdre calmly held up her palm to Crawford. "Levi, Lynette says that you're the father of her teenage son?"

"What!"

"She says she became pregnant after you coerced her into sex? She says her marriage has ended because of it? She's already submitted her son to a DNA test? – For which the firm paid? – And, if you will submit yourself, then she's willing to settle with you, and the firm, out of court. Are you willing to take a DNA test?"

Open-mouthed, Levi stared at Deirdre. He stared at Lynette, who had tears in her eyes. He looked back at Deirdre. "I don't have anything left to say to you people." Then, as if to admonish the invasion of his privacy, he bent over the table and slammed his briefcase shut. He walked toward the door.

Before he got there, Deirdre spoke one more time. "Levi?" He turned just enough to look at her. Crawford had moved behind the desk and was dialing the phone. "If Lynette's allegations are true? Then they substantially predate your claim for medical leave of absence, and we have grounds to terminate you for cause. Bob Cohen's office will contact you. I've contacted our long-term disability insurance carrier? They may deny further coverage, and you may owe back the money you've already taken from them. I assume they'll contact you."

Levi turned to leave here, presumably for the last time in his life. At the door loomed Giant Jimmy. "Right this way, Mr. Monroe." Jimmy motioned toward the elevators.

Levi paused. He glared back at the others. "Are you sure you want me to have nothing left to lose? Are you really sure?" No one answered. He stepped through the door. Halfway to the elevator, a hand caught his elbow. It was Lynette. She moved close and spoke meekly, trying to be private.

"Levi, I'm so sorry," she offered. He said nothing, feeling only hatred for her. She snared the back of his hand and shoved something in it. A box. A small, flat box wrapped in grocery-bag paper. "Marilyn made me promise to get this to you. I didn't mail it because I wasn't sure what was in it and I didn't know if it should be sent here or where. So I brought it. I hope…" He jerked his hand away, clutching a box from his dead friend, a box delivered by Judas.

Five minutes later Deirdre stood with Lynette at the elevators on the forty-fifth floor, waiting for Jimmy, Lynette's escort to the limousine. Deirdre's blood was up, her body impatient to dance, eager to rejoin Crawford, to share the kill, to howl, feeling wonderful, feeling … sexual.

"Stay in town as long as you like," Deirdre jabbered. "Do you have friends here?"

"Not really." Lynette was holding her purse with both hands in front of her crotch, staring blankly at the base of the elevator door.

"Oh. Well, stay as long as you like. If you want to see a play or a ball game or anything else, just call the hotel concierge and charge it to your room. We'll cover it. Enjoy yourself a little." Lynette looked at her oddly. The elevator bell finally chimed and Jimmy emerged. "Call if you need anything," Deirdre chirped. She shook Lynette's hand and scarcely waited until the door closed before snapping about, her body abuzz. She wasn't aware of people looking or not as she strode through the field of secretary desks. It was all she could do to keep from hopping, a rare feeling indeed. She had done it! She had delivered to Crawford his enemy's body on his enemy's shield, a shield Crawford could make use of. Lily was nowhere to be seen when Deirdre stepped into Crawford's office. From behind the big black desk, he was grinning too.

"Close the door," he said. She did. "Lock it," he said. She did. He walked around the desk, straight at her, his eyes on hers. He didn't slow until his arms were around her, hugging her tight from the shoulders, from the waist, low from the waist. He was hard. She felt it on her leg. For a split second it shocked her, but *okay*, she thought. *Fair enough.* She pressed back, a little. "Nicely done," he said over her shoulder. He released her, holding her shoulders in his hands at arms' length. "Nicely done."

"Thank you," she said, beaming. *And now you can thank me by moving me to New York.* Retreating behind the desk, he responded right on cue.

"Listen, I've got some calls to make. It looks like I'm out here indefinitely until this division is either fully dissolved or Monroe is replaced. I haven't decided which yet. We've already saved millions." Much of which he would pocket, he didn't say. Nor did he congratulate himself on positioning Levi to hang for Crawford's felonies. There was prudence in the unsaid. "I'm staying at the Nikko. Why don't we meet there for dinner at seven? We've got plenty to discuss."

Yes, she thought. "I'm available. I'll just work here until then. There's a lot to tie up. Easier to do it here than from New York. I don't want to leave loose ends for the next person."

At that exact moment Crawford's eyes went cold, save for the flicker of mistrust. "I've decided to go another direction on that. I need you out here."

From somewhere in Deirdre's gut, a floor caved through and blood fell from her face. That moment, she would come to recall, was the instant dark unions dissolved and dark confederacies formed. Crawford had failed to pay an assassin.

42

HOMECOMINGS

Hello darkness my old friend
I've come to talk with you again

PAUL SIMON

For most of eleven hours aboard United Flight 19 from Heathrow to San Francisco, Dusty slept. Angela couldn't help but grin at the spent eighteen-year-old. He had been the perfect traveling companion – exuberant, funny, smart, thirsty for new experiences. He had been a joy, never a burden. For that matter, while she was away she had felt no burden of any sort. She had laughed. She had lived. Most of their time was spent in Rome, a good choice, in retrospect, for staying inundated with art, architecture, and history by day, fantastic food, wine and, for Dusty, discothèques near the hotel by night. Even Angela had gone out, once. It nearly went too well. Flirting was another Italian art, and masterfully practiced day or night, she decided.

The trip had been the ideal anesthetic to thinking. Angela had done enough of that on the flight there. It wasn't as if there was any more to decide. She finished her wine and asked the attendant for another. It was just plain sad.

At SFO, she hung with Dusty long enough to transfer him to a Delta flight that connected through Salt Lake City to Billings. At his gate, he thanked and hugged her repeatedly, and she told him to brush his teeth, no kidding. She'd see him soon.

At the driveway of her house – rather, the house – as she paid the driver, Levi appeared wearing cargo shorts, wagging like a golden retriever, jubilantly fetching bags. As she turned, he suddenly put his arms around her and kissed her, startling her, and she didn't quite kiss him back.

"How was your flight? God, it's good to have you home!" In the last few weeks – had it only been weeks? – Levi's limbs had grown rangier, his face had thinned.

"Good." She looked past him. The lawn had gone to seed and sported pimples of fresh dirt.

He grinned at her. "We're out of gas for the mower, but I'll get some today. Well, maybe not today. I went to Wal-Mart yesterday – did you know there are seven in the South Bay? – for gopher traps. I haven't set them yet." He smiled. "Wanna help?" he joked.

She busied herself looking at the lawn and the house. "Not tonight. I'm pretty tired."

They stood, him clutching bags, her holding her purse and jacket, waiting for each other to lead the way to the house. Finally she went.

She flopped her jacket over the banister and went to the kitchen. On the counter was a pile of mail and unread newspapers.

"I was thinking maybe we could go out for sushi," he said, "if you're not too tired."

As she sorted through the mail, she sensed him eyeballing her. "Just let me settle in for a while. Okay?"

"No problem." He chirped.

"What's this?" She was looking at a flat little package addressed to Levi.

"Oh, that was addressed to me by Marilyn, from Billings. Before she died. The office there finally got it to me. I thought you might want to open it with me. You know. A mystery thing." She set it back down. "I'll take your stuff upstairs," he said. "Be right back."

Angela put down the mail and reached for a wine glass. All the cupboard doors were slightly open. She closed them. She took an open wine bottle from the refrigerator and poured a glass. Straightaway she drank most of it and refilled it, leaving it on the counter while she made for the bathroom. The downstairs water closet was something of a showpiece in which she had taken pride, having herself designed the cabinets and selected the sconces, the burgundy-veined marble. Perhaps if she had taken less pride she wouldn't have lifted the new throw rug. Perhaps she would have thought it simply Levi's touch of hominess. But she did lift the rug. And she could not believe what she saw. Across the marbling – rather, bled into it – ran new colors of meandering lines and straight ones, and more straight parallel ones, and bars and swirls, and grotesque outlines, and coils and coils, in colors – three colors – no, four, five! – five colors of ink! She sat, aghast, and peed. She wet a washcloth and scrubbed, but only perfunctorily, to prove what she knew already: these stains did not wash off.

Back through the kitchen she scooped up her wine glass and carried it into the family room. At a big chair, she stopped, frozen upright. Nothing around her seemed from her life. Not the formal furniture or the Waterford and Baccarat knickknacks. Not the thirty-five thousand dollar per room catalogue collections of furniture. Not the Persian rug … should she lift it, check the floor under? Why? What would it matter? These … *things* … seemed a burden, almost an obscenity. She was embarrassed for herself. Not even her Bob Ross painting over the fireplace seemed hers any more. Dead things. In an ill-lit corner, tucked beside a sofa table, a digital alarm clock peeked green-eyed from the shadow, and a wadded blanket played pedestal to an ink-smudged pillow. A scrawled-up plume of paper rested on top, a hundred feathered-out pages that had been a notebook before it was scrolled, this way and that, a million times over until it curlicued east and west as if a madman had wrestled it for directions time and again. Levi called out from the kitchen. She took another slug of wine. "In here," Angela said.

He walked in. "What are you doing in here?" She noticed now the many inks on his fingers. He put his arms around her and this time hugged until she hugged back.

He dropped his arms with a look of discovery. "You smell like the wind."

She smiled weakly. "I don't know. Just thinking. Resting." At this moment, his smile was almost too pitiful to take.

"Thinking about what?"

"Did you draw on the floor of the bathroom?"

He looked sheepish. "Oh, that. I thought I was using those white board highlighters, the ones you use for school, the ones you can wash? I screwed up. They were Sharpies. Can you believe it? Pretty dumb, huh? Duuuh." He grinned, overplaying it. "I called the tile guy already. Sorry about that."

"Oh, Levi." She took a sip and looked at him. "I was thinking I don't belong here."

"I know what you mean. I've been thinking the same thing." He talked too fast. "We're not *from* Silicon Valley, not that anyone here is, and who needs the pressure? Or expense?"

God, she thought, *please* stop looking so warmly at me.

"I've decided I'm not ever going back to Bookman Stuart – maybe not even back to the business. I was never of it, you know, just in it. But you knew that." He sat forward animatedly. "Let's sell the house. Let's blow this popsicle stand," he grinned and carved an arch with his arm. "You know, the only thing holding housing prices up here is funny money from Internet stocks and options and mortgage liar loans. It can't last. There's no actual profit being made. Shares and options will tank, and 98 percent of people can't afford a median house on their income alone. Unemployment's bound to surge, and the unemployed can't buy houses. When the housing crashes, this place'll become Silicon Crater. *Especially* if there's another earthquake – like after '89. Let's sell now. The high-tech industry is drunk. Homeowners here are in denial. Like Denver and Houston before oil crashed in the '80s." He looked expectant. "Let's get out now." She didn't talk. "Housing crashed here from, like, '89 to '95 because it had run up too far too long, you know, wages up 3 percent a year, prices up 25 percent. The math *can't* keep working. You know what touched that decline off? The '89 quake – not that it wouldn't have plummeted anyway. What if we have an earthquake now and..." He halted. "Ange?"

A thick moment congealed. She sipped wine. Looked at the alarm clock. "You've been sleeping in here."

He scarcely looked embarrassed. "Yeah. Sometimes. What's wrong?"

She ran out of things to look at so she closed her eyes and tilted her head back. "Oh, nothing. I'm just tired."

He touched her knee, then rubbed it. "So. Do you want to go to bed?"

Bucking at the thought, she said. "Not right now." She fought an impulse to brush away his hand. *Dammit!* She didn't *want* to hurt him ... hadn't – ever. But *he* did this, not her, to both of them. She had worked so hard for so long to not notice that she was exhausted from not noticing.

"Well. Why don't I have a glass of wine too, while you wind down?" As he went into the kitchen, he kept talking. "Maybe we should go on a road trip," he said loudly, "you know, in a car. Maybe we should check out places to live *other than* Montana. Warmer places. Like Colorado or Arizona. I hear Sedona's nice."

When he returned to the room, she began to cry.

"You could teach anywhe..."

Levi stood motionless before her. She recognized dread in his eyes, but she couldn't feel it. Only sadness. Sadness for this final loss. More clearly than ever, she realized she had said goodbye to the man who had been her husband long ago, and this, now, her last goodbye, was not at all to him.

She was acknowledging the end of something more personal, not apart from herself, a discreet, intimate presence that she had, for years, stubbornly refused to unlove. She was saying goodbye to *us*.

"No," he quietly said.

"I'm going home, Levi. And I don't want you to follow me."

"No," he said, more fully. "It's not the truth."

"I'll help you in any way I can, but I can't stay here. The truth is I can only hurt as much as I can love … and I just can't hurt anymore. The truth is that there's nothing sadder than the truth. You can have whatever things you want. I'm sure you'll be fair. I'm going home."

Through gusts of anguish on his face, he was only able to say, "I love you. I love you." She stood, and as she climbed the stairs to unpack, he said, "I love you."

Minutes later, she heard him leave the house. She watched out an upstairs window as he strode to the car as if he had somewhere to go. After an hour or so, he returned and told her again, with great conviction, he loved her, and that he could be however she wanted, wherever she wanted. As the gloaming grew late, he posted himself at the bottom of the stairs for a long while, leaving the lights off as the day drained, waiting to confront her. When she finally came down, she stood her ground. He left again. He returned again. In the middle of the night he came to her bed, wanting to make love. When he lay down, she rose and went downstairs. A half-hour later he followed, so she returned to their bed again, leaving him on the couch.

For the first week of preparations for her move back to Roundup, Levi tried many times, with no hint of success, to change her mind. In point of fact, Angela was surprised how things happened without thinking much at all, as if working through a to-do list. She stopped by the school district office to tender her resignation and meet with the human resources director about benefits. On Friday, Kathy and their principal took Angela to lunch.

During the second week Levi avoided the house if Angela was there. He disappeared for long periods while she packed. She went to her dentist, her gynecologist. When she paid bills, she set up an accordion file for Levi, parking it on the island in the kitchen. The morning before she left, she shopped for groceries and filled the freezer with pizzas, Hungry-Man dinners, and vanilla ice cream. She stocked the pantry with canned vegetables, soups, and stews.

A book-size box had appeared on the counter, Tiffany blue, with a tiny card bearing her name. It read, "Sometimes you can fix things you love." She did not open it. She saw Levi drive by, but he didn't come home that night. At noon the next day, Angela met Geno's Delta flight at Minetta San Jose airport. Hoping to say goodbye to Levi, they waited at the house until 3 o'clock. He never showed. Finally they struck out, Angela driving her loaded car behind Geno in the U-Haul. That night, from Reno, Angela called Levi to say they were stopping. It just felt odd not to call. She left a message.

Levi lay on his side, naked on the cool bathroom marble, clutching a photo of Angela and catching her eye in it. He thought about the day they moved into this house from their first house in the Valley, how big and empty it was, how their furniture suddenly seemed spare and each piece was assigned an outpost until others could be bought and settled in. He thought about the Bob Ross painting and how happy Angela was when she got a job. He thought about trips to the clinic and the baby that never was. About atonement. Retribution. How souls that can't be blended get tangled from trying and how pain untangles them and makes more pain. If you're not careful. Or kind. He remembered when Kathy and Bob came to dinner and Angela interrupted him in this bathroom – *in the bathroom, for Christ's sake! Made fun of him! Made him trip, cut himself!* He'd guessed right that night, months ago, about his blood … that it would stain the wicked, stone face. *Crimson dried russet that can't wash off of – should never wash off of – that face. Done! No turning back. And russet had turned … gray … everything gray – the bedspread, the paintings, the leaves waving at him through the window. Everything!* He had been expecting it. For years. His only surprise in its relentless pursuit was that it had taken so long. It had taken his world. It had taken Angela. He gave himself to it.

He thought how Angela and his mom might hug, console each other, then he recoiled at the image. *It's a trap. It's a prison, their pain. They'll be okay. Fine. In not long. I am too.* Something felt wrong. *They'll be relieved. Eventually. But they'd only admit with their eyes, never admit to each other. First Dad'd talk in soft tones that dress up vindication like sorrow, like "it's sure too bad." Then throw around words like "big shot," but carefully. And Crawford'll puff up, the smug son of a bitch. He'd win. He'd win. But it's so hard to keep trying – and the tension, and the words and the words and the words and the words … for everyone.* Levi melted with exhaustion. *Too depressed. Tired. Too tired. They say you're not strong enough at the bottom … to do it … have enough strength to give a shit. Huh. The tile needs regrouting. Here and there. All right. Okay. Okay. It's time.* He tried to concentrate, to rally. To rally enough.

To Angela's picture, he said, "I'm sorry. Sorry for my … *before.* Sorry for *our* before. I'm sorry for my scars and stains. And shame. And the suits. Stupid suits. They don't matter. People see. *You* knew. Thank you for waiting as long as you did." He found himself staring at the scar on his knee, crinkled lead crepe, not like before – nothing was. He marveled at the delicate skin of the scar. He dragged the heavy iron pistol sight hard across the old wound, filleting it open. He felt nothing. He thought about stains and why they work, why they won't go away, as he caught the blood in his fingers. He pinched the wound, worked it until his fingers were awash. Soon they became sticky, like with deer blood, tacky between his fingers. He carefully spread the digits, and it pulled his skin into webbing. He touched his branded palm. Gray. He regarded his forearm, *naked, naked, that's not how it was.* So with two stiff fingers, he smeared a wavy, bloody cross the length of it. The marble effigy on the floor was watching, cold and hard … judging … so he bloodied it, pressing firmly to gather energy from it, enough energy. Levi pinched his knee tighter and it flowed, and he swabbed with his fingers and began to finger-paint a graph across the marble face. He blurred his eyes, but it wasn't coming … the vision. Nothing. In growing frustration his fingers poked the effigy, and swirled, again and again, and spiraled and coiled, and smeared and coiled again, until the tile was sloppy, the face in the floor screwed with blood, and Levi slapped down his palm, disfiguring the face with his disfigured print. Now he just wanted its energy. Its help. He felt only … fatigue. The image had grayed, and changed, somehow … the man gone … or morphed. He stared insistently, insistently, insistently – and it reddened. Not a man. It was … *Lam* … and Levi was … watching. Hiding. "I'm sorry! I was afraid! I'm sorry! I'm so sorry!" With confusion and crisp fear and gummy fingers he steered the barrel of the gun to his forehead and concentrated.

It wasn't until the fourth ring that Levi grew vaguely cognizant of the phone. From an answering machine, his own confident voice offered to take a message.

"Hi. It's me. I'm sorry I didn't catch you at home. I don't know. Maybe you're listening. Anyway, I'm sorry we didn't get a chance to say goodbye.

I just thought I'd let you know we stopped in Reno for tonight. Maybe I shouldn't've called, but, you know … old habits. Anyway, I think Dad wants to play the slot machines." There was a long pause. "Thank you for having Mom's pearls restrung … I …" Pause. "Please be okay. I need you to be okay. I've loved you – forever – and I will – forever." Another pause. "Well, I probably won't call tomorrow. We hope to make it to Pocatello, or Butte, if we make good time. Dad doesn't want to drive behind RVs through Yellowstone. My cell phone is on if you need to talk. I'm so sorry, Levi. I love you."

Levi looked at the gun and the bloody muzzle, sharpened to surreal detail. Desperation and rage rose and possessed him, their energy whitening his knuckles around the handle, their pressure splitting his chest and face from within, ripping him utterly. Suddenly, violently, clumsily, he hurled the pistol into the bedroom, where it caved into drywall on the other side. *Lam.*

43

EXPATS

The cruelest lies are often told in silence.
ROBERT LOUIS STEVENSON

It was not quite 8 A.M. Lily's voice rose from the phone speaker. "Deirdre, Mike Sandler's office is returning your call,"

It had been raining for days, so when Deirdre went to close her office door before she took the call she thought nothing of Lily wearing her trench coat. With Crawford out, Lily could have come in late. Or maybe she was going to Starbuck's. Deirdre returned to her desk. With both hands, she squared her laptop. She took a breath and lifted the receiver. "Deirdre Oliver."

"Please hold for Mr. Sandler," said Sandler's whiskey-voiced assistant, slapping Deirdre on hold before she could reply, as always. Did she do this to everybody? The woman had always made her feel defensive, like a neighbor who knew you'd snuck in their house but couldn't prove it. Deirdre regarded the stack-haired broad as a battle-ax, but she decided consciously, starting right now, to like her. Until further notice.

"Mike Sandler." His voice sounded mildly perturbed. Maybe not.

"Uh. Mike. Hi. This is Deirdre Oliver. She probably told you that? Anyway, I don't want to take much of your time, but I've come across some very sensitive information? Big issues, big, and, well, given that we don't have a national director of HR yet? – that's who I would usually share this with, God knows I don't want to disturb you – "

"Listen, you need to go through Gary."

"Um, well, that's just it, you see, I, uh, you see Gary … Could I come to New York and talk with you? I think there are things you should know. There are others here who know them, too." It was a gamble, she knew. In fact, there were others who had information, information that could collectively sink Crawford, but she was almost sure no one else had put the pieces together.

When the time came, Deirdre would recruit their testimony, in any way she needed. After all, she knew many things. Still, it was possible no one would throw in with her. Especially Lily. Too principled. Yes, Lily would take special finesse, but at the end of the day, Deirdre surmised, one could count on Lily's hate for Crawford. She could gather them all. She bet on it. "You should know. I'm worried about the firm? The whole firm?" Sandler's silence lasted through four breaths. *Shit*, she began to panic – she *never* panicked. *I shouldn't have called!*

To her surprise, when he finally spoke he sounded more contemplative than anything. "I have a better idea." He didn't seem mad at all! Not even surprised. More like, *oh God ... in league? With Crawford?*

Seven blocks away Lily Fujiwara removed her trench coat before she sat in the lobby of the NASD offices. So this is where her packages had been going for more than a year – packages with copies of client complaint letters, internal memos, and Franklin calendar pages taken from Gary Crawford's day planner with attached phone messages.

In her lap, her soft leather briefcase bulged with the last of it: her notes on conversations Crawford had from his car with Abhaya Ramakapur, among others, and printouts of Deirdre's dirty correspondence. In her pocket, she carried digital copies of every conversation recorded in Deirdre's laptop, the existence of which she would keep to herself for now. She wasn't sure what laws she'd broken to acquire it. The letters were the main things, and the payout lists, sent to Crawford's home address. There were letters to outside parties and outgoing e-mails. Lily had printed those, had them with her. She laughed to herself that paper trails had become safer – slower to duplicate and easier to shred – than electronic trails.

The law shielded Lily from being accused of stealing direct correspondence. The Securities Acts demanded that all correspondence at brokerage firms be supervised and kept, in paper or digital form, for six years, subject to internal Compliance audit review and to review by regulatory bodies at any time. If Deirdre claimed Lily came about correspondence surreptitiously, she would further damn herself. Not only was the correspondence evidence of Deirdre and Crawford's guilt in breaking any number of laws – securities, civil, and criminal – but to protest that the correspondence was not meant to be seen, supervised or filed would prove intent and exacerbate Deirdre and Crawford's legal footing. When Lily lit the fuse on the investigation by anonymously sending client complaints to the NASD, she knew the NASD and SEC might subpoena other relevant records, such as outgoing and internal correspondence. The day the subpoena came, Lily herself had taken it from the server's hand. From there, she simply followed the court's order. Except for the flash drive. As she sat there, she was unsure why she'd brought it, for now the SEC or perhaps the FBI would seize Deirdre's laptop, based on the evidence so far. One document – the Abba letter - should do it. Lily would, here and now, claim she'd innocently seen a letter on Deirdre's laptop screen which ostensibly was sent to Bookman Stuart from Abba. She thought it was an email, she'd say, so she printed and filed it. It wasn't until she read how it falsely implicated Levi and Joy Parnell in the scheme to earn interest on the improper float on other people's money did she realize it was a forgery. Yes, on this day she would prove that Deirdre had, in fact, invented the letter. How Lily came about it was a small lie for a greater good. Yet Lily took no solace in her betrayal. *Betrayer,* she thought, *a clumsy word.* What Lily could not prove, for all her access, was that payoffs to Abba had actually occurred. She knew who could.

Lily edged her fingers inside one briefcase side pocket, tenderly drawing across the small, flat box encasing the Purple Heart. *"In loyalty, honor,"* she quoted her mother who had quoted her father, then added her own. *"but never honor for loyalty."* From another leather pocket, she removed a business card that read: *Lily Fujiwara, Assistant Vice President, Divisional Administrator. Bookman Stuart:* the firm she long-ago adopted as the lattice into which she wove purpose, friends, even family – people who for decades had recognized her, praised her, defined her. But who was left to remember her dedication anymore? The notion of institutional loyalty had become a vestige of some pagan religion that B-school zealots had callously and naively exterminated. There no longer existed any memory or sentiment for past fidelity. In their smug, green objectivity, they had codified behavior, reducing ethics and moral sway to pretend dogma recited in executive speeches and HR brochures. So now, absent practiced judgment, in the anonymity of immensity, men like Crawford flourished. Still, she felt ashamed. *Traitor. A harder, more elegant term.* She extracted her remaining ten business cards and slowly tore them in half.

The receptionist showed Lily where to find a wastebasket for her scraps, and Styrofoam cups for the coffee. Sometime later Lily discovered herself cradling a cup at her lap, still full but tepid, when a door from a conference room opened and two women emerged to greet her.

"Hello." The stout, Mediterranean-looking one held a homemade coffee cup with *I'd Rather Be Gardening* painted on it. "Are you Mrs. Fujiwara?"

Lily stood and offered her hand. "Yes. It's Lily. You must be Fran."

"I am." Fran smiled comfortably. "I'd like to introduce you to my counterpart at the SEC, Julie Pennington. As I said in my email, Julie and I are working together on this investigation." The women exchanged pleasantries. "We'll be using one of our conference rooms." She indicated the way. "Is your attorney joining us?"

"No. I've decided I don't want an attorney for now."

"Okay. As I also mentioned, someone else has joined us, another friendly party from your organization. Joy Parnell. Are you still okay with that?"

Lily thought of how carefully she had presented herself over time, and how managers, young and old, had sought her unofficial counsel and treated her as Mother Confessor. She remembered how some of the same people mocked Joy. She thought of how, from this point forward, in her colleagues' view, she and Joy would be forever linked. In Lily's mind, it was at that moment that she drew a curtain on the past and many of those from it. Then she thought of her husband, the land they had purchased in the Central Valley and sunshine. She nodded to Fran. "I am fine with meeting with Joy."

"Joy doesn't know you're here yet. Before we go in, I want to ask you if you've fully considered what effect this will have on you, on your career, on the careers of others. I don't want you to feel coerced or unduly reticent in any way."

In an instant, Lily reflected on her career. She thought of Crawford's, Deirdre's, Levi's. Her eyes set. "Dead is dead." *In loyalty, honor, but never honor for loyalty*

"Okay then."

As they walked down the hall, Lily regarded Fran's cup. "You're a gardener. My husband and I are gardeners. We hope to do more of it soon. In the Central Valley."

"I envy you being so close to retirement." Fran smiled. "Though if my husband retires first, I might keep working just to keep from killing him." When they entered the room, Joy was at the conference table.

"Lily, I believe you know Joy Parnell."

Joy had been typing an email into her Blackberry, and now her thumbs moved in a frantic display of the importance of finishing – for Lily. Yet she didn't seem surprised. While Lily held her shoulders back, Joy pushed the last button with affected flair and then aimed her jaunty smile at Lily and stood, virtually reeking with gladness at their reunion.

Fran spoke. "First, I need to reiterate to both of you that you each should consider hiring private counsel. Do you want to do that before we continue?"

Both women said no. Julie Pennington nodded to Fran.

"Okay, then. Please sit. Mrs. Fujiwara – Lily – there is certain information about agreements and complaints between Bookman Stuart executives and clients, both corporate and private, we have discussed with you. What you weren't aware of – nor was Joy for that matter – was that Joy was simultaneously providing us with faxes and other evidence involving *executions and transactions* in client accounts and Bookman Stuart *profitability and bonuses*. We don't yet know how much of this information we can legally use, and I remind you again that you should each seek legal counsel." She paused. "We only have a few questions of you two together, but first I want to commend both of you for your integrity and courage in coming forward."

"No need to thank us," said Joy, sitting primly. "I just can't work at an organization that doesn't have integrity."

"Please understand, Ms. Parnell," said Pennington, "that no one is alleging that Bookman Stuart is devoid of integrity. In fact, we are not without their aid at very senior levels."

Joy looked at Lily. *Senior levels?* "Well," said Joy, "I know Lily feels the same way. We've worked together for years, and she's the best," and she smiled. "We're a team, huh?"

"Perhaps you can work together one more time," said Pennington. "There's something we want you to do."

Lily smiled sickly. Perhaps for the clever, dead isn't dead.

44

BIG GAME SEASON

Black as the devil,
Hot as hell,
Pure as an angel,
Sweet as love.

CHARLES MAURICE DE TALLEYRAND-PERIGORD

It had been sixteen hours since Levi drove away from Saratoga at sunrise. His return there was immeasurably far away. Oddly, it was liberating not knowing. The first six hours, through the Bay Area, Sacramento, past the Sierras to Reno, were congested and slow. Then, a few miles east of Reno, about where truckers met whores at the Mustang Ranch, traffic vanished, as if the desert was some great moat protecting *his* America from invasion by those whom and that which he had finally escaped. He punched the speed control up to 80 mph. He stopped only for gas. He ate at the wheel. His back ached. Again in the dark, past Pocatello but before West Yellowstone, he gassed up at a truck stop. As the waitress filled his thermos he said, "I'm on my way home. Roundup, Montana. Ever heard of it?" The old gal hadn't and peered dubiously out the picture window at his California plates. "I worked for a while in California. Man. You can have it. I'm going home to take care of my mom. Tough when your parents get old." She charged him $2 and said good luck with your mom in a way that meant it.

To keep his mind alive, Levi listened to AM talk radio until he lost all signals in the pitch black envelope of the Gallatin canyon just north of the Park. No other cars. No trucks. Within touching distance of sleep, he didn't notice the ebony bull bison in the road and barely swerved in time to miss it. But fifteen miles later, the narcotic of the wee hours was back. He gripped the steering wheel and nearly bounced his chest off the horn, again and again, determined to shake off the drowse. A mile more and he did it again. The temperature gauge in the dash said it was 28 degrees outside. Figuring the bison were behind him, he sped up. Still hours from dawn, it was too late and too early for deer to be moving. He was driving straight through, he told himself, come hell or high water. Once dawn broke, he'd be okay. He would keep the promise he made all those years ago, to Lam. When he left. What was it he said, exactly? *I'll be there if you ever need me. I promise.* "I lied," he whispered. "Didn't mean to." Other than with money, he had never been there. Perhaps he had known he was lying when he said it. "But it's not too late." *This is one thing I can still do. She's got Russ for everything else, and Dusty. How old is he? But she still needs me. Lam still needs me.* He hoped. *I can still keep my promise. She needs me to help with mom.* And truth be told, though not aloud, he needed them too. But right now he needed some rest or he wouldn't make it there at all. What difference would a few hours make now? He would stop in Bozeman or Livingston. He rolled down the window and stuck his head into the frigid wind, leaving it until his forehead ached.

It was late afternoon on a warm autumn day in the back roads of the Bull Mountains as a storm of dust erupted in the wake of a rattling pickup. A dead three-point mule deer rocked in the open truck bed, its chest cavity split and held open with a stick, field-dressed, with a bloody hunting tag stuffed into its ear. Flecks of dirt had cemented to the sun-dried membranes of its eyes, and its protuberant, leathery tongue had escaped its mouth too late. From the cab, Donny looked back and noticed that the chest cavity was powdered with dust, and the lid of the cooler had bounced loose, exposing the heart and the liver and the beer.

"You might want to slow down, bro. Beer's getting warm." he said to Tommy.

The thighs of their pants were stiff with dried blood. It had been Tommy's kill, but Donny had fished for the organs as he teased Tommy about its size.

They had started hunting at dawn. By the time they stopped at noon, the coffee was gone and Donny still hadn't filled his tag. He was getting owly about it. They sat in the sun and finished off the ham sandwiches and pop, and by the time they got back to hunting, they had removed their sweaty hats and unzipped their orange vests. In late afternoon, Donny became reinvigorated, aware that big game would be up and moving toward haystacks and water. So they drove with the windows down and a shell chambered in each rifle propped between them, safeties on, and shared the pint of whiskey Donny had stashed in the glove box.

Donny pointed. "Turn to the right here."

Tommy looked dubious. "I don't think Russ and Lam will let us on the ranch."

"We ain't gonna get on the Johnson ranch. Nothing saying we can't hunt *around* it. They don't own the whole fuckin' county." Donny took a long pull on the bottle.

"I'm just saying…"

"I know what you're saying. Just drive."

They parked at the ridge of a coulee that ran parallel with the Johnsons' fence line. Standing by the truck, Donny adjusted the knife sheath on his pistol belt. Quite a few men wore pistols when they hunted, ostensibly to shoot bears or rattlesnakes. Tommy thought it was folly. "If you loaded it with hollow-points for bear, you couldn't hit a snake," he would say to Donny, "and if you loaded it with snake-shot, it's no good for bear. Why don't you just file the front site off so it won't hurt so much when the bear shoves it up your ass."

As they surveyed the ravine, Tommy asked, "How do you want to work it?" The ridge across the coulee laid at least a football field from where they stood, and the wooded slopes descended steeply until they met at a spring-fed stream 100 feet below.

Donny looked at the inclines and grinned at Tommy. "Why don't you work south just below that ridge," he pointed across the gully, "and I'll work just below this one."

"You're one lazy son of a bitch," Tommy said. Rifle in hand, he began picking his way down through the pines and prickly-pear cactus, knowing Donny would stay put until he climbed up the other side.

When Tommy was well committed to the descent, Donny opened the door of the pickup and took out the whiskey bottle. There was about an inch left in it. He downed it and tossed the bottle in the grass. He looked away from the gully, across the barbed-wire fence to Russ and Lam's ranch, over the tops of 300 yards-worth of sage brush, toward a small herd of Black Angus grazing on dry grass. Among them was a horseman; a half-mile farther, a ranch house. Donny rested his rifle on the hood of the truck and looked through the scope. It was Russ. He frowned and gripped the stock tighter. "Pow," he pretended.

Donny lowered the gun and glared. As he cleared his nose and throat and hocked, he saw Tommy just below the far crest of the coulee. Tommy pointed upstream, and Donny took the cue and waved. He descended his own ridgeline until his head was no longer profiled against the sky. The men turned south and stalked carefully through pine needles and loose rocks along the walls of the gulch.

Soon Donny could no longer see Tommy, but he knew where his brother must be. They'd hunted together for decades. Still buzzed from whisky, Donny leaned at a perilous angle as he walked horizontally along a rubbled game trail that scarred the hillside, occasionally reclaiming his balance by popping his open hand off the uphill gradient as though it were hot with rattlesnakes. Knowing the speed at which Tommy would work the other side, he matched it. One of them was bound to spook a deer toward the other. It didn't take long.

For only an instant, a swollen, organic rushing sound. Donny paused. *Just wind.* Then a dry crackle, like breaking spaghetti. Next, from farther away, Tommy's wintry whistle – a buck. Donny flipped off the safety. Soon there was more noise from below, pulses of crushing undergrowth, climbing fast, up the coulee wall below him. Donny raised his rifle to where the sound would meet the path, above a tree, thirty yards away. He knew the animal would make the game trail, hesitate, then either turn away from him or toward him. All was quiet for a moment, then, from around the tree, two deer trotted out and froze, nervously, facing him. It was a doe, a mule deer, and a large fawn. "Dammit," he whispered, and let off the trigger. The deer scampered upward. Donny reset the safety and set the butt of his rifle on the ground. He'd chew Tommy's ass for this. Frustrated and a bit dizzy from the whiskey and the rush of excitement, he took off his hat and wiped his forehead. That's when he saw the buck.

A massive five-point, the biggest he'd seen in years, barely hesitated on the trail where the doe and fawn had crossed before it charged farther up the slope. Donny dropped his hat, raised the rifle and aimed, pivoting as the animal moved, holding his fire. "Come on, you're a stupid muley. Stop and look," he whispered. He knew their behavior. When the buck crowned the ridge, it stopped and turned to spot its adversary. Donny squeezed on the trigger, but it was locked. He had forgotten to release the safety – a child's mistake, or worse, a tourist's. By the time he flipped the button, the buck had vanished over the horizon.

"Dammit!" He slung his rifle around his shoulder to free both hands to climb as fast as he could. He stumbled, shoving his hand onto cactus. "Fuck!" he screamed with his mouth closed and kept climbing. As he crested the ridge he saw the buck 100 yards away. It jumped the fence between the gully and ranch house and headed across the sagebrush flat. Donny hustled to the fence and steadied his rifle on top of a post. He found the trophy in his scope. As he clicked off the safety, he took a deep breath. Then he heard galloping hooves.

"I don't think so, partner," Russ called out loudly. He pulled up his horse ten feet from Donny, on the other side of the fence.

For a long while, the men stared at each other with hate they could taste. Russ's hand rested calmly on the shortened shotgun scabbard that was strung near the horn. He kept his horse facing Donny while he casually untied the barrel at the saddle's breast collar. With sharpening senses, Donny monitored Russ's steady hands, even as he arced the rifle from the fencepost with ominous care. Adrenalin cleared his blood of alcohol.

A walkie-talkie on Russ's belt crackled to life. "Russ, do you copy?" Lam was hailing from the base station in the ranch house kitchen.

Without taking his eyes off of Donny, Russ drew the radio from his belt and fingered the switch. "I'm here."

"Supper's in a half-hour. Levi called. He just got to town, and Dad drove in to meet him. I don't know when they'll get here, so I'm not holding supper. Should I set a plate for you?"

Donny met Russ's stare, senses raw. The wind wandered, the smell of sage and horse sweat became bracing. The horse ripped grass from sturdy roots with its teeth.

"I'll be there," Russ answered and re-clipped the walkie-talkie to his belt.

"Dusty, do you copy?" Lam again, but no answer. "Russ, will you grab him for supper and tell him to turn those headphones down?"

"I hear you, Mom," Dusty's voice broke in. He was home from college for the weekend.

Donny looked at the walkie-talkie, then back at Russ's eyes.

"Finish up the barn and be here in half an hour," Lam said.

"Copy that."

Squared off the horse's chest, Donny stood ready, rifle suspended at thigh level. His thumb rechecked the safety. It was off.

"You might want to think about your next move," said Russ. "Your reputation's already worked itself loose."

Donny squeezed the stock and his eyebrows floated down. "So what's it like being told what to do by someone who wears panties?"

Russ was expressionless. "Maybe you should ask your brother," he said slowly. With that, Russ tipped his hat and gently tugged the reigns, presenting his back and the horse's ass to Donny. The horse walked away, slow as you please, picking along through prairie dog mounds, toward black cattle and sunlit grass.

"You fuckin' asshole," Donny yelled. "Why don't you bring your candy-ass to this side of the fence?" He was still being ignored. "Because of *your* fucking shit I can't even see my kid no more. *Come on*, candy-ass, why don't we see how you fight without a sucker-punch?"

Forty yards away, Russ continued to dawdle on.

"I'll bet you don't fight no better than your fucking wife."

The horse stopped. After a long moment, Russ turned slowly in the saddle and tipped his hat back. He smiled at Donny and blew him a kiss, and then turned and continued away with presumed impunity.

Under his breath Donny spat, "You arrogant son of a bitch!" He raised the gun and lined up the shot. He breathed in and held it. The trigger was slick with sweat. As the cross-hairs centered between Russ's shoulder blades, Donny's pulse quickened. He should just *pop the uppity bastard*. He quickly stole a look across the coulee, spotting for Tommy. *Fuck.* He couldn't. To be sure, again, he sighted Russ in. His eye drifted from the scope to the ranch house, *the one Lam had connived her way into* – so he adjusted his aim. Again he scanned that area, but saw no one. He scoped Russ once more and imagined blasting the kiss off his face. His rage began to nova inside him. Through hot light, he flashed on the face of his daugher; wondered if he'd ever see her again as it is; *not if her bitch mother had anything to do with it*. On the other hand, no matter *what* had happened, he loved the girl and there *was* a chance, and he *was still her dad*. What about Dusty? The scope left Russ's back and pointed at the barn. Donny saw movement inside. Moments later, a man rolled a wheelbarrow out twenty yards and dumped it. The kid. *Russ's new kid. At least that's the way the prick acted. Lam, too.* But Dusty might be *Donny's own* kid, Lam had said as much – yet Donny couldn't have *them* either. He'd lost everything, and *that fucking cowboy had everything, even a goddamn family. Fuck it!* He swung the muzzle, sighted, and fired.

The high-powered bullet entered Russ's lower back, tore through a kidney, and exited his abdomen, striking his horse in the head. The team imploded to the ground. The horse flailed until it stood again, riderless, and staggered in circles. Russ lay prostrate. Donny kept his scope trained on the body for a full minute. It never moved. *Fuck! Tommy!* Donny's eyes darted down the fence-line. No one. He was a half-mile from the pickup. He turned and dropped his gun, picked it up and ran thirty yards to the ridge, and scanned the gulch. The report of the shot had quickened Tommy's step, and the younger brother splashed through the spring at the bottom of the gully and had started up Donny's side. Donny yelled and motioned right, trying to send Tommy toward the truck. When Tommy waved and continued straight up the slope, Donny skied down on lose stones and dirt and met him at the game trail, insisting they follow it back.

"Did you hit him?" Tommy gulped an urgent breath. "He was one big son-of-a-bitch."

"Yeah. I hit him." Donny strode away quickly, pulling Tommy along the slope.

"So what are we doing? Can we drive to it? Why are we going back?"

Donny kept walking fast. "Uh. I'm not sure. It was on the other side of the fence. I think I gut-shot it. It ran toward the ranch house." His mind raced. *This is bad.* "We need to go ask permission to go after it. It'll probably lay down somewhere and die." He was out of breath. "We need to see if we can get it." He broke into a trot.

"Hey. Slow down. First, there ain't no way in hell they're going to let us on their land. And if that thing *does* lie down, there's no hurry getting to it. We've got maybe an hour and a half of light left."

At the truck Donny slowed only long enough to jerk the warm six-pack from the cooler into the cab. *Nothing! I've got nothing left!* The words sliced through his mind. *Nothing left!* And any facility he had to sort emotion from reason simply flayed into shreds.

Tommy removed his sweaty cap and started the engine before he fully took in Donny's face. "Shit. Are you okay?"

Donny guzzled and smiled wryly and kept pinching the bloodstiff thighs of his pants and rubbing his hands on the seat.

"Listen, we don't have to go to Russ and Lam's. It's just a deer. Why don't you relax and let's forget it?"

"No! I mean, I'm okay. Let's just get the goddamn deer." He finished the beer and crushed the can. "I'll do it. You can wait in the truck. Just drive." He threw the can out the window.

Tommy looked again and shook his head with deep reluctance. "Oh, this oughta be fun."

In the fog of half-sleep in the back bedroom, Virginia heard the phone ring in some other part of the ranch house. Late afternoon. It was time to get up anyway, so she commenced to lie the minute longer it took nowadays to gather her strength. From the kitchen came cooking noises as Lam put down a pancake turner and answered the phone. Virginia could smell potatoes frying with onions and black pepper. She could hear the sizzle. Good. She liked fried potatoes. A moment later, as Virginia opened her eyes, Lam, in an apron and a hurry, poked her head into the room that had become Virginia's makeshift hospice.

"Mom. It's Levi. He just rolled into town from California and he's getting gas. Dad caught up with him at the station." Frank had driven into town early to meet Levi and lead him out to the ranch, knowing full well that Levi could find it on his own and knowing full well the real reason was to stop at Geno's for a beer. "He wants to know if we need anything. I told him cereal and pop. Can you think of anything?" From her pillow, Virginia shook her head no, pointing to the phone at the same time and mouthing the word *Him*. "She says just you," Lam relayed. "She must need her meds adjusted. I'm cooking supper but I ain't holding it for you so hurry up." Virginia smiled at her kids playing and watched until Lam hung up. "He'll be here in twenty minutes," Lam said, then scurried down the hallway toward the sizzling sound.

Virginia pulled her bony frame to a sitting position on the inflated mattress. She paused to catch her breath. The deep vibration of the mattress air-pump taunted her serenity, but the forgiving mattress was less punishing on the ulcers of her papery skin. Russ and Lam never complained about the noise. Or anything else. She hadn't wanted to burden them, but the process of dying was physically inconvenient. Being near Lam made the most sense. Without a home or homecare insurance, Virginia had little choice. Frank came along, with hope at first of a chance at reconciliation with Lam. Lam made him sleep in the bunkhouse. It didn't really bother Virginia. She was tired of him always looking at her and looking at her, like she was supposed to answer some clumsy question or at least ask him to get her something just to help his feelings. For crying out loud. It was exhausting.

As she sat there breathing – a damn chore all by its lonesome, breathing – she decided to unfold the walker and try to push the thing to the kitchen. Lately each time she snapped open the contraption, she wondered if it was worth it. But she liked watching Lam cook. Besides, she didn't want people eating in her room. When they did, they always ate with too much enthusiasm, especially Frank, like it was normal as dawn to eat in a room that smelled like a dead thing, and we'd all jump up after we'd licked our plates, good to go do the dishes. You wash, I'll dry. Just plain stupid. Though she enjoyed companionship, she wouldn't suffer stupid. On the nightstand, from atop a white cardboard garment box she had taped and labeled to Levi, she scraped off her glasses. There were two cups – one with orange juice and a straw and another with water and her teeth. She hefted one and sucked through a straw. Since they took her salivary glands, her mouth was chronically dry.

Virginia's face warmed in tangerine light. The late sun hunkered lower nowadays, shined stronger through her window. To her, the most beautiful part of the day had always been its last hour, especially after harvest time, when people slowed and paid attention while God danced a little. As she gazed out, she savored the formal pines of the piedmont, gloriously backlit, wading in ginger and red confetti left by deciduous trees, promising to deliver nature's cache of green through winter. With the first real snow overdue, she felt lucky for the moment.

As trees bristled up with wind she noticed, a mile or so away, a plume of dust chasing a pickup her direction. Dusty was in the barn. Russ was on horseback. Everyone was accounted for, and Lam hadn't mentioned company. Virginia pulled the robe from the foot of her bed, wrapped herself in it, dropping her arms into the sleeves like twigs down drainpipes. As she tied the belt, the pickup pulled into the yard and stopped, slinging beyond it a front of dust and rock music. It was the Zupicks' truck. Hastening, her feet searched for slippers. The engine stopped but not the music. She watched Donny get out and walk funny toward the house, quick, like he was sneaking into court late. Just as quickly he was out of view. Must be Tommy behind the wheel. Herky-jerkily, she unfolded the walker.

As Virginia fought to stand, the kitchen screen door banged on its frame and sent a tremble through her. Lam would never have asked him in. Grasping the walker with both hands, she rocked forward and back into the mattress – once, twice – and finally launched up and locked her knees. There was shouting. She shuffled and pushed into the back hallway and peered toward the kitchen.

She gasped and covered her mouth, but her trachea hole wheezed. Down the hall, by the fridge, Lam stood tensed, feet planted, her fist clutching the handle of a kitchen knife. Donny loomed into Virginia's view.

"Leave," Lam roared. "Now!"

Donny too wielded a knife, a shorter one. Lam backpedaled deliberately, away from Virginia but facing her, drawing Donny between them, his back to the hallway. Lam hit the microphone on the base station. "Russ! Dusty! Mayday!" and Donny lunged from Virginia's sight, noisily body-checking the kitchen table.

A report came back from Dusty. "I'm sorry, Mom, what was that?"

Dusty! Virginia thought. *In the back barn.* She swung the walker in a half circle, and tilted down the hall, past the gun cabinet, toward the back door. *God save Lam, Please! God save Lam!* She struggled with the door handle. Through her feet, the thump and quake of heaved furniture. *Is this it, God? Is this why I caught the cancer? To be here? Now? To see this? To be punished? Damn you!*

"Ahh!" Donny screamed, and Virginia's ears moved. "Bitch!" Lam was fighting. Virginia pulled the door free, twisted her walker to give it room, and felt a tumble of crisp air. Finally space to move again, she raised the walker, sliding its tennis ball feet over the sill, driving open the screen. Russ's pickup was twenty feet away, and, beyond that, his horse sat queerly, like some grotesque dog, grinding its head against the barn. The barn was open, but no sign of Russ or Dusty. Faint rock music, but not from the barn. *Lam.* She had to help Lam. *God, please. Help.* She would draw Donny away. She would do it! If it's not too late … Virginia slammed the screen door with all she had, nearly toppling herself, banging the door loudly off of Lam's scream.

"Russ!!" Then nothing.

Terror commanded Virginia's arms as they shook in spent protest. One foot dragged like an anchor to her dizziness. Her stomach convulsed. She pushed fiercely. Behind her, inside, more furniture sounds, sounds getting closer. He was coming for her.

Virginia collapsed over the walker's frame. *I could never make the barn.* Again, her head rose, and, panting hard, she reached the fender of Russ's pickup. A knee gave out, and one armpit drove to the frame and exploded in pain. Precious seconds went by in semi-consciousness. Her hand was bleeding. From around the house, music thumped from Tommy's pickup. In the house, thrashing … closing in. Donny was searching rooms for her – for everyone. *Move!*

The door of Russ's rig was three feet away. She hugged the walker and drove her foot against the ground until the tennis balls plowed trenches through the dirt. Her arms and ribs seared with agony. She pushed again, vomited, and pushed again. Finally she was able to reach the door of the pickup. When she pulled on the driver-side handle, her bloody fingers snapped away from it. She tried again and opened the door and wrapping her arms on the steering wheel she pulled, and kicked the walker out of the way. As she dragged one knee onto the floorboards, she heard the back door slam. Her vision caved to the center, a white, roiling bull's eye, as she pulled her shriveled belly across the seat.

"Where *you* going, you old bitch?"

As Donny bellowed from ten feet away, her palm slapped the floorboards and hooked under. She forced her trembling hand under the seat. Two seconds later, a presence at her feet and an exploding metallic rattle as Donny flung her walker across the yard.

"Your whole fuckin' family's finally getting what you deserve." Between her legs his knee pinned her robe to the seat, and he jerked a fistful of cloth at the nape of her neck. "First Russ, and then your bitch daughter. Hear that? That's right! If they're still kickin' they won't be for long after I finish you. What do you say about *that*, you crazy old bitch? Sss-sss-sss. Nothing! You fucking mute! At least you won't scream when I gut your ass! But you're sure as fuck gonna look at me! *Look at me!*"

There was a clicking sound under the seat.

"Welcome home, son," Frank said as Levi closed the gas-cap door of his SUV. Levi just smiled at the scrawny man and got in his car to follow his dad to the ranch. It was later than he had hoped, but he was there. That morning at the Bozeman Holiday Inn Levi had woken up later than he intended, but he felt strong for it, a strong that became invigoration as he rolled out of Roundup behind Frank's old orange pickup. They drove past the sagebrush fairways of the golf course, beyond the adjacent shooting range, up the hill past the turn-to-the-windsock airport. *Fuck, it's been long time,* he thought. This *was* home. *Family. Mom. Lam. Maybe even Dad. Like what Angela always said.*

A few miles north of town Frank turned west off the highway, into the sun, under the tree-trunk arch at the ranch entrance and onto a gravel road etched into the land that would eventually ribbon its way to the ranch house. Levi followed him up a long, washboarded rise, hanging back far enough to avoid rocks and dust. At the crest, the sun broke glorious. Levi dropped the visor. A mile off was a cluster of buildings: two barns, what was probably a bunkhouse, and a ranch house attended by a cluster of pickups and a car. *I can't believe it,* he thought. *They're right there. I'm here.* He felt butterflies.

As the road descended, Frank accelerated, slightly at first. Levi pressed the gas pedal a little harder, matching Frank's pace. Abruptly, Frank sped up again, as if being yanked forward. A storm of dirt and gravel jumped at Levi's rig, causing him to drop back. It took a moment for the dust to clear so Levi could see what Frank saw – a truck bearing the logo of Zupick's gas station – and another moment for it to register that this might be trouble. Levi hit the gas and fishtailed an instant on the loose gravel. He saw Frank plow to a stop by Zupick's truck and saw a man get out, as Frank did. At first they stood talking, the man tipping the brim of his hat back – Tommy, it was Tommy Zupick – but as Levi pulled up, Frank's arms stiffened like the wings on an old bantam rooster, his neck craning forward as if in disbelief. Tommy reached in his truck and rock music stopped. Frank pointed urgently at the house as Levi got out.

"Levi! Donny's in there! Russ ain't here! And –"

Frank's tone delivered a cold bolt to Levi's chest, scattering emotions as he broke into a trot toward the ranch house, Frank and Tommy in tow. Levi ripped opened the screen door and then the door to the porch. A stride later he opened the door to the kitchen. A light haze of smoke filled the room, the smell of burnt onions and potatoes, the sound of them burning. A chair was on its side. The table, set for a family dinner, was badly askew. From under it, from a source unseen, a blackish-red slick the shape of melted crayon reached out to him. "Shit, no!" Levi heaved the table into the cavity of the room, launching dishes and silverware in every direction but the one he was going.

From the dark pool streaked a tangle of hair, a sticky mop from the head of a woman with a blood-smudged face. She wore an apron with flour-sack lilies, strained to the side with shiny wet oozing through it and her once-clutching hands and the open filets on her forearms. "Oh, my God!" Levi yelled as Frank came through the doorway. Levi dropped to his knees, spreading her hands away and replacing them with his own. He barely looked, but felt the wound as he applied pressure. "Call an ambulance! Call an ambulance," he screamed as his ear came to her face to check for breathing.

"Jesus Christ!" said Tommy, "I didn't know. I didn't know!" He snatched the phone off the wall.

"Your mother!" Frank exclaimed and tried to wrestle around the table to the hallway.

"What?"

"Her bedroom," Frank gestured. "She's down there."

"No!" Levi said. "Get down here. Now!" Frank stopped, confused. "I'll go! I'll go! Get down here. Get down here!" Frank knelt quickly and Levi pressed his father's palms to his sister's gut.

At that very moment, from somewhere out back, the forceful crack of a magnum pistol slammed against the house and rang down the hall to the kitchen. The men flinched. By the time Tommy said *Oh shit,* Levi had vaulted the table and was sprinting for the back door. Outside, he nearly tripped on the aluminum bones of a walker. A few yards away, a pickup with an open door. A man's boots stuck out, toes toward the dirt. Blue smoke wafted in the cab. A boot shuddered.

Virginia had felt no pain as Donny manhandled her, flipping her over on the seat. In that moment, she noticed nothing in the cab of the pickup, and nothing outside – only the polished wooden handle in her hand and her mind's tight tunnel to Donny's blood-smeared face – first menacing, and then astonished. Donny saw the gun before she could use it. His fist released her robe and clipped her chin on its way to seize it. He just missed. Her arm swung up like a mallet, the barrel of the Smith and Wesson cracking his nose, coldly, hollowly, splitting the thin flesh. As his big-eyed face recoiled a quarter turn, his hand hesitated but a few milliseconds. Long enough. She squeezed the trigger. What menace that existed there above her exploded into a spewing funnel of pink and gray and white.

The concussion extinguished Virginia's every sensation except a sort of dense, underwater ringing. In less than an instant, she talked to God, praying her family would live, telling Him thank you if they did. Suddenly, she knew. She knew the answer. *Thank you for the cancer, God. For bringing me here now. Sorry I cussed.* She was vaguely aware of the firecracker smell of spent powder as warm, vile wetness leaked on her face, her throat, her lap. It was a long moment before her body decided to pull for air, and it fought poorly against the weight of the corpse on her chest. The last thing she saw was blood, bone, and brain on the roof of the cab.

"Oh, God, Mom," Levi cried out as he dragged Donny's body off her, hefting limbs and ass in urine-soiled pants, gripping at a blood-soaked collar, yanking until the carnage crumpled heavily at his feet. The cavity in its skull gaped up at him, propelled him into the truck's cabin. "Don't die, Mom, don't die, don't die." He began mouth-to-mouth, frantically, guessing at the details, tasting the cancer, sharing it, desperate to donate life.

By the time the sheriff and ambulance arrived, Dusty, sobbing and pleading, was choking his unconscious mother's arms with tourniquets as his grandpa applied pressure to her abdomen. Before the life-flight helicopter from Billings arrived, the EMTs had already determined that her cranium was fractured.

It didn't take long for Sheriff Tuffy Jankovich to locate Russ. The steers had surrounded him like curious toddlers. Russ lay on his back in black mud, a melon-sized rock atop his exit wound, apparently put there by him to stem the bleeding before he passed out. To reach him the ambulance rocked over badger and prairie-dog holes, lurchng and settling like a creeping rabbit.

Lam and Russ were flown to Saint Vincent's Hospital in Billings.

Virginia was taken by ground ambulance to Deaconess, where she treaded in a sea of narcotics for two weeks, during which time a nursette with a thirst for Jesus instructed loudly and hourly, coma or no coma, that "you need to roll to prevent bedsores and take Jesus as your personal savior." It didn't help. Virginia's face soon morphed into a waxy replica of itself. Yet, the nurse persisted. In the end, or not long before it, Frank and Levi noticed Virginia's hand move – delicately, but sentiently – as though writing. Levi threaded a pencil between her fingers and thumb, and helped her hold the point to her spiral notebook. Her milky eyes split open a bit, trying to focus. With Ouija board touch she feebly wrote, *"do this do that do this do that this ain't funny no more go fuck yourself."*

It had been 100 years since Frank and Levi found anything funny. This, they agreed, was funny. The head nurse reassigned her young subordinate to the other end of the floor and then told Virginia they were moving her to a "skilled cursing facility." Virginia did not stir, but Levi thought he felt her smile.

Two days later, with Frank and Levi at her bedside, Virginia passed away.

45

Cowboys and Indians

Things said or done long years ago
Or things I did not do or say
But thought that I might say or do
Weigh me down, and not a day
But something is recalled
My conscience or my vanity appalled

William Butler Yeats

The family that owned the furniture store in Roundup owned the funeral parlor next door. Its small chapel was nicely appointed, seasonal horn of plenty notwithstanding. Virginia's funeral was standing room only. Up front, beside a pew, Lam sat in a wheelchair between Levi, in a chair, and Russ, who sat stoic and wan on the bench, a walking cane on the floor behind his boots. She held hands with both of them. Down the bench sat Dusty, Angela, and Frank, and the EMT that returned Lam to Billings.

An hour later at the snowy United Mine Workers cemetery, the preacher's careful psalms were punctuated by shutter clicks with implied apologies of news reporters from Billings. Afterward at Geno's, there was a crowded potluck reception to celebrate Virginia's heroism. Angela helped tend bar. Proper folks sat or stood around with toothpicks on stained paper plates until they had tithed a polite amount of time. A few others had come to close the bar, and did. Geno accepted no money that night. Lam and Russ paid for the funeral. For his part, Levi ordered the pink granite slab, big as any rancher's, which would be his mom's marker.

For weeks afterward, the family members numbly circulated between the ranch and the hospital, all tarrying at this bleak junction in their lives, unable to discern direction and queerly avoiding any consideration of the need for it. Dusty, Frank and Levi abandoned school, work, lawsuits to help

Russ run the ranch. No one talked much. On rare occasion, Russ would give Levi advice, half-expecting it to be accurately implemented.

Repetitive activities – chores, meals, visits to Lam – made days interchangeable; and singular events – the discovery of Lam's pregnancy, Russ mounting a horse again, Thanksgiving – were inevitably marked as a week or a month or some period of time after *the incident*. The big day Lam came home from the hospital was adopted as an oblique proxy from which to measure time, a second, less tragic reference point. That made two, so the world stayed fairly flat.

After a while Levi nearly forgot why he had driven to Montana in the first place: aside from his mom and Lam, he had been cut off from Angela, anyone else who gave a damn, and his money. His waning assets were frozen during the SEC probe and operating the California house had sucked him dry. For all he knew, his riding lawn mower was still on his lawn, out of gas.

Things had a way of settling. When Virginia died, Levi moved into her room at the ranch house. It was morbid, but he found some odd comfort in having morbidity to push against. He told Lam and Russ he would stay on only until he straightened a few things out in California, he said, a couple weeks tops. Then his mind set about concocting scenarios in which Angela might consent to see him. After all, here he was. Minutes away. For weeks. And for weeks she showed no interest. A couple times he fetched a small tan package from his suitcase, reading the label addressed to him while listening to her phone ring and waiting vainly for her to answer. He left messages saying he still had the mystery package from Crazy Marilyn to be opened. Angela ignored the bait, never returning the calls. Meanwhile he tethered himself to the ranch, desperate to prove useful. He even scrounged up passable work boots and old gloves from the bunkhouse. He kept saying he was there to help out. He never mentioned that it was safer than being alone.

Over time Levi did become more help than hindrance, and a nugget of pride formed from earning his keep. His hands got stronger, though the gray scar on the one became ulcerated from use and was forever weeping through the bandages on the thin skin. At the end of each day his back felt sore when he pried off his boots, but his shirts were getting tighter at the shoulders as a byproduct of muscle re-alloyed with labor. One evening Lam caught him on his way to the shower and poked fun at his farmer's tan, but in her voice he heard approval. Russ, half recuperated, said thanks. Even Dusty was warming to him.

On the second straight day of Indian summer in early December, the landscape on the ranch was muddy but clear of snow except for scalloped pockets on the north side of hills and benches. It seemed every critter on the landscape woke for a short, joyful dance, especially prairie dogs and the myriad of cottontails, mice and burrowing owls that lived in their tunnels. As if to make life perfect, only rattlesnakes and bugs stayed underground, except in the barn where Dusty got bit through his T-shirt by a horsefly. Everyone agreed it was unlikely, but he showed them the welt. They said they'd be damned. Still, big snow was coming, so Russ decided to take the truck out and have Levi and Dusty ride in back to fetch a few alfalfa bales the combine had missed and redistribute them where the breeding cattle could use them. It was to be short work over by the makeshift rifle range, so they took along guns and ammo for fun.

Russ only yelled back once at Dusty, with implications toward Levi, for screwing around. Levi had complained to Dusty about the bandage and blisters on his palms. Then he said how the bales smelled like green tea ice cream. Dusty had called him Aunt Sally and turned up his DiscMan, so a man's contest erupted to see who could throw a bale farthest into the truck bed. The bragging rights went back and forth until Levi won twice in a row, at which time Dusty called him a pussy for wearing gloves, so Levi took them off and a wrestling match ensued. Russ had driven fifty yards before he realized he had no crew. Finally he circled around and got out, much to Levi's relief, given that Dusty was on top and demanding he say *uncle*, of all things.

"You two ain't got the sense you were born with," Russ said. "Never did."

Levi and Dusty stood and adopted a look of contrition until a chunk of mud fell off Levi's butt. Russ got back in the truck.

"Good thing your dad came back," Levi said. "I'd a kicked your ass," and they laughed. Then Dusty straightened his DiscMan and quickly lost much of the mood. Levi noticed, gingerly pulling his glove back over his bandage. A while later he pushed Dusty off the back of the truck, but the boy's spirit would not be lifted.

At the rifle range, the men propped some bales against rickety sawhorses that stood at 50, 100 and 150 yards from an old stock tank, pausing at each to slip a target under the bailing twine. Next to the stock tank two gray posts supported a plank shelf, chest high. They set up there. Russ and Dusty insisted

Levi shoot first, to Levi's unspoken disappointment. He had stopped thinking of himself as a guest and had hoped they had too. Not yet, he guessed.

"Here. Try mine," Dusty said, and handed him a .30-.30. "The safety's here." He pointed, sincerely thinking Levi didn't know. Over the next few minutes, Levi's shooting only reinforced the suspicion. Each round only kicked up dust high and/or left of the targets at 50 and 100 yards. Sheepishly he said, "We never owned a scope. I prefer open sites. Let's see Mom's gun."

Russ looked far too understanding, like a man placating his wife's brother. Dusty unzipped a marred leather scabbard that had begun to rot at some creases, and pulled out a lever-action firearm. Its original steel butt-plate now over-jutted a stock that had been sanded too deep. On the hexagonal muzzle, the bluing had worn from the ridges. Levi casually cradled the gun like a lance and assessed the targets, never looking down as he loaded it – five in the clip, one in the chamber. He closed the lever and dropped his elbows on the plank like he'd just finished lunch. He took an easy breath and raised the rifle. Six shots reported, three at 100 yards and three at 150, each separated by the sure mechanical clackety-clock of Levi deftly cocking the lever.

When Levi pulled back, Dusty was staring through binoculars. "Wow."

"Chuck fucking Connors," said Russ.

"What?" said Dusty.

"*The Rifleman.* Old TV show. Watch *Nick at Night*," Russ said, and he examined the relic.

"Dad wasn't around much," said Levi, "but Mom knew this gun. It was her dad's."

It was at that moment that Dusty asked a question that wiped the echoes from the air. "Do you guys know who my dad is?" No movement. No wind. "I mean, no one's closer to Mom than you two. Maybe not even me. I don't want to hurt her, and I won't say you said anything, and I don't care what the answer is – but do you know?"

Levi was first to fidget. He rested the gun on its butt. That drew the boy's attention, and Levi's mind raced to assemble something … important … comforting … sage. Dusty looked hopeful. Several long seconds passed, the verge of too many, before Russ finally spoke.

Russ took the binoculars from Dusty and smiled. "Yeah. I know who your dad is." It was the deepest of promises, and he held the boy's gaze until warmth moved Levi's skin. Dusty smiled back at Russ, and then at Levi. "Go check the targets," Russ said.

"Yes, sir," and he bound off down the range.

Levi watched Russ watch Dusty. "You were at Stanford when she got pregnant."

Russ never looked away from the boy. "That's not what he was asking."

Less than five minutes later, Dusty returned, hat cocked back, paper targets from 100 and 150 yards flapping in his hand. The two inner, black circles of each target bore three holes, some intersecting. Speechless, Dusty handed them to Levi.

"I'm crap with a scope," was all Levi said.

On the way back to the ranch house Russ drove circuitously, idling at places where the cattle might take cover when an Arctic Freight Train roars through. The other two men dropped a saltlick and a few more bales. Levi was pleased to see Dusty's mood high and playful, so when his nephew scooted a bale to the back of the truck, Levi pushed him off again. Dusty kept his feet, barely, and hustled back onto the bed, retaliating by throwing Levi's gloves overboard. Russ ignored them, rocking up front as the truck crept over badger holes and prairie dog mounds on its way to the barn.

Dusty edged closer to the cab, acting as though he needed to say something to Russ, but changed his mind at the last moment, slipping into nonchalance. Levi suspected nothing. In the barnyard the brakes squeaked to a standstill, and Levi stood against the momentum, preparing to dismount. At the instant his hand clipped onto the corroded side-rail and he bent his knees to jump, Dusty delivered a jolting body-check from behind. Levi's free hand ripped the DiscMan from Dusty's waist as his other clenched around metal melted jagged by rust. The blow was too much. Levi launched – hips, shoulders and head – off the back of the truck. When his arm jerked straight, his hand flexed around serrated rust and the bandage ripped away, taking with it a four-inch swath of skin and more. By the time his knees hit the ground, his palm was surging wetness like a pregnant sponge, and Levi drove his bloody hand into the dirt.

"Holy shit!" Levi bellowed. He rolled up onto his ass, body curled tightly around his wound. Dusty bent beside him, apologizing rapid-fire.

Russ sauntered up disgustedly and snatched the hand like a broken tool, inspected it. He picked the broken music-player from the ground. He handed it to Dusty and walked toward the house. "Not the sense you were born with. Take your uncle in for a tetanus shot. When you get back, tell your mom why you missed supper."

Russ took to sending Levi to town on errands while he and Dusty performed all actual labor on the ranch. Levi tried to mitigate his embarrassment by resolving to make optimal use of his trips to town. He scoured the grounds, taking unneeded inventory – the kitchen, the workshop, the barn – from which he created shopping lists for the approval and vague annoyance of Russ and Lam. In Roundup, Levi hung flyers advertising the sale of the two houses that his parents and Lam had lived in. Geno scared up one potential buyer by talking up the property over the bar, but the court controlling Levi and Angela's assets during the investigation wouldn't allow Levi to carry the buyer's mortgage personally. Levi dropped by Wells Fargo and learned the buyer was in bankruptcy. Every day Levi made seemingly purposeful tracks. Mostly he was just driving around. Occasionally he circled Central School where Angela was substitute teaching. Sometimes, late in the evening, he looked for her car behind Geno's. He never saw it, and that bugged him, but then he heard she had traded her Lexus for a Ford, making plausible that she had been sleeping at home all along. It was something. So again he called Geno's home to talk with her about having coffee. Geno said she wasn't there, and no, he didn't know when she would be. So one night Levi drove through town at 2 A.M., out past Geno's. No Ford.

When he got back to the ranch, Levi lay down in the bedroom he shared with the memory of his mother. It occurred to him that the last day he saw her was the last day he saw his wife. He hated to think he buried both relationships on the same day. He couldn't sleep. Nothing about him seemed to interest Angela, not even Marilyn's mystery box, there on the moonlit dresser. He gazed at it a while. He sat up, turned on a lamp. He held the package, shook it. On one end of it, he carefully popped the tape. *Ah, hell with it.* He ripped the paper clean off, exposing a cardstock box. He lifted the lid. A small and stained handwritten note lay on top. Under it, a key with a silver be-be chain and a squirrel-foot fob. The note said simply, "*Dear Levi, I tried to call but you were busy. I asked Lynette to get this to you instead of waiting for you and me to talk. I can think of no better courier. Take this key to First Interstate in Billings. I left a safe deposit box for you and the* *authorization for only you to open it. Also, please make at least a $5 donation to the Yellowstone County Parks Save the Squirrels Fund. The address is on the other side of this. Warmly forever, Marilyn. P.S. Please excuse this note if it smells like Salsbury steak."*

Sunrise ached with questions: what's in Angela's head, what's in the safe deposit box, was he a hindrance on the ranch? He couldn't bear another day of conspicuously doing nothing. So he tossed Marilyn's key box on the car seat and headed for Billings.

At First Interstate's big branch downtown, it took a few minutes to validate his California driver's license and get clearance to open the safe deposit box. A bank official escorted him into a caged area and inserted the necessary second key. Then Levi was given a private nook to examine the contents of the modest steel box. Inside was but a single envelope; in it, a one-page hand-written document. He read it. He reread it. Again. And again, for fifteen minutes. He read it again in the parking garage. He tried to decide what it meant – to him.

Right off, he was not ready to drive back to Roundup, so he drove the other way, toward the West End, trying to re-sort and reconfigure. Maybe it didn't matter anymore. He walked around the shopping mall for an hour, wanting of nothing. Waiting for nothing. Without fully formed intent, he was sucked into a bar across the parking lot where he drank beer and watched people play video poker – housewives, delivery men, truants, the unemployed. He began thinking. When he was within a drink from not being okay, he ordered another. Had Crawford really done this to him? Had they all? Deirdre? Joy? Lynette? Was there no way to push back? Even if he could, why would he? When he wrapped his hand around the bottle, a shoulder brushed his. He looked up. From inside the mirror he gawked back at himself, sitting on that barstool in the afternoon on a workday. Sitting beside him was a woman his age with chew in her lip. She winked at Levi and ordered one. "Are you together?" the tender asked. God, no! Enough, already! Levi slid his beer in front of her and put a twenty on the bar. Time to do something, dammit. Stand for something. By the time he reached his car he had his phone out. Seated behind the wheel, he scrolled through the list of contacts. He stopped at one he had never used. He checked his watch. In California it was 3 P.M. He pressed SEND.

"Ramakapur," a voice low and confident announced from the other end. "Abba, this is Levi Monroe."

"Levi. I forgot I had offered you this number. I must say, I am surprised." Levi heard Abba ask someone to excuse themselves in a lilting voice that seemed more Indian than he remembered – because of Levi's recent seclusion in the ethnic homogeny of Montana, he supposed.

"Me too. I called to talk about options. Your options. Do you still need a pile of money to save the planet?"

"We all need to save the planet, Mr. Monroe."

"What could you do if you knew a stock would fall from 50 to 15 in a matter of days? What could your friends overseas do? You know, the ones that can't be traced."

It was a damn gamble to be so brazen. Levi knew if it were him getting this call, he'd hang up, perhaps call whoever was running the investigation. After all, maybe Abba needed a scapegoat too. *Screw it*, he thought. *Can't make things worse.* "If I give you information that compels your friends to short a stock overseas, put them in a position to make a billion dollars in a few days, I need a favor from you." Again there was silence. Levi wondered if the call was recorded. *So what.* "I need you to contact the FBI, I think, whoever handles securities situations with foreign nationals. I need you to produce records that incriminate Gary Crawford."

"Mr. Monroe, I don't know what you are talking about. Further, even if such records existed, hypothetically, I would be arrested by your FBI."

"Not if you were in India." Again, the quiet time grew. "You said it will cost billions to save this planet. Billions to save the ones you left behind. You asked what is a person willing to sacrifice. What about you? What if you placed another big bet that won? The biggest. You could be in India, saving the planet. But this time, with the billions to do it." Levi knew his only hope was that this guy drank his own Kool-Aid. "Hell, if Gore wins the election, you'd be pardoned."

"If records existed of this sort, what makes you think you yourself will not be arrested?"

"I'm tired of powerful people fucking people who can't stop them. My consequences are mine. So, Abba, what about karma?"

46

SCARGAZING

These fragments I have shored against my ruins.
THOMAS STEARNS ELIOT

Twelve hours later, in the cold, early hours of morning, Levi lay on the bedroom floor in a sleeping bag, back turned on the puddled bladder of a disinflated hospital airbed, its dissembled frame stacked aside like bones of regret. For long, successive nights, Levi had watched the stars leach light from the waning moon while he considered courage and character. Finally, this night, the moon was used up entirely, a no-show, and the stars strutted across the sky, casting into the room only enough light to render ghostly the gauze strap round Levi's hand. He stared at the bandage. He could settle it. It was time. Before any hint of dawn, he resolved to return to California. In the cold outside, nothing stirred. No creatures. No wind. He eased up the light switch so it wouldn't click, put on his pants and socks, and packed up.

Later, but before the crystal predawn melted, he heard Lam opening the kitchen. She insisted that he eat breakfast. He watched her robe-tented body shamble painfully around the kitchen. Bacon crackled in one pan as she broke eggs – *pap-snap-bwah, pap-snap-bwah* – over another while a pot steamed with something else. Three able-bodied men drank coffee and listened to the farm and ranch report on the radio. Levi's patience frayed at the absurdity of tradition. So he rose and put the half-emptied egg carton in the refrigerator. Lam rebuffed him, closing the fridge before his hand was through. "You'll get your bandage dirty," she said. So he sat and drank coffee and tried to put in perspective the number of cattle-on-feed.

Lam didn't eat. "A touch of morning-sickness," she said. As the men ate, Russ and Dusty asked Levi interested questions about the route he intended to take, remarked that the mountain passes were probably clear, and asked if he'd gas-up in Pocatello or Twin Falls. If he took his first stop in Butte, they were sure he could make Twin Falls – maybe even Jackpot. Meanwhile

Lam packed a cooler with bananas, chips, and two tongue sandwiches with mayonnaise and pepper, as Levi liked, and filled a thermos from the steaming pot. Eventually Russ and Dusty begged Levi's pardon, saying he was the last guy they had to tell how much work was waiting. It was meant as a compliment, but they came off a bit too buoyant. They shook hands, and the cowmen headed for the cows, leaving Levi with his sister.

After a moment of silence Lam said, "You can stay, you know."

"Nah. I've already overplayed my hand." Levi said, holding up the bandage. She rolled her eyes. "I have things I need to do there." So he stood in the kitchen, thermos and cooler in hand, promising to return them. She said she wasn't worried. "What's in this thermos?" he asked.

"Oh. Virginia stew."

Levi smiled. "Must be pretty old. Mom didn't do much hunting this year." The unintended joke made him flush with embarrassment.

"I made some and froze it a while back. I heated it up. Anyway, it's my recipe now. I can cheat and call it what I want, dammit."

"*Aw - verr*," he said like a child. "I'm tellin'."

It delighted her and her laugh sounded good. "Oh, and don't forget her rifle. She wanted you to have it. I think she held out hope you'd move back here." She steadied herself with the back of a chair and shifted her weight. His turn.

Levi turned solemn. "I'm sorry," he said. "I'm sorry I wasn't there for ... you know. All the time I spent pushing you away, and then on the day I wanted to be here, I'm too late."

"You did fine," she said. "You did all you could. I'll be okay." Truth be told, she wore the blush of every expectant mother, even now quietly boasting the satisfied peace of a woman who could tell how she looked.

"Have you picked out names?"

"Russ likes Cody for a boy. I like Emma for a girl. It was his mom's name."

"Very pretty." He looked at the cooler and then looked up. "And I'm sorry I didn't do more when we were kids. I'm sorry I left you. I know I said I'd be there, but—"

"Stop." Lam's eyes were glassy, her voice soft. "You know, one of the nasty, shameful little secrets is that when you're a little kid, it doesn't always hurt. When grownups find out, they think it does — they *need* to think it does — but it doesn't … always. Adults are horrified – including me, now that I'm grown. But when you're a kid, and it creeps in deeper over time, you don't think that way … and you don't talk about it. When it's happening, it can even feel good. That's part of the problem. You can become addicted. So sometimes you actually ask for it … literally. Sometimes –"

"Lam, don't…"

"No. It's true. You don't know. I mean – maybe *you* know – but *people* don't know. You *want* to be touched. Like it's love, or hell, it just *feels* good. It's not until later that you find out *how* sick and wrong it is, and the memories get more sick and wrong and *horrible* as you get older, so *horrible*, even if it stopped a long time ago. Then you think *you're* horrible, and that everyone knows, even if they don't." A long moment before she straightened resolutely.

"All those years," Levi said, "…when I stayed away … I didn't want to see you because … and I guess I didn't want to see who you were with … like, if I didn't look, I didn't have to face that I could have *done* something. And maybe even I had wanted you … to be mine."

"I *don't* need to hear this."

He looked down and shook his head. "I didn't want to be him! Oh, shit."

"You weren't him! You aren't him! Look, I know he hurt you. I mean, I *know* it hurt. You know – pain. You worse than me, I think."

Lam made Levi put down the cooler and thermos and took his hands. "You saved me. I remember. I remember you saving me. I remember when he called for me, you went in there sometimes … and he left me alone."

"*Jesus*, Lam, *stop!*"

"You did save me. Even after you left. You gave me hope. To Mom, too. I wish we hadn't been so needy."

He felt like hugging, but felt uninvited, unworthy. She must have sensed it, for she pulled his hands to start him toward her and wrapped and hugged him hard. After a while, she broke abruptly. "Oh!" She began to shuffle away. "Wait here for a minute." Her small steps loosened a bit as she disappeared down the hallway. Levi sighed. Less than a minute later she returned with a tattered gun case and a square, white cardboard box the size of a cookie sheet. "Here." She handed him the gun case first. "It's mom's rifle. The pistol from … is in there too. The sheriff gave it back. I don't want it here. I thought maybe you could … Anyway, there's this too." She gave him the box.

For a moment Levi held the box like a sacred artifact he was seeing for the first time. Across the lid was scrawled *To Levi, From Mom.* He quietly laid it on the table and felt along the edges for tape. He cleaned a butter knife on a napkin and slid it along under the perimeter, and opened it. Inside was a blue denim jacket with a leather collar. It was lined with padded, cross-stitched flannel. He slowly lifted the garment by the shoulders, and held it up to himself for size.

"At first Dad thought it was for him," Lam said, "but she was making it for you all along."

He put it on. It fit well. Inside the box was an envelope. He opened it.

My Darling son,

I could never give you much of anything, and it seems like you gave plenty to me and everybody too. I wish we could've spent more time together, but I know you got your reasons. I want you to know I love you, and always did. So does Lam and your dad. That's what we have that's worth something. That's what we can give you if you take it. We can wrap ourselves around you and love you when it's cold. No one has to know. That's why I made this jacket. Well, I made the lining anyways. It's full of little bits and pieces of the things that have kept us warm just like love. Love is free, but it comes in bits and pieces and doesn't seem like it holds together too good, but that's wrong. You just have to be willing to gather them and wrap something around them to hold them together. When love comes from your family it holds together better than anything and you can wrap your own self up in it whenever you want no matter how long you didn't. So this coat is love, ok? Don't worry about nothing before or after this. Just love, okay? God will show you the rest. I know you felt like you were supposed to be there for Lam when she was little, especially when I wasn't because of drink, but you were little too. Then you was gone when she had Dusty, but I was there then. Dusty turned out good. Now your sister is having another baby. I can't help think He still ain't called on you yet. To do good for good people. Nothing else matters.

Love you,
Mom

PS. Your dad loves you too.

Neither Levi nor Lam could talk. They stood, hugged, and bawled. In a long while, Levi wiped his eyes and nose. He held out the jacket and felt the lining. "What's in it?"

Levi thought Lam's shoulders and face had little tremors, and he thought she was going to cry again, but as the tremors got bigger, she began to laugh and blew a snot bubble. "Lint!" she cried, and she belly laughed and sniffed.

"What?" Levi was smiling through red eyes, the answer not yet registering.

"Lint." She took a deep breath. "From Mom's dryer and from mine. Lint from my shirts, and Dad's pants, and Dusty's gym clothes, and … and Mom's *underwear!*" At this point, she lost all control. "She had us all save *lint!*"

They laughed and laughed, and they cried, and laughed some more. And just when they thought they had about worn it out, they laughed again. Levi laughed until primordial threads floated in his vision like ghostly little fibers. Finally, they wound down, and the floaters drifted toward the door.

"Wait." Lam nervously held out a paper clip of currency. "Take this. Please."

Levi stood with no empty hands, full of embarrassment. "I can't take money from you. I'm fine. I'll stop at an ATM in Billings."

She gently closed in on him and slipped the cash into his new jacket pocket. "Your ATM card didn't work in town. It won't work in Billings. Besides, it's a loan. You'll pay me back."

"How did you know …?"

"Roundup ain't that big." She looked at his hand. "You need some more gauze?"

Levi looked. "No. Not really. I'm about healed."

"Then maybe you ought to let it breathe. Set the cooler down." She took his wrist. With her other hand she unwound the gauze like it was no big thing, slowing on the last layer. There was no scab, just baby skin. She paused, and then looked at his eyes. "It's pink!"

"Yeah." They regarded it in stillness. "All this time. Just slice it away. Voila. Normal." He held it up, smiling. She rolled her eyes. "Okay, still scarred. But pretty-er – ish."

They laughed one last time, and hugged. He pushed out the door with the cooler.

The cold singed his nostrils like smelling salts, sucking his focus forward in time to now. The bunkhouse roof glowed with moonlight. No window was lit. He imagined Frank watching them from the shadows. He tried to pull it back, a last warm moment, shrugging inside his new jacket, feeling it everywhere: arms, back, belly. It was no good. Then he remembered. He went back in and brought out the gun case. Frank flashed in a bunkhouse window. Sensation blended with dread. Some things are never set straight. *No.* He forced himself into the present. *Love* this *moment. Embrace these gifts, now.* He knew what was coming ... in the other world. What he would set right there could not be done with a lint jacket and Virginia stew.

47

NIGHT

*Out of the night that covers me
Black as the Pit from pole to pole …*
WILLIAM ERNEST HENLEY

A soft, twilight drizzle varnished the Bay Shore Freeway by 3-Com Park, giving each rushing headlight and skittish taillight a shimmering doppelganger. Levi's SUV, still thickened with road grime, climbed the hill near Candlestick Point toward San Francisco. The radio played *White Christmas*, all rich and velvety. He sang along, holding his chin down as men do when they sing like Bing, and, as men who hold their chin down do, thought he sounded pretty good. Despite the duet, he drove purposefully, as eager as he was anxious, wondering where to stay tonight.

A few miles later he exited at 4th Street in the direction of downtown. Holiday traffic thickened near the stores around Union Square, but he had allowed plenty of time. Dinner wasn't until eight. He planned to enjoy the seasonal lights, peruse the stores, and listen one last time to the carolers. This city knew how to Christmas. As he parked underground, he remembered his and Angela's first Yule by the Bay, how they window-shopped for toys at F.A.O. Schwartz, her gleeful crescent eyes. For old time's sake, he would make it his first stop. Before getting out he gazed at the passenger seat. He fingered the tattered book that lay there, wondered how long he had carried it. Wondered at its reality. Resented its testimony on sanity. Then he reached under the seat to check his other cargo, looking only with his fingers. Best not to look until morning. He would settle things on this trip, make things right, do good, one way or another. *Nothing to lose. Nothing else matters.* He knew now that nothing ever had.

Levi eschewed the elevator, instead bounding up the stairs to the street with an ease that pleased him. The work on the ranch, however unskilled, had pumped the capacity of his legs, his arms, his lungs. A minute later, on the sidewalk corner of the Square, misty rain collected on his hair and trench coat and on the humped umbrellas podded up around him. He stared kitty-corner at the three-story pile of enormous alphabet blocks stacked child-like up the wedge of the F.A.O. Schwartz building. Only when a woman bumped him did he realize the light had turned green. "My wife loves that store," he said, pointing. The woman had passed. During Angela's first time in the store, Levi watched her big eyes lasso toy after toy, pulling herself along, giddy, speculating rapid-fire about kids at school and the fun it would be to shop for a child of their own – at least one, she had said. He had heard the store might close. From this memory rose a morose urge to visit other spots on the Square – ones where he had shopped for her each Christmas – Gump's, Sak's, Tiffany's – and drink free hot spiced cider. For at least a decade he had felt the first spark of holiday spirit while shopping for Angela, usually around December 23rd. If he were honest, this walk was indulging his melancholy more than cherished memory, as if this act, too, was finishing the unfinished, tying things up. He pressed on, strolling the Square's perimeter. He stopped and admired the great, central Christmas tree, observing faces of kids and oldsters and lovers. Beyond it, the St. Francis Hotel. Only last year he had talked Angela into celebrating the Millennium there. They had bought tickets to the party, rented a room. Made love.

Catching himself in the wrong part of the past, he shook his head like a drowsy trucker. No. No more sorry. Save Angela, most of what he missed – had mourned over, for Christ's sake – wasn't even real. The title. The parties. The trappings. Had *never* been real. Isn't that why he had come back now? To kill ghosts? In retrospect, only Angela stayed true. Even though she had been immersed *in it*, just like him, she never became *of it*. As he did. Biting coins. Weighing them. Suddenly the Muppets were singing *Marley and Marley* in his head. A Christmas Carol. A rush of embarrassment raided him. His hands had found the folded money in his pockets. Lam's money. "Irony can be pretty ironic sometimes." *Marley and Marley (beat – beat) Marley and Marley.*

Dinner would be held at Postrio, Wolfgang Puck's restaurant on Post Street. As he walked, Levi tried to guess who would be there other than Sandler and Lily. Abba had lit the fuse. Lily had called him. How long would tonight take? "Doesn't matter." Wasn't going home anyway. Maybe he could stay at Lily's place. Inside, the host escorted him along copper handrails, past modern art and glass sculptures, to a private patio room. There were six people waiting, three that he knew – Sandler and Lily, as he expected, and … *Joy?* Who were the others? *Cops?* Levi blanched. Maybe he wouldn't need a bed at Lily's after all.

"Hello, Levi," growled Sandler. "Come in. Let me introduce you."

Next, as though it was their honor, all six people stood. Lily hugged him, pulling back an impressed expression. "Hm. Finally got some exercise," she said to him in a private voice. Levi's eyes asked her questions. Joy sang out ringingly, "Hello, stranger!" He noted breadcrumbs and drinks on the table. They'd talked some already. Never one for chit-chat, Mike Sandler, his broad-lined face now seeming something from home, introduced Levi to Fran Abondolo of the NASD, Julie Pennington of the SEC, and Special Agent Chestnut, a hulking FBI man. They were curt, professional. No clues. As Levi took his chair at one end of the table, opposite Sandler, Fran handed him a folder.

Throughout the evening, Fran took the lead. She said there were three parallel investigations – the FBI having opened theirs only last week. She referred to the documents in the folder, only a sampling of evidence they had amassed. There was more they couldn't share yet. At first she spoke dispassionately, laying fact upon fact, a criminal pre-mortem.

For more than an hour, Pennington held tensed, her blonde hair pulled back formally, her pretty, hard face sporting the carnivore eyes. Agent Chestnut was silent altogether, writing with impractically thick fingers, his shirt cinching tight when he turned a page. It was oddly distracting. *I can take him,* Levi joked inside.

At no particular cues, Joy nervously floated "So true," or "I concur," like cartoon balloons for her bobble-head nods. Lily sat primly, nibbling from time to time. Sandler ate.

To Levi, the corporatesque tone and cadence were dreamlike in familiarity. Conjuring his formal business persona was uncomfortable in its ease, too form-fitted from wear to forget, no matter how long neglected. But however easy the fit, the topic at hand was surreal.

For 90 minutes, Levi mostly assimilated the pieces. He asked a question or two. From time to time he was referred to the evidence folder before him. According to Fran, Crawford had perpetrated felony theft through securities and banking fraud. In commission of these crimes, he had co-conspirators. That constituted racketeering as defined in the RICO Act. He was provably guilty of stock manipulation and interstate wire fraud. Along the way, he violated state and federal wiretapping and right-to-privacy laws – the only true surprise to Levi so far, other than the sheer fantasticality of this moment.

When Fran said that much physical evidence had been furnished by Lily, Lily cast her eyes down. Levi looked at Mike, ready to scrap.

Mike held up his hand. "I know what you're thinking, cowboy, but save it. The firm has no whistle-blower complaints here. Not for Lily, not for Joy." *Joy?* "They did what's right. We're representing them. If you want to bust someone's balls, you'll get your chance."

"Maybe we can talk about the options you got from EcoPulse, Mr. Monroe." FBI said.

"What options?" *What options?* "He offered some, I declined."

"You're on their records. Maybe it's true. Ramakapur won't answer that yet."

"We'll get to that." Fran held her tack. Not surprisingly, there were client complaints. Some evidence had just been stumbled upon serendipitously, as things tend to go. Then, to Levi's amazement, Fran said they had copies of Deirdre Oliver's personal notes regarding Crawford and others, including himself. "Paradoxically," Fran said, "this helps you."

Patience spent, Julie Pennington broke loose with all the finesse of an ice pick. "We want you there when we take Crawford down. Tomorrow. We require it." She hung there. "We think you can get him to say things, incriminate himself. Yes or no? It's your boss's idea."

Slowly, Levi felt a big grin grow across his face. "Mr. Sandler is not my boss."

"I'll leave that up to you two," said Pennington. Mere feet away, Sandler grinned back. "Please know, Mr. Monroe, that we may be able to proceed without you. I'm sure you are familiar with Abhaya Ramakapur, the founder of EcoPulse. As it happens, because of Mr. Ramakapur's work in energy independence and environmental cleanup, he has friends in high places. We've talked to Ramakapur, as has Mr. Sandler. He can be a friendly witness. Maybe for you, if Crawford goes down. It seems EcoPulse was delaying distribution of checks from Bookman Stuart to their employees. However, Mr. Sandler maintains," she eyed Sandler dubiously, "that he and Mr. Ramakapur agreed that the delays were ordered by Bookman Stuart via Crawford in order to assure the accuracy of the checks. If so, Mr. Ramakapur is off the hook for collusion to delay settlement. At most, he'll plead guilty to some lesser charge and get a slap on the wrist. In exchange, Mr. Ramakapur will testify that Crawford solicited from him a list of names of people Ramakapur thought should get shares of hot issue stock. It's not illegal to ask, as long as you don't get paid. We can't prove Ramakapur was paid, so he's off that hook on that. He will then testify that Crawford tried to use the fact that stock was directed to Ramakapur's friends to blackmail Ramakapur and EcoPulse into further holding up distribution of checks so Bookman Stuart could make more money on improper float. Do you follow me?" Levi did. "The long and short of it is that in exchange for immunity, Ramakapur will help us get Crawford for wrongfully delaying settlement, improperly directing stock, and for extortion."

Levi looked at Sandler. "I'd like to talk with Abba."

"He's in India on business," Pennington said. What she didn't know is that Sandler had, just as Levi had before him, discussed with Ramakapur how Bookman Stuart stock would get crushed when news of Crawford's fraud became public. She also didn't know that Ramakapur's agents overseas had already borrowed hundreds of millions through Bookman Stuart's overseas subsidiaries and shorted Bookman Stuart stock through another firm. As a hedge, they had even shorted EcoPulse. In exchange for Abba's tailored testimony, Abba would receive Bookman Stuart's lone *mea culpa* on all violations, plus untold profit from shorting the stock. Bookman Stuart would buy its own stock at basement prices. Sandler already had the board authorize a beefed up buyback program. When Bookman Stuart began to buy, Abba's cohorts would cover their short position and go long, accumulating millions of cheap shares. When it was time, Bookman Stuart would pin the problem on Crawford, its rogue officer. The stock would recover. Voila. Billions. All this Pennington didn't know. And she didn't know Ramakapur would return only when the trial was over, and a pardon granted. Or maybe never.

Pennington went on, "In the morning Sandler will have breakfast with Deirdre Oliver, where, given her desire to win a promotion, it is hoped she will unwittingly corroborate some of the evidence against Crawford, thereby opening a legal door to her records and implicating herself."

When Agent Chestnut said he could fit Sandler with a wire, Levi couldn't help but laugh. Sandler good-naturedly said go to hell. "After breakfast, Sandler, Oliver, Crawford and some local managers are scheduled to meet regarding regular business," said Pennington.

"That's when," Levi decided. "At that meeting. That's when I help."

Pennington and Fran looked to Sandler. Chestnut looked put out. After all, they were the law. But in court they needed the firm as a friendly to make it all stick. They needed Levi.

Sandler looked at Levi, assessing. "I'm not his boss," Sandler said to all. That was that.

"In addition to criminal filings," Fran added, "the NASD will charge industry rule violations against Crawford. We'll tack on supervisory negligence."

Levi sat, simultaneously electrified and stunned. Tonight he had expected, at best, to tell his side of the story to Sandler before he dealt with Crawford tomorrow, on his own terms. But this. With what Crawford and his minions had done – the humiliation, the madness, the failed career and marriage – fuck 'em. *It all never needed to happen, never!* If not for them, he would have been … been what? Like he was? A year ago? Two?

"Something else you should all know," said Sandler, "Gary has been named in a sexual harassment suit. The firm will handle that in civil court." Levi regarded Joy, wondering.

"That's a thumbnail summary," Fran concluded. "Do you have any questions?"

Levi did not.

"We asked you here as a friendly party to the investigation. I wasn't sure you'd help us. I, for one – I know Julie feels this way too," Pennington appeared emotionless, "– would like to express my deepest regrets for the damage or pain this investigation may have caused you."

"That doesn't absolve him." FBI said.

Levi nodded his acceptance, thankful they could not possibly know what was under the seat of his car. "I had planned to see Crawford anyway, though he didn't know it."

Agent Chestnut was piqued.

"Nothing big," Levi lied.

Finally, they outlined tomorrow's plan for Levi. They gave him three envelopes. The walls bulged with anticipation. "How do I get in?" Levi asked, "Into the building. Past security? I'm not an employee."

"We'll meet you in the lobby," said Chestnut, almost surly now. He added for everyone, "Having three agencies in this case is bad enough – no offense."

Offense already taken. "And the State Department will be a genuine pain in the ass. But civilians dictating tactics? Monkeys fucking footballs. What could go wrong?"

On his way to the car, Levi walked slowly on a damp sidewalk, in and out of lights from restaurants, hotels and residences that box-lit the spitting rain. He opened the folder, read a wet-freckled page of Deirdre's stolen notes given only to him. Lily had slipped it in. According to the notes, Crawford had told Deirdre details of Levi's crumbling marriage, secrets Crawford couldn't know, confidences Levi had shared over time, pillow talk, with one person. Wincing at himself, he blamed no one more for his betrayals. For Joy. He checked his watch. "Ten more hours." He took a deep breath, coaxing himself to relax. "Nothing left to lose, no one left to take it." He threw the folder on the passenger seat. Conceiving no destination, but far too wound up to sit still, he drove out of the garage. There was thinking to do.

Levi drove to see the tree at Ghirardelli Square. He walked again, imagining. *What to say?* He walked to the Buena Vista Café and Bar for an Irish coffee. On his second one, he began to assemble thoughts and notes. Rearrange his presentation. He timed it in his head. *Too long. What to leave in, what to leave out?* A pretty bartender flirted with him. To his surprise, he flirted back. *Nice girl,* he thought, *eyes like Angela's.* With that, he paid the tab and left.

Before midnight he rolled down to the water, turned east along Fisherman's Wharf, past festive Pier 39. He continued, driving slowly, circling clockwise along the water. In this season, along with much of the San Francisco skyline, the Embarcadero Center towers were soaring boxes outlined in brilliant white lights, morphing the high-rises into silhouettes of generous presents, gift-wrapped in black. By the time he circumnavigated the waterfront to Pac Bell Park, he had it worked out, not that things like this go as planned. Elsewhere in his head, without intention, he had been tracing the night's route, a spiral on an imaginary map, coiling clockwise, the clean side of the rug. He didn't punish himself for the black thought, psychotic symbolism or not. *It will be over,* he told himself. *After tonight, it's over.* His cell phone rang.

"Levi? It's Joy. I just wanted to call and say it was good to see you again."

His betrayer. His Mata Hari. His fault. Perhaps it was his culpability that, even now, made him pity her, for Levi could not make the slut label stick to her image. But neither could he reciprocate. "Thanks."

"Lily said she got you a room in town tonight."

He didn't respond.

"Are you staying at the Nikko?"

"Yes."

"I know you … you might think … Well. I'll just ask. Do you want some company?"

"No." He hung up.

Levi turned right and dove deep into the Financial District and the Hotel Nikko. "Do good for good people. Nothing else matters. And fuck the bad guys, no matter what. No matter what, Gary, you've made too many people be who they hate to be. No more."

48

DAWN

The rat is in the trap, it is in the trap,
And attacking heaven and earth with
a mouthful of screeches like torn tin.

TED (EDWARD) J. HUGHS

At 6:30 A.M., before he hit the street, Levi made a stop in the hotel's underground parking garage to retrieve what he wanted from the car. Two minutes later, on a financial district sidewalk, Levi carried in his baby-pink hand the scroll-wadded notebook, the totem he had honed and communed with for years, at last unafraid that the inks with which he stained it must stain him as well. He checked the envelopes in his breast pocket, creeping through memories. Above him, in the rain-cleaned sky, once-vain stars humbled in the red-orange blush of dawn.

It was not yet 7 A.M., but markets were tied to the New York clock and the streets already effervesced with morning city sounds – cars, voices, retiring garbage trucks. A siren yowled over by Market Street. Across from the waiting rose-granite tower, exhaust and rancid alley smells blended with wafts of baked goods and Starbucks coffee. Levi ducked in. He lined up with people on phones reading newspapers, bought a tall Christmas blend. From his windowed perch, he watched the familiar skyscraper vacuum people off the street. He recognized few faces, knew fewer names than before. Streisand sang *Silver Bells*. Occasionally he checked his watch, tracing the tattered friendship bracelet from Angela.

Across the way, Lily entered the building. Next, smoking-manager from San Rafael showed up. Two minutes later, the East Bay managers popped up from a BART subway hole. He didn't blame them for avoiding the Bay Bridge. Soon Joy and the other Peninsula managers walked up. Probably carpooled, Levi guessed. He knew Crawford would already be inside, eyeing folks judgingly as they arrived. No one was ever sure for what.

Out the window to the right, Sandler's face materialized, three feet away and closing. Deirdre Oliver flanked him, jabbering shrewd-sounding observations, overplaying her power-walk, hair popping on each step as if spanked on top. Levi's blood surged. Sandler's eyes met Levi's but didn't let on. Levi's eyes flashed fight, taunting Deirdre to look. She did not. They passed. Fine, then. Better, even. And then, on the corner, as she and Sandler readied to cross, she spied him. He was sure of it. Maybe. He rose. She showed nothing until they mounted the curb on the other side. Then, as Sandler turned for the building, she glanced back, directly at Levi. Even at sixty feet, her confusion was palpable. He hooked her stare with a smile. Her face died. When she kick-started her stride, she stuttered, hustling to Sandler's side. For her, more flight than fight. "Swallow hard, asshole," he said. "Your special breakfast is about to repeat on you."

Levi had to hand it to Sandler. Even now, in what would surely bring the firm public disrepute and client defection, the man moved with unreadable ease and confidence. No nonsense. No hurry. Canny of the treacherous ambition Deirdre veiled with competence, luring the disingenuous assassin to her payment. Levi imagined their breakfast, Deirdre cutting Crawford's balls off, occasionally picking at Levi's tainted legacy like carrion. All the while Sandler grappling, using the weight of her aspirations to tip her, to spill out dark secrets about Crawford. "Stanford, my ass," Levi whispered. His voice woke him. It felt late. He downed the last of his coffee, grabbed his booklet, and headed in.

The distance across the lobby was farther than he'd remembered. He didn't see his allies at first, so he approached the turnstile designated for visitors. Maybe they had left word.

The guard asked for a day pass. Levi had no day pass. "Step over here while I call Mr. Crawford's office," the guard said.

"No, no," Levi said as if not wanting to be a bother. *Can't spook Crawford.* The guard's body squared with suspicion. Levi played scenarios in his head. Lily would probably answer. What if Crawford overheard? What if Deirdre had already said she saw Levi? *Crap.* Just then, from behind the immense lobby Christmas tree, Giant Jimmy's great head and offbeat nose buoyed above the sea of incomers, picking a trough and wading over in it. *Shit. Not good.*

"Mr. Monroe," Jimmy nodded down at Levi.

"Jimmy." *Fuck, this is it. Busted. Crawford rides away. Dammit!*

Jimmy reached and Levi flinched. He had something in his hand. A badge. "Here's your day pass." He clipped it on Levi's pocket. "Your friends arranged it."

"Oh. Uh, where are they?" Through Levi's momentary relief bled genuine concern. He couldn't do this alone. He had no authority, nor did Sandler or Jimmy or anyone else but the cops, to detain Crawford. If this went off before they got there, Crawford could bolt, would bolt, maybe even have time to leave the country.

"I'm not sure. They said they'd catch up with you." Jimmy smiled. "Get'em, Cowboy."

Levi smiled. He pushed through the turnstile and settled on the elevator. Here again. He remembered the ride up twenty years back: his hope, his surety of purpose, of auspicious beginnings. He remembered Joy's immensity of hair, her big, plastic smile. She had changed. Only Lily seemed timeless, forever dignified, smart, grounded. The ride back down that day had been a true counter-cycle, descending floors on sinking spirits. Eager to go home. To Montana. To Angela. He had discerned back then that Crawford was bad news – crooked, predatory. *Were my senses no more than common? Common.* The word felt good. And Crawford was no more than a common criminal – one of at least two Sandler now had treed up on the 45th floor. *Deirdre, too, and maybe a couple of managers. But not Joy. Poor Joy.* "Where the hell are the cops?"

The door opened on the 45th floor. Levi inhaled and sallied in. Five strides later, a field of secretaries, caught unaware, ground still. One dropped something. The girl from Fresno waved as if spying a cousin at the mall. Lily met Levi halfway. "Where's the cavalry?" he asked. "I don't know," she whispered. A meeting kicked off in the VIP conference room thirty feet behind her.

"Thank you all for coming in today." Sandler sat behind the speakerphone at the head of a long table surrounded by eleven other businesspeople, his back to floor-length windows displaying a magnificent morning on the Bay. Deirdre, laptop at the ready, sat to his left, Crawford to his right. "We'll try to finish and get you folks back to your branches soon as possible."

"I'm not going to bullshit you. I know you're all aware of the ongoing investigation by the regulatory bodies. If you're not, you're too out of touch to manage." Crawford's eyes warned everyone to pay attention – Joy, smoking-manager, the East Bay guys, the Peninsula crew. "There's a lot of speculation out there about what has occurred within this firm. If you're part of that speculation, you're wasting your time and the firm's. Stop it. That said, I'm not stupid. Neither is Gary, here, or Deirdre. If we're going to get beyond gossip and get the hell back to work, it's time to remind you folks what's expected of our officers. What you can and can't do. People have gutted their own goddam careers. After today, no more bullshit." They understood.

Manicured, wrinkle-free, and cocksure, Crawford nested into what he chose to understand from Sandler's comments: that any residual loyalties or sympathies for Levi were about to be smothered. He had no chance to know of Deirdre's breakfast, of Levi's proximity.

An epiphany pulled Deirdre's frame straight – Sandler may well sack Crawford right here and now – with an audience! What balls! She chilled at her good fortune. No more little package deliveries, no fucks by threat or indenture. No more Sen-Sens. And most importantly, no more obstacles. She stared pleasingly at Crawford's face, reminding herself to clean out her purse.

In this room only Joy knew, and for the first time, she was sick for it. She filled her glass with water and drank it half down, her grip damp.

Sandler went on. "Some things happened in this division awhile back. No one in this room should be proud of it. It looks like it started with some funny business in our stock option exercise unit, but I suspect, if you backtrack on the dealings of the responsible parties, there's an abundance of unethical bullshit that went on before it. Well, that's not us."

Crawford looked scornfully at Joy, who deprived him of her attention, fixed on her water glass. Without regarding him, she raised a hand to her jaw, drew along it with her finger. He let his eyes drift away, but something yanked them back. *Her nail.* The short one – nearly grown out. His brow tightened at the insolence, but only for an instant. No matter now. She stared at her glass, hiding there in fear, he presumed. Joy, this trampy suck-up, would be little use to Sandler now, Crawford thought, because Sandler had swallowed the bait. And now that Deirdre Oliver and HR were fully under his thumb, he had access to far more secrets than Joy could ever screw out of people. Besides, it was for insurance that he had masterfully positioned Joy in management on the Peninsula in the first place. If his stock option cult was disrobed, she, as with Levi, would be his proxy sacrifice. His sin-eater. He smirked until he realized Sandler was still chiding on to his, Crawford's, constituency. These were Crawford's people. Time to show control. "What Michael and I are saying is that we – the firm – and we, who lead it, are principled. We demand that of you as well. Let's do the right thing, people."

"Thanks," Sandler said, dry and flat. Joy and Deirdre caught it. Between keystrokes, Deirdre stole a glance at Crawford, relishing his impending demise. Next, she side-glanced at Joy, the pimp's whore, at once surmising Sandler must sweep out all the trash. Whether Joy went down with Levi or Crawford, Deirdre was good either way. Just then, Joy did something odd. She reached over and touched Deirdre's hand – no, her finger – the one with the short nail, pausing on that digit as if readying to roll it for examination. Deirdre, raising it in recoil, exposed the F key, the irony of which, once realized, she feared was not hers alone. An instant later, Joy confirmed it, unfolded her own fingers softly, holding out a still slightly blunted one until Deirdre was sure. The whore was pointing … at her.

Smoking-manager's eyes clicked stupidly. He nodded at everyone, on everyone's side so far, especially the side of right, whichever that came out to be. Others seemed bored to pain.

"Well, it's gotten more complicated than we first suspected," Sandler said. "You probably know that the NASD is involved, and the SEC. Turns out the FBI has jumped in to help out."

Deirdre's fingers slowed on the keys and Crawford sat straighter. "I didn't know that…"

"It just came up," said Sandler. "You'll get all the details. Right now, the important thing is to help the investigators from all three enforcement teams. If – rather – when they show up in your offices, you're to give them anything they want. Usually that will be access and copies of records. You'll meet them today. They are just outside that door." He pointed a pencil, having every reason believe they were there. They were not.

"Here? They're here?" Crawford exclaimed. "Why the hell are they here? How did you…" Crawford's ears reddened. "Mike, we shipped the salient divisional files to outside counsel in New York months ago. They've already provided copies to the NASD and the SEC."

"They think they missed a thing or two." Sandler's tone gave no hints, no handle to grab.

Crawford reached to retake any initiative. "Um. I'll go talk with them." When he put his hands on the table to stand, Sandler touched one of them. He leaned into Crawford's ear.

"You might want to wait on that," Sandler said softly. "They're the cranky type." They looked at each other. A moment burned until Crawford's scalp retreated a full half-inch. Another passed before he pulled back, leaving two moist prints on the tabletop.

"As I mentioned," Sandler was addressing statues now. "The complexity of this scheme is considerable." He looked at Deirdre. "Are you getting this down? I wouldn't want you to miss anything." In this, Deirdre chose to find reassurance of her immunity, the palpability of which betrayed her. She began typing in earnest. Sandler appeared to enjoy himself. "I want to bring into the room the individual who's been working with these and related issues and laws longer than anybody, someone who brought this mess to our attention long ago. We ... *I* dropped the ball then. Anyway, he can tell you what we know so far." *He?* Deirdre and Crawford both heard it. They had met the investigators from the NASD and the SEC, had conference calls with them. They knew the investigators were women. Sandler watched. He pressed the intercom button. "Lily, can you break for a second?"

It took a minute for her to answer, "Sorry, Mike, I was away from my desk."

"Please send our first guest in."

Joy saw herself in her water glass. Deirdre read her laptop keys. The door handle moved. Smoking-manager's eyes ping-ponged from Howdy to Doody.

Levi came in.

"What?" Crawford said, jumping up. "This is unacceptable! Mike, this man is the focus of ... I simply will *not* sit with this *con man* in the room. And I don't think it's fair to ask others to." For support he looked at Deirdre, her face open wide like a big-mouthed jar, and then at the two older managers, men with secrets.

Sandler leaned in to whisper, motioning Crawford to come in close. Even at that, with the voice of a whale's lament, words carried. "Let's hear him out, shall we? What's to lose?"

Crawford's lips parted, but no words left his reddening face.

"Before my friend gets started," Sandler said to all, "it's important to say a few things. First, it is clear now that Levi left under an unfair cloud of suspicion. Because of that, we've been working with him behind the scenes for a while." By a while, he meant twelve hours. "Second, he's shown more honor and balls than anyone can ask. And no one knows this business better. He's the smartest person in this room." With a puff from his nose, Crawford posted his disagreement. "Maybe we can learn a thing or two. Mr. Monroe, the floor is yours."

Levi placed his booklet, his file, and two envelopes on the far end of the table. He stared at Crawford, too cold for the thin man to hold. *Okay,* Levi told himself. *The cops aren't here. So you can deal with me. Let's see how much it'll take.* "Most of you don't do a great deal of stock option exercise business – Joy has the bulk of it." Joy wouldn't look. "But all of you do a little. All of you know the firm makes money on float. Well, too much money. From inside the firm, a system of illegal payoffs was devised to improperly delay payment to individual customers who exercised options and sold stock. I ran some rough calculations. The ill-gotten interest increased management bonuses by over a million a year, the bulk of which went to one executive." Levi smiled tauntingly.

Crawford sprung to his feet, "How dare you insinuate…"

"Sit down, Gary," Sandler said. "We're not his boss. Just ask him."

"I will not sit! I will not be insulted by this con – this *mongrel.*" Crawford reached for his pen and pad, making a show of walking out.

Levi edged into the path between Crawford and the door. *Not yet, you son of a bitch.*

Sandler stood, foursquare with Crawford, inches away, and spoke quietly, sternly. "If you leave now of your own accord, you will have no claim to $20 million in stock and options the firm holds for you. If I dismiss you, your contract provides for negotiation. What's your pride worth? Your call."

"It's all right, Mike," Levi said. He tensed, daring Crawford his way. "Gary, you may leave now." *Come on, you fucking whore, stay for the money … or dance with me.*

"I beg your pardon? You insolent son of a…" He truncated the thought, guessing abruptly and badly at Levi's strategy. Crawford had a weak hand, but Levi bet that, like any bully, he'd meet insults with defiance – until he ran. "All right." Crawford sat, forcing a superior look around the room. "Spin your tale, with all the strength and elegance of cobwebs." Then he grappled with forced stoicism. Strapped down by the law at the door and $20 million, he stirred afraid and bitter, a liar in an electric chair with his victim at the switch.

Feeling anything but the victim, Levi spoke on. "It appears that the conspirators moved money across state lines, maybe even internationally, through bank wires and by mail, making this case Federal. But stealing from clients and paying off corporate officers with hot stock through dummy accounts were not the only crimes – legal, moral, or ethical."

"There was forgery – documents and e-mails regarding the options scheme and other, unrelated collusions. As a case in point, when the NASD began their investigation, incriminating e-mails were concocted and sent from my workstation to conspirators outside the firm in order to leave a trail pointing to me. I wasn't the only target. The same thing happened to some of you." Levi looked at Deirdre, who was stiff, her mouth open soundlessly. She had indeed, under the guise of HR audits at various branches, sent incriminating e-mails from managers' terminals while the managers held staff meetings on benefits. It was easy to erase the e-mail from the manager's outbox so he wouldn't know he was framed. "Further, devices installed in the personal computers you keep in your offices tracked your keystrokes. Private information was gathered on each of you about your finances, your true thoughts, what websites you visit, your health issues, even what personal *relationships* you have."

"You are fucking kidding me." The senior-most manager looked from Levi to Crawford.

"New York was mistakenly given transcripts of your keystrokes. Remember the third-party vendor the firm ostensibly hired as a perk to give managers free IT service for their personal PCs? It was actually an independent security company. They thought they'd contracted with the firm itself, not some rogue individuals within it. They were so pleased with their contract that they called the firm president's office in New York to see if they could go national. Karl – you remember Karl? – took the call. He attained copies of your keystrokes."

Deirdre blanched. She started shutting down her laptop. Crawford, though, suddenly relaxed somewhat, as if a thought had just delivered him.

What are you thinking now? Levi wondered. "Additionally, not only were the records of your office and cell phone calls watched, but the same security company was hired to call your home phone service provider and pretend to be you. Your home phone records were acquired."

"Can they do that?" smoking-manager asked with affable, measured outrage, apparently having decided for the moment that Levi was ahead in score.

"Be aware," Crawford answered with pedantic, lazy arrogance, "that accomplished liars braid plausible elements with vagueness. His cobweb will fashion into a hangman's noose."

"Who the hell talks like that?" goaded Levi. *Come on. I want a rise out of you, but not the kind the investigators want. Come on.* Crawford ignored him. "There's your trouble. You talk. You might struggle with class more than others here, but why shame yourself by showing it?"

Crawford slapped his hands on the table as if to push off, and Levi thought he had him, but Sandler stopped him. "Go on, Levi," Sandler said in a cautioning tone.

"It's called pretexting." The other managers had become rapt mannequins with blinking oversized eyes, but Crawford gathered himself. *I need to push the bastard harder,* Levi thought. He gave Crawford a sublime, self-satisfied look. Crawford smiled back in kind. No dice. "Collectively, this invasive pattern could only be motivated by three things – the intent to catch you doing something wrong," counting with rising fingers, "the intent to blackmail you, the intent to frame you. Hopefully that's only happened to me so far." This was the first time Joy met anyone's eyes, as if to plead *me too.* Levi felt a pang of remorse at his rough handling of her call the night before. "By the way, you know if you leave the firm voluntarily or through malfeasance, all of your deferred compensation – over a million for most of you – returns to the firm. What you may not know is that your supervisor, at the divisional level or higher, pockets 15 percent of that in bonus for recaptured profit." Every head turned toward Crawford.

"Oh, pu-lease, Mr. Monroe," Crawford groaned, cocksure and imperious. "You've been in trouble for quite some time. You have an abundance of motive to deflect your guilt. You lack proof. Why should these people, the regulatory bodies, or anyone else believe you?" Crawford was smug in the bet that he and Deirdre covered all their tracks, left no direct evidence against themselves. That fact alone would stop the firm from proving wrongdoing, fired or not, long enough for him to collect his deferred compensation.

"I don't think the proof will take too long," said Levi.

Lily eased into the room and snuck the door shut.

Crawford addressed Sandler. "Okay, Mike. For whatever erroneous reason, you have attempted to humiliate me. Cards are on the table. If you don't fire me, I'll stay on indefinitely while my attorney deals with the firm over my deferred comp. If you do fire me without provable cause, my contract calls for the firm to pay my deferred to me within thirty days of dismissal, plus a severance package. I don't think you or that idiot with the Columbo complex can ever prove anything. Keep me and pay me. Fire me and pay me. Now it's *your* call." Crawford stood, buttoning his suit jacket with consummate leisure.

Sandler nodded to Levi.

Levi glanced to Lily with the secret, implied question, *Are they here?* Almost imperceptibly, she shook her head no. *Shit! This fucker will bolt, sure as hell, rather than go to jail.* Lily snuck back out. "First," Levi said, "we have Lily's transcripts of your phone conversations from your car, including those with Abba Ramakapur."

"That's impossible. We were never required to keep those files, so we didn't. They were shredded ages ago, not that it would—"

Levi cut him off. "Lily kept copies. Gary, not only are there ways to acquire physical evidence, but there are copies of incriminating notes in your own handwriting."

"What?" Crawford sneered, less sure now what was a bluff. "You have no access..."

"As you know, last week your assistant, Karl, filed a sexual harassment suit against you." Levi let this marinate for all parties for a moment. Sandler looked put out. "Sorry, Mike. It slipped. Anyway, *Gare*, Karl, a firm employee, was given access to everything in your office when you made him your assistant. No files were marked personal; some had correspondence in them — thus, correspondence files. The firm is obligated to supervise correspondence. You yourself carry a supervisory license. If you check the Securities Acts of 1933 and 1934—"

"I know damn well what the acts say!" Crawford bellowed. "So I'm damn sure you'll never be able to use my private notes for anything." His befuddled face said he wasn't sure at all. "Karl's a fruit, and it's clear as hell his motive is as tainted as yours and this entire charade!"

By this time the managers were drowning in mixed emotion, a blend akin to fear and disbelief. They had semiconsciously pushed away from the table, nesting far back in their chairs to evade the line of fire between men who hated each other.

Levi chuckled, light and dismissive. "You might like 'fruit', but I believe Karl prefers '*gay*.' You should also know the regulatory bodies have corroborating testimony from people in this room." He let Crawford hang on it. *Almost there.* "Joy, for one." Deirdre exhaled audibly.

"Who, your lover? That's what she is, isn't it?" Crawford tried to sell it to the crowd, but there was no bid. In his confusion, it was all the mud he could grab. A sling and a miss.

"I think you mean 'isn't she.' But if that were true, one would wonder by what means you came to know it." Counterpoint. "And you might have noticed I said 'people' corroborated. This morning Deirdre Oliver gave direct testimony to Mike about your stock option dealings."

From her trance, as though jolted awake by a sickening bolt of fear, Deirdre's head jerked wildly from Levi to Sandler to Crawford to Levi and so on, blinking, blinking.

"What?" Crawford screamed at her. "What!"

"I know what's legal under labor law," Deirdre protested at Sandler pleadingly, "and you, you can't treat me this bad."

"Badly," Levi offered.

"What?" She was fully disoriented now.

"Badly. It's an adverb." Now, with an amused air of full sardonic provocation, Levi piled on. "I know what you're thinking, Gary: Deirdre wants a promotion you won't give her, so she wants you fired." To her gasping mouth, Deirdre rushed a trembling, agitated hand. "Even so, I think her verbal testimony is sincere. Besides" – *and the envelopes, please.* He slid two envelopes down the table, their names on one each – "her sincerity will be tough to impeach, even by her, when the investigators read the notes on her hard drive. She might even be self-incriminating. In the envelopes are subpoenas for her records – business and private – and yours." Two managers scooted farther back. "The FBI says your personal telephone service providers will get one too."

Crawford bolted up, his voice loudly cracking. "Okay, you want trouble?"

Yup. It's time, thought Levi. "If I want more shit from you, I'll squeeze your head."

In a frenetic explosion of rage, Crawford lunged for Levi, frisking inelegantly around his colleagues' chairs. "You son of a BITCH!" It was Levi's payoff. From indelible rote, from skill forged in a bare-fisted town of miners and cowboys, sprung perfect martial timing. Just as Crawford arrived, lunging wildly, Levi's arm reached its full extension. At their combined speed, his fist met Crawford's oncoming chin. There was a deep, satisfying snap. Crawford crashed back, tumbling across the senior-most manager's lap.

Near the floor, scrambling to his knees, Crawford's suit coat roiled with elbows and shoulder blades, like so many cats in a sack. He screamed at the floor, searching frantically. His mouth sprayed blood like a gummed-up atomizer. "My toof! You broke my fucking toof! OwAhg! My jaw!"

"That went well," Sandler said.

Levi shrugged and rubbed his hand, pleased his cut knuckles would bear a new scar.

Sandler pushed the intercom button. "Lily, we're ready for the others now."

Levi began to explain, "Mike I don't think…" when a muscular man in a suit was already flying through the door. Fran and Pennington filed in behind. Giant Jimmy blocked the door. "Gary Crawford," Sandler nodded to indicate the guy on the floor, "this is Special Agent Chestnut of the FBI."

"Good," Crawford cried out, giving his body to Chestnut, allowing the man to lift him as a parent lifts a fallen child. The bloodied man jabbed a finger toward Levi. "He attacked me. You see! Ow." His jaw. "You see!" Crawford smeared his fingers with blood from his mouth and held them in outrage at Chestnut. "Arrest the son of a bitch!"

Chestnut pulled rubber gloves from his pocket.

"A dozen people in here would testify it was self-defense," Sandler said. "In addition to that, Agent Chestnut had streaming audio." He emphasized *streaming* as if to show the youngsters that the old guy knew a little something about tech-talk.

"Where ..?" Levi began at Chestnut.

"One floor below," Chestnut answered. "Didn't want to worry the help." He nodded quickly toward the secretarial bullpen, as if he had better things to explain. "Gary Crawford, you are hereby under arrest for racketeering and wire fraud. I'm sure there'll be more. Please empty your pockets on the table.

Jimmy, would you arrange a medic for Mr. Crawford?"

"But..." was all Chestnut allowed from Crawford before spinning him toward the table and emptying his pockets for him; a car key, a wallet, a phone, and a red tea-bag size foil of Sen-Sens, its torn top stapled shut.

By this time Julie Pennington had flanked Deirdre. She dumped out Deirdre's purse on the table. Deirdre looked aghast. Pennington was reveling in her craft. "Don't worry. You're under arrest, too." Strewn before Deirdre was her cell phone, teeth-whitening strips, and two extra absorbent tampons. Also within the menagerie lay a sugar-wafer-shaped flash drive and a red tea-bag pack of Sen-Sens – stapled shut. Pennington held up the Sen-Sens to Agent Chestnut. "Look, Todd, they're twinsies," managing through Deirdre's horror to make her blush. "Ms. Oliver, you can put everything else back in your purse. It'll be held for you at the jail. But I'll take this for now." She picked out the flash drive. Deirdre's eyes stayed locked on the Sen-Sens. Pennington saw them. "Why don't we have a mint?" she said and snatched away the packet an instant before Deirdre's hand got there.

"No!" Deirdre cried, tears bursting from her eyes. Pennington broke the foil around the staple and reached in. She extracted a tiny zip-lock bag, about an inch square, filled with white powder. "It's not mine! It's his! I picked it up for him!" She jammed a finger at Crawford.

Pennington handed the bag to Agent Chestnut who, as a cuffed and bloodied Crawford stared down, pulled open the stapled bag from Crawford's pocket. The contents were identical.

Like everyone else present, Levi was stunned. Some looked like they'd give anything to get out of the room. Levi had paid plenty to be there. It almost seemed worth it.

"You bought this for him?" Chestnut said in the tone of a friend.

If Crawford saw the trap, he made no move to save her.

"Yes," Deirdre howled. "It's his."

"Was he going to pay you back? For what you spent?"

"Yes! Yes! I don't use that crap! It's his!" Her top lip was shiny with snot.

"And to think it was just possession up to now. Now it's sale."

"What? No!" she cried. "No! I wasn't selling. It's not like that!"

"Why don't we stop talking now?" Agent Chestnut said. "You need an attorney."

With that Chestnut read Deirdre Oliver enough charges to arrest her for now. He read her rights while Jimmy covered the door. She too was bound with plastic cuffs.

"Please note, Gary," Sandler boomed, "in light of evidence of your malfeasance, you are both hereby fired. If you have benefits questions, please contact your HR representative."

Chestnut guided Crawford to the door while Pennington flanked Deirdre. Jimmy stood behind them.

"Anything else, Mr. Monroe?" Jimmy said, getting in a rare dig directed at Crawford.

"Huh?" Levi was standing with Lily. He had almost forgotten. The chart book – his chronicle of craziness. Even now, he discovered himself rolling and re-rolling it in his hands, unremembering of picking it up. With so many painful pages inspired by Crawford, he had planned to jam it down the malefactor's throat – or at least into his hand – a grand, public gesture of triumph! But ... it felt silly. Who would get it? Surely not Crawford. No one. He strode powerfully at Crawford until Agent Chestnut moved as if to intercept him. Close enough. "How's that dignity working out for you?" Levi glared at Crawford. "Don't worry," he whispered. "It's a gated community." Then he looked at Jimmy. "I don't work here, Jimmy, but thank you for asking." He returned to stand by Lily.

"Let's go," Jimmy motioned through the secretarial field, toward the elevators. "Please stay together." Agent Chestnut looked at Jimmy as if to say, that's enough.

"Yoshi owes me a dollar," Lily said. Levi was stumped. "Deirdre *does* kill after mating."

Sandler and Fran debriefed the managers. It was best to tell the press nothing. A statement would be out by day's end. Generally, it was best to be frank with employees – use your judgment. Things would be rough for a while. Sandler said to do what investigators say. As he spoke, the branch offices of the two senior managers in the room were being served subpoenas.

All the while Levi sat self-possessed in a chair against the wall. Lily sat beside him, taking shorthand. At adjournment, the managers proceeded slowly past them with the air of a funeral reception line, shaking hands with mixed pleasure and regret at seeing Levi again under such tough circumstances. Each wished him well, hiding as best they could their secret shame for things they did or should have done.

"He always did seem a little crazy," whispered smoking-manager loudly. "I think it was the pressure." Then the managers were gone.

Sandler hung back with Levi. "Merry Christmas, young man."

"Thank you, Mike. Happy Hanukah."

Mike nodded. "Listen, I have calls to make. One is to get you your money. I'm sorry it's not sooner. But I'm not done with you. Can you make it back in tomorrow for lunch? We're going to start that home loan division – without the help of Ilsa Crawford. Maybe we'll partner with Countrywide or Bear Stearns. Lehman. Maybe we'll buy some loan brokers. Commission when we lend, another commission when we package them and resell them to the street. Lay off all the risk. This could be big. Billions." Levi said he'd think about it.

On the way out, Levi stopped at Lily's desk. "How's the stock?"

"Down five points on heavy volume."

"Kill the firm, save the world," he said. She didn't get it.

He did think about Sandler's offer, all the way to the driveway in Saratoga. He killed the engine. He reached under the passenger side and slid from under the seat a stained and bulging holster.

49

Love You Like I'm Crazy

I long to talk to some old lover's ghost,
Who died before the God of love was born.

JOHN DONNE

Summer in the Bull Mountains had just begun. It had drizzled all night, but now the sky was brittle blue. The windows and doors at Geno's were open to air the place out. A light, fresh breeze and proud, rain-washed sunlight poured in, branding the floor by the booth under the plaque that read, *Fires and Firearms Strictly Prohibited.* There Levi and Angela sat with steaming cups of coffee. The saloon wasn't yet officially open for the day – only one patron was at the bar, an out-of-stater who marveled at the stuffed animals as he responded to Geno's questions with answers that Geno stabbed into a state computer that promised to spit out a waterproof fishing license.

"I bet the winters around here are pretty tough," the man said.

Geno scratched the white hair on the back of his head. "I'm sorry? What?" he grabbed the TV remote and muted CNN.

"The winters here, they're tough?"

"Ahck. You don't know winter. When I arrived here as a boy – *those* were winters."

Angela sat tall and smiled at Levi, her white tank top trimming tan, fit shoulders. "You look good."

"Thanks." Levi did look better nowadays. He had changed shirts three times that morning, hoping she would notice. "I been punchin' dogies on the ranch." Unlike her, he had worn his wedding ring. He slipped his hand under the table. "You look good too. You cut your hair."

"Do you like it? It's lots easier to take care of."

He raised his eyebrows. "Yeah. It looks nice." He leaned forward and looked warmly at her. "Really nice. You always look beautiful. Man, it is *so* great to see your face," he wanted to stop himself, but couldn't. "I feel like I can finally breathe."

She smiled. "How's your dad?"

At her tone, something dipped in his chest. It was … *nice* – apropos of a high school reunion. *Okay, she's taking it slow. Don't crowd her. Give her room.* Levi leaned back and slowed. "He's weak, but he's all right. At least he's harmless. He misses Mom, like all of us. His heart bothers him, but he's smoking again. These days I think he's more nervous around Lam and the baby than she is around him." This exchange was less buoyant than he'd intended. "She's bringing him here in a few minutes to go fishing with me." He had badly wanted their first conversation to float above the all the crap. *Lighten up.* He whipped up a fresh smile. "We'll probably drive up to Checkerboard, if we leave early enough. If not, we'll stop at Two Dot." Inside, another urgent bubble forced its way out. "*Man*, you've got beautiful eyes. I mean, I think about them all the time, but it's incredible to look into them."

"I don't know how good the fishing will be. The water's pretty high." Belatedly she touched his hand to thank him for the compliment, patted it twice but didn't linger there. "So your attorney called and said the house sold. That's good news."

He decided to assign his hands a place to be. They surrounded his coffee cup. "Yeah. I was afraid there wouldn't be much left once we pay the lawyers. My attorney says he thinks the SEC will release whatever funds we have left." *Should I be discussing money now? No. It's not the point. It cheapens the point.* "Turns out I'm not guilty. Go figure." He looked away from her, catching himself. He looked back. "It doesn't matter – the money. We … ummm … you and I … I mean, either one of us … can build it back up. If they ever sell, we'll make a little something on the houses here in Roundup, and you can decide what we do with it."

"Don't worry about it. I'm okay." She sounded too relaxed, light even, for her comfort to be false. This plucked in him a fiber of dread.

"Sandler released my deferred comp. He even credited interest and paid our … my legal fees. Presto-chango – we're rich again. Well, it's possible we will be, if the stock ever comes back. He's been great. He wants me back." It hung there. "Though I don't know in what role. Maybe president of their new mortgage division, and related investments. Says he'll give me 'space and permission.'" He searched her eyes for buy-in.

"I'm not surprised. You deserve it."

"We deserve it." *Christ, Levi, move on.* "Did you know there's a cave on the

West Bank with a two-headed goat and a four-legged chicken? It's a museum. They charge money."

"So we've heard. We don't have a four-legged chicken." She looked toward the bar. "Dad looks good, doesn't he? I'd like him to take more time and travel – he *still* hasn't seen Italy. Just keeps coming in here." She chuckled softly. Shook her head. "He won't get out. Ever. Not even to church. Instead of going to Mass, now he watches the Catholic channel out of Billings." She raised her eyebrows and tightened her lips. "Gotta love him."

Levi shook his head as though bemused, as though he could be bemused just as easily as the next guy. "Well, anyway, it's good he can take care of himself. I mean, not needing anyone to live with him or anything. He really *should* travel. You could watch the bar while he's gone."

Angela laughed, floating her cheeks up on her eyes, splendid as ever. Her neck was smooth and strong. "Oh, *hell* no. My bartending days are long gone. Besides, I have a contract with the school district this fall. I keep telling Dad he should sell the place."

Geno took money from the fisherman and rang it up. They watched as the man walked out the door. Geno hauled the remote to the far end of the bar, the end by the door, and raised one big buttock onto that stool, and then the other. He pointed the remote to turn up the sound when the screen door opened again with the push of a shoulder from a woman holding a baby.

"Say hello to Papa Geno, Emma," the woman sang, waving the baby's forearm like a pudgy little wand. "Hi, Papa Geno." It was Lam. She let Geno give the baby a big smooch and then raised her eyebrows and headed for Levi and Lam.

"Is this the new baby!" Angela cooed, holding out her arms as if for a gift. "Is this little Emma? She's big!"

Lam beamed and handed Emma over. "She loves Gerber. This is my Emma. Aren't you, Emma. Aren't you. Yes, you are."

Levi had been preempted, though happily so. He hadn't made sense of this reunion with Angela yet, at least he hadn't for Angela, and seeing his sister, that lovely strong woman, with little Emma made him swell with pride and, yes, joy, despite himself. He touched something in his back pocket, hoping he wouldn't be taking it out.

"I left Dad in the car," Lam said, looking at Levi but side-smirking Emma and newly dubbed Auntie Angela. "Your car. He says his feet are swollen and he'll wait there 'til you come out. Anyway, he's been babysitting lately, but maybe not any more." She darkened, focusing on Levi. "We need to talk."

Levi studied her eyes and what he saw scared him. "Should we talk now? We can go out…"

"No. It can wait. Call when you hit town. Before you get to the ranch. I'll come in."

Levi didn't want to let go, but she said it could wait, so it mustn't be urgent. He stowed his concern for now. Lam wanted him to. So he did. For now.

Lam touched his arm. "Really. Have fun fishing." She looked for concurrence.

"No problem," said Levi. "We were just finishing up. Could you ask him to wait in my car?" At first Lam looked like she had just said that, but then she made an I-get-it face. Angela was allotted another sixty seconds with the baby and only gave Emma up for a promise of dinner next week out at the ranch. Levi and she grinned until after the screen door closed to frame Lam and Emma walking into sunshine.

Levi waited until Angela settled. "I owe you an apology," he said.

"For what?"

"Remember Deirdre Oliver? Well, when they went through her records – her computer – they found an entry she made to her log that indicated she may have drugged you." Angela looked quizzical. "In the Caribbean. When you jumped in the pool." Angela's face dumped as though it were the last thing she wanted to remember. "I thought you should know. I'm sorry."

Angela spoke next. "How are Lam and Russ?"

Levi had released his coffee cup and captured an ashtray, which he sent spinning between his hands. "They're both doing great. Considering. I mean, they still deal with some issues from the … incident. But they've healed pretty well, especially since the baby, though no one sleeps now – except Dad. He's in the bunkhouse. No one talks about that day much, but I don't think anybody feels that there's anything left to say." He trapped the ashtray and looked at Angela until he held her gaze. "They're very much in love, you know. More importantly, they love each other. You know. I think that's why they've healed so well."

For a very long moment, they breathed shallowly. Each blinked once. *Maybe she never heard. Maybe…*

"Have you heard from Lynette?" She looked at his ring.

He closed his eyes. She had heard. "No. We're not in touch." *But it was a long time ago. A lifetime. And it's time to set the record straight about Lynette's oldest child. There must be a chance. She* must *still love me. After all, she's here. Seeing me. Being nice.* He took a deep breath and pulled an envelope from his pocket. "I want you to read something. Marilyn left this for me. I didn't get it until much later. Basically, Lynette sat on it." This was it. If he were to have any chance with Angela, he had to drag the topic into the light. Had to be earnest, honest. He slid over the envelope.

She placed her hand on it. "Do I really need to read this?"

"Yes, please." He waited while she read. It was a copy of a thank-you note to Lynette's doctor.

"Did you say Lynette sat on this? Did she give this to you?"

"Not exactly. Lynette mailed the original from the Billings office. Marilyn's job at that time included copying all outgoing mail. NASD rules. She was crazy diligent about rules. If someone gave her any mail already sealed, she opened and copied it, then resealed it and mailed it. Well, she opened this one. As you see there, Lynette had a paternity test a long time ago. It showed all of Lynette's kids had the same father." He let that sink in. "See, she didn't accuse me until after Marilyn died. She did it to save her job, or get a settlement. Who knows? Doesn't matter. This is what was in Marilyn's safe deposit box. Can you believe it? God, Marilyn was great. Anyway, Lynette actually delivered Marilyn's package with the safe deposit key to me in San Francisco the very same day she lied to Crawford and cut the legs from under me."

"Let me get this right," Angela said. "Marilyn had Lynette deliver a package to you that ultimately told you that Lynette was lying to everyone regarding an illegitimate child? And the admission to the lie is in Lynette's own writing? And there was a key?"

"There is no illegitimate child. And, well, a key and a safe deposit box, yes."

Angela roared with delight. "God, I love that woman! Ooooh. And I'm happy for you about the test. Ha, ha. Ooooh." She wiped her eyes. "I am happy for you."

"Uh, me too. I hope you see that… Well, that I wasn't… I showed you this because…" He looked at her. She looked kind now. Kind! Should he say more? No. No. Enough said. "Angel, I love you."

A very long moment passed.

Angela watched her father watch TV. Absentmindedly she said, "Billings also has a Mormon channel." She looked at Levi. "I heard about Crawford. Hard to believe a guy who loved himself so much could hang himself."

She doesn't love me. Go on, got to move on. "The day before he was to appear for sentencing. I don't think the prospect of jail suited him. Especially if the cell block got advance word that he lost a sexual harassment suit to a man named Karl. Men get lonely in prison."

"That's disgusting." Levi could tell she appreciated the irony. "And did I hear his elderly mother found him? In her house?"

"That's what they say."

"Yeeesh." Angela contorted her face. "So, how long will you stay at the ranch?"

"I'm not sure. Lam says I can stay as long as I want. But I'm moving out soon as money is settled and I figure out what to do. Soon."

"I'm sure that won't be much longer." It sounded like her telling a child they'd get the hang of reading if they hung in there. "Do you think you'll go back to California?"

He snorted. "I can't imagine. Though I probably *will* help drive Dusty to the Bay Area in the fall. You heard he got into Stanford? Wants to study archaeology. That kid's spent too much time in the sun."

"That's what I heard," she said in sing-song. "Is he going to wrestle?"

"I don't think so." Levi sipped his coffee. "I think the little shit got in because he's smart."

"Like his uncle." She smiled. "You should go to college."

He took the praise and advice with a dose of melancholy. "I got a call from Abba Ramakapur, the EcoPulse guy, the one trying to 'save the planet?' Anyway, I think he wants to hire me. He's in India now." He let that sit a moment. "Sandler wants me in New York."

At this she looked genuinely impressed. "You mentioned that. Are you going to go?"

Levi looked for a hint in her face, something saying *Please stay*, but he saw no such message. "I don't know. Maybe. Something feels wrong, though, like the world's tipping. New York seems like, I don't know. Like a fulcrum. Dark. Maybe I'll try to find a job here, start a business, or become a financial advisor. You know, independent."

"*Here?*" She raised her eyebrows. "Let's see, the World Trade Center of Roundup," she teased. "Maybe if you got a space on Main, by the barber shop. It's busy there. Babe, if you stay in Montana, you should at least be in Billings. Nobody lives here."

Babe? Okay. He smiled and looked at his mug, then back at her. "Not nobody. Anyway, Billings has changed since gambling. They kind of Winnemucked it up. But Roundup's become downright charming – on Main." He drew a breath and leaned forward. *Babe.* "You know, we need to talk some more. Maybe we can get together when I get back from fishing. I don't think Dad can make it more than a couple hours. Besides, I don't want to drive back in the dark."

"Oh. I'm sorry. I can't. I have plans."

His hope began to fray. He nodded. "Babe, should I try to meet you some other time?"

"Probably not."

He realized *Babe* had been a slip of the tongue. Innocent on her part. He nodded again, his façade dissolving completely. "Is there … is there someone else?"

"Let's not talk about this."

"Well? Is there?"

"If you want to know if I'm dating, the answer is yes."

He looked away. "I see. Just one person?"

"Levi," she was shaking her head. "I don't want to talk about it."

"I see." He blinked and drank. "Can I call you?"

She breathed in deeply. "Yes. You can call me."

"Is there a better number than your dad's? I can't seem to catch you at home."

"Just leave a message. I'm in and out."

"Yeah," he said quietly, "I've tried that."

"I know. I'll be better about it. I will. Just call if you need to." She reached across the table and squeezed his hand. "It *really is* great to see you. I'm so glad you're doing well."

He cupped her hand with his two. "I love you, Angela."

"I know." She smiled at him. "I really should get going."

As she sat up, he released her hand. He cleared his throat, and with a big, fake bravado said, "Hey. Me too. I've got my own things to do – important things – and don't you forget it. So quit holding me up, missy." He stood. "You're always holding me up."

She stood with him, took his hands in hers for a moment. She put her arms around him and they hugged like they loved each other. Finally, holding hands, she retreated half a pace as if to get a good look at him. Her eyes welled. "Tell your Dad hello. Everybody else too."

"I'll tell them," he managed to say. "You can tell them yourself at dinner next week."

She nodded. "Love you like a crazy." A fresh swell of wind surged through the screens.

He squeezed her hands once. "Hard to undo crazy," he whispered. "Love you like I'm crazy."

"Smells like wind," she whispered. He turned and strode out the door. Angela walked to the end of the bar and slid up onto the stool next to her father. Geno was watching CNBC. He coarsely manipulated a paring knife through an apple and popped a wedge into his mouth.

The news anchor sounded tongue-in-cheek. "Well, it's mid-2001 and doomsayers seem to have crawled out of the hills to prognosticate. Today 'Web Bot Technology,' a group using sophisticated language monitoring programs to measure large-scale changes in word use on the Internet for the purpose of predicting world events before they happen, say that sometime in the next few months an event will occur that will negatively change the way Americans live forever. They say their predictions rise from charting pre-conscious human behavior and identifying cluster points that indicate people's future actions. They're considering supplementing the evidence with photos posted on the Internet. And just when you think you're safe ..."

"Levi told me to sell everything," Geno said.

"Everything? Did he say why?"

"Nope. Don't matter to me anyhow. Like you said, he's magic."

"You're going to cut your tongue." Without resistance, Angela took the knife and apple away from him. She began to carve pieces and lay them on the bar, but something on the television stopped her. Behind the anchorwoman was the EcoPulse logo.

"Speaking of temperature, tired of worrying about global warming? Want to look on the bright side? Well, here's something you can do about it. Move. That's right, move! A team of prestigious scientists funded by Abhaya Ramakapur, the founder and former CEO of EcoPulse Biotech who now resides in India, and Bookman Realty, last month's meteoric spinoff of

Bookman Stuart Holdings, have determined where land prices are bound to skyrocket right along with those summer – and winter – temperatures." The screen split, half of it showing an Indian man in a suit. "We'll have Mr. Ramakapur, live from Bangalore, right after this break."

"See, Dad. That's what you should do with your stock money. Buy land, here in Montana. We're about to become tropical." She reached up and turned the volume down, and then handed Geno the last piece of apple.

"What?" he asked.

50

THE BOTTOM OF THE SKY

As if our birth first sundered things,
and we had been thrust up through into nature like a wedge,
and not 'till the wound heals and the scar disappears,
do we begin to discover where we are,
and that nature is one and continuous everywhere.

HENRY DAVID THOREAU

As the SUV floated and fell along the road, Frank stretched out, pushing his swollen ankles as far from himself as he could, heedlessly making footprints on the opposite door as he leaned against his own, which was unlocked. Levi drove upstream on Highway 12 from Roundup, where the Musselshell wasn't so warm that the trout had not surrendered to catfish. After fifty miles, right by Shawmut and Dead Man's Basin, the pavement showed signs of drying, and Levi suggested they fish the reservoir because the river was swollen and murky.

"I'm not so goddamn old that I have to sit behind a can of worms at a man-made mudhole."

Levi looked dubiously into the rearview mirror. "What's in the Folgers can in the cooler?"

"Those weren't for me, smartass. I thought Dusty was going with us. I dug those for him. Besides," he added, "they've practically drained Dead Man's to dredge the channel."

So they continued west. Garish sunshine that had all morning been dammed up behind pot-bellied clouds now poured down in abundance, strobing through a picket line of riverside cottonwoods that ran up to infinity. They rolled past dewy pastures harboring raiding parties of white-tailed deer, lazily undercutting last year's haystacks. The car banked along a blacktop arc with eight white roadside crosses marking eight dead travelers.

They briefly slowed in Harlowton, as if party to a funeral procession for the town's dead rail-yards.

A few miles farther, Frank read a sign. "Two Dot, Pop. 76. Let's fish here."

"We've got time, Dad. Let's go to Checkerboard. Thirty miles."

"The water looks good here," said Frank. "Why don't we put in at the bridge? Me and Dusty've caught some nice fish there. Not just browns, either. Rainbows. Nice ones."

"Huh." Levi held his speed. If they went on to Checkerboard, he could plant his dad on the lakeshore where the old man could cast various directions and distances without having to walk to find a new hole, freeing Levi to fish the North Fork or Checkerboard Creek. At Two Dot, with Frank incapable of wading the willows or the river, he would be stuck at a single hole in the river. And the river wasn't that big.

"I gotta piss," said Frank.

"Fine, Sally," Levi quipped. He pulled off the highway, down a gravel road a couple hundred yards and across a bridge, where he eased off the gravel, rocking into long grass. He followed ancient puddled tire ruts alongside the fat river. Where the ruts and road petered out, Levi parked, surrendering to the decision of whatever vehicle and parties had visited here before. At the side of the car, Frank faced the willows and peed. At the hatch, Levi put on his denim and lint jacket, leaving the front buttons open. He rolled new hip-waders the color of boiled peas up his legs. He snapped one rubber thong from each around his belt loops.

Frank joined him, smoking a cigarette. "Waders? Since when were you such a pantywaist?"

Levi handed Frank a fishing vest, smelling of scales and blood. Levi's was crisp new canvas with snow-white badges of wool at either breast where he could hang flies if he wanted to. He poked his arms through. Frank noticed.

"That's lovely," said Frank. "Won't dirty your laundry-lint coat. Lovely."

Levi pointed to a stretch of river thirty yards away where water charged into a massive hole under a cutbank as tall as a man, where it boiled dark, hard and deep, rethinking its course before heaving out 90 degrees to the left. "Looks pretty high," he said. An understatement. "But it pools up there. Why don't you set up over the top of it? You can cast up into those rapids and shoot it down into the hole. Pretty cloudy. I'd use a silver blade. Something heavy – a Panther Martin, a #3 Mepp, to get deep. If they don't hit it, you can switch to sinkers and whatever's in this coffee can. That pool's bottomless below the bank." He repointed to the bend in the stream, diverting Frank so he could sneak the shabby chart book from under the seat into the big pocket of his vest.

With one eye closed to smoke, Frank lipped the cigarette while he assembled his rod. He'd always been a spin-caster. "I may not be book-smart, but I've done a helluva lot more fishing than you. I think I'll figure it out. But thanks for the advice." Frank feigned a grin so they could both pretend that no offense was intended or taken.

Levi balanced his rod hip-high, pointed forward, on his middle finger, just in front of the reel. He waited.

Frank seemed to fiddle aimlessly. His rod. His lure book. He checked his swivel, accomplishing nothing. Finally, stamping out his cigarette, Frank's patience was the first to bleed through. He snapped open the lid of the cooler, jerked out the Folgers can. "Fine!" he said, and spanked the cooler lid shut. "Let's go." And he began his march to the bank, saying *Fine!* once more, not so much under his breath.

Levi took a lawn chair from the rig and closed the hatch. He walked fast enough to catch Frank as the old man crept up onto the cornice of the five-foot-high cutbank to assess the water. "Don't trust that edge, Dad. I saw it from the road. It's undercut."

Scowling, the older man dropped the can of worms as if they weren't his and took the lawn chair from Levi, who settled into watching, studying this man, waiting, as one waits when they hold a car door for a grandparent. Frank spoke at the unfolding chair. "Got any more advice?"

"I was just…"

"You were just what? Gonna jump in front of me? Take the first couple of casts? Get there first? Well, don't sneak around. I can't stop you no more." That was true enough, Levi noted, as he watched this bag of bones his father had become. Frank rattled the chair into position at the cutbank's edge and then rattled it back a foot, to no special spot. Scooted it six more inches. Dumped himself into it. He snatched his pole and tin can and began to rig his line. An awkward moment finally popped. Frank loosened. He twisted the chair and himself halfway round to face Levi while he wormed his hook. He looked up, making Levi's eyes avert, so Frank focused out on infinity. "Gawd, those are pretty mountains."

Levi looked. The beauty seemed to wash holy down the landscape, covering it and them. "Yeah. The Crazies. Didn't they name them after some Indian woman?" Levi purposely misspoke as he often had as a boy to make his dad feel smart, to inflate his mood. To stave off madness. But Frank no longer scared him. This time, it was simply a gift.

"Nope. She was white. The Indians messed up her husband and kids, leaving her alone up there." He pointed to Loco Peak, white-capped and surrounded by thunderheads. "Went crazy as a loon. Scared the hell out of the Indians. Some say she killed the ones that attacked her family." For a long while they stared reverently. A spectral wind whispered into the river-sounds. "I think her name was Virginia," Frank said. He checked Levi, grinning a grin that reflected back. Frank closed the swivel on the leader of a bare #6 hook. He leaned for the Folgers can as Levi sat on a rock beside him.

"You've changed," Levi said.

"You don't say?" Frank said without looking up.

"I used to be afraid of you." Levi spoke from within himself. "All my life I didn't know who you were. I was just afraid. Now you seem … real … like my father. Now I don't really know who I am."

Frank was grappling with a disobliging worm, staring it down. "I been gonna tell you this. Lam too. I'm sorry for the things I done." He pinched the writhing bait, skewering another length of it. "Your mother stopped me, when you was about nine. I don't mean from hurting you – I stopped that myself, believe you me. I mean from hurting me. Killing myself." He let the end of the worm wiggle and reached into his vest for a jar of salmon eggs. "She was stronger than me. That's where you got it." He dared a glance at Levi. "I guess I never told you how my step-dad came at me. But she saw it. Her dad came at *her*. If you had it, you can see it in others." His voice was wrapped only in water and wind. "I was ten when he gave me this tattoo." Frank brushed up his sleeve, let it fall back down. "Sewing needle and ink. Just like his. He kept comin' 'til I left home. *Your mom* knew. She never told *nobody*. And I never forgave him. I never really gave a shit how he got that way, and I don't know if he finally changed or not. In *my* head, he never changed, even after he was dead. I never let him be no different. I kept the dark parts alive, stared at 'em. So I stayed so mad and messed up at what he done to me that I did it too. To Lam mostly. I built a mountain of wrong, 'til I hated *me* just as much as I hated him." Frank looked. "That's why I almost done it – killed myself."

Levi stared, covering his surreal disbelief, afraid if he talked his father would stop. Frank had beaded one orange egg onto the fishhook. He began work on another.

"When you left, I yelled and hollered at your mom. I was gonna jump you about it first chance, tell you you better never set foot back round here. I almost did that day your mother made me go into your office in Billings with her and Lam – the day you hid us from the governor like garbage. But your mom said she'd be damned if I was gonna mess up any chance of us being a family again. She told me yous kids'd suffered plenty 'cause of me – and her – and I was gonna keep my mouth shut." He sighed and softened. "Far as I know, Lam never said nothin' bad about me to your mom. But like I said, if you been through it, you can tell. Your mom knew. She knew I hurt yous kids when you were little. I used to try to keep her drunk then. She should've hated me. I know Lam never forgave me neither; she don't trust me even now. I'm sure that's why I'm in the bunkhouse and you're in the ranch house. I ain't stupid. I hope I live long enough for her to forgive me. I think your mother let it go. Maybe she found somewhere to put it. And maybe you did." He fixed on Levi's eyes. "Can you forgive me?"

It felt odd. Only odd. Nothing else. Levi wondered if he should be shocked at it, put right out there like that. Or perhaps thankful for the chance to forgive. Wow. Family. When he wasn't looking, had he forgiven his father? For everything? Or had he only squandered years looking, worrying that Frank would rub off if he was allowed too close. It had been a very long time. And one can only control oneself. One can only forgive oneself. With a word from Levi, Frank could forgive himself. Levi looked softly at the small, sorrowful man. "No. Not yet."

Suddenly Frank looked tired. Sorrowful, and tired. "Lam neither. You make somebody hate you and they might get over it someday. Maybe there's enough time for them to. But it ain't so easy when you make them hate themselves. Ain't no such thing as that much time."

Levi wanted to say something, but couldn't. He simply couldn't.

"You want to see who you are?" Frank went on. "Look at them dark mountains." They both looked. "There's two ways to feature them. You can look at great big dark mountains, or you can look at the bottom of the sky. One of them will be how you see yourself, and the other might be how people see you. If you stare at the worst you ever done – or what people want to *think* you done – you'll be standing at the bottom looking up at the dark mountains you built that are covering up and stealing your sky. You won't never see over the top of them or around 'em. You'll be in the shadow every day and miss the heavens at night. But if a man tries, I think you can just *know* the dark parts are there without staring at them or watching them grow. Just climb them instead. Just do. Use them to stand on … and then look right up at the light, always. I believe all that dark and that shadow can become the bottom of a guy's sky, and a guy don't ever have to *have* no top. Maybe, if that's true, you'll be tall enough to see what your mom called 'what God has in mind for you.' I think it could work – if you can treat your pile of dark like a perch. I could never stop staring up at my mountain of wrong, scared to death it was growing faster than I can climb. I'll never know. Son, if you don't want to end up like me, then make your dark mountain be the bottom of your sky."

He regarded Levi and pointed at the Crazies. "And one more thing. Sometimes, when you stare a long time, your vision gets funny, and a bright gap lights up between the top of the mountains and the bottom of the sky – like a fluorescent blanket laid between them. See?" He pointed again. "Stare a minute." He waited. "See? That's hell's corona. Well. My advice is don't talk to people about seeing that. We already think you're crazy." Frank smiled big. "Oh, don't look so damn serious. Get out of here so I can fish. And don't cast right above me." Frank turned the chair toward the river and cast upstream, into roiling water, letting the bait drift into the massive hole below him. Talk was over. Frank was fishing now.

Levi stood for a moment. Numb. No thought of where to go. After a while, he found himself walking downstream, pulled by gravity along a cutbank that sloped thinner until it melted into old riverbed tufted with willows and tall, wet grass. He glanced back. It dawned on him that he had left no monster up there, no boogeyman. Nor could he sense of one inside himself, only the hollow from it, a collapsing shape littered with mishandled artifacts. He felt at once liberated and disoriented. Hopeful – and wary of self-deception. Such a great distance between then and now. A safe distance? With a growing sense of triumph, the world in-between – the one where Crawford and posers skulked and conspired as though they or any of it mattered, the one with amorphous integrity – seemed childish: delightfully, laughably insignificant. Adults playing dress-up with preposterous import. He felt pity – *pity* – for souls taken by illusion.

At once the air smelled crisper and spicier than ever, as though astringed by truth, the damp foliage earthier, fresher. Sunshine burned good. A light heavy step scared up a buck from its bed in the tall grass, starting Levi into laughter. Fifty yards later, he nearly stepped on a skunk before it waddled, tail raised, into the underbrush. "Yes!" he hollered. He looked up. Into the boisterous water, he yelled, "Thank you, God!"

Levi looked back from a distance at his father, the little man in the lawn chair, small as a bean, perched atop the sandy overhang with his Folgers can, watching the bobber bob. Fishing as a child fishes. Fishing. Levi's focus drifted appreciatively down the water toward him. Beautiful living water. He paused, reading it as fishermen do. High, fast, muddy. Glorious and beautiful. He couldn't give a shit if he ever caught a fish. He cast without intention and, as happens that way, straight away found a wet snag. "Ah, hah!" he confirmed. He turned his back to it and walked, fist tightening around the straining line to keep it from breaking off inside his reel, feeling it plead until, poof, it slackened. Broken and free. Broken and free. "Ah, hah!" he delighted. The perfect excuse to go sit with his father. Just one thing before he did.

He unzipped the big pouch in the back of his vest and reached in to grasp the colored helter-skelter wad of crackling scrolls. Without ceremony he cocked it back like a shredded baton and heaved it with all he had at the most raucous section of water. The pages opened wildly to the wind, flailing, and it fell pathetically into a meandering ribbon of stream within the stream. No boil. Just wet. It made him laugh. That would do. That would do. Time to see his father. So he turned into the tall grass, keeping a sharp eye for critters.

Levi emerged dampened and started up, along the slope of the embankment. Halfway up, about thirty yards from the top, a toppled lawn chair rose on the near horizon. No Frank. Levi looked toward the car but the doors were closed. Frank wasn't there either. Probably went to find a bush, Levi told himself. A few steps later, Levi spotted the red Folgers can, also tipped on its side, having vomited a dune of black dirt from its mouth. He squinted. Walked faster. "Dad?" he called. No answer. Only the water on the rocks and the wind in the grass. His heart and legs quickened. At ten feet, the wind whistled through the lawn chair. Beyond it Levi spotted Frank's body, prostrate, stretched precariously along the ledge. "Dad?" Levi yelled as his pole fell from his hand. He broke into a run. No response. Frank's rod lay as if tossed from him, his face and one arm hung fully out of sight, over the edge of the bank. Levi collapsed at Frank's side, driving his knees into the earth, and clutched Frank's far shoulder and back pocket, pulling at denim and flesh to roll him over, roll him back.

"Let go of my ass, God damn it! Let go! I got a fish here! Let go! A damn big one." Frank tossed back his head above the ledge of the bank, unable to look at Levi. A vein in his neck bulged. "I was trying to horse him up this bank and he snapped my line. 'Bout time you lollygagged your ass back here. Listen, I got hold of the line, but it's snagged under water, and he's under the damn snag. If I let go I'll lose him."

Levi collapsed back onto his heels, his hands dragging across Frank's body, and was overcome. He silently wept, urgently erasing tears from his face and eyes with the chill-reddened heel of one hand. Colors blazed. His hands, his golden shirt, his green waders – *everything* gleamed brilliantly. *Everything.*

"Did you hear me?" Frank's voice came from below the ledge. "I need your help, dammit! Hurry up. I been here forever and I'm damn tired!"

Levi dropped to his belly near Frank's head and peered over the edge. Several feet below, the fish flashed violently, a quickened rainbow at the water's surface, and then drifted lumpishly under, as exhausted as Frank. Levi looked at his dad's face, nine inches away, a face ripe with disgust.

"What the hell! Are you crying?"

"No. No. I just thought…"

"Oh, for Christ's sake. I *know* what you thought. And I *will* expire if you don't get your ass in gear. Go to the car and get the net."

At that moment the bank surged from their collective weight. A fissure opened at their bellies. Frank started, but Levi was much quicker, peeling back two feet to safe ground and yanking Frank's pocket again, this time urgent enough to tent the man's hips off the ground. Frank yipped. "Shit!' He had lost grip on the line. The fish was gone.

"Look what the hell you done!" yelled Frank. "Who the hell…" and Frank moved his hand back and captured Levi's. "Let go of my ass."

Levi let go, little realizing he had it in the first place. He backed up a step on his knees. He stood. With herky effort, the man before him rolled over. "It's just a fish," Levi said.

"That's cause it's not your fucking fish."

"Hey, I was only trying to–" but he cut short as Frank labored to stand, his back to the stream.

When they were squared off, Frank panted, "I know what you was trying to do." The older man struggled for breath but it was coming back. "Okay. Fine. I know you didn't mean no harm." After another suck of breath, Frank said. "Okay."

"Okay," Levi said, smiling tentatively.

Frank smiled back. "Okay. You saved my life. Big deal. You almost killed me, then you saved my life." Levi warmed at the father he saw before him. "Some hero. Next time," he smirked, "keep your hands off my butt." They both laughed. "I know you and Emma don't forgive me yet, but that doesn't mean you can touch my butt. If anything, you oughta know I prefer girls." Frank smiled again. This little old man with his awful little joke. This little man. This awful …

"What did you say?"

Frank's face melted some. "I said … hey, I didn't mean nothing. I mean … Come on. I was only trying to … Come on. Why do you need to …? Okay, I'm sorry. I'm sorry, okay? I just wish, I just wish you and Lam would forgive me, okay? It was a joke."

Levi stared. At once he saw what he was looking at. He heard what he heard. "Did you say, me and Emma?"

Frank's face took on the seeds of alarm. "No. No, that's not what I said. That's not what I said. Okay, I admit … That came out wrong, but that's not … Why don't you two just forgive me? That's what your mom wanted. You know that. Can't you forgive me? Can't you? Damn, son."

What his mom wanted. Frank's words broke like a stone through time-soiled glass. Starkness flooded in, demanding focus, assimilation of facts and images, of memories and truth. What his mom wanted. Levi chased echoes. "Lam said you might not be babysitting anymore."

"Oh, hell. She's got things in her head that just ain't … they're ridiculous. Now she's taking the baby to a doctor, just because of a red spot in her diaper. Ridiculous. How'm I s'posed to know what's the matter. How'm I…" and then for Levi, Frank's voice became white noise.

Red? My God. Forgiveness? Family? God's purpose for him? He tried to grab onto purpose. Purpose. Family. His father. Slowly Levi's hands clasped denim at his ribs, pulling open his lint jacket. He confirmed the lining, recalling the letter his mom wrote. He had read it many times. Knew it. *I can't help think He still ain't called on you yet*, it read, *Do good for good people.*

Nothing else matters. When she wrote it, Lam had been pregnant. Purpose. At once, he understood. He gazed upon Frank. Lam was a woman. Dusty a man. Strong. Emmie was only a baby girl. Lam's precious baby girl. Forgiveness. Promises. Redemption.

As if to absorb the onslaught of rage, a great, warm tide of purpose washed through Levi's mind and chest, calmed him, leaving behind, oddly and for the first time in his life, a sober promise of peace. Peace. Levi decided. Slowly he rummaged in a pocket of his fishing vest for a tiny ziplock bag and removed from it his fishing license. "Do you have a pen? You've got everything else in that vest."

Frank bypassed questioning the off-topic request, eager to move on to anything else. He handed a pen to Levi, venturing not a word.

Levi wrote on the waterproof paper, retracing his words so they'd hold. Then he bent and righted the Folgers can and placed it on top of the paper, leaving both on the ground. Frank looked quizzical now, but as Levi rose his body relaxed and he offered Frank a glowing look that said the worries were gone. In turn, Frank accepted the distance from blame and softened his guardedness.

"Forgive me? Do you? You know I ain't done nothing but love that little girl. You know that. Right?" Frank nodded like he wanted Levi to. "Right?"

Levi raised his palms toward his father, and then his forearms. Levi's arms opened wide. Frank appeared to battle a reluctant look. Levi opened farther. He walked gently toward his dad. Frank turned his face to the side.

"Oh, for Christ," Frank started, shifting his weight as Levi approached. Before he could raise his arms to accept the hug, Levi wrapped his arms around Frank. "All right, that's—" and Levi tightened his arms. And tightened, like rungs on a barrel. "Son, I can't..."

Levi stepped forward, back-walking Frank toward the cornice.

"What are you...? You're gonna... What the hell are you doing!" Frank's eyes darted.

Shuffling, closer and closer, six inches at a time, Levi crowded his father toward the sandy ledge. Now Frank wrestled in earnest. Their feet crossed the fissure, stubbed onto the cornice. Sand slabs shifted. The older man thrashed, growing wilder, wilder, kicking a fishing rod into clacks and rattles. Fishing line tangled at their feet. Levi crowded.

"What the hell are you doing? You crazy son of a bitch! What are you doing!"

Levi stopped, as if to answer. He stopped, and looked in his father's eyes. Yes, these were the eyes of his father. Dear God, his only father. Levi could see the roiling pool over his dad's shoulder. Frank was climbing him like a cat now, and Levi stopped him to check his face again. Then, surely, Levi held tighter. The ledge lurched, and through his feet Levi heard the deep snaps of popping roots. Above that, a frenzied knee searched hard for Levi's groin, and again.

"Stop it! Stop!"

Levi thought of what his mother had said, about purpose. The letter, that morning in Lam's kitchen. He saw Emma's face. Little Emmie's face. Lam's Emmie. His Lam's Emmie. *Lam.* At that moment, as the sand gave way, Levi spoke one more time, with calm and clarity. "I promised," he said. "I told her I would be there."

Levi tightened his grip with the strength of certitude, as though he would never let go. He planted his feet and bent at the waist toward Frank. They plunged, he with his father, into the cold, angry water.

Levi rolled onto his back, pulling his father deeper, deeper away. Water flooded his sinuses, biting inside his head. At his legs a cool vacuum sucked, hungrily, drawing water into boots that became full and leaden. Frank struggled in fits and starts. Collapsing. Erupting. But Levi held. Sinking. Washing. In the green depth, they met a driftwood skeleton. Levi searched it with his feet. There. He locked to it, pulling himself and his past even deeper, squatting there, on the driftwood trunk. Waiting. Frank bit his chest. Levi clenched his father's neck. Through pain and asphyxia, he squinted up, past his captive, into the dayglow above. Frank emptied loudly and pulled in breath of river. Levi allowed a moment to pass before he did the same. And as their shiver subsided and the cool settled in, Levi Monroe reached up from his mountain, offering his scars to the bottom of the sky.

■

PROLOGUE REDUX

For her, Roundup, Montana, like Wall Street and Silicon Valley, never really existed in black and white or even sepia tone, though photographic images and personal retrospect may have recorded it that way. It had color and contrast. On thirty-below-zero days, the sky was always cobalt blue with a brilliant yellow bullet hole. After winter storms, the run-down Bull Mountains were blinding white, pocked with evergreen. The slough-green Musselshell River girdled the hills from tumbling north onto the plains. Grasslands that had sustained cattle since 1881—and the bison before them—were verdant in spring and gray-gold in summer and fall. The veins deep under Roundup ran coal black, and the ones above, crimson red.

Through the middle of the last century, most of the men in town were coal miners with Old Country names like Wilhelm Johnig, Kavka Bublivich, Cian O'Reilly, or Izroc Ketanna, and they went by Shorty or Red or Izzy. They named their children John or Kathleen or Betty or Charley. Some had never attended school, becoming trapped there in the mines by their ignorance and their accent, disoriented by their addictions, or buried beneath the propaganda and prejudice of two world wars. Straightforward and iron-tough, they bloodied each other regularly and their families occasionally. They drank and stayed married to resilient women of practical grace who saw to it that they wore their one set of church clothes when they were told to, who endured the profane to protect the sacred, and who rose above dispossession to hold up children so that they might see beyond shacks and mines and dreams played out.

Now, under sandstone hills, among weed-stumped plots, this daughter with a daughter of her own stands upslope from a pink granite cemetery marker. In one hand she holds a note written on waterproof paper, in the other, the hand of her child. "Thank you," she whispers to someone else. "Thank you." She pockets the note as though it were the heirloom it has become. In a swoop, she hoists the child to her shoulders, tickling the young girl's fancy. As they walk to the car, they point at big clouds and divine their magical shapes, marveling at the bottom of the sky.

About the Author

Born in a rural Montana coal and cow town, William C. (Bill) Pack grew up in an environment beset with all of the attendant difficulties. At 15 years old the courts emancipated him. At 16 he dropped out of high school. At 17 he married and at 18 he became a father. He worked variously as a truck driver, bartender, fry cook, and advertising salesman. When he was 21 he began a successful career as a broker with Merrill Lynch in Billings, Montana. A few years later he was divorced and broke.

With his brokerage license and GED, Bill transferred to Northern California where he rose to become the youngest Executive VP/Divisional Director at Smith Barney Shearson (later, Citigroup Smith Barney). His business and financial acumen became renowned. Bill ran a division managing many billions of dollars and met regularly with past and current chief executives of the largest financial firms in the world. He spoke to thousands of investment professionals and investors, shared podiums with CEOs, a presidential chief economic adviser, a governor, the executive director of the California Treasury's Debt Advisory Commission, and many other notables. Bill served a prestigious three-year appointment with the NASD (now FINRA), the S.E.C.'s partner in regulating Wall Street.

Along the way, through Menttium 100, Bill volunteered as a mentor for female executives at both Hewlett Packard and JPMorgan. He has worked at and financially supported many charities, most particularly women's and children's advocacy groups.

When Bill became seriously ill at 43, he quit the financial world to pursue lifelong goals. He took the SAT college entrance exams and earned acceptance into Stanford University where he became Stanford's lone undergraduate director for an archaeological project. He won the Annual Reviews Prize in Anthropological Sciences for his thesis and graduated Phi Beta Kappa. During college, Bill published a poem, and shortly afterward, his first short story. *The Bottom of the Sky* is his first novel.

Bill Pack is married with four grown children. When he's not in Montana, he lives in Northern California.